# The Strange Voyages of Jacques Massé and Pierre de Mésange

# The Strange Voyages of Jacques Massé and Pierre de Mésange

by
**Simon Tyssot de Patot**

translated, annotated and introduced by
**Brian Stableford**

A Black Coat Press Book

ISBN 978-1-61227-370-9. First Printing. March 2015. Published by Black Coat Press, an imprint of Hollywood Comics.com, LLC, P.O. Box 17270, Encino, CA 91416.

# TABLE OF CONTENTS

## Introduction

*Voyages et aventures de Jaques Massé* here translated as "The Voyages and Adventures of Jacques Massé," was first published anonymously in several different editions bearing the date 1710, some versions bearing title pages stating that it was issued in Bordeaux "Chez Jaques l'Aveugle" and one that it was published in Cologne "Chez Kaincus" The typesetting of three Bordeaux title pages differs, and the typesetting of the entire text bearing the Cologne title page is also distinctive, while the copies now available on line include several that have no preliminary title page at all. The copies containing preliminary title pages also contain a "letter to the editor," usually bound at the front but occasionally at the back, suggesting that the text and the supplementary materials were printed separately. The resulting puzzle has caused considerable comment among bibliographers. Both title-pages are certainly fakes, there being no such publishers, and the likelihood is that the text was actually first printed in the Netherlands, although the "Cologne edition" might be a pirate edition produced elsewhere. Several sources suggest, on the basis of various items of indirect evidence, that its actual first publication date might have been 1714.

The reason for the text's anonymity and the concealment of its actual place of publication is presumably the risk it was running of being considered heretical, and thus attracting persecution. The attribution of the book's authorship to Simon Tyssot de Patot (1655-1738), first made in 1740, helps to explain the sensitivity; Tyssot was a Huguenot whose family had been forced to leave France before he was born and was subsequently forced to flee England as well, with the result that he spent most of his life moving around, mostly living in various locations in the Netherlands, where he worked as a teacher of French and Mathematics, including a long spell at the Athenaeum in Deventer.

The second text included in the present volume is generally known as *La Vie, les aventures et le voyage de Groenland du Révérend Père Cordelier Pierre de Mésange*, and it was first published in two volumes dated 1720. The preliminary title page bearing that title states that it was published in Amsterdam "au depens d'Etienne Roger, Marchand Libraire, chez qui l'on trouve un assortiment général de Musique" [at the expense of Etienne Roger, Bookseller, at whose shop a general assortment of Music can be found]. Although that page does not cite an author, the remainder of the preliminary material contains a dedicatory epistle signed "S. Tyssot de Patot," so the text in question is definitely his work—and no one who has read the two books attentively can possibly have any doubt that the earlier volume chronicling the adventures of Jacques Massé is by the same writer. Page one of the second text, in both volumes, gives the title as *Voyage et découvertes autour du pole boreal du Révérend Père Cordelier Pierre de Mésange*, and that is the title I have abridged slightly for the translation in the present volume, "Discoveries in the Region of the North Pole by the Reverend Father Pierre de Mésange" (the term "Cordelier," which I have omitted from the title of my translation indicates that the priest in question is a Franciscan.)

Although a previous English translation of the first book, by Stephen Whately, appeared in 1743 as *The Travels and Adventures of James Massey*, and is now available for consultation on line, in wanting to translate the second text, I thought it worthwhile to preface it with a new translation of the first, given that they are thematically complementary and are even more interesting when read in juxtaposition than separately. The pair that they constitute is a truly remarkable achievement, marking a highly significant watershed in the evolution of literary accounts of imaginary voyages. Although the adventures of Pierre de Mésange are dated a year after the publication of Daniel Defoe's *The Life and Adventures of Robinson Crusoe* (1719) they were obviously written beforehand, with no knowledge of that work, or of the tidal wave of imaginary voyages that its example inspired, aided and abetted by Jonathan Swift's satirical account of the travels of Lemuel Gulliver, first published in 1726.

The 17th century had seen the publication of a number of accounts of actual voyages of exploration, but most such voyages had been extremely tentative by comparison with what was to follow in the eighteenth century. Dutch explorers had mapped much of the northern coast of what they called "New Holland," but had rarely attempted to land there, let alone explore it, although the privateer William Dampier did so briefly in 1688 and 1699; the island in question was still *terra incognita* for a further century until the English began to the colonization that eventually transformed it into Australia. The island of Tahiti had also been sighted, but there was no record of anyone landing there, and it was not until the latter half of the eighteenth century that the great French explorer Louis de Bougainville, who landed there in 1768, would establish its native society as a key exemplar in the mythology of cultural evolution, in a context provided by Jean-Jacques Rousseau—who was only eight years old in 1720.

Tyssot was, therefore, writing in an era when the possibility of finding more vast islands, as yet unheeded as well as unexplored, was still entirely plausible. As Pierre de Mésange points out at one juncture in a ringing speech, nobody yet cared about exploration for the sake of scientific investigation, and the European invasions of the East Indies and Americas had been guided entirely by the quest for commercially valuable commodities and the lure of gold. The adventurous French navigators and explorers of the seventeenth century, without exception, followed the contemporary tide by heading for the Indies and Americas; only victims blown off course and shipwrecked, like Jacques Massé and Pierre de Mésange, ended up anywhere else—and hardly ever lived to tell the tale.

The first and greatest of all the accounts of heroic voyages available as exemplars to Tyssot, *Livres des merveilles du monde* (c.1300; tr. as *The Travels of*

*Marco Polo*) was the story of a mercantile expedition, as was the epoch-making tale of the equally heroic expedition mounted by Marco Polo's greatest admirer, Christopher Columbus. Columbus also loved the first great fanciful imitation of Marco Polo's account, the imaginary and somewhat fabulous account of the travels of "Jehan de Mandeville", called in English translations Sir John Mandeville, which was penned in the mid-14th century by an author never conclusively identified, although the most likely candidate is a Flemish monk named Jean de Langhe, whose wrote in Latin as Johannes Longus and in French as Jean de Long.

The literature of imaginary travel had, however, only made significant progress since Mandeville's oft-reprinted adventures in the subgenre pioneered by Thomas More's *Utopia* (1516), in which voyagers gone stray and shipwrecks are employed as a literary device to grant witnesses access to a number of significant "ideal societies" in the seventeenth century, most notably Tommaso Campanella's *Civitas Solis* (1623; tr. as *The City of the Sun*), Francis Bacon's *New Atlantis* (1627) and the Duchess of Newcastle's *The Blazing World* (1668). In the early decades of the 18th century, therefore, attitudes to navigation and exploration had not yet undergone the profound metamorphosis that they were to undergo when the idea of "Enlightenment" as the Great Work of the human mind got a serious grip on the European imagination.

Tyssot would undoubtedly have been aware of some examples of the Utopian subgenre, and the imaginary societies visited by Jacques Massé and Pierre de Mésange are not without elements of comparison calculated to make European society seem a trifle sorry and more than a trifle sick, but neither the author nor his imaginary alter egos were social reformers. They were, however, pioneers and evangelists of Enlightenment, not merely in the sense that they have an insatiable appetite for discovering "curiosities," but also in the sense that they are ever avid to spread the knowledge they possess and to operate as fervent disciples for the training of minds by mathematical logic and the acquisition of new knowledge by means the methods of science. Among the literary genres to which Tyssot's works made a substantial foreshadowing contribution, which include the quintessential Enlightenment genre of the Voltairean *conte philosophique* as well as the Vernian scientifically-informed traveler's tale, not the least important is the hybrid genre of "the popularization of science"—a project that both Massé and Mésange see as a kind of mission.

Written in the early years of the 18th century—whatever the actual publication dates of the two texts were, the elements of the portmanteau texts might well have been commenced before 1700 and were probably works in progress throughout the next two decades—the adventures of Massé and Mésange were produced at the crucial juncture of the "Age of Reason" and the "Age of Enlightenment," and help to illustrate a significant transition in ways of thinking and the accumulation of knowledge in relation to what Massé or Mésange would call "the system of the world." Although Simon Tyssot de Passot was contemporary with Isaac Newton, and Newton first published his *Philosophiae Naturalis Principia Mathematica* in 1687, neither Massé nor Mésange, whose adventures mostly take place before that date, has heard of the English philosopher, and it is entirely plausible that their author was also completely unaware of his work, which was not popularized in France until after the publication of his own texts. The two voyagers are, in consequence, thinking and acting in advance of the influence that the Newtonian world-view and its associated scientific theories was to have in the history of ideas.

The late 18th century was to see the publication of several highly essays in the popularization of science cast as imaginary voyages, including *Le Voyageur philosophe* (1761) by "Monsieur de Listonai" [1]—also published in Amsterdam for fear of dangerous accusations of heresy in France—and *Le Philosophe sans prétention* (1775)[2], which seem bizarre today because their chemistry is anchored in the theory of the four classical elements and theories of combustion that antedate the discovery of oxygen, but at least their physics has taken aboard some Newtonian notions. Tyssot did not have that advantage, and the science that Massé and Mésange endeavor to explain to their various listeners is therefore primitive to an even greater degree.

Indeed, Tyssot had only one significant precursor in the relevant subgenre written in French—albeit a *tour de force*—in Bernard le Bovier de Fontenelle's *Entretiens sur la pluralité des mondes* (1686; tr. as *Conversations on the Plurality of Worlds*), which seems in retrospect to have completed the intellectual victory of the heliocentric Copernican "system of the world" over the geocentric system inherited from Aristotle, in spite of continued diehard opposition from conservative elements within the Church. Significantly, however, Tyssot's heroes do not regard that dispute as conclusively settled; although they are convinced Copernicans themselves, they take it for granted that almost all their interlocutors are not, and strive to persuade them of the truth.

From the viewpoint of the 21st century, of course, Tyssot's attempts at scientific popularization seem absurd, because we now know certain vital truths that his heroes did not. The lecture that Mésange delivers on the explanation of the phenomenon of weight is not merely mistaken in its entirety but is bound to seem utterly perverse to anyone familiar with the concept of gravity, but that only serves, in a way to make it even more intriguing in its ambition and misguided ingenuity. As with many aspects of these and many other texts of the same sort, the wonder is not that they are done well, from a modern viewpoint, but that they were done at all. Theirs is certainly an eccentric virtue, but it is nevertheless a very real virtue, and an unparalleled one. It is not only their physics and geography that Tyssot's books seem woefully primitive, but also their

---

[1] tr. as *The Philosophical Voyager*, Black Coat Press, ISBN 978-1-61227-367-9.
[2] tr. as *The Unpretentious Philosopher*, Black Coat Press, ISBN 978-1-61227-136-1.

narrative technique, but in that aspect too they were ground-breaking and highly distinctive.

Analogies can certainly be found between Tyssot and Daniel Defoe and one or two other pioneers of the modern novel, but in many respects his two imaginary voyages were utterly unlike anything written before, and they certainly illustrate the explorations and innovations that paved the way for the rapid sophistication of prose narrative technique that was to follow in the next half-century. While they were being penned, the twelve volumes of Antoine Galland's *Les Mille-et-une nuits* (tr. as *The Arabian Nights*), first issued between 1704 and 1717, must have been emerging from the presses, and the unusual narrative structure of Galland's work presumably lent some useful encouragement to Tyssot's equally idiosyncratic development of portmanteau narrative, specially the more elaborate usage deployed in Pierre de Mésange's account of his adventures. The evolution of that technique is very marked and clearly visible when the two texts are juxtaposed. The second text exhibits a strong interest in the nature of narrative and questions of reliability and import inherent in history and storytelling.

Both of the works in this volume, like many other foundation-stones of the modern novel, take the form of fictitious autobiographies, and carry forward aspects of the genre of "spiritual autobiography," in which authors excused themselves for the apparent vanity and narcissism of recording their lives with the implication that their humble experiences might provide a useful exemplar of the evolution of moral wisdom. Traditionally, that evolution had progressed in the direction of committed faith and trust in Providence, whose eventual consolidation provided a climax and denouement of sorts, but the whole point of Tyssot's works is that blind faith is a deceptive trap and trust in Providence, although perhaps psychologically necessary, essentially hollow. In narrative terms, the fundamental assumption of both texts is that life is ultimately anti-climatic and its only denouement is death; in the meantime, it is long and tortuous, and essentially flat, devoid of meaningful achievement no matter how much movement and endeavor it involves. That developing awareness in the consciousness of both Jacques Massé and Pierre de Mésange gives the tone of their narratives a remarkable quality of laconism, which reaches an extreme in the manner in which the latter deals with the most horrific incident in his life, not only in the mater-of-fact description of the event itself, but in the way that no subsequent reference is made to its physiological or psychological effects.

In spite of the flatness of the two narratives, however, there is a marked evolution between them, which becomes obvious in the matter of justification. Jacques Massé (whose name could be translated in context, as "accumulation," although the word is nowadays used to refer to a push-stroke in billiards) is a Catholic intensely interested in religion, and the puzzles that arise from his intensive reading of the Bible—such questions as the whether *Genesis* ought to be construed literally or as a set of parables, and whether its chronology is trustwor-

11

thy—and although he draws upon his knowledge of philosophy, mathematics and physics to help him work his way through those problems, they always remain his central focus of interest.

When Massé is stranded for a time in the imaginary civilization at the heart of an unknown austral continent, although he is interested in all aspects of its culture, his primary focus is on the differences between the natives' religious beliefs and those current in Europe, including their alternative version of the myth of Adam and Eve, and the influence of that variant myth on their social history and attitudes. Massé never does make up his own mind, and remains a passive listener to the various alternative views presented to him—although that does not prevent him from being imprisoned by the Inquisition, in whose dungeon he whiles away time by listening to the exemplary autobiography of a spiritually-troubled Chinese convert to Christianity—and he is careful to dissent from the various unorthodox view he hears, although Tyssot obviously knew that the narrative strategy in question would not save his text from accusations of heresy. The most extreme of the novel's challengers of orthodoxy is Massé's atheist companion in his eventual slavery, who acquaints him with the fiercely anti-clerical "Fable of the Bees" which surely would have invited persecution is Tyssot had been known to be its author; the narrator's objection to it is conspicuous in its half-heartedness.

Somewhat by contrast, the spoiled Franciscan monk Pierre de Mésange (whose surname could be translated, albeit loosely, as "fallen angel"), is not primarily interested in religion. Religious bigotry is a perennial fact of life for him, and a perennial source of trouble, but his most intense interests are secular, inclined toward matters of mathematics, physics, cosmology and history. Many of the interpolated stories making up the elaborate portmanteau narrative are supposedly taken from the written history of the polar continent where he spends many years, although several of them look suspiciously like stories that were originally set in the known world before being adapted to that context, and the vast majority of the anecdotes related to Mésange by the people he meets elsewhere are devoid of any theological or doctrinal implications.

One of the significant thematic bridges between the two texts is, however, theological in nature, connecting the seemingly-arbitrary appearance in the early pages of Massé's narrative by the Wandering Jew with the remarkable visionary narrative attributed to the folklore of the polar continent, in which a character bearing the suspiciously atypical name of Raoul discovers a subterranean portal to "the abode of the blessed" (i.e., a posthumous paradise). What connects the two is a conviction that resurrection, as described by the Wandering Jew in his account of events in Jerusalem following Christ's crucifixion, and Raoul's account of the abode of the blessed, must logically involve the provision of the soul with a new physical body significantly different from the carnal envelope employed for earthly existence. Neither narrator labors the point, and from the viewpoint of the author it is obviously a purely hypothetical logical exercise, to which he cannot add an atom of faith, but its situation within the overarching narrative of the two texts is nonetheless significant, and illustrative of the directional thrust of the author's mentality.

It is obvious, as Mésange's narrative proceeds, that he becomes gradually less interested in the actual substance of the stories that he hears and tells, and increasingly interested in the psychological quirks that they reflect, and the reasons for their ability to seduce the interest of listeners. Like its predecessor, and not by virtue of mere coincidence, Mésange's account of his life and listening acquires a particular fascination in its later phases with confidence tricks and impostures, not unconnected with the author's awareness that his texts are themselves impostures: accumulations of artifices embedded within artifices, sometimes stacked two or even three deep. Whether they are parables, fables, speculative fictions or mere tall stories, the stories are always told and carefully enfolded in the interests of prompting the quest for the truth via skepticism, ingenuity and intellectual ambition: the march of reason toward enlightenment. In that context, in the particular era of their publication, the two narratives are truly fascinating works, fully deserving of classic status in the evolution of imaginative fiction.

Simon Tyssot de Patot might have published another anonymous text in 1714, a pastoral romance falsely represented as a translation from Latin, *Les Amours et les aventures d'Arcan de Belize*, although bibliographers are divided as to whether to attribute it to him or to his contemporary—presumably a relative—Petrus Cornelius Tissot de Patot, who put his name to several medical treatises written in Latin. What is certain, however, is that Simon Tyssot de Patot published two more books after the adventures of Pierre de Mésange, to which he put his name, both in 1727. *Oeuvres Poétiques Tome I* was apparently intended to be the first of three volumes of his poetry, but was the only one actually to appear. The other, *Lettres choisies*, might consist of two volumes but the only one available for consultation on line is *Tome Second*, and the evidence for the existence of a *Tome Premier* seems a trifle thin, so it is possible that it was so marked in relation to the volume of poetry rather than another volume of the same work. The prefatory essays contained in the first book, which are framed as letters, and the more extensive letters contained in the second, reveal opinions that some critics thought indecent and atheistic, and Tyssot was apparently unable to continue teaching in Deventer thereafter, as well as being unable to publish any further works.

The poems contained in the former volume are long philosophical meditations framed as religious fantasies, with themes drawn from the Bible or the Apocrypha, and cast in rhymed verse: "L'Histoire de la sage et très illustre Reine Ester, espouse du grand Assuerus, roi de Perse" [The Story of the Wise and Illustrious Queen Esther, wife of the great Ahasuerus, King of Persia], "Le Triomphe de la patience, ou L'Histoire du Saint Homme Job, prince arabe" [The

Triumph of Patience; or, The Story of the Holy Man Job, an Arab Prince]
"L'Histoire du pieux et bon homme Tobit." [The Story of the Pious and Good
Tobit], "L'Histoire de la belliqueuse Judith, fille de Merari, native de Bétulie"
[The Story of the Bellicose Judith, Daughter of Merari, Native of Bethulia],
"L'Histoire de la chaste et vertueuse Susanne" [The Story of the Chaste and
Virtuous Susanne] and "L'Histoire de l'Idole Bel et du dragon" [The Story of
the Idol Bel and the Dragon]. The second item, re-examining the book of Job, is
more than two hundred pages long, almost book-length in itself. The poems are
not atheistic—God routinely features in them as a loquacious character—but
they are defiantly irreverent and ironic. Taken in isolation, they probably give a
biased impression of Tyssot's poetic endeavors—the second intended volume
was apparently to have consisted of an extensive reworking of the ancient Greek
pastoral romance of Daphnis and Chloe, which adds plausibility to the idea that
he might also have written pastoral romance in prose—although their satirical
skepticism presumably gives an accurate impression of his philosophical stance.

Throughout the 18th century, books in French that could not obtain the
necessary royal license for publication in Paris, including classic works by Mon-
tesquieu and Voltaire, were frequently printed in Amsterdam, usually anonymously or pseudonymously, and sometimes advertising fictitious places of publication. Tyssot de Patot might well have been one of the founders of that curious tradition, but his own usage of it illustrates the fact that it was by no means
an unproblematic procedure. It did allow him to obtain a measure of posthumous
celebrity, while permitting him to remain partly hidden during his lifetime, but
there can be no doubt that had he been able to publish freely in his own homeland, he might have written and published a great deal more. On the other hand,
the resentments and personal difficulties that led him to identify so strongly not
merely with his heroes but with the legendary Wandering Jew and such inventions of his own as the gypsy genius Beronice, were presumably the sharpest
spur urging him to write anything at all, and to triumph over all the obstacles
making it difficult for him to reach an audience. Perhaps the adventures of
Jacques Massé and Pierre de Mésange could not have been written by anyone
but a rootless exile, and could not have been published anywhere but Amsterdam, in the partly-disguised form in which they appeared—in which case, a debt
is owed the author's actual and potential persecutors as well as to his own idiosyncratic intellect.

It is perhaps worth adding a footnote to this introduction, in view of the
fact that the attribution of the adventures of *Jacques Massé* to Simon Tyssot de
Patot has been challenged recently—although the attribution has been robustly
defended against that challenge by other commentators. The process of translation inevitably brings a translator into close contact with the style and mind-set
of the writers he translates, and for what it may be worth, the fact that I spent
several weeks in intimate contact with the two texts contained in this volume has
left me without the slightest shadow of doubt that they are the work of the same

14

author. In addition to all the thematic and attitudinal links, certain stylistic quirks associated with the frequency and the fashion in which certain words and phrases are employed, including and especially *nonobstant* [notwithstanding, or "in spite of"], *incontinent* [incontinent(ly)] and *de sorte de* ["in consequence of which," or "with the result that"], are common to both texts, albeit becoming gradually more marked as the two narratives progress. I do not think it possible that those similarities could have arisen in any other way than as a consequence of common authorship.

These translations were primarily made from copies of the texts kindly provided by Jean-Marc Lofficier, the first in the form of a Word file and the second a pdf file of a scan of the Etienne Roger edition. In both cases, however, I also had recourse to the various electronic versions available via *gallica, archive.org*, the Hathi Trust and Google Books, in order to fill in gaps or to assist with passages that were difficult to read.

I have made very substantial alterations to the layout of the second text. Although there are two paragraph indentations in volume one, the entire Etienne Roger edition is, in essence, set as a single long block of text, the only breaks, apart from the arbitrary division into two volumes, being blank lines inserted before and after various quoted letters and the two lectures delivered by the narrator. It is not inconceivable that the author wanted the text to be set in that way, but it seems far more likely to me that the printer did it off his own bat, in order to cram the text into the minimum possible space. At any rate, it makes the original text very awkward to read, especially in long passages of dialogue where no textual indication is given when the narrative switches from one speaker to another. I have therefore arranged the text in conventional paragraphs, separating out items of dialogue in the manner that is nowadays standard, and have introduced a number of text-breaks where the narrative skips significant intervals of time, although I stopped short of numbering the "chapters" thus produced.

Brian Stableford

# THE VOYAGES AND ADVENTURES OF JACQUES MASSÉ

*Chapter I.*
*In which is treated the Profession and Embarkation of the author,*
*and the first shipwreck he suffered on the coast of Spain.*

The life of a man has such narrow limits, and the number of years that he can employ in the cultivation of the sciences and the perfection of the arts is so soon elapsed that it is necessary not to be astonished if the progress he makes concludes with so little achieved. The brevity of life is not, however, the only obstacle that is opposed to the natural desire that we have to know everything; the privation of worldly wealth is another, which is scarcely less considerable. It was just when I was about to finish my studies that experience taught me that verity.

The inclination that I had had since the cradle for belles lettres, antiquities and rare and strange things that I saw being brought from distant parts of the world caused my father to send me to school early. The facility with which I learned my lessons was extraordinary; my diligence and my memory procured me the prize in every class. The praise that my masters gave me, combined with the affection that my parents appeared to have for me redoubled my enthusiasm; I gave myself no rest, and employed my time so well that at the age of eighteen I understood Greek and Latin very well; I had passed my examination in philosophy and was well advanced in mathematics when my father, David Massé, who was a ship's captain, had the misfortune to be blown up along with his vessel, owing to the imprudence of a sailor who had accidentally set fire to the powder-store.

That fatal blow struck our family in 1639, on the same day that our army was beaten by the Spaniards at Thionville,[3] which seemed to have happened expressly to give me a firmer memory of it. And as the good man was bound for the Senegal trade[4] and the majority of the crew were to his charge, my mother suddenly found herself widowed, with five children, and almost entirely destitute of worldly wealth.

---

[3] 7 June 1639, during the Thirty Years' War. Thionville was then in the Spanish Netherlands, but is now in Lorraine in northern France.
[4] i.e, the Slave Trade.

That disgrace did not frighten her; as soon as she received the news she sent for us and said to us, in a virile fashion: "Children, the greatest of the misfortunes that can happen to human beings has just happened to you; at the same moment you have been deprived, in the person of my dear husband, of all your wealth and your father; but don't be alarmed by that, because Providence has miraculous ways of sustaining its creatures."

She went on: "Learn by this fatality not only to rely on the arms of the body; the good God will not abandon you. Since the means that remain to me are insufficient to raise you as we had planned, see for which profession you have the greatest penchant.

"For you, Jacques," she said to me, "I am of the opinion that you should embrace the career of surgery. It seems that your father's example leads you to love travel, and that art will favor your design."

In the same way she proposed to the older ones what they ought to undertake; each of them consented, tearfully, and applied himself to it successfully.

My mother, who was from Hesdin, where her parents still lived, quit Abbéville and went to reside there. I was delighted to see that, contrary to my expectations, many people were interested by her misfortune. One of her brothers relieved her of one child, a friend took another, and she was promised twenty places, which would permit her never to want for anything. There were even some who wanted me to change my sentiment, so that I could pursue my studies in order to have greater scope and be better able to help her, in time, to raise the innocents who were not yet able to do anything; but my resolution was made, and my inclination was not to stay there.

I took my leave of the family and our closest acquaintances, who saw me leave with regret, and took the road to Paris, where I arrived a few days later.

The grandeur, the magnificence and the diversity, combined with the tumultuous competition of an innumerable multitude of people of every sort, which I found in that fine place, stunned me at first. All the objects that were presented to my eyes seemed new; it was as if I had only just been born; and Monsieur Rousseau, master surgeon, to whom I had been recommended, was occupied for twelve or fifteen days continually replying to the questions I asked him in order to content my curiosity. He also did me the favor of taking me to Marly, Fontainebleau, Saint-Denis, Saint-German, the Louvre, the Tuileries and several other places that excite the admiration of strangers.

Scarcity adds value, whereas abundance diminishes prices; I finally became accustomed to regarding all those beauties with indifference, and from indifference I passed gradually to disgust; with the result that, abandoning all those curiosities to idle individuals, I began to apply myself with care to the art to which I was destined.

Monsieur Rousseau had a great deal of practical skill, and even more experience; the frequent cures that he achieved gave me further enlightenment every day. Along with that, I did not fail to spend several hours a day on the languages and sciences that had been my occupation previously. I was all the more excited by that because philosophy and mathematics seemed to have become fashionable; all honest men were applying themselves to them, no matter what their age or condition.

A treatise on conic sections appeared, attributed to a son of Monsieur Pascal, a lawyer in Rouen, which astonished many scholars.[5] I was curious to read it, but I found things therein that seemed to be beyond the range of a boy of sixteen, since in places it surpassed Apollonius. Many people shared my opinion, especially when they came to consider that the father of the pretended young author was himself consummate in that science, so the majority concluded that the father, being established, had wanted to do honor to the son by giving him an entry into the world.

Whether or not that was the case, however, it is certain that the younger Monsieur Pascal had a vivid imagination, a great deal of penetration and no less judgment, as became clear subsequently. Monsieur Morin,[6] to whom I took the liberty of addressing myself, and who received me in the most honest fashion possible, immediately procured me the acquaintance of Monsieur Desargues, Monsieur Mydorge[7] and several other mathematicians, who spared me a good deal of work by the fine manuscripts that they communicated to me, and the clear and economical methods that they were kind enough to impart to me.

By means of those learned individuals, I was even able to enter the home of the Reverend Father Mersenne.[8] That skillful man was a great help to me in the intelligence of several questions of physics and metaphysics. As he had close links with Monsieur Descartes, who was then in Holland. I did not propose any difficulty to him that he did not clarify for me sooner or later. He was the one who first put in my hand the celebrated philosopher's six meditations.

The desire to learn to demonstrate the existence of a God, the immateriality of the soul and its real distinction from the body caused me to read them with all the attention of which I was capable; but I admit frankly that I was not satisfied. His method for the good guidance of reason, and the search for verity in the sci-

---

[5] Blaise Pascal's essay on conic sections was first published in 1639, although only a few copies were printed. His father Etienne Pascal (1588-1651) was moderately famous by that time.

[6] Jean-Baptiste Morin (1583-1656) was a professor at the Collège Royal, the predecessor of the College de France, in 1639.

[7] Girard Desargues (1591-1661) and Claude Mydorge (1585-1647)

[8] Marin Mersenne (1588-1648) was resident at the convent of L'Annonciade in Paris in 1639; four years earlier, he had set up the Académie Parisienne, which put most of the world's leading mathematicians in touch with one another and helped to foster the rapid advances made in that period. The other mathematicians named were all members, as were numerous astronomers and philosophers, including René Descartes.

ences, his dioptrics, his meteors, his world, and, in general, everything I had seen of him, charmed me, but if his metaphysics, I say once again that nothing came back to me but the subtlety of the reasoning.

I was forced to conclude that we ought not to venture beyond the range of our limited intelligence, and only to entertain material bodies, limiting ourselves to explaining the nature, the appearance, the number, the properties, the changes caused by movement, and that which can be most profitably observed, for the good of society, for intelligence and the advancement of human knowledge, without getting involved in trying to render manifest, and, so to speak, visible, subjects that are hidden by their nature, and which will probably be objects of our faith and admiration forever.

It soon appeared that I was not alone in that sentiment. An unknown author published an anonymous book in The Hague, in which he claimed to devastate Monsieur Descartes' philosophy. At the same time, Père Bourdin attacked it by means of public theses.[9] Then the objections appear of Messieurs Hobbes, Gassendi, Arnaud and others, on the subject of his metaphysics.

As I was interested in the author, I was curious to see all that I could of these disputes; that took up a great deal of my time. My master often reproached me; he claimed that I was neglecting the principal in order to attach myself to things that could not be of any great utility to me, several of which did not have universal approval. He even went so far one day as to reproach me for having set forth on the road of atheism, in that I had already embraced an opinion that had been newly condemned by the tribunal of the Inquisition, in the person of Galileo, who had been confined in the prison of the Holy Office after his treatise on the circular movement of the earth, in accordance with the principles of Copernicus, had been burned by the executioner.

In order that those reproaches should not discourage me completely, they were carefully seasoned with praise for the considerable talent that I had for surgery, and the knowledge that I had acquired in spite of the time that I devoted to other occupations. Finally, seeing that he was incapable of giving me an aversion for those beautiful sciences, he formed the idea of embarking me in marriage. He had a very pretty niece, who, following the death of her mother, ought to have considerable wealth, which he never stopped mentioning to me. He often gave me to understand that he would not be sorry if I had her for a wife, and that, being old, he was quite capable of leaving his shop entirely to me, which was very well stocked—but that was not where I was bound.

---

[9] Pierre Bourdin (1595-1653) was one of numerous attackers of Descartes's philosophy, as set out in the *Discourse* and *Essais* of 1637 (the *Meditations* were not published until 1641, but Descartes was discussing them with Mersenne by letter in 1639). The reference to an anonymous book published in The Hague might be to the criticisms of Descartes published by Jan Stampioen, who was resident there, although he normally signed his works.

Perceiving my indifference, he became much cooler in my regard than he had been before. From then on he began to neglect me, and to hide things from me that I could only learn from him, with the result that after my two years of apprenticeship I went to Dieppe, where I remained for a further entire year with Monsieur La Croix, who was also, indubitably, a very skillful master.

I shall not amuse myself here by reciting the petty adventures that I had in either of those cities; I do not think them sufficiently considerable for that. I cannot, however, pass over in silence the fact that, in the meantime, a man arrived in that maritime location whom the vulgar call the Wandering Jew. My master, who was curious and easy-going, after having talked to him several times when the occasion arose, invited him to dinner in order to have the pleasure of hearing him talk for several hours.

The first thing he told us was that he was a contemporary of Jesus Christ, whom he had seen crucified with his own eyes. "My name," he added, "is Michob, formerly a domestic servant of Pontius Pilate. That Roman judge having pronounced sentence on Jesus, I approached the supposed criminal and said to him: 'What are you still doing here? Did you not hear your sentence? Go on; what are you waiting for?' On which that holy man replied to me: 'I shall go, but you shall remain here until I return.'

"That was," he said, "more than sixteen centuries ago; I hope that will be the greater part of the time that I must wander the earth. The greater number of people seek to live; there are few who would not wish to add a century to the term they have already passed, if that were within their power, but for myself, I wish with all my heart that I had died a thousand years ago."

As the odd fellow spoke all sorts of languages, and had in consequence a good memory, and had done nothing but travel, it was a pleasure to hear him talk about a thousand things as clear and evident verities that remote centuries have only permitted us no envisage confusedly, and in a very uncertain manner. There was no corner of the world to which he was not certain that he had been. He named several kingdoms and republics in the vicinity of the two poles, of which we had never heard mention, but which, according to him, would soon be discovered. All the courts of the world were known to him. He was not ignorant of the slightest circumstances of the most remarkable revolutions to which empires had been subject since he had been in the world. Moreover, the most remove incidents appeared to him to be as recent as if they had just occurred.

The junction at which we were all ears was when he began to tell us about the saints who were resuscitated at the crucifixion of Jesus Christ. All Jerusalem, he said, was in panic when the rumor spread that those who were in the cemeteries had seen the earth move in several places, sepulchers open without anyone laying a hand on them, and naked bodies appear, and make a thousand different movements.

"The fear," he continued, "occasioned by such an unexpected spectacle caused fever, and even death, in several of the witnesses. The boldest, however, saw it through to the end, and they were marvelously surprised when, a short while later, they saw human creatures emerging entirely from their tombs and fleeing with great urgency through the multitude, which opened to give them passage, letting themselves fall to the ground, as if all of them had to go to occupy their places.

"No one could see," Michob added, "no matter how attentive they were, what sex the resuscitated individuals were; they all appeared to be the same height, the same age, and similar in girth, not bearing any mark by which they could be distinguished from one another; their bellies were flat, and seemed as if they were attached to the loins; several kept their mouths open, but no teeth could be perceived therein; and their rounded and uniform fingers seemed entirely devoid of nails. That led to the conclusion that all the excremental parts, and those that serve us for grinding, receiving and dissolving aliments while we are subject to death, do not accompany us into the other world—where they would not, in fact, have any utility."

Finally, according to what he said, no one had ever known positively what had become of those individuals; the rumor ran around, however, a few days later, that they had withdrawn to Galilee, where they were to confer with Jesus Christ, and would be taken from there to the abode of the blessed.

As is easily believable, that curious subject-matter did not fail to give rise to a long conversation. It was midnight when our guest left us, and my master, in spite of the conversations that he had had with him elsewhere, would gladly have retained him until the next day.

As the magistrates treated him as a visionary, people put very little stock in what he said, so he was not at all dangerous and he did not ask anything of anyone. The poor people and a few credulous and superstitious women, who regarded him as a prodigy, furnished him sufficiently with everything that he needed; in addition to which he did not remain long in any one place, and effectively did nothing but wander the world.

His departure, combined with all the fine things that I had heard him say about foreign lands, augmented even further the natural desire that I had to travel. I communicated my design to Monsieur La Croix, and, as he had already done me the favor of carefully publishing at every opportunity the progress that I had made in my profession, I had no difficulty of joining as a surgeon the vessel of Captain Le Sage, which was going to undertake a voyage to Martinique.

We left Dieppe on the twenty-first of May 1643. Our ship only carried four cannon, and the crew consisted of fifty-two men. Although the captain was a Huguenot, he was nonetheless a perfectly honest man, equitable and extremely devout. He would not permit a single day to go past without everyone being present, morning and evening, at public prayers, which a student of theology named Pierre Du Quesne led with much zeal and education. Speaking for myself, I can say that I immediately conceived a high esteem for the young man, and that I had not known him for a fortnight when I had reduced the respect that the monks had inculcated in me for the saints of paradise.

Misfortune did not want me to profit for long from the salutary lessons that I received in that agreeable company. Twenty-seven days after our departure, having reached the latitude of Cape Finisterre, it was perceived that our ship was taking on much more water than usual. The carpenters, who were immediately alerted, applied all possible diligence to discovering the cause of the disaster, but in spite of their great zeal, and the pumps that were operating day and night, it was impossible for them to find a means of preventing it.

After thirty-six hours the water had risen to such a height that it was pouring out of the portholes. The captain, seeing that there was no remedy, had the two launches put to sea and commanded us to arrange ourselves in the larger one, taking absolutely nothing but money, which we did not have in great quantity. Monsieur Le Sage was still aboard, with the mate, the pilots and four young midshipmen, who were not there for their pleasure, when the ship sank like a stone. Although they had been preparing for that eventuality, they had not intended to endanger their persons. Still being within range, we gave them all the help of which we were capable, but could not prevent the loss of one of the four boys, named Colombier, a native of Picardy, who had not yet reached the age of fifteen.

We were obliged to reconcile ourselves to that loss, and determine for what coast it was appropriate to head, for we had to try to reach land in less than two days. The wind, which was blowing from the south-east, was not at all favorable for that. What was more mortifying was that we had very little food, as much for having poorly understood the meaning of the captain's words as because we had not had time to furnish ourselves with any. We were also destitute of a compass to guide us.

The sky was tranquil enough, the sea calm and the weather agreeable, but everyone was apprehensive for the future. However, we made every effort to get closer to the shore, by taking sightings of the sun by day and the stars by night, without being able to observe that we were making considerable progress, with the result that we were beginning to despair of our salvation. A thick fog that fell on the third day contributed not a little to that.

It was in those conditions, when it was impossible to see more than two feet, that the small launch drifted away from ours. The captain having perceived that, by virtue of the cries that we uttered reciprocally in order to inform ourselves, pressed the debilitated oarsmen to make further efforts to catch up, but they succeeded only too well, for having crashed into our small boat, those who were in it were so alarmed that they all stood up at the same time, imparting such a shock to it that it overturned. We had a great deal of difficulty rescuing them, and even more in making room for them. We were all on top of one another, and we had had absolutely nothing to eat for twenty-four hours.

Finally the good Lord desired that toward noon, the day star having dissipated the fog, we discovered several sails heading toward us; the joy that agreeable sight gave us is inexpressible. We immediately turned toward them in order to go to meet them; three or four hours thereafter they reached us, and Captain Davidson received us favorably aboard his vessel. It was out of Portsmouth and was escorting a convoy of seventeen English merchant ships heading for Lisbon.

As our guts had not yet had time to shrink, and as the physicians that we consulted on that score opined that there was no danger in eating and drinking at our ease, we were brought food, and everyone took pleasure in seeing our chins move. Everything that was served to us disappeared as if it had been thrown into a well. It was only when we were full that we felt sated.

A profound drowsiness immediately followed the repose that we finally accorded to or jaws; I doubt that there was one of us who did not sleep for at least twenty hours before being woken up. After a second meal we felt completely recovered. A ship's lieutenant who spoke French wanted me to give him details of our misfortunes, by which he seemed touched in places, and in others could not help laughing.

Finally, we arrived in port and were able to set foot in land in Lisbon on the first of July, without having lost anyone else except Colombier.

## Chapter II
## *Of the Author's Sojourn in Lisbon, etc.*

Lisbon is situated near the mouth of the Tagus, in an extremely diverting location; it is surely one of the most beautiful cities in Europe. Commerce is very considerable there, which renders it very populous and rich. According to the approximate calculation I made, it must contain more than twenty thousand houses. There are thirty-five or forty gates, for the convenience of the inhabitants, and I am greatly mistaken if it is not two full leagues around.

A certain Monsieur Du Pré, a surgeon by profession, was the person to whom I addressed myself, as a man who had a thriving practice, and could give me work. Indeed, the worthy man received me with open arms. I had not been with him long when I noticed that he was Reformed; he only went to mass very rarely, but he often read sermons to his children, and a Sunday rarely went be without him subjecting them to a detailed catechism. For his part, he soon recognized that I was nothing less than a bigot. He admitted to me that he kept a Bible in his home for the instruction of his family; he even brought for me to see.

I must not lie; the first time that I read it, which I did in a very short time, I took it for a rather badly-concocted romance, the fables of which I nevertheless considered sacred. *Genesis*, in my view, was pure fiction, the laws and ceremonies of the Jews a badinage of vain puerilities, the prophets an abysm of obscurities and ridiculous gibberish, and the gospel a pious fraud invented to lull young women and common minds.

What shocked me from the start was to see the creation of light of precede the luminaries that produce it, without which there would have been nothing but darkness and obscurity. Then I latched on to the necessity of laboring and dying, which was only imposed on man, it is claimed, in consequence of his crime. After that came the sentence pronounced on woman, to give birth in pain, and on the serpent, to crawl on its belly, as if it had previously had limbs; the rainbow, which was placed in the sky after the deluge, in order to banish the human dread of perishing for a second time beneath the waters; the mercy that Heaven granted Lot to leave Sodom, in order to allow him incontinently to commit double incest with his daughters thereafter; the loves of Pharaoh and Sara the wife of Abraham, and the rape of the same person in decrepit old age by Abimelech, king of Gerar; the frequent dialogues of the creature with his creator; the passage of the Red Sea and many other miracles made for the Jews; the ass that was made to talk in order to say so little, and a thousand other difficulties of that sort embarrassed my reason prodigiously.

I could not understand that effects could occur before their causes; I had learned the contrary in school, and daily experience had so frequently confirmed the verity in the works of nature that I did not even deign to make the slightest reflection thereon. It appeared to me to be no less absurd that humans would have been immortal if they had not disobeyed God, since I could not see any appearance that the order and constitution of their parts had undergone any alteration since receiving life. And it did not seem reasonable to me that the earth had been in a condition to produce fruits continually in the same abundance without being cultivated, unless it was entirely different in nature from what it is presently, which is not plausible.

A hundred voyages that I had read assured me that in general, the women who inhabit the East Indies, Africa and the Americas, in the equatorial regions, suffer little pain when it is a matter of bringing a human creature into the world. In that regard, those of Brazil ordinarily go to deliver near to a spring river, where they wash themselves, clean the infant and then take it to their husbands, who go to bed, swaddle the child and receive the felicitations, while the woman occupies herself in going to fetch and prepare food for them. Instead of which, among the peoples who live in the polar regions, the members of the female sex suffer greatly in those circumstances and often perish as a result, from which it follows that they vary in proportion to the climate and the constitution of individuals. That is found even in animals, which have not sinned, and are nonetheless subject to these various changes.

Finally—for it would require long volumes to exhaust the matter—knowing the cause of the rainbow and its grandeur, as well as its colors, and having made artificial ones a hundred times myself, as is easy to do by scattering a quantity of water with which one has filled one's mouth in all directions, in a place opposed to the sun's rays and beyond which there are no very bright objects, and in several other ways, I had difficulty believing it when Moses talks about it as a previously-unknown meteorological phenomenon.

Nevertheless, all these obstacles did not deter me entirely; I attempted to read the holy book a second time, on the condition that as I went through it, I would ask my master for explanations. He consented to that, and we were embroiled in argument every day. The worthy man often became angry with me, and I got off lightly when he only called me libertine, stubborn and incredulous.

"It is not astonishing," I said to him sometimes, "to see a host of swimmers following the rapid course of a vast and profound river, since that is no less agreeable than easy, but as soon as it occurs to one of them to turn his back on the rest, head upstream and advance with promptitude toward its source, that action surprises the observers. Some consider him with admiration, others gaze at him enviously; above all, his companions are jealous; they are bursting with resentment and omit nothing that they are capable of imagining to decry and defeat him, because what he is doing is an evident mark of skill and vigor on his part, and pure laziness and weakness on theirs.

"It is the same with the sentiments we have on the subject of the sciences, and principally that of religion; those that we have acquired from birth remain with us, and we absolutely cannot abide others; everything that is not in conformity with them displeases us, and one passes infallibly for a brainless individual or a blackguard from the moment when one speaks about departing from them. I tell you, however, that, in the same way that I have a much better opinion of a man who swims against the current of a torrent than one who allows himself to be borne along insensibly by its waves, I make an infinitely more advantageous judgment of the penetration and solidity of the mind of the man who examines everything, and sometimes opposes himself to opinions received for a long time, which others have inherited from their ancestors and only conserve because of their antiquity or their authority; because it rarely happens that one departs from the common way, given that there are few reasons to do so, but many incentives not to deviate from it."

During our first conversations something else occurred that gave rise to further dispute. The captain of a ship that had brought a few negroes from Africa made a present of one of the best constituted to one of his friends, a man of consideration and great means, but capricious and difficult. The negro, having remained for some years in the home of such a rigid master, and having suffered a thousand indignities, lost his self-possession and resolved, no matter what might happen, to take his revenge in the most dangerous fashion.

To that effect he went to the local apothecary and, under the pretext that he was extremely inconvenienced by rats, asked for two or three sous of arsenic. Scarcely had he left the shop in order to deliver a few messages with which he had been charged than the apothecary sent word to the Monsieur that, since his Moor had just come to obtain rat poison, it had occurred to him that he knew an admirable composition to exterminate such vermin, and that if he wished, he would send him the recipe immediately.

That message astonished the Monsieur, who was anxious by nature, and who remembered very clearly that he had maltreated his domestic severely the previous day. He summoned him in order to ask him what he intended to do with the poison, and swore by all that he held sacred that he would take away his life if he saw any evidence in him giving rise to the slightest suspicion.

It happened that the valet was not there. As soon as he came back, a maid-servant, gripped by the fear of seeing him beaten severely, warned him secretly about what had happened. The unfortunate man was scared, and, not feeling sufficiently brazen to support the examination to which he was destined, he slipped upstairs quietly, and without further ado, hanged himself.

Meanwhile, his master was becoming terribly impatient to see him; he sent several people to look for him in the places to which he had sent him; finally, he was quite astonished when, an hour later, a lackey came to report that he had found him hanged in the grain-loft.

The rumor of the tragic action spread through the quarter; my master went running, as to the house of one of his principal clients, and after having conversed with the Monsieur, he begged him for many reasons to act in such a way that he could obtain the cadaver. As he had credit, the Monsieur made no difficulties about assuring him that he would get it, and kept his word the same day.

As soon as it was in our hands we carried out a formal dissection. All the body parts were disposed as in the body of a white man—at least, we did not notice any difference—but what surprised us equally was that immediately below the epidermis we discovered an extremely slack and delicate membrane, which my master had never perceived elsewhere and of which I had not heard any mention.

He immediately reported that discovery to a famous physician of the city, who yielded to his pleas; that clever man did not seem as astonished that I had imagined; the same thing had happened to him on a similar occasion, although that had been unique in his lifetime, having never had any other negroes in his hands. Thus, we judged that it must one the veritable cause of the blackness of that species of humans, in that the tunic in question doubtless softens and absorbs rays of light, as, on the contrary, a sheet of quicksilver applied behind a Venetian glass reflects them and sends them back whence they came. That gave rise to arguments regarding the origins of Ethiopians, which does not seem to be the same as that of other humans, in view of that remarkable difference.

Following that principle, I tried to insist on consequences that were nothing less than a complete inversion of the system of the sacred author that we were discussing, but they closed me mouth, saying that there are many things that God wants us to admire, but forbids us to investigate in depth.

I took considerable pleasure, regardless, in hearing that doctor talk about the operations of the human body. He spoke Latin like Cicero, and was no less accomplished as an orator than Demosthenes. Everything that he said charmed me, because he only expressed things in forceful and well-chosen terms, and strove to make everything clear and intelligible.

I shall not amuse myself by giving details here of the long conversation that we had on that fine subject; I will only say that we pointed out to us three things that generally extend over the entire body: one external, which is the skin, and the others in the interior and most hidden parts of the mass, to wit, the veins and nerves.

"The skin," he said, "is necessary to the animal, in that it covers all the limbs. Like a shell, it is what encloses and envelops all the parts, in such a manner that it is capable, if one accustoms it appropriately, and one does in relation to the face and hands, of protecting us against the insults of the air.

"The veins and arteries, the little streams in which the blood flows, the veritable principle and immediate cause of life, take their origin from the heart and extend through the entire machine, with the consequence that it is not possible to prick it in any location, however small it might be, without piercing some of their branches, which is visible by the vermilion coloration of the humor that then leaks out.

"Finally, it is obvious that there is no place where nerves are not encountered, and one can easily convince those who attempt to deny it or who hold it is doubt. Those nerves all come, without exception, from the brain, where, like so many cords, rods or hollow tubes, they have one of their extremities arranged in such a way, one after another, that they form collectively a sort of sphere, in the middle of which is located an extremely sensitive and delicate little glandule, attached at its base to an infinite number of imperceptible arteries, which bring from the heart a prodigious quantity of spirits, which maintain it in a continuous agitation, and are ready to cede to the slightest foreign movement.

"Assuming, then, that these nerves, or the tiny fibers of which they are composed, are filled with spirits, as in fact they always are while one is alert, whereas they are partly deprived on them for as long as sleep lasts, if it happens that an object of some kind collides with the external end or some other part of the tubes, it is evident that, being full and in consequence taut, the other extremity, which is the brain, must feel the shock, and communicate that movement to the gland, which one cannot dispense with establishing as the seat of the common sense; it is neither more nor less impossible than supposing that I am holding in my hand a thousand ends of threads, attached together, and that someone pulls one of them, which I perceive incontinently, but without being able to distinguish the place from which that attraction came.

"As experience has taught me since infancy that the blows, cuts and other inconveniences that my body receives ordinarily come from outside, every time I feel the slightest agitation in one of my parts, I cannot help attributing the cause to some exterior agent, and believing that it is really the extremity of some nerve, and not any other of its parts, that has been touched. And we are naturally so strongly preoccupied with that sentiment that people who have had the misfortune to lose an arm, for example, proclaim loudly of the pain they feel in the fingers of the hand that they no longer have, and no other place—which is confirmed by experience every day.

"Thus, whether it is the impulsion given to the optic nerves by rays of light, or to the nerve-endings in the tongue by tiny particles of food, in accordance with their shape and movement, or to the mammillary apophyses called odorant, by imperceptible particles emitted by bodies, or any other fashion whatsoever, it amounts to the same thing: the organs might be different, but touch is the sole and unique cause of all the perceptions of which we are capable.

"In consequence, it appears that those who have fixed the number of the senses at five have not known nature very well, any more than a few others who, not knowing in which of the five categories they ought to place hunger, thirst and the pleasure of amour, have counted as far as eight; since it seems clear, by virtue of what we have just said, that there is definitely only one.

"I can say more," he continued. "It would not be difficult for me to demonstrate, with the aid of a geometrical figure, that it impossible, considering things rigorously, as perfectly as our nature can permit, to have more than one perception at the same time, and that when two or three occur together, they are necessarily confused, just as experience informs us that of all the parts of an object we envisage, there is only one that corresponds to the optical axes, which see perfectly and distinctly, the others only being perceived in proportion to their proximity to the center. Our ideas, or images of thought, are no different from our perceptions, for although one can make two species of them, which we distinguish by the terms conception and imagination, it is certain that touch is the sole cause of both; it is the unique source of all human knowledge, and even of our reason, which is fundamentally only the assembly or dissociation of names that we have imposed by common consent on substances, such as they appear to the senses—which is to say, in conformity with their qualities, and not their essence.

"Other animals, having organs similar to ours, doubtless also have the same perceptions; it is only their greater or lesser extent that can make a difference. Thus, animals have reason, and they are deprived of it, than can only be a consequence of their lack of speech, in order to give names, as we do, to the things that movement renders capable of affecting them; for in meantime, they are perfectly able to distinguish them."

A loud scream uttered by the maidservant at this point abruptly interrupted our physician. While bringing an armful of wood from the loft, the poor girl had lost her footing and had fallen down the stairs. We all rushed to help her, and found that she had broken her right leg. After witnessing the first apparatus that was applied to it, the doctor went home, to my great regret, since, in addition to a few objections that I was ready to raise, I would very much have liked to hear the conclusion of a discourse as curious as the one with which he had been entertaining us, and which would, according to all appearances have had consequences that are not within the grasp of everyone. The regret was all the greater subsequently, because I never found an opportunity to renew it and to persuade the amiable man to discuss the same matter with me.

Setting all that aside, I must say that, although Monsieur Du Pré was nothing less than a philosopher, his small enlightenments were no great help to me; and that the commentaries of Monsieur Calvin, which he put in my hands, made very little contribution. In consequence of that, I had occasion to remark that the creation of light can mean nothing, except the formation of the subtle matter of which the stars were composed on the fourth day, and that if Moses speaks of day and night before that, it is by anticipation, as he says elsewhere that God had made humans male and female before he came upon Adam in a profound sleep and formed a companion out of one of his ribs.

I also understood quite easily, with regard to the punishments that he imposed on our first parents, the rainbow, etc., that they were both natural signs to begin with, which God the changed into signs of institution, as we see happening, shortly thereafter with the holy sacraments of baptism and communion. As for the term commencement, which is at the beginning of Genesis, that did not cause me any difficulty, although many people are embarrassed by it; I knew full well that in philosophy, it is necessary to distinguish between internal and external terms, just as one distinguishes in geometry between an external and internal dimension, if it is permissible to express it in those terms—which is to say that it is necessary to differentiate between a measured and contained magnitude and another that is not.

My bedroom, for example, has dimensions; that is incontestable, but speculation alone can fix its contents; one must add practice to that, and make use of some common measure that people have agreed beforehand, in order to be able to say at a given point how many feet and inches, or square inches, it contains; by that means, the dimensions, which were initially internal and hidden, become external and known, in relation to external measurements that have served to determine its contents.

All natural entities, therefore, have an internal time and an external time; their interior time is duration, by which they remain in their actual and veritable existence and which extends from their beginning to the end; their external time is the duration of the earth, in that its movement is employed to measure it, with the consequence that the external time of one thing is in relation to its interior time as measure is to the thing being measured.

Before the birth of the world, we can only have the idea of an abstract internal time because there was then nothing existent except God, the being of beings, whose duration has no beginning or end, and cannot properly be defined or measured; but from the moment the sun appeared in the firmament, and the earth was imagined rotating on its axis, around which it is carried in a certain space of time from west to east, each of those periods has been given the name of the natural day, and the lesser parts of hours, minutes, etc., just as one calls the composite of seven days a week, one revolution of the moon from west to east a month, one of the earth around the sun a year, etc. These common measurements enable us to designate time by rendering the internal that is its nature external for our usage. There is no marvel if, not going beyond that, we limit ourselves to that principle and only count time since there have been measures appropriate to fix duration.

The solution of these difficulties facilitated the acquaintance of others for me. I began to perceive the spinal nature of the great work of redemption, the connection and relationship between the parts of the Old Testament and those of the New; how the antecedents and the consequences are reciprocally dependent on one another; with the result that, at the third attempt, I concluded that the creation of the world, the fall of man, the threats the promises, the deluge, circumcision, dreams, visions, the passage of the Red Sea, ceremonial laws, the prophecies and everything remarkable that happened in the Kingdom of Israel were merely types, allegories, emblems, figures and shadows, which only related to the new alliance, which only shone by the light of the gospel and of which Christ was the veritable body.

My host was charmed by this metamorphosis; he admired it, as if I had passed through a chill that had caused me to regard things with scorn to a zeal that no longer permitted me to consider them with anything but esteem. Everything that I did attracted his applause; he had never seen my like.

As nothing is perfect in this world, however, one thing remained that afflicted his heart. I was naturally blond, and my mother had accustomed me to wearing my hair long, covering my shoulders; that shocked Monsieur Du Pré.

"Is it possible," he said to me several times, "that a boy who has so much disposition to resolve the most difficult passages of the scriptures cannot see that Saint Paul positively forbids wearing hair long, and that he even considers it shameful for a man to nourish and care for it?"

For a long time I treated the remonstrations he made to me as jokes, but seeing that he was speaking to me about it more seriously every day, I said to him one day in my turn: "Can it be, Monsieur, that you are unaware that, just as the variation in the seasons of the year obliges us to dress differently according to whether it is hot or cold, the changes that occur in society require us to observe different maxims?

"Once," I continued, "long hair was a mark of subservience; when a slave was freed his head was shaved, as a sign of the liberty that had been accorded to him; it is that to which the prophet is alluding. Under the law we were slaves of sin, he meant, but we are liberated therefrom under grace; why should we still wear the marks of our former servitude, as a woman does who is under the dependency of her husband? In those times, there were still slaves; presently, the usage is banned among Christians. I know that the text says that it is nature that shows us that we ought not to make a display of our hair, but it is necessary not to take that term rigorously; in this instance 'nature' only signifies custom.

"Naturally, we have nothing superfluous; hair has been given to us for the protection and conservation of our head and the upper parts of the body, as the fingernails re the weapons that have been provided for our defense. It is, therefore, not nature that enjoins us to cut the one and bite the other, it is what we call fashion, decorum, and certain civil laws established among peoples, which have eventually come to be regarded as natural. That fashion presently authorizes long hair; I do not think that I am doing any harm in following it, especially now, when a large number of sensible people, and the majority of theologians, admit that it is a matter of absolute indifference."

All of that was incapable of satisfying my master; in order to content him it as necessary to permit him to make use of his scissors, and to shorten my hair at least to the level of the ears. That change caused me some pain, but after all, what will one not do in order to have peace and live in harmony with one's neighbor? In fact, that complaisance completed attracting his amity so fully that he would have given me his blood if it had any use for it; his person, his family and his property were all at my service; I only had to call upon it.

In addition to these advantages, which were already very considerable for a foreigner, he procured me the acquaintance of several of his intimate friends, among others, an agent of a Dutch company, who was one of the nicest fellows I have ever known. He spoke French well enough, and understood his religion perfectly, so I had occasion to converse with him every time we met, which happened as often as was possible for me. I had the pleasure moreover, that he accommodated me with everything I needed, without wanting to permit me to importune my master, who, was, however, accommodating and full of good will. He never treated anyone, without obliging me to join the party, which had the disadvantage that he treated so well that one usually felt the effects two days later.

Once, he drew me into so much debauchery that I was gripped by a violent fever the next day, which truly nearly killed me; in the space of the three weeks I had it, I became as thin as a skeleton, absolutely no more than skin and bone, and my physician despaired of my recovery. I finally got myself out of it, however, by means of a well-organized diet, and while I gradually recovered, I never ceased making mature reflections on the severe laws that nature observes so punctiliously toward poor mortals. After having recognized that there are few excesses that she does not punish, I concluded that frugality and temperance are the veritable means of always having a free mind, and sheltering the body from all the ills to which almost all of us are subject which caused me to make a firm resolution to be wiser in the future than I had been in the past, and never to do anything for which I would reproach myself subsequently.

Van Dyk—that was the Dutchman's name—had reached that sentiment before me, but his generosity when he regaled his friends sometimes obliged him to relax, and not to put into practice the pious lessons that he scarcely failed to give when he put himself out on behalf of others. Eventually, however, I got him to agree that it was better to pass for economical than liberal and generous when health is at stake.

In the meantime, that honest man had an unfortunate experience that caused me just as much chagrin as him. He received a letter by which the wife of one of his merchants instructed him, in her husband's absence, to give her nephew, the son of Monsieur Heudde, who had departed for Lisbon, everything that he might need to continue his voyage; and that a full and itemized account should be sent to her, which she would settle.

About a fortnight later, Monsieur Heudde arrived at Van Dyk's house accompanied by a valet, who, like him, was rather poorly dressed. The first thing that he asked what whether he had received a letter from his aunt sent some time ago; the factor having replied yes, he started recounting many details about several people of his acquaintance; then he talked about the plan he had made of seeing Portugal, traversing Spain and then of passing through the realm of France, eventually to return home via the British Isles. Finally they reached the money that he would need to travel through so many countries. Van Dyk told him what he thought, and after having exhorted him not to make any unneces-sary expenditure, he also recommended him not to undertake anything that was beneath him, since he had instructions to furnish him with everything necessary, not only in Lisbon but in all the places he was to pass through—which would not be difficult, since he had very good connections, directly or indirectly, in most of the large cities of Europe.

Monsieur Heudde seemed very edified by this compliment; he contented himself with a sum of five hundred francs and a few useful addresses, and after having stayed for a few days, he continued his journey. Van Dyk, who was exact in matters of business, immediately sent news to his principal of what had passed between him and her nephew, and the route that he had taken.

A week later, however, he was surprised to encounter Monsieur Heudde's supposed valet in the street, and, having asked him why his master had not yet departed he was even more astonished learn that he did not know him and did not know what had become of him.

"A few days ago," he said, "I arrived here from Bordeaux with the design of going to America; the Monsieur to whom you are referring was on the same ship; he proposed that I serve him for the time that he was in the city, on condi-tion that he gave me twenty sols a day and expenses. He paid me for the week, bade me farewell, and I haven't heard any mention of him since."

That speech alarmed my friend somewhat, and although he had no certain-ty as yet of having been duped, he took the precaution of writing immediately to the people to whom he had recommended his voyager, and asking them not to give him anything until further notice. That protected him against the possibility of further losses, but not that of his three hundred ducats. The reply came from Holland that they did not know what he was talking about and that the pretended Monsieur Heudde appeared to be a rogue, doubtless in search of a gallows.

Although the damage was not considerable in proportion to the conquests that Monsieur Van Dyk had made, it afflicted him nevertheless; he employed all possible means to discover the thief, but all his pursuits were futile, and I do not know whether he ever heard any more about it, because I left shortly thereafter

Although I was perfectly comfortable, it is necessary to admit that I ob-tained no great pleasure from being there. The income I received was very me-diocre, and my principal aim was to see the country. The friends I had made and my master's reputation facilitated the means to leave.

*Chapter III*
*Of the Author's Second Voyage, and his Shipwreck*
*on an Unknown Coast*

I found the opportunity to join a Portuguese vessel that was to go to the East Indies in the company of three other vessels. The man in command was named Dom Pedro. It was only carrying twenty cannons, but the crew consisted of a hundred and forty-seven men, among whom there were numerous Frenchmen, all of whom understood the Portuguese language. Everything being ready, we set sail on the fifth of June 1644, in very favorable weather.

The first misfortune that befell us was in the person of our captain. He was, in fact, a man of consummate experience, but he was brutal and debauched. On the tenth day after our departure, when he had, as usual, taken a strong dose of eau-de-vie, he lost his temper with one of the sailors, to such an extent that he wanted to pass from threats to blows. The mariner, who was inconstant, started laughing and fled. Irritated, Dom Pedro pursued him with a crowbar in his hand, swearing that he was going to break his neck. While they were running after one another, our officer tripped, and after a few pirouettes, fell so heavily against the capstan that he broke his left arm three inches above the elbow.

With that, I was summoned; I examined the injury and found that the bone had snapped completely. After mature deliberation I decided that it was absolutely necessary to resort to the saw. In spite of all that I was capable of saying to the patient there was no means of persuading him to undergo that operation, and he swore that he would rather die than resort to such an unpleasant extremity. It was necessary for me to agree, reluctantly, to treat him as he wished, but what I had anticipated transpired two days later. The wound became inflamed, gangrene set in, and my patient died five days after his fall.

The crew was extremely alarmed by that loss, which seemed to us to be a bad omen; it was necessary, however, to reconcile ourselves to it. Honors were rendered to his body; then it was buried at sea to the sound of a canon.

We continued, however, to make good progress; small storms blew up from time to time, but nothing dangerous. The greatest misfortune that overtook us was that we were separated from the other vessels, with which we had no further contact.

Having reached Ascension Island, we perceived that our water supplies were badly polluted, so it was decided that we would call in at Saint Helena, fearing that the number of our invalids, which was considerable, would be further augmented if we deferred landfall until we reached the Cape of Good Hope.

When we could already see the island in the distance, however, and were congratulating one another, we saw a waterspout, which appeared to us to have the girth of a large barrel, within cannon-shot of our ship. Having only seen the

35

phenomenon in paintings and read about it in the accounts of voyagers, I studied it with all the application of which I was capable, and concluded that it must be an effect of an agitated region of air driven vehemently in the vast extent of our atmosphere, which had just encountered another kind of turbulence moving in the opposite direction, resulting in a downward rotatory movement, thus forming a cylinder, which elongates instantly as soon as it touches the surface of the water. The sea being then subjected to high pressure outside that location, it follows necessarily that, as we see in the matter of pumps, syringes and suckers, the matter corresponding to the center of the column rises up.

That happens rapidly and forcefully enough to lift up large fish. We were all astonished to see the sky, serene as it had been, swiftly covered with thick clouds, which obscured the air in a trice. The wind commenced blowing horribly, the sea was stirred up, the waves swelled, and one might have thought that nature was angry, threatening to drown us all. The sailors were in great haste to furl the sails as soon as possible, with the sole exception of the bourcet pacifier; and, having changed course, we pitched and rolled for a long time. In the meantime, the vessel was carried away with such violence that it was necessary to renounce the mainsail again for fear of being driven on to some deadly reef.

I cannot bring myself to describe here in detail, following the journal that I kept of it, everything that happened to us during that frightful tempest, which lasted twenty-two days; that would require several sheets of paper, and would cause the reader nothing but compassion and sadness. It was not only the few women and children we had aboard who uttered howls capable of melting hearts of stone; the majority of the men were gripped by fear to the depths of the soul.

Not a day passed without out suffering at least one death. We lost our pilot and the bosun; only the ship's captain—the former first mate—remained who was capable of steering the vessel well, and he too was quite ill. During that cruel storm we were constrained to throw into the sea, at various times, a dozen of our cannons, and everything that we could of the cargo; we also lost the majority of our anchors and we drifted for a long time at the mercy of winds and currents, without knowing any longer where we were going if it was not the ocean bed.

Finally, by virtue of a particular bounty, God decided that the twenty-third day would be as mild as the others had been cruel, and we ran aground off a shore that was completely unknown to us. After having calculated the height of the sun at midday, examined the clocks and corrected the estimate so far as was possible, we found that we were in the region of the sixtieth degree of longitude and the forty-fourth of austral latitude—which is to say, about a thousand or twelve hundred leagues from Saint Helena.[10]

---

[10] This location is not very far from that of the Falkland Islands, where the first recorded landing, by the English captain John Strong, was in 1690.

As the largest of our launches had been carried away by the waves, which had passed over us a thousand times, we were very glad to have conserved the smaller one. It was immediately put to sea, and after having given thanks to God for having spared our lives, we began to unload the best clothing and everything else that would be most necessary to us on land.

We made use of a few paltry sails to make two tends. Other cut tree branches, with which they constructed huts, where the remains of the crew, which consisted of ninety-five individuals, were lodged.

There were about forty of us who were as well as circumstance permitted. One party was left in charge of the ship, the other went foraging. Never had forearms, powder and lead been more useful to us. There was game of all sorts in abundance, among others large birds heavier than guinea-fowl, which were plump and very succulent. Nor was there any shortage of fish, because we had a good provision of nets, hooks and other instruments appropriate to fishing. Turtles were scarce there, but they were large and good. We captured a few, which must have weighed between four and give hundred pounds, which gave us all sufficient to eat. The flesh appeared to us to be excellent, and the fat surpassed in delicacy the moist precious foodstuffs in the world; we made use of it for all purposes: for sauces, on bread, for burning, and generally for everything for which it might be needed. We also found a river two hours away, in an easterly direction, which furnished us with good fresh water.

These refreshments notwithstanding, two more of our men died, but the others did not take long to recover. Meanwhile, our vessel was finally unloaded, and it was observed that she was afloat, with the consequence that we towed her to the aforementioned river. As soon as she was ashore, the carpenters examined her very closely, but they found that there was no apparent hope of returning her to a state in which we could use her to continue our journey. It was, therefore, resolved with common accord that we would dismantle her completely and built a smaller vessel, with which we could reach Africa.

The captain wanted us all to take turns at that work, but we persuaded him that we were not all equally adept to the task, and that it was necessary for someone to provide and cook the food necessary for the maintenance of so many people, so ten people were set aside or that. The nine who were assigned to it with me were skillful; one party became, so to speak, hunters by profession and the other fishermen. As can easily be imagined, we did not have a great deal of trouble, in a country like that, in finding enough for our company to eat.

Those agreeable occupations, in which another might have taken great pleasure, only charmed me for a few days; I soon wearied of the métier. The desire I conceived to penetrate into a country where it appeared to me that no one had ever been before caused me to make the resolution to abandon my comrades, but I did not want to accomplish that reckless design alone. The two crewmen who appeared to me to be the most resolute, to whom I communicated it, were delighted by my proposition. They confessed to me that they had each had the same thought independently, but had not dared to confide it to anyone else. Thus, the affair was concluded with an oath not to reveal the secret, and, having all promised sincere mutual amity and fidelity, we went to bed, with a view to setting off as soon as possible.

*Chapter IV*
*The Author leaves the rest of the Company with only two comrades*
*and penetrates with them into the unknown land.*
*The obstacles he encounters en route, etc.*

The next morning, the twenty-fourth of September 1644, on the eleventh day after our arrival, we each seized a good hatchet, which we put in our belt, a rifle, and everything we thought necessary for an enterprise of that nature. Without seeming to be doing anything, at first, we went into the woods, drew away from the others, and advanced with long strides toward the south-south-west.

We covered at least four leagues before talking about taking a rest. La Forêt—that was the name of one of my comrades, the other being named Du Puis—saw a grouse a hundred paces away and killed it; while he plucked it, Du Puis and I cut brushwood and made a fire under a tree. To one of the branches of which I attached a stout piece of string, and then attached our fowl to it, which was soon roasted in that fashion. We dined lavishly; only water was lacking, and we had to put that off until later.

We set out again, and found a hollow in which there was a pool, which was not very clear, to tell the truth, but seemed excellent to us. We filled our flasks, but did not have to use it, for a league and a half further on we found a stream that contained the most beautiful water I had ever seen in my life. It was about two feet deep, and cut directly across the route that we had decided to take, with the aid of a little solar quadrant that I had in my pocket, and which was a great help to us.

Having no bridge or any other commodity, we took our shoes off and waded across the rivulet, which we left with regret after having drunk our fill and made provision for the future. We found no trace of humans or large animals; there was nothing anywhere in the eight or ten leagues that we had covered before sunset but sand, heather and forest. Finally, we made camp at the foot of a mound where the bushes were so thick that we would be sheltered from the wind as if under a tent. We finished eating what we had conserved from our midday meal, and went to bed as best we could.

When we awoke the next morning, we were surprised to see that the whole sky was covered and that we were threatened with heavy rain. We thought it appropriate to hollow out a shelter in the little hill, which was sufficiently steep at the place where we were, in order to protect ourselves from the weather. In fact, it did not take long, with the aid of our hatchets instead of spades, to prepare a small lodgment. The rain did not begin to fall until about eleven o'clock, however, so we had time to spare to massacre a few quail and other small birds, mostly unfamiliar to us, which would supply us with enough to eat for a week; there was an innumerable multitude there, and the majority allowed themselves to be felled almost without moving from their place, which caused us to conjecture that the place could not be inhabited.

In the end, we were constrained to remain in that place for four days, which seemed to us to be longer than four weeks spent elsewhere. We were recompensed subsequently, however, since we enjoyed more than a month of continual good weather thereafter.

After emerging from our refuge, we began to discover high mountains. For fear of not finding enough to sustain us, we laid in a supply of meat for several days. We were not mistaken in our conjecture; one might have thought it a veritable Greenland, so dry and arid was it, and in many places there was no grass, no bushes and nothing else that might give pasture to the smallest animal. We came across very few of them; even the birds became scarce—from which it is easy to judge that we passed our time rather badly. If we has not come into little valleys from time to time, filled with trees laden with a few paltry fruits, and water with which to slake out thirst, our lives would have been in danger.

On the evening of the ninth day of our march, we arrived in a low-lying region where a little torrent was visible about a quarter of a league away, descending from a crag into a hollow, from which it then discharged into a marsh, which formed a semicircle and extended across the valley as far as the eye could see. The banks that enclosed the beautiful water were high but not very steep, which made us think that it was not as swollen as in another season of the year. I approached with the intension of going down to it, but when I was only a few paces away, I was astonished to find the ground beneath my feet suddenly lacking. I sank into it to my armpits.

My comrades, seeing that I was stuck there, burst out laughing and came to my aid. At the same time, ten or twelve large birds about the size of geese with beaks as broad and long as a hand, launched themselves into the air, sounding the alarm with a quacking that was their natural sound, and which must have been audible at a long distance.

Before we could count to a hundred the sky was black with the creatures. That extraordinary multitude, combined with the furious racket they were making, frightened us; we had absolutely no idea what to think, especially when some of the company, screeching like the damned, plunged vertically toward our heads, as if they wanted to dismember us. Although we fired a few shots at them, bringing several of them down, they continued just the same. When we saw, however, that they did not want to do us any harm, and were even beginning to beat a retreat, we went down the slope in order to refresh ourselves.

Du Puis ascertained that the place where I had sunk was a nest to which a number of the birds had retired; beside it there was another, and then a third, approximately ten or twelve feet apart. The openings of these subterranean dwellings were oval in form, the smallest diameter being about a foot. Being the smallest of the three of us, I searched the third; I found the place to be about the size of a small bedroom, more than eight feet square and at least three high.

There were fifteen nests around the perimeter, built of small leafy branches cemented with clay in the form of a rounded basket. Each nest contained six speckled eggs as large as a fist. In the middle of the lair there was a trough much larger than the nests, filled with a substance divided up into little round balls, some larger than others. I imagined at first that it was their excrement, but, curiosity having led me to lift a little to my mouth, I found that it tasted excellent, surpassing our best macaroons, to which it bore some resemblance.

My comrades, who had the same desire as I had to discover novelties, had each descended into a similar lair, where they found things disposed in the same fashion as I have described. The only difference consisted in the number of nests, which was more considerable in some than others because they were not the same size. We understood that there were so many of the birds because they multiplied so copiously, and there was no one to destroy them.

Scarcely was our first surprise over than another subject caused us one that was infinitely more considerable. It was one of those caverns that we found a hundred paces away. It had an entrance that it was impossible for the birds to have made: three large stones a foot in diameter placed in the soil beside one another, formed a threshold, and the two uprights, four feet long, tapering at the top, were formed of large stones weighing more than a hundred pounds each. Other stones were arranged one on top of another inside, sealing it entirely.

Those productions of the human hand caused us to hesitate as to whether we wanted to be there or not. We would certainly have liked to see animals of our own species, but we feared not being treated very well. In that uncomfortable uncertainty, we nevertheless drew closer, but calling out, and making sufficient noise to be heard by anyone who was inside.

La Forêt, weary of all the grimaces, told us to stay outside, hatchets in hand, while he forced the obstacles and went through the entrance, with the intention of going in to see what was behind them. He carried it through, but when he was inside he found that it was too dark for him to be able to see anything. What he told us when he came out was that a man could stand upright inside, and that the apartment was habitable; he had even felt a bench of sorts at the back.

With that we ran to discharge our wrath on the first trees that we had left in passing a short distance away; we cut as much wood as we could carry and built a fire with it in front of our cave; then all three of us returned to the task in order that we would have a provision adequate to last us through the night.

When the fire was well alight we went into our bedroom, which was twice as large as the others. It was properly paved with selected stones, and there was indeed a bank of grass all around it, but the most formidable object, which we saw at the same time as the bank, which was to the left, the side most sheltered from the wind, was the carcass of a human being, skeletal in form from head to toe. Above it there was a kind of slate, fairly smooth and sunk into the terrace, on which was engraved, in large Greek letters:

*Oh Lord, holy and strong, holy and immortal, have pity on us.*

I shall not amuse myself here by listing our various conjectures, and the different sentiments that we had on that subject, since they are easily imaginable.

The hunger that we were feeling, however, made us take two of the birds that we had killed and pass them over the flame in order to burn off the plumage instead of flaying them, as we had done so frequently, because we reckoned the skin to be one of the best morsels—in which we were not at all mistaken, since, having gutted and washed them, we put them under the embers, where they were swiftly roasted. We had had so little to eat all day that we left almost nothing but the bones. The birds were fat, succulent and very tasty.

After having supped well we bedded down as best we could, leaving the dead man where he was, without touching him, because we wanted to examine him more closely the following day.

It was not yet broad daylight when our impertinent birds recommenced their din; some were emerging from their holes, others returning to them, and with so much noise that it was impossible for us to sleep any longer, although we would have liked to do so. We waited for the sun to arrive, however, before getting up.

Our presence did not alarm the fowls at all; they all worked at their tasks as if they were being paid a wage to do it. We saw some of them emerging with beaks full of earth, which they had doubtless excavated from the most irregular parts of their hollows, in order to make them larger or neater. Some of those arriving were coming to furnish materials appropriate to build their nests, but most of them were carrying the fragments of cracknel that I had found so tasty the previous evening.

We climbed the slope in order to see where they were obtaining that food. As soon as we had raised our eyes we perceived, within musket-range, on a little rise, three objects of the same girth and height. We moved toward them in order to see what they were, and found that, in fact, they were three truncated cones about eight feet high, five in diameter at the base and about three at the summit, constructed in a very orderly manner with stones neatly arranged one atop another.

The mere sight of three monuments, so rare in a deserted region, did not content us, and we set about demolishing one of them. When we had removed about a foot and a half's thickness of the uppermost stones, however, we uncovered the skull of a human being. After that, the bones of the shoulders appeared, and then the arms: in brief, the entire carcass, all the way down to the feet. We could have done as much for the others, but we contented ourselves with uncovering the head of the cadaver that was under the second, since it was probable that there was another under the third.

While we were reflecting on all that that with a kind of admiration, I discovered characters around the third cone, made of little stones about the size of a pigeon's egg, arranged in the soil. I took them for the letters in the Hebrew alphabet, named, in the following order: Koph, Vau. Lamed, He, Teth, Lamed, Koph, Pe, Gimel, Vau, Beth, Thau, Sajin, Koph, Mem, Lamed, Alep, Sajin, Samech and Reseh, but not accompanied by dots or any other marks that might facilitate reading them. I made every effort to decipher their significance, and have thought about it a thousand times since, but have never succeeded in getting to the end, in such a way that I could grasp the meaning.[11]

There was something similar around the other two monuments, but I did not take the trouble to uncover the stones, on top of which we had dropped others, because I did not think it worth the trouble. All appearances suggested that it had been a very long time since four unfortunates, like ourselves, having wandered around without finding any place apparently better than this one, had stopped here and hollowed out a cavern in the same fashion as the birds of which I had spoken, or perhaps appropriate one of their nests, and had died there one after another—firstly those who were under the monuments, and then the last one, on the bench, where we had found him, and whose clothing and flesh had been consumed by time, so thoroughly that not the slightest relic of them remained.

What confirmed that thought further was that not far away, there were a great many straight trees, like rushes, whose branches were all arranged in tiers, the first of which commenced four feet from the ground, by my measurement; there were twelve of them, each as thick as an arm and seven feet long. In the second tier, three feet higher up, there were eleven, six feet long. In the third, two and a half feet beyond that, I only counted ten, even shorter than the preceding ones; in the fourth, at a proportionate distance, nine, and then eight, even, sex, five, four and three—after which came the summit of the tree, in the form of an acorn the size of an egg.

All the branches of those pyramidal trees were like as many ostrich plumes—which is to say that they were garnished with thin leaves like the filaments of two pinions. From one end to the other, and all around the extremity of that down, there was a border as thick as a writing quill, and above each row of branches a ring surrounding the tree, the first one thicker than a finger but becoming smaller as they approached the top. Both of them were composed of the excellent foodstuff of which the big birds seemed so fond, and which he believed to have served our poor pilgrims as bread.

Instead of simply tasting the bread, as I had done the previous evening, we threw ourselves upon it, my comrades and I, like poverty upon society; and it was the prerogative of the most skillful to climb up to the places were some still remained—for many had been stripped. Finally, we ate so many that we were

---

[11] A conundrum is evidently being presented to the reader here, but it is not easy to solve, not knowing whether the solution is likely to be in Hebrew, French or some other language.

full up, and found it so toothsome that Du Puis was already talking about building a tabernacle and dying there, like the good people testifying by their bones had done. During the time that we were conversing, however, we were also gripped by such a great drowsiness that we could hardly lift our feet to take a step.

I was the first to let myself fall to the ground; the others followed suit a moment later. Not one of us lost our judgment; our limbs alone were numbed, although even our tongues had difficulty serving us for proffer speech. We remained in that state for two hours before going to sleep; the slumber lasted until midday.

Du Puis, who was the first to wake up, found his right hand resting on something that appeared to be naked, smooth and about as thick as a thigh. He thought at first that he had rolled over in his sleep on top of one of us, but as he recovered his senses, and having opened his eyes in search of clarification, he was gripped by a mortal terror on seeing between him and La Forêt a snake more than twenty-five feet long. He became even more paralyzed in his limbs than before, unable either to move or to speak. However, the snake abandoned the place, coiled round one of the nearby trees, and set off after the cracknels in its turn.

With that, my friend recovered his courage, pushed me, and, having woken me up, showed me that frightful monster. Although I still felt debilitated, I got up instantly, and started running away as fast as I could. Du Puis imitated me, and in response to our cries, La Forêt did not take long to do likewise. We were delighted that the monster had not swallowed us, and that fear contributed in no small measure to persuade us to decamp as soon as possible.

It took us all night, however, to recover.

*Chapter V*
*The subsequent adventures of the Author and his two friends,*
*until their entry into an inhabited region.*

We found ourselves fresh and hearty when we got up, which resolved us to lift camp. So, scorning the terrestrial manna that had debilitated us to such an extent, we only made a good provision of roasted birds, and having bid farewell to the monuments, we set off again across country.

By then we were a good fifty leagues from the sea. That evening we tried to eat, for the first time that day, but our appetite was not sufficiently great, even though we had marched a long way and had passed a mountain by seven or eight leagues. Three entire days went by before we could take anything, which made us think that the bread of the tree must be extremely nourishing, and that it might be very good, taken in moderation.

Meanwhile, the route was getting steadily worse. A great consolation to us was that the nights were fine and the days were becoming longer as we got further into the spring of the region and got further away from the equinoctial line. The sky seemed to us to be more charming, the landscape more cheerful, and they furnished the subject matter of the bulk of our conversation.

Du Puis, most of all, seemed charmed by the sun, which never ceased to cover us, from dawn to dusk, with its agreeable rays.

"I can't lie," he said to us one day, "if I weren't from a country where the people are lucky enough to have been instructed in the knowledge of their creator, and I'd never heard talk of the Being of Beings, the torch of these skies would be, without contradiction, the soul and unique divinity that I'd consider worthy of my adoration, not only because it most agreeable object visible in the world, but also because, without its help, no plant or animal could subsist. Everything languishes as soon as it goes away, and it presence renders vigor to that which appeared to be dying."

"You are not the only one," I said to him, "who has that sentiment. There are entire nations that evoke the beautiful star as the first cause of all things; and even those who have recognized a sovereignly perfect being cannot help giving it epithets that mark the esteem in which they hold it sufficiently. Orpheus called it the eye of the sky, Homer that which sees all things, Heraclitus the fount of celestial light, Saint Ambrose the beauty of the heavens, Philo the idea of eternal splendor, Plato the soul of the world. King David exalted its excellence marvelously, especially in his eighteenth psalm, and the holy men of the Old and New Testaments had no scruple about representing it as the model of the divinity, as they called it in a hundred places, the orient of the heavens and the sun of justice."

"I don't care what others have said about stars," La Forêt continued, "I pray to God, and if I have any veneration for creatures it is only in relation to the creator, who is worthy of being admired in his works; but what surprises me about to sun is the two opposed movements that it is said to have: a daily movement from the orient to the occident and an annual movement from the occident to the orient."

"It's true," I said, "that those two movements are directly contradictory to one another, if one attributes them to the sun, as almost all the ancients did, but nothing is more natural if one attributes the two movements to the earth, which makes a great circle round the sun in the space of a year and turns once about its center, or its axis, in twenty-four hours, exactly like a ball, or, if you wish, a turnip that you have pushed from one end of a path to the other; for at the same time as the turnip advances toward the end of the path it also makes several rotations on its axis.

"The earth does the same, and its two different movements have always served humans to measure the time of their duration. The rotation it makes about its axis produces our day of twenty-four hours and the time it takes to make its great circle around the sun makes our year of three hundred and sixty-five days and six hours, within a few minutes.

"It's true that that measure for the year has not always been equally known to all nations. The Egyptians, the Chaldeans, the Jews and other ancient peoples counted their years differently, and some made them longer or shorter than others. Some of them regulated their years in accordance with the course of the moon rather than that of the earth, and several nations do the same today.

"The calendar that is presently followed among the nations of Europe, which has come from the ancient Romans, has not always been so exactly regulated as it is now, for in the time of Romulus, the founder of Rome, the year, which ought to have been the time the earth employs in making its great circle around the sun, was only three hundred and four days, comprised by ten months. March, May, July and October had thirty-one days, the others only thirty. Numa Pompilius, his successor, added fifty-one to that number, so that the year then had three hundred and fifty-five days. He also removed one day from each short month, which he added to the fifty-one, and from their sum he instituted the month of January, of twenty-nine days, and February, of twenty-eight.

"Finally, Julius Caesar, the first of the Roman emperors, having consulted the most skillful astronomers of his time, with their consent, changed the year, which was almost lunar, into a solar year by adding another ten days, which he distributed in such a way that January, August and December each had two and April, June, September and November one. As that was still not sufficient, however, because the year is three hundred and sixty-five days and six hours, less eleven minutes, that monarch decided that every four years there would be a year of three hundred and sixty-six days, and that day would be placed between the sixth and seventh Kalend of March—with the result that there were two sixth

Kalends of March in such a year, which was called bissextile because the sixth day was counted twice before counting the next.

"That correction, accurate as it seemed, nevertheless caused a error in the calendar in the long term because the year was then too long by about eleven minutes, with the result that whereas the sun entered into its term, as they said, at the spring equinox on the twenty-fourth of March forty-five years before the birth of Jesus Christ, it entered it on the twenty-first by the time of the Council of Nicea in the year three hundred and twenty-seven, and the eleventh in the time of Gregory the Thirteenth in 1582. The Pope having noticed that, he removed ten days from that year, between the fourth and fifteenth of October, because there were no festivals of important saints in that period. And to make sure that the same abuse would not recur, with the consequence for the equinoxes that they would follow a retrograde movement through all the months of the year in time, he ordered that in future, for three centuries running, there would be no bissextile year at their end, but only at the end of the fourth; from that it follows that four hundred and three Gregorian years equal four hundred Julian years."

"I'm very grateful to Monsieur Du Puis," said La Forêt, "for having occasioned that discourse, because I've wanted to know for a long time what is meant by a bissextile year, by the old and new style, and to know the veritable cause of all those changes."

It was necessary, in order to content them, also to explain several times what is meant by the terms epact, golden number, solar cycle, Roman Indiction, Ides, Kalends and almost everything that it is necessary to know to compile an almanac. What caused them most admiration was when I assured them that the sun, which appears so small to us, is undoubtedly much larger than the entire earth.

"Assuredly," La Forêt said, "that surpasses the imagination, and I believe that everything you've told us is pure fantasy."

Du Puis, who outbid everything that his companion could allege in that regard, dared to treat me as extravagant because I sustained their it was all true, with the result that it was necessary for me, reluctantly, to provide some clarifications in order to give them some satisfaction on the subject.

"I admit," I said to them, "that it is impossible to determine exactly the size of the celestial torches; all those who have done so, and tried to impose their results upon us, have been presumptuous. The instruments of which we make use in order to measure the parallax of the sun are too small and too poorly divided in relation to the prodigious distance of the star. I have never seen an astrolabe divided into minutes, and it would be necessary to divide it into seconds, and perhaps into lesser fractions; that can't be done, or it would be so large that one would not be able to make use of it.

"A proof that one can easily be mistaken without that is that, exact as astronomers have been who were not content with speculation and wanted to reduce the question to practicality, they are so greatly abused that the difference of opinion between their opinions is capable of making one doubt whether they even have common sense in wanting to present their sentiments as the truth.

"Tycho Brahe, who seems to have traveled the heavens as Christopher Columbus did the earth, assures us that the sun is one hundred and thirty-nine times larger than the globe we inhabit. Copernicus sustains that the number goes as far as a hundred and sixty-two. Ptolemy made it a hundred and sixty-six, Father Scheiner four hundred and thirty-four, Wendelinus four thousand and ninety-six, and one of my tutors went as far as three million times greater than the same earth. We do not know its size for certain, therefore, but what is certain is that it is much more extensive than this large body, however vast it appears to us.

"First of all, if one supposes it equal to the earth, it is evident that its rays, skimming the exterior parts of that sphere, would leave as they continue a cylinder of obscurity behind it, the sides of which would be parallel, with the result that the planets that pass through that shadow, not receiving any light and having none themselves, would be eclipsed.

"If the sun were smaller, its rays, after having grazed the earth, would spread out as they went on, and would form a truncated cone of shadow of which the base would be the firmament and the summit the part of the earth opposed to the sun, from which it would follow that an even greater part of the sky would be obscured and that all the planets one encountered there would be unable, as had just been said, to return any light.

"Now, there is only the moon that ever appears to us to be eclipsed; thus it appears that the sun must be incomparably larger than the earth, since its rays, having grazed that large mass, reunite a little beyond the moon, where by the cone formed by the shadow of the earth concludes in a point."

To that explanation I added a figure drawn in the sand, to facilitate their intelligence of it.

"I confess," Du Puis said then, "That that is demonstrative, with regard to the cause, but as for the effects of which you speak, the lack of the planets, I don't understand at all. I didn't even know that eclipses were ordinary and natural."

"Indeed," I went on. "There's nothing mysterious about them. The planets are opaque and solid bodies, which resemble the earth, and which many people believe to be inhabited. They only give light by reflection, after having received it from the sun. It follows that we only have an eclipse of the moon when it is rising on one side while the sun is setting on the other, and the two heavenly bodies are consequently in opposition, the earth being directly between them, preventing them from looking one another in the face."

"But if the sun is the source of light," La Forêt interjected, how does it lose it, in its turn, at certain times? Whence come those failures, which alarm the world so much, and what returns its former glare?"

"Just as the interposition of the earth causes eclipses of the moon," I said, so the interposition of the moon also obscures the sun—which is to say that every time the moon is in conjunction with the sun and passes between the sun and the earth in a straight line, it performs the function of a curtain, which hides the beautiful star from us. But that privation cannot last very long because of the different movement of the bodies. The circle that the earth describes around the sun is incomparably larger than the one the moon describes around the earth, and instead of the latter advancing about thirteen degrees is a day, the former one crosses a little more than one in winter, and slightly less in summer, with the result that they are soon disengaged from one another."

"What!" said La Forêt. "Does the earth move more quickly in one season than another?"

"Yes, in appearance," I said. "The difference is about four minutes, because, the earth being much more distant from the sun in summer than in winter, it necessarily seems to be moving more slowly during the long days than during the short ones—just as a carriage that is only fifty paces from our eyes seems to be moving more rapidly than it does at a hundred paces."

"But since it's a matter of paces," said Du Puis, "doesn't the same fire make itself more felt at a distance of two paces than ten?"

"Undoubtedly," I replied.

"But if the sun, which is hot, is closer to the earth in winter than in summer, why is the heat not regulated in accordance with its distance? Why is it that we are trembling with cold in the period when we ought to be sweating in large drops?"

"Well said," I retorted. "That objection makes it evident that ignorance and reason are not incompatible. However, in thinking that you've caught me out, you've made a mistake. I can't prove to you that there is neither heat nor cold in the world, nor light, odor, sound, colors or any of the qualities that we perceive in bodies; that would be too difficult and you probably wouldn't understand, because it depends on certain knowledge of which you don't even have the principles. I'll content myself with saying to you that there is, properly speaking, only one sort of matter, but which, depending on whether it is fixed or in motion, produces certain effects in us, by means of our organs, which we attribute to bodies, which leads us to call them hot, cold, luminous, colored and so on, even though, effectively, sound, color, taste etc. are in us and not in the bodies, just as the pain that is produced by a pinprick is on us and not in the pin that has caused it.

"Note, in any case, that your comparison is not accurate even in the sense that you want to employ it, because the summits of the Alps, which are closer to the sun than the feet, remain covered in snow in summer, while everything perishes of heat in their valleys, which are further away, the true reason for which—in order not to pass over it without some brief explanation—is that the air is so subtle a league from the earth that, no matter how agitated it is, it does not have the force to dissipate the slightest bodies, whereas at its surface, it is so gross that it is capable of shaking the most solid particles and causing what we call excessive heat."

"All that's very well," said La Forêt, "but I beg your pardon for telling you that you haven't yet concluded anything with regard to winter and summer."

"That's true," I replied. "That's a question of another kind. When the sun is nearer to our zenith, as in summer, although it is further away from us, it nevertheless sends us its rays almost perpendicularly, whereas in winter, when it remains closer to the horizon, the majority of its rays, which can only arrive obliquely, rebound from the surface of our atmosphere and very few pass through to reach us. It is, however, in the greater or smaller number of those rays that heat or cold consists, as is easily proved by ardent mirrors and lenses, whose effects are always proportional to the quantity of rays of light that the assemble."

In the course of these pleasant conversations, which were made more with a view to passing the time that augmenting the number of philosophers, since it would have been necessary to take another tack to succeed in that, we nevertheless made considerable progress. In the end however, it was necessary to change language.

Thirty-five days after we had quit our troop, when we estimated that we had covered about a hundred and thirty leagues, we suddenly found ourselves on the shore of a lake that seemed to us to be vast in extent. That obstacle astonished as, and we remained irresolute for some time as to what we ought to do. On the one hand, we talked about turning back, and on the other, of staying there, of lodging ourselves as best we could in order to spend a few days there.

In the end, we decided to advance to our right, and to skirt the large expanse of water to see whether we could find its limit.

After walking for seven or eight leagues, we began to se land on the far side, and were delighted that as we went further, we were always better able to distinguish objects. On the other hand, we perceived that we were gradually moving into a marshy region where the ground was soft, tremulous and had a very bad odor. The whole area ahead of us was flat and smooth; we could not see any issue, and we could not take a step, no matter which way we turned, without sinking up to our knees.

No matter how I encouraged my companions, there was no means of going on, it was necessary, reluctantly, to retrace our steps, and although we were very weary, we were obliged to travel more than two full leagues before we dared to stop, because we were wet, and until then we had not been able to find wood to make a fire capable of drying us off.

After we had rested sufficiently we made the decision to keep going to the left, to see if there was any impediment in that direction. We therefore marched for four days in succession, until we arrived at a forest filled with oaks of an extraordinary height and girth. We hesitated as to whether we ought to go into it, and only did so on the condition that we would only move away from the lake to the shortest possible extent.

That did not last for long, however; we had only covered three petty leagues when he found ourselves at the foot of a mountain so steep that no animal would have been capable of scaling it. The rock even advanced into the lake, the waters of which were sometimes agitated, probably having eroded the foot. We skirted that cliff in the other direction for a whole day without finding any place that rendered it accessible to us; there was nothing but precipices and frightful heights.

At the frightful aspect of so many invincible obstacles, patience abandoned us; my two comrades made me very telling reproaches for having engaged them to take that bad step.

"I confess that we have reason to complain of our misfortune," I said to them, "but you have to consider that nothing happens by accident; there is doubtless a Providence that directs everything at its will. As that wisdom has bought us here, it will also suggest to us the means of getting out of it, one way or another. It is certain that God never abandons his own, no matter where in the world they may go; if we put our confidence in him, he will come to our aid. You know that it was not lucre or glory that drew us here; we have nothing to lose, as so long as we can conserve our lives, we have everything that we would have had at home. Let us not resent the fact that we have arrived here; our principal goal is to travel, and to discover novelties, which give us pleasure. I shall not despair of going further, and of finding one day something that will give us the means to live happily.

"Let us not waste time," I continued. "Let us return to the lake, and see if we can find a means of crossing it without too much danger. Fortunately, we have our hatchets, and there's wood here in abundance. We wouldn't be the first people to make a journey by raft. If we go on to the end, I hope for a more fortunate discovery thereafter. Thus far the country is uninhabitable; it's humanly impossible that it should be the same everywhere, and who knows whether we might not eventually find some civilized people, who will recompense us by their honesty for the fatigues and dangers we have suffered in order to unearth them, and to inform them, if they do not know, that there are other people than them in the world."

No matter what I told my comrades, it did not satisfy them, and I was convinced that if they had seen the slightest possibility of finding our crew where we had left them, they would undoubtedly have staked everything on trying to rejoin them. It was, however, necessary to decide on another course of action.

We returned to the lake, and considered several places before agreeing on the one from which we would try to make the crossing. Those comings and goings consumed eight days, however, and it was only on the ninth that we began to put our hands to work.

First we cut down ten trees seven or eight inches in diameter, from which we removed the branches and cut them to a length of twenty feet. Then, having put them in the water, we attached them together as best we could, partly with interlaced rushes but principally with the bark from the branches of willows, which grew in large quantities on the edge of the water, whose fibers we could braid to whatever length we desired. Afterwards we prepared a further twenty smaller trees, which we arranged and secured at right angles to the first. Finally, we put a third stage on the second, orientated in the same direction as the first. We also made five oars, or paddles, which took us longer than all the rest.

While we were all occupied in our carpentry, La Forêt told us that he had seen something moving in the rushes on the edge of the lake. Indeed, we immediately saw, as he had, that it must be an animal of considerable size. Du Puis and I both primed our rifles, and having loaded four bullets we fired the first of them together, keeping a third shot in case of necessity. Experience had taught us to do that en route, where we had nearly been torn apart by bear on two or three occasions because we had exhausted our fire.

We had scarcely lowered our weapons when we were extremely surprised and alarmed to hear frightful howls and to see a prodigious stirring in the reeds. We remained in suspense for some time, wondering whether we ought to go and see what it was, but after having considered what we had heard, and thinking that it was probably the effect of a mortal wound, which had rendered the animal incapable of defense, we reloaded our rifles and gradually approached, albeit while trembling, the place where it was thrashing around.

At first, when it saw us approaching, it redoubled its cries and made great efforts to escape our pursuit; its fear gave us heart, and La Forêt, seeing it raised its head, launched his shot so accurately that it went clean through, and laid it out stone dead.

Nevertheless, we stayed there for a few moments more before daring to go any closer. Seeing that it was no longer moving, however, we began by touching it with our fingertips, and having pulled it out we recognized that it was a kind of otter, although it only had two short limbs at the front, which one of us hand broken with the first volley, making it impossible for the animal to flee. It must have weighed at least a hundred and fifty pounds.

We set about skinning it, and then we roasted the best parts. The flesh was good with a taste reminiscent of our ducks.

The next day, which was the thirteenth since we had arrived there for the first time, we resolved to cast off and set forth. The weight of our raft meant that we went very slowly; two of us took shifts paddling while the other rested. Fortunately, the air was very tranquil. The weather was agreeable as possible, and I can say that we took pleasure in the journey, which we had undertaken without knowing what would become of us.

It was surprising to see the infinite multitude of fish that there was in the beautiful lake; some were leaping to one side and others collided without vehicle on the other; there were even a few that followed us, with their heads out of the water, shaking their tails in a manner that almost suggested that they wanted to testify the joy they felt in seeing us. That mute game sometimes rendered us so attentive that we remained inactive for long periods. We caught several of them in our hands, which we immediately returned to their element, and we could have taken as many as we wished.

What increased our joy considerably was that toward dusk, when we had lost sight of the shore that we had quit, we discovered the one toward which we were heading. That agreeable sight gave us new strength; we labored almost all night, and I suspect that it was after four o'clock in the afternoon of the following day when our raft ran aground.

As soon as we were ashore we thought it appropriate to make use of the apparatus we had brought with us in order to moor our raft, including stakes or tree-trunks and large stones with which to drive them into the ground, having been uncertain that we would find better materials elsewhere and might be forced to spend several days in the same spot. In any case, we were so fatigued by our navigation that we camped a hundred paces away and stayed there until the following before continuing our route.

We had scarcely covered half a league when we came into a wood s dense as those were had encountered previously, but which we had pierced in less than two hours. It was then that we were suddenly stopped by rocks that had no more slope than a wall.

That new barrier caused further disputes among us; my comrades were murmuring extremely, and I encouraged them as I usually did. It was even necessary for me to assure them that, instead of my ideas being so confused and incoherent during sleep that I rarely saw the denouement of my dreams, I had had one the previous night whose coherence and circumstances were so particular that it must infallibly be a very advantageous augury. With that I invented a few fictions, which, although they were rather poorly concocted, nevertheless had all the effect that I expected of them.

"In the morning," I said to them, "at about an hour before sunrise, I seemed to hear a voice as loud as thunder, which said to me: 'What are you doing there, my child? Get up and walk; your deliverance is at hand.' At the same time, a young woman appeared before me, clad in white garments, with hair hanging loosely over her shoulders, a laughing face and legs bare to the knee, holding in her hands an artistically and delicately-woven wicker basket filled with rare and delicious fruits, which she invited us to eat.

"To my left there was a field covered with sheaves of the most beautiful wheat that the earth bears, and to my right there was a tree, in the trunk of which there was an opening, from which a clear vermilion liquid was flowing impetuously, which embalmed the atmosphere with its odor. I turned round to see what there was behind me, but, perceiving a hideous monster bristling with spines and thistles, I was gripped by such horror that, even though its back was turned toward me, I could not help waking with a start."

To that dream I added a favorable explanation, which contributed not a little to stiffening our legs.

While skirting the mountains, moving eastwards, we eventually discovered a cleft in which we were able to climb. I cannot describe the trouble we had in reaching the top. When we had succeeded in doing so we sat down to recover our breath and to have something to eat.

When we got up again we perceived soon afterwards a pool about a quarter of a league in circumference, bounded on one side by steep spurs of rock, some of which even overhung the water, and on the other side by a kind of narrow flattened dyke, which had a precipice to the right whose bottom was undiscoverable.

Those frightful objects rendered me as mute as a fish; I no longer felt that I had the strength or courage to say anything, and I confess frankly that I desired then, with all my heart, that I had not set forth on the adventure. There was no apparent way to descend from where we were, and it seemed too risky to me to pass over.

In the embarrassment in which I was, I made a considerable effort to climb up to the summit of a rock that we had left behind us. As soon as I succeeded, my dolor suddenly changed to an excessive joy, when I saw that immediately beyond those heights a flat terrain appeared, intercut by channels, on the banks of which there were trees planted in an orderly fashion. It even seemed to me that I could glimpse livestock in grassy meadows, and further away, large bodies that appeared to be human dwellings.

I made signs to my comrades to follow me, and signaled to them with my gestures and various contortions of my body that our deliverance was nigh. The desire that they had to learn the good news led them to imitate me. They thought as I did, crippling themselves before being able to reach me, but they were incontinently consoled in the same way for their labor, and agreed without hesitation that the region was incontestably inhabited.

The only difficulty was reaching it, and that difficulty seemed to us to be insurmountable. From the height where we stood we considered everything around us attentively, but, nothing accessible having been revealed to our eyes, we helped one another to descend, and came to examine the pool and the precipice again.

For myself, I was convinced in the opinion that, however risky it might be, we ought to retrace our steps in order to cut wood in the forest where we had spent the night, drag it up as best we could and make use of it to make that small crossing. Du Puis, on the contrary, thinking my proposal almost impossible of execution, said the passage between the lake and the precipice appeared to be two feet wide in the narrowest stretches, and that we could therefore easily contrive to pass over it—and that he was fully prepared to act as our guide.

I was delighted by that solution, and did not fail to support it by means of examples from the Pyrenees and the Alps, about which I had read in several voyagers' memoirs. La Forêt, however, who said that he was subject to vertigo, protested that he would not follow us whatever happened, but that if we were determined to cross over, he would rather do it by swimming. The other immediately agreed with him, and offered to carry his clothes, and mine too, if I wanted to take to the water with him.

What was said was done. La Forêt and I undressed and made a parcel of our clothes. Du Puis, having taken charge of it, set out to cross over. We left our hatchets and rifles behind, the latter no longer being useful to us in any case, since we only had three charges of power left, but on condition that if he found the passage less dangerous than we imagined, Du Puis would come back for them.

As we were both good swimmers, La Forêt and I soon reached the other shore because we had chosen the narrowest place, whereas, Du Puis, who had taken our clothes, was obliged to make a rather long detour before reaching his passage. As soon as we came ashore we ran to meet him, and were very glad to see him coming boldly toward us.

By an inconceivable fatality, however, which I shall never cease to regret as long as I live, when the unfortunate fellow was no more than ten paces from safety, a splinter of the rock that was carrying him suddenly broke away, with the result that the ground was lacking beneath his feet.

Horrified, we saw him disappear, crying: "Oh Lord, have pity on me!"

We went forward precipitately to see what had become of him, but alas, we could not see or hear the slightest sign.

I beg the charitable reader to pause here momentarily, and reflect seriously upon our disaster. The despair that we felt on having lost our friend, combined with the pitiful state in which we found ourselves, having no clothes to cover our nudity, nor any human means to sustain our bodies, depressed our minds so much that we thought a hundred times over of throwing ourselves head first after him, and thus finishing in an instant the sorry course of such a misfortunate life.

*Chapter VI*
*Of the discovery of a beautiful land, its inhabitants, their language,*
*mores, customs etc., and of the esteem that our author*
*and his comrade enjoyed there.*

Meanwhile, the cold gripped us, because the sun was at the extremity of its course: two powerful motives for us to think about our retreat. We descended the mountain easily enough, because there was sufficient slope. At the foot there was a wide and profound ditch, which it was necessary to cross once again by swimming; it was one of the barriers of the land, where no bridges had been built to facilitate entry or exit.

The further we advanced into the terrain, the more beauty we discovered; a thousand different indications assured us that the country was inhabited. The animals we thought we had seen from the mountain were, in fact, goats, which were grazing in meadows where the green grass hid them partly from view.

Finally, we came close enough to the flocks for the goatherd who was guarding the nearest one, who was lying on the ground, noticed his animals stretching their necks, seemingly having some object in view that was causing them astonishment. He stood up, and as soon as he had perceived us he started running away as fast as he could, imagining—as we subsequently learned—on seeing two men naked in the dusk, coming from the direction of the mountains, that we must be rabid. His goats stampeded in the same way.

Shepherds, who were looking after sheep not far away, did not know what to think about that disorder. They had enough courage, however, to gather to-gether into a band of seven or eight, and they came to find out who we were.

As soon as we thought we were within range, we put our hands together and tried by means of all possible indications to move them to compassion. They came forward, and seeing that we were naked and unarmed, came to within four paces of us, each with a heavy staff in his hand, and started speaking to us.

I told them in Latin, French and Portuguese—a language of which I had learned sufficient while living in Portugal—that we were two honest Europeans who believed in God, raising my finger toward the heavens and then striking myself on the breast.

Whatever efforts and grimaces I made, however, I knew by their mime that we could not understand one another—with the consequence that I threw myself at their feet, than then, starting to tremble and extending my hands, I tried to insinuate to them that I was cold and had a strong desire to warm myself.

With that they conversed among themselves briefly, without giving any in-dication that they wanted to do us any harm. Finally after an extensive consulta-tion, they signaled to us to follow them, and took us to the home of a venerable individual, who, after having cast his eyes over us, commenced by giving each

56

of us a large robe, which covered us from head to toe because it had a bonnet attached to the top in the form of a hood.

He then started to interrogate us by means of signs, as to whether we had come from the Orient or the Occident, or some other part of the world. We replied to him in our own language and by means of the best gestures of which we were capable, that we were neither angels nor demons having come from the heavens or the abyss; that we were reasonable animals like him; that we had passed over the sea in a wooden machine of extraordinary dimensions, which had nevertheless been wrecked a hundred and fifty leagues away; that out of all the crew, three of us had searched for a shelter, with the intention of spending the rest of our days there; that one of us had perished on the way in the most tragic manner, and so on. We then begged him to have pity on us, to put us to work and give us life.

I do not know whether he understood very much of what we were saying, but at least he seemed moved, to the extent of shedding tears. We were given supper, and an hour later were shown to a bed where he could sleep. All of that was done in a manner so honest that we were charmed by it.

The next day there was a comedy of seeing people come in crowds from all directions in order to see us. Everyone looked at us with astonishment, and no one could understand where we had come from or by what means. Those visits lasted at least a fortnight or three weeks.

By virtue of listening to them speak, we began to understand a few words of their language. The first one we learned was *Mula*, the one they had the custom of pronouncing whenever they raised their eyes or a finger to the sky, proffering us the name of God. We learned the terms for eating, *At*; drinking, *Bŏskin*; sleeping, *Kapan*; walking, *Pryn*; laboring, *Tian*; yes, *Tŏto*; no, *Tŏton* and a quantity of others, which we eventually found to have the significance that we ought to have conjectured to begin with.

What gave us a great facility in rendering that language familiar to us was that it had only three tenses in the indicative of each verb: the present, the indefinite or composite perfect, and the future; that they had no imperative; that their subjective was only found in the imperfect and the former perfect, with the infinitive and the participle. Also, they only had three persons for the plural and singular combined. Thus, for instance, they conjugated the verb to eat, *At*:

*Present indicative*
Ata: I eat or we eat
Ate: You eat
Atη: He eats, or they eat

*Perfect indicative*
Atai: You have eaten, or we have eaten
Atei: You have eaten

Atηi: He has eaten, or they have eaten

*Future*
Atao: I will eat, or we will eat
Ateio: You will eat
Atηio: He will eat, or they will eat

*Imperative and Infinitive*
At: Eat

*First Imperfect of the Subjunctive*
Atain: I would eat, or we would eat
Atein: You would eat
Atηin: He would eat, or they would eat

*First future perfect*
Ataif: I will have eaten, or we will have eaten
Ateif: You will have eaten
Atηif: He will have eaten, or they will have eaten

*Present participle*
Atai: Eating
*From which are derived the words*
Ataiηs: Eatery or Kitchen
Ataiŏs: Manger or animal feed
Ataiŏ: Cook
Ataius: Eater, etc.

Their alphabet is composed of twenty characters , including seven vowels, a, e, I, o, u, η, ŏ, the sixth corresponding to the Greek *eta*[12] and a seventh distinguishing *ou*, and thirteen consonants: b, d, f, g, h, k, l, m, n, p, r, s and t. The same consonants also serve as numbers, b being 1, d 2, f 3, g 4, h 5, k 6, l 7, m 8, n 9, p 10, pb 11, pd 12 etc. dp being equivalent to two times ten, or twenty, fp three times ten, or thirty, fb thirty-one, etc., pp ten times ten or s, a million, ps, ten million pps, a hundred million, ppps a thousand millions, etc., always adding an extra p.

It is necessary to remark that their nouns and verbs also describe one another in the same way as "cat" and "catty," etc., in English. Their declinations are also very easy, for example:

---

[12] The Greek eta, η, was originally a consonant analogous to h, but eventually became a long e, finally tending toward a variant of i.

*Nominative*: Brol, male sheep or ram; Brolu, female sheep, or ewe; Brolη, sheep (rams or ewes) in the plural, etc.

*Genitive*: Brul of the ram; Burula, of the ewe; Brulη, of the sheep (plural), etc.

*Dative*: Brel, to the ram; Brela, to the ewe; Brelη, to the sheep (plural), etc.

What is admirable is that there are no exceptions in the conjugations and declinations of the language, and that as soon as one knows the variations of one verb or noun, one also knows all the others, and that variation simply consists of adding an a to the infinitive to make the present indicative, as one makes At into Ata, Bukin into Bukina, etc.. To nouns one adds an a to the masculine indicative in order to make it feminine, or a η when one wants to change it into a common plural, as the preceding example shows.

Given that, it is easy to understand there is nothing surprising in the fact that after six months we understood everything that was said to us, and could make ourselves understood—but let us return to our original subject.

A few days after our arrival we were woken up one morning by an extraordinary racket that was being made in the house. We got up to see what it was, but although we had been observing the slightest details of their actions, we did not understand the urgency that they were testifying, from the smallest to the greatest. All that we could do was guess that a lot of people must be coming to dinner, because a lot of poultry had been slaughtered and there was an abundance of food in every part of the kitchen.

At ten o'clock, the entire family went out; our patron, who was marching in the lead, was carrying a huge cock; we followed him with the others.

As we went past the bridge over the canal we saw that all the neighbors were doing that same as us; at the same time, those on the other side of the water were also coming out of their houses, each with a cock. The man who lived opposite exposed his in opposition ours; the others were doing the same, each one having arranged things so that the person who lived on the other side was in confrontation with him.

It is incredible with what courage and animosity those animals fought; sometimes, one flew up into the air and fell upon its enemy's back, often carrying away of clump of feathers; a moment later the other lay on the ground and attacked its adversary's underside, sinking its beak in as far as it could. They sidestepped, turned somersaults, and never gave anything away, either in vigor or in cunning, until the weaker was forced to cede to the stronger and fell, whereupon the victor tore it to pieces, and stepped back, crowing its triumph. The combat in which ours was engaged lasted until midday; others finished earlier, but there were some that only finished an hour later.

My host, whose bird had been killed, went to take the master of the victorious bird by the hand, congratulated him on his victory and took him to his house; all their children and domestics wasted no time in following them. What had been made ready in the other house was brought to ours; everyone sat down at table, and I can say that I had not partaken such a feast in a long time. We were assuredly at a meal fit for a king, and the toasts were not forgotten; unfortunately, we did not understand them.

The next day, our people were no less alert; as soon as the sun rose they emerged from where they were, and the young man of the district—which is to say, the eldest son of each family—picked up a straight, polished tree-trunk, like a ship's mast, which they went to plant in the middle of the canal, in a hole or groove constructed on the bed with stones, expressly for that purpose.

Thick ropes had been attached to the tops by means of fitments, and all these ropes were then stretched and twisted around various trees planted on the water's edge. In order that there should be no jealousy or grounds for complaint, each rope had a knot at an equal distance from the mast. At the top of the tree, which was thirty feet above the surface of the water, a round plank had been nailed, on which there was an eagle, whose two feet were separately attached with strong twine to two iron crampons driven deep into the wood.

When everything was ready, they waited until two o'clock in the afternoon. Then the same young men returned, and each seized one of the taut ropes at the location of the knot. At a signal given by our host they began to climb as best they could. The first who arrived in the vicinity of the eagle immediately tried to master it, but they were received in a hostile fashion. As they had bare hands and were not even permitted to cover them they were obliged to endure thrusts of the beak, which bloodied them. Each of them could only make use of one hand in the attack, holding on tightly with the other. On the other hand, the eagle was so tightly secured that it could not rise up less than two feet into the air.

Thus, instead of the combat only lasting a few moments, as I had imagined at the beginning, I saw no appearance of an end to it after two hours, when the end of the day was not far off. However vigorous the attackers were, the situation they were in was too violent; it was impossible for them to keep going for a long time. Some rested as best they could; others let themselves fall into the water, where they were immediately assisted by people who were standing by for that purpose in little boats.

Finally—I think it was about six o'clock—there was an enraged flutter of wings, as one of the troop had cleverly seized the eagle and broken one of its legs in his teeth. Another who pushed him then forced him to let go on pain of taking a tumble, took hold of the animal in both hands, and threw himself head first off the rope. His weight combining with the effort, the eagle was dismembered, the leg that was attached remaining hanging from the tree, and the young man fell into the water with his prey in his arms.

At that fall the audience redoubled its cries of enjoyment, as if it were a matter of wholesale salvation. Those who had got wet went to change clothes, and soon came back to the home of the victor, where everyone complimented him. They supped there together, and spent a part of the night enjoying themselves, while the fathers of the families also treated one another reciprocally, having what one might call a very good time.

The third day was also spent in games, dances, races and agreeable diversions.

We had no idea what all that signified, but we saw thereafter the same ceremonies were observed every year, at the full moon preceding the solstice of Capricorn, throughout the realm. The young man who carried off the eagle for that year had the choice of all the girls in the district in case he wanted to form a household, with the consequence that none could marry anyone else without his permission—which he hardly every refused; thus one might say that all of it only terminated in a simple formality and a singular honor for the triumphant competitor.

At other full moons throughout the year, they also held cockfights, went out in gondolas in the summer and in sleighs in the winter, partaking for two days in all the innocent pleasures of which they were capable except for that of the eagle on the mast. For the rest of the month, everyone was at work, and there were absolutely no other festivals.

That whole time having run by without doing anything, we made it known to our patron that we would be glad to have some kind of occupation. In the beginning he did not seem to be listening, but on seeing that we persisted in wanting to be employed, we were given wool to clean, wash, beat and card, not knowing whether there was anything else we could do.

We soon grew weary of that métier. La Forêt, who was a clockmaker by profession, would rather have had a file in his hand and to be working on the movement of a watch, but there were no such machines in the neighborhood and it would have been difficult to give them an idea of them.

Having perceived our discontent, they tried to make use of us in maneuvering a small fleet.

As there were twenty-two houses in our village or canton, of which I shall give a description subsequently, that fleet had to consist of twenty-two boats. Each father of a family organized the crew of his own and supplied it with the provisions necessary for four people for a voyage of three weeks. All sorts of goods and merchandise appropriate for trading were loaded into these boats, such as, for example, ropes, pulleys, wheelbarrows, hatchets, hoes, mattocks, spades and other instruments for moving earth, but manly robes and other garments made of wool or linen.

We were then in the month of December and, in consequence, in the middle of summer and the moist beautiful season of the year. As the billy-goats in that country are very large and their strength is equal to that of our horses, they make use of them for most carriages; each boat had four of them, two of which hauled for about two hours while the others ate or rested in the boat. When their turn came they were put on shore again, and so on, alternately, for fifteen or sixteen hours a day, which was approximately from sunrise to sunset. The night was spent in sleep or inaction, for there was then a halt.

It was impossible for my comrade and I to be surfeited by the sight of the beauty of that enchanted country and the riches with which the land was covered. The orchards were ornamented with beautiful trees, some in flower and others laden with the most excellent fruits in the world; the fields were covered with wheat, barley and other cereals; the grassy meadows filled with goats and sheep of an extraordinary size—akin to horses and cows, which I never saw—and all that was neat and orderly, with a regularity that enchanted us.

The whole country, as far as it extends—which is, as we learned later, a hundred and thirty French leagues from east to west and at least eighty from north to south—is divided into cantons or villages. These cantons form perfect squares, whose faces are about one thousand five hundred paces, or an Italian mile and a half, all having around the perimeter a straight canal twenty paces wide, which separates them, with a royal road to either side twenty-five wide, where there are two rows of trees in the middle, forming a pathway of twenty-five feet or five geometric paces, in order to have the edges free for the commodity of the animals employed to haul the boats.

Each canton is further divided in the middle by a ditch of twenty paces, and a road of twenty-five to either side, with trees planted in the same manner. The length of these roads, or half-villages, contain eleven habitations, each one more than a hundred and thirty geometric paces wide at the front and about seven hundred deep, which are also separated by small five-foot ditches, parallel to the smaller side of each demi-canton. At the head of each of these habitations, or alongside the ditch that divides the village into two equal parts, there is a single-story house sixty feet wide with a path through the middle from which one can gain access to all the bedrooms, stables, barns and other apartments.

The reason why they have no upper floors is that they are subject, albeit rarely, to violent winds that knock the houses down, for they are not built very solidly. All of it being disposed in the manner that I have just described, it is easy to understand that there are twenty-two habitations or houses in each canton, which are situated opposite one another, all of the same size and height, eleven on one side of the canal and eleven on the other. At each extremity of that watercourse there are bridges, both for communication between the two demi-villages and for passing from one village to another; there is another in the middle of each canton; they are all made of stone, of very fine architecture and perfectly maintained.

Of the twenty-two families two are distinguished. One is that of the Papŏ or priest, and the other that of the Kini or judge of the canton; they are in the middle, opposite one another at either end of the bridge. Those houses are the only ones that have an apartment at the back as large as the entire house, one of which serves as the church, the other the courtroom or senate. But we shall perhaps have an opportunity to talk about that other part later; let us return to our voyage.

We were *en route* for nine days, and when we were seven or eight leagues from the place where he had to be, we began to discover the uplands; nothing was to be seen from then on but mountains, which seemed to rise up into the heavens and whose summits dazzled us by virtue of the brilliant whiteness of their snow, by which those great masses are covered all the year round. The canal on which we were traveling terminated two petty leagues from the higher ground; it was necessary to stop there. Part of our company remained in the boats; the rest set off for the mountains.

Before arriving there it was necessary to pass through a beautiful forest.

The continual metallic din that we heard as we advanced made me think more than once about Vulcan and his Cyclopes. The whole atmosphere resounded with hammer-blows, and one could, in fact, have sworn that we were only a few paces away from the workshop of Mont Gibel or the anvil of Brontes, Pyracmon and Steropes.[13]

We were not entirely mistaken in our conjectures; the men we discovered soon afterwards were not unlike giants and demons in appearance; some of them were monstrous in stature and others as hairy as bears, and there was not one who was not as black as a Scottish coal-miner. The members of our company immediately addressed themselves to a director to tell him the canton from which we came, which was the third of the first line, named Rûs —for it is by number and a similar name that they are distinguished from one another. They also told him what kinds of merchandise we had brought, and what we desired to take away. Then they introduced my comrade and me to him, apparently asking him to show us all the places worthy of being seen by people who had never been there. Immediately, he gave an order to one of his attendants to accompany us everywhere. Five of our company joined us.

The first thing we were taken to see was a wide gulf of immense depth. It was an iron mine, which had been worked for thousands of years, and from which all the matter had been removed, which had formed other mountains nearby.

Descending into the hole on the left there was a stairway, which the workers had carved into the rock as they dug down. Although the steps were wide and shallow, I would have had great difficulty going down it. In front of it there was a wooden machine fitted with a large cross-beam, to which they had attached a pulley three feet in diameter, which served to extract the ore from approximately half way down the pit, where a platform had been built, to which

---

[13] Brontes, Pyracmon and Steropes were three Cyclopes who worked in Vulcan's forge, according to Virgil's *Aeneid*. In Hesiod their Greek originals had been called Brontes, Steropes and Arges. Mont Gibel was a classical name for Etna in Sicily.

other workmen pulled it up from the depths, by means of a number of baskets that those down below filled as they descended.

To the right, on the other hand, no one was working; everything there appeared to be in disorder. Our guide, seeing that I was leaning over to consider the irregularities made me understand by signs, as best he could, that five months ago a large section of the rock on that side, which had perhaps been excessively hollowed out below, had been detached and had fallen, crushing three hundred and sixty individuals working on that side.

After we had examined that place, he took us to see another from which coal was being extracted in the same manner, but which is much richer than that found in England, and even that of the region of Liège, since it burns for an entire day, and those who burn it only put it into the hearth once ever twenty-four hours. Between those two mines there was a pool of mineral water that was boiling continuously; it serves to clean all the dirt from their bodies, their clothing and their tools, but it is not used to cook foodstuffs because it gives them a nasty taste. The iron that they temper in that hot water becomes impenetrably hard, and is much better than our finest steel for making springs.

I had never found any difficulty in understanding why the mineral waters of Aix-la-Chapelle can have the degree of heat that is attributed to them, because they pass through long subterranean conduits, where sulfurous and bituminous deposits are doubtless abundant in the bowels of the earth, which, being themselves in great agitation, communicate a part of their movement to the waters in passing. Here, though, I could not see anything similar, merely a small lake in which water was collected, and into which, in order to replace that which was dissipated, as much by exhalation as by the usages that were made of it, a stone tunnel, which nature seemed to have made expressly for that purpose, discharged a trickle of crystal clear water as thick as a little finger—and which, far from being hot, was as cold as marble. That caused me to believe that there must be a terrible spirituous fire beneath it.

We also went to see the workers who separated the iron from the ore, the furnaces where it was melted and the forge where it was wrought or formed into bars to be wrought later. All of that was so similar to what is done in Europe, however, that I do not believe that I ought to describe it here. I understand clearly, from what I was subsequently told, that the whole of that chain of mountains, which served the beautiful country as a barrier, is the store from which the people extract a part of their wealth and things which are, for the most part, useful in society, like stones for building, others for making chalk, salt—which, although different from ours is nevertheless very good—fine tin and red copper, albeit in very small quantities, which also cost a great deal of difficulty and many human lives.

While I was occupied in considering all these curiosities, our workers labored at unloading their merchandise, bartering it, and loading up those that they had orders to obtain in its stead, which was done by mean of sleighs or little long and flat carts pulled by two, three four or as many as ten billy-goats, or by porters. So many people were employed in that work that it was completed in a very short time, even though there were long distances to cover—with the consequence that we were there for less than two full days.

We brought our guide back to our boats, where we treated him as well as we could, and gave him so much to drink that at the first step he took to go back he fell full length and hurt his shoulder, so badly that he pain he felt drew the name of Christ from his lips. I was surprised by that expression, and I would have liked to know how he had learned to know the savior of the world, but for want of knowing the language, it was necessary to limit my curiosity to helping him up and making sure that the injury he had suffered was not very dangerous, until I was able to investigate.

As we were on the point of casting off in order to return to our village, it occurred to me that if, instead of going via the same canal by which we had come, we were to go along another about two or three cantons away, we might perhaps see novelties that would give us pleasure and compensate us from the time that we would have lost and the trouble we would have taken. I communicated my idea to La Forêt, and he and I contrived to make the others understand. The good folk were so honest that they consented to our proposal without hesitation.

With that we planned a westward course, but when it was a matter of attaching our goats, the oldest of them, who had been leading them, so to speak, for forty-two years, and had followed that same path I don't know how many times, seeing that we were leaving the usual route, started playing up diabolically; it was impossible for the guide to retain the animal, which made so many leaps and somersaults that it broke the rope that was tethering him, and set off in flight at top speed. Twenty people hastened to run after it, shouting at the top of their voice bidding it to stop. The cries having been communicated to others, someone thought that he ought to try to make the goat turn back. The impetuous animal threw himself into the water.

The banks at that point were high and steep, and there was no way for it to be able to climb out. Our guide having been informed of the fall, he came running with three or four others to see if there was any means of getting his billy-goat out, and, perceiving from a distance that it was swimming along the channel, he placed himself a few paces in advance, and bent down very gently. Just as the goat was passing by, he threw a noose over its head and caught it by the horns.

At the same time, the billy-goat took fright. It launched itself toward the other bank, pulling our man in after it, as much because the rope had become coiled around his body—I don't know how—as because he preferred to allow himself to be dragged rather than let go. Immediately, the alarm was redoubled; people came running from all directions, and while everyone was urgently occupied in helping our comrade, the animal advanced as far as one of the stanchions of the nearby bridge, where it was able to get back on land and ran away, in such a manner that no one could see it any longer, and we had no absolutely idea what had become of it.

I was particularly enraged by that loss; I would have given a finger of my hand to be cut off, because I feared that our patron was going to look at us with an unkindly eye and might take it out on those who had been obliging enough to listen to us. We continued on our new course nevertheless, in spite of the resistance that the other goats put up, although that was only temporary, for as soon as the leaders built up some momentum, the others followed them like lambs.

That was of no profit to our voyage, however; the country is so uniform that it is worth as much to see one part of it as to amuse oneself travelling the whole. The only real diversity to be observed is in the faces of the people, as everywhere, and even though there had been some pleasure to obtain from that, the anxiety we were suffering would have prevented us from participating in it.

We were quite astonished on our arrival, however, when we learned that the billy-goat had been in the stable for a week; the skillful runner had covered the ground in thirty-five hours. Such agreeable news dissipated our chagrin entirely, and we laughed wholeheartedly by dint of seeing the others laugh.

The next day the boats were unloaded; all the inhabitants of the canton were there.

The judge takes possession the bill of lading that has been brought, and, having examined everything, he has each of the interested parties take what belongs to them. It is all accomplished in such an orderly fashion that not the slightest item is mislaid. To recompense him for that trouble, each household sends him, the day after, a late of the best fish caught in their waters, half of which is consumed in his house and the other half in the priest's lodgings, where the fathers of the families help him to dispatch it. It is an honor for those gentlemen, but they pay for it dearly, since all that they can conserve of that fish is not worth half as much as the sauce that generosity leads them to add to it.

Finally, everything was concluded and it was a question of returning to our work—not that anyone gave the slightest semblance of caring. On the contrary, we could see so clearly that no one was paying much heed to whether we did anything or not. Because we did not want to be reckoned as idlers, however, we would have liked someone to employ us for something else.

La Forêt, who was even sicker of working on the wool than I was, tried to make our host understand that, being a clockmaker by profession, if the other cared to furnish him with the necessary metals and implements, he would make him a machine that would indicate and chime the hours, in whatever divisions of time he pleased, and which all the inhabitants of the village understood.

As for me, who could not be of any help to them with my medicine, because the herbs of that country were mostly different from ours, there were very few minerals and they had a mortal hatred of being bled, all that I could do was

66

applaud what my comrade said in the hope that I might be able to work with him on the same project.

That proposal appeared marvelous to the judge, who sent for the priest in order to communicate it to him immediately. They had, in fact, heard mention of our clocks but they had only formed a rather confused idea of them, and no one thus far had ever seen one. Thus, they asked us without further ado to start work as soon as we could, and spared us nothing, all the more so because their manner of dividing time is mechanical and extremely awkward.

They take a piece of string, one end of which they pass through a metal ball, while they attach the other end to a wooden board, in such a way that it serves as a pendulum three feet and a sixth long, or thirty-eight inches. Having set it in movement they count as far as seven thousand two hundred oscillations, which, because of the length of the string, are as many seconds, and, in consequence, a twelfth part of the natural day, or two of our hours. I will say shortly what people they use to count the oscillations and to cry the hour throughout the village, as is done in many places in Europe during the night, particularly in Holland, where they pay men for that purpose they call *clappermans*.

We were given the materials necessary for our work. La Forêt ordered some of the tools that we needed, and made the others himself. Finally, we set to work, but not in a manner to become fatigued, since we only finished our clock after some seventeen months.

No one would believe the admiration with which everyone regarded us. They could not understand how the machine worked by itself and sounded all the hours of the day. By that time, we were so accomplished in the language of the country that we could explain as easily as in French, and we told them that it was necessary to build a small clock tower on the house of the judge or the priest, in order to put the clock where everyone could hear it chime. What was said was done; the slowest hastened to follow our instructions, and many people did not cease to work with us until the product of our labor had been put in its destined place.

Returning to the people of whom they make use to look after the pendulums and inform others of the time of day, it is necessary to know that until then, no one had ever been condemned to lose his life. Crimes were forbidden there, and criminals punished, but not put to death. They imagined that, the life of a man depending uniquely on the God that gave it to him, it is not our prerogative to take it away, for any reason whatsoever, not even for having killed his father and mother. I told them that it was a maxim that almost all the human race observed, and that our law, which we believe to have been dictated by God himself, expressly commands it, but it only irritated them and gave them a horror of people that they did not know but thought unworthy of the light.

It is not plausible, they said, that a man who killed another could be in his right mind; it would outrage all those of his species who can think. But when people were encountered sufficiently extravagant and cruel to deprive a neighbor of a life they had not given, it was necessary to leave vengeance to the Universal Spirit—that is what they call God—and not to anticipate that right by imitating his barbarity under the specious pretext of obeying divine law, which are fundamentally nothing but the ordinances of a distorted tyrant.

Every person, when it is a matter of firming a society, can transfer to another, as to a prince or sovereign, the rights and authority that nature has given them over themselves, but cannot give him any power over their life. It is God who, by means of our fathers and mothers, has made us without our participation, and since we have not contributed in any fashion whatsoever to our being, it is just and legitimate to leave to the same God the right of unmaking us, and to limit ourselves to putting to death other animals, which he seems to have left at our disposal.

Following these principles, they contented themselves with imposing on everyone the punishment that they thought proportional to the crime. Blasphemy against God is the most enormous sin among them; those who commit it are mercilessly condemned to work for the rest of their lives in the depths of a dark mine, where the sunlight will never reach them. Murderers, adulterers, lechers and those guilty of grand larceny are treated in a similar fashion, but some work at a higher level than others; some are there for ten years, others more or less, in accordance with whether the crime is aggravated and the person mature and intelligent.

Peccadilloes are punished less severely, and those who commit them rarely leave the village. Some are employed in fishing and mending nets, which occupies many, because their waters are populous and they eat fish in large quantities; others care for paths and trees, some dredge the canals. Girls and women take charge of the pendulums, at which they are relieved every half-day, and young boys go out to cry the hours—which is done from the time that the sun reaches its meridian until it returns to it. All of that is for a certain time, after which their liberty is returned to them.

I said just now that blasphemy is the offence most severely punished; that gives me the opportunity to say a few words about the poor fellow who, after having served as our guide to the mines, had proffered the name of Christ when he fell over, as if to appeal for his aid. When I was in a fit state to talk to everyone I let few opportunities pass to inform myself in regard to things I wanted to know. One day, I was recounting to our patron the circumstances of the voyage we had made to the mountains, and, having mentioned that individual and what he had said, I asked whether they knew of a Christ among them.

He replied that three or four hundred years before, a number of people had come to their country for similar reasons to those that had brought us; that the last one who had arrive had been a grave man clad in a long robe—in brief, in such a fashion that it was easy for me to deduce that he was a monk of some mendicant order.

"That man," he continued, "was intelligent, and even a scholar. He arrived in a canton not far from this one, but did not stay there for long. As soon as he understood a little of our language, he set off on foot, often changing village. My great-grandfather, from what he told my father, lodged him here several times, and took a great deal of pleasure in hearing him talk. He did nothing but preach morality to everyone; he often talked about a resurrection and a happy immortality after this life.

"Furthermore, he asserted that God had a son, engendered of his own substance a long time before the world, who had manifested himself to humans several centuries before, born of a virgin—or someone, if you wish, who had never known any man; that this man-god had conversed with human beings; that he had suffered death like a brigand, in order to merit by that eternal life for other humans who wanted to embrace his faith; and finally, that the person in question, who was named Christ, had risen from the dead himself, and had seated himself in the heavens at the right hand of his father, in order to govern the heavens sand the earth with him until the end of the world.

"As that doctrine pleased many people, he found many who took a singular pleasure in hearing it, while others were scandalized by it. That eventually reached the ears of the king. He was summoned to the court, and after having been carefully examined, he was condemned as the worst of blasphemers to end his days in the depths of a mine, where he died some time afterwards. Because he had the word Christ on his lips until the very end, a few of those who were working with him imitated him—and what you have told me about your guide," he concluded, "is certain evidence that that happened among us."

Although that discourse alarmed me, I could not help saying that I had the same belief as that man, that the precepts of the religion I professed brought me to that, and that I was surprised that people as wise and as charitable as they were could resolve to treat a poor holy man so inhumanely, whom heaven had doubtless sent to them for their salvation.

"Politics," my host replied, "probably played a major part in it. Princes do not like great changes in religion, for fear that they might suffer in consequence, or that it might be prejudicial to the government. But it is also sure that your sentiments are repugnant in many respects, and that this Christ both excites revulsion and embarrasses reason prodigiously."

"I admit that it is an incomprehensible mystery," I told him. "We believe it, however, and we believe it with all the more confidence and firmness because we see that it is advantageous to us to believe it, because of its influence in the economics of salvation, apart from the fact that it is a truth of which a thousand eye-witnesses have given evidence, and that God himself has revealed it to us."

"It must be the case," said the judge, "that you live in very fortunate climes, since the divinity communicates with humans there—our, to put it better, it must be the case that the people of your society are very vain and presumptuous, to have the impudence to publish loudly that the Universal Spirit lowers itself to the particular and familiarizes itself with an earthworm. That appears to me to be insupportable, and if that same God took the slightest interest in his glory, he would not fail to punish your pride rigorously.

"But before I engage further in this discussion with you," he continued, "tell me, I beg you, how this revelation was made? Did God speak to you directly, in person, or did he employ the heavens, the earth or some other creature for that? In what manner did he proceed?"

"I don't know if it's worth the trouble of talking to you about this matter," I said to him. "I see that you're so distant from our sentiments and so little disposed to give the slightest credence to our dogmas, that I'm afraid that your incredulity might excite your anger, and that might cause me trouble."

"You have nothing to fear," he replied. "I'm your friend, and an honest man; I will allow you to say anything you wish, and simply conserve the right to judge it as I please."

"On that condition," I told him, "I would like to tell you the little that my age, my education and my art have permitted me to learn about it. But for fear of taking things too far, or talking to you about things that you probably know better than I do, tell me, if you please, beforehand, what sentiments you have of God, the world, human beings and their origin, as well as their dependency and what they ought to expect after this life."

"You're right," the old man replied. "I shall satisfy you, in regard to myself as an individual; it's impossible that my confession should be general, since there are perhaps no fewer people than opinions.

"I believe in an uncreated substance, a Universal Spirit, sovereignly wise and perfectly good and just, an independent and immutable being, which made the heavens and the earth, and all the things that exist, which maintains them, governs them and animates them, but in a manner so hidden and no disproportionate to my nothingness, that I only have a very imperfect idea of it.

"However, seeing the necessity of its existence, and the dependency that we are in with regard to it, we believe it to be an indispensable obligation to render our homage and adoration to it, only to speak of it with respect and only to think of it tremulously; that is the principal part of our religion. The other is to render continually our actions and graces for all the blessings we have received, without any pretention for the future, much less after death, since then, no longer existing, we will have absolutely no need of anything. And it is for that purpose that we assemble every morning in the home of our priest, as you have witnessed several times since you have been in our midst."

"It's true," I replied to him, "that you are very punctilious in giving God an hour of your devotion every day of the year without interruption, in which you are much to be praised; but I think it strange that you reject prayer entirely, and that you make no distinction between the days. As for us, we employ six for our domestic affairs, and give the seventh to God, and to the exercises of our religion."

"We do not think," he said, "that one day is any more excellent than another; they are undoubtedly all equal, and although we only spend one hour of the morning in our churches, we nevertheless devote the rest of the day to the Universal Spirit, mediating upon its grandeur at every moment and admiring its bounty toward all of its creatures. As for praying to it, that is absolutely futile, in addition to the fact that it would be akin to doing violence to it, for being immutable by nature, it is evident that it cannot undergo any shadow of change."

At this point someone came to inform the judge that the Timnŏ—which is to say, the governor, steward or satrap—was there to receive the canton's tribute. We have already remarked that each village consists of twenty-two families, who are governed by a bailiff; ten cantons form a government, of which the oldest of the bailiffs is Timnŏ and president of the other nine, in the assemblies that they hold in order to administer justice and regulate the policing in the ten villages. In addition to that there is the sovereign court, to which the ten governors delegate one of their number once a year, which assembles for twenty days or more, never fewer. The king presides over that illustrious and numerous assembly, where he conserves regal rights, and to which all other tribunals can appeal when it is principally a matter of the punishment of some major crime.

The steward who had come to receive the gift of the people was very well received by our host; a magnificent meal was made or him, to which the priest and the two village assessors were also invited. In the conversation they did not fail to mention the clockmakers. The governor was curious to see our machine; he admired the invention and lavished a thousand praises upon us; but it would have been better for us if he had known nothing about it, since in the end, no good came from it—as will become evident in due course.

*Chapter VII*
*Curious conversation between the author and the judge*
*and priest of his village, on the subject of religion, etc.*

After the satrap's departure, the judge, who still remembered our conversation very well, was impatient to hear me explain the religion that I professed. In order to have a more favorable occasion for that he invited the priest to dinner the following day for that express purpose, and my comrade and I made up the party.

The first thing that gave the Papŏ reason to speak was to see us pray to God before the meal. As his sentiment was not unknown to me, and I had already talked about it with my host, I contented myself with telling him that the idea I had of God, as a sovereignly powerful and perfectly good being, led me to implore his blessing for the food he gave me to aliment my body, being persuaded by reason and experience that his word sated infinitely more than bread.

He criticized me for that in almost the same terms as the judge, attempting to elude the strength of my argument by the example of the people of his nation, and the majority of animals, who were no less nourished by what they ate than us, who made that ceremony, with the result that the prayer was reduced to absolute insignificance.

"We shall not bother to dispute that," I told him. "It's a question that will be resolved soon of its own accord, which only depends on a few other verities that I shall place within your reach. In the conversation that I had the other day with our judge, he admitted to me that you confess unanimously the existence of a perfect God. Assuming that verity, which it would otherwise be very easy to prove to you by several incontestable arguments, above all the one attributed to a certain Saint Thomas, which he called the path of causality to the efficient cause, since that path brings one inevitably from effects to a first cause, intelligent and necessary to the production of everything."

"I know that," said the priest, "and it would be necessary to be deprived of reason to doubt it."

"Well," I continued, "it's obvious that it is that same God, and no other, who created the universe—which is to say, the heavens, the earth and, in general, everything that exists."

"As to that," the judge put in, "I don't understand it very well; nothing can be made from nothing."

"You're right," I replied, "with regard to us—but with regard to God, it's a different matter. One cannot, without contradiction, posit matter coexistent with God, for there would then be two infinities, two independent beings, and it's claimed that that is incoherent. But let's leave infinite things, which our beyond our range. I think it fundamentally sufficient to know that God made everything, without going to the trouble of asking out of what, how and at what time.

"We have a book," I continued, "which informs us of all that. Moses assures us there that God did everything by means of his word, about six thousand years ago, and that he took six days, after which he rested from his work."

"What did he do on the first day, then?" asked the judge.

"After having created the heavens of the earth, he said 'let there be light' and light there was, etc. On the sixth day he created man from clay, and breathed the respiration of life into his nostrils, etc.

"Having made him capable of discernment, it was just that he lived under his dependency, and recognized him as the sole master of the universe. He gave him power over everything there was on earth, and only forbade him to touch a single tree that was planted in the middle of the garden of delights, where providence had established it.

"The submission he had for his creator would doubtless have prevented him from contravening his orders, but the woman he had been given as a companion, being weaker and more curious than him, allowed herself to be carried away by her passion; she put her hand on the admirable fruit of the tree, tasted it, and found it so excellent that she gave it to her husband. That wretch was unfortunate enough to eat it, and to incur in consequence the punishment imposed upon him of dying an eternal death—which is to say, of suffering eternal punishment after death: a harsh and surely insupportable punishment in proportion to the sin and the one who had committed it, but which was nevertheless proportionate to the majesty of the person offended."

In that fashion I ran through the story of creation, the deluge, the patriarchs, Moses and his brother Aaron, and the miracles that had confirmed the verity of the story. I told them about the prophets and their predictions, principally in relation to the Messiah, the advent of the savior, how he was the son of God, and in what manner he had ransomed us of the punishment that we had merited in the person of the first man, our father. Finally, I made them see the necessity of prayer, as much by what nature indicates to us as by what holy men said about it, in particular Jesus Christ. Finally, I talked to them about the resurrection of the body, of which souls would resume possession, and of an eternal and blissful life that the son of God had earned us by suffering an ignominious death on the cross."

It must be admitted that they listened to me with a great deal of patience. It even seemed that they took pleasure in it, and that they acquiesced to the greater part of it. But I was very surprised when the priest looked at me very seriously and asked me whether I believed all that.

"Yes, certainly I believe it," I replied. "Those who doubt the law of Moses die without any mercy; and the apostles assure us that one cannot doubt the verity of Christ's words and all the economics of salvation without danger of eternal punishment. But that is not the force that leads me to it; it is really the evidence.

73

"What would you say to me," I continued, "if I were to name to you, not only that which you have kept most hidden, but everything that you will do and will happen to your country? If I cured the sick, resuscitated the dead, passed over the sea with dry feet, split rocks with a simple rod in order to cause enough water to spring forth to slake the thirst of an entire people, and accomplished a thousand similar prodigies, would you not say that either I must be God, or at least an instrument of which God was making use to contrive so many different miracles, since there is nothing human in all of that?

"Well," I went on, "that is what the prophets, the apostles, and Jesus Christ most of all, have done, as I have insinuated to you just now—with the consequence that we have no reason to doubt the verity of what has been left to us in scripture."

"Your conclusion is not just," interjected the Papŏ. "Have you seen all these wonderful things?"

"No," I replied, "but it is not always necessary to see something in order to believe it. You have never seen Europe, the realms that comprise it, their wars, their religions and their customs; you believe, however, what we have told you about them because you take us for honest men, and two or three other voyagers before us have informed your ancestors of very similar things. When a fact is supported by the testimony of several individuals of probity, one has no more reason to hold it in doubt. Now, the facts of which I speak are not simply confirmed by a sufficient number of pious and sage individuals, but by hosts of witnesses, by entire nations, who cannot be suspect, since there are some whose religion is different from ours, and who are our enemies, fit for burning. Those people, who are the Jews, know how God appeared to our forefathers, sometimes in dreams, sometimes in a burning bush, often as a cloud by day and a column of fire by night, who led them, and stopped where they were to camp in the wilderness[14] into which he had led them himself, in order to go and take possession of a great country that he had destined for them. Certainly, after such

---

[14] Author's note: "Mention has been heard of an English scholar who has recently made a dissertation in which he endeavors to prove that there was nothing miraculous or even extraordinary, about the column of fire that led the Israelites through the wilderness; and to show by the best ancient and modern Authors that it has always been the custom in these sorts of deserts to make use of fire to direct the march of armies, or multitudes, by sending out guides ahead of them, in such a fashion that the troops can see the smoke during the day and the flame during the night. He claims that the person who had the direction of that fire and who served the Israelites as a guide was none other than Hobab, the father-in-law of Moses, which he tries to prove by verses 29 and 30 of Chapter 10 of Numbers and several other passages in Holy Scripture." The reference might be to Henry Hammond, whose Biblical commentaries were criticized by Jean Le Clerc in a book published in 1699.

strong testimony, it seems to me that we would be quite wrong to be incredulous."

"Speaking ingenuously," said the judge, "there is something surprising in all that, which, although supernatural, nevertheless appears quite plausible."

"Not as much as you think," said the priest. "You know how our ancestors have been taken for dupes, almost in the same manner, by the subtlety and violence of our first kings. Parchment is available for writing at any time, and the punishments inflicted on those who do not give their consent to pretended facts that are told to them as truths force people to be silent who would otherwise have taken pride in contesting them."

He fixed me with a stare and continued: "That creation you have just described to us is a pure allegory, which I find rather crude of its kind and fabricated by an author very ignorant of the nature of things, to the extent that he makes effects precede their causes—since, according to what you have said, light was created on the first day, and the luminaries from which it comes on the fourth. It is certain, moreover, that the idea of a god who labors and who rests can only be swallowed by very primitive an ignorant peoples, whom one wants to master, and of whom this Moses of whom you speak claimed to be the temporal lord, while his brother Aaron had a boundless domination over their consciences."

I dare not describe the manner in which he treated Jesus Christ and his mother; but on the subject of the soul, the spiritual substance within us—of which, they said, they had no notion—I cannot help remarking here on one of the difficulties that came to the priest's mind in the matter of the resurrection of the dead.

"It is certain," he said, "that the earth is composed of an innumerable quantity of tiny particles, the figurations of which are extremely different; that can be seen by the diversity of objects that the same soil produces, certain particles, which are appropriate to form one species of fruits, being not at all apt to the production of some others. That which is good when made with copper is worthless when constructed in iron. Hence, if one sows wheat for several years in succession in the same field, one eventually finds that all the particles of matter appropriate to produce wheat for us having been employed, and none remaining, that field will produce no more wheat, unless, by means of compost, one brings others to it.

"Let us apply that example to human beings. The particles that are appropriate to make human flesh are no more infinite than those of cereals, and there is no doubt that in our realm, there is only sufficient to form a determined quantity of individuals. Make that number as large as you please, but I do not think it equals that of all the people who have lived since the beginning of the world.

"I will say more," he added. "I don't know whether one can suppose, with justice, that there are enough of those particles to sustain the humans born within a mere ten centuries, Those who have studied the nature of things even a little know that, just as the hair and the nails grow, wear away and fall, the external parts of the fibers of our bodies also wear away while the blood feeds and augments the interior fibers. It is indisputable that some dissipation occurs every day by transpiration alone; but there is this advantage: that the particles of which one is derived on the one hand serve as reparation on the other. In consequence, if everything we lose could be transported to another country, without any coming from elsewhere to ours, it is plausible that, as sometimes happens, famine and morality would necessarily follow, in order that the particles of those who die could serve for the growth of others, until no more remained.

"From that I conclude," he said, "that if there were resuscitation, it would be impossible for there to be sufficient particles appropriate to the construction of human beings to afford it to all those who have lived, even if it were only necessary to form bodies of very mediocre stature—and God alone knows where he would find sufficient for the others, since it appears that if all those who have expired in the several million years that the word has existed were to be formed into a mass, it would, so to speak, surpass in magnitude that of the earth from which they have taken their origin.

"Let us clarify this paradox by an approximate calculation. In this country we have 41,600 villages. In each village there are 22 families, of an average of nine persons each, so each village contains nearly two hundred inhabitants, making 8,323,000 in the entire country. Let us give each human body, considered in the form of a parallelepiped, five feet of height and half a foot of width and thickness, on average; I obtain from that, at the least, as can you see, that on the day of resurrection there will be 8,323,000 bodies containing about 10,400,000 cubic feet of flesh. If we suppose, finally, that the number of human beings is renewed every fifty years, it will require 208,000,000 cubic feet of flesh for the humans who have lived during a thousand years, and 2,080,000,000 for the society of ten thousand years. Continue that multiplication and see where it goes.

"But what would be the case," he continued, making a great exclamation, "if the opinion if the opinion of a few clever men is true, which, as you have said to your host, passes for constant, that the majority and perhaps all animals are only composed of an innumerable quantity of tiny creatures that have life and movement, with the consequence that in a volume the size of a grain of millet there are thousands of them, which, in spite of their smallness, are nevertheless individuals of the same species as those that have engendered them, and which ought in consequence participate in the same advantages as the others, even though they surpass them in size to the same extent as the highest mountain differs from a grain of sand? Then it is manifest that your sentiment is ridiculous, and even a contradiction, which leaps to the eyes."

"You speak of thousands of years," I said to him, "as if they were as many minutes; in your understanding, the world must be very ancient."

"I am making use of a definite term to designate an indefinite number," he said. "It is necessary not to take it too precisely. Whether the universe is ancient or not, it does not change the nature of things. It is constant that we believe in a time immemorial, which we cannot express either in numbers or in words."

"You are not the only ones who are mistaken in that regard," I said. "The Chinese among us extend their chronologies more than forty thousand years, without counting the time that has not been registered prior to that. The Egyptians, among others, went at least as far. An ancient philosopher named Plato mentioned an Egyptian priest who, in conversation with Solon, told him that nine thousand years had elapsed since Minerva had built Saïs.[15] Diodorus Siculus counted twenty-three thousand years between the time of Osiris and Isis and that of Alexander the Great. Diogenes Laertius speaks of a term of forty-nine thousand years, during which they calculated all the eclipses. They claim to have observed the stars for a hundred thousand years, according to what Saint Augustine says; and according to Cicero, they extended that number as far as five hundred and seventy thousand years.

"All that, however, is advanced without foundation, following a principle of vanity, by which they wanted to place themselves above the other nations of the earth. For our part, we refer to Moses, who assures us that the world was born approximately six thousand years ago. And certainly, if one takes the trouble to reflect even a little, it is impossible to call that verity into doubt. An incontestable proof that the world is not very ancient is that we have no history that goes back further than four thousand years. The arts are, for the most part, very new. We do not know of anyone prior to five hundred years ago who had any knowledge of the navigational compass, the printing of books, gunpowder, firearms, telescopes, microscopes and other fine inventions. We know that even the usage of money was unknown to the first writers. Chiming clocks, watches, glass, paper, tempering steel and an infinity of other things are of recent date. Thus I conclude that in this matter, as in others, it is necessary to believe in the word of God."

"I have already said," the priest replied, "that no one emancipates us from determining the age of the world. We are persuaded that it had a beginning, but we do not know when. All that I can say is that the time in question is extremely remote. The first man has not been identified, and none of us knows anything about him. All that we know is by means of tradition. The majority of the arts that you have just named are unknown to us, but this region is no less ancient than yours for that; we might be here for another million years without knowing them, because we have no need of them; it is not impossible that others have

---

[15] Sais was a city in ancient Egypt; according to Herodotus it was the burial-place of Osiris; he associated its patron goddess, Neith, with Athena, the Roman Minerva, as did Plato, who cited Sais as the city where Solon found the story of Atlantis, and Diodorus Siculus. The cult of Neith was said to date back to the fourth millennium B.C. Diodorus alleged that Athena built Sais before the deluge that supposedly destroyed Athens and Plato's Atlantis.

existed in the same way for a long time before us. Necessity, or the existence of other similar things, have caused the invention of things in a hundred years of which no one has ever had occasion to think before in as many centuries. No consequence can be extracted from all that.

"What I know is that from father to son, we always say that the years of our duration are unknowable. In fact, it is certain that notwithstanding the prodigious quantity of wood that we burn, the mountains of coal that have already been leveled are so considerable that if one wanted to make the calculation, that alone would be capable of confirming us in our sentiments. But what is more remarkable is that around seven thousand years ago, at the top of one of those mountains, on digging down thirty feet from the summit, an iron hook was found weighing more than one thousand five hundred pounds, who we still have, and which the strangers that we have had here from time to time have assured us to be one of the machines of which use is made to stop large vessels—from which it follows that before us, the ocean has been in possession of this beautiful country, and that our highest mountains were perhaps then only reefs.

"In addition to that, who can tell whether the arts that you claim to have discovered were unknown to those who preceded you? I notice very clearly here that sciences grow old; my great grandfather was much more knowledgeable than my father in astronomy; I know even less than them, and according to what they say, the enlightenment we have is only darkness by comparison with what their ancestors knew. It is the same in other families. There are sciences that are cultivated in certain times, as if they were fashionable, and which are completely neglected in others; they can even be so completely forgotten that those born afterwards find no trace of them, and sometimes take them up thinking that they are their first authors."

"That might well be the case in your realm," I said, "where you have no communication with the other peoples in the world, but among us, if sciences perish in one place because of war and fire, or because of the idleness of indifference of some—of which we have examples—they are brought to a higher degree of perfection elsewhere by the diligence of others, and I do not know that anything very considerable has been lost of what was known in the past. On the contrary, we discover new things useful to society every day."

I tried to explain to him the apparent contradiction that he found in *Genesis* in relation to the heavenly bodies and light, and show him that he was mistaken with regard to the resurrection, but he mocked me and all my arguments; he did not want to admit the power of God anything that he did not believe to be necessary.

"Why," he said, "resuscitate people after this life? What necessity is there in exterminating the human race, in order to revive it thereafter? If Christ was God, could he not have exempted humans from that death as well as the other? And on what would we subsist if we were all alive? There would not be enough to feed us in the entire land."

"The body will be different in nature," I interjected. "We shall neither eat nor drink, nor be subject to any natural infirmity—and in addition to that, God will transport us into the heaven of heavens, where we shall be sated by his glory."

"What! You'll be lifted into the heavens? What idea do you have of the heavens, then, my friend?" He went on: "For our part, we believe that the air that we breathe is infinitely more gross than that which is above us, and that the further one gets from the earth, the more subtle matter becomes. That being so, the heaven of the blissful must be like a void by comparison with the inferior heavens, in relation to the matter that fills hem. Thus, adieu lungs, since one will not breathe any longer; adieu the larynx, for speech; adieu the intestines; adieu, in brief, to the whole body, which the blood will no longer refresh; throw it into a warm fever, which will consume it in no time. But supposing that one conserves all that, like a useless burden on which one will repose, what will sustain those heavy material bodies?"

"They will be sustained by the omnipotence of God," I replied.

"You're wearying me with your power of God," he said. "I can see that you practice in your religion what we observe in the mysteries of nature; when we cannot give a reason for something, we say that it is the result of some hidden mechanism. Once again, I do not doubt the power of God, but I do not think that it is necessary to invent chimeras in order to be obliged to have recourse to it. If you made a paradise of sensualities, it might pass; but a place denuded of everything, where the body enjoys absolutely no pleasures, where there is no object capable of affecting the senses, no odors to tickle the sense of smell, no foodstuffs to tease the palate, no musical instrument to divert the ear, nothing to consider with which the eyes can be diverted—that is assuredly marvelous. It requires good faith to be so extremely sensual, since, notwithstanding the eternity that you attribute to your soul, and which you believe to be capable of subsisting independently of the body, you would rather embarrass it again and charge it with a frightful weight, which you want to make good for nothing, than leave its elbows free and abandon that mass of flesh to the corruption from which it absolutely cannot be exempt."

"It is not the soul alone," I said, "that determines good or evil; the body and the mind contribute to it too; it is necessary that they participate equally in the rewards or punishments of which the sovereign deems them deserving."

"All that," he said, "is incapable of persuading me. Our bodies do not remain the same for a moment; no man has ever reached the age of twenty-five years without being deprived of everything that he brought into the world. The blood, the flesh, the skin, the nerves and even the bones have diminished on the one hand only to be augmented on the other; the entire machine renews itself over time. Our inclinations vary too, according to age and constitution. One is often very debauched at thirty and extremely pious and retiring at sixty.

"With which of the two bodies will one be resuscitated? With the old, stiff, curbed and debilitated one that has lived virtuously, and all of whose actions have served as exemplars to adolescents and have been the edification of mature individuals? Or will it be the young, upright, vigorous and agreeable one that has deserved to be sent to the mines twenty times over? You can see that whichever way one turns, one is extremely embarrassed, and it appears rather as if the person who was the author of that opinion has not anticipated all the inconveniences.

"If I were to be resurrected I would be indifferent to what particles the body would be composed of when rising; for it is the same thing as the soul, and I would establish as constant that it would be in a certain state and not a certain place, which would render us happy. But all that is mere bagatelles, unworthy of a man of common sense.

"It is necessary that I admit, however," he added, "that I still don't understand what you mean by a soul, a spiritual substance, deprived of all matter—or by a mind constituted purely by thought—but nevertheless enclosed in a body, which that faculty is limited to pushing, or making it act according to its will, outside of which it could exist as before. As the idea that you form of it is agreeable in that it flatters you with another life after death, I am not surprised that there are people who acquiesce in it. They are doubtless intelligences of the common order, but it enables them to be happy. Wellbeing consists more often than not in pure imagination.

"Those who are filled with the thought that death is merely a passage to a glorious life must quit the world with less regret than others—especially those who have as much attachment to it as people seem to have in your homeland—and already to sense the aftertaste of a pretended eternal felicity. In consequence, it is the same for them where it is true or not, neither more nor less than, supposing that I have ten thousand *Kala* in my coffers that I shall never need, and believing them to be composed of the finest metal that can be taken from our mines, when they are only iron, my contentment would be no less perfect for it."

My companion, who was devout, was enraged to hear that pagan call into doubt the mysterious of a religion founded on the pure word of God. Several times he made me understand that he had difficulty controlling himself and that he wanted at least to retaliate with formal passages from the Holy Scriptures. I always deflected him, however, because the other, denying their divinity and even pretending that they only consisted of poorly concocted fictions, would only have shocked him by saying more about them.

I told them, however, with the design of alarming them, that not only was I persuaded of an eternal bliss for those who did good works and who had faith, but that there was also a punishment and an inferno prepared for the wicked and the incredulous, and that everyone would infallibly be treated in accordance with whether they had done good or evil.

"You have already told me that," said the priest, "but it is an error no less gross than the preceding ones, for it renders God the cruelest of all beings, to have created humans in order to damn them eternally under the pretext that they have infringed one of his commandments—and a commandment that simply consisted of not eating a fruit, which certainly caused me to shiver. I deny that anyone is capable of doing good or evil in respect of God, and I ask you seriously whether you believe it yourself?"

"Indubitably I believe it," I said, "and it seems to me so obvious that one cannot doubt it with shocking common sense. Are lewdness, murder, theft and blasphemy not crimes that offend the majesty of the omnipotent?"

"Not at all," retorted the priest. "First of all, if lewdness were a sin, God would be the author of it, and what is worst, of incest, since, according to you and your great Moses, there having only been one man, it follows that their descendants must have committed numerous incests before the number of living beings was sufficient to permit them to avoid it. And let no one tell me that it was then a necessity, since it would have been no more costly for God to have made a hundred individuals than to create only one. We are all children of the first man; among us there are degrees of consanguinity; before God it is not the same thing.

"Women and wealth were common in the beginning, as air and water still are at the present time. Men, who seem to have been made for society, decided, in order to avoid the disorder they observed that the community in question produced, that it would be good if each father of a family had at his sole disposition one or several women, a certain extent of land and a determined number of livestock. People were obliged in consequence, with unanimous consent, to make laws, which imposed penalties on those who did not observe them. In consequence, if anyone is offended by the transgression of those laws, it is really society, or the chiefs who represent it, and not the Universal Spirit, which cannot be offended by anyone in any manner whatsoever.

"One can say the same about theft and murder, in which I only wrong, strictly speaking, the individual whose life or property I have taken. As for blasphemy, although we punish it more rigorously than the other sins, it is not because we imagine that God is insulted by it. Not at all—that would be an infirmity in him, if he were capable of it. We are the only ones who are capable of suffering ingratitude, and the blackest ingratitude of that a man can commit is to outrage or lack respect for the author of his being, and all the benefits that he is capable of receiving therefrom; and that is also a bad example for children and inferiors, with regard to their fathers and masters.

"I conclude from all this that there are in human actions something akin to the qualities of bodies, which, in effect, are only considered in accordance with the combinations, relationships and comparisons that we make between them. Thus, for example, the same substance can sometimes be considered immense and sometimes negligible. A mountain is not great or small while my understanding, making the abstraction of all other matter considers it alone and indivisible, or if I suppose it to have no other relationship with other bodies, including my own. But if, thereafter, I consider it as a whole composed of an infinity of tiny grains of sand, it is obvious that it then appears to me as immeasurably vast compared with one of those little particles. It is not the same if I look at it next to another mountain of a similar size, with which I can deem it equal; and it will be extremely small when I compare it to the mass of the entire earth. Finally, the terrestrial globe will itself become nothing but a mathematical point in relation to the entire universe.

"It is the same with our actions; in themselves they are nothing, or, if you wish, they are all indifferent. If they become good or bad it is perhaps only in relation to certain institutions, like those about which we have just talked and by which they must be measured, so to speak, in order to know their exact value."

"You do not believe, then," I said, "that God, who is a God of order, and who hates confusion, has prescribed rules for humans himself, and given them laws in accordance with which they are obliged to conduct themselves and regulate themselves?"

"In the manner in which you think," he said, "no, I don't believe that; that was not necessary, since the Universal Spirit has given humans a will and an understanding, to regulate themselves, as you can see that we do. As there is no pride, jealousy or desire to reign among the beasts, God has not subjected them to any civil laws; there would be no more need for them among reasonable animals than among brutes, but as soon as someone wanted to abuse the weakness or the generosity of others, they were forced to invent punishments for those who transgressed certain regulations, and those regulations multiplied as the frenzied license of a few turbulent spirits gave rise to them."

"All that you say there," I retorted, "is true, but you will pardon me if I dare to say that I deny that God plays no part in it. It is not reasonable that Providence has produced a reasonable creature only to abandon him entirely thereafter; he is the father, and he also wants to be the director and the protector; common sense dictates that, and his word—for I always come back to that—assures us of it so positively that it is not possible for us to doubt it.

"I wish to God," I exclaimed then, "that you could see that word! It bears so many marks of the one who dictated it that you would be the first to read it with veneration if it fell into your hands; and I do not despair that it will be brought to you one day, either by some unfortunate or by a entire nation, which, by an order from heaven, will come to establish it among you in order to facilitate the conversion of such an honest and human people."

"I would be delighted," he replied, "to see this book about which you talk so much, but I would be very sorry if it were brought to us by a multitude of people, which your laws, holy as you believe them to be, would not prevent from tyrannizing us. We prefer that things remain as they are. Only be content with your lot, as you see that we are content with ours, and you will be happier than in fact you are.

"But let's talk about something else," he continued. "It seems to me that the time to leave has come; I shall retire. Adieu."

After the priest's departure were continued to converse for a little longer about the immortality of the soul, the resurrection of the dead and eternal life, because the judge had acquired a taste for it—and I noticed, if I am not mistaken, that it would be easy to bring those people to have the good sentiments of our religion.

Before quitting us, my host asked me whether I had seen the ardent mountain when I was at the mines.

"I haven't even heard mention of it," I told him.

"Apparently," he said, "it wasn't burning then; otherwise, they would not have failed to point it out to you."

"I would have been glad to see it," I replied, "but it's not a rarity in our homeland. There is Hecla in Iceland, Etna in Sicily, Vesuvius in the kingdom of Naples and several more such mountains, which also burn at intervals, but one cannot approach them very closely, even when they are not burning, because of the sulfurous exhalations that emerge from them, the prodigious quantities of ash that surround them and the danger of sinking into the earth at various places, with is soft, tremulous or lacking in solidity."

"Perhaps," he put in, "the Europeans who have been here before you have said the same thing to our ancestors, and that is the reason why the people have been disabused of the error they were in relative to the cause of the prodigy. What is certain is that simple folk have always been of the opinion that, God having created the world and then decided also to make beings possessed of movement and life, had installed a laboratory beneath the ardent mountain, which contained a crucible of prodigious size, with a high bar in the middle, which divided the orifice into two, and that the bar in question was connected to a lamp.

"The great workman, they said, filled that vessel from time to time with earth that he took from behind it, instead of which there is a great lake there now; and when that earth had become liquid by the force of the fire, he extracted a small portion of it by means of a hollow tube, which he used for that purpose, on one of the extremity of which he only needed to blow for an animal immediately to appear at the other end, which he sent forth.

"He had only made a small quantity when he noticed that his lamp had set fire to the mountain under which it was hanging. That unexpected inconvenience immediately made him change location, for fear of setting the whole earth ablaze. He had not been searching for long when he found a deep fissure between two mountains, which he judged appropriate to fill with water in order to work beneath it, fire having no purchase there.

"As that water soon attained a very considerable degree of heat, therefore, which first changed it into vapor, he pierced the nearby neighboring mountain in order that a stream of fresh water could be distilled therefrom, capable of tempering the ardor of the boiling pool—which is doubtless the same one you said that you had seen, and which still retains the same properties.

"It was added to that tale that God, having finished forming all the living creatures there in the same manner, with the exception of humans, which originated elsewhere, as I can relate to you another time, at leisure. Finally, it was claimed that the matter that was in the crucible being in a violent agitation, sulfur, mercury and the other greasy and metallic parts, which emerged in fumes, had been carried rapidly under the vaults of all the nearby mountains, which they had penetrated, some in the form of coal and others as iron or minerals, and metals that we find there."

That fable, primitive as it is, and doubtless invented in honor of chemists, gave me occasion to believe that glass had not always been unknown to them and that there had once been blowers among them. At any rate, the conversation ended there, because it was getting late and everyone was giving evidence of wanting to go to bed.

A few days after that conversation, the priest also wanted to give a meal to our host, to which we were also invited.

He then offered us apologies for having got a little too carried away in opposition to our opinions. By way of remedy he asked La Forêt, who had read the Old and Testaments more times than I had, to give him the most detailed account that he could off the contents of the Bible.

My comrade did so, and he thanked him for it, testifying that he was very satisfied by it, although I knew full well that he was only laughing at it—unlike the judge, who seemed to me to be extremely edified, with the consequence that the affair might have gone a long way if we had remained together.

To my regret, however, Heaven did not want that.

## Chapter VIII
### The author is taken to the king's court.
### He describes here the origin of those monarchs,
### the royal palace, the temple, etc.

The satrap I mentioned previously, who had come to levy the tribute, then went to take it to the king. While conversing with him, he told him how he had seen two strangers in one village who knew how to make machines that measured time perfectly and divided the natural day in to two times twelve parts. What was most admirable, and of great convenience for the inhabitants, was that every hour there was a metal bowl on which a hammer fell, marking by a certain number of strokes what part of the day had been reached.

The king seemed surprised by this report, and expressed a desire to talk to us. In fact, we were quite astonished one day to see two of the prince's domestics arrive to ask our host for us. Not knowing what pretext he could use to retain us, he reluctantly placed us in their hands.

Although we were deeply sorry to be leaving the judge, in whose house we had been infinitely better off that I could have wished to be in Europe, we nevertheless allowed ourselves to testify our joy at the honor the king was doing us in sending people in quest of us. We asked our guides several times what the cause of it might be, but they protested to us that they did not know. All that they were able to tell us was to assure us that people were talking about us at court as great individuals, and that we would certainly be well treated.

The disputes we had had nevertheless left me with a few anxieties. I feared that the king might have been informed of them, had been incensed by them and wanted to treat us as seducers, or people who were working to overturn the government, which came to the same thing.

We had no sooner arrived than the king summoned us to his presence. After having made our reverences, we wanted to kneel down talking to him, in accordance with the advice we had been given, but he did not want to permit it. He had a little stool brought for each of us and commanded us to sit before him. Everyone else who was there was standing or kneeling. The king was sitting in a magnificent armchair elevated by three steps and covered with a magnificently sculpted dais.

He asked us where we had come from and how we had entered his country. It was necessary, in order to content him, to give him an exact account of all our petty adventures. He seemed to be very pleased that our misfortunes had procured him the pleasure of our company. Finally, he came to the chapter of our science, in which he was extremely interested.

After telling us that he had learned that we had made a clock in our village, he made us understand that that his principal reason for summoning us was to ask us to make one for him too, with a promise to recompense our labor with his most tender amity and anything we desired of his person. We replied, with a profound bow, that we were not accustomed to being treated in that fashion by our sovereigns, that it was a great honor that his majesty was doing us in finding us worthy to be employed in his service, and that we would acquit ourselves with the least possible difficulty.

With that we were taken to a beautiful apartment, which was to be ours, where everyone took care to serve us and accommodate us as if we were great lords. The very next day we gave orders to have the tools fetched that we had left behind; we had a few others made as soon as my comrade ordered them, and we set to work as soon as possible, because the king was impatient to see us busy.

The monarch who governed then was named Bustrol: a wise, modest, sociable man who, if he is still alive—as I hope—makes himself distinguished less by ostentation and grandeur than by his striking virtues. His robe is the finest goatskin, tinted with a red dye found in the country; it is large and ample, with insets a foot wide at the bottom and at the top of the sleeves. His bonnet has five corners, with a copper globe on top an inch and a half in diameter, which is the principal mark of his royalty, if one excepts his gravity, his stature and his fine bearing.

The satraps also dress in red robes, but they are made of wool, and are smaller in every respect. The other men, without exception, have woolen robes of mixed colors. The judges are only distinguished by their bonnets. As for the women, they all wear dresses or veils of fine linen, in addition to which they put on underclothes, in accordance with whether the season obliges them to cover themselves to a greater or lesser extent. The king's children have no prerogatives above others; people have a little more deference for them, but that is not obligatory; only the eldest is almost as highly-considered and is dressed like his father, except that he does not wear any globe.

The king can have as many as twelve wives, who are chosen for him, or whom he chooses himself, from among his entire people when he makes a tour in order to be seen; and no one dares refuse him one, even if she has been promised to someone else. The governors can have three, the judges two, and the people one. Priests are also permitted to have two wives at once, but, simultaneously or not, they are only allowed a total of two in their lifetime; if they die before him, he is forbidden to remarry.

The most magnificent thing that the king has is his house; it is situated in the middle of the royal canton, which has the same extent as the others. The frontispiece is facing north-north-east; it is thirty-six geometric paces wide and twenty deep. The first story of the palace is ten feet above the level of the country, divided into several high-vaulted apartments, and pilasters have not been spared there; nothing is to be seen there but marble of various sorts and colors. The pavement is red, the pillars black and the vault white.

The second story being elevated by twenty feet, there is a staircase outside, before the portal, in the form of a demi-oval, of twenty steps, each half a foot deep, in order to go up to it. One initially enters into a vast antechamber, behind which is the king's audience chamber. From the antechamber one passes into two wings, one to the right and the other to the left, which divide the body of the edifice into two, in such a way that on each side there are two sets of two magnificent halls, making a total of four on each side, and ten apartments in all, with the most beautiful ceilings in the world, and paneling that surpasses in its sculpture everything that I have seen of the most curious.

Above the second story there is a third, divided almost in the same manner as the previous one, except that instead of the audience chamber, there is the room in which his majesty sleeps. After that one reaches a platform covered in tin, with a balustrade all around of solid bronze, wrought and pierced in a very artistic manner. In the middle of the platform there is a round pavilion covered in copper, so highly-polished, like everything else, that one cannot look at it directly without hurting the eyes when the sun is shining on it. Above it there is a globe twenty feet in circumference, on which a square-based pyramid has been set, one foot wide at the base and five in height. That mast is carried by twelve pillars of agate. There is nothing in the entire building but marble, agate, jasper and similar exquisite stones, marvelously polished and worked; the whole is constructed in accordance with an order closely resembling the Corinthian, save for the hollow columns, which are more Tuscan.

What they lack in that country is glass; they make use instead of skins of Polη, which they are able to scrape and prepare in a certain manner, which endures eternally, and gives such free passage to light that it is as bright inside the rooms as outside. It is that parchment with which they fill their windows instead of latticed panes. Although it is beautiful and effective, however, it has to be admitted that our glass windows far surpass it.

Behind the palace there is a dome of the Roman order, five hundred feet in diameter, also covered with copper, of the same materials, and of equal magnificence. That place serves two purposes, as the Temple and the Senate. The king's throne is on the southern side, opposite the door, elevated by six feet on a four foot pedestal which is covered with a magnificent stage, for it is certain that those people surpass the Turks infinitely in the weaving of their carpets.

In the middle of the ceiling is a copper sun of excessive grandeur; the body of it is perhaps ten or twelve feet in diameter, but its rays extend for a long way. The cone above the dome is broad and tall. All of it is made of copper and carried on six stout columns or towers, in each of which there is a staircase leading to the galleries of the superb edifice.

All around the canton continuous dwellings have been built, with pavilions at their corners and two on each side or face, at an equal distance from one another, in such a way that there are twelve in all. Twelve arcades have also been constructed between these pavilions, which are as many open gates to leave the canton via twelve bridges with sculpted copper balustrades, opposite one another. Finally, above these dwellings, which are for the king's twelve wives and some the domestics of the court, there is a gallery running all the way around, supported by columns of jasper, covered with tin like the rest of the buildings—except for the copper-lined pavilions—and of an extraordinary beauty.

The gaps between these buildings are filled with obelisks, pyramids, statues on magnificent pedestals, pots filled with all kinds of flowers, depending on the season, and cages full of birds with all kinds of plumage, which produce very diverting songs—everything, in fact, that might offer some diversion to the senses; which makes the location into a veritable enchanted paradise.

The canton to the south of the house is a park filled with goats and deer—which are small in that country—and particularly with a kind of animal called Polη, which has long hair, a single horn on the head, two flat ears as large as a hand, a short but very broad tails, and large flat feet, which allow it to stand upright more often than not. The size of the animal is similar to that of a small donkey; the flesh is very delicate but it is rarely seen other than in the king's park—which is a great pity, because there are few people who have any scruple about eating it, although it bears a strong resemblance to a human and appears, in truth, to be endowed with some reason.

The canton in the direction toward the equator, with is our north, is a patchwork of flower-beds irrigated by a thousand small artificial springs. The two to the right and the left are destined for fruit trees, vegetables and edible herbs. Beyond these five cantons there are a further twenty, twelve of which are for the queens, their children and their domestics and the other eight for cultivation and pasturage.

The kings revenues consist, very year, for each head of a family, of a copper coin the size of a guinea, which they call *Kala*, of which I have made mention elsewhere. One on side is engraved "Our hearts to God" and on the other "Our wealth to the King." I cannot specify what these coins are worth, but I noticed that people in that country make as much of one as we do of a louis d'or. The common currency is made of tin, and there are coins of all sizes, as in Europe, each with a different mark. With that single coin all the charges of State are satisfied; it is a small contribution for the individuals, but as there are 41,600 villages, or 41,575 leaving out the twenty-five of the royal house, that nevertheless brings in 831,500 *Kala*, not counting the judges and priests, who are exempt—which is, honor excepted, the only recompense they receive for their responsibilities.

I learned, however, that matters had only been regulated in that fashion for 345 years. Before that time, royalty had been, since time immemorial—or, in their own terminology, eternally—in the same family. Those kings had called themselves sons of the sun and the earth. That birth gave them a great deal of ambition, and the children all became worse every day than their fathers had been. They had reached the point of demanding homages and adoration from their people. They abused their wives and daughters as well as their wealth, and spoke of nothing less than having their throats cut when they showed the slightest sign of not being content with their tyranny.

Finally, fortune determined for those wretches that, by a certain fatality of which I never knew the details, a Portuguese arrived, who, having learned their language, told them that after having been shipwrecked on the coast of their continent, as we had been, he had established himself there with his comrades, all of whom had died within four years except for one. With the latter he had resolved to travel up a river that discharged into the sea nearby, with the aid of a small skiff they had salvaged. He added that they had been traveling for eight months, and that after having overcome inconceivable difficulties that had reached a chasm in the mountains from which that river emerged, as from its source.

They tried to get into it several times, but it was so gloomy, and there were so many reefs, bends and obstacles of every sort that they had despaired of getting through. They finally succeeded in their design, however, for after having covered more than two leagues underground they arrived in that country, so weary and exhausted they no longer had the strength to move, In consequence, having landed, and that one having come ashore, the other, while trying to do the same, fell backwards into the boat, which drifted away from the bank at the same time, so that the one who was on land could not reach it, and he had the displeasure of seeing it return into the chasm, from which it never returned.

The priest to whom he related that was no less astonished by it than he had been by his arrival; he made him repeat the story several times, to see whether there might be any revealing flaw in it, but was finally unable to doubt such a detailed narration and informed the judge of it. The latter communicated it to the principal individuals of other neighboring cantons, with the result that in a short time, the whole realm knew that their kings had been bandits and blackguards, in that, under the pretext of a particular and miraculous birth, which raised them infinitely above their subject, they treated them as slaves and were on the way to considering them, in time, as dogs.

Before six weeks had passed, they shrugged off the yoke; the king was dethroned and sent to the mines for life. They elected in his stead the oldest satrap in the land, with the promise of allowing his children to reign after him, so long as they were humane, virtuous and equitable.

Although that exiled prince was wicked, he was nevertheless in a position to complain, because he protested until death that he had believed himself in what was published about the origin of his ancestors, of which he knew nothing except by tradition. Nevertheless, that gave a great deal of ambition to the family, which claimed by virtue of it to be infinitely above other mortals—which, in fact, was bound to inflate them, and imprint in their people a very profound respect for their persons so long as both parties were convinced of the truth of it.

This is the story, as it was told to me by people worthy of faith in their assertions.

"God," they said, "has existed for all eternity; the heavens and the earth are not so ancient. As soon as the universe was created, the earth, which is an animate body, was charmed by the striking beauty of the sun, and became madly amorous. She made various attempt to rise up to it, but her leaps were futile; the weight of her mass was an obstacle to her leaps and she could only raise herself a short distance.

"The sun perceived her stirring and her prodigious agitation, took pity on her, covered himself with extremely dense clouds for fear of setting her on fire and consuming her completely, and approached her, penetrating her with his rays to the depths of hers entrails, and immediately withdrew.

"The earth conceived immediately; three hundred and sixty-five days and a quarter thereafter, hers belly opened and she gave birth to a man and a woman, both of a surprising beauty and majesty. Those two charming individuals having advanced in the direction of a country where they found an innumerable multitude of all sorts of trees laden with excellent fruits, they were curious to travel all over the territory that they found accessible.

"Finally, having reached the austral extremity of the vast country, they found it limited by impracticable mountains. It was there that Mol, and his wife Mola—for that was what they called one another—came into contention, she wanting to turn right or retrace their steps and he, on the contrary, being of the opinion that they ought to make an effort to get through. In consequence, having become angry because he saw himself being obliged to renounce his plan because of the obstinacy of his wife, he kicked the rock so forcefully that he made an opening in it, from which water flowed in abundance, and formed a stream that went to precipitate itself into the cleft from which the two twins had emerged. That cooled the womb of the earth to such an extent that since that time, she has no desire to join with her lover the sun, and thus has never had any other children."

They added to this beautiful story that it was from those two individuals that the inhabitants of their land had descended, and that they believed it to be the only place in the world to be inhabited. As soon as the Portuguese arrived, and told the story of his adventures, they knew full well that they were not the only people in the world and that the earth's pretended childbirth was only a fable—of which the revolution I have just mentioned was the consequence. Since that time the kings and their subjects had lived in great tranquility and harmony; they praised one another very highly.

In fact, I always saw that the people had an infinite respect for their sovereign, and that, reciprocally, the present king testified to the urgency of giving evidence of his affection for all those who approached his person. He was generally civil to everyone, and for us, in particular, it is certain that his civility was boundless.

## Chapter IX
### Which contains several very curious conversations
### between the King and our Author

It is inconceivable how assiduous that monarch was, in the beginning, to observe the hours of our occupations. He was all eyes to gaze at us, and often became all ears in order to listen to us, when we told him how people lived in our homeland. Above all, he took an indescribable pleasure in hearing about the sciences, and particularly philosophy, in which he was keenly interested. We were rarely together without him asking me some question of physics, mechanics or astronomy.

What pleased him a great deal was the Copernican theory, and I can say in his praise that I did not have much difficulty in making him understand all the different movements with which it is necessary to credit the earth in order to satisfy the apparent movements discerned by vulgar opinion, distinguished by virtue of daily movement from west to east and the annual cyclic movement of the sun, by that of the fixed stars and by those of vibration, once attributed to the crystalline heavens.

Having taken a ball and marked it with the principal points and circles of a terrestrial globe, I showed him how the earth rotates from the occident to the orient about its center in one natural day, and at the same time around the sun, which I placed at the center of the system, in a space of three hundred and sixty-five days and six hours, less eleven minutes. I then pointed out how that annual movement was not made about the equator, but following the ecliptic, because the axis of the earth, instead of being perpendicular to the plane of the annual circuit, is inclined on either side to an extent of twenty-three degrees and thirty minutes, which we call the movement of parallelism.

After that, we talked about the fourth movement, caused by the greater or lesser impulsion or haste that the earth suffers in accordance with the locations it passes in its course, by virtue of which its axis is sometimes raised or lowered be a few minutes, and, in consequence, the ecliptic seems at certain times to be closer to the equator than at others. That can be explained perfectly well by subtle matter whose turbulence it enters and passes through, but I did not want to get into that subject, which might perhaps have caused him difficulty, or at least demanded more time.

Finally, we talked about the fifth movement, which comes from the earth, in the part of its course that is most distant from the sun, having a greater arc to travel than the one that is diametrically opposite, not completing its period so rapidly. That difference is the basis of the part of the firmament that we judge to be passing from the occident to the orient in a certain space of time. Inasmuch as that portion appears greater or smaller, in proportion to whether the earth is more or less distant from the center of its near-circle around the sun, that causes an irregularity that Ptolemy attributed to the first crystalline—which makes the sixth movement.

As for the calculation of eclipses, the prince understood it like Copernicus himself. He reasoned very well with regard to comets, planets and meteors, and that which is most agreeable in physics, but he was absolutely ignorant of the cause of the tides of the sea, of which he had difficult hearing mention, and he only ever heard with admiration the reasoning of the proportion of the distances covered in a determined time by falling bodies, the oscillation of pendulums, the force of levers and, in general, everything regarding statics.

Firearms were also utterly unknown to him, and he would have held them in high esteem had it not been for the evil uses made of them. Nothing made him shiver more than the occasional accounts that I gave him of our wars and the bloody battles they caused. He could not understand how people could be mad enough to run in that fashion to the massacre and destruction of their own species, for such slight reasons, when there was often nothing at stake but the interests, ambition or caprices of a single man.

It was nearly four hundred years ago, he told me one day, that the king then reigning had been declared inept because, under the pretext of his origin and a miraculous birth, which distinguished him from other men, he treated his subjects arrogantly.

"One might have thought," he added, "that his vanity would have caused him to undertake great endeavors in order to maintain his position, but far from it; he only attempted to employ speech to disculpate himself and appease the anger of those who sent him to the mines; he obeyed immediately when he learned that it was the will of his people. And I swear to you that, instead of exposing armies to the fury of my enemies, I would a thousand times rather become the least in my realm than to conserve my sovereignty at the expense of a single human life."

"I admit," I replied, "that war has something cruel and inhuman; however, it is often just, and then God authorizes it, and the evidence that he takes pleasure in it is that he calls himself the god of armies."

"O heavens!" the king interjected. "What are you saying? You shock me by speaking in that manner. You are certainly fortunate not to have spoken those words before one of our judges; stranger as you are, you would be running the risk of passing your time very badly, since, in accordance with our principles, you ought not to have expressed such an enormous blasphemy."

"I beg your pardon, sire," I replied, incontinently. "The holiest of men, who have written our law, affect in several places to describe the divinity in that fashion. They attribute to him alone the winning of all the battles that the Jews sustained against those whose countries they conquered, and made him appear at the head of their troops like a formidable general, who lays low all those who come to meet him. I do not believe it to be culpable to imitate such great men,

and to have veneration for their lives, their precepts and their sentiments; however, I have so much respect for your person that I would prefer to observe eternal silence than to give you any cause for discontent."

"What!" said the king. "Your legislators use that language! Assuredly, I
find that extraordinary—that a God who, according to you, forbids the shedding
of the blood of a single individual, authorizes a general butchery of entire nations. There is doubtless much that is human, much passion and much cruelty, in
your laws; the thought alone makes me shiver. Let us not talk about it anymore,
for fear that I might say more than you would like to hear. I find much charm in
your sciences, but your religion and your maxims are not agreeable to me."

"That's because you don't understand them, sire," I replied. "I have no
books, and I am not a good enough theologian to convert you, but we have a
thousand Doctors among us capable of showing you so many marks of sanctity
in our Bible, and demonstrating its contents so clearly, that you would be forced
to give your consent to it, neither more nor less than to a mathematical demonstration."

"Well, until we see one of them," the king replied, "tell me how the armies
that you mentioned just now are composed, in what manner they are enabled to
subsist, how they fight, what recompense victors have and what profit reverts to
the widows and orphans, whether these wars have and end and whether there is
ever peace among you."

"Rarely, sire," I said. "The earth is extremely large by comparison with
your empire; there is an infinity of such kingdoms in the places from which we
come. So many great lords cannot live together for very long in perfect intelligence; the interests of royal families, more than individuals, often cause quarrels. Jealousy, the desire for aggrandizement, rank and religion—which is different in each country—are all subjects of rupture, which often only end after a
great effusion of blood. We have an empire named Spain, in which an intestinal
war broke out some time ago that lasted a hundred and sixty years, and which
cost the lives of a million men.

"The dominant religion of that country, and the one where I was born, is
Christianity, which differs extremely from all others; those who profess it do not
all have the same sentiments in every regard. The greater number of them claim
that it is not sufficient to worship God, the creator of the heaven and the earth;
they also want to evoke dead saints in order that they will intercede on our behalf in paradise. The prelates of the church impose the necessity of believing in
a purgatory, which is a place filled with fire and sulfur, where, after death, souls
must burn and suffer for a certain number of years, one more, another fewer, in
accordance with the crimes they have committed, in order to be in a condition to
appear pure and stainless before the throne of God. That same Church engages
people to confess that Jesus Christ is alive, in flesh and bone, and as great as he
was when he was crucified, in a host, or morsel of paste the size of the palm of

my hand, which the priest gives to each lay person on certain days of the year destined for that ceremony, etc.

"Some people cannot reconcile these maxims with common sense, nor with the precepts contained in the sacred book of our laws, believing in conscience that they would be wrong to observe them. The clergy, which perceived that disorder in the church, set up a severe tribunal, which imposed heavy penalties on those who emancipated themselves to reform the divine religion. It is necessary to add to that there were also ecclesiastics who extracted money from the people in return for reciting efficacious prayers, by means of which they claimed to be releasing the souls of their ancestors from purgatory. The officers of the king also charged them with new taxes every day, with the result that the most resolute of the inhabitants, wanting to shrug off the yoke, formed secret cabals and determined to assure themselves of a few mature cantons, or cities, of which they were the masters.

"Because of that, commerce declines, laborers languish for want of work; a foreign prince sets himself at the head of the malcontents. Other monarchs, jealous of the King of Spain, who only sought his abasement in order to rise above him, join forces with them. Companies of artisans are formed, who are glad to serve in return for subsistence. From those companies of approximately a hundred men, which each had their officers, regiments are formed, and of those regiments armies, which are commanded by generals experienced in the profession of war. They are carefully furnished with weapons, uniforms and all kinds of munitions at public expense, for which the magistrates impose subsidies.

"When everything is ready, cunning and a thousand stratagems are employed in the interests of surprise; eventually, battle is joined, and after fighting all day, it is frequently found that the greatest advantage of the victor is to have held the battlefield, at a cost of fifteen or twenty thousand combatants, whereas the enemy, having retreated five hundred paces, has only lost half as many. If one defeats the other entirely, he takes advantage of his victory by gaining territory and towns, which he sometimes puts to fire and the sword. Meanwhile, the defeated party tries again to fortify itself, either by raising new troops or contracting alliances with other princes, whom it attracts to its cause. They come to blows again, where fortune decides, sometimes for one side and sometimes the other, until the treasures and the men have vanished, for then they are forced to come to an accommodation, which lasts no longer than some turbulent individual desires, since pretexts for renewal are never lacking."

"But what is done with these troops?" asked the king.

"They are thanked," I replied.

"That is all very well for the discharge of the people," he continued, "but are men who have become accustomed during the war to libertinage and, doubtless, all kinds of sensual pleasures, good to be employed for anything else? On what do they subsist when they are no longer drawing pay?"

"I've already told your majesty," I said, "that the world contains an infinite number of countries governed by different princes; when conflicts cease in one place, they usually recommence elsewhere; the soldiers go to seek employment there; if not, each returns to his profession. I admit, however, that there are many who, having lost the habit of working, or who have no trade, go begging from door to door, with the women and children whose husbands and fathers have been killed, or abandon themselves to brigandage in order to live more comfortably. Some become highwaymen, others forgers; some associate with debauched women and help them to rob, and sometimes to murder, people who frequent vile places. Finally, there are intrigues that they practice in order to obtain good times, which oblige honest men to use a great deal of precaution in order not to be trapped, and often fail to escape. I could confirm this verity by a hundred examples that would make your hair stand on end, but one alone will suffice for the present to give you an idea.

"About eight months before I left Paris, a famous city that is the capital of the most beautiful kingdom of Europe, a parliamentary counselor passing by carriage along a side road where there was little commerce saw in the distance a well-dressed young woman who was extending her arms, putting her hands together and looking alternately at the heavens and the ground, showing signs of a veritable despair. The sound of the horses' hooves having caused her to turn round, she suddenly pulled herself together, wiped her face and continued her route at a slow pace. The counselor did not take long to catch up with her, and stopped alongside her.

"'What's wrong, Mademoiselle?' he asked her, in a very honest manner. "I saw you weeping; has some disaster occurred in your family? Speak boldly; you have fortunately fallen into god hands. Many people would try to take advantage of your distress, but with me there is nothing to fear. I'm an honest man; I have credit and good will; if I can be useful to you in any way, I shall apply myself to it with all the zeal of which I am capable.'

"Although she was only sixteen or seventeen years old, she initially adopted a serious expression, sustaining for some time that nothing was wrong and that there was no need to offer her his protection, that she was grateful to him, but all that she wanted from him was to be allowed to go on her way. Finally, however, after long persistence, that was only the effect of the gallant man's charity, she abandoned herself once again to tears that she could not hold back.

"'Yes, Monsieur, you're right,' she said. 'I'm not in possession of myself; my mind is in confusion; I'm roaming the streets and it would not take much to drive me to desperate extremes. I'm the only daughter of a father who adored me; my desires were a law to him, which he took pleasure in observing in every respect, with the result that I never asked him for anything that he did not immediately grant me.

"'It was a year ago that God took him, in the prime of his life; our separation caused him a thousand times more pain than the loss of his own life. The displeasure that he had in leaving me caused him to recommend me to his wife with hands joined. That stepmother promised everything that he wished; she embraced me in his presence and promised by an oath accompanied by a torrent of tears to make me eternally part of her most tender amity.

"'Alas, the poor man had scarcely closed his eyes than I became the object of her tyranny. Not a moment when by without her desolating me with insults and threats—threats that she often accompanied with blows; and today, after having greatly mistreating me, she threw me out of the house.'

"'That is violent,' said the counselor. 'You undoubtedly have cause for complaint. Enter my carriage, if you please. It's necessary that I bring you together again, or at least that I know the cause of such dangerous dissent.'

"It was not without difficulty that he persuaded her to take him to her home; she was very apprehensive of being seen there; her stepmother's anger caused her to tremble. It was, however, necessary to convince her.

"The window's house was fine in its appearance; a high wall with a coaching entrance and a large courtyard separated it from the street. The counselor, having asked whether Madame was available, was taken into a beautiful carpeted room, where she came to find him a moment later.

"He was surprised to see a woman of about fifty come in, tall, beautiful and kindly, with a mild and engaging physiognomy and having a bearing more like a queen than the wife of a citizen. After a few reciprocal compliments, he gave her an exact account of his meeting with her daughter, represented its consequences, and, having asked her to forgive the liberty that he was taking in interfering in what was essentially a domestic matter, he asked her in a very civil manner to tell him of what their difference consisted.

"The lady thanked him for his generosity in taking such a charitable interest in her family, put her stepdaughter in the wrong as much as she could, and finally, in consideration of the arbiter, summoned the demoiselle. Madame begged her pardon, and they made reciprocal promises, one of them to be obedient henceforth and the other to be more indulgent, and to have all the tenderness and regard of which a mother is capable—to the great contentment of the counselor, who applauded himself inwardly for being the author of such a good work.

"With that, the girl was sent away, and it was then that Madame began to exalt the obligation that she had to the counselor. She begged him to permit her to make the acquaintance of his wife, in order to have the opportunity to profit sometimes from his salutary advice. She asked him to extend his complaisance so far as to honor her with his company for dinner, all the more so as the table was already set and, having invited guests, she was in a position to regale him with three or four fine dishes.

"That compliment was proffered with such good grace that the counselor allowed himself to be persuaded. He told his coachman to leave, to tell the people at his home not to expect him, and that he would return in two hours. Meanwhile, the lady absented herself, with his permission, to give her instructions.

"He walked around while awaiting her return; having gone back and forth two or three times, he casually leaned his elbow against a tapestry as he turned round; the gap that he felt excited his curiosity. He found that there were two loose panels in the tapestry, one a foot in front of the other. He lifted up the outer one, and shivered when he saw the naked and bloody body of a man, who appeared to have been recently murdered, lying full length on a bed of straw fitted into the wall.

"That horrible spectacle, which threatened him with a similar fate, caused him to make a hurried exit from the room. Someone saw him when he was already in the middle of the courtyard; he called out to him, begging him not to be impatient and to stay, saying that Madame would rejoin him momentarily, and that everything was ready to be served—but all those fine words were not capable of making him turn back. As he fled he told the other that he had remembered something, which would not suffer any delay, that he would come back, and that in any case, they had not begun to eat, and there would be plenty left.

"He was followed all the way to the door. As he went out, four burly cutthroats came in, doubtless appointed to recompense him for his kindness—but they were a little too late, and the worthy man had escaped their ambush. The old procuress and the young whore had played their roles in vain."

"Assuredly," said the king, "that is a stratagem capable of surprising the most skillful man in the world, but what happened thereafter? Was there no search for them, in order that their punishment should serve as an example to similar rogues?"

"None," I replied. "Those who have taken such steps have come out of it badly. Bands of those sorts of people are so numerous that the slightest displeasure caused to one of them is doubly avenged sooner or later by the others, day and night, on you and yours, in any manner whatsoever."

"And all of that is the fine fruits of the wars to which you are exposed?" said the king. "I pity your lot; by that account you are nothing but the prey of the wicked, slaves, and miserable victims of the ambition and interest of your sovereigns. The dogs are more fortunate in my realm than men in your regions."

"You reason according to your principles," I said, "and we act in accordance with ours; everyone approves of his own sentiments, and all those contrary to them are shocking."

"It's true," he went on, "that education has a great ascendancy over our minds. Our ancestors would have sacrificed themselves rather than doubt the excellence of their origin. The sun had engendered them; they had been born of the earth. Today we would send anyone who wanted to sustain that opinion seriously to the mines. What we suck with our mother's milk we retain; the first lessons of out tutors are the strongest; they put down profound roots, which contrary winds of sentiment have difficulty in shaking."

"But with regard to your ancestors, sire," I put in, "did they never find anyone who, having examined the nature of things carefully, found difficulty in that supposed miraculous birth? For after all, it leaps to the eyes that the union of the sun with the earth was impossible, and that those two lifeless creatures, being destitute of intelligence and sentiment, are incapable of the effects so inappropriately attributed to them."

"Assuredly there were some," replied the king, "but no one dared open his mouth to say so. The people, who were prejudiced in favor of the fable, would have been capable of tearing them to pieces. In addition, the kings made use from time to time of a rather extraordinary stratagem to defeat them, which contributed more than a little to fortifying others in their opinion. They had built a subterranean tunnel from the palace to the temple, which ended beneath my pedestal, where there as an extremely deep shaft. When someone was accused of having proffered some shocking remark against the birth of the first man, which was treated as blasphemy, he was obliged to appear before the court, where the satraps never failed to condemn him to the mines.

"The king, who wanted to pass for clement, immediately annulled the sentence, which he claimed had not been pronounced in conformity with the rules of equity, since, he being both a member and the leader of the council, the judges had probably been inclined to his side rather than that to the accused—from which he concluded that it was necessary to summon the Universal Spirit to the tribunal in order to deliver exemplary justice to which of the two of them was in the wrong. With that, he fixed a full assembly for midnight, summoning the Senate, along with all those who wanted to witness the spectacle, not forgetting to go to his throne at the appointed time.

"One of his sons, brothers or close relatives brought the criminal before him, with his hands tied behind his back, and made him sit on the pedestal and the place that had been marked. Then the king, keeping his eyes lowered, pronounced four lines in a loud voice, which I have rendered into our language thus:

"'My mother, I know that you are equitable

"'To doubt it would be hazardous

"'Please engulf instantly, of the two of us,

"'The one that Heaven knows to be guilty.'

"At the same time, the man who had hidden beneath the theater adroitly withdrew the bolt securing a trap-door made expressly for that purpose in the pedestal, and caused it to drop with such rapidity that the poor victim, who was on top of it, fell like a thunderbolt, without having time to realize what was happening, into the shaft beneath, from which he never returned.

"All that was done so promptly, with so much dexterity, that the accursed trap seemed to open and close instantaneously, so that even when everyone was close at hand, it would have been difficult for them to perceive the deception. In order to play their role with all possible security, however, they were careful not to illuminate the place very well—in addition to which, the pedestal was high enough to prevent the satraps and other observers, who were on their knees, from seeing what was happening on top of it, and the interested parties who were present, pretending to see the earth open, made a great deal of noise, crying out as loudly as if they were veritably afraid of being swallowed alive along with the guilty party."

"But how were these impostures discovered?" I asked.

"The king's priests," Bustrol replied, "seeing their master banished and the face of things completely changed, proposed, on condition that no harm was done to them, to reveal everything pernicious that they knew. Although they did not know of any similar event in their time, they were nevertheless party to the secret, and had been engaged by an oath, by which they had been constrained, to assist in those cruel executions. The subterranean tunnel is still there; I can show it to you whenever you wish. As for the shaft, it has been filled in, and the trapdoor changed into a slab continuous with the rest, such as it is now.

"There was a second imposture of which they were aware, which had been practiced at various times. When there were great debates between the sovereign and his subjects, and he feared some evolution fatal to his family, one of the interested parties was sent in secret to climb the stairway in one the columns supporting the dome, and slipped quietly between the cap and the platform. When the council was assembled, he started shouting with all his might through a hole made for that purpose, which was connected with the center of the copper sun in the middle of the edifice: 'My son is right, and you are wicked!'

"That voice, which resounded everywhere like thunder, surprised the audience extremely, and never failed in its effect. Perhaps there were some among them who were not exempt from doubt, but the majority would have sworn that it was the sun that had proffered those words, and suspected that only those who were above the slightest suspicion would be exempted from a severe punishment."

*Chapter X*
*In which the ceremonies practiced in the country in association*
*with births and deaths are seen, as well as the manner*
*of administering justice and several other remarkable things.*


A domestic who came in at that point, very excited, interrupted our conversation. He had come to inform the king that the Mela had just given birth to a male child. It was only two years since he had taken his first wife, and was twenty-seven. I say that in order to make the remark that the king cannot take a wife until he is twenty-five, and must take the others before thirty, even though females are nubile at twenty. In the meantime he had married twice He had two daughters from the first and one from the second. That one had just given him a son, whose father was the marshal of one of the neighboring cantons, was the third, and as she was the legitimate queen, we will distinguish her from the others by calling her Empress, in accordance with the custom, which only gives that title to whichever of the sovereign's wife gives him an heir to the crown.

We congratulated the king on the birth of the young prince, and made him understand that we ardently desired him to be able to reign happily after him. He gave evidence that our compliment pleased him, and to convince us of it further, he invited us to follow him, in order to witness the ceremony of giving the child a name.

He went out, accompanied by two of his brothers, his cook—whose employment is highly considered there—and his butler.

The Empress was waiting for us in a bed that was as magnificent for its sculpture as because of the other ornaments with which it was enriched. As soon as she saw him she sat up. Care was taken to cover her shoulders with a red goatskin mantle covered with insets and embroidered garlands, lined with snow white ermine. Having asked the king of permission to kiss his hand, she expressed the joy she had because God had given her a son, since by virtue of that she had the honor of becoming Empress of such a great kingdom.

With that a chaplain came forward, who, following the orders he had been given, thanked God, on behalf of the king, the queen and all the people for the grace he had just accorded to them. I can say that his eloquence, combined with the submission and zeal with which he acquitted it, penetrated to my soul. He extended himself for some time on the negligibility of humans compared with the infinite grandeur of the monarch of the universe, on the continuous care that providence takes of its creature, notwithstanding that disproportion and the immense difference separating such different beings. He remarked on the constituents of that care, and it was then that he spoke about the virtues necessarily required by a good king; how providence had give them one, worthy in all respects of the sincere love of his people. He talked to us about the young prince, who had just been accorded to them, the obligations that he would have, along with many benefits, and concluded with a million actions of grace-with the result that the pious speech went on for at least an hour. Then the king's child was brought in, and named Baiol—which is to say, "benign."

Immediately afterwards, we were served dried and candied fruits, with honey that certainly surpasses the best American sugar. We also drank some excellent hydromel and other liquors, which lost nothing in comparison to ours, except for wine, of which they are absolutely desolate, there being no vines in the country.

The ceremony of the consecration of the Empress was postponed until after her lying-in, which would last eighteen days—but as it only consists, like the preceding one, of actions and graces, I need not bother to tell the story of it. Furthermore, it is not only in the king's palace that it is observed but in every canton in the realm, as soon as the news spreads.

Speaking of news, this is the place, if I am not mistaken, when I ought to remark that every day, each canton sends two men, between noon and one o'clock, along each road to neighboring cantons—thus eight in all, because there is no canton that is not in the middle of four others, and linked to them directly, except for those as the extremity of the country. On these roads there are marked pillars, set at an equal distance from one another, by means of which travelers know where they ought to go, and the distance is such that those sent forth can easily be heard, with the aid of speaking trumpets.

If something extraordinary happens at the court, which can be expressed in a few words—as, for instance, that the king has died, married, fallen ill or had a child, etc.—those sent forth proclaim it to their neighbors, and those to others more distant until it reaches the most remote, which happens so rapidly that in less than an hour, everyone in the realm knows it. When there is no news, they content themselves with saying that all is well. In the same way, when a canton has something to communicate to the courts, the sentries make use of the same means in the reverse direction.

If there are messages or parcels, there are messengers for that, who leave the court at five o'clock in the morning for the nearest villages; the latter put others *en route* at six, who hand over those who go even further at seven, and so on. For large burdens, boats are used, which also proceed in a very orderly manner, without it costing a penny, because every father employs his children or his domestics, in turn, for that purpose.

A short while after the Empress gave birth, the deputies of the satraps came to court to administer justice or put things in order. That assembly lasted twenty-two days, and many affairs were settled, with the majority of which I can say without vanity that I played an indirect part.

As the delegates only assembled in the morning and the afternoons were devoted partly to pleasure and partly to the examination of facts relevant to the next day's session, the king could not help coming, as usual, to spend a few minutes to spend a little time with us, and to tell us informally—on which he never failed to ask us what would be done in such cases in Europe.

One day, he told us that a young man from a remote canton, having often been maltreated by his father, who seemed to hate him mortally, had taken the opportunity, when they went out fishing in a gondola, to tip him into the canal. Seeing him on the surface, he had struck him in the head with his oar, for fear that he might climb back in and punish him for his temerity.

The father, who had been knocked silly to begin with, soon recovered his presence of mind; he knew how to swim perfectly, so, sensing danger on the surface he had allowed himself to fall to the bottom, and having found his footing there, returned to the surface a little further way, whence he started swimming with all his might for the other shore in order to escape his son's fury.

As the one strove to flee and the other hesitated as to whether to pursue him in order to break his skull, an old pine tree planted on the edge of the canal, following the description I gave earlier, suddenly fell like an inert mass, enveloping the boy and his gondola in its branches.

The old man, who had reached the far bank in the meantime, seeing the tree covering his boat, so that he could no longer see his child, was moved to compassion and did not doubt that the fall must have been fatal. In order to make sure of that, he went immediately to knock on the door of the nearest house, and, having had everyone resting inside roused—for it was early in the morning—he told them what had happened to his boat, a large rotten tree having fallen upon it so impetuously that he had been thrown into the water and his son crushed.

At that news, everyone there rushed out in order to see the disaster; three of them set out in their boat to go to the boy's rescue, in the case that he was still alive.

The latter, sensing that he was trapped without knowing how, and not having dared until then even to open his mouth, perceived the people who, unable to see what had become of him, were parting the branches of the tree zealously, started weeping and shouting: "Don't kill me, Father, I beg you. I was wrong, I admit; I merit an increase in your hatred; it's my fault that you're dead now, but I beg you to forgive me."

The more desperate his cries became, the harder the other strove to clear a way through to him, and the more terrified the wretch became that someone was coming to kill him. "Mercy, my dear Father, mercy!" he cried again. "It wasn't my true self; it was an accursed fit of wrath, a wrath I detest, that led me to lay a sacrilegious hand on your person; in the name of God calm down."

The father, who heard all that, did not know how to react; he would have liked to punish his child, but as he did not want others to know his reasons, that was impossible. Although the gondola was finally detached from the branches of the tree, and the young man saw the multitude of people who had come running to his rescue in response to the spreading news, and would doubtless not have allowed the father to sacrifice him to his vengeance on the spot, he made so many movements and contortions, and pronounced so many words that he accused himself in the presence of a hundred witnesses.

Thus, it was not in the power of the father to disculpate him, as he had desired to do. A few other fathers who were there, fearing the consequences, seized him and took him to the judge, who, having summoned the father, confronting them and examining them separately, condemned the child to labor in the mines for twenty years.

The father did not like that judgment; he knew in his conscience that he had provoked his son to ire by the rude treatment he had meted out to him; attributing the cause to his despair, he had him counseled clandestinely, appealed to the satrap of the government, and then to the court, if the former confirmed the initial sentence.

"The satrap to whom the case was referred," the king concluded, "did not want to decide; thus, it will be debated tomorrow in my presence, but, in truth, I don't really know what to say about it."

"How old is the young man?" I asked.

"Twenty-two," replied the king.

"Well, sire," I said, "he would die in my homeland; nothing would be capable of saving him from that; but since you're not so severe here, the son detesting his action and begging forgiveness with all his soul, and the father confessing to having given rise to his recklessness, I believe, with all the respect that I owe your majesty, that it would be sufficient to have him whipped with rods and condemned to wear an inscription on his forehead saying, in large letters: *rebel against his father*. On condition of good conduct, he should be absolved from that shame after a year."

"Your advice is excellent," said the king, "and if my opinion is taken into account, that is the punishment that will be imposed on the delinquent."

As soon as the council was assembled, the case came up, and everyone gave his opinion. Some wanted to confirm the sentence that had been passed; others claimed that the young man ought to make honorable amends and have his right hand cut off before being imprisoned. There were some who wanted him to be sent to the deepest mine for life. The king, however, having heard all their opinions, proposed his own, which was approved by the company and carried out the same day.

The two parties expressed their thanks to the court for the favorable judgment pronounced in their favor. The king, who wanted to give me the honor, told them that that they if they owed gratitude to anyone, it was properly to me, to the exclusion of anyone else. In fact, the worthy people came to thank me in the most honest and humble fashion in the world. They went home immediately afterwards, where, so I was told afterwards, they lived together in perfect harmony.

It is hard to imagine how much consideration that bagatelle won us among the deputies. The judgment of Solomon was a small matter by comparison with ours, and if we can believe what was said, we could have been appointed as extraordinary members of their body.

When they returned for the following diet, our work was nearly complete; everyone took pleasure is coming to see it, and could not weary of admiring its beauty. La Forêt could engrave very well, and also knew how to gild, and he had learned the fashions of the country so well as to be able to gild with copper, which is far more beautiful than it is in lands familiar to us, and the smallest piece has an admirable gleam.

Our new timepiece surpassed admirably the one we had made for our canton. It was another matter altogether a year later, when people saw the clock mounted in the dome of the king's house, with six quadrants round the rim, which not only indicated their hour but the minutes, which we had omitted from the preceding one. In addition, the basin or bell, made of tin and copper mixed together, was three times as large and of much better resonance.

In recompense for that fine work, the king honored each of us with a satrap's robe and gave orders that we should be shown the same deference. We were treated, in consequence, like princes. The cooks and the cellar-master made sure that nothing was ever lacking at our table: beer, cider, hydromel and ōŋs, which is a delicious beverage of which one can drink as much as one likes without any inconvenience, made from a fruit admirable in every fashion, with the form of a Spanish melon, and we no more lacked water than a river. There was a kind of ragout, tarts and pastries that we were given every day; and as partridges weighing at least four pounds and Tōtŋ, which are burly poultry, of which I have made mention before, were very common, there were few meals when we did not eat game—not to mention the excellent fish that were served without fault every midday.

We were taken for excursions three days running by the king himself, clad in his ceremonial garments, which is the greatest honor that the monarch does his subjects.

One morning, when we were passing to the west of the temple, a young boy who had gone to see his father working on the dome, having run to the balustrade in order to see what the noise from down below was that was made as we passed by, fell over and was killed.

That unexpected fall caused the king, who never let me rest, to raise an objection against the circular movement of the earth.

"Something has just come to mind." he said to me, "that didn't occur to me before. If the earth is turning, as you have tried to convince me, it seems to me that although that child's fall did not last long, he ought to have come down some distance away from the wall of the edifice, instead of being within arm's reach of it, if I'm not mistaken. For after all, the terrestrial globe is large, and, supposing that it completes a rotation in twenty-four hours, it is necessary that its parts pass by extremely rapidly"

"That's easy to determine, Sire," I interjected. "One terrestrial degree contains sixty miles, as you know; one only has to multiply that distance by three hundred and sixty to obtain the circumference of the earth at the equator, 21,600 Italian miles, or 21,600,000 geometric paces. Now divide that quantity by twenty-four hours and the nine thousand miles resulting from that operation by sixty minutes—in consequence two hundred and fifty feet per second, and more than four in a tierce, which is the smallest interval that a body can require to fall from the top of that high building.

"However, Sire," I continued, "you ought not to consider the air as independent of the earth; it rotates with it, exactly as the water of the sea does, with is confined within its own limits; it is a down that envelops it, both are part of the great whole; in consequence, falling into one or the other is, in that respect, exactly the same. There is, however, another reason, confirmed by experiment, which informs us that anybody descending by virtue of a simple movement, or what can be considered as such, must fall on the point to which it corresponds at the first moment of its fall.

"Suppose, then, that I am on top of one of the highest masts carried by European warships, and that I drop a metal ball of whatever size you wish. It is constant that it will always remain the same distance from the mast, until it hits the deck, no matter how rapidly the wind and the tide are bearing it away. From that it follows that the body does not fall perpendicularly, as it seems, but necessarily follows a parabolic line—for which the reason is that, although it seems to be descending in a simple motion, it is nevertheless participating in two simultaneously, to with the artificial movement made by the ship relative to the plane of the horizon, and the natural one from top to bottom.

"That is so true that if, at the moment when the ball is released, the vessel were to stop dead, we would see that it would not fall alongside the mast, but some distance away, as often happens among us to cavaliers who, in mid-gallop, are borne by a capricious horse, which suddenly stops at the sight of some object of which it is afraid; for then, continuing in that movement, they emerged from the stirrups and hit the ground some distance in front of their horse. And it is also for the same reason that good hunters, who are perhaps not ignorant of all this, rarely fire on a moving target without following the bird for a few moments with their weapon, in order that he bullet or arrow acquires a sideways movement that causes it to describe a curved trajectory, by means of which it will hit the target."

"I understand all that," said the King. "There's nothing extraordinary in it, since the same thing happens to anybody that is impelled violently, from whatever height, along a line parallel to the horizon, for it is evident that from the moment that it emerged from the hand that has thrown it, it starts to fall, and, as you say, in order to reach the ground, it must describe a line similar to those made by the section of a cone that is parallel to its opposite side."

"You're right, Sire," I replied, "but there's something admirable in that, which passes for a paradox among many people. It consists in the fact that if one makes use of one of those machines, which are so common among us, known as a cannon, directed horizontally at one of the highest towers, and at the same time as the cannonball is released, one drops a ball of the same fall and composition as the cannonball; notwithstanding the fact that one is fired at a distance of a mile and the other simply falls in a perpendicular straight line, they will hit the ground at the same time."

"Indeed," said the king, "that is surprising; and I confess that that never occurred to me. However, I can see very well, now, that it must happen like that, because no matter how far the bullet travels, the movement from up to down must follow its course nevertheless, and be no less rapid for it. But these fine examples still don't enlighten me sufficiently with regard to the movement of the earth, and how it comes about that such a violent agitation doesn't shake it into a million pieces."

"Well, Sire," I replied, "take a jam-jar made of white clay, round in form, whose edges are squat and perpendicular to the bottom. Put an inch or two of water into it, and into that water a small quantity of copper filings, fine sand and grated red wax. For want of glass, which you don't have here, cover the jar with a securely-attached lid, then seal it with a little clay on the pivot of one turn of the earthenware, and set it in movement. As soon as the jar has made a few rotations, if you lift the lid, which has only been out on to prevent the water getting out during its agitation, you will see that all the particles of matter that were put inside have come to arrange themselves against the edges of the vessel: evident proof that if the heavens, which are represented here by those edges, were turning, it would be necessary that the earth quit the place it occupies in order to go and arrange itself against their concave surface, or their ultimate extremities.

"Another incontrovertible proof, which confirms the first, is that if the rotation were stopped, in such a way that the heavens, or the side of the vessel, was no longer turning, the water, continuing its movement, and therefore tending proportionately to draw away from the center of the jar in which it is contained, forces the particles of copper , sand and wax—which is the lightest of them—to quit the sides where they were, so to speak, stuck and approach the center, where they form a round mass, the deepest region of which is the copper, the second the sand and the outermost the wax. Hence, it appears that it is sufficient that the subtle matter that surrounds the earth should be agitated to oblige all the terrestrial particles to assemble into a globe in the vicinity of their center. That also enables us see, I will mention in passing, that it is impossible for a stone thrown into that subtle matter to remain there for long, but that it must, for the same reasons, abandon the aerial regions and return toward the other substances of its species, which is what is properly meant by weight."

"Certainly," said the king, "you have often told me about vortices, changes that the astronomers observe in the different aspects of the planets, the movement of the sun around its own center, the spots that cover its surface and confirm that movement because they change location as it advances, as well as the periods that the others describe, either around themselves or around it; but I have not yet heard anything as compelling as what you have just told me. You would give me pleasure by making the machine of which you speak for me, in order that, by examining it closely, we can understand it even better. But it is desirable that the lid you put on the jar should be transparent, in order that what is happening inside the vessel can easily be seen without removing it."

"I shall carry out your orders, Sire," I replied, "And if your parchment cannot serve that purpose I'll replace it with a round hole an inch of two in diameter, which I'll make in the middle of the lid. I think the rest will suffice to prevent the water from gushing out in its greatest agitation."

In the meantime, one of the king's brothers fell ill and died. I thought that I would see something particular at his funeral, but I was quite astonished not to observe the slightest circumstance more than in common burials. The entire ceremony consists of putting a robe of fine linen on the deceased, which is attached at the neck and tied in the middle of the body, the knees and the feet. Then he is placed on a stretcher, which two men carry away, preceded by the dead man's four nearest relatives and followed by two men and their wives if the he was married, or otherwise by four young people, two of each sex, who weep along the way and talk to one another about his god qualities. When they reach the extremity of the habitation in which the dead man lived, he is laid in a ditch dug expressly for that purpose and covered over afterwards, on which a small wooden pyramid is placed, marked with the name and age of the person buried there; after which, everyone returns home and says no more about him, as if he had never existed.

The king's brother was treated in the same way; two of his other brothers—for the prince is exempt from it—with his mother and one of his sisters, formed the procession, and the mourners were people were only there to pay lip-service. It was then that I learned that it is forbidden to the brothers and sisters of the kings of that country to marry; that is only permitted to the eldest son of the royal family, and even he cannot have more than one wife before he becomes king.

With regard to wives, I ought to relate here how our monarch found one in my presence, worthy of wearing the diadem. For some time he had been planning to visit the west of the kingdom, but he wanted us to go as a party, and the work we had in hand was too important in his eyes to be interrupted. It was necessary to wait until it was finished, and that took a long time. Then bad weather arrived, and then the assembly; finally, that passed and we were in the finest season; the king wanted to take advantage of it.

He assembled a small crew, and only took ten people with him to form his retinue. He was riding in a magnificent two-wheeled chariot pulled by four white goats, each of which had a long black beard and horns of prodigious size. His retinue and his baggage were in two gondolas, in each of which there were four oarsmen, and four others to relieve them.

I was delighted to make the journey, because I had not yet been in that direction. The majority of the inhabitants of that edge were occupied in making bricks, pottery and all kinds of porcelain, depending on the propriety of the soil to different endeavors.

We did not pass through any village in which everyone who was able to do so did not come out to see the king; he sometimes got down deliberately, and walked slowly, in order to give them the time to consider him at their ease.

One day, when we were in a place where the people were so densely crowded that it was difficult for him to could not get through without dispersing them, he saw a young woman, the sight of whom charmed him. He commanded her to come closer, and, after having considered her and found her even more charming at close range than at a distance, he summoned her father. He asked the man how old his daughter was.

The worthy man, having already promised her to someone else, and suspecting the king's intention, did not know what to reply. After hesitating momentarily, he said: "Sire, she is not yet nubile, and, in consequence, can neither be sold nor given away."

The girl, who liked the idea of being a queen better than being the wife of a carpenter—which was the trade of the fellow to whom she was due to belong— spoke up, and said: "It's true, Sire, that I'm not yet nubile, but I shall be twenty in two days' time."

"Well," said the king, "we'll wait, my good man, until the term has run out, in order not to infringe our laws. Bring your daughter to the court the day after tomorrow, in order that I can make her my wife, and see to it that no one approaches her."

"Although the old man felt very honored to have the king for his son-in-law, he was nevertheless sorry at being unable to keep his word to the other— which I wanted to record here in order to show the simplicity and rectitude that reigns among those people. Pηo—that was the individual's name—did not fail to be in the designated place within the time that had been specified to him.

Three days after our arrival there he requested an audience and presented his daughter to the king personally, in the presence of his chaplain, who immediately gave thanks to God. The wedding celebration lasted three days, after which Pηo returned home, with a hundred Kala—copper coins—as payment for his daughter. The poor young woman, however, who had not yet had smallpox, was afflicted three months later and died of it.

The number of people carried off by that pestilential malady is prodigious; there is not one in ten who escapes it. The majority of those alive have never had it, and however old they are, they are so unlikely to be exempt from it that they rarely die of anything else. If it were not for that, the land would apparently be exceedingly populous, instead of which, at present, it is by no means the case, in proportion to the bounty of the soil and the purity of the air.

Little time went without the King making further conquests, with the result that, four years after his first marriage, he was already enriched by seven wives. My comrade and I attended all those solemnities, where we had our fair share of the pleasures to be obtained there.

Everywhere we went, people never failed to praise us on the subject of our clocks, in which I had played the lesser part, as was known to many people. To obtain recompense for that, I told the king that we had been glad to ornament his palace with a machine with which he had been generous enough to appear content, but that if he desired, I would make him another to place on the frontispiece of the temple, which would not be subject to any change, and which the sun would regulate by its own course.

"I can understand," the monarch sad, "from the little astronomy that I know, that it would not be impossible to divide an artificial day into as many equal parts as one might wish, by means of the shadow cast by some object in the presence of that star, but we have had no one until now, so far as I know, who could apply himself to that."

"Before I work on it," I replied, it will be necessary for me to examine toward which part of the word the façade is orientated."

"That isn't necessary," the King put in. "I know that it is inclined to the north-east by twenty-two degrees thirty minutes, and what is more, I know it by experiment."

"Pardon me, Sire," I said, "if I take the liberty of asking you what method you employed to assure yourself of that verity."

"I had constructed for that express purpose," the King replied, "a perfectly uniform board, on which there were several circles taken at different openings of the compass, and in the center, which was common to them, I placed a perpendicular stylus or rod of smooth brass wire, at the end of which was a button as large as a hazelnut. I placed that square instrument against the wall of the temple, on the ground, and leveled it off, which was easily done by pouring a little water on it.

"All that having been prepared, I waited, the sun having risen a few degrees above the horizon, until the shadow of the button on my stylus fell on the circumference of one of the circles on the board. I marked that place with a dot. Then I marked another point where the shadow fell in the afternoon on the opposite circumference of the same circle. I divided the arc between those two points into two equal parts by means of a straight line passing through the center of the stylus. That line is the meridian of the place where I carried out the operation. Inasmuch as it is twenty-two and a half degrees from perpendicular to the façade of the building, and it is inclined to that extent toward the east, it follows that the frontispiece of our temple is orientated as I told you."

"There are several means," I said, "to obtain the same result easily, but that one is one of the best I know. Well, then, I shall make you a vertical quadrant in accordance with that inclination."

"No," said the King, "since it's only a matter of drawing the lines, you must give me the pleasure of involving me in its construction."

I consented willingly to his request, so we made a quadrant eight feet wide by six high, and another horizontal one of copper, which was placed on an octagonal pedestal of agate in front of the king's palace; both had the signs of the zodiac.

Those two machines gave rise once again to much admiration on the part of those who saw them; I do not doubt that they have rendered as much service as the others after our departure, since there was no one in the kingdom who, far from making similar ones, was even able to entertain them.

La Forêt, penetrated by all the civilities that he received daily, as well as me, from the whole court, and also wanting to testify that he was not insensible to them, set to work thereafter on a pocket watch, without saying a word to me, and before I became aware of it he had finished the work.

Although he worked better on a large scale than a small one, a watch in a country where none had ever been seen was a jewel of inestimable value. As soon as he had finished it he went to the King, and, after having complimented him on the obligations that we had toward him, he took the watch out of his pocket and begged him to accept it from his own hand, as a sincere mark of our just gratitude. The King, having been shown what it was, was astonished by it. He admired the beauty and utility of the little machine, and protested that its maker would never ask him for anything that was at his disposal without it being granted.

## Chapter XI
### Continuation of the adventures of the author and his comrade, until their departure from the court.

As the King often went to see his wives, it did not take long for him to show his watch to them; there was not one of them who did not admire the genius of its maker. Although they had seen the clock a thousand times, and every one of them still seemed transported by astonishment, that was nothing, in their opinion, by comparison with the pretty instrument that, in spite of its smallness, nevertheless had all the same mechanisms, and indicated the parts of the day as clearly as the large one.

Among others, Lidola, the King's second wife, made great attempts to become its proprietor, but the King, who did not want to let go of it, and who could not have done so without exciting jealousy among all those ladies and even causing the Empress chagrin, pretended not to hear her.

In order to avenge herself for that lack of complaisance, the queen, when there was a question of receiving the King after supper, during which he had informed her that he was coming to spend the night with her, as he often did, having more affection for her than any of the others, she pretended to be indisposed, and asked the King not to come to see her that evening. Having not suspected anything, he sent for news of her in the morning, and did the same several days running.

Finally realizing what was going on, and that not only were his messengers coldly received but that she gazed at him with a coldness capable of freezing him when he saw her in passing, he had a clear suspicion of the fly that had bitten her. He gave no sign of it, though, and, wanting to see how far the indifference would go, gradually neglected his visits, and attached himself so strongly to his most recent queen that he almost no longer went to any but her.

La Forêt, who was as completely unaware of all this as I was, was surprised when, one evening, as he was walking in the galleries, he heard someone call his name. He turned precipitately in response to the voice and was suddenly struck by the sight of the most beautiful woman he had ever seen in his life—for she was uncovered, contrary to the local rule that does not permit married women to be without a veil, which covers almost all of the face, wherever men are present. He stood there staring at her, without having the strength to ask her what she wanted.

"You're astonished, handsome genius," she said. "Don't be alarmed; I only called out to you in order to express the pleasure I have in seeing you every time you go past my apartment, and to give you this *Miadu*"—which I shall henceforth call a melon—"here, take it, adieu." Having proffered these words, she let go of the fruit, went away and shut herself in with her jealousy.

La Forêt was neither insensible nor ignorant, but he did not know what to think about that sally. As he had not been skillful enough to catch the melon, which had fallen on the ground, he picked it up without saying anything, brought it back to our room and told me what had just happened to him.

Immediately I took the melon, wanting to slice it with a knife, and perceived that it had been opened very subtly near the stalk. That caused me to cut into it with precaution, for fear of spoiling something if there were anything inside it. It was certainly not little seeds with which the excellent fruit was filled, as it usually is by nature. A scroll of fine parchment occupied its capacity. This is what it said, in the language of the country:

*I have seen you pass before my windows a thousand times, but have only rarely heard you speak. The judgment that I have made of your intelligence by your detached expression and your rare remarks makes me curious to hear you talk at my ease; it seems to me that you would not say anything that was not beautiful. Be prepared to satisfy me. Tomorrow I will wait for you, without fail, at my door; do not neglect to be there at the first stroke of your curious machine after midnight, and you will oblige*

*Lidola.*

Reading that note alarmed me. I explained the reasons for that very seriously to La Forêt, but everything I could say was futile. He was tall and well-built, as vigorous as a man of thirty can be, and not hostile to the fair sex. The amity they king had for us made him believe that he had too much trust in him to imagine that he would attempt anything with one of his wives, and, without regard to the consequences, he resolved to take advantage of the opportunity, at whatever cost.

What embarrassed him more was his lack of eloquence, and the small talent he had for polite expression. His birth was somewhat obscure and he had little experience of high society. Ignorant of fine manners and having a better opinion of me than himself, he wanted me to take the first steps and bring things to the point that he desired. Apart from the fact that his stature was very different from mine, however, since he was a head taller than me, and I was also too plump to be mistaken for him, I had no desire to embark on an affair of that nature. All of that, however, was incapable of putting him off.

The next day he dressed himself as neatly as he could, provided himself with everything that a gallant man ought to have when visiting his mistress, and searched his mind for everything that might contribute to pleasing her. He went out in that apparel, after having bid me adieu, and was at the appointed place on time. The beauty, who was apparently all ears, having heard him coming, came to open the door to him quietly, and, after having made him a sign to observe a profound silence, took him into her room.

She was in negligent state of undress, which was nevertheless very ostentatious, and the negligence seemed to owe its origin to pure artifice. A veil of fine linen, in which art played infinitely more part than substance, covered her head and shoulders, but, whether by hazard or design and skill, under the pretext of making use of that same veil and pulling it up or down in order to cover that of which modesty seemed to command the concealment, she often allowed glimpses of her beauty that would have capable of inflaming a heart far less susceptible of amorousness that La Forêt's, which could not resist those charms. His eyes dazzled by the sight of so many marvels, as if he were enchanted, he did not have the strength to open his mouth, notwithstanding the firm resolution he had made to talk well.

Seeing that her lover was not saying anything, Lidola uttered a deep sigh, and, casting a fatal glance at him, said: "I love you, handsome stranger; I had intended to spare myself the trouble of saying that aloud, believing that it would be easy for you to divine; your silence has overcome to my modesty; I'm ashamed of having uttered the word. Take note of that declaration, and remember that it is necessary to be discreet when one wants to be fortunate with ladies."

"Don't reproach yourself, Madame, I beg you," replied La Forêt, very respectfully. "My silence has an eloquence that ought to persuade you sufficiently of the sentiments of my heart." He went on: "If your presence has robbed me of the usage of speech, it has only been to consider with more leisure the delicacy of your charms. Words are not always timely; there are moments when the eyes express themselves far better than the tongue; one can be ignorant of the art of divination, and know by their movements what the soul is thinking. I was wrong to be silent, I admit, but I am glad not to have spoken, since the most beautiful expressions of which I would have been capable of making use in a language that I only understand in a very imperfect manner would scarcely have drawn from your beautiful mouth in a century what silence has procured me in an instant.

"What! You love me, Madame? O Heaven! To what excess of joy is such a tender confession not capable of bringing me? Who would ever have believed that a queen could ever lower herself to showing so much generosity to the least of her slaves. Continue, I beg you; I shall limit the greatest of all my desires to that, since it will doubtless not be permissible for me to think about anything else."

As she was about to reply to him, a chambermaid, entering abruptly, alarmed our lover; he could not imagine what would become of him, and his surprise was so great that the efforts he made to hide did not prevent him from being perceived.

Lidola, however, showed no semblance of fear, adding to his confusion.

"I have ordered that a few fruit preserves should be brought, and a cup of hydromel," she told him. "You see how my orders are carried out; I hope that you will find something you your taste in this bowl."

La Forêt, who was more avid for amorous tenderness than honeyed sweetmeats, was angry that an importunate witness had interrupted their conversation. He would rather have spent the time in dalliance that waste precious moments eating. It was necessary, however, out of complaisance, to admire the extent of her civility. He even expressed his gratitude to her.

The beauty, who did not want to neglect anything in demonstrating her affection, picked up half a peach, which she lifted amorously to his mouth. Then she took it away from his lips, half-consumed, and ate it with an inconceivable avidity. Another time she made him eat a morsel that she held between her own beautiful teeth. In sum, there was no teasing in which she did not indulge in order to augment her new lover's passion.

The days were then about sixteen hours long, because the sun was not far distant from the sign of Capricorn, and that place is situated at fifty-one degrees twenty minutes of austral latitude; with the result that they were still frolicking when the darkness—or rather the twilight—disappeared and the celestial flame was on the point of gilding with its rays the enamel of the florid countryside. The demoiselle was the first to notice it, and warn the queen.

La Forêt was annoyed, and even went so far as to address reproaches to her for not having fixed an earlier time, since, in his view, it was not worth the trouble of coming only to stay for a moment.

"Although I am slightly at odds with the king," the charming Lidola replied, "I'm sure that he won't neglect me for long; the desire might take him to come to see me in the morning; and even when that does not happen, there are other people who keep watch on our actions; it would be bad for me if anyone saw you leave my apartment. Let's play safe, and retire this time. If you have another pocket watch, like the one you've given to the king, make sure to bring it another time, in order that it can indicate to us what we have to do; we might not always have people with us who would think to warn us."

As she concluded that tender speech, she put her arms around his neck, kissed him tenderly, and suddenly drew away.

Time passes rapidly in such agreeable circumstances; La Forêt, however, had not lost his mind to the extent of not knowing how urgent it was to withdraw. He took out a Kala, which he gave to the girl, and, recommending himself to her care, returned very quietly to his own apartment.

The first thing he thought of doing on his return was confiding to me everything that had happened in the company of his mistress. Never had any man, to hear him, traveled so extensively in the territories of amour in ten years as he had just done in an hour. In sum, he was in possession of everything, and no longer lacked anything but the final enjoyment.

"O Heaven!" I exclaimed then. "How credulous lovers are, and how easy it is for amour to impose itself upon them. La Forêt, La Forêt, you are playing a game that you will infallibly lose. Gambling, women and wine have a beautiful appearance, I admit, but too much frequentation is dangerous; they offer brief pleasures, the repentance of which is long, and their greatest sweetness often changes into bitterness; they only pay in false glamour; those who delight in it are dazzled, and ordinarily mistaken. Remember what I said to you yesterday; you are engaged in an affair of which you will repent more than once."

I was moralizing in vain; everything that I could say was futile. My friend could only envisage the pleasure with which he was being enticed, and turned his back on the consequences. He was already lost in all the pleasant ideas that his mind was capable of formulating. The poor man was so completely blind that he could not see the precipice into which he was on the brink of falling; he had nothing clearly in sight but his dominating passion. His wounded imagination was perpetually showing him his beauty in his arms, and he spoke to her frequently, as if he were in bed with her.

Finally, he spent the time that remained to him pleasantly enough in his bed, for, although he scarcely slept, he had reveries of the kind that give more pleasure than slumber, and which have the advantage that, while delighting the mind, they do not diminish the strength of the body at all.

Three days passed without La Forêt receiving any word from his mistress; that interval threw him into anxieties that turned his thoughts upside-down. He often went over his entire conduct, and if he found anything with which to reproach himself, it could only be having been too respectful.

I had not noticed before then that the women of the palace had any penchant for gallantry; they seemed to me to be too simple by nature for that, but I began to see by virtue of that specimen that there is hardly anywhere where more is known, when it is a matter of making men fall in love, and that if they did not reveal it, it was only because their laws are extremely severe for those who break the rules that marriage seems to impose upon them.

And let no one think that kings and satraps are subject to less inconvenience than the men of our nations, because, those gentlemen having more than one wife, each of them exerts herself to gain the good graces of her husband, and when she does not succeed, that gives her occasion to attach herself to the first subject who presents himself.

But let us get back to our love story. On the fourth day, before noon, when the King came to spend a few minutes watching us at work, I thought right away that he had definitely got wind of something. Looking fixedly at La Forêt, he said to him: "You're suffering some chagrin, my friend; your face is not as it has always appeared to me before, and if I can judge by your eyes, the interior of your machine is not in a very tranquil state. Have you fallen in love with some beauty of the canton? Love makes great ravages in a short space of time.

"You're blushing," the King went on. "Tell me boldly what it is; although you're a foreigner, and of a religion very different from mine, I assure you that I will do everything for you that is within my power. You cannot aspire to any free individual to whom I cannot find a means of marrying you. As for amusing yourself casually, I advise you not to do it; all my credit would not be capable of saving you if you were caught in the act. Perhaps gallantry is rife among us, but at least it is hidden, and you're not unaware that it's one of the articles of our law about which judges are least relaxed; for any adultery, even I could not obtain a pardon."

"It is right, Sire," said La Forêt, who had had time to collect himself, "to be severe in that chapter, especially with respect to important individuals. If I had the power, a gallant king would be less exempt from punishment than others, since, unlike his subjects, who are obliged, for the most part, to restrict themselves to a single object, he has the liberty to take a full dozen, and the consequent pleasure of having in his home all the diversity that he could find elsewhere.

"It is, however," he continued, "a happiness that I do not envy Your Majesty. Although I have neither a wife nor a mistress, I am no less content for that, and if I appear slightly more exhausted than usual, that is doubtless because I have not slept very well these last few nights, for otherwise, I'm perfectly healthy."

"I am, moreover," he added, "infinitely obliged to Your Majesty for the desire you have to render me happy, and even to think of helping me to establish myself. If ever the time comes when I want to marry, I swear to you, Sire, that I shall refer the matter uniquely to your choice."

"Let's talk about something else, La Forêt," I put in. "It's not yet time to think about that."

"It will be whenever you wish," the King said, with good grace. "You know the privileges that the robe you wear gives you, so you will have nothing much for which to reproach me."

With that, the King withdrew, and we ate, making various reflections on the conversation we had just had with him.

La Forêt, however, never let an afternoon pass without taking a tour of the galleries. Lidola often took pleasure in seeing him pass before her windows; she followed him with her eyes until she lost sight of him.

The chambermaid, for her part, never ceased exploring in search of some news that might be advantageous to them. Finally, she came to tell her that she had just encountered the King walking with the Empress. The queen concluded that he would infallibly spend the night with her, which seemed all the more plausible to her because that indication had never failed, and without hesitating as to what she ought to do, she told her maidservant to try to encounter La Forêt and tell him in passing that she would be waiting for him at eleven o'clock.

The young woman did not take long to carry out her mission; she encountered him nearby as he was retracing his steps, approached him as closely as she could and said to him as she passed by: "Come to see us an hour before midnight."

I dare not describe the joy that he had on hearing those agreeable words; I would be afraid either of saying too much to be believed or not saying enough to give an accurate idea of his transports.

He finished his shift so rapidly, and with such scant attention to what he was doing, that he was at home before he knew it. Needless to say, he was not thinking at all; he did not even want me to speak to him.

The few moments that remained to him were employed in his toilette; he consulted his mirror a hundred times, which, being only polished steel, gave him the apprehension that he would not be seen without its stains. He washed almost his entire body with scented water, trimmed and reshaped his moustache, combed and recombined his black hair, and, finally finding himself as handsome as Adonis, he wished me goodnight and left.

The maidservant was on sentry duty. As soon as she saw him appear, she pulled him into the antechamber, where there was no light, and told him to slip into her mistress' apartment.

Lidola was lying in a perfumed bed, which embalmed the whole house; her hair was loose, her upper torso bare, with the left breast uncovered and the arms free; her posture was that of a drowsy person who was nevertheless not asleep. La Forêt made so little noise when he came in that she did not perceive him. The unexpected sight of so much grace rendered him almost motionless; even his eyes, fixed on the body of the charming Venus, remained still. A hidden desire, however, on which he was incapable of making the slightest reflection, caused him to take a step forward in order to see her at closer range; she was like a magnet, attracting him in an imperceptible manner, the power of which was so effective that he would finally have stuck to her in spite of his efforts.

Meanwhile, the adorable beauty casually opened her eyes, and seemed extremely astonished to see her lover so close to her bed. She blushed, sat up, and covered herself with a veil, which she picked up from a chair.

"You surprised me," she said, "and you have apparently seen things that you ought not to have seen."

"Yes, Madame," he said "Destiny has wished, and not you, that I have had an opportunity to contemplate your beauties, which have ecstasized my thought. That will not diminish in the least, however, the respect that I owe you, although it has infinitely augmented a passion that I believed incapable of going any further."

"You merit a punishment nevertheless," said the beauty, "for not giving me any indication of your presence immediately. But why have you come so soon; it must still be broad daylight, and I only invited you for eleven o'clock."

"You were taken by surprise," La Forêt replied, "and you're reproaching me for my slowness; I have, however, come at the right time, although you did not expect me to be here already."

"You're mistaken," the queen said. "Consult your watch; it will inform you that you're wrong to resist me."

"I have no watch," La Forêt said. "I only made one of them. On occasions of this kind, my head is a clock of the minutes; it is never wrong by a moment."

"You have no watch!" retorted Lidola. "It's surprising that you are deprived yourself of jewels that you make for others. If I had the talent to make such pretty machines, I would not want it to be said that I did not have one for my own use, and another at the service of my mistress."

That compliment mortified our Frenchman somewhat; he knew very well what that reproach meant, and was angry that he had not foreseen it.

The queen, who saw that he was embarrassed, did not think it wise to leave him in pain any longer. "I'm joking, La Forêt," she said, "And it seems to me that you're seeking to respond seriously. Sit down on my bed. Time is precious; let's not spend it uselessly."

At the same time she tried to take hold of his hands, but amour rendered him so weak that a sigh escaping the impassioned follow cast his head on to the bedside. Matters accelerated, and the two young hearts did not doubt that the moment of their felicity was on the point of blossoming—but fortune, envious of their joy, changed all their hopes to mortal anxiety in a trice.

The king loved Lidola, with a violence a increased by not having seen her for such a long time, which had reached such a pitch that they could no longer bear it, and, because the news of her indisposition that she had put around once again had increased his anxiety, he had resolved to keep her company that night. The servant, who was still standing guard at the shutter, heard a confused noise in the distance like a number of people, initially entered into doubt, because it was not yet midnight and the king never went to bed before then; finally, seeing the company approaching, she ran precipitately to raise the alarm.

"All is lost, Madame!" she cried. "The king is only a few paces away."

Warmed up as our two lovers were, the blood froze incontinently in their veins. La Forêt did not know what to do; it was necessary to take advice immediately. It was promptly resolved to put him in a cabinet connected to the rom.

Scarcely was he inside than a domestic, coming on ahead, knocked on the door. The chambermaid made him wait for as much time as she judged that it would have taken her to get up, and, those sorts of visits having happened more than once, she did not put on any pretence of being surprised. As the King was close behind he came in almost as soon as the door was opened.

The queen, who heard him coming, did not have any difficulty putting on the expression of someone in distress; the dread that she had, for herself and the gallant, contributed not a little to that. For his part, the King, convinced that she had not recovered, was not in the least suspicious on seeing her more discomfited than usual. He lavished more caresses on her than ever, and told her that, in spite of the poor state in which he found her, he intended to spend the night with her.

"Sire," Lidola replied, "you do me a great honor, but I am scarcely in a state to give or take pleasure; If fear that the slightest agitation might do me harm, and I believe that I need rest."

"I don't want to inconvenience you," the King replied. "If you can't tolerate my company, I'll go into this cabinet; there's a bed in there; I can lie down on that, having resolved to spend the night here."

That response, which the beauty had not expected, alarmed her. Immediately, she offered apologies for the coldness she had shown him, the cause of which she attributed to her illness, and she began to caress him in her turn, inviting him eagerly to undress.

As soon as he was in bed and the domestics had gone, the chambermaid found a means of going into the cabinet, in order to consult with the prisoner as to what steps needed to be taken to set him free, but she was very surprised to find that he was not there. There was no door except the one she had come through, and the windows, which were closed, did not appear to have been opened.

While the chambermaid was occupied in looking under the bed and the other items of furniture in the room, the lady's embarrassment with regard to her lover led her to call out to her in order to obtain news of him, under the pretext of asking her to plump up her pillow and fetch her something to drink. She was relieved, however, as soon as she heard that he had disappeared, even though she did not know how—with the result that she slept tranquilly enough for the rest of the night.

For his part, La Forêt, believing that the King had only come for a moment, had shut himself in provisionally. He was extremely disappointed when, a short time later, he heard that he intended to spend the night with his wife, or at least in the cabinet where he was if she could not tolerate him beside her.

It was then, as he admitted to me more than once since, that he was gripped by a fear whose like he had never felt. He could not go through the room where the king was without the risk of being seen; he thought that the windows of the apartment were fitted with iron bars, in addition to the fact that it was to be feared that he might make a noise opening them, and even more by jumping into the canal that the cabinet overlooked.

Having rejected those possibilities as rapidly as possible, he found no better expedient than letting himself down into the water via the hole in the watercloset where he was hiding and swimming away.

Fortunately for him, the room where I was sleeping was on the ground floor, and had an outside wall. He rapped with his fingers on one of my windows. I suspected immediately that things had not gone well. I got up right away, and when the widow was open he leapt in promptly, got undressed with equal swiftness, and got into bed, where he gave me a detailed account of his nocturnal adventures.

"You see, my dear boy," I said to him, "how love and fortune toy with you; they rarely see eye to eye, and if they reach agreement, it's only to deceive us doubly. Believe me, abandon such a dangerous game. I've already told you that playing it will surely doom you."

"Don't talk to me about that," he replied. "She's worth the trouble. Even if I can only kiss her once, I won't care anymore about dying. What embarrasses me more is that I can't satisfy her; she's asked me for a watch, and I don't have one to give her. It will take me at least a week to finish the one we have in progress."

"She's asked you for a watch?" I repeated. "That suggests that her love is interested; and if you satisfy her, how do you expect her to make use of it? The King, who will be the first to know, will also want to know where she got it. The mystery will be discovered, and adieu the two lovers."

"In truth, you're right, my friend. I wasn't thinking so far ahead. But after all, it's necessary to finish it. Between now and then we'll find some expedient that will get us out of trouble; love is too ingenious to abandon us on such a fine road."

At the same time, five or six loud strokes on the bowl of our clock, delivered with a great deal of precipitation, caused us to shiver forcefully; we could not imagine what that might mean. Then we remembered that we had advised the King to give orders that that means by used, as in Europe, to raise the alarm, warning the inhabitants of the canton that something to the disadvantage of the quarter was happening, in order that they could all come running and attempt to bring a remedy.

A man who went by immediately afterwards shouting "Fire!" at the top of his voice, extracted us from one anxiety and plunged us into another. Not knowing where that inconvenience had struck, we leapt out of bed, and each put on a wretched robe which we tied tightly around the waist, with the intention of taking vigorous action with the others.

As soon as we were outside who remarked that it was Queen Lidola's house that was on fire. Ladders were brought from all directions, and by means of water kept there by discretion, the flames were prevented from reaching the neighboring apartments, with the result that the damage was not considerable.

As the fire had stated in the cabinet where La Forêt had hidden, we had no doubt that the chambermaid, while searching for him, must have allowed some spark to fall on to the bed, or some other item of furniture made of combustible material, and had caused the conflagration.

Meanwhile, the king had withdrawn as soon as a domestic had announced the news. We went to him immediately to express our chagrin, but he only laughed, and told us that neither the fear nor the loss merited our compliment, especially with regard to a man of his nature, which was not capable of the slightest disturbance.

The Queen had no sooner recovered from the alarm that the unfortunate blaze had caused her than she put her hand to her pen and traced a second letter to La Forêt, the gist of which was as follows:

*My chambermaid has already set out on campaign; I know of your retreat and have a strong suspicion of the means you used to effect it. The situation was dangerous, at least as alarming for me as for you; the fire that subsequently took hold in my cabinet, by virtue of the imprudence of my servant, was nothing by comparison. Let it not deter you, however; we will be more fortunate another time. Be constant and tranquil. I will tell you when the opportunity arises, and will take my precautions so well that at our first sight, I shall be glad to have the opportunity to testify to you formally that I am truly your friend,*

*Lidola.*

It was not difficult for the messenger of love to slip this note into our lover's hand. He rarely failed to pass before the house of his mistress at breakfast, at midday and in the evening. She could encounter him and speak to him whenever she wished, because no one looked at them very closely.

Meanwhile, La Forêt had set to work very seriously on his watch, and labored with so much zeal that it was ready by the fifth day. It was extremely dainty, the engraving of its case was beautiful in its perfection, and the exterior was matched by the workmanship within. Dusk had not fallen when he went out with his machine in his pocket, and, having encountered the person of whom he was in search, he put it in her hand, asking her to give it on his behalf to the Queen, to whose good graces he always recommended himself.

If ever a person testified to joy it was Lidola at the sight of that pretty watch; we can be certain that she kissed it a thousand times and congratulated herself on having succeeded so well in her intrigue.

Instead of that beautiful pledge of love hastening the happiness that he expected as a recompense, he heard absolutely no more mention of anything. The chambermaid, who had once sought him out eagerly, affected to avoid encountering him; she fled as soon as she perceived him in the distance. That behavior caused him anxiety; and as he had no reason to suspect the lady, he imagined that the girl was shocked to see her mistress so well recompensed, when he had not, so to speak, yet had anything in reparation for all the trouble that she had taken.

Finally, sometime later, when he had almost stopped thinking about it, he was astonished when the same girl came up to him in a place where there we no witnesses, and, after having uttered a sigh, said: "You've been wretchedly deceived. I'm very sorry for you and I strongly detest the unjust procedure of my mistress. Everything she has done until now was simply to obtain a watch from you; now that she has it she has instructed me to tell you that she sees too much difficulty and danger in receiving you at home, that she is in despair, that the dolor she feels in expressible, that she will surely die of chagrin, and many other songs, that are really only deceptions."

"The king came to the house yesterday," she continued. "While chatting, he heard the watch ticking, and immediately asked what it was. There was no way to avoid telling him. He seemed surprised, and wanted to know how Madame had come by the jewel. It would have taken more than ingratitude, she confessed to me herself, to accuse you of having sent it to her, with the intention of making use of that means subsequently to try to corrupt her, and that you had tried to do so already. For fear of embarking on a course of action in which she might have been as much at risk as you, however, or at least at risk of having to give up the watch, she told him that I had found it and that she got it from me—whereupon he summoned me and asked me whether that was true. The signals she gave me with her eyes at every word made me see that she was in trouble and that it was necessary to say amen to everything."

"'Well, if that's so,' said the king, 'I know to whom it belongs and it's only just to return it to him.'

"'I've already tried to do that,' said the Queen. 'As soon as my girl found it, I suspected that it must belong to the strangers, who made yours. I sent it back to them immediately, but when my servant to them why she had come, they protested that they would never take it back, and that their plan had been to make them for the Empress and all the other queens.'

"That," the chambermaid added, "is how things happened; you might be hoping for some recompense for your present, but I don't think you'll receive one in your lifetime."

"It's sufficient," said La Forêt, "for me to thank you, my dear child; I shall undoubtedly remember this, and take my measures accordingly."

It was then after supper, so La Forêt did not delay in returning to his room. He went to bed without saying a word.

"You're pensive, my friend," I said to him. "What's the matter? Are things not going as you desire?"

"Certainly not," he replied. "They're not going at all. I've just learned something that had never occurred to me." And with that, he told me everything that the girl had told him.

"Well," I put in, "didn't I tell you? You have, however, got out of it better than I thought. Now, you can see the consequences of the affair, which are that it's necessary for you to make watches for all the king's wives as quickly as possible, under penalty of incurring their resentment, and perhaps even the hatred of the monarch, who might well suspect you, if you don't do so, of having wanted to ingratiate yourself with the most beautiful of his wives—to which the slightest rumor of your being seen outside at a undue hour, or in the water, or climbing in through our window, if anyone has the slightest wind of it, might contribute a great deal.

"Devil take all women," he said then, angrily. "I'll never trust one again, no matter what quality she might be."

"Fine," I said. "Getting carried away won't solve anything. So far as I can see, it's a question of taking action at least to gain a little time. We need to ask the King to let us go to spend the summer at our first village, and then we'll see what we have to do next."

The next day the King came, as usual, to see what we were doing. He teased us about the adventure of the watch. La Forêt confirmed everything that the chambermaid had said, but added that because it was hot, and he worked more comfortably in winter than in summer, he would like His Majesty to agree to our spending a few months in our former canton.

"With all my heart," said the King, and having ordered that we be given a hundred coins, he wished us a good journey.

We immediately went to say our farewells. The cook, with whom we were on very good terms, was one of those to whom we thought we ought to take our leave. The man seemed nonplussed by the confession we made him of our resolution. We both took that as an effect of his amity and the fear he had of losing us for a long time, but we were very surprised when, finally opening his mouth, he said to us, with evidence of his great astonishment: "You're going away, sirs? Have you really thought about what you're doing? Do you know what people are saying about you, or don't you know? God forbid that I should suspect you of the smallest bad action; you've never given me any occasion to, and you've done nothing that I know of—but not everyone knows you as I do. If you take my advice, you'll justify yourselves before changing cantons; otherwise you'll run the risk of passing for arsonists. Those who are spreading the rumor will triumph in your absence, and who can tell whether those who doubt it at present won't then believe it."

"Arsonists?" I said. "Are we accused of wanting to burn everything before we go?"

"No," he replied, "but it's claimed that La Forêt is the man who set fire to Queen Lidola's house."

"We're much obliged to you for your kind warning," I said to him, "and we'll take steps to discover the cause of such an ill-founded insult. I don't think it will be difficult to purge ourselves of it."

As soon as we were outside, I said to my comrade: "I'll wager that someone saw you at the house at an undue hour on the night of the fire, and that's why some ill-intentioned individual has drawn that conclusion to your disadvantage." I went on: "Let's go to see the King. Let's make overtures to him, and see what he has to say."

As soon as the monarch saw us he said: "What's the matter, my dear friends? Have you not been given the money I assigned to you, or do you need more? What do you lack? Tell me frankly, I implore you."

"We have no need of anything Sire," I interjected, "except the continuation of your good graces, but we are desolated by what we have just learned and will remain inconsolable at your feet until Your Majesty has given us satisfaction. We've been accused of wanting to reduce the royal canton to ashes; if we're guilty, we deserve to be punished; if not, the calumny is atrocious, and we hope of your clemency that the man who has invented it will be given an exemplary punishment."

"Bagatelles," said the King. "I known about it for several days, but I paid so little heed to it that I didn't deign to mention it to you. To content you, however, I'll seek information as quickly as possible."

In fact, those who were given the commission acquitted it with so much diligence, one way or another, that they were able to discover within an hour who it was that had first invented the lie; it was one of the King's grooms, a man of probity, wisdom and exemplary modesty.

The King yielded to our solicitation to summon him to our presence, and asked him what had led him to proffer words so prejudicial to our honor.

"I had been ill for several days, Sire," here said. "The court physician, whom I consulted, ordered me to take medicine. That beverage had purged me, and it was still having an effect thirty-six hours later. Being thus obliged to relieve myself at night to satisfy the necessities of nature, I heard a loud noise in the canal, which my bedroom overlooks, at the entrance to the next canton. Curiosity made me put my head out of the widow, and as it was not very dark, I saw a man who, having reached the bank, climbed out opposite the Queen's house, shook his clothes, and started running toward the Temple bridge. With that I opened my door quietly and ran after him as fast as I could. Having observed him from a distance, going alongside the Senate, I saw him rap with his hand on a window, which someone opened for him shortly afterwards, and the climbed into the house by that means. I knew that was the apartment of these gentlemen; their stature and a certain air that they have that is particular to them, was not unknown to me. Shortly thereafter, Lidola's dwelling was on fire."

He concluded: "I wonder, Sire, "if, given so many circumstances, my conjectures we so poorly founded, and whether someone wiser than me might have been deceived by them?

"There was an appearance, I admit," said the King. "However, it requires more than that to form an accusation." He turned to La Forêt. "But before deciding anything, what do you have to say to that?"

"Nothing, Sire," my comrade replied. "Everything that he has reported is true; only the conclusion is false, so I only reproach him for not having had sufficient charity. My comrade is an astronomer, as you're not unaware. He taught me some time ago to know the principal stars. The desire that I have to improve my knowledge of that science often leads me to get up at night in order to see whether the sky is clear, and when it is I go for a walk in one of the four neighboring cantons, because the buildings are lower than those here, and do not shield the view of the stars as much.

"I went out that night for the same purpose, with the result that, having cast an eye upon Sirius and Procyon, and, wanting to walk while observing their situation and distance, I unfortunately fell into the canal without thinking. Stunned as I was by the unexpected tumble, I remained there for some time trying to pull myself together, letting myself drift without knowing where I was going. Finally, I caught hold of the bank, where this honest man saw me, and from where I took, as fast as I could, the most direct route to my room, into which I climbed through the window, as much because I didn't want to wake our servants as not to show myself in a condition that would doubtless have made them laugh.

"You can see, Sire that we agree perfectly in our depositions, but the cause of my immersion was quite different from the one that the worthy groom attributed to it. I hope that he will now be sufficiently convinced of my innocence. I'm sorry that the misfortune in question has given rise to such a bad judgment against me. Properly speaking, my carelessness is the cause of it, and that's why I don't wish him any harm."

"I'm obliged to you," said the groom, "and I beg your pardon for the offense that I've caused you. I certainly regret it; I can see that I was too precipitate in jumping to a conclusion; it will teach me to be more restrained another time."

"Are you both content, then?" said the King.

"Yes, Sire," they replied.

"Well then," he said. "Clasp your hands, and let no more be said about it."

With that, we took our leave again and withdrew, as content as kings, La Forêt with his presence of mind and me with the honesty of our prince, and that we had got out of trouble so cheaply.

The next day we departed, not taking anything but a robe each, and a few trivia of which we believed we had an absolute need. We had money, we were known, and society there is very hospitable, so we had no reason to fear that anything bad would happen to us.

The King, however, remembered that he had not asked what vehicle we intended to use, and he sent a domestic after us in order to implore us to make use of the best one that he had for his own use, with the threat that if we did not do so, he would not be content with us.

We were half a league away when the messenger caught up with us; he tried with all his might to oblige us to turn back, or to say how we wanted to be conducted—by chariot or gondola—so that he could accommodate us immediately, adding to every statement that it as his majesty's will.

We thanked him for his kindness, and begged him to tell the king that we were embarrassed by all his generosity toward us, that we would willingly take advantage of the offers that he was kindly making to us, but that we had a desire to walk, and not to pass through any village without spending enough time there to make the acquaintance of the judge or the priest.

That response did not content our man, who only left us with regret and perhaps fear that the King might believe that he had acquitted his mission poorly. One can judge by that specimen, which I mention in passing, whether we had reason to complain of our lot, and whether, with the exception of my comrade's unfortunate adventure, we were not, in fact, lucky. It was not only at court that people had a particular regard for us; there was nowhere along our route that people his not hasten to treat us with civility. One might have thought that they had express orders to receive us as the foremost individuals in the realm.

Finally, on the seventeenth day after our departure, we were delighted to encounter two domestics of our judge and our priest, with a canoe laden with saucepans, mattocks, picks, hatchets, bows and garments, with the food supplies necessary to make the voyage to the copper market.

They told us that that the two men had taken it into their heads to ask us to make another clock, much bigger than the first, with a bell in proportion, of which they wanted to make a present to the satrap of their government, in order to smooth the way for them each to be accorded one of his daughters for their sons. The daughters in question, it was said, were consummately beautiful. And as copper would be necessary for that, they had sent the domestics to the mines to trade for it with everything they had given them to carry. They were furnished with very good provisions, and had been given permission to take as long as necessary for their journey.

That news augmented my comrade's chagrin more than a little. "What!" he said. "I've run away from one place to avoid the continual labor in which they wanted to engage me, and they're preparing another in the one where I was hoping to rest? I'd rather the Devil took me away from this nation than give them one more thrust of the file. What's more, if we amass anything here that we can take home with us, in the case that we find ourselves comfortably off one day, our recompense will be limited to metal coins that are only worth fifteen sols a pound in Europe.

"Let's turn back," he continued. "I'd rather risk a hundred lives, if I had them, to get back where we came from, and try to return to our homeland, than stay here any longer."

"You can't think so, La Forêt," I said to him. "You're not giving enough thought to the obstacles we'd have to overcome. We had great advantages when we came that we don't have now. There were three of us, all with firearms, and necessity was pressing us. It's quite different now. Believe me, my friend, let's stay where we are. It's a matter of occupying ourselves for part of the day; we'll be all the more liked for it, and one can't always be doing nothing. Wherever we are, we'll need food and clothing; we have twice as much here. Let's not imitate the people of our nation whose humor doesn't permit them to stay where they are. We wouldn't be far from here before we repented of our folly."

In sum, I extended myself at length and broadly on the difficulties that opposed our return—but it was all futile. He told me straight out that he would go alone if I were obstinate in not wanting to go with him.

Well, then," I said, "since you're inexorable, and, on the other hand, I've resolved not to abandon you, it's necessary to take the opportunity of this boat by the horns, and try to make use of it to escape through the frightful cavern." That was what they still called the place by which their first king claimed that the earth had given birth to him, as I have written previously.

While we were making this plan our two laborers became impatient to see the end of our dialogue. I told them that there we were in some doubt as to whether we ought to return to the village or go with them to the copper mines, where we had not yet been, which would result in our keeping them company.

They gave clear evidence of their joy, and to give them more, we resolved to go to the first canton to buy a few flagons of the best liquor they had; we also obtained a few more food supplies, and at the same time we persuaded them to steer toward the river, under the pretext that, having only seen one part of it, we desired to examine its banks from top to bottom. We assured them, too, that we would help them alternatively in hauling and rowing, and furnish them with all the things they needed, if the current—which was not very rapid there, because the country was almost flat—slowed down our voyage by a few days.

The poor fellows consented to everything we proposed to them. There was only one difficulty that embarrassed them slightly, which was that both of them were from a canton a few miles away and they had wanted to go that way in order to embrace their relatives.

I immediately made them understand that, far from interrupting their design, we would facilitate it. "Go now," I told them. "Spend two or three days at home, while we move forward in small stages, and afterwards you'll be hauling with the current, where you'll soon catch up with us."

They were charmed by my complaisance, and I was delighted not to be obliged to think of a means of getting rid of them in some other fashion.

*Chapter XII*
*The Author leaves the beautiful country.*
*The means he uses to get out of it;*
*he finds on the seashore a part of the crew*
*with whom he was shipwrecked on the shore of the continent, etc.*

As soon as those worthy folk had left us, we set a course toward the river, always remaining in the divisions of cantons in which there were no houses. I do not know whether it was two days that we were traveling continuously, but it was not far from midnight when we found ourselves one evening at the end of the canals.

We had not thought, and no one had had told us, that at the end of every canal there is a lock, which serves to maintain the water at the desired level. That accursed passage alarmed us; it took us nearly an hour to discover how to open the gates. On the other hand, it was fortunate for us that the waters on either side of the gates only differed in height by a couple of inches; if the difference had been greater, we would never have been able to get out.

We finally got ourselves out of difficulty, but we were dog-tired. It was, however, necessary to go on. The operation would have been hazardous to carry out by day, because no one was permitted to enter the river without the permission of a judge, as much because of the fishing as to observe the laws forbidding inhabitants to go beyond the limits of their territory. By night, on the other hand, there did not seem to be any danger of being seen by anyone at all.

We only had the extent of three cantons to pass—which is to say, about four and a half miles. La Forêt, animated by a greater zeal than me, was also more exhausted than I was; I told him to take a little rest, since only one of us was required to man the tiller.

I steered into the middle of the watercourse, and, as the weather was mild and tranquil, our boat went downstream without any motion being sensible. That tranquility, combined with the fatigues that we had been obliged to undergo, made me so drowsy that I could not remain awake no matter how much effort I made to keep my eyes open. However, we made progress nevertheless.

To tell you whether we were fortunate enough always to remain a long way from the shore, or whether we sometimes collided with the bank, is not within my power; we slept in such a manner as not to be easily awakened. I have never known exactly how long that slumber lasted; it is probable that it would have lasted long enough to allow us to recover, but misfortune dictated that it should be abruptly interrupted.

A frightful impact that our poor little boat made against a rock threw me out of my seat. I fell so stiffly on to the bench in front of me that I mutilated my face. My comrade got away with waking up with a start, with the fear of not knowing where he was, and what the great racket meant; he had even forgotten that we were on the water.

"Oh God!" he cried, suddenly. "What's that? Where am I?"

Although I had hurt myself badly, I could not help bursting into laughter.

"Are you there?" he said to me. "Where are we, pray? It's darker here than in Hell."

"Don't ask me," I replied. "I don't know anything certain. The only thing of which I'm convinced is that our boat has just bumped into something that made me fall in such a way as to break my head, and if my conjecture is correct, we must be in the hole that we have to go through."

"I was so deeply asleep," he said, "that I didn't remember any longer that we were in a boat. Good God, it's black here—I believe you're not wrong to think that we're underground."

"Grab hold of an oar," I said, "and feel around the place where we're stuck. We must have stopped somewhere, because I can't sense any movement, even though the water is flowing every rapidly, if I can believe my hand. The passage is definitely narrow here."

La Forêt was brave, but that frightful chasm astonished him, and he hardly dared move. Already, he would have been glad to have stayed where we were.

When I saw that there was nothing to be obtained from him, I moved forward carefully, and by means of my hands and the oar I was holding I recognized that we were caught between two spurs of rock.

"Come on," I said to him, then. "There's no harm done. We're where I said; I can feel the vault of the mountain with the tip of my oar."

With that he got up, but whatever efforts we made, I believe that we remained there for three hours getting ourselves out of that accursed trap; after which we went straight ahead.

The whole place was full of reefs, which doubtless came from splinters of the mountain that were detached from time to time and rendered the passages almost impractical. We suffered continual impacts, sometimes with the bottom and a moment later against the sides, with the consequence that it would have been advantageous to us had the boat not been moving so fast—but we could not stop it.

Meanwhile, the passage narrowed further and further as we went forward, to such an extent that there was no means of passing through. The blood rose to my face then, and in the belief that we were absolutely doomed, I thought about hitting La Forêt over the head to avenge myself for the disaster that he had procured for me without any a necessity. But I remembered just in time that I had once thrown him into a similar predicament, and that this one was merely the consequence of our miserable precedents.

"We're stuck, my friend," I said to him. "I don't know how we're going to get out of here. If we'd veered to the left just now we'd doubtless be in open water, and if we could go back a little, I don't think that it can be far away—but the current is too rapid here."

With that, he took a sounding, and found that the passage was only three or four feet deep. Without saying anything, he undressed, and threw himself into the water.

"O Heaven!" I cried. "What are you doing? It seemed to me that I heard you fall into the river."

"Have no fear," he replied. "The fall was voluntary. I'm going to examine the width and the depth of the strait."

He was only twenty paces away when he conjectured that he was at the point where the two branches came together again. He came to tell me that agreeable news, and added that we were indubitably at the narrowest point.

With that I made my way along the two sides and, having remarked that there were only two projections where the rock would not allow us to pass, I started attacking them with great blows of a pick and hammer, with the result that in two hours, I had demolished one of the spurs.

That exercise, together with all that we had already done, had exhausted me extremely. We ate some food in order to give us a little strength, and rested until we were in a fit state to resume work. La Forêt, imitating me, tried to smash the rest of the obstruction blocking our passage, but, either because the rock was harder or he was not acting with as much vigor as I had done, he remarked that he was not making much progress. It was necessary to help him, and we took turns at the task.

We were occupied with that for a long time, and little more remained to do when we heard a confused sound, like that of voices, approaching us. We remained silent for a few moments, in order to listen more attentively. Finally, we recognized that it was people, who were coming toward us.

"Assuredly," I said to La Forêt, "our flight wasn't so secret as not to be noticed. Perhaps the day was well advanced before we entered the cave-mouth, or someone spotted us from the canals. At any rate, it's quite likely that the court was informed by midday, and that the King commanded that people be sent to capture us. Can you hear how they're coming forward?" I continued. "They'll soon be at our heels. What do we do now?"

"In truth," said La Forêt, "my opinion is that we fight until the last breath; we have instruments here that will serve very well for that—for if we let them take us back, I fear that they'll do us a bad turn and send us to the mines."

"No," I replied, there's no danger of that. "The King is too mild-mannered to treat us in that manner; our works give him too much pleasure for him to want to deprive himself of us by banishment. In any case, we can say with considerable plausibility that we set out on the river with the intention of examining its banks, that misfortune overtook us in the dark, that our boat came untied without our perceiving it and that we were carried away by the current to the place where these people found us. They'll laugh at the petty misfortune, and will be delighted to have come to our rescue in such a timely fashion."

As my comrade opened his mouth to reply, we saw a light. They were undoubtedly no more than thirty paces away from us, and in the same arm of the tunnel in which we were engaged—but there was a bend at that point, which ensured that, in spite of the torches they had, they had not discovered us. Having come that far, their boat, which was apparently wider than ours, had suddenly become stuck; they were giving evidence of being in difficulties.

"What are we going to do now?" said one of them.

"What we're going to do," replied another, "is get ourselves out of here as best we can, and try to get past to the left, as we would have done if you'd listened to me."

"We can do whatever you please," said the first, "But for myself, I imagine that whatever we do will come to the same thing; it's probably twelve or fifteen hours since the people we're searching for passed this point, and they must be a long way away by now, or they've perished somewhere, as we nearly have several times. If you share my sentiment, we'll go back and say—which is true— that we met obstacles that prevented us from going any further. The King, who would dearly like to bring them back, doesn't want any violence done to them. You know that we've been charged with asking them honestly to come back, and letting them go in peace if they don't want to do that.

"We could also say, if you like, that we caught up with them but in spite of all our insistence, it wasn't within our power to make them return, because they weren't happy among us, their maxims being too different from ours, and they wanted to see whether there might be a means of getting back to their homeland, where they could exercise their religion in complete freedom, whereas here they didn't even dare to talk about it, as they testified on several occasions. Come on, let's agree on the way as to what we ought to say."

We stayed where we were for some time without daring to budge although we could no longer hear them, because we feared that they might change their minds, and that, if they heard our hammer blows, they might come back. From the tranquility we were in, we passed easily to drowsiness, and finally went to sleep.

When we woke up, we began hammering again with all the more urgency because we were not warm and we were as fresh and hearty as if we had slept in a good bed.

Thus, we finished breaking the projections that had stopped us, and we opened the passage by the strength of our arms. We then found things as my comrade believed them to be, for we soon found ourselves in open water, but in a place where a thousand echoes resounded, sending back a thousand times the words that we pronounced, with an inexpressible force.

That prodigy, which would doubtless have charmed us on another occasion, frightened us then; one might have thought, in good faith, that there were as many demons cleaving the air with their monstrous voices; the fear that gripped us prevented us from talking for a long time. We were then going very slowly, and in the meantime we began to hear another confused sound, which was somewhat reminiscent of distant rumbles of thunder. Our fear, which was already very considerable, nevertheless increased further; it does not take much to complete the trouble of a man who believes himself to be in danger. We both racked our brains to figure out what it was.

We were not very far away when we judged that there must be a place where there was a steep slope, where the water was falling like a torrent, causing the racket we could hear. That was when our doom seemed to us to be inevitable. I did not think at the time about the Portuguese about whom we had been told who had previously passed that way; if I had thought about that, I would not have given myself so much pain.

As we had ropes, I thought it was time to make use of them; as quickly as we could we gathered together ten or twelve mattocks and crowbars, which we tied into a bundle as tightly as we could, and threw the improvised anchor into the water.

The remedy was effective; the bed being smooth, our device hooked on to a good place, in such a manner that we only moved forward in proportion to the rope we paid out.

After some twenty-five brasses, my comrade, who was more often in the bow sounding with his oar, and feeling the two sides to see whether there were any obstacles to our passage, suddenly shouted to me to hold firm, that water was falling from above and that he was already wet through.

With that I called him, and after having agreed that the water we had heard, which was doubtless the same as the water he had just felt, could only be coming from high up the mountain, and precipitating through some fissure into the river where we were, we resolved to go back and recover our anchor.

We were scarcely half way when the cable broke, although we were not making great efforts to go upstream. It was necessary to reconcile ourselves to that loss; there was no way to repair it, and it was not considerable at that juncture. I only thought about steering laterally in order to avoid the impetuous fall of the torrent, which we feared.

By plying the oars, La Forêt aided my tiller to take us close to the rock; thus we went by as fortunately as possible, not without getting wet but without any danger of being swallowed up by the frightful swell and seething that the great quantity of water caused in precipitating from so high. It is probable that we would have been sunk if we had passed on the other side.

The rest of the route that we had still to cover was not nearly as dangerous as the preceding stretch; God gave us the grace of bring us within sight of the issue, so we thanked him wholeheartedly when our eyes began to readjust to the light. We were so joyful that the strongest words in our language were not adequate to express it.

We were not, however, able to set foot on land immediately; in the beginning, the walls of the lugubrious mouth were too steep for that, and we were obliged to go downstream for another three miles, after which we landed to the left, in a grassy place, which nature seemed to have made expressly to delight us after having escaped so many visible dangers.

The provisions with which we had commenced had brought us to that point marvelously; we were assured of a good meal and did not spare the cider. It must have been at least two o'clock in the afternoon, so far as we could judge from the height of the sun—from which it appeared that we must have been under that tenebrous vault for about thirty hours.

From there we continued our route as best we could. The river has prodigious bends; it is filled with rocks at the water level, and of all sorts of heights, and islets which form as many as ten or twelve narrow and difficult passages in places. There are even dangerous waterfalls. Nevertheless, as we got through them all without any misfortune, and without anything so extraordinary happening that it is not easily imaginable in a navigation of that sort, I shall not bother to describe the circumstances for fear of wearying the reader.

I shall only say that, about thirty leagues from the sea, the river divides into two branches, of which we chose the smaller one because we wanted to keep to the left and it seemed to us that the other would take us too far out of our way. It was at the fork in question that a large salmon leapt out of the water, to a height of seven or eight feet, and fell back into our boat, where we received it joyfully, in the hope of making a god meal of it—which, in fact, we did, for several days.

In spite of our diligence, however, our voyage took a full month. The joy that we felt at heading toward our homeland—without, however, knowing whether we would reach it—rendered us indefatigable; we scarcely took any rest. One might have thought that a vessel was waiting for us to take us to Europe. But alas, when we arrived at the mouth of the river, we suddenly found ourselves at the end of our hopes. A frightful trajectory presented itself to our eyes, the passage of which seemed forbidden forever.

While one is on land one seeks and invents means to overcome the obstacles that present themselves; there are hardly any so troublesome that one cannot get over them with a little patience and hard work; but the pitiless ocean even takes away from those it stops on its edge the desire to make any attempt to cross it.

Five years had passed since we had quit these coasts to go and seek our fortune. We had, in truth, survived many dangers and extraordinary fatigues, but we had also had many diversions, and I still would not want, at the present time, to have missed seeing such a beautiful kingdom. On the contrary, I have regretted having quit it a thousand times. My comrade, who was the cause of that, did not know what to say at that point. The poor devil was utterly disconcerted.

It was, however, necessary to resolve to do something.

The season was still good, and we were fortunately furnished with a number of good things; it was only nails of which we did not have a large quantity. I opined that the first thing we ought to do was to lodge ourselves as best we could. The hatchets and mattocks that we had brought served us very well for that. In a kind of clearing of marvelous size, therefore, which was fifty paces from the river and thus from our boat, we built a large triangular hut, to which we removed all of our baggage.

The bows that we had brought were also very useful for hunting, without which we might have run the risk of dying of hunger. The birds were not as tame as we have found them to be previously; it needed a good deal of skill to catch them.

What gave us some trouble was making fire for the first time, because we had lost our flints, and the fire we had conserved went out on the day before our arrival. The place where we were was full of sand and seashells, and it took us several days of searching a long way inland before we found stones that could get us out of difficulty. Once we had them, it was not difficult to accommodate ourselves; we had linen, which we were able to dry in the sun, and we had no lack of metal. Having plenty of wood available, we took care not to let the first fire we made go out, with the result that there was no longer any danger of seeing ourselves destitute for very long, for there were always entire trees to burn.

We remained in that location for about eight months, living on our hunting. Sometimes, to kill time, which seemed to us to be mortifyingly long, we got into our boat and used it to make a small excursion, either on the river or at sea, the weather and the tide permitting, or we climbed the highest hills in order to see whether we might discover in the distance some stray vessel, which would be able to extract us from our wretched solitude.

Finally weary of staying in the same place, we resolved to travel a few leagues westwards, with the intention of seeing, not only whether we could recognize the place where our ship had been wrecked, from which we could not be very far away, but also whether we could discover anything new.

We took enough food for several days, and having got up early in the morning, we advanced toward the shore in order that, always staying close to the sea, we would not go astray. We marched with sufficient resolution to have covered more than fifteen leagues by the evening of the following day, if I'm not mistaken.

The shore was very uniform; there was no diversity of objects capable of rejoicing sight. We climbed dunes, which were of a considerable height there, and always beheld the same thing, as far as the eye could see. A fresh wind blowing from the north-east obliged us to camp by night in the shelter of a hill, where the sand had conserved a good deal of the heat that it had obtained from the sun during the day. At dawn we moved inland; there was more diversity there, but, on the other hand, the paths were much poorer. If we had wanted to load ourselves with game, we would only have had to shoot in any direction, because we had good bows and there were all sorts of animals in abundance.

Finally—I think it was the fifth day after our departure—it was some two or three hours after midday when we arrived back at our river. As we were some distance from the sea, we found ourselves at least a league and a half away, but we immediately recognized several indications that were familiar to us. We were glad, because we feared having gone too far astray. The short distance that we had to cover seemed nevertheless to be extremely long to us, including a detour that we could have avoided, although it had been voluntary, and we were delighted when we perceived our hut in the distance, because we assumed that we would be able to rest there at our ease.

Soon, however, we were gripped by a frisson that nearly chilled our blood, when we saw that our boat had gone. We thought at first that we had not moored it securely, or that the agitation of the water had broken the rope that secured it. The curiosity to know what had become of it immediately made us pick up our pace. We cursed the day when we had decided to undertake the fatal excursion, which had deprived us of the commodity we obtained from the little machine; we had even began to accuse one another reciprocally of having first made the proposal, when La Forêt, who was walking to my left, having casually turned his head toward the hut, which we were passing a few paces away, suddenly cried, shivering with fear: "Oh Lord, what's that? Some frightful monster is hiding in our hut!"

I turned round instantly, and saw with the greatest astonishment a large animal lying on its side, of which we could only see the back, and which we judged by its fur to be a bear.

I cannot lie: the sight of such a ferocious animal, as that one appeared to be, terrified us. Simple bows like those we had were not weapons sufficient to attack it, but we nevertheless considered the possibility that we ought to approach it very quietly, get as close as possible, and both unleash an arrow at the same time, and then reload our bows instantly, in order to be ready to stop it with another if it still had the strength to come at us. The fear we had of failure, however, and being torn apart thereafter, caused us to continue quietly on our route, persuaded that if it woke up, it would be more likely to head into the woods that toward the sea shore.

One might have thought, seeing us run, that we had not made use of our legs for a week, so much had we forgotten the fatigues that we had suffered. Fear carried us like the wind, without looking to the right or the left, with the result that, always veering toward the river, we found ourselves three paces from our boat without having seen it beforehand, and no longer giving it a thought. That unexpected sight immediately brought us back to living in the moment; we approached it, but having found it moored, in a different fashion from the one we were accustomed to use, we thought we had found another object of surprise.

135

Our boat was dirty; the oars and poles were not in the state in which we had left them, In addition to that we noticed a kind of net at least three brasses long, in the form of a bow, with ropes attached to either end, part of which was a lowered into the water, and which had been used for fishing—which was confirmed by several small dead fish, with which the device was surrounded, which those who had made use of it had negligently thrown into the water.

These various effects of human industry led us to conclude that we were not alone there; it was merely a matter of finding out what people they might be. It was impossible for us to imagine them as sociable and civilized; appearances made it plausible that they might be cannibals.

We were, however, very hungry; we had nothing left of the food we had take with us and the three birds we were carrying were raw; it was necessary to cook the if we wanted to eat them. There was still a fire next to our cabin; we could easily see the smoke, but the bear prevented us from getting close to it. The daylight was fading; it was necessary to decide on some action if we were to sleep in our home. We resolved to go along the river as quickly as possible in our boat, until we were level with our hut, and then howl and shout loudly, in order to frighten the animal and cause it to run away.

We did, in fact, everything we had planned, but instead of putting a bear to flight, we were surprised to see two men running out, clad in furs down to the knees. Although the river, which was fairly deep, separated us, we were nevertheless afraid, and remained on our guard. They came closer, and seeing us both in robes, one of them started shouting, asking who we were.

"O Heaven!" I said, then. "That's Normand—I recognize his voice." I replied: "We're friends, and perhaps more than you think."

"Pass then, in the name of God," they said to us, "And don't let our clothing alarm you. We're poor unfortunates, abandoned by God and men, but Christian and civilized."

It requited no more to oblige us to join them. Tears flowed from my eyes as soon as I discovered who they were; the great change in them had prevented us from recognizing them. We embraced reciprocally with marks of inexpressible affection, weeping with joy like children.

We went back to our hut together, where they offered us a few roasted fish, but our hearts were so constricted that we could not eat anything. One might have thought, to see us, that we were stone statues; only our eyes remained mobile; all that we could do was look at one another, in a fashion that revealed our astonishment.

Finally, having recovered slightly, they persuaded us to have some food, and after they had reproached us a thousand times for having abandoned them without warning, and we had protested that none of them had doubted that we must have been torn apart by ferocious beasts, they asked us where we had been for such a long time and what had become of Du Puis. It was necessary to content them by giving them a brief account of our journey. They wished a thousand times that they had been in our place; to hear them, we had made a terrible mistake in leaving such a fine place.

"Let's not talk about that anymore," I said to them. "You don't know yet the tenth part of what I'll tell you later. La Forêt is the cause of the fact that you see us here; had I been alone I would never have thought of returning to my life. Tomorrow, you can tell us how you come to be here in our hut, and how you've survived for such a long time in this place, far from any commerce. For the moment, I need to sleep, and in truth, I can't stay awake any longer."

Indeed, I slept like a log, and our savages had been up and about for four hours before La Forêt and I awoke.

Scarcely had we greeted the day when we resumed where we had left off. Normand wanted to know more than I had related to him, and we were eager to learn about their adventures. It was quite warm then, for although we were in the middle of autumn—or, if you prefer, the month of May—the sky had been serene for several days and the weather was mild and pleasant, so we went to sit down in the shadow of the hut.

"Four days ago," said Normand, immediately, "desiring to bathe, I asked my comrades if any of them wanted to go to the river with me. Alexandre was the only one who decided to accompany me. Although we each had a bow, we didn't plan to amuse ourselves hunting. A brightly-colored fowl, however, of an extraordinary size and beauty, having taken off in front of us about half way, we deviated from our route in order to chase it. One might have thought that the bird of good omen wanted to bring us here, for as soon as it was within range it took off again in a straight line, without veering to the right or the left. That lasted until we were able to stick our heads into your hut, so to speak, and we discovered the little boat. Then the fowl disappeared, and we didn't give any further thought to what had become of it.

"Objects so rare in a country like this caused us astonishment. At first it occurred to us that some unfortunate vessel had been wrecked in the vicinity, and that a few people had saved themselves, so we didn't see any difficulty in presenting ourselves at the entrance to the hut. Seeing that, in spite of the noise we were making, no one appeared, we both went inside, and found a number of things that confirmed what we thought. My comrade wanted to go back nevertheless, and come back again tomorrow with more men, but I obliged him to say, principally because I was curious to meet the owner of a dwelling so artistically made.

"To pass the time we made a big wicker scoop in the form of a semicircle, and with the aid of your boat we made use of it successfully to land fish in places where there was a steep bank and the river had encroached on the land. On the third day you arrived, and we had, thank God, found one another, at a time when we were scarcely thinking about it."

*Chapter XIII*
*Concerning what happened to the rest of the crew*
*during the Author's absence, and the continuation*
*of their adventures until their departure from the country.*


"You know, at any rate," he continued, "that when you left, we were occupied in building a ship to transport us. In the beginning, everyone worked on the vessel with a great deal of enthusiasm, but as we saw the work advance, the zeal of our men diminished. The smallness of the vessel frightened the majority; in addition to that we gradually got accustomed to these austral coasts, and few days went by without our discovering something new and useful to sustain life. Five months went by before the little boat was acceptable."

"How acceptable?" I put in, "and where, pray, did you get the necessary supplies?"

"The captain," he said, "had very carefully conserved the greater part of the provisions. There was plenty of smoked bacon, butter, oil, salt, biscuit and candles. The rest consisted everything we could gather here appropriate to sustain the human body. When everything was ready, he assembled the crew and ordered all those who wanted to go with him to make the decision.

"'I don't want to force anyone,' he said, 'but for myself, I'm going to try it. The voyage is dangerous, but it's necessary to hope that the one who has protected us so far will look after us in the future.' Some of them made the determination right away, others didn't know what to decide. Finally, sixteen of us decided to stay here together, after the others had promised us on oath to employ their credit and their prayers to persuade the king of Portugal to take pity on us and to order the first vessel departing for the greater or lesser Indies to come and pick us up from here. We only parted with great regret, after shedding many years.

"They raised anchor at daybreak one morning, with a mediocre south-south-westerly wind, which carried them away so forcefully, with the ebb tide making a considerable contribution, that we had lost sight of them within two hours. That favorable departure made us envy their fortune, and we wished that we had gone with them, since we couldn't doubt that if that persisted, they'd arrive at the Cape of Good Hoppe in a short time. The wind remained steady for two days, but around midday on the third it turned. On the fifth and sixth we had bad weather, so we couldn't tell what had happened to the good people.

"No longer being attached to the sea shore, we went to establish ourselves in a valley situated about four petty leagues from here. That place, which is irrigated by a stream with an abundance of fish, is certainly very pleasant; a great many root-vegetables grow there as large as beets, which are excellent when they're well-cooked. In a south-south-easterly direction there's a wood of considerable extent, from which we obtain an abundance of apples, pears and other very agreeable fruits. The other side furnishes us with as many peas and broad beans as we need.

"Our captain had left us all the instruments he could do without; we had firearms, lead, powder, ropes, hatches, picks, hammers, saws, nails, thread, needles, matches, pots, saucepans, cooking-pots and other utensils. We loaded up all that baggage and went to build two very accommodating huts in the place, which bear a certain resemblance to peasant houses, and we covered then so well with rushes that we had no fear therein of wind or rain.

"We had been living there for about a year, without going very far afield, especially to the right, or westwards, where we were confronted by nothing but sterile heights; no one had yet taken it into his head to climb all the way to the summit. One day, three of our comrades decided to go hunting there, and to see at the same time whether they could discover anything new. It took them about three hours to get over the mountain; from there they went into a dense wood, where they covered several leagues without any sign of emerging from it. Uncertain as to whether they should go back or push on, one of them said that he could hear confused voices that sounded human.

"That surprised the others somewhat, but they nevertheless advanced in that direction, and having put their ears to the ground they discovered that he was telling the truth. Two were of the opinion that they ought to take a closer look, but the other opposed it on the grounds that they could only be savages, who would not give them any quarter if they fell into their hands. As he said that, they spotted, a hundred paces away from them, through some brushwood, a big fellow clad in animal skins, who had doubtless seen them, apparently running to tell his companions that there was a capture to make. At least, that was what they thought, so they didn't think that it was a good idea to wait for them, and they retraced their steps, taking to their heels as fast as they could.

"Experience had taught the that it's necessary to keep an eye on the sun and the stars when one goes into a forest that isn't familiar; they had taken such good care to do so that they emerged at almost the same place where they had gone in. When they reached the high ground they paused to draw breath; there was no longer any danger of their being cut off, as in the woods, where, perhaps by reason of panic terror, they had imagined several times that they had heard sound like those of people pursuing them..

"We knew when they arrived back that they had been frightened; they were distressed and soaked in sweat, as if they had emerged from water, but we were not expecting what they told us. We were extremely alarmed by such an unexpected story, and we honestly did not know whether or not we ought to abandon everything and go to camp on the other side of the river. The most resolute encouraged the others, based on the firearms that we had.

"Personally, I was of the opinion that we ought to fortify ourselves; three or four campaigns that I had once made had taught me how necessary it is to take precautions against an enemy; people rallied to what I thought it was necessary to do. That evening we were content to post sentinels for fear of being taken by surprise.

"At daybreak the following day I marked out a square thirty-five geometric paces long, which surrounded our two houses. We immediately set about making considerable earthworks, and began with a simple parapet four feet high, to cover us from the blows of attackers in case they decided to search for us there. We heightened and enlarged it thereafter, so that the rampart was twenty feet long and six feet high, with a five-foot parapet on top. The earth that we employed for that gave us a ditch sufficiently wide and deep. On the face opposite the mountain I left a gap six feet wide, which I covered with a little spy-glass, and where there was an exit provided with a traverse.

"All of that was finished in seven weeks, but in the meantime we had not seen any sign of anything, and we couldn't help sometimes mocking those who had given us such a fright. In the beginning, no longer dared go out in search of provisions; then they made no more difficulty about it—but that didn't last long. Two of our men who had gone out foraging at daybreak had the misfortune not to come back. Perhaps they had been imprudent enough to expose them more than the others had—at least, they had talked about it several times. Their loss gave us a great deal of anxiety; that circumstance led us to put palisades around our fortress.

"As we were occupied in that work we saw a troop of people coming down the mountain at a rapid pace. That sight surprised us, especially at a time when three of our comrades had gone hunting, so that there were only eleven of us. I ordered my men to load their rifles, and not to fire until the enemy had reached the ditch, where we would salute them with a discharge of at least five shots.

"When the fellows were within range we saw quite clearly that they were savages. There might have been seventy men, all tall and well-built, covered in animal-skins to the knees and carrying bows and arrows. Most of them had clubs five or six feet long. Apparently, the rogues had been spying on us before coming in a troop, because they didn't seem to be in the least surprised by the work we'd done. None of ours showed himself; a big leafy branch that I'd put at the place from which I was observing them prevented them from even seeing me—with the result that they thought that they could take us by surprise, and approached as tranquilly as possible.

"In that fashion they reached the edge of the ditch. There they stopped, not knowing with way to turn in order to get all the way to the fort. I didn't think I ought to give them the time to examine the place at close range, so I told five of my men to fire cleverly over the top and reload as quickly as possible, in order that we wouldn't be without fire. They acquitted themselves so well that they dropped three of them.

"That blow frightened them; they didn't know what to attribute the sudden collapse of their comrades to; they'd certainly seen the fire and smoke from our guns, but I very much doubt that they'd discovered those who fired them; they thought it must be lightning or some demon that had struck them—at least, the frightful cries they started to utter, looking at the sky, made us think so.

"'Let's take advantage of the wretches' fright,' I said to my comrades. 'Let the other five fire.' That discharge, together with the shot I added to it, knocked over another two; that redoubled their astonishment. Then we all showed ourselves at the same time, screaming like the damned. The first five fired a second volley at the same time, and laid two more on the ground.

"We could have exterminated them all in that manner, but they weren't crazy enough to stay there any longer. Seven of the strongest each picked up a man, and they started running as if an army were chasing them.

"The three absentees from our band weren't so far away on the other side that they couldn't hear us shooting; they knew well enough that something must be happening, since we weren't men to burn our powder without great necessity. They spent some time hiding under a bush with the game they had; toward evening they moved forward and were delighted to see from a distance the sentinel patrolling the parapet, expressly in order to show that there was no danger.

"The dread we had that the rascals would come back stronger and more resolute made us finish our palisades quickly. We also put pointed stakes on the rampart, for want of a parapet. As well as that, it was decided that some of our men would go in turn to the dunes to get the two small cannons that our captain had left there. We had a lot of trouble dragging them as far as the fort, and it took us a long time. Then we laid in a supply of little pebbles, with which our stream was well-provided, in order to make grapeshot. In the meantime, we heard no more mention of anything.

"Eight months passed like that, and we had almost stopped thinking about the wretches when one Sunday, at midday, when we were eating our meal, the sentinel sounded the alarm. With that I came running, and God knows how astonished I was to see the mountain covered with a swarm of enemies, coming like a pack of hungry wolves intent on devouring us.

"I won't lie; the bravest of us was trembling with fear; we had no doubt that the rogues were resolved either to be victorious or die, and that that would take all the precautions necessary to carry out their plan.

"They approached calmly; I was of the opinion that, like the first time, we ought to hide, and wait to fire until they were on the glacis, but the majority thought differently, and that it was necessary to intimidate them right away, making use of the cannons, since we had them. In fact, as soon as we saw them three or four hundred paces from the fort, the first gun was fired. We couldn't see whether the shot had any effect or not, but they stopped dead—whereupon we fired the other, which carried several of them away, according to one of our comrades who stuck his head over the edge claimed to have seen.

"At any rate, that didn't frighten them. On the contrary, they resumed marching, coming on at a fast pace. There were at least four hundred of them;

that number of resolute men was too superior to ours. As soon as they were within range we started firing as fast as we could. All of that didn't deter them, and in spite of the losses they took, they came as far as the palisades, in front of which some of them bent down and the other climbed on to their backs, throwing themselves over with great promptitude, and a frightful fury.

"Our cannons loaded with stones worked wonders, but notwithstanding all that, if they'd decided to attack us from several sides at once, instead of just the one, we'd have been doomed infallibly. Our fraises were a great help to us; they had no implements capable of pulling them away and they were only able to break two of them. That opening allowed two of the boldest to climb up as far as our parapet, while the others got into position to follow them, but three of ours threw themselves at them and ran them through with swords, causing them to fall from top to bottom.

"Finally, the fury faded away, and the sight of three or four of the biggest beginning to beat a retreat started a stampede. After three hours of combat they abandoned us with infinitely more rapidity than they'd come toward us.

"We were delighted with that fortunate deliverance, which we could certainly count as one. The next day we went out to see the carnage that we'd wrought. We found seventy-two dead and thirteen unfortunates who were still alive, whom we finished off with musket-butts. After having dug a big ditch we threw them all inside, for fear that their stink might infect the air and cause us some malady.

"One of those who had gone up on to the parapet to punish the audacity of the most reckless, who were attempting the escalade, had received an arrow in the thigh, from which he recovered not long afterwards; his was the only wound we had sustained.

"That skirmish redoubled once again the cares that we took for our protection; we still feared our beaten enemies, because we were apprehensive that time hadn't made them any wiser, but we haven't seen them since, nor heard any mention of them—nor of our two comrades, who the rascals must surely have massacred and eaten."

"Speaking of eating," I interjected, "it seems to me that it's time to think of sounding the dinner-bell. If you think the same, let's go and eat. Afterwards, we'll see what we still have to tell one another."

"Everything that's happened since then is unworthy of your attention," said Normand.

"Are you all still alive?" I asked him.

"Certainly not," he replied. "Four died two years ago, and there's another who's very poorly. Perhaps the sight of you will help to lift his spirits. I'm sure that he and the others will be delighted to see you. Let's go and see them, I beg you; we still have enough time today; the poor folk won't know what's become of us."

Although we were still very weary from the fatigues of the previous days, after having had a bite to eat we set forth. The sun had set some time ago when we finally saw the shelter, but the sky was serene and the moon almost full. I could not help laughing when, a hundred paces from the fort, we heard the cry; "Who goes there?"

Normand replied: "Friend"—but that wasn't all.

"Only two of you went out," said the sentry, "and I can see more of you. Officer—call out the guard."

With these words Le Grand came out, rifle in hand, to find out who we were. I was charmed by that fine guard, all the more so as I was coming from a country where no one knew what a "guard" was.

Normand, who had gone forward, declared who we were. The others, who were still apprehensive of being taken by surprise, came closer, and said yes—whereupon they all came out to fall upon us, and nearly smothered us with caresses.

After that it was necessary to recommence the story of our fortunes, and hear harsh reproaches for not having taken advantage of them.

"What are you looking for, my friends," Le Grand said. "Treasures and empires? What need do we have of anything but adequate food and simple garments? You were in a place where you enjoyed both those advantages at the same time. Everyone there is equal, there are only a few people for whom the others have a little voluntary deference, because of their virtues and the care they take to administer justice among them. You were even friends of the King, who nourished you with the fat of an abundant and fertile land—a land of benediction and peace, from which soldiers as well as executioners are banished, where human blood is sacred and sheltered from the rage and tyranny of the great—what more do you want, pray? Go wherever you like, you'll never find as much elsewhere. But that's the weakness of the greater number of men; they're rarely content with what they possess; in whatever state and whatever place they find themselves, they always think it necessary to change it in order to be happy."

"All that moralizing is futile," said La Forêt. "We're out of it, and we're not going back, even if we have to die of starvation elsewhere."

"He's right," I went on. "When mistakes are made, there's no point in thinking about them anymore, unless it's to serve us as examples for other occasions. If similar good fortune happens to us another time, perhaps we'll be better able to profit from it."

The next day we went in quest of the rest of the baggage, which we had left by the river, and of which we believed we could still obtain some utility. We came to join the others, with the intention of ending our days there.

I was very glad to see the good order that was being maintained within the fort as regards mores. It was forbidden, under pain of correction, to utter the slightest dishonest word. There were prayers in the morning and the evening, in which everyone participated, because, although they were mostly Catholics, they lived together as if they had the same religion. They all professed to love God and their neighbor as much as themselves; everyone took his turn to go out for provisions, to do the cooking, to stand guard and all the rest; the others strolled or occupied themselves as they wished.

It was easy enough to accommodate ourselves to the maxims of that little republic. The sick man who was there got better, with the result that our society was composed of twelve individuals.

We spent twenty-seven months together without there being any considerable change among us, but then one of our comrades died; his name was Gascagnet and he was a Cévénois. He had been extremely discomfited by asthma for years, which had rendered him as thin as a stick. When he died I asked for permission to open him up, which was granted to me willingly. I made use for that operation of a few rusty razors and scissors that my comrades had conserved.

I found the cadaver's lungs almost devoid of fluid, as dry and retracted as a sponge. The tracheal artery was hard and inflexible, and large enough to have passed an egg through. The liver was green, and one of its lobes was granular, the other attached to the kidneys, which seemed to be extensively ulcerated. I found four stones the size of a plum-stone in the bile duct, which was as yellow as wax. As for the heart, it seemed as sound externally as one could wish, but having opened it up, I found an opening in the medial septum the size of a sou, bordered by a membrane, which had doubtless been formed there to prevent it from closing.

I confess that that surprised me, but having reflected somewhat, I conjectured that the man having always had difficulty breathing, and his lungs, in consequence, not being sufficiently refreshed, nature had tried to remedy that as she substitutes in other ways for children who are still in their mother's womb, and who are not, in fact, breathing at all, so that the circulation of the blood takes place within them in a manner quite different from the subsequent one. There the blood contained in the veins is carried from the extremities of the body to the heart, which it enters by means of the vena cava, is discharged into the right cavity, from which it passes into the arterial vein and then into the venous artery, and from there into the left cavity of the heart, from which it is transported to the extremities of the animal by the aorta, which is connected by its branches with those of the vena cava. In this case, on the contrary, the blood that emerged from the right cavity passed immediately from the trunk of the arterial vein into the aorta, while it passed immediately from the vena cava into the trunk of the venous artery, entering therefrom and dilating in the left cavity of the heart.

I noticed nothing extraordinary in the intestines. The urethras and the kidneys were full of granules, in consequence of which it was not surprising that the poor body was always complaining, and the man had died relatively young, being no more than thirty-four years old.

We buried him in the counterscarp.

Not six weeks after that we had a horrible earth tremor, which was followed by a tempest as furious as any I have ever seen in my life. The mountain to the west of our fort split in two from the summit to the foot; at the same time, a torrent of muddy water emerged from it with an extraordinary impetuosity. Fortunately, it did not come down directly toward us; otherwise our earthworks would have been greatly at risk. That deluge lasted until the following day; our entire valley was under water, and for three days we were unable to travel in the vicinity.

When the bad weather passed and our meadows dried out, we climbed the mountain in order to see some of the ravages that it had caused. We found that the opening that I have just mentioned was at least twenty toises, or a hundred and twenty feet, wide at the bottom, and more than fifty at the top. I was the first to notice that a spring near the summit had disappeared, and when I saw the others looking for it, I recited this impromptu verse:

*You are no longer, beautiful rain,*
*A fatal turbulence has closed your flow;*
*Heaven, when its wishes, will ease my pain*
*And one day put an end to my sorrow.*

That change surprised us all, but what astonished us more was that half the forest, which was down below on the far side, had sunk, and instead of trees there was now nothing but a lake of vast extent.

Those prodigious events gave us occasion to admire the works of Providence. The captain was sad at the loss of the spring, because we had often gone to seek diversion in its vicinity and it had been very easy for us to draw fresh water from it, which was marvelously pure and clear. He could not understand what relation that the jet of water had to the split rock; the others were even more astonished than him.

"Don't you see," I said to them, "that to make such an opening in that huge mass, it required the little particles making up the two halves to be squeezed together, and the conduits through which the water passed, which formed that little jet, to close up, in the same fashion that the pores of a sponge close when it is squeezed."

"I don't know whether you're joking or not," one of them said. "One might almost think so by your expression, but what you say there seems quite plausible."

"Of course I'm joking," I replied. "There's a natural and physical reason for what you're admiring, of which no one who has the slightest smattering of philosophy is unaware."

"We don't know what philosophy is," said Le Grand, "but if you think that we're capable of understanding you, give us the pleasure of philosophizing with us about our spring."

"I'd like that," I said. "We have nothing else to do at present—but on condition that it doesn't obtain me a reputation for pedantry."

I went on: "The globe that we inhabit is composed of a vast number of different tiny particles. The principal ones are the terrous and the aqueous. That composite rotates around its own center in twenty-four hours."

"What!" Le Grand interjected. "The earth turns?"

"Yes, yes," said La Forêt. "I've heard him explain that phenomenon so clearly elsewhere that there's no way to doubt it."

"Clearly enough to please you," Le Grand retorted. "I never believe anything to the prejudice of my senses and Holy Scripture, where one finds a quantity of formal passages that positively ruin what you're putting forward."

"Your senses often deceive you; that's easy to prove," I continued. "As for what is in the Scriptures, it's certain that the objective of the Holy Spirit has never been to render us mathematicians and philosophers, since it would otherwise have taken care to clarify the parts of *Genesis* on the subject of creation that embarrass many people, and which a priest of the country where La Forêt and I have been noticed as soon as he heard mention of them. It even neglected to teach us the true proportion of the periphery of a circle to its diameter, when it treats the sea of copper that Solomon put into his superb temple, and states it there, in accordance with vulgar opinion, as thirty to ten, or twenty-one to seven, instead of which it is twenty-two to seven, or very nearly, as is easily demonstrated in mathematics. God simplifies things in order to make himself intelligible, accommodating himself to human language; when he speaks in his own fashion, it's impossible for him to hear him; what he says are mysteries that we cannot penetrate. All that is easy to understand and does not create any difficulty here.

"Supposing therefore, that the earth turns, the most agitated particles must be those that draw apart from its center with the greatest impetuosity, as it is easy to prove by numerous beautiful experiments. That being the case, water— which, in addition to the movement of any body that is impelled, has a particular one that renders it liquid—must, in consequence, go on ahead. Afterwards comes the air, which is another liquid composed of particles that are much more subtle and more agitated than those of water, which also makes it go on head and form around the terrestrial globe a kind of cushion, which makes up our atmosphere, and extends to a distance of about two leagues above the surface of the earth—and it is, to mention it in passing, that atmosphere in which rain, now, lightning, thunder and, in general, all meteors are formed."

"Wait," said Le Grand. "According to your philosophy, the bodies that are the least in movement, ought to remain the closest to the center of our globe. The aqueous particles are in greater movement than the terrestrial ones, so water

146

ought necessarily to cover the entire surface of the earth, and we ought to have a continuous deluge—which is not the case."

"The objection is good," I replied, and it is assuredly the case that if God, in his omnipotence, flattened the mountains reduced all heights to the same level as the valleys, dry land would not appear anywhere. It is an argument that can even be used to for the possibility of a universal deluge, were it not that the text speaks before and afterwards of mountains. But you ought to consider that nature cannot always take her course freely, because of the obstacles that prevent it. The waters of a river must, in accordance with the laws prescribed for them, follow the slope of its bed; however, it often happens that an impetuous wind stops them, and even drives them back toward its source. The mountains and rocks that providence has formed are barriers that the ocean cannot cross, as liquid that is in a vase cannot surpass its rim; but if the rim is lowered, as I said just now about the mountains, you will immediately see it overflowing. I shall return to my subject, then, and say that there is no void in the world."

"No void in the world!" Le Grand interrupted. "Ah!"

"I give in," I said.

"No, I'm wrong to interrupt you so often," he retorted. "Continue, I beg you; you're right to stop me, for I know that I was about to say something stupid. I shan't say another word today."

I continued: "As soon as a few particles of air or fire, more subtle and more agitated than the others, rise up, it's necessary that an equivalent quantity of others descend at the same time, which take their place. That causes a certain tension in the water, which causes it to fill the slightest intervals that those tiny particles can penetrate. Now, it's necessary to know that the majority of mountains are hollow toward the base, as you can see in this one now that it has been opened, and inasmuch as the earth is porous, full of crevices and conduits, it happens that the sea invades these passages and comes to fill up these hollow mountains to the level of the ocean."

"I understand you." said Le Grand. "It's unnecessary to say any more. "You mean that, the sea being as high as the highest mountains, as everyone admits, and which is easy to see when one is on the coast, the air that presses the water of the ocean forces it to pass through the low conduits of the earth and to rise up to the summit of rocks, from which it emerges in trickles that form the springs in question, exactly as the liquid that one pours into a vase in which there is a pipe or an arm, when it rises to the level of that arm, emerges therefrom if there is the slightest opening."

"That's certainly reasoning philosophically," I replied. "Your conclusion is very good; it's a pity that your premises are unsound. It's not true that the sea can only be as high as its shores; if that were the case we'd soon be sunk. It's a popular error whose cause is known by those who only have the first elements of optics. This is the fact of the matter.

"The water, having reached the foot of a hollow mountain, is warmed up by the sun's rays, which penetrate that far, and it rises in vapors to the vault, where the particles of water collect, as the water in a boiling pot forms droplets inside its lid, and those drops form trickles, which emerge through any opening that they find, and make what we call a spring, and several springs a river, which takes the water back to the sea from which it came—which is, in consequence, only circulating, like the blood in the veins of a living animal."

"Well," said La Forêt, "what do you say to that? It's nothing yet, however; the explanation is clear, but it depends on other knowledge that I've heard deduced elsewhere, which it's necessary to have in order to understand fully."

"Other knowledge or not," retorted Le Grand, "I think all that is very good, and I'd like our doctor to tell us in the same way about the formation of meteors. That must be extremely diverting."

"It would be more useful," I put in, "if I were to give you a smattering of mathematics. I've learned enough of it; that science might be useful to you, if we ever get out of here; at least it will help you to kill time."

They all agreed to my proposal joyfully. Only Le Grand, who was avid for knowledge, shook his head.

"You've put in one clause regarding physics," he said, "that doesn't please me at all. I'll willingly treat the works of nature, but it's necessary not to demand too much of one's masters. Only have the generosity, before finishing this agreeable conversation, to tell us what sentiment you have regarding the deluge. From the manner in which you talk I doubt that you follow the vulgar opinion; confess to us frankly whether you believe it to have been universal or particular."

"As salvation isn't dependent on the choice one makes between those two alternatives," I replied, "I have no difficulty in yielding to the reasoning of one of my regents at college, who sustained loudly that it would be impossible for all the water in the world to cover the earth to such a great height as the text seems to insinuate."

"But isn't God omnipotent?" Le Grand interrupted. "And in any case, isn't it said that the sluice-gates of the heavens were opened?"

"Undoubtedly," I said, "but the theologians haven't proved any miracle here; if that is what it was, I don't have any objection to raise. I don't deny that the one who created the universe can make new water whenever he wishes, but I sustain that if he created waters then, he annihilated them afterwards. As for the sluice-gates of the heavens, that's a poetic and metaphorical expression, of which the author makes use to bring out the excellence of the subject."

"Why," said someone else, "if there's a heaven of fire, couldn't here also be a heaven of water, which would be like an inexhaustible reservoir, of which providence could make use on occasion, either to dampen the earth in times of drought or to inundate certain lands?"

"As for that," replied Le Grand, "it's a pure bagatelle; the first is a fiction of ancient philosophers, the second an infantile chimera, although I've heard it alleged by reasonable people. For after all, where can one place an aquatic heaven? If one puts it above the firmament, it has no liaison with the earth; if one places it below, it's impossible that it wouldn't hide the fixed stars, since the slightest mist robs us of the sight of the sun. It's not necessary to seek the remedy so high, but it's necessary to begin with to consider that if it rains for six or eight hours solidly in a place, everything there is flooded. Now, it's only necessary that it rains everywhere with an equal force for forty consecutive days, and then it seems to me that the matter wouldn't have so much difficulty."

"You can't think so," I said. "When there's a great deal of humidity in one place, there's an excessive dryness in another; what the sun elevates in one place, the clouds carry elsewhere. If it were to rain with so much violence, it would first be necessary for the entire oceans, so to speak, to rise up in vapors, and even then, everything that fell would only be sufficient to refill the basins from which the water was taken to form the clouds. It would need many others to cover the entire globe to a height of fifteen cubits above the Alps and the peak of the Canaries, mountains that might be two leagues high. You can see that it's impossible.

"There is, however, another difficulty, which is the size of the Ark. My master of mathematics had the curiosity of taking the dimensions of that large vessel, and calculating its capacity. Then he examined Pliny and consulted all the accounts of voyagers, in order to make an accurate list of all the different animals of which we presently have knowledge. Finally, he calculated how much food all those animals and eight people would need in a year—but when all that was added up, the volume was so great that the vessel couldn't remotely contain it. I'll leave aside the animals of which we haven't yet heard mention, which are doubtless large in number."

"But are the measures of which Moses speaks well known?" said Le Grand.

"Yes," I replied. "The cubit of which the text makes mention was a foot and a half long; and in order that you don't think that we're talking at hazard, you need to know that the ancients, seeing that men are not equally tall and strong, and that, in consequence, the proportions of the parts of their body must be different, agreed, instead of making use of them for their common measures in commerce, to take four grains of barley arranged in a line for the lateral measure of a finger, four of those fingers making a palm, or three inches, and twelve inches, or sixteen fingers a foot; from one and a half of those feet they made the cubit, and of five feet the royal or geometric pace, instead of the common comprehension of only two and a half feet. The rod is twelve feet; the stade was composed of a hundred and twenty-five feet, and eight stades were an Italian mile—from which you see that the principles of measurement invented by the first humans passed to the Greeks, to the Romans and several other nations.

"Given all that, it's easy to conclude that the deluge of which Moses speaks was not universal with respect to the earth, but only with regard to humans. The world was in its infancy; they had not had time to multiply and spread far and wide. God inundated the land that they inhabited; it was unnecessary to submerge all the others. Thus, it was sufficient for Noah to conserve the species of livestock that were in those countries; the Ark was more than sufficient to lodge them; and all the other difficulties vanish. For it's common enough for the sacred writers to make use of the expression 'the whole world' to indicate a part of it, as witness that place where's it's said of Joseph and Mary that everyone in the world had to be counted. No one is unaware that 'the whole world' was limited, at the most, to the countries that were under the government of the Roman emperor."

With that, everyone retired, resolved to plunge into the study of mathematics and profit from my lessons.

In fact, we commenced the next day with the elements of Euclid. Although it was years since that author had passed through my hands, I had taken so much care to pass frequently through my mind the principal contents of his six books that however scantly I recalled his ideas, I rarely hesitated over the demonstrations that I made. From that we passed on to geometry, in which I was not, in truth, so expert, apart from the fact that in order to treat it in depth we would have required books and instruments, which we had little chance of recovering. Finally, we finished with fortification.[16] I would also have liked to teach them a little algebra, but Le Grand was the only one who wanted, from time to time, to apply himself to it, and even he became discouraged as soon as we got to quadratic equations.

We spent years on those beautiful sciences, with the result that there were no smooth and sandy places that were not filled with geometric figures, especially in the dunes and along the sea shore, where we often went to walk.

One day, when we were there and the water was rising in little waves, when we had taken the opportunity to converse about the causes of the oceanic tides, we were extremely surprised to see, to the west, an object that we had been unable to see before. Our sentiments were initially divided on the subject, some suggesting that, the water being low, it was the tip of some rock that was protruding; others contended that it was a small cloud; Normand assured us that he had seen the same thing before; and the rest argued that it was a slip.

In order to make sure, I fixed two arrows in the ground, which made a straight line with the object, and, having positioned myself behind them, I immediately ascertained that it had changed position, and therefore could not be a

---

[16] In the 17th century, because of the applications of geometry and calculation in planning and constructing fortifications, "fortification" was included as a branch of mathematics in many educational programs, as was "gunnery" (i.e., ballistics).

rock. We then applied ourselves to observing it very attentively, to see if it changed its shape, as clouds ordinarily do, which extend, augment or dissipate over time. Having not seen any change in the space of half an hour, except that it was magnified very slightly, we concluded that it absolutely must be a ship, which Heaven had sent us to extract us from our tedious solitude.

The wind freshened slightly, and it was not yet midday, so there was some hope of seeing it approach before nightfall, since it was skirting the land. La Forêt, who was more fearful than any of the others that such a rare and unexpected commodity might escape us, opined that four of us should set out in our boat—which we have taken care to put into the hut we had built on our arrival, and of which we had made scarcely any use in the twelve years since we had first put it there, thus conserving it well, in association with the care we had taken care to maintain it—and row out to meet the ship, for fear that it might draw away from the shore without those manning it being informed that we were there. That negligence would deprive us of a good fortune that might never arrive again. His sentiment was approved, so we went to put out boat into the sea, where La Forêt and three others climbed into it.

As we only had two oars they worked in shifts, but with so much vigor that we soon lost sight of them. Meanwhile, the large vessel drew closer, and we were beginning to make out her sails when we observed that the sun was approaching the horizon. We had at least a league and a half of ground to cover before reaching the forest lodging that we had between our fort and the sea, and the moon would be rising late. Those considerations made us think about retreating. We eventually arrived at the first shelter, where we found a few leftovers of the food we had brought in the morning, which were very timely.

Although we were tired it was impossible for us to close our eyes; there was not one of us who was not feeling mortal anxiety. The next morning, we returned as directly as we could to the ocean shore.

When we arrived we were delighted to see the large ship at anchor, about a league out to sea, and at the same time, two launches coming toward the land. We went to the place where they would reach the shore.

The captain of the ship, not knowing the men who had come to his vessel, had retained two of them; their comrades were serving as guides to eight others who had come in their own boat to investigate us.

Immediately, we were ordered to go and fetch our baggage, and to come back as soon as possible, because the sea-bed there was not appropriate for anchorage, and if the slightest bad weather blew up they would be at risk there. Six crewmen accompanied us; having reached our fort we charged ourselves with what we thought it best to take, the rest remaining for the savages, if they ever acquired a desire to return.

Diligent as we were, night fell before we reached the ship. La Forêt had already informed the captain of the properties of the land we were quitting—or, to put it more accurately, he had take care to paint a picture of it as disadvantageous as he could—in consequence of which, having no great desire to see it, he immediately set sail. That gave us occasion to give thanks to God for taking us away from the wretched place where we had been unfortunately wrecked eighteen years previously.

*Chapter XIV*
*How the Author passed from the austral lands to Goa,*
*where he was handed over to the inquisition;*
*the story of a Chinaman he encountered in that prison,*
*and the manner in which they got out of it.*

The captain of the ship was a Spaniard, which was not belied by any of his actions; he had in every form the pride and the genius of his nation. Thus, however much I desired to know by what fortuitous circumstance the vessel had been led to the shores of a land devoid of commerce, it was impossible for me to find out. There was not a single man in the crew who knew anything, and I dared not address myself to that boor in order to obtain information, for fear of being received like the others. The surgeon, however, who spoke a little Latin, told me one day that they had come from the American islands, to which they had escorted a number of merchant ships, and carried orders on the subject of four or five ships that Monsieur le Chevalier Tyssot, the governor of Surinam, had had arrested for reprisals, and the release of which was desired—after which they had immediately set a course for the austral lands, where they had landed twice.

"On the first occasion," he continued, "nothing was found worthy of the captain's curiosity; at the second descent we made, perhaps seventy or eighty leagues from the place where you were, of the ten men who were sent ashore, only two returned, who were those that had been left to guard the launch. The others had been attacked by the inhabitants of the country, who had pursued them to the dunes, where their comrades had seen them overtaken and hacked to pieces; they had difficulty escaping themselves because the tide had gone out and their boat was on the strand. We had intended to disembark again where we found you, but the account you gave us of the vicinity put our captain off. That causes me to presume that he has had a secret order from our king, or some company, to see whether there was any means of making a fortunate discovery on these coasts."

He added: "I don't know whether he has given up or not, but I seem to have heard that we're going directly to Goa."

Indeed, I remarked, without knowing the reason for it, that we had entirely abandoned the lands from which we had come and were heading north-eastwards. We could not, however, conclude our navigation in a single haul; it was necessary for the captain to put in at the Île de Bourbon, situated east of Madagascar, from which it is five or six degrees distant. We stayed there for ten days to renew our supplies and take on fresh water.

During that brief sojourn, our sailors never ceased to have as good a time as their purses would permit. The day before our departure a group of them went ashore and got drunk; there was among them a native of Seville, about thirty-five years of age, and very handsome, who had a large moustache, which he was continually stroking, and of which he took more care than the rest of his body. In spite of his drunkenness he got back to the launch, but had no sooner climbed into it than he fell asleep. The others who were with him, having joined him, started pulling and shoving him back and forth, in order to excite one another to laugh. A young Portuguese, who was in little better condition than him, wanting to do his bit, quietly took out his scissors and removed the left-hand section of the Spaniard's moustache.

That action caused them to shiver; everyone criticized him loudly for his imprudence, and immediately predicted that no good would come of it. Indeed, the following morning, having learned from some blabbermouth who had played the trick on him, he came to the capstan, where the other was working to raise the anchor, and without saying a single word, plunged his knife into his chest, all the way to the hilt.

The Portuguese, feeling himself wounded, lifted the lever that he was holding and landed such a prodigious blow on the Spaniard's head that he fell down stone dead, while he made three or four pirouettes and then fell face-down, shedding almost all his blood in the space of a quarter of an hour and dying in my arms.

Thus, we lost two brave men at the same time, to the great displeasure of the captain, who took the opportunity to swear that the first of his men that he saw behaving foolishly, he would punish in a manner to make him remember it. That did not, however, prevent us from putting on sail, and we arrived at Goa gladly on the thirteenth of April 1663.

That famous city is situated on an island that bears the same name, at least fifteen miles in circumference, at the mouth of the River Mandovi. It is enriched by a fine harbor, a celebrated arsenal and an incomparable hospital. Having no engagement on our vessel, the captain had the generosity of permitting me to establish myself there and exercise my profession, without claiming anything for my passage. For the most part, my comrades left in the same fashion, and went their separate ways.

A hostelry was indicated to me where the host made me welcome. I had not been in his house for an hour when he graciously offered to let me stay there gratis, until I had found a house I liked in which to reside. I supped with a great appetite, and went to bed early.

It was hot, so, having mechanically approached the edge of the bed, my left arm slid off and hung down, almost to the floor. When I had been there for at least four hours, in my deepest slumber, something soft and warm, which came and went along my arm, caused me to draw it up again, without sleep permitting me to perceive enough to make any reflection.

The arm having fallen back shortly afterwards, the same thing happened again, and several more times in succession, until, finally having woken up completely, I was surprised to see a phantom moving about the room, which seemed to me to be as large as a calf. Blood rose to my face; I could not imagine what it was; and although I took it as given that everything that was said about witches and apparitions was only old wives' tales, having closed the door of my apartment firmly and not knowing that there was any other bed than the one I was lying in, I nevertheless began to doubt the verity of my hypothesis.

Meanwhile, that frightful object, after having made a few turns, came back directly toward me. With that, I recoiled; I moved in one direction as it advanced from the other, and, believing myself to have already reached the gap between the bed and the wall, my astonishment, which was already extreme, increased considerably nevertheless when I felt something moving behind me.

I cannot tell a lie; I was in mortal anguish on finding myself besieged on all sides. My heart was hammering in an inconceivable manner; I was having difficulty breathing, and there was not an inch of my skin that was not dripping with sweat. Finally, at the same moment when one of them made as if to throw itself upon me from one side, I heard a voice from the other, which said to me: "What's the matter? Are you ill?"

At those words I uttered a frightful cry, which communicated the anguish I was in well enough.

"Have no fear," someone said.

"Who are you?" I retorted, trembling.

"I'm Juhan," he replied. "A sailor on the vessel on which you've just arrived."

"Devil take you," I said. "You've given me a shock that will doubtless cost me my life. I'm half-dead already, and if no one brings me help it's impossible that I'll escape. How the devil did you get in here? And who else is in the room with you?"

"No one," he said, "and if you can see something, it's only our captain's dog, which followed me here yesterday evening. "

"A dog?" I said. "Is it as big as a donkey?"

"It's the big black barbet that you've seen a hundred times," he replied. "Fear magnifies things; it's doubtless appears bigger to you than it is."

"That's the rascal, then," I said, "that came to lick my hand three or four times before I was fully awake. But once again, how do you come to be crammed in next to me?"

"He captain went to supper with one of his friends," he said. "He kept me there until ten o'clock, they told me to come and lodge here for the night. When I came in the host told me that he had no place to give me, but that if I'd come an hour or two sooner, I would have been able to accommodate myself with a foreigner who had arrived on the *Santiago*—and having obtained further explanation, I realized that it must be you.. So, after having told him that we were from the same ship, he permitted me, on the word that I gave him that you wouldn't complain, to take my place beside you."

"All that would have been perfectly all right, my friend," I replied, "if you had taken the precaution to speak to me when you came in."

"I wanted to do that," he said, "but you were sleeping so tranquilly that I thought it would be a crime to interrupt that sweet repose."

Those circumstances reassured me greatly, and I felt myself gradually recovering my spirits. Nevertheless, the shock had been too great not to do anything about it. As soon as it was light I had my Portuguese get up and instructed him to fetch a surgeon. I got him to open a vein and take out five or six ounces of blood. Thus, thank God, I was acquitted for the fright I had had, but it was assuredly such as to surpass all those that had gripped me before.

My host, who almost did not recognize me, was afflicted by the incident, although we laughed about it afterwards and no one came to the house that he did not divert with it.

Ten days later I obtained lodgings opposite the Dominicans, who have a very fine monastery there. In the short time I had been there I had had the good fortune to effect a few cures, which made me well-known to honest folk. One of the monks that I have just mentioned, who fell down a staircase and broke his leg, sent for me. Although the bone was broken I healed it so well that after two months he was walking as freely as he had done before.

That did me a great deal of good. The monk only had to make a few flattering remarks about me, and all those in his order took pleasure, as well as him in having me in their company during all my hours of leisure, when it was necessary for me to entertain them with the story of my voyages. In addition to that, they recommended me wherever they went, so my practice was augmented from day to day, which brought me a good deal of money, so that I was already flattering myself that I would amass considerable wealth in time. My star, however, ingenious in my oppression, provoked a new trouble that nearly cost me my life and which caused me a great deal of chagrin.

The inhabitants of Goa practice a mixture of all sorts of religions. There are pagans, Jews and Mohammedans there. The Catholic religion is the dominant one, and there is no other public exercise. The clergy there are very rigid, and the people extremely superstitious. It is necessary not to imagine however, that that stems from a principle of devotion; most of them are crassly ignorant and the others excessively debauched; the women, most of all, have a reputation for inconceivable lubricity.

Finding myself at ease, and frequenting their companies, I often allowed myself to jest about those eaters of crucifixes and drinkers of images who believe that they can cut a purse with impunity with one hand, so to speak, provided that they are holding a rosary in the other. A man of my profession, enraged at seeing me so much in demand, while he had difficulty earning a meager living, having heard me make such speeches several times, was rascally enough to denounce me for heresy to the Inquisition, which is certainly the most terrible and the most unjust tribunal in the world.

A few days later, as I was going to the governor's house, where I had been summoned to bleed one of his domestics, I was only fifty paces from the house when an officer ordered me to follow him. Four guards who were accompanying him immediately surrounded me, and having seized me by the collar, took me to prison on the twenty-sixth of June 1669, where, like the worst of criminals, my feet were immediately put in irons.

There were more than twenty of us in one accursed dungeon, where there was no light. There was a deep hole in the middle, the edge of which was at floor level, which was destined for the prisoners' necessities, but they hardly dared approach it for fear of falling in, with the consequence that everyone deposited his ordure where he could, and there was an intolerable stink.

The first day of my detention passed in regrets and moans, at being deprived of my liberty and in the apprehension of shortly feeling the effects of the tyranny of the most pitiless judges in the world. Seeing thereafter that all of that would do no good, however, I thought that the best way of dissipating a part of my chagrin was to converse with others about indifferent matters.

With that aim, I addressed myself to most of my fellow prisoners. Some did not understand me because I was not speaking their language, and the others were so beaten down by misery that they did not deign to reply. Only one man, more patient and sociable than the others, seeing me rebuffed on all sides, said to me in Portuguese:

"You've been given a poor welcome, but you ought not to be surprised by that; it requires a fortunate temperament and a great firmness of soul not to let oneself decline in a place like this, especially when one has been here for some time. For myself, thank God, I'm of an age to be able to suffer a great deal, and I'm so resigned to the decrees of Providence that I laugh at all that men can do to me."

"Those are good qualities," I said to him. "Very few people are capable of such resolution." I added: "Of what religion are you?"

"I'm a universalist," he told me, "or the religion of honest men. I love God with all my heart, I fear him, I worship him, and I try to do treat my fellow men, without exception, as I would like them to treat me."

"That's well and good," I said, "but you're doubtless of some communion; one rarely reaches the age where you are without declaring for a certain party."

"No," he said, "I make no difference between one society and another; there is none that does not have its beauties and its stains, and I'm convinced that there is no road on which I can be damned or saved."

"Assuredly," I said, "your language confirms me in the opinion that I have held for a long time, that there's as much diversity in the thoughts as in the faces of men."

"That's true," he said, "not only with regard to each man in particular but with regard to all the days of life; what we conceived yesterday in one manner we envisage today in another; the mind, as well as the body, is subject to a thousand changes."

"I'm Chinese," he continued, "the son of a rather well-to-do father, who took great care of my education, with the result that if I have no great enlightenment, it's entirely from him that I acquired it. A Jesuit missionary named Du Bourg, having heard mention of him as a generous man whose family was numerous, found the means of introducing himself to our home. The man was not only civil, but seemed exemplary in his piety; we took and indescribable pleasure in hearing him reasoning. He gave each of us a catechism and asked us to read it attentively. After that he gave lessons at our house twice or three times a week, in which it is necessary to admit that the father neglected nothing for our instruction.

"As the matters with which he dealt at first were not greatly confused, because he only talked in general about the fall of man, his redemption by the son of God and eternal bliss, we acquired a strong taste for his lessons. Eventually, however, two or three months having gone by, the ecclesiastic, who proceeded by degrees, and had not wanted to alarm us, began to explain the prophecies and to set out the mysteries of the trinity and the incarnation. My father's mind did not take long to rebel. He could not understand how reasonable men, who boasted of being enlightened by revelation, could not see that their religion is enveloped by the thickest darkness of paganism.

"'Is it not surprising,' he said, 'that people take pleasure in being blind, to the point of having a horror of those who make them see that the principal maxims and most essential dogmas of their religion are poverties, puerilities and impertinences, which, according to themselves, have been the scandal of the Jews and the folly of the Greeks. Above all' he said, 'I shiver when someone tries to persuade me that a sovereignly perfect and immaterial being engenders another corporeal god, equal to him, for all eternity; and that there is yet another god, an independent spirit, who proceeds from the father and the son; each of the three being a distinct person, and yet all three of them only making up one perfect god. Assuredly it is making a strange chimera of the most simple and least divisible being in the world.'

"The Jesuit would have liked not to have gone so far; he tried to remove that obstacle by the ordinary methods of theologians, but, not being able to reach a conclusion, he made use of this comparison: 'Imagine,' he said, 'a tree that bears fruit uninterruptedly. In that tree, I find three things that bear a strong resemblance to the holy trinity. I remark there the relationship between the trunk and the father, because the branches and the fruits are its products; the branches are like the son, in that they are produced by the trunk like so many arms or means to distribute to humans all that proceeds from the trunk. And the fruits are like the holy spirit, in that they come to us from the trunk and the branches like so many assurances or testimonies of their bounty.

"'I admit that when it is a matter of eternity, there is no more apparent resemblance, because it is not possible to find a proportion between the finite and the infinite, however ancient and extensive the former might be. It is true, however, that when one examines the pips or seeds of the fruit of the tree with a good microscope, one observes, not only a tree already formed with its branches, but even its fruits, albeit with a certain amount of confusion: a veritable emblem of the divinity, considered during and before the creation of the world, since there it only appears as a tree in its entirety, without distinction of branches and fruits.

"'Now, to get from there to my objective, it is evident that whatever difference one makes between the trunk, the branches and he fruits of a tree, essentially there is none; they are in truth different parts, but all those parts together only constitute a single whole. One can say that the trunk is not the branches and that the branches are not the fruit, but I sustain that the distinction is not real—which is to say that the three things cannot subsist independently, as when they are assembled. To make a tree complete as we imagine it, it necessarily requires the assemblage of a trunk, branches and fruits; however, each of them has its particular usages: the first, to say it once again, creates or produces; the second carries, deploys and donates; and the third confirms, by its presence and its operations, the belief that one has in the second and the first. There is one same substance represented by various aspects, one agent that operates in various ways, but which is fundamentally only one, and cannot be considered as several without an evident contradiction.

"'God is only one in essence, but in the economics of salvation he is considered as the author and father of the human species; in redemption one regards him as an obedient son, submissive and humble, who satisfies his father's justice; and when it is a matter the application and distribution of his grace, one treats him as the holy spirit.'

"'In that manner and no other,' my father interrupted, I understand what the term trinity means; but there is something else hidden therein, and you would not have made so many detours without it; all these fashions of acting do not please me. Once you appeared to me to be an honest man; now I considered you as a rogue.' And, taking him by the arm, he expelled him from the house once and for all.

"Then he turned to us. 'Do you not notice,' he said to us, the absurdity there is in the reasoning of this sophist? By his own account, this Jesus of whom he had preached to us so much, and whom he makes the equal of God, did not even have enough credit to pay, by means of his ignominious death, for the debt that the first man had contracted by eating the fruit whose usage had been forbidden to him; since Adam, who had been, according to him, created to live eternally, merited by that eternal and temporal death; and Christ only guaranteed his posterity against the first of those deaths, of which we do not even have any certainty, and of which the majority of nations is unaware; in addition to which he was unable to redeem that which we know by experience, and which, according to him, was imposed upon us as a punishment.

"'And what is even more noteworthy than that is that the redemption in question was only made on onerous conditions, much more difficult to execute than those to which the Jews were subjected under the former dispensation. The Israelites, according to the Christians themselves, were limited to doing good works; the law only demanded of them aspersions and other similar ceremonies; but under the new alliance, faith was added to the good works, and a faith that has to be firm enough not to call into doubt any of the mysteries of the religion, in spite of the fact that they defy reason and common sense. For myself, my children,' he added, 'I renounce such bizarre sentiments; I absolutely do not want to hear any more mention of them'

"I was twenty-two years old then, and was, in consequence, at the age of discretion. Infatuated as I was by the sanctity of my teacher, I thought in all conscience, in spite of what I had just heard that I ought to profit from all favorable opportunities to receive salutary instruction from him. There were several places where he had made proselytes, and which he frequented assiduously. I took my opportunities to attend his assemblies; he seemed charmed, and it seemed to me that I was profiting considerably from his instruction.

"Although my steps were taken with a great deal of precaution, I could not avoid my father perceiving them; he made me very tangible reproaches, and forbade me, under penalty of his indignation, to keep company with a man who, according to him, had nothing in view but his pleasures, a vain glory and the eventually ruination of our family. My father was of a nature not to suffer any republic in his children; it was necessary to obey or run the risk of being chastised.

"Six months went by without my seeing the monk more than three or four times; that was an insupportable mortification for me, so that one day, having told me about a voyage that he was about to make to Goa, I informed myself as to the route that he was going to take, and, without saying anything to anyone, I left two days after him and went to wait for him fifteen leagues away. The good man was delighted to see me, but when I told him what had led me to join him, it would not have take much for him to refuse to receive me in his company, because of the consequences. I was obliged to assure him on oath that I would sustain until the end—as was the truth—that he had had no part in the escapade, and that, at the peril of my life, I would always try to disculpate him.

"When we had arrived here, I begged him to find me someone in whose house I could live, in the capacity of a domestic. It did not take Father Du Bourg long to procure me the position I had requested; he placed me with a certain Signor Pelciano, a Portuguese physician whom he knew well. That honest man had a great deal of consideration for me, and took so much care to teach me his language, that I was able to speak it in a very short time, my ordinary occupations notwithstanding. He also took a singular pleasure in instructing me in his belief, but as he was less devious than the Jesuit, I was repelled by many things, either because they seemed to me to be ridiculous, or because they seemed to me to embody a manifest contradiction. I even had difficulty in reconciling your chronology, which limits the birth of the world to a term of approximately six thousand years, with ours and that of the Indians, which extends it, with much greater plausibility, to an almost infinite distance.

"In addition to that, I found myself extremely embarrassed by the choice I had to make between one or other sect, when I learned that Christians, as well as others, are divided into a number of societies that are sufficiently different in their sentiments to cause an irreconcilable hatred between them, and to damn one another reciprocally; and even within each of these companies, there are I don't know how many different opinions. My master, to whom I put my doubts, and who employed all his rhetoric to enlighten me in their regard, wanted me to prefer the Roman religion to all the others, apparently because it was the one that he professed, but, being shocked by the ridiculous superstitions that appeared to me to obsess those of that communion, I immediately asked him to tell me, in all conscience, what he advised me to do.

"'Well, my child,' he said to me, 'stay as you are; if not, throw yourself in the direction I which you find the most advantage. I cannot make use of the authority of Polybius,[17] a famous historian about two hundred years before Christ, who claimed, as he explains in his sixth book, *that the gods, as well as punishments and recompenses after this life, are only chimerical productions of the Ancients, which would be quite unnecessary if one were able to form a Republic that was only composed of wise men; but since there is no State in which the People are not disorderly and wicked, it is necessary to make use, in order to repress them, of panic terrors of the other world, to admit them and believe them, and to conform with them entirely, under pain of passing for reckless and deprived of the usage of reason.*

"That great man was a pagan, and it is not just to cite him among us on a fact of such consequence, so it will suffice to tell you that it is the maxim of the great as well as scholars to accommodate oneself to the times and the circumstances. It does not matter in which church and with which people one worships God, as long as one serves him with respect and veneration. He alone is the common father of all men; he will want to grant them all salvation. It is not the name of Catholic, Calvinist, Lutheran or Anabaptist that saves people, it is faith and good works. The person who lives well is agreeable to God, wherever he is to be found; the Providence that sounds hearts and loins known full well how to

---

[17] A Greek historian of the Roman Republic, Polybius (c.200 B.C.-c.118 B.C.) insisted on the necessity for documentation, the consultation of eye-witnesses and ideological neutrality in the writing of history, and thus became the great exemplar of modern historians.

distinguish one of the faithful from a hundred thousand of the impious and rascally.

"Most of the differences that divide humans on the subject of religion are not as essential as ecclesiastics claim; it often does not matter whether they are admitted or rejected, and if any of them are of consequence, it is still certain that no one can see inside us; it is easy to march with stupid people, and even imitate their external grimaces, without sharing in their ridiculous sentiments. Religion is no more attached to one particular place; it's no longer on a mountain or in Jerusalem that we worship; God is no longer paid in the blood of a heifer or contortions of the body; *My son*, he cries to us, *give me your heart*.'

"'That seems very reasonable to me,' I replied. 'I thank you very humbly for your advice; and, following those principles, I shall be content to conserve the title of Christian without attaching myself positively to any sect.'

"Since that time," the Chinaman continued, "I witnessed all divine services in the voyages I made with Signor Pelciano without any scruple and without causing any scandal to anyone."

"But why, then, were you put here?" I asked.

"In truth, I don't know," he replied, "unless it was for having spoken a little too freely about the mystery of the incarnation, for I remember clearly that I conversed publicly about that matter three or four days before my imprisonment. I shall never be quiet, for although I call myself a Christian, and am one, in fact, I don't claim that in prejudice to the author of all things. Jesus Christ himself, if he were here, would forbid that.

"However great a man the divine prophet was, it suffices to believe him the most excellent son of God, and it is to insult him to attribute that title to him by nature. One can even say that he is veritably our mediator, because he has indicated to us the road to salvation and the means of following the route. His morality was incontestable pure, his life holy and his teaching divine; he confirmed that truth by his death; but that he is omnipotent and eternal God, of the same essence as his father, and yet personally distinct from him and engendered for all eternity, conceived immediately of the holy spirit or God himself and born of an immaculate virgin, is not what he claimed but what others have said of him, with the greatest injustice in the world.

"It is true, as my master said a hundred times, that the Scriptures introduce God saying, while speaking to him: *You are my son*; but they add immediately thereafter: *I have engendered you today*. As for the term 'virgin,' it's certain that it also signified 'young woman' in the original language. In any case, there are many people who claim that it is distorting the text to want to appropriate those passages to Jesus Christ.

"Finally, I should say to you that even the miracles that are attributed to that great individual ought not to be taken literally, but in a figurative sense, as one also understands the parables of the gospel. Thus, for example, the temptation, which appears ridiculous and impossible if it is taken literally, has no meaning, unless it is that kings and princes, who rise like mountains above other mortals, the ecclesiastics, those directors of consciences who preach in temples and sacrifice on their altars, as well as the poor idiots who retreat into deserts, are no more exempt from temptation than anyone else, but that there ought not to be anything that is capable of deflecting them from their duty and preventing them from rendering their homages to the monarch of heaven and earth.

"The demoniac is a repentant fisherman, and the swine into which the demons that possess him are wretches who abandon themselves to all kinds of soiling and drown in vice. The faith of the faithful appears in the example of Peter, when he walks on the water; his incredulity when he sinks into it; his virtue in wanting to follow his master into the most evident dangers; and his infirmity in denying him at the moment when a simply woman accuses him of being of his company when he is in the hands of his enemies.

"In brief, all the extraordinary events, the curing of the lame, the one-armed, the blind, the paralyzed and other similar incommodities, as well as the resurrection of the dead, of which the story of Christ's life make mention, ought to be understood spiritually; for then there is no difficulty in explaining Scripture, and those to whom it seems ridiculous or mysterious would find it intelligible and easy—as is the Old Testament too when one puts it on the footing of only considering it as a composite of emblems, allegories, metaphors, hyperboles, typical events and comparisons invented for the consolation and instruction of the children of God."

"What you have said there," I interjected, "would be capable of furnishing us with material for a long time, but I think it would be quite futile. All that I can reply to you is that the Jesuit Du Bourg is a subtle politician and your master a Portuguese Jew; as for you, I consider you as a volunteer, or a free individual, not as an enlisted soldier. So long as a man is not engaged to a captain, he is permitted to serve whomever he wishes, without anyone having any objection to raise, but from the moment he is enlisted, he cannot quit his company without the permission of his chief; if he deserts, he is culpable, and is punished in accordance with the law.

"You say that you are a Christian, although you are not necessarily one until you have not abjured paganism and embraced the party of your choice among the Christians; you are not, strictly speaking, subject to any censure, and I am convinced that if those detaining you knew you, you would not be here for long. Fundamentally, you are not under their jurisdiction, and there is complete liberty in this city for all sorts of nations. Show that to your judge when you appear before him, adding to it, however, that you are Chinese, and without making any mentioned of Christianity, and I have no doubt that you will be acquitted, and not subjected to any punishment, as you deserve."

"If I ever get out of their clutches," he said, "I assure you that I shall not fall into them again. I have, thank God, what I need to live in my own land, and I can live there perfectly well in the manner that I propose. Even if our domestic affairs do not give me any occupation, so long as my father is alive, I have what I need to spend my time making telescopes and microscopes."

"How microscopes?" I asked him. "Where have you learned that science?"

"In the house of Signor Pelciano," he said, "who is as skillful a man in that as there is throughout the Indies. Father Du Bourg has dabbled in it too, and even claims to excel in it, although fundamentally, he does nothing of value. The microscopes that I make magnify in an inconceivable manner, making a grain of sand appear the size of an ostrich egg, a fly seem as large as an elephant, and the objects most imperceptible to sight discover themselves distinctly to the eye.

"What I admire a hundred times over is to see with the aid of that little instrument that our bodies are covered with scales, overlapping one another, as on the back of a carp. Thus, my master holds it to be a maxim that the air we breathe is a subtle water, which only differs in degree from that of fish; and I even think that our gross air is composed of particles grosser in proportion to subtle matter than those of water are, relative to them. That idea is supported by experiments that I have seen him carry out several times, and which you might not be sorry to know.

"He takes two bottles, one full of water, into which he put a few fish, and the other of gross air, into which he puts birds, mice, rats, squirrels or other small animals; then he pumps the water out of one and the air out of the other. By observing then with certain lenses, slightly hyperbolic in shape, one sees that there is less difference between the particles of water emerging from the one and the particles of air that remain in it than there is in the other between the particles of air and the parcels of subtle matter; to which one can add that the fish live for longer in the first than the small animals in the second. But those sorts of lenses are difficult to construct; at least, I have not yet been able to succeed as is necessary.

"To that, I have heard it objected that, having put a live sparrow for example, into three different jars, hermetically sealed, the first filled with water, the second with air and the third with subtle matter, it has always been remarked that the flesh of the animal has been corrupted in a matter of days in the first, while not the slightest alteration has been observed in the others after several years. From that, it seems to follow that particles of air must be grosser and more efficacious than those of air, since otherwise it would happen by degrees— which is to say that if water corrupts flesh in eight days, air ought to do so in sixteen and subtle matter in twenty-four, supposing equal differences; instead of which one finds that only water is capable of the operation. It is apparent, however, that the grossness of the particles plays less part in that dissolution than the figure and agitation in the agent, on the one hand, and the arrangement of the same particles in the patient on the other; since there are bodies, such as oak-wood, that are conserved long in water than in air, while fire, on the contrary, dissolves an ash-tree in a day, which water cannot do in a century."

"That's curious," I said, "but do you know what sentiment your doctor has with regard to the production of animals?"

"He believes," he replied, "that there is none, other than that achieved by generation, whatever argument can be invented in favor of the contrary. For that purpose, the example is offered of fruits inside which worms are found, without any indication appearing that they entered from outside, but that does not raise any difficulty. To clarify the matter it is necessary to remark that flies and similar insects ordinarily squeeze themselves into openings that they find in trees and plants, as much to take shelter from the insults of the air as to find nourishment when they are in sap, with the result that happens that the eggs of such vermin are found at the place where a fruit will form, the closest of which are surrounded by the first drop of the humor that emerges for its formation, remain enclose therein, and live there until the fruit is ripe enough for the hatchling to find its sustenance there. When the provision is exhausted, it pierces the obstacle that arrests it and emerges.

"To support that sentiment with an incontestable proof, one only has to cast one's eyes over an oak-gall, and examine its production carefully; one will see something surprising. The gall is an excrement, or, if you prefer, a kind of small fruit, which grown on the leaves of oak trees in that fashion. There are certain black flies that lay their delicate eggs in the appropriate season on the undersides of the leaves of those great trees, for fear that they might be burned by the ardor of the sun; as soon as the little creatures are hatched, they start browsing the cover that gave them shade, piercing the veins in order to nourish themselves on the sap that emerges in large enough quantity. If it then happens that one of those creatures finds itself surrounded by a droplet that has enough consistency, it remains there while the drop is fixed, grows and finally becomes a fruit about the size of a pigeon's egg, and only comes out when it had become a fly, or when the fruit that it has, so to speak, produced has become so desiccated that it can no longer serve as nourishment.

"He confirmed that opinion by other arguments that I don't remember, and concluded that of he did not do that, it would be necessary to believe, because of the unfortunate consequences, which could easily lead once again, when it is least admitted, with Lucretius, that the sun and the earth are the sole authors of all animals, without exception, which would be insulting to God."

Three weeks after my imprisonment I was taken to the Holy Office. My judge having asked my birthplace, my age and my religion, to which I replied immediately, implored me to declare myself the subject of my detention, since he had no better way of getting me out of the affair promptly, doubtless claiming that it is necessary to act with regard to that tribunal as one does before God— which is to say, confessing one's sins oneself in order to obtain mercy.

I protested that that I had not done anything, or said anything, for which I ought to reproach myself, or that anyone could legitimately criticize; that God was the witness of my innocence, and that it could only be someone ill-intentioned, or perhaps jealous that my affairs were going well, who had done my the bad turn of accusing me of some crime that I had never committed. Finally, I gave him to understand that I had high hopes of his bounty, and that if he sought information regarding my life, he would soon be convinced of the verity of what I said.

A fortnight later, the same thing happened again, and so on seven times over, after which the inquisitor told me that since I did not want to confess of my own accord the verity of the crime that I had committed, by which means I could recover my liberty, the declaration would be read to me. At the same time, the secretary read the depositions, which consisted in that I had spoken with scorn of the images of saints, the crucifix, purgatory and the infallibility of the Holy Office.

"What do you say to that?" said the judge.

"I admit," I replied, "that seeing the disorder of the majority of the inhabitants of this city, I could not help saying in several places that I was surprised to see that people who would have been ashamed of passing before a crucifix, often doing so in a abject manner, without making a profound reverence, or neglecting for once to prostrate themselves before paper images, had no scruple about wallowing in the ordure of the most infamous vices that can be committed in a society of reasonable human beings.

"It is also true that I have spoken of purgatory as a place I which I do not believe to be necessary, because it is sufficient for a Christian to be convinced that the blood of the savior cleanses him of all his sins. And as for infallibility, I do not think that it can be attributed to anyone except God alone, all men being sinners, in accordance with several formal passages of Holy Scripture.

"I confess," I said, "having spoken in such terms, but God knows that it was with a view to rendering glory to his name, and by virtue of the reaction of horror that I had of so much libertinage, where people pretend that piety and sanctity reign to a very eminent degree, without, however, having any intention of shocking religion or the Holy Office."

"You emancipate yourself too much, my friend," retorted the inquisitor. "However, if you had confessed all that in the beginning, it would not have been any worse, although you would have been no less guilty."

Meanwhile, the secretary, who had written down my confession as a formal deposition, commanded me to sign it. With that, sentence was passed on me; I was condemned to the galleys for life, and all my property confiscated.

We were approximately five hundred unfortunates who emerged on the eight of January 1670 from that redoubtable place, some to be exiled, as was the Chinaman, and some to be whipped. There were also three to be burned alive, because they had been accused of magic, including a poor old man of eighty-three, whom two different orders of monks had deprived of a very considerable inheritance by extorting from the unfortunate man's brother a testament by which they entered into possession of everything that he left after his death, under the pretext of extracting his soul from purgatory sooner.

That unjust procedure had so embittered the old man that he could not help testifying his chagrin, and hurling fire and flame against those he believed to be the authors of the injustice—on which they fled, having imposed on him actions worthy of wolves, and not having ceased to pursue him until they had seen him reduced to ashes.

*Chapter XV*
*Of the departure of the Author for Lisbon;*
*how he was captured and taken into slavery,*
*and what happened to him while he was a slave.*

I was taken to the ship where the captain had orders to put me in the hands of the Inquisition of Lisbon; thus, we departed the same month for Portugal. I was told on the way that the galleys to which I was condemned were a discipline, in which the prisoners were employed in hard labor, because the Portuguese had no seaborne galleys. That consoled me slightly in my woe; it seemed to me that it was no small thing to see myself delivered by that from the oar and the cruelties exercised by the tyrannical officers supervising the convicts enchained in their vessels.

Our navigation was passable; we had the best weather we could reasonably hope for during the journey. The most remarkable thing that happened to us was that on the twenty-third of March, a gust of wind seized our vessel by the top of the mainmast with so much violence that it nearly tipped it over; the crew believed that they were doomed, and I then saw impiety change instantaneously to words of devotion, which lasted until the turbulence had released us.

Eventually, a long time after we had passed the Canaries—it seemed to me that we had reached in thirty-fourth degree of boreal latitude—one morning, at daybreak, two pirates suddenly appeared, which set about bombarding us in a lively manner. Although our voyage had been fortunate, there where nevertheless many sick men aboard; we battled for nearly two hours, during which we had twelve men killed and seventeen wounded.

I beg God's pardon, but I was delighted to see us fall into the hands of those corsairs, since I hoped by that mans to recover my liberty sooner. Things did not, however, go as I thought. The captain ransomed his ship for a sum of money, and its vanquishers were content to take thirty of the most robust and healthiest men—including me—whom they took to Sercelli, a small town on the Mediterranean twenty leagues from Algiers, and four from the River Miromus. We disembarked there on the eighteenth of July, and were sold to the highest bidder.

My owner was a master ship's carpenter, a man of means who had at least thirty men in his service. In the beginning he only made use of me for coarse work: fetching and carrying, and serving the workmen whatever they needed, was my occupation. Afterwards I helped in careening vessels, caulking, sealing and rigging them. There was a big difference between that estate and the one I had enjoyed during my sojourn in Goa before my detention, but when I remembered what I had suffered in the Inquisition's prison and what was in preparation for me in Lisbon, I estimated myself extremely lucky.

In fact, I had a perfectly good master; as I did what I could, he spared me as much as was necessary to me. The lodgings were good, the food even better, and he never said a bad word to me. That made me reflect a hundred times on the idea that we give children in my homeland of barbarians and Turks; it seems, the way people speak of them, that they are devils; however, I can say in their praise that I found among them as much charity, humanity and good faith as among Europeans—and even, I dare say, more—with the consequence that I would not have had any regret about finishing my days among them.

Providence was, however otherwise disposed, and the means with which it served me in order to get out of it were quite remarkable.

As nothing is perfect in this world, as much as my owner liked me, the overseer, who as a renegade, a native of Vienna in Austria by the name of Schilt, hated me mortally. There was no bad turn that the traitor would not do me when it as a matter of saving appearances, so my master, who saw clearly enough what he was dealing with, but who needed the man, was forced, in spite of his own inclinations, to get rid of me. I was sold to a rich and opulent lord who lived in the country some three leagues away from the place where I was.

That lord had a son aged twenty-seven or twenty-eight, who was mad and often enraged. He had intervals when he was rational, but others when he tore his clothing, sometimes broke his chain, and would have been capable of dismembering anyone who appeared before him, or of taking his own life if he were not prevented from so doing. A love affair had caused that havoc; he had been infatuated with a girl who had not wanted to listen to him, had first become a dreamer, and ultimately his head had turned. It was necessary that someone should be with the unfortunate day and night, and desirable that the someone in question should be mature, prudent and strong, in order to be capable of watching over all his actions. I was sufficient in one instance and not entirely destitute in the others, so I can say that I adopted an approach that pleased my superiors considerably.

I had not had him in my care for six weeks before I could do with him as I wished, except when he was furious, when he had no respect for anyone. All that could be done with him then was to keep him firmly attached and not let anyone near him to whom he might do some damage.

That house—or, to put it better, that superb palace—was accessible to all the honest people in the surrounding area; there were always stranger there. One day, a pacha arrived who was received with very particular expressions of esteem and consideration. He was lodged in a very magnificent room overlooking the main courtyard.

Toward the middle of the night, the gentleman was woken up by a prodigious racket, with which the whole room resounded. Pacha as he was, it nevertheless frightened him; he lifted his head, looked around, and finally spotted an animal lying on a Turkish rug at one extremity of the room, which he could not make out very clearly. He was on the point of getting up to examine it more closely or to shout for someone to come to see what it was, but while he was hesitating, the object suddenly got up and advanced toward his bed, dragging a heavy chain after it. With his clothing all ripped, a beard covering half his face and his head bare, he bore more resemblance to a demon than a human being.

That spectacle chilled the pacha with fear, and he remained motionless. That was not all, however. The phantom was not content with making twenty circuits of the room; he came to throw himself down beside the pacha and remained lying there for half an hour with without doing or saying anything. Having then got up, he went out, slamming the door behind him.

Morning having come, my owner was astonished not to see his guest appear; the morning meal had been ready for a long time, and they had arranged to go for a walk in order to work up an appetite. Finally, at about eleven o'clock, he went a domestic to look in quietly and see whether he was still asleep.

That man, having opened the door and slipped into the room, advanced toward the bed slowly, and saw the poor pacha with his eyes open, as pale as a corpse, with all the signs of a man almost devoid of life. He turned around, ran to his master and reported what he had seen. With that the whole house was alarmed; people ran to the sick man from all directions, spoke to him and examined him, but could not get a word out of him. No one doubted that he was dying.

However, someone having decided to put a dab of wine-spirit on the palms of his hands, his temples and beneath his nostrils, they observed that he was beginning to come round. Shortly thereafter they obliged him to take a finger of eau-de-vie by mouth, which did him even more good. He recovered consciousness somewhat, and after having uttered a deep sigh. He said "O Heaven! What a terrible night!" He addressed my master: "I'm scarcely obliged to you, my lord, for having put me in a place where sorcerers come to hold their Sabbat."

"What do you mean?" asked my master. "Have you had bad dreams? We drank a little yesterday; perhaps you're not accustomed to excess; it might have disturbed your brain and produced disagreeable objects in fantasy. Come on, it's nothing. It's only necessary to recover a little courage; a good meal will remedy everything."

"It's necessary," he said, not to blame the wine or the brain; it was no more an imagination than a dream; I was assuredly in my right mind when the devil appeared to me. He stayed in my room for two hours, and even came to lie down on my bed for a time."

"But my lord," said my master, who was beginning to suspect something, "what form did this devil take?"

"It had the face of a man," the pacha replied, "and in spite of the poor light entering through the windows, I noticed that it had nothing but rags on its body; its expression was lugubrious, its cheeks hollow and..."

"Don't say any more," my owner interrupted. "I'm sorry for this accident; it's necessary that I tell you, to my great regret, that the man you saw is my son."

An order having been given to bring him, the pacha came down to earth as soon as he saw the individual. "I can't deny, he said, that this is the same man that I saw last night, and who troubled my mind to such an extent."

He proffered those words in a fashion that caused the madman to burst out laughing, and gave him occasion to recount himself everything he had done in that regard.

That annoyed the pacha, and he asked whether there was no one committed to his guard, and having received the answer yes, he demanded to see him.

I was fetched immediately. When I was presented before him he said: "Is it you, dog, who watches over the actions of my host's son?"

"Yes, my lord," I replied to him.

"And for what reason did you let him loose last night?" he asked.

"He was not attached," I replied. "For several days he had been quite well; that had led me to be less exact in his regard than I usually am; I did not did not have any anxiety about going to bed after him; in the meantime, he went out, and, so I've learned, came to alarm you. I'm assuredly in despair. I beg your pardon; it won't happen again."

"It won't happen again, accursed dog," he said. "I believe that, at least in my regard, for I won't come back. I have a great respect for those to whom you belong, but you're fortunate that I'm in a state to get up; I might have had difficulty in recovering my self-possession, and you would have run the risk of having your head cut off. Get out of my sight, wretch that you are, and pray to God that I never see you again."

Then, addressing himself to my master, he said: "If you want to give me pleasure, my lord, you'll pass judgment on this wretch immediately, in order that I hear no more mention of him."

I had only been living in the house for a few months; the other domestics there did not hate me, and my master has a good deal of consideration for me because of the care I gave his son, who gave me a great deal of difficulty. It was nevertheless necessary for the good man, for the sake of complaisance, to get rid of me.

It was taken to the city to be sold to the first comer. I learned there that the overseer I mentioned earlier had died, so I had inquiries made of my former master as to whether my services might be agreeable to him. He was glad to recover me, and I was delighted to re-enter the service of a person who had had every imaginable regard for me while I was living in his house.

About three months later, the pacha, accompanied by a company of important individuals, came to visit our carpentry. I recognized him at a hundred paces; his threats had made such an impression on my mind that I immediately fled as fast as I could.

He suspected that it was me, because, having found himself much better the day after his vision, and his fit of anger having passed entirely, he had asked what had become of me, and having been told, had expressed chagrin at my departure. In fact, he learned that he was not mistaken and ordered that someone run after me and tell me that he wanted to speak to me, adding that he gave his word not to do me any harm.

Notwithstanding that assurance, I approached him tremulously; he noticed that and started laughing, doubtless to reassure me. He asked me several indifferent questions, to which I responded with all the submission of which I was capable. Finally, he asked me whether, if my master wanted to let me go, I would not be glad to return to the lord that I had quit because of him.

Having made him understand that it did not depend on my choice, I had nothing further to say except that I was perfectly content where I was.

"Stay here, then," he said. "It's at least as agreeable to be in the company of sane men as to be eternally guarding a demoniac." And having given me a coin with which to drink to his health, he sent me back to work.

That little adventure was not the only one that happened to me during my slavery, but since the others had nothing extraordinary about them I shall pass over them in silence. As for the disputes to which I was often subject, to the point of sometimes being obliged to come to blows, the story would be so vast in extent that it might bore the reader.

The Turks are ignorant, for the most part; I never heard anything from them but cold mockery of our crucified God, which I endured patiently because, on the one hand, they did not believe in Christ, and on the other, being on their dung-heap, I could not hope for anyone's protection. I had difficulty containing myself, however, when I was assailed by renegade Christians.

Among others, there was a suggestive Gascon who was the boldest atheist, or deist, that I have ever seen. He was angelic in his mildness, but when he indulged in mockery he turned everything to ridicule, and confused our greatest mysteries with the reveries of the Jewish Talmud and the legends of the Roman church.

"My father," he told me one day, "was murdered while going on a pilgrimage to Notre Dame de Lorette—a fine recompense for the good Catholic that he was. My mother, who made a profession of the reformed religion, was dragooned and massacred for being stubborn in not wanting to obey the orders of the court. As for me, I was captured by pirates which trying to go from France to Holland, so, in order to avoid persecution I unfortunately fell into slavery."

As I not only found a good deal of intelligence and knowledge in that young man, but also much gentleness and good will—for all those who knew him in that place praised his benevolent and helpful nature very highly—I had a great compassion for him, and tried several times to bring him back from the dangerous sentiments he had with regard to religion. We had frequent conversations on that topic, and I had high hopes of being able to bring him back to the

172

path of verity in time, but an unfortunate accident took away his life before Heaven had permitted me to bring that charitable endeavor to a conclusion.

It would take too long to report here all the disputes we had together, so I shall just touch briefly on a few of the principal points.

When I reproached him for his change of religion and the profession he made of the Mohammedan faith, in which he did not believe, he replied to me that after having carefully imagined all the different religions that had come to his knowledge, he had found nothing in any of them that could satisfy a reasonable person; in consequence, he saw nothing that ought to prevent a sage man from conforming, at least externally, to the dominant religion of the country in which he lived, in the same way that one adopts the habits, customs and manners of a country in order not to appear ridiculous by virtue of one's singularity.

"And since I had the had the means of attracting more confidence and consideration among the people of this land by conforming to their mode of religion," he said, "I would have been foolish to deprive myself of that advantage by a stupid attachment to another, which is a hundred times more absurd and impertinent than that one."

I replied to him that I was extremely surprised to hear talk of that sort from a man brought up in the Christian religion, and who, by virtue of his profession, ought to know it better for having studied it in depth.

"It's for exactly that reason, my friend," he replied, "because I've examined it well, and discovered all its weakness and ridiculousness, that I speak of it in that fashion. But it appears that, mature in age as you are, you have not yet shaken off the prejudicial yoke of education, and you hold hard to what you learned from your nurse or your curé, without examining it in depth."

I told him that I had traveled more and seen more of the world than he thought, and that I had heard the arguments people of different sentiments in matters of religion but had never found any so worthy of God and appropriate to humankind, and who had as many marks of truth as the Christian religion; and that my profession had not permitted me during my youth to study the controversies of religion in depth, as he had, but that I was nevertheless able to defend against attack the principal truths of the Christian religion: the existence of God; the creation of the world; the immortality of the soul; the fall of man; the redemption of the human race by Jesus Christ; the truth and divinity of Holy Scripture, which serves as the foundation of all the rest; and the necessity...

He interrupted me. "That's enough," he said, "and if you can defend those articles, I'll grant you thereafter anything it pleases you to add to them. We'll begin with the last, if you don't mind, and go back by way of the others to the first. You know that Christians are not all of the same sentiment with regard to Holy Scripture. Some hold that it is all inspired, down to the slightest word; others reject that sentiment and only sustain broadly, with regard to its material, that the Holy Spirit so guided the writers of the sacred books that they were unable to commit any error in the facts they recounted or the doctrine they taught. Tell me, I beg you, which of those two opinions you intend to sustain?"

"I am not for the first of those two opinions," I told him, "and it seems to me that it would be necessary to be deprived of reason to sustain it, no matter how inattentively one has read the holy books. But the latter is supported by convincing reasons. I shall not insist on the great antiquity of the first books of Holy Writ, although you will admit nevertheless that they are the most ancient monuments there are in the world and that they were written before the art of writing was known to other nations; but the marvelous things that are contained in those writings, the miracles that God worked to confirm the revelation and the predictions of the holy prophets, the accomplishment of which had been seen in large measure, while that of the remainder is awaited, are things that surpass human understanding, and of which only God can be the author."

"You do very well," he told me, "not to insist on the antiquity of your sacred books, because you would obtain no advantage from it, for a romance or an imposture can be as ancient as, and more so than, a veritable history; that proves nothing. However, I'm far from according you the great antiquity that you claim for those books, and I defy you, or anyone else, ever to prove that any of those books existed before the time of Esdras—which is to say, a thousand years after Moses, who, according to you, must have written the first books. Also, by reading the books attributed to Moses attentively, one finds a great number of passages which were evidently written a long time after him."

He cited a quantity of them, which I shall pass over in silence here to avoid tedium.

"But from your argument," he said, "founded on the marvelous things contained in scripture I draw a conclusion entirely contrary to yours, for the more a book contains of marvelous and extraordinary things, the more subject it is to caution. That is the way that you would judge any other book, and if you don't judge this one in the same way, that is purely an effect of your prejudice—which is very evident, since it has just turned into proofs of the verity of a book that which would serve to remove all belief from it if it were judged without prejudice.

"As for the miracles of which you make mention, they are only reported in the book of which you want them to be the proof, so they ought rather to serve, as I have already said, to cause its rejection. Any objective and unprejudiced man only receives a relation or history of things past in accordance with the degree of plausibility that he finds therein, and holds it to be false, or romantic, to the extent that he sees marvelous and extraordinary events, for nature has always been the same at all times, and the truth has always been simple and natural.

"With regard to the predictions of which you have spoken all the accomplishments that are reported in the same book as the predictions prove nothing, except that they are parts of the same romance and that they were fabricated at the same time, and for those that are claimed to have happened since, the events have so little relation to the predictions for which they are supposed to pass as accomplishments that it is only the force of prejudice that can enable any conformity to be found."

He cited a large number of examples to support what he had said, but I shall pass over them in silence here.

"Furthermore," he said, "if you knew the history of the canon of that Holy Scripture, both of the Old Testament that you obtained from the Jews, an ignorant and superstitious nation if ever there was one, on the truth and authenticity of the various parts of which they cannot agree among themselves, and of the New one, such as it is presently admitted by the majority of Christians, you would see so much ignorance, superstition, uncertainty and embarrassment therein, that you would be ashamed."

With that he went into the history of the canon and the manner in which it had been formed, and the time when that was done. He talked about the factions and disputes among the members of the Council of Laodicea and several others with regard to the different gospels, acts, epistles, etc. that different churches or societies of Christians had received as veritable, to the exclusion of others; the difficulties and embarrassments that arise in that matter, and how some rejected what others received, with the reasons on either side. I was astonished to see that the man knew so many curious things, as if at his fingertips.

I proposed another argument that I had heard employed by men of the reformed religion to prove that the Holy Scripture was inspired by God—to wit, that those who participated in the grace of God, on reading the Scripture, found themselves so penetrated by it that they were unable to doubt that it came from the Holy Spirit. But as I wanted to act frankly with him, I admitted that I had never found any great force in the argument, because it was of no use to those who did not feel that effect of the reading of Holy Writ.

"You're right," he replied, "to reject that proof drawn from a supposed interior conviction, for it is only a consequence of the prejudice with which one is previously imbued in that regard. And only proves the enthusiasm of those who claim to feel it. Furthermore, if the argument were sound, it would prove the divine inspiration of the Koran, for I can assure you that I see every day among good and zealous Mohammedans, and you can observe it yourself, that there is as much, and perhaps more, interior conviction among them as among the most devoted and the most zealous Christians. And everyday experience enables us to see clearly enough that interior persuasion is capable of leading people who allow themselves to get carried away by their imagination to the greatest extravagances.

"However," he continued, "whatever idea you might have of God, who, according to you, is the sovereign master of the entire universe and who is able to dispose all parties as he wishes, can you believe that in order to make his will known to the human species it was necessary for him to employ obscure, ignorant or fanatical individuals to write books, or prophesy, or preach in a remote corner of the earth, among a troop of ignorant people, without savant and civilized nations having any knowledge of it? Do you think that is the best means of communicating to all men such a necessary thing as the will of God?

"Has not the one who created everything and arranged it all to his pleasure, without anything being able to prevent him, not put everything in the state in which he wanted it to be? Is not his will that we call the order, the course and the voice of nature? To suppose some other particular will in that infinitely perfect being is to suppose change and imperfection, which is contrary to his nature. And to suppose that he communicates to certain persons, and hides from many others, certain rules to which he wants all humans to confirm, is to suppose an unjust partiality that is unworthy of him.

"Thus, one must surely conclude that everything that is called divine revelation in one country or another is veritably nothing but an imposture founded on the weakness of humans in general, invented by those who want to impose certain views upon them with certain designs."

I replied to him that if humans had dwelt in the state of perfection in which the creator had first put them, perhaps they would not have needed a revelation to serve as a regulation for their actions, but since they had lost that happiness through their own fault, they were so spoiled and inclined to evil that they not only needed revelations but also the particular grace of the creator in order to...

"Stop there," he said. "I see that you're going to tell me the story of the fall of man and all its consequences, such as the corruption of human nature, original sin, the redemption of the human race, etc. That can be, if you wish, the subject of our conversation for the rest of the evening.

"Your theologians," he went on, "are right to say that mysteries are the reefs of human reason, for assuredly, the enlightenments of reason and common sense cannot understand them at all. But before going into the particular examination of these articles, permit me to tell you a fable that I obtained from an Arab philosopher who had traveled a great deal. He said that he had made it up in order to give his friends an idea of the mythology of a certain nation that he had seen. It is *The Fable of the Bees.*

"'There was once,' he said, 'on an island in the ocean, a great and powerful king, sovereign over the entire island. His power was so great that no other king equaled him in authority, and all his subjects were so submissive to him that he only had to wish for something for it to be done. His will was so much the rule of all their actions that they could not do anything that he did not want them to do. His bounty was as great as his power, and his wisdom was great as both; in brief, he possessed all the perfections to a sovereign degree.

"'The king had planted the island, which he had found desert, had filled it with inhabitants and animals of every sort, and had organized its cultivation, with the consequence that it produced everything necessary both for the maintenance and for the agreement and pleasure of all the inhabitants. The royal palace was the largest and the most magnificent that one could imagine, situated in the middle of the most beautiful gardens that had ever been seen.

"'That monarch, who understood everything perfectly, formed a plan of everything that nature could produce of the most beautiful, and then gave the order that it should be carried out immediately, for such was the extent of his power that even inanimate things conformed exactly to his will and immediately followed his orders. There were parks, meadows and woods, all of an admirable beauty, filled with all the kinds of animals, birds and insects for which one could wish, either for utility or for decoration.

"'I would have a great many marvelous things to say if I wanted to go into detail regarding all those animals, and so on, and it is for that reason that I shall content myself with telling you the most remarkable thing that I learned about a single species of insects: bees.

"'There were a great many bees on the island, and as the king's concern extended to everything, he made sure that there was an abundance of flowers everywhere, to nourish the bees. But in one corner of the flower-beds in the king's garden, there was a certain species of flower that he forbade the bees to touch, not because the flowers were harmful to the bees, or because the monarch cared more about them than any other species of flower, but because he wanted, so I was told, to test their obedience.

"'Some time after that, it happened that some of the bees, forgetting the order, or not caring overmuch about it, sucked nectar from those flowers. The king perceived it immediately, and was so irritated that he resolved to exterminate all the bees on the island, even swearing, so great was his anger, that he would not spare a single one.

"'Later, however, when the greater part of his anger had passed, he regretted having passed such a rigorous sentence, and some residue of pity for the poor bees persuaded the monarch, who was fundamentally good and merciful to search for a expedient to get him out of the difficulty.

"'The king had an only son, whom he loved infinitely more than anything else in the world, and he wanted him to be the mediator to make peace between himself and the bees. In order that the peace in question could be made in a fashion appropriate to his royal dignity, however, without injuring his honor and his justice, which were implicated in the maintenance of the oath that he had sworn, he wanted his beloved son to bear the full penalty due to the bees, and to that end, he made him into a bee too.

"'That metamorphosis having taken place, the son went in the form of a bee to one of the most unruly hives in the whole island, where the advised the other bees to be more circumspect and more observant of the king's orders, but in vain; they mocked him, maltreated him and stung him so much that in the end, he died. And the worst of it was that, at the same time, he had to suffer al the indignation and wrath of his father, the king, who wanted to avenge the bees' fault on him.

"'As soon as the son was dead, he went back to his father, and set about interceding on behalf of the poor bees, whose debt he had paid and whose punishment he had borne—which he continued to do, with so much success that the king had pity on some of the bees and forgave their faults, provided that they attached themselves entirely to his son, as many entire hives had already done.

"'One does not see those favored bees making more honey or being more comfortable than the others, but the reason for that is—as they told certain hornets that introduced themselves into all their hives in considerable numbers—that they would be better able to feel the benefits that would come to them after they were dead.

"'It was those hornets who informed the bees who wanted to listen to them of that whole story, with an infinity of details that have not been mentioned here. In the different hives, the story and the circumstances are so various that some receive it in one manner and some in another, and some of them do not believe any of it. The latter were threatened by the hornets with exceedingly rigorous punishments after their death, instead of which the bees that follow their advice will then receive great rewards.

"'When anyone says to the hornets that it is evident that all bees, when they fall dead, fall to earth and are consumed, being reduced to dust or mud, they reply gravely that it is only their bodies that are consumed, but that their hum, which is something different from their bodies, will enjoy the rewards or suffer the punishments with which they are threatened. For they make them believe that when a bee that has followed the hornets' advice, and has given them the greater part of its honey, comes to die, its hum will go straight to the king's palace and contribute to filling the great audience hall with a music that the monarch in question finds very charming, so they say. Instead of which, the hum of a bee that conducts itself in a different manner will go after its death to a great vault underground, where it is chilled by cold and makes a very different noise because of the infinite pain it suffers there.

"'There is an infinite number of similar chimeras that the hornets never cease to inspire in the poor bees, for being dispensed with laboring, and living on the labor of the bees, their entire occupation consists of inventing things to frighten the bees and keep them in dependence—in which they succeed so well that one sees an infinite number of those poor insects so occupied which apprehension as to what might happen to their hum when they die that they are unable to take pleasure in eating the honey they have made, or doing anything necessary for the sustenance of their life. And when bees who scorn those chimeras apply themselves to their labor, and do not lend an ear to the hornets, they excite the other bees against them, and often make them kill them, or at least expel them from their hive as dangerous and seditious individuals.

"'It often happens when the hornets are divided among themselves that all the bees in a hive take one side or the other, and, animated by the hornets, they hurl themselves upon one another with so much violence that half the bees in a hive are killed because they have not conceived the hornets' chimeras in the same fashion as the others. Sometimes, the hornets even engage entire hives to make war on other hives, in such a fashion that one sometimes sees several thousand killed on each side, uniquely to sustain the chimeras of their hornets against those of the others.

"'The bees, for the most part, expose themselves willingly to that slaughter, on the assurance that the hornets on both sides give them that they will thus be rendering a great service to the king, who will be grateful to them, and admit their hum to the big room, in preference to that of many others. For they claim to know the orders and the will of the king much better than the other bees, because certain hornets, they say, who lived several centuries before them, learned them from the king's own mouth, and have transmitted them, engraved in part on fragments of wax and in part on the basis of the reports of their predecessors.

"'It is on that foundation that the hornets have usurped so much authority over the bees throughout the island—because the hornets have invaded almost all of the hives—and have extended their tyranny to the point of rendering those poor insects utterly miserable. They forbid them to such nectar on certain days from flowers whose usage they are permitted on other days, and forbid them to labor to make their wax and honey on certain other days, because, they say, the king wishes it thus.'"

After he had finished his impertinent and ridiculous fable, which was much longer than the report I have given of it, I told him that I could see the objective of it quite clearly, but that I would talk about it another time, because it was then too late and it was necessary for us to separate to go to bed.

I thought a great deal that night about the means I could use to bring that man back from his errors, and I formed a plan in my head from which I hoped to obtain success. That was to commence the first conversation that we had together by establishing the existence of a God, the author and creator of all things, and then to deduce from that great truth the other principal verities of religion. But as I have already said, God, in his sage Providence, did not wish my project to be carried out, for some time afterwards, the poor fellow, when carrying a heavy beam with another man, tripped and had his head crushed by it, with the consequence that he died without having time to recover consciousness.

I regarded that as a just punishment of Heaven, because he had made such a bad usage of his intelligence and his knowledge. I even took care to point that out to other libertines like him, but they only mocked me.

At any rate, I had been in Sercelli for fourteen or fifteen years when one day, while occupied in sealing a ship, I discovered a place near the middle, two feet from the keel, that was badly damaged. The repair that was required there was considerable. In order to do that work well and durably, I was obliged to go into the vessel, where there remained a quantity of large stones that are used, along with gravel, to ballast ships. While moving those heavy objects, which were in my way, I discovered a packet larger than two fists, rolled up lengthways and tied up with string. The fear I had that someone might perceive that I had found something caused me to hide it as quickly as possible in my hose. At midday, after having eaten, I drew apart in order to see what it was.

The first envelope consisted of a sheet of painted cloth; inside it there was a tube of stocking-silk, and in that tube there was a blue slipper, in which there was a purse containing three hundred and eighty-five beautiful guineas.

My first concern was to hide my treasure in a safe place where no one would take it into their head to look for it, and notwithstanding the great joy that I felt, I was very careful not to give any indication that I was richer by a single sou than before.

About six months later, the English consul, who was resident in Algiers having business in our town, came with two other young gentlemen to see about having some boats built. One of my comrades, needing assistance at that moment on moving a mast on which he was working, called on me to lend him a hand.

On hearing my addressed as Massé, Mr. Elliot approached me and asked me where I was from. I replied to his question.

"I have a good friend, a silk merchant in London," he said, "who is from the same place, and whose name is Jean Massé."

"I know," I replied, "that I left behind a brother who was also named Jean, who was six years younger than me, but as that was about fifty years ago, and I haven't received any news from home since then, although he's probably a relative of mine, it's impossible for me to say so for certain."

"What you tell me," he interjected, "makes me believe that you're brothers, for the man of whom I speak is about sixty years old, and he has often talked to me about a brother he regretted deeply, whom he believed to have perished a long time ago."

With that it was necessary for me to tell him in a few words by what fatality I had become a slave in Africa, after which he offered to write to my brother in order that he might look for an expedient to get me out of there for my old age. I declared to him then, in confidence, that I had money.

"If that's so," he said, "I'll find the means to release you; but it's necessary not to make any semblance of it. Let me take care of all that, and don't get involved. Adieu."

I kissed his hands and recommended myself to his good graces.

A month later I was astonished when my master summoned me and, having taken me by the hand, said to me: "I'm delighted, my friend, that you're going to return to your homeland. Mr. Elliot has negotiated your ransom with me; go to join him in Algiers. I wish you a fortunate voyage."

On those words I embraced him, and thanked him for his bounty, and for the regard he had had for me from the day of my arrival to the moment of my departure. We both wept as if we were close relatives.

With that, I took my leave of my comrades and immediately went to Algiers. The consul received me in the most honest manner in the world. I paid him the thirty-five guineas that he told me my liberty had cost him—which was, in truth, very little, but his credit and my age had been taken into account.

## Chapter XVI
*Containing the sequel to the adventures of Pierre Heudde,*
*who was mentioned in Chapter II,*
*and the author's arrival in London.*

I stayed for a month in Algiers before embarking for London. In the meantime it happened that a Turkish pirate brought a French galley to Algiers. Mr. Elliot immediately obtained a list of its crew in order to see whether there was any name known to him among the convicts, and who was from his homeland. He read it in my presence, and seemed astonished to find the name of a man that he had known quite well in London.

The name of Pierre Heudde was no less surprising to me; he noticed that and asked me the reason. His curiosity engaged me to tell him the story, after which we both went to the place where the galley's rowers were imprisoned. As soon as we arrived he asked after his man and I sought out mine. The man he desired to see had been wounded in the combat and had died a quarter of an hour before; the other was immediately produced.

"You name is Pierre Heudde?" I asked.

"Yes," he replied.

"Have you ever been in Lisbon?" I continued.

"Perhaps," he said, "but it must have been a long time ago."

"That's true," I sad, "since it must have been if I'm not mistaken, 1643 or 44. There was then a certain factor there named Van Dyk. Did you know him? You've gone pale, but there's no danger in it for you, although you must admit that you played a dirty trick on him."

"I can't deny it," said the convict. "He was the man from whom I stole a sum of three hundred ducats. I beg God's pardon for that enormous sin, and others that I've committed; I've been punished for them sufficiently in this world, and I hope he'll grant me mercy in the other."

"Spoken like a Christian," I said, "and you're fortunate that Providence has given you the grace of being repentant of your sins. But tell me, please, why and when you were condemned to the galleys?"

"The memory of it makes me shiver, Monsieur," he replied, "and I'd like you to exempt me from a story so unedifying, which can only renew my chagrin."

We praised him for his worthy sentiments, but I persisted on my request, in which I was supported by the consul, with the consequence that he was persuaded.

"Well, Messieurs, I'll tell you," he said, "as much to give you evidence of my obedience as to subscribe to the just punishment of my crimes.

"After the theft that I made from Mynheer Van Dyk, I embarked for Nantes, where, under the name of Vander Stel, posing as a nephew of a famous wine merchant of Rotterdam, I immediately made the acquaintance of all the Dutch businessmen there. I can't describe all the kindness that those good folk showed me; scarcely a day went by without me being invited to magnificent meals at the home of one or other of them.

"In the meantime, a commissioner from Languedoc arrived, who had dealings with many of the people I frequented; that gave me the opportunity to make his acquaintance. He kept company with me gladly, and as he was a gambling man he was delighted to find that I had the same disposition. Sometimes we played games of chess, and often spent entire evenings playing piquet, but always without inflicting any heavy losses on either side.

"Eventually, having gone to see him one day, I had the good fortune to find him alone in his room, where he was becoming impatient at having no one with whom to pass the time. He sent for the cards, and we set about playing a game of ombre. He was good at the game, but I surpassed him in skill. Whether by design or not, he incited me to drink more than usual; I was delighted by that, because I had no doubt that a large quantity of wine would prevent him from discovering so soon that I was cheating. In fact, I won fifty pistoles from him in less than four hours. He seemed astonished, and asked to get his revenge at lansquenet.

"That was exactly what I was waiting for. I put on a semblance however, of not being very well-versed in the game, and told him that unless fortune favored me as it had before, it was impossible that I would not lose my shirt. At this point my man began to get more enthusiastic than ever. We played for high stakes, and although I let him win from time to time in order not to put him off, by midnight, when we parted, I had won more than three thousand écus, which he counted out to me two days later in honest coin.

"That coup completed my affairs marvelously. I sowed five hundred ducats into a strip of chamois leather, with which I made a belt that I wore under my shirt, and, the commissioner departing in one direction, I took the road to Avignon in the other. On the way I equipped myself with a valet and resumed my former name of Heudde.

"The expenditure I made in that new abode made no one doubt that I belonged to the top flight of society. I had no scruple about introducing myself to the best company, where people where pleased to receive me. After two or three weeks, I happened to encounter casually in the street a young woman of about twenty, of the most excellent beauty that I had ever seen in my life. I let her pass by, and when she was fifty paces away from me I turned round and followed her at a distance until she went into a house. With that I gave orders to my valet to inform himself surreptitiously as to whether she lived there, and who her parents were.

"He came back fully informed and told me that her father was a Jew, a jewel merchant who made large transactions. The next day I went to find him, under the pretext that I wanted to buy a small diamond for twenty-five or thirty pistoles, and in order to enter into a narrower commerce with him I told him my name and birthplace. I added that I knew several Jews in Amsterdam, and named a few that were not unfamiliar to him. In sum, I omitted nothing at all that was capable of gaining me entry to his home, without him mentioning either a wife or a daughter.

"That first visit succeeded so well that I hazarded to attempt a second. I did indeed buy a ring, on which that usurer must have made a profit of at least a third, but that was not a significant affair. The hope of a more considerable profit led him to invite me to come and see him often; I took advantage of that civility, and also took the step of treating him from time to time in my hostelry.

"Everything was going well, but I could not see that it was advancing my scheme, so I concluded that it was necessary to adopt another approach. As I was meditating on that, it happened, fortunately, that at our next meeting he was accompanied by another Jew. I led them gradually to the subject of the difference of religions, which engaged us in a dispute. I put on a semblance of having been ignorant until then of the force of their arguments and the weakness of ours with regard to the Messiah. The hope of making a convert easily caused them to consent to our seeing one another as often as we could, in order to treat the matter in depth.

"With that I asked them if I might witness their public worship; they opened their synagogue to me with joy; I had myself instructed in their religion, and eventually, convinced of my errors by the verity of their principles, I was circumcised and became a Jew. As soon as that was concluded I was solemnly initiated into all their mysteries; I had entered everywhere, and the fair sex, who regarded me as a saint, following the example of the men, made me party to their amities and their courtesies.

"For my part, there was no complaisance of which I did not make use in their regard; above all, I showed a respectful deference for the beautiful Jewess, which was not disagreeable to her. In addition, I put myself on the footing of often making her little gifts, which she received with pleasure, and which her mother did not disdain. It was only the father, who, having considerable wealth to leave to his only daughter, but being no less miserly for that, did not look upon that petty commerce with a kindly eye.

"Meanwhile, I played the rich Monsieur, without, however, indulging in extravagance. That manner of living surprised him; he was eager to know by what means I obtained the wherewithal to live; he asked questions left, right and center without being able to obtain the slightest information. When I saw that, I sent my valet to a Jewish goldsmith in order to ask him to sell me a couple of crucibles, without telling anyone.

"The jeweler frequented the house in question, with the result that three days later, my valet was astonished, on having gone to my friend's house to see whether he had the leisure to receive me, to be regaled with a glass of his best wine, and, the matter of the crucibles having been raised, to be slyly asked what I was going to do with them. My fellow, whom I had schooled in advance, initially feigned ignorance in order to make him believe that there was a mystery, and finally, after much interrogation on the one part and protests on the other that his master would break his neck if he ever told anyone, he said that the secret—which had to remain between the two of them—was that I made use of a method for augmenting gold that I had from one of the foremost chemists in Europe.

"That confession, which seemed ingenuous, and plausible, did not fall on stony ground. Mascado—that was the jeweler's name—was delighted to have discovered the secret, but he did not know how to make use of it in order to persuade me to take me into his confidence. He began by sounding me out as to the quality of my effects, whether they consists of money, houses or land, and what I did to obtain coin for living expenses; he offered to let me have some at a good rate. He asked me whether I intended to travel indefinitely, and whether if might not be more advantageous to me to settle down. I replied to all of that in a vague enough manner, not calculated to satisfy him.

"Seeing that he would get nothing from the master he addressed himself for a second time to the domestic, and by dint of promises and a small present he made him he was assured that the next time I settled down to the great work he would be informed.

"Ten days later I fired up my crucibles, and even though I was wearing little more than a shirt I was so hot, by virtue of plying the bellows that vermilion was no redder than my face. Meanwhile, my man had run to Mascado's house to tell him what was happening, under the pretext that I had sent him out to buy a few drachms of aqua regia—so that scarcely had he returned than the other came looking for me. The maidservant who had answer the door came to knock on mine and told my fellow that someone wanted to speak to me, and that she had already said that I was in my room. I pretended to be annoyed and sent the valet to say that I couldn't see anyone.

"The Jew took no notice of that and came in brazenly to where I was. 'I beg your pardon, sir,' he said, 'being very retiring before your conversion I thought you were occupied in some religious observance, and for fear that an excess of devotion might render you melancholic and pensive, as it seemed that you might become before long, I took the liberty of coming in without being introduced, with the design of chatting to you for an hour and inviting you to send the evening with my family. But what are you doing here? Have you become a chemist? What do you have in those crucibles? In faith, I believe that you're in search of the philosopher's stone.'

"'Let's talk about something else,' I said, seemingly very embarrassed. 'It's necessary to have some occupation in this world'—and so on, for it's not necessary to relate the whole dialogue that we composed. The conclusion, after many detours, and on condition that he did not say anything, was that I knew how to multiply gold. 'I ought not to hide from you,' he said, 'that I was surprised by your expenditure, without it appearing that you obtained any money from elsewhere, and that you had not spoken to anyone to supply you with any. But is your science assured, and does it never fail?'

"'The next time I work,' I said, 'I'll allow you to see the experiment.' A few days later, I gave him a time and told him to bring ten ducats. In my presence he threw ten gold pieces into one of my crucibles, while I put my multiplication powder in the other. Then I mixed it all together and stirred it well with an iron road, which was hollow, and into which I'd put fifty francs' worth of powder, sealed with a little wax with which I'd closed the opening, and which melted incontinently, augmenting the mass of metal by the same sum that I'd put into it.

"The time fixed for the operation having elapsed, I put the little ingot resulting from the fusion in his hands. He immediately took it to his friend the goldsmith, who told him that the gold was as pure as one could see. He was charmed by the secret, and began by urging me to work every day. I replied that I'd made enough money, that it was sufficient for me to occupy myself when it was necessary, and that as I had no hearth or home, I had no need to amass great treasures. In addition, it was difficult to prepare the powder I needed and there was a risk, while making it of a deterioration in health, unless one had a sizeable laboratory and all the instruments appropriate to working on a large scale.

"You're doubtless yawning, Messieurs, on hearing all these details, although I'm omitting many others for fear of boring you, which might not be disagreeable at another juncture. To cut the story short, he did not wait for me to raise the subject of marriage; he found matchmakers who came to me with the proposition. I wanted, however, everything to be done formally. Being assured of my facts, I asked the beautiful Jewess' parents for her hand, which they accorded to me with marks of entire satisfaction, and took me incontinently into their home.

"We had scarcely been married when my father-in-law began to talk business. 'You have a talent, my son,' he said to me, 'which it is necessary not to bury; let us act while we have the commodity and amass wealth for ourselves and our descendants. I immediately inclined in his direction, and we resolved to establish our laboratory in a house that he had six miles from the town, in order that we could work there in peace without anyone seeing us. But I had no more multiplication powder and it was necessary to make more; and because that took time and required considerable expense and a great deal of difficulty, we decided to make enough of it for at least a million in one go.

"With that I gave him a list of the substances that went into the compound, the greatest quantity being mercury. I thus made him believe that I required marine and mineral salts, antimony, pearl-seed, coral, the ashes of a heifer, the antler of a stag, the horn of a narwhal, the eyes of lobsters, the tusk of an elephant, the blood of a dragon, the claws of eagles, birds of paradise, the beaks of American parrots, the heads of vipers, the bones of a camel, the tail of a crocodile, the head of a porpoise and the rib of a whale, all the metals and the majority of minerals. It was necessary for a determined quantity of each of those to be infused for five days in the urine of a ewe, mixed with a third of its weight of the dung of a gray cow that had been steeped in the water of the Rhine for nine days—that being the square of three—and that the cube of that number, being twenty-seven days or a periodic month, was the time that had to be employed in calcinating the mass and reducing it over a slow fire, into the pretended projection powder.

"All that did not frighten the worthy man; the hope of a great profit made him envisage as easy what another would not have thought feasible. It was therefore a matter of searching for what I demanded of him. Some of it was found in Avignon and the surrounding area, the rest had to be obtained from Holland, where one can, in fact, acquire everything there is in the world. I then made him understand that gold that had once passed through my hands could not be multiplied again, so that he needed to try to accumulate large sums, either by borrowing at interest or obtaining it from his friends, whom it would be easy to offer a share of the profit.

"The goldsmith was the first one that he let in on the secret, and who begged him to take five hundred louis on whatever conditions he wished. Several others did likewise, but always in secret, and everyone swore not to reveal anything whatsoever, even to their own wives—with the consequence that each of them was absolutely ignorant of what the others were doing. As he received the gold it was taken to the house in the country, where I was often occupied in putting things in order.

"Finally, when I saw that everything was on the point of being ready, I told my father-in-law and my wife that I was going to put the final touches to the work, but that as it required a great deal of application, and I would need at least three days, I begged them not to come to interrupt me before that time. I went out, closing the door, after having seized a jewel-case in which there were at least sixty thousand livres of gems.

"As soon as I arrived at the farmhouse I went to get some sleep; then, having got up at daybreak, I loaded up all the coins that were there, told the farmer that an affair of the greatest importance about which I had not thought sooner summoned my to Arles, and that if my wife arrived after three or four days as she had promised, he should assure her on my behalf that I would cut my visit as short as possible. And I mounted my house, and bade him farewell. As soon as I was out range of the peasant's eyes I turned the other way and took the road to Lyon.

"After arriving in that famous city, it happened that the Marquis de Villeneuve came to supper in the hostelry where I was lodging. I told him that I was a Dutchman, of the Wassenaar family, and that I was a cornet in the service of Their Highnesses, but that having had the misfortune to kill an ensign in the regiment of the Prince of Orange's guards in a duel, who belonged to a very influential family, I had been obliged to abandon my country for fear of the consequences, but that what was consoling for me was that I had not left emptyhanded, as well as being furnished with good letters of credit.

"With that the cavalier treated me with a thousand courtesies. 'I know your family, Monsieur,' he told me. 'It is considerable in the Low Countries; and to show you my esteem, if you want to form a company at your expense in the cavalry regiment that I'm on the point of raising, it's only a matter of making you a captain. I'm leaving for the court; we can make the journey together, and I'll do my best to make you agreeable to the king.

"'I'll take you at your word, Monsieur le Marquis,' I said—and, taking from my little finger a five-hundred-écu diamond furnished by the jewel-case I had taken, which had already dazzled the colonel's eyes several times, I added: 'And I'll make you a present of this into the bargain.'

"The next day I had a coat made trimmed with a hundred pistoles. I sold my horse, acquired a valet and, having furnished myself with everything necessary, we took the coach that conveyed us to Paris. We had not been there long when my patron expedited my commission and recommended me to think as soon as possible about raising a company. Monsieur de Saint-Jean, who was my lieutenant, advised me to go with him to Joinville in Champagne, where he was well-known, and where, according to him, we could find men and horses at a reasonable price.

"Indeed, scarcely had we been there six weeks than we were almost complete. But in addition to the excessive expenditure that I made in every manner, I had the misfortune that my rogue of a valet from Avignon, whom I had paid very poorly for his trouble, and who was from that locale, having caught sight of me in passing, recognized me. The scoundrel, as much by a principle of vengeance as with a view to being liberally rewarded by my wife, immediately sent news to Mascado.

"That wily Jew exercised such diligence, and employed people so powerful, that not only was I arrested and put in prison shortly thereafter, but having been accused and convicted of the ultimate rascality, I was deprived of all my remaining property and condemned to the galleys in perpetuity.

"That, Messieurs," Pierre Heudde concluded, "is how the course of my infamous debauchery came to an end. You can see that my slavery has been long. The pleasures that I had do not equal the punishment that I have had to endure.

The One who governs all willed it thus; I suffer his chastisements with patience, until he has the generosity to put an end to them."

We pitied him his unfortunate lot, and Mr. Elliot having given him the value of an écu, he assured him that in the dispositions he anticipated, he would try to render him service. We would have liked the unfortunate to tell us his birthplace and parentage, but he did not want to tell us, so we withdrew, admiring the sage conduct of the Omnipotent with regard to his creatures, good and wicked.

I paid so little heed to Algiers during the sojourn I spent there, and was so incurious in passing through its quarters, that I marveled, as soon as we were at sea, on discovering beauties there that had not come to mind. The charming city is situated in the form of an amphitheater on the slope of a high mountain, in such a way that one can see the whole of it at a glance, although it is large and contains more than a hundred thousand inhabitants. There was not time, however, to return to examine it, and I had little desire to do so.

The season was agreeable and we had such a fortunate crossing that I did not feel the slightest discomfort. Eventually, I arrived in London—that famous and magnificent city, which effaces by its luster all that I had seen before—on the fourth day of the month of May 1694, aged seventy-three years, but strong and vigorous for my age.

The first thing I thought of was to get myself dressed, because I did not want to show myself to my friends in the garments that I was wearing. My host spoke French, and I asked him to send in quest of a tailor for me who also spoke my language. The man in question having come and having taken me to a refugee merchant, while we were occupied in looking at cloth, a man came in who, as soon as he had cast eyes on me and heard that I was a barbary slave, was seized by a hemorrhage, which lost him more than twenty ounces of blood; there was no means of staunching it.

Everyone applied what remedies he had, but seeing that it was all futile, and that there was even talk of sending for a surgeon to open a vein, I took his little finger on the side of the nostril that was bleeding and tied it very forcefully with thread between the nail and the first joint. That remedy, which never failed me, but which few people are capable of using well, took effect, and was admired by the company. The merchant, who knew the individual, had a glass of eau-de-vie brought to him. Having taken it from the hands of the maidservant, he said: "To you, Monsieur Massé; it's necessary to repair a little, with these spirits, a part of the loss that you've just suffered,

Although he was young when I left home, he had nevertheless conserved a few features, which enabled me to recognize him immediately, even though he was extremely scarred by smallpox."

"Your name is Monsieur Massé, then?" I said to him.

"Yes," he replied. "At your service."

"Do you know Mr. Elliot, the consul in Algiers?" I asked him.

"Very well," he replied.

"Well," I said, "here is a letter that he asked me to give you."

He took the letter and started to read it, but when he reached the place where mention was made of me he put it down precipitately on the counter, against which he had learned, and threw his arms recklessly around my neck without pronouncing a single word.

No matter how much effort I made to regain possession of myself, it was impossible for me to utter a word for a long time; we remained stuck together like two stone statues, and I believe that we would both have died of joy if someone had not taken the trouble to separate us.

"You've emerged from slavery, my very dear brother," he said to me, with tears in his eyes, "and you're doubtless destitute of worldly goods. Heaven has blessed me for both of us; come to my home to enjoy the rest of your days, and my abundance, and your liberty. It is just that you govern in your turn; I, my wife and my children will now be your slaves; I want you to command in my house, and I will be the first to obey you."

I tried to reply to his civilities, and make him understand that a man of my age, would not be a very agreeable object for young people, and that it would be better for me to go into the house of some stranger, who would be obliged to suffer my infirmities by paying him, but he interrupted me immediately, and, having instructed the tailor to finish my suit as quickly as possible, he took me to his house.

All that I have said about my brother was nothing by comparison with what his family did. My sister, his wife, and my nephews and nieces could gladly have eaten me alive. They gave me a beautiful apartment to lodge me, and a domestic to serve me in all my necessities.

Le Grand, one of my traveling companions, having learned of my arrival, did me the grace of coming to see me. He told me how, after having quit Goa, he had gone to the island of Java, where he had had the good fortune to be introduced to Monsieur de Saint-Martin, who had introduced him to Mynheer Van Reden, the governor of Batavia, and the means by which he had had occasion to profit from the lessons in mathematics that I had given him by exercising the functions of engineer in several favorable employments, which had put him in a state to live honestly for the rest of his days. He also told me that La Forêt had died in those regions in easy circumstances, but he did not know what had become of the others.

If it is necessary to render justice to that gallant man, I admit frankly that his frequent conversations contributed not a little to reminding me of a quantity of circumstances of which I no longer had the slightest idea; and that although there is much that is missing from this relation that would have appeared herein had I been able to conserve my journals, or had greater commodity in recovering accurate memories, without him it would have been even less complete.

If I have forgotten many things, I have, on the other hand, not advanced anything that I have not witnessed, or which did not come to me first hand. And

I would have given this relation of my voyages to the public ten years ago if powerful reasons, two in particular, had not prevented me from doing so.

The first of those reasons is that my brother, having had a share of large farms in France, had fared so poorly there that he had been obliged to abandon everything and come to establish himself in England, where he makes as little fuss as is possible, for fear that news of him might reach the court and cause trouble for him.

The other is of lesser weight, and affects me in particular. I feared that my book might give some insatiable monarch the desire to want to conquer the realm whose description I have given, and force me to serve as a guide to those who would be employed for such a difficult expedition. I am weary of voyaging, and my age no longer permits me to support the fatigues that I once endured. My nephews have been charged with taking care of this manuscript after my death, with the consequence that by the time it is seen, everyone can be convinced that my brother and I are no longer in the world.

# DISCOVERIES IN THE REGION OF THE NORTH POLE BY THE REVEREND FATHER PIERRE DE MÉSANGE

Birth and death are two extremities through which humans are indispensably obliged to pass; they are the entrance and the exit of all flesh, the great as well as the small. Of whatever quality one is, from the moment one has a commencement, one has a story that is tending infallibly toward an end; it is necessary that a moment follows the repose, and although that happens in one subject with more brilliance or less toil and trouble than another, fundamentally, it is the same thing, since there are two extremities between which it is necessary to have a middle.

On the other hand, one can say without any risk that there is an infinite difference between the course of some and the duration of others, either in terms of time or with regard to the incidents to which we are subject while we exist. We often see that on the one hand, there are some who expire in the same instant that they begin to breathe, and on the other, some who live for a century. The days of some are fortunate without interruption, and the years of others are nothing but a tissue of afflictions and disappointments.

My fate has been to live for a long time and to be unfortunate to excess; misery has been my full share. I was born in lowliness; I have lived in agitation; and I am at risk of dying in poverty.

An obscure birth and an abject and servile life are rarely the object of public curiosity; that attention scarcely awakes save at the strident noise that is ordinarily made by heroes, the bellicose actions of great men, or that that which is judged to be positively interesting. However, as there are no rules without exceptions, despicable as I might be in myself, I am convinced that if one takes the trouble to peruse this treatise from end to end, one will find adventures therein worthy of a singular admiration, and discoveries which, notwithstanding that they are entirely owed to hazard, will give pleasure to the majority of those who read them, although it is certain that had the treatise been of such great extent and as explicit as it would infallibly have been if it had come to my mind to begin it sooner, and if I had not, unfortunately, lost my journals, it would have been a considerable volume. It will be seen at the end of the work where I have composed it, and the reasons for which all the facts are not reported therein with as much exactitude as a delicate intellect could have wished.

To enter into the matter, order requires me, if I am not mistaken, to commence with the time and place of my birth. I am French by nation, born at Viviers in Cévennes in 1639, strong, robust, of good complexion, and very well-constructed. Physiognomists and Chiromancers came to our house every day to measure the dimensions of the parts of my body; they protested unanimously that they had never seen one better proportioned.

I had, according to them, a face exactly as long as my hand, measuring from the extremity of the middle finger to the base of the palm. Nine times that length was the extent of my body, either in height, from the soles of my feet to the summit of my head, or in width when my arms were extended horizontally The height of my forehead was equal to the length of my so-called index-finger, and everywhere of the same width. I had well-cleft eyes, and just as long as the space from the mound of Mercury to the second joint of the little finger. The nose and the mouth were the same size, the cheeks and hands of equal width. The lines of my forehead were long, straight and broad: certain marks of good fortune, enjoyment and intelligence.

What confirmed that prognosis was the proportion of the parts of my hand, the breadth of which contained precisely four times the space between the Mounts of the Sun and Mercury, just as nine times that distance was exactly the length. The thumb and the little finger were equal, the solar finger equal to the index finger. The life-line was broad straight and firm, accompanied by fortunate branches, and was joined to that of the head beneath the middle of the Mount of Jupiter. The same line, which is that of the heart, was so well-connected to those of the lungs, the liver and the stomach that they all seemed to have one and the same origin.

The breast, the stomach, the belly and, in a word, all the parts of my body were, so they said, so perfect in every regard that I could pass for a veritable masterpiece of nature. Those who knew my horoscope claimed that I would live to a decrepit age, succeed in great employments, become extremely rich and be happier than one can imagine.

Events have shown that the science of these pretended scholars had no foundation other than vanity, and consisted of nothing but simple conjectures. My father, who loved me madly, nevertheless listened to those charlatanries with pleasure. He flattered himself with great hopes in my favor, and imagined that he saw in me more disposition to cultivate belles-lettres than inclination to exercise, like him, the difficult métier of cloth-cutter or to devote myself to commerce. He was careful to make me spend my youth in schools, where, I do not know for what reason, my masters baptized me with the nickname Cordelier.[18] I was known by that name to all the inhabitants of our town.

The monks of that order took the opportunity to befriend me and, seeing me thereafter as destined to embrace the religious life, persuaded me in spite of all that my parents could say to deflect me from it, to take the cloth and to join their ranks. I was then twenty-six years old—which is to say that I was in the

---

[18] Construed literally, Cordelier means rope-maker, but it was also the familiar term for Franciscan friars, because of the rope girdles that they wore. It is presumably the latter meaning that the teachers and townspeople had in mind when giving the narrator his nickname, which proved fatal, although the shadow of the other might nevertheless remain relevant.

most beautiful and agreeable age of life, when one ordinarily has the most gaiety and vigor. However, I can truthfully say that, notwithstanding that I was the only child of our household, that I had been brought up preciously and delicately and with all possible tenderness.

I immediately applied myself so forcefully to devotion that, observing the most rigid rules of our society with exactitude, and leading a life so austere that my father and mother, suddenly changing their sentiments, praised God for having given me the grace to quit the world in order to work for my salvation and theirs; and, reflecting on the past, they convinced themselves that all the predictions that had once been made on my behalf had found their accomplishment there, in that I suddenly entered into possession of honors, treasures and the most precious wealth that the Creator can accord to his creature.

I served, in fact, as an example of all the zeal there was in our Convent; I was cited in families as Saint Paul is cited in churches. But patience; let us not render odious the matter I am treating, by permitting me to stop there; it is not appropriate that, in imitation of certain Preachers, who affect to preach themselves, and whose personal qualities often form by themselves the most essential part of their sermon, I should make my panegyric here and write a book in my praise.

I shall content myself with saying simply that the same things that attracted the esteem of some made me hated by others, and gave jealousy to many people. One of the brothers of the Convent, named Jacques Surcel, was of that number; he wished me harm without my having merited it, and without knowing what approach to take to satisfy it. Having eventually remarked that in my prayers I was ordinarily careful to address myself particularly to the Blessed Virgin, he resolved, in order to turn me to ridicule and to get me away from the Convent for some time, to appear to me in the guise of Saint Francis.

He chose a Friday for that, when he entered my cell between midnight and one o'clock, enveloped in a shroud that covered him down to the floor. I had been praying all evening and had been overcome momentarily by drowsiness; I was sleeping lightly when I awoke with a start and was surprised to hear a voice that said to me:

"Pierre de Mésange, your wishes are granted; I am your patron, known to all good and veritable Catholics under the name of Saint Francis, who sits before God, and am sent here to announce to you on the part of Jesus of Nazareth that you have been received in grace. Only one thing is lacking to render you perfect felicity and elevate your glory above all that is sacred in Paradise; that is that you have never been on Pilgrimage, and that that act of religion, so necessary to advance your salvation and so essential to Christianity, has never even entered your thoughts. Get up, gird your loins and depart promptly for Loretta. It is there where Our Lady, the immaculate Virgin, to whom you never cease to pray day and night, will appear to you and will give you, with her blessing, one of the veritable nails of the crucifixion of her adorable son. Have you understood what I have said?"

"Yes, Holy Father," I replied, "but your presence astonishes me; I can only look at you with difficulty, and hear you trembling."

With that he disappeared.

I cannot lie; that vision caused me tremendous anxieties and gave great embarrassment to my mind. After having thought seriously about it, however, I was convinced that it must have been a dream, which had immediately succeeded my great drowsiness, and I believed that all the more because, having had my imagination full of Saint Francis, whose help I had implored, and on whose life I never ceased to meditate night and day, it seemed to me quite natural that my brain, during sleep, had conserved those traces. Thinking that, I made no semblance of anything, and did not want to talk to anyone.

The pretended saint noticed that. So, a week later, at precisely the same time, he did not fail to pay me a second visit and to make me the same compliment. Then being well awake, I decided, one getting up, to communicate the prodigy to a monk in whom I had great confidence, and whose nature was less credulous than intrepid.

"Keep silent," he said. "Don't mention what has happened to anyone; assuredly, it's a trick that someone is playing on you; you're sincere and someone wants to abuse your simplicity. Believe me, Saint Francis is very well where he is, and the repose that he is enjoying scarcely permits him to come to trouble yours. I doubt that he goes to any trouble for us. At any rate, I believe that I can glimpse the veritable cause of this unjust procedure. Let us exchange cells in the evenings without anyone noticing, and I shall see for myself what is going on."

The Saint, indubitably impatient to see me leave, did not wait so long the third time. He came back the following Sunday and, having expressed himself almost as before, protested loudly that he would not see me again, and that if I deferred the execution of his order, I would not take long to feel the effects of divine vengeance.

My friend, who was lying down, observed the messenger at close range, with the result that when he saw that he was on the point of leaving, he only had to leap upon him and seize him round the body, crying: "Who are you, Rogue, who come here under the appearances of a divine Mercury, to bring us positive orders from Heaven? I know you, if I'm not mistaken; you can try to disguise your voice, but I've heard you sing elsewhere."

At these words the other tried to escape from his hands, but he did not have the means, the one who held him being determined not to let go.

"Speak," he said to him, "or I'll stun you with blows and make a din capable of alarming the entire Convent."

I was listening in the meantime, and, my apartment being adjacent to the one in which the two actors were playing this comedy, I approached in order to see what was happening.

Brother Jacques heard me, and, fearing to be discovered, made new efforts to get himself out of trouble quickly, but, seeing that he could not do so, he seized a knife that happened to be close at hand, with which he stabbed downwards, trying to prick the person holding him, with the design of making him let go. In the meantime, misfortune determined that the other, wanting to throw him to the ground, pulled the arm so forcefully that the knife entered to the hilt into the lower abdomen.

That deadly blow had an immediate effect.

"Oh God!" cried my friend. "Murder! Help! I'm a dead man!"

At these cries I ran forward fearfully, with the stub of a candle that had served me while reading for the best part of the night, and I saw two men, as embarrassed as one another. The disaster completed my distress.

Brother Jacques did not know what to do in that fatal juncture; the blood was flowing from the wound in great gouts; he and I tried to close it, but it was futile, and it was in vain that he implored assistance.

"Wait," said the one who had struck the blow, eventually. "I've had an idea; the remedy is effective; I'll soon bring you relief."

Pronouncing those words, he left us, ran as fast as he could to the Porter's apartment and told him that one of the Brothers had just been afflicted by a dangerous hemorrhage which threatened him with losing all his blood in a short time, and that it was necessary to let him go out to consult a skillful man who was among his friends, who had an admirable recipe for such inconveniences.

Scarcely had he disappeared than the patient lost consciousness; that further accident redoubled my anxiety; I feared that the poor man might die in my arms, and that, having got him mixed up in the affair, I would be presumed culpable. So, without hesitation, I went to the Convent door, which had been left on the latch until the other returned.

As soon as I was in the street, I transported myself, with all the rapidity of which I was capable, to the home of one of my aunts, from which I sent someone in quest of my father. I told him what had happened to me. His opinion was that I should stay there until he found out how things worked out.

My Brothers, meanwhile, having been informed of what had happened in our community, sent a domestic to our house, who said to the person who opened the door that it was not necessary for me to bring remedies, and that I to return, since there was no more to be done. That message was immediately brought to me.

"I'll wager that the poor man has died," I said, then. "The Criminal has run away; in his absence I might perhaps have difficulty rendering the justice of my cause evident and avoiding some harsh punishment. Let someone find me clothing; I would rather go elsewhere swiftly than run the risk of being punished for a crime that I have not committed."

Everyone approved of my resolution, and they supplied me with money and all that was necessary.

At daybreak I went to Orange, after having given instructions that I was to be kept informed by letters, which would be sent to me under an assumed name, of everything that they thought ought to be communicated to me.

They did not fail, in fact, to write to me every day, but it was always the same thing; it consisted entirely of letting me know that whatever trouble they took, it was impossible to learn anything about the event, which was not so extraordinary. The Monks of the Convent were keeping it so well hidden that no more mention was heard of it than if nothing had happened at all, apparently for fear that it might cause a scandal and give the public a distaste for mendicant monks capable of such extravagances.

In that state of uncertainty, assuming that it was a stratagem invented with the design of making me fall into a trap, I took the road to Bordeaux, where I found a ship with a cargo of wine, plums, grapes and other similar gods, ready to depart for Middelburg, the capital city of the island of Walcheren in Zeeland.

The captain of the ship, whose name was David Leskes, gave me all imaginable consideration; we ate and drank together, and were always in one another's company. He was a man who enjoyed life, who ate well, but he also cost me a good deal; when one want to have pleasure, it is just that the purse feels it; the recompense ought to be proportional to the good offices that are rendered to us.

Our voyage was fortunate enough; we had mild and tranquil weather until we were above Flessingue, where a turbulent wind nearly capsized us, the mizzen mast snapped in the middle, and an anchor and a sailor who was holding on to it fell into the sea and were lost. The most experienced seamen though the vessel doomed, but we escaped with a fright.

After having passed through the strait and gained, with great difficulty, the haven or channel that extends from Arnemuiden to Middelburg, we were imprudent enough to run aground at high tide. The ship did not suffer any damage, however, and it only cost us the trouble of unloading part of the cargo into boats that we had brought expressly for that purpose, which took us an entire day.

As soon as we were on land I obtained directions to the house of a Catholic sieve-maker, where I was made very welcome. The man did not lack intelligence, and he knew everyone in the town; there was nothing he did not know about its ins and outs. His enlightenment, as well as his faith—which, as I had already made him understand, was mine—gave me occasion to consult him about what I could do to subsist in that foreign land, where I could not expect any help from anyone, not even my parents, whom I did not want to be charged with the cost of a folly. I told him naively what I was, what I knew and the desire that I felt to remain in that agreeable abode, if I could earn a living comfortable there.

"If you were reformed, Monsieur," he replied, "you could easily start a French school; you're quite capable of it, from what I understand, and at present, there isn't a worthwhile one. It's a profession that is sufficiently esteemed here, above all when one is competent and gives the impression of it; people would have confidence in you and you'd be able to settle comfortably here. But as a papist, as we're called by the people of this nation, I don't think you'd be given permission."

"It's necessary to try," I said. "The worst that can happen to me is that I don't succeed, and then it will be time to think of something else. It's not a matter of stocking a shop or commencing some wholesale trade, for which one needs credit and collateral. A pen-knife, a ream of paper and a box of quills is sufficient to set up in business."

With that we went in search of Monsieur Tibaut, in order to ask him if he would be kind enough to permit me to live under his protection, to form a small establishment and to teach French to young people. The Burgomaster, doubtless giving no thought to religion, and perhaps assuming that I was of the common opinion, agreed to my request.

"In order to risk nothing, however," he said to me, "if you'll take my advice, you'll begin by taking a room with some individual, in order to show what you can do and to see whether you will have enough occupation, before renting a house and putting yourself to the expense of buying furniture and everything necessary to a household."

I thanked him very humbly for the favor that he was doing me, and assured him that I would do my duty so well that he would have no reason to refuse me the continuation of his benevolence. My host had a fine apartment, which overlooked a little courtyard, from which it obtained a good deal of light, and he generously offered it to me at a very civil price, with the sole view of giving me pleasure, until it became clear what progress the business would make.

I took advantage of his honesty, put up a sign outside the house without further hesitation, and started the school. I had only undertaken the métier for a fortnight when I thought my fortune was made; children flocked to me from all directions, and I praised God for having destined such a fine refuge for me.

Suddenly, however, when I was no more thinking about that disaster than the hour of my death, I saw birds of the most evil omen enter my room: an accursed cripple by the name of de Long, the Minister of the French Church, accompanied by a one-eyed wretch who was introduced to me as his Rector.

One might have thought to look at those Tartuffes that they had come to announce better news that than Angel Gabriel had once brought to the Blessed Virgin Mary on the day of the Annunciation. The Pastor put on the finest expression and played the dirtiest game. He approached me smiling.

"Well, Monsieur," he said to me, "you have pupils in sufficiently large number, for what I see; I'm assuredly delighted, and I hope it will be further augmented. You have not, however, been in the region long enough for me to know whether you belong to the Flemish assembly, for I have not yet see you in my church—although you are French, if I'm not mistaken?"

"Yes, Monsieur," I replied. "I'm from Languedoc, and I do not know Flemish, as you can easily persuade yourself by the fact that I only know your tongue and also affirm it; but thus far I have been so busy in taking care of my everyday affairs that I have not yet seen any church or tavern,. My host will be my witness that I had formed the design of coming to pay my respects to you today, after school, and I'm sorry that you have anticipated me."

"You're of the reformed religion, then," he said to me.

"Undoubtedly, Monsieur," I replied. "It is evident that I would not have dared to do what I am doing if I professed another."

"Show me your attestation, if you please," he said.

"I have none, Monsieur," I replied. "Affairs have embroiled me, which have not given me time to ask for one from our Consistory, but if it is necessary I offer to put one in your hands within a month, or six weeks at the latest."

"To speak frankly," said one of the Messieurs, "you are a trifle suspect, for not only is it asserted in the city that you are a papist, but you have all the appearance of a Monk. Don't pretend; tell us the truth; in any case, it cannot remain hidden."

My conscience was already burdened by the fact that I had just indirectly denied my true religion; it was impossible for me to hedge any longer, in addition to which I could see that I was dealing with people who would give me no quarter.

"It is not possible," I replied, "that those who hold me suspect can do so other than by pure conjecture, for I assume that there is not a soul in the entire Province who knows where I come from, or what I am; but if what you imagine were true, would it raise any obstacle to my establishment? Are we not in a free country, where everyone is permitted to earn a living, provided that he does so in an honest manner and without doing any harm to his neighbor? There is no question here of religion; I do not represent myself as a Theologian, I do not want to dogmatize or tell anyone how to live; I am only teaching how to read, to write, to calculate and to speak French, and if there happen to be lovers of geography or mathematics, I shall do my best to give them a general idea of their principles and explain their elements"

"Fundamentally, you are right," interjected the Cantor, who appeared to me to be a man of common sense, "but it is not permitted for an individual like you or me to dictate laws to a entire people under the protection of whom we place ourselves; it is necessary, on the contrary, to accommodate oneself to theirs and follow their maxims rigorously, under penalty of punishment or incurring disgrace. If you were to plead in favor of Catholics before the tribunal of reform, and attempt to have the members of that communion enter into the professional guilds or other associations of the town, you would undoubtedly lose your suit. Schoolmasters have their separate association, and they will never admit you to it until you have proved that you belong to the dominant religion, and in order that you make no mistake, I want, as Dean, to warn you that if they do not speak to you first, and you wait six weeks before you present yourselves to them and satisfy their regulations, they will impose a heavy fine upon you, which you will be obliged to pay without delay, unless you decamp."

"I did not know that, Monsieur," I said. "I thank you for your kind warning; I shall try to see them first; it is only just that I accommodate myself to their manners. And as for you, Messieurs, I shall also try to satisfy you, as is only reasonable."

"You would do well," the Minister continued, "and it would be as well if you did not take long about it."

With that, they retired.

My host, who had witnessed that dialogue looked at me compassionately. "Your affairs are going badly, Monsieur," he said to me. "It's necessary to become a Huguenot, or at least put on a semblance, or you'll have to shut up shop. Monsieur de Long is violent, and he's one of those Ecclesiastics who never lets go. Monsieur Pervilé is more moderate, but he follows his interests, since he exercises the same profession. I say it again; you won't succeed unless you turn your coat."

"Turning my coat," I said, "is something that I have no desire to do; I can no longer dissimulate; the best thing to do is to go in search of my bread elsewhere."

In fact, at the end of the week, I embarked on a beurtman for Rotterdam, where I was one of sixty passengers. We had such a favorable wind that, in spite of the fact that it was between nine and ten when we cast off, we arrived in port the same day before seven o'clock had chimed, even though we had remained at anchor for two hours between Tergoes and Willemstad waiting for the tide.

I went to lodge at the Three Scissors, the establishment of a certain Du Prat, who dabbled in brokerage and also served food. To his contentment, I did not want to expose myself to treatment similar that I had received in the place from which I had just come. I set myself up as a language tutor and went to teach in private houses.

Two Danes who were lodging with me began to occupy me for a hour a day; they recommended me to others do not think the first month had expired when I had at least a dozen disciples, who each gave me a ducat every twenty-eight days, with the consequence that it would have been quite wrong to complain of my fortune.

I had been living in that famous city for about eight months when a rather extraordinary adventure, which happened to a Frenchman, gave me a new reason to move.

A gentleman from the region of Gex named Monsieur Chalet, having heard mention that Monsieur Tyssot, who was one of his relatives, had quit France under the pretext that people of his religion were beginning to be persecuted, and had gone to life in Delft, traveled to see him there. He was treated very well by him for several days, according to the account that he gave us on his return, but the ingrate had a soul so base that, on his departure, whether because of a natural penchant for theft, as I have known others to have, or simply to avenge himself for the fact that, being short of money because a letter of exchange on which he was replying had not reached him on his travels, his friend had refused him a hundred écus that he had asked to borrow, he had stolen a silver goblet of eight or ten ducatons, which he found within reach, and which the children were using to drink after a meal.

As no one in the house suspected him, he was not rigorously observed, but when he had gone and the goblet could no longer be found, someone said that they had seen him stuffing something into his trousers that he had taken from the table immediately before the porter had came to pick up his suitcase to take it to the boat.

Monsieur Tyssot did not want to believe it of him, so he first sent for the barrow-man in order to make no mistake, and having learned that he had seen him leave for Rotterdam on the eight o'clock boat, he took the one that left ten o'clock in order to run after him. He was able to describe the person so well to the people to whom he addressed himself with regard to the route that the thief had taken that he was directed to the Ramestraat and straight to us. Our host, who received him at the door and from whom he learned that the man he sought was in the house, took him to our room, where we were just sitting down to dinner.

As soon as he saw Monsieur Chalet, he said: "Well, Cousin, here you are."

"Yes, Monsieur," he replied, blushing and somewhat nonplussed. "What have you come to do in the city, and why didn't you tell me that you wanted to come so soon after me? We could have traveled together; I would have had the honor of your company and the time would have seemed shorter."

"I didn't know then," said Monsieur Tyssot. "Something came up since then that made me take the resolution to follow you, in order to say a word to you in private."

"Very well, Cousin," he replied, "if it is urgent for me to go out with you; if not, I beg you to sit down and aid us in the dissection of this guinea-fowl, which seems to me to be not at all bad."

"It's not a matter here of invitations," said his cousin. "We're in a public place, before a table to which, by paying his fee, any honest person can be admitted. There's a soup that smells good; I must mount an assault on it with you."

After having discussed the food briefly, the conversation turned to the war that was then being fought with England, everyone offering his own opinion of it, and things were said on that matter that might give pleasure to the Reader if I could remember them and if the circumstances of the three naval battles that took place between the islanders and the Dutch had not been described perfectly well by the authors who have written about them. I shall content myself with saying in passing that the Batavians then recovered all the glory that they had lost in the times of Cromwell, not only in that they beat their enemies soundly in the second battle, but because they were then bold enough to sail up the Thames and descend on Chatham, where they ruined so many vessels that the English were constrained to make peace via the mediation of the King of Sweden.[19]

As soon as the meal was over, the Messieurs got up from the table and went into another room. I do not know what they said to one another, but I learned subsequently that the young man had been scolded, although he feigned ignorance to begin with, and that shortly afterwards, having gone to visit his clothing, among which the goblet was found, he protested that it had been a mistake. He begged his friend not to say anything to anyone, since, society being naturally inclined to speak ill, it would be impossible to prevent gossip, and his honor being questioned, in spite of his innocence.

When they returned we resumed drinking. Monsieur Tyssot, having looked at me several times, seemed curious to know who I was and what I did. I told him where I was from and my profession.

"You're a language teacher?" he said. "Have you many pupils?"

"No," I replied. "I had a good number once, but unfortunately, instead of increasing, it's diminishing every day."

"Do you speak Flemish?" he asked, in Latin, apparently to test me and to see if I were involved with a métier that I did not understand.

"No, Monsieur," I replied, in the same language. "I might have learned something of it while I've been here, but the company of persons of my own nation, whom I frequent every day, on the one hand, and the scant advantage that I imagine I would be able to obtain from it, on the other, have cause me to neglect to apply myself to it thus far."

"You're wrong to stay in this city," he told me. "Since you're not unaware of the language of scholars, it's necessary to abandon the sons of merchants, to whom you're not appropriate, and go to join men of study. If you'll take my advice you'll go to Leyden; I'm convinced that you'll do better there than here."

I thanked him for his good advice, and promised to act on it as soon as it was possible for me to do so. Indeed, six weeks later, I was in that famous academy, where I lodged with a very honest man who said that his name was Patri.

The multitude of foreigners who were then in that place gave me the opportunity to meet a great many people, and in a matter of days I had a larger practice than I had ever had in Rotterdam. There were several who, in addition to French, wanted me to give them lessons in Mathematics, but I dared not do so for fear of making enemies. Monsieur van Schoten,[20] who was then the Profes-

---

[19] The Dutch Medway raid that resulted in the burning of English ships at Chatham occurred on 20 June 1667.

[20] The reference is presumably to the Dutch mathematician Frans van Schooten (1615-1660), an important popularizer of Descartes' system of analytical geometry who inherited his father's position as professor of Mathematics at Ley-

sor of that science, was very friendly toward me, the majority of my pupils came to me by that channel, so I was careful not to disoblige him. On the contrary, I often went to consult him in the difficulties I encountered in Astronomical calculations and algebraic equations above the quadratic.

Eventually, I decided to frequent the colleges assiduously for two or three semesters. There was only one man, if I'm not mistaken, who was from Gueldre and whose name was Mynheer Smeenk, to whom I gave a few lessons in Geometry, on condition that not a soul should know anything about it. The only reason that led me to do that, was that notwithstanding the trouble the poor fellow took, he could not comprehend one slightly difficult proposition on which several relationships depended, and his Master had often reproached him before his comrades for the obstinacy of his conception when he had admitted ingenuously that he did not understand it, or asked more than once for a repetition.

There were then a considerable number of clever Doctors in the university and a large affluence of young people of all nations, but I can say in all sincerity that I had never seen a human prodigy similar to the one in whose company I found myself casually one day in the house of one of my best friends. We were having a little party, and he had been invited, without my being aware of it, to take part, and the word had been passed around to deceive me agreeably.

It began with a gazette that the great genius had taken from the maidservant, who had brought it to the Messieurs, because, he said, he liked to read the news, especially when he had nothing else to do. He started reading aloud, for the benefit of those who wanted to listen. I was charmed by the grace and pronunciation of the agreeable reader, and admired the Gazetteer, who expressed himself in the finest terms of the French language. As soon as he had finished I thanked him in particular for the trouble he had taken, and praised him for having acquitted it so well.

Shortly thereafter he got up, and the others did likewise; insensibly, following their example, I also moved, and had drawn closer to the table. Seeing the gazette open at the place where it had been put down, I was seized by a desire to reread the article on France, in which there was mention of the death of a great man, whose name escapes me. I picked it up but was astonished to find that it was in Flemish, because it seemed to me to be the same one that had been read a moment before. It was necessary to conclude, however, reluctantly, that I had been mistaken, and thus, without saying anything, I put it down and picked up a small book that was alone there, and which contained Terence's *Andria*. I riffled through it and read two or three pages, but without paying much attention.

Half an hour later, as usually happens in pleasant company when there is nothing to do but chat, play and drink it happened, either by chance or deliberate

---

den, but if so, it is anachronistic in juxtaposition with the previous reference, as he would have died some years before the raid on Chatham.

contrivance that Beronice, as the learned individual was called, having gone back to the table picked up the comedy that I had just seen, playfully, and started to read in Greek.

*What is this?* I then thought. *Is it magic, or am I dreaming?*

"It seems to me," I exclaimed, "that writings metamorphose as soon as Monsieur touches them. Just now he read us a gazette in excellent French that I found immediately afterwards to be written in Flemish, and now he's reading in Homeric Greek what I've just seen expressed in Latin. Assuredly, it's beyond me."

At those words everyone stated laughing, and after having left me in suspense for a little while, I stood there nonplussed when I was told that the person was actually a chimney-sweep, devoid of a home and hearth in society, having, like Melchisedek, neither a father, a mother nor a genealogy. He had never wanted to say where he came from, except that his fatherland was the habitable earth; he only remained in one place for a few days, passing from one country to another, and spent his money as he earned it, without wanting to be subject to anyone, not to live in the dependency of anyone whatsoever.

There was no language that he did not understand and did not speak perfectly, and the most admirable thing of all was that not only, as we had just seen in experiment, could he read a French, Italian or Latin book in Dutch, Spanish, English or any language he wished, but he could read verse as prose if one wished, and fluently, without ever hesitating, in the most eloquent fashion in the world—with the result that all those who heard him were ecstatic. If he had wanted to be a Professor of History at Leyden, he would have been one three times over; the offer had been made to him there and in several other places, in vain. He was a libertine,[21] who did not want to subject himself to anything, and who found himself in the condition that he was in, where he had no measures to take with anyone, to be the happiest of living men.

I stayed for more than four years in that agreeable city, where I amassed nearly three hundred ducats, but in spite of all my fine physiognomy, the fortunate lines in my hands, the just proportions of the parts of my body and the favorable planet under which the disciples of Cardan declared that I had been born, I was constrained to leave it in a very precipitate manner.

A gentleman from Overyffel who, if I remember correctly, was named Monsieur de Linteloo, had treated seven or eight of us who were among his best friends; it was about two o'clock in the morning when we left his room and our stomachs were not empty. Unfortunately, we encountered a poor soldier near the

---

[21] The author does not use the term "libertine" as it is now frequently used, to mean someone with loose morals, but simply to mean a lover of freedom, in both ideas and actions.

fish-market who, having had too much to drink, had the imprudence to shout at us: "Verda!"

The member of our company who was the most intoxicated of all, a native of Frankfurt and the nicest fellow in the world, took umbrage at that.

"What, Cheime," he said to him, "dare you familiarize yourself with people like us? We'll teach you a lesson, rogue." At the same time, he drew his sword.

The soldier, who was brave, drew his own, and they commenced fencing, the blades clashing all the way to the hilt.

The apprehension seized me that they might kill one another, and I threw myself between them in order to separate them, but by an inconceivable fatality, at the moment when the German thrust, and ran the soldier though, my blade went into his arm. Seeing a man fall on one side, and having thrust so solidly on the other that my blade had struck had enough to enter into flesh that had resisted considerably, I thought in good faith that I had committed murder.

With that, I promptly took to my heels and, without consulting anyone for fear of being arrested, I ran to the port at Harlem, where, having slipped quietly into the water I passed over the city moat, partly wading and partly swimming, and took the road to Amsterdam, leaving my host all my possessions, which were worth at least four hundred francs, as well as fifty ducatons in cash that I had lent him at various times.

I spent a few days in that Metropolis of the World, so called because of its wealth, its magnificence and its trade, and then embarked for Hamburg at the earliest convenient opportunity, for fear that I might be pursued and captured if I stayed any longer where I had gone to earth.

Having arrived in that populous city, I went in search of an uncle, who, according to what I had heard my mother say a hundred times, must be very well established there. My efforts were futile; I did not find him, and no one could tell me anything about him. Seeing that, I left the Golden Arm, where I had lodged temporarily, and rented a room from a tailor from Liège named Pequet. He had numerous workers, because he was much in demand, and kept a rather good table, which was why I took up residence with him for the sum of two hundred francs, all in, for a year.

I resumed my former métier, which was as successful there as in Leyden, but which I did not exercise with any great pleasure. Although my affairs went as well as I could desire, I still regretted Holland; I had found a frankness and honesty there that I despaired of ever finding anywhere else. Given that, it will not seem surprising that I was cut to the quick when the news reached us that England had declared war of Holland under several vain pretexts, which gave sufficient evidence of the genius of that superb nation—such as, for example, a few insulting medals that the King sustained had been struck with the intention of shocking, the old dispute about the flag, the Surinam affair, and others of a similar kind.[22]

I was afflicted by a violent fever, the agony of which I can still remember, when the news spread that the Very Christian King, in imitation, had just done likewise. I knew that a good number of the frontier towns of the United Provinces were very poorly fortified and deprived of any kind of munitions, committed to the care of Governors or young and inexperienced officers, and that in general, their troops were very ill-disciplined. The Estates General were not unaware of all that; that is why they omitted nothing in their power to avoid the unfortunate consequences of such a menacing storm. They urged the Bishop of Münster, who was armed like the other Powers, to tell them frankly what he was planning, but unsuccessfully. They offered France to submit to anything she cared to impose for her satisfaction, if she could show that there was any legitimate cause for complaint. Nor did they neglect anything to appease England, which seemed more animated; neither of them even wanted to listen.

I feared that such powerful enemies might subjugate that flourishing nation, where all the wealth in the world was accumulated, and that it would cease forever to be the veritable refuge of poor foreigners and the seat of liberty.

Finding themselves in extreme difficulties, they thought they ought to commence by ensuring themselves of a Leader in whom their soldiers could have confidence, and, knowing of no one more beloved by the nation than William of Nassau, whose ancestors had been the first founders of the Republic, the States of Holland and West Friesia decided to elect that young lord as their Captain General. A short time thereafter he was created Stadthouder of the Seven United Provinces, notwithstanding the perpetual edict of the year 1667, by which it was expressly stated that the responsibility in question should never be conferred on anyone, and in spite of the power of the de Wits, who were declared enemies of the House of Nassau. The People, by contrast, who loved the family, could not suffer anyone taking up the reins of Government other than the Prince of Orange.

The name de Wit, above all, seemed to be held in such abomination that new libels against the entire Louvestyn faction appeared every day. That hatred was sensibly augmented when the rumor went around immediately afterwards that Ruart van Putten, the brother of the Dowager de Wit, had tried to persuade a surgeon to assassinate the new Stadthouder, for fear that he might block his schemes and raise an obstacle to the aggrandizement of the family. The accusation was thought sufficiently well-founded for the person to be arrested, and confronted with his accuser. Although the latter sustained loudly that the decla-

---

[22] The English declared war, in association with the French, in what became known at the third Anglo-Dutch War, or the Franco-Dutch War, on 6 April 1672. 1672 subsequently became known in Dutch history as the *Rampjaar* [Year of Disaster] because of the depredations of the French army.

ration was true and that it was proven by circumstances that seemed incontesta-ble, the Burgomaster, who was put to the question was put, refused to admit anything and the Court was content to deprive him of all his employments and banish him in perpetuity from the Province of Holland.

At first, that sentence shocked people. If he was innocent, they said, then he was being treated badly; if he was guilty, then he ought to lose his life. The Dowager, however, who was perhaps not sorry that her brother had got off so lightly, went to the prison in a carriage to collect him and take him away before anything worse befell him.

Misfortune determined, however, that a bourgeois discontented with what had happened in their regard, having encountered them by chance as he was going into the sad place, started shouting at the top of his voice that, since the two traitors were together, it was necessary that they should not escape. At those words, several other inhabitants of The Hague joined him; they forced the doors, went up to the place where the two victims of the State were, and obliged them to come out. As soon as they were in the street they were set upon, and instantly beaten to the ground. As soon as they recovered consciousness, the clothes were ripped from their bodies and torn apart, and they were dragged naked to the gib-bet, where others hung them by their feet.

As everyone wanted to participate in that sacrifice, in which the latecomers always outbid their predecessors, it rapidly transpired that, not being content with that treatment, the crowd cut off their noses, ears, fingers and shameful parts, which were sold thereafter to the highest bidder, and transported out of the country. Finally, their entrails were torn out, and the excess of rage went so far as to bite them and eat morsels of their flesh.

Meanwhile, Louis le Grand,[23] who had set out on campaign with an army of at least a hundred thousand combatants, made incredible progress. In very little time he took Orsoy, Wesel, Burich, Rees, Emmerik, the fort of Skenck, Rhinberg, Doesburg, Utrecht, Arnhem, Sutphen, etc. The Bishops of Münster and Cologne, on the other hand, rendered themselves masters of Grol, Brevoort, Deventer, Zwol, Kampen, Hasselt, Steenwyk and several other places. The con-sternation was so great that the Magistrates of towns, far from waiting to be formally afflicted and putting up the slightest resistance, sent the keys to their gates to the enemy as soon as they came within twelve or fifteen leagues.

The States, seeing that they were on the brink of ruin, sent ambassadors to the King of France, then camped near Utrecht. The dispatched others to the King of Great Britain, but those princes made such demands, which seemed to them so exorbitant, that they did not even respond to them, and could not, in fact, ac-cept without rendering themselves slaves to those two Crowns. That did not,

---

[23] Prince Louis II of Condé, subsequently known as "the great Condé." His allies included Christoph Bernhard von Galen, Prince-Bishop of Münster, and the Archbishop of Cologne.

however, prevent things from getting worse. Conferences were held thereafter, in which very great offers were made to the victors. On the other hand there were men on campaign, who never ceased to remonstrate with the Emperor and other interested Powers that if they waited for Louis to render himself master of the Low Countries, they could not fail to fall under his domination one day and see him succeed to the Universal Monarchy that was the unique object of his ambition.

Their remonstrations had the anticipated effect; several Princes joined the side of the United Provinces. The Troops that we set on the march immediately provided a diversion and permitted the Prince of Orange a breathing space. That sudden change did not please France, which was running out of men and money, with the consequence that, seeing herself threatened by an infinite number of enemies who were coming from all directions, she abandoned the major part of her conquests in no time at all.

That procedure, which was unexpected, gave courage to the Allies, who were getting stronger by the day. The man who had excited them made proposals in his turn, but they no longer wanted to hear talk of anything but war, and it was only after many entreaties that they contented to the Peace, which was finally concluded and signed at Nimegen in 1678, to the great contentment of many honest people—at least, for me in particular, it was an inexpressible joy.

It has always been natural to me to have a mortal hatred of carnage and the shedding of human blood, especially between peoples who believe in the same God, and whom Christianity commands so strictly to love and concord.

Another reason I had to be content was that my affairs were going as smoothly as possible, so that in due course I found myself in possession of more than two thousand five hundred francs. Instead of that capital, which was considerable for a man like me, naturally leading me to make a little more expenditure and live generously, I became more economical every day, in such a manner that instead of always keeping my money in a strong-box, it occurred to me to invest it and draw some interest from it.

I spoke to my landlord, and he advised me to put two thousand francs in an annuity from which I would draw twelve and a half percent, but, having been unable to convince me to do that, he found me a Merchant in whose hands he imagined that it would be as secure as in my own. I entrusted that wretch with five hundred ducats in god coin, but I never received a sou; he went bankrupt a few months later and fled so far that I never knew what became of him.

That fatal blow took away my courage entirely; I entered into a kind of despair, and without consulting my friends I went to join a whaling expedition, even though I had a great aversion to cold and water. I provided myself sufficiently with everything that was necessary for the voyage, but it left me without a sou; on the contrary, I still owed a few hundred francs to my landlord, for which I left him a few clothes that I no longer needed, but which could compensate him in case I never saw him again.

The vessel on which I took ship was commanded by a Captain named Hans Jurien Peppel. We cast off at the beginning of May in the year 1679.

Having emerged from the Elbe we continued our navigation in weather as favorable as we could have wished. That lasted until we had reached the Arctic Circle, where we had to endure violent squalls for three or four days, which always kept us in suspense.

That great agitation was followed by a calm, which unfortunately caused us to lose a lot of time; one might have thought that we were eternally fixed in the same location.

Finally, having reached the seventieth degree of latitude, a frightful tempest attacked us, and separated us from several ships of which he had not previously lost sight. That evil weather transported us to between Greenland and Nieu-Land,[24] about twelve degrees from the Pole, and within sight of certain lands that our sailors said were limited by Schuyl and Vogel Hoek.

As I had not been much at sea and those regions were entirely new to me, every object I discovered gave me cause for admiration, but nothing astonished me more that the cold of the season, by comparison with what I had experienced elsewhere. The mountains of ice that we discovered in various places caused us to shiver, and our Captain said that it was a small miracle that we had succeeded in coming so far without being broken a thousand times over.

It appeared that the horrible wind that had seized us, while advancing us so considerably toward the Boreal Pole, had cast blocks of ice on one side and thus opened up a passage for us on the other. That seemed all the more probable when, as soon as the weather calmed down, we were astonished to see that we were surrounded by ice on all sides. Turning back was absolutely prohibited to us.

We were all trembling with fear; the Captain did not see any chance of ever saving his ship. He sent a few brave men accustomed to that métier to see whether there was any place in the surrounding area where a passage remained free.

On the fifth day we were there, two of them came back, who declared that, according to all appearances they had been stopped three of four leagues from there by an area of sea that extended as far as the eye could see, which might well furnish a means of reaching one of the nearest islands.

With that, the ship's officers assembled, and after much discussion, they resolved that the large launch would be unshipped and as much food put in it as possible, and it would then be dragged over the ice toward the place where the separation had been discovered. If difficulties came up on the way that appeared

---

[24] The island subsequently called Spitzbergen, in what is nowadays known as the Svalbard archipelago.

insurmountable, they would attempt to return; if not, they would press on. Many of the crew thought that enterprise exceedingly bold, and inevitably dangerous, but on seeing the Captain ready to attempt it, the confidence they had in him determined them to follow him.

Two Dutchmen, one from Leyden and the other from Edam, preferred to stay on board, with three Walloons and me, to whom the low Germans, in the minds of whom we all passed for Frenchman, did not even deign to make the slightest overture of their design. We were so ignorant of the reason for which they were quitting us that we did not even think of joining their party.

We were then in the longest days of the year. The Sun, which was always over the horizon, gradually began to make the agreeable warmth of its penetrating rays felt. The ice was visibly melting, or sinking, with the result that in a short time we were delighted to see an opening before us that extended as far as the eye could see. Our crewmen, however, did not come back, and I had no idea why that might be; it had already been thirteen days since then had left us before I suspected anything.

Although we had no commander on the vessel, I could not help remonstrating with my Dutch comrades that Heaven seemed to have opened a passage to get us out of our predicament and continue our journey, but they were content to shake their heads at me and say that it was in the opposite direction that we needed to go.

Three days later, seeing that nothing had closed up in front of us, they told us to help them put on a few sails, in order to take advantage of the weather, and see whether, after advancing a little way, an issue might appear to the right or the left by mans of which we could tack southwards I was delighted to see that it was working out well, without thinking about the route we were taking. Although I was not unaware that the further we advanced they less likely it seemed that we would ever see our homeland again, it seemed to me that there was nothing more mortifying than crouching in the same place, and that it was better to act than stand with folded arms, even if it was only to make the time—which seemed to us to be frightfully slow—pass more rapidly.

We moved slowly, without feeling the slightest agitation, but, having the wind behind us, we nevertheless made progress. That continued until we finally discovered land. The sight of it gave us pleasure, and although the ice-floes had for the most part abandoned us, we were no longer thinking about anything but breathing country air and seeing whether it might be possible to stay for some time in that new land.

As we talked about the different objects that we conjectured that we might encounter in that uninhabited desert area, subject to an almost continuous winter, the wind changed, and simultaneously brought about such a change in our circumstances that in less than an hour we saw ourselves besieged on all sides by ice floes, which one might have thought were being forged in our presence.

That new accident frightened us; fortunately, the agitation of the air was not considerable, and our ship was not yet in danger. Not knowing what would become of us, we decided to make use of the crystal sheet to transport ourselves to the shore, from which we would only draw away by three miles at the most.

When we had climbed the dunes, the country seemed to us to be flat and uniform; we could not see any mountains. Everything seemed to be fearfully sterile; we could only see a few fugitive malnourished plants protruding like gravel, and they were in very small quantity. In compensation, the water appeared to us to be full of fish; one might have thought that it was alive everywhere. After we had walked for a while we returned to our shelter, where he had a good meal after the fashion of mariners, who are content with a meal when they can eat fatty peas, after which we went to bed.

When we awoke we returned to the land, to which it seemed we had moved closer by a third, carrying rifles, because we had perceived that there were animals there of which it was necessary to be afraid. We had not been there long, in fact, when we did indeed discover a bear the size of a small ox, which came toward us shaking its head, often rubbing one of its paws, which seemed to be covered in blood.

"What does this mean?" I said to my comrades. "That animal is bleeding, as if it had been wounded by some hunter."

"Bagatelles," they replied. "There have been inhabitants in Greenland since time immemorial, who live, for lack of any other aliments, on fish and salt water."

"That's true, but this isn't the same thing. It's not credible that humans could live so far from the equator in winter."

"But there's no doubt, too, that here are frightful monsters here, since that one has found something stronger than itself."

As it came closer, the Dutchman who had been charge with the command ordered us only to fire two at a time. The Walloons, who had spent years in the service, also said the same thing, for reasons that I was obliged to approve.

It succeeded marvelously. As soon as the formidable animal was within range, two of our people fired at it, and hit it, each of them breaking a leg, one fore and one hind—which caused it to fall over.

Having got up again, with much difficulty, it set itself in a sitting position and set about howling like a demon. While the two that had fired reloaded, two others approached the huge beast and laid it out, in such a manner that it was no longer seen to shiver.

As we surrounded it, and were deliberating as to what to do with it, we were extremely surprised to see five men emerging at a distance, coming around a small eminence that was no more than four hundred paces away. They were tall and well-built, lightly clad in furs from head to toe, each with a bow suspended from his side and holding a staff in his hand as long as a half-pike, which seemed to be burned or ironclad at both ends.

As soon as they saw us they stopped dead, seemingly as surprised as we were by such a glimpse. They stayed there for at least a quarter of an hour, as if they were immobile.

We had reloaded, and were resolved, in case they came closer, not to show them anymore quarter than the bear. It subsequently seemed that they had more humane sentiments in our regard; the good people did not wish us any harm; they merely feared that we might do some to them.

Their dread was visibly augmented when, a fox having emerged from its lair between them and us, they saw one of our men put it down with the first shot he fired at it. They doubtless thought, thereafter, that we had lightning in our hands, and it only remained for us to strike them with thunderbolts. Such a prompt execution frightened them so much that, without further consultation, they fled with such rapidity that they were soon out of sight.

"Not good, Monsieur," said one of our Dutchmen then, "not good for us in the ship."

"I think you're right," I said. "Those fellows, frightened as they seem, might well come back in a state to maltreat us. It's true that we have a good refuge, but what use will that be to us? You can see that the safest thing would be to try to go back the way we came as soon as the wind is favorable and the ice retreats. Before going aboard, however, we need to take a quarter from the rump of our heavy beast, with the design, if we find it good, of coming back in search of the rest before some hungry wolf steals it from us."

The ice-floes had accumulated in that location on top of one another, which rendered the going difficult, but we carried back eighty or a hundred pounds of flesh. As soon as we were on the ship we cut up that piece of meat and roasted a part of it in a pot. We had never eaten bear meat before, but we found it tender and tasty.

Scarcely had we finished our meal than we heard a confused noise that alarmed us. We immediately went up on deck with our weapons, and God knows the amazement with which we were struck when we saw thirty or forty armed men coming straight toward the ship. Some had cutlasses and iron-tipped staffs, others large clubs, and several of them were carrying bows.

I must not lie; we thought we were all doomed; it did not appear possible to us that six men could resist such a large number. Nevertheless, on the assumption that they would give us no quarter, or, if they spared us, then it would only be with a view to fattening us up in order to massacre us in cold blood in the future, we resolved to sell our lives as dearly as we could and die with our swords in our hands rather than expose ourselves to the mercy of a cruel troop of cannibals.

When they were a hundred paces away from us we raised our weapons, and signaled to them with our hands not to come any closer. Those who had seen us seven or eight hours earlier were undoubtedly in the party, for we saw one of them representing to the others, with words and certain movements, the noise and prompt execution of our rifles.

That account of the threat we posed scared them; they dared not come any closer, but in order to testify to us that they meant us no harm, some of them raised their fingers in the air, as if to take Heaven as a witness that they had no evil intent. Others made inclinations of their body down to the ground, and some opened and closed their arms, as a sign of the desire they had to embrace us. In brief, they gave us all the signs of amity of which they were capable—and all that was accompanied by cries and words that doubtless related to their good intentions, but which, being proffered in a language that we did not understand at all, nevertheless rendered them suspect in our eyes.

Our Commandant, who did not trust them at all, shook his head at all that, and signaled to them that they should turn back.

They found our apprehension quite understandable, for in order to take away its cause entirely, they took all the weapons they had—swords, staffs clubs, bows and arrows—and threw them over the ice toward our vessel, folding their arms to signal their impotence to do us any injury and making gestures inviting us, while smiling, to go toward them.

When I saw that, I said to my comrades: "Assuredly, I suspect that those people, Barbarians as they appear to be, are not acting in good faith, but my opinion is that we should surrender to them and implore their mercy, given that, if they are obstinate in wanting to capture us, it's impossible for us to avoid falling into their hands. Even if they are crueler than we imagine them to be, perhaps the curiosity to know who we are and where we come from might easily lead them to spare our lives in order to find out."

Everyone agreed with me, and with that, we set down our arms in imitation of them, and, having lowered our hands, signaled to them to advance.

Never have I seen anyone as welcoming as those people seemed to be; they rubbed their hands with joy, and without giving any evidence of suspicion they advanced toward us. Immediately, we gave them a ladder, and one of the troop, for whom the others seemed to have a great deal of deference, climbed up it.

He had no sooner set foot on board than he approached the Dutchman who was in command, which he had apparently noticed, and after having given him his hand, he embraced him and kissed his cheeks as if he were his brother, after which he did the same for the rest of us, saying:

"Mela tay vani fiou ksan ataa." Which means, as we learned subsequently: *Be welcome, my friends*.

Then, without permitting the others to climb up, he invited us politely to follow him.

We wanted to obey him immediately, but he obliged us first to pick up our weapons and asked us by means of sign language whether there was anything else that we wanted to carry. We contented ourselves with taking our rifles and a little powder and lead.

When we were down below, all the others greeted us in the same fashion as he had done, and, having picked up all their possessions, they led us away.

Although the good people seemed sincere to me, I admit frankly that I had grave doubts about my salvation. It seemed to me, naively, that we were being led to the slaughter.

When we reached land, they turned to the left, where we eventually reached much higher dunes, which were not those we had seen on the previous days. A white bird the size of a river duck, which passed in front of us, gave one of our men an opportunity to fire. The unexpected shot caused all our guides to shiver; they were incontinently charmed thereafter to see the animal fall out of the air, dead, before their feet.

The chief of the band approached the man who had fired respectfully, and testified that he was curious to touch a machine capable of such a prodigious effect. The rifle was handed over without hesitation. The poor man handled it and considered it with as much veneration as a devotee touching a relic, and returned it with the same marks of submission.

Meanwhile, we were still advancing, and I do not think we had covered a league of distance when we quit the shore, where we had discovered a line of peaks that extended much further than the eye could see. Immediately afterwards, we saw low objects that were rather reminiscent of old buildings, or the ruins of demolished buildings.

"I don't know where all this is going," I said to one of our Walloons, who was alongside me, "but I'd swear that we were approaching a fortress that has been smashed by cannon fire, or which lightning has entirely blasted."

"It does indeed resemble a sacked location, a destroyed Jerusalem," he replied. "We'll see shortly what it is."

We soon realized that what we had taken at first for simple stakes were, in fact, good and strong palisades, fitted at the top with hooked iron spikes and joined together by strips of the same metal, with a dry but broad and deep ditch, very steep in front, which surrounded the islanders' subterranean dwellings.

We were similarly agreeably surprised to see that what had appeared to be buildings were little domes with balconies and chimneys: the entrances to houses excavated below ground level.

First we passed through a strong barrier that was beyond the ditch, before reaching a second, which formed part of the perimeter of an area that had the form of a rectangle, one of whose sides might have been ten miles long and the other six, as we found out later.

We were surprised to find so much order and magnificence in a place where there ought, in our view, be nothing but confusion and misery. Everything that was presented to our eyes was neat, well-maintained and rather beautiful in its architecture. The diversity of a thousand different objects contributed to making the long route that we had to travel seem shorter.

Eventually, we found ourselves before a magnificent porch, where there was a stairway thirty feet wide, by which we descended into the most beautiful cave in the world.

That superb apartment is five hundred paces long by three hundred wide and fifty feet high, with a very precious paving of large slabs of white stone. Opposite the stairway by which we entered there is another, as well as two slightly narrower ones at the other extremities. High on the walls, every ten paces, there is a ventilation shaft, and in the middle there is a dome about fourteen feet high and a hundred paces in circumference. Underneath that dome there is a superb throne, where the sovereign sits every time it is a matter of administering justice, or pronouncing some decree in public.

In each face of that rare edifice there are several streets, ten, fifteen or twenty paces wide, which extend to the extremities of the city. To the right of the first staircase I mentioned is the dwelling of the king, to the left that of the queen. All those major streets are traversed by others, also excavated with precision; they lead to the inhabitants' houses, which are in the depths in as many vaulted caves, a great many of which have a stairway leading to the surface, covered in a manner so methodical and extraordinary that rain, wind and snow are absolutely unable to enter. There are ventilation shafts and chimneys everywhere.

Every individual dwelling has a ten foot pillar before his door on which there is a lamp, which burns all the year round without interruption. The Senate, where the throne is located, is also filled with light-sources, in the middle and around the perimeter, which the consequence that it is almost as bright there as bright daylight in our homeland. I admit that that would be a great expense in the southern lands of Europe, but in addition to the fact that it is not the same thing there as we would see elsewhere, even if it had cost double, it would nevertheless have been necessary to do it, unless they had resolved to be eternally in darkness.

On the other hand, it would be impossible for humans to live in such a climate if the houses there were built in the same fashion as those in France, for instance. Being near the North Pole, those who have the slightest smattering of astronomy know that from the autumn equinox to that of spring, they do not see the Sun. One can deduce from that how unbearably cold it must be. They shelter themselves from the discomfort they suffer by retiring into dwellings like theirs; there is no means more efficacious. Their summer, which lasts six months, during which, as if in recompense, they never lose sight of the beautiful Star, is agreeable enough; for the six weeks or two months after the beginning and before the end, the weather there is fine, and one might almost describe it as warm.

In addition to the Lamps, which are an indispensable necessity, there is another commodity for the inhabitants, which is that at intervals, in the middle of the street, there are deep wells, accompanied by drains and sewers, by means of which water and other wastes flow away without causing the slightest stink.

When we first entered that hall, those who had accompanied us, as well as a crowd of other spectators, at whom we looked admiringly, stayed outside. Only the leader of the troop took us into the audience chamber and signaled to us to stay there while he went into another room.

A few minutes later he came back to fetch us, and escorted us to the King's chamber. The Monarch was there, beside a mediocre fire, covered in furs like the others, except that his were finer and ornamented by little white objects in the form of stars, to which was added a crowd of the same species, which he wore between his shoulders in the same way that the bodyguards of our Kings bear their coat of arms or some other mark of distinction on their uniforms.

The respect with which our introducer—to whom we had seen the others show so much deference—spoke to him made us believe that we were dealing with a great Lord, so we prostrated ourselves at his feet, but he made us get up immediately, and began to question us.

There was no Latin, French or Flemish there, so I did not understand a single word he said. When he saw that neither of us understood, he made us a sign to show him our rifles. We gave him one that was not loaded. He examined it for a long time, and I could see that he thought it an admirable invention.

I learned later that he had asked us whether we wanted to settle in his country, if that was agreeable to us; if not, he would have permitted us to go back, if we were able to do so—but at the time we did not understand any of that.

When he had made a sign to us to withdraw, we were taken into a room constructed like the others—which is to say, vaulted, with a chimney, benches around the walls, one of which is broad and hinged, like a soldier's bunk in a guardroom. That bench is covered in the skins of wild animals, which serve as a mattress, and there are others nailed along the edge, which serve as covers; all that is accommodated in such a manner that one can be as warm as one wishes.

There is no wood in the city except for the King's house, and for fuel the inhabitants burn coal. A small fire was made for us, because it was a little cold.

Until then, everything had gone very well, but difficulties arose when it was a question of eating the food they brought us—undoubtedly with the design of testing us, and seeing whether we could adapt to their manners, for we were treated better afterwards. It consisted entirely of a wretched morsel of smoked meat and a few slices of dried fish, which substituted for bread. Although it was not very appetizing, our Dutchmen, who had been at sea since childhood, found the meat sufficiently to their taste; they made considerable inroads into it. The others did not seem so enthusiastic, like me they went to work slowly. Nevertheless, we filled ourselves tolerable well, because we had a good appetite. As for the fish, it was impossible for me to take, but the others, who tasted it said that they had no doubt, if we were obliged to stay there—as every appearance suggested—that we would get used to it in time.

After the meal we tried to get a little sleep, but not without great anxiety, because, although it was a great consolation to have fallen into the hands of civilized people, which we had not expected, the difficulty of returning home, or of living with people we did not understand, whose maxims were opposed to ours, in a harsh, uncomfortable country very difficult for us to inhabit, troubled our minds to such an extent that we were in a state of continual agitation.

When we woke up, we were given more to eat and were then showed the door and instructed to take up our rifles. I honestly thought that we were being expelled, which, in the state we were in, would have further augmented my anguish.

As we went out, the King joined us, and we smiled with a good grace. He was accompanied by his court, which consisted of about twenty people, and forty soldiers, whose leader was the man who had brought us from our vessel; that was his Lieutenant and favorite.

First they sounded a horn, which was an instrument made of thin iron in the form of a ram's horn, with an ornate edge; and everyone picked up his weapons. That apparatus caused me to change my mind, and I conjectured that we were going hunting.

As soon as we had been commanded to follow the company, we loaded our rifles and went to take up our positions, with half of us at the front and half at the rear.

Scarcely were we outside the city than a wild boar, which was in the ditch, started running away from us. With that, six men peeled off and ran as fast as they could in order to get ahead of the animals and force it to come toward us— but they could not succeed in that aim. The fellow was undoubtedly a wily bird; although they tried to frighten it, they made haste to scatter and let it through when it charged, without any of them doing it any harm.

My companions were enraged not to have gone forward to show the King that they were more adroit those people, who had unleashed their arrows at the heavy beast without killing it. It was too late; it was running with an inconceivable rapidity and it as impossible to catch up with it.

For more than an hour we did not see anything; finally, we discovered two white bears of monstrous size, but as they were a long way off we divided our troop into three bands. The king stayed behind with twenty-four men and two of our men, while the other two platoons moved to the right and the left, each with two riflemen. I was with one of those detachments.

Having separated, we waited until we were both beyond the place where we had seen the ferocious beasts, and then we headed straight toward them, spreading out so that we formed an arc eighty or a hundred paces wide. The other group did the same. When the savage vagrants saw us approaching, they placed themselves back to back, one facing one way and the other the other way, and started growling, as if to excite one another to combat.

The Walloon who was with me was an admirably good shot; he would not miss a coin the size of an écu at twenty-five paces, and as I had more faith in him than I had in myself, when I saw that we were about sixty or seventy paces from the enemy, I signaled to those who were opposite us, but considerably further way, to bear left and then told him to fire. The shot succeeded so well that it broke the skull of the bear that was looking in our direction. Although stunned and mortally wounded, it uttered a frightful scream, but, having staggered three or four steps, it fell flat on the ground and did not move again.

At the frightful spectacle, its companion took fright and started running in the opposite direction, but it was not given time to run far; two shots rang out from the other platoon, which imposed on it the necessity of stopping. It lived for a few more moments, however, and it required two or three mighty blows with clubs to finish it off, for fear that it might still do some damage.

The King seemed charmed by the surprising effect of our weapons. He took us all by the hand to show us how content he was, and gave us all the signs of amity of which we believed him to be capable.

The bears having been skinned and cut into quarters, eight men took charge of the meat and two others the furs, because we had no vehicle with us— as often happened to them, for the King wanted to harden them to labor, and was indefatigable himself.

As we went back we killed another two foxes, which were also taken to the kitchens, and another wild animal with the form of a mole, about the size of a rabbit.

As we were moving along the sea shore we saw our vessel, and we tried to make the Monarch comprehend that we had more weapons there like the ones that we were carrying, and that if he cared to give us permission, we would go in quest of them. Not only did he consent to our request, but, after giving orders to those laden with prey to return to the city with an escort of six well-armed men in case of any unfortunate encounter—always likely in the region, which is filled with all kinds of rightful monsters—he came with us himself, accompanied by the rest of his men.

When we reached the ship, he put his hands together to mark the astonishment caused to him by a floating machine of that size. He went inside, and visited all its sections, of which there was not one that did not surprise him.

Once he was content, we all loaded ourselves up—except for him, who only took a rifle—with things that we thought might be useful to us: ropes, kitchen utensils, weapons, powder, lead, etc. Then we agreed by signs to come back shortly with enough men to carry away the sails, the food supplies and everything that was not too heavy, or attached to the vessel, which we would also bring to shore as soon as the ice had retreated.

We did not have to take the trouble; three or four hours thereafter, the wind changed, and carried away all the ice-floes, and apparently the vessel too, unless it sank; for when we returned we found no evidence that it had ever been there.

That loss touched us keenly, and it was then necessary to resolve once and for all to remain there for the rest of our days, and to learn the local language as soon as possible in order to be able to communicate with the people.

On our return we were served a dish of fresh fish, which was rather good, and piths instead of bread or dried fish, as before. A pith is a kind of truffle, a fruit that grows underground; it is usually the size of a sweet or Portuguese orange, but irregular in form, although approximately round. It is good, floury and very nourishing, and keeps for years without spoiling. What is also admirable about it is that the People have the secret of distilling a liquor from it, which is as strong as our eau-de-vie and tastes delicious. It is the only beverage they have, except for fresh water and salt water, which some of them drink almost indifferently.

We were each regaled after the meal with a small cup of that pithson, as they call it, apparently to console us for our loss, since it was not usual. I had not seen it before, and it is only taken rarely, as, for example, to celebrate some festival or when someone is ill.

As there are no idle individuals in that numerous society, it was not surprising that every twenty or thirty hours, we had to go hunting—for we were no good for anything else. I was astonished to see the prodigious quantity of foodstuffs that arrived incessantly from all directions. Some people came laden with piths, others with fish or meat; some brought wood, or coal and iron that others had extracted from mines; the quarries especially, provided work for a large number of people. Those who remained at home worked on the buildings or maintaining public works, preparing whale oil, which they obtained in large quantities in order to have something to put in the lamps all the year round.

The women melted the fat of terrestrial and aquatic animals, of which use was made in preparations, and among which there was a kind of salmon that they called diros, which grows to as much as a hundred pounds, and which supplies an oil better by far than olive oil; I have never tasted anything better. They sowed threads of gut, of all sizes, of which they made use for many purposes, for want of other materials, but principally for making fishing nets.

Everything they have is common to them, and they share in it in equal proportions; the King has a tenth part, which serves for the maintenance of his family his guards, and poor people who, because of malady, old age or other infirmities, are not in any condition to work and have no relatives to take care of them.

In sum, there was not a single soul who gave himself any respite. I recovered from my astonishment, however, when I had recognized subsequently that they only have three months to make provision for an entire year, since for the rest of the time the sea is frozen, the land hard and covered in snow, and the air so harsh that it is often impossible to expose oneself without having one's nose or ears frozen; when one goes abroad it is necessary to be extremely cautious, or to be in continuous movement.

Let us note, in addition to that, that nothing is done without difficulty or without risk to life, for although no one goes anywhere without a strong escort, or being armed to the teeth, the number of ferocious beasts of several species is so considerable, in spite of the continual war they make on them, that there are few days, so to speak, on which one does not hear mention of some disaster.

To my great regret, I saw one fatal experience overtake one of my Walloon comrades about a fortnight after our arrival. We had gone out twenty-eight strong; poor Petit Jean—that was what we called him—wanting to do his business, was imprudent enough to let us go on and to post himself ten paces from a pool we had skirted. One could not have counted to a hundred before a Blings, a vile creature formed somewhat like a crocodile, emerged stealthily from the water and seized him from behind with so much promptitude that the diligence with which we responded to his frightful screams and ran to help him was futile. The poor fellow was dragged into the depths before we had time to get near him.

There were often combats between men and beasts, which were extremely cruel, were often fatal on one side or the other.

Meanwhile, the good weather passed insensibly—I say "good weather" by the standards of the place where we were, for it would not have counted as such in France or Italy. It is true, however, that there are very few storms in that region; the sky is almost continually serene as long as the sun is above the horizon, which is from the twentieth of March to the twenty-third of September—which is to say, six entire months. Rain is not frequent then and the wind not very violent; even though the day star never reaches an elevation more than twenty-three and a half degrees above the horizon during the entire interval, its continual presence warms the air so considerably that it is sometimes as warm as in the torrid zone.

As I say, however, the beautiful season passes, and we had the chagrin of seeing the torch of the world plunge into the ocean and say adieu to us for an entire half-year. It is necessary not to imagine, however, that in its absence one can see absolutely nothing; total obscurity only lasts for about six weeks or two months, and at other times one can see, more or less, by virtue of the twilight after the sun has sunk beneath the horizon.

The King, his court and all the people went out to witness that sad spectacle. At the moment of the immersion everyone threw themselves face down on the ground, uttering frightful howls and screams. Some wept, others moaned; there were some who struck their heads or chests with their fists; in brief, one might have thought that it was everyone's life or salvation that was going.

That ceremony lasted at least an hour, after which they went to close all the barriers and avenues of the city, with the design that no one would go on to the surface except when necessity required.

Until then we had not yet dressed in the manner of the country, although our clothing was in a rather poor state; we were each given two vests and two long robes of soft and well-prepared hides, lined with fur inside and out. The undergarments, culottes and camisoles, as well as stockings and shoes—which were all of a piece and shaped like boots, without knee-pads—were made of the same fabric, as was the bonnet, garnished with ornaments, which came down over the shoulder. Even with all of that, there was no means of surviving for long in the open, or outside the houses where nothing is proof against the rigor of the air in the middle of winter.

As I was accustomed to exercising my memory to learn foreign languages, I perceived from day to day the considerable progress I was making in that, and I can say without vanity that before the Sun had reached the Tropic of Capricorn, not only did I understand everything that was said to me, but I could also express myself and render myself intelligible.

Having been informed of that, the King sent for me; that prince appeared charmed to hear me talking to him in his own language. Curiosity led him to ask me numerous questions about the lands where I had been, to which I replied in a manner that gave him so much pleasure that he sent for a cup of pithson, which we emptied together.

That familiarity pleased me, and in order to have the opportunity to cultivate it, I tried to recall the ideas of some of the things I had read, especially with regard to history, in order to engage him by that means to distinguish me increasingly from the commonplace.

I succeeded in my design; before long, he could no longer get by without seeing me. He wanted me to tell him everything that I knew, and he was no less ready to communicate to me the things that it occurred to me to ask him. One day, he went so far as to ask me to have dinner with him. His Lieutenant and the Colonel of his guards were also in the company.

I told them many things that struck them with astonishment, but I confess that what they told me also surprised me.

We commenced with their religion, which was limited to believing in, loving and worshiping an omnipotent, perfect Being infinite in every way, and to showing everywhere and at all times striking marks of their humanity to other men, of whatever nation they might be and whatever sentiments they might have. Then there as a matter of explaining the idea they had of Providence, in which they were extravagant, in the manner of Spinoza, in the school of whom they seemed to have been raised, since they only understood by it what we would place under the term Nature.

Leaving that matter aside, therefore, from which we could obtain neither edification nor advantage, I asked them when and how they had come to inhabit climes so distant, and so contrary to human nature. That expression shocked them, and it was necessary to beg their pardon; they could not imagine that there was any country in the world where people were better off, more restful and had so much pleasure as in theirs, so much force do habit and birth have in making agreeable to some what others envisage as intolerable.

"It is not a matter of preoccupation," said the King's Lieutenant, whose name was Bardan—the King's name was Ayamu—"but I should like to know what a reasonable person could want better in life than what we have here in profusion. One might perhaps say to me that six consecutive months of night is something frightful, that the cold to which we are subject is violent, that we are inconvenienced by monsters, that commerce with the nations is absolutely forbidden to us, and other similar things; but what is that by comparison with the advantages we enjoy over the peoples who live in the vicinity of the tropics and the equator?

"There is as much light as darkness in the space of a year over the entire earth; what you gain in France in summer for example, you lose in winter, everything evens out; a night of six months is sad, I admit, but one cannot deny that a day of half a year has charms that cannot be expressed. What is the small difference we have from the beasts of the fields, of which we are still the masters, by comparison with the continual wars that you have with your fellows and the frightful massacres that you entertain? There are three other cities like ours on this island, fifty or sixty leagues apart, with which we trade, but with which we do not have the slightest dispute. And as for the cold, we have no fear of it; our clothing, our houses and fire protect us from its ravages.

"We are, furthermore, provided with good meat, excellent fish, pure water and a liquor that surpasses the ordinary beverage of the gods. Add to that that we have pretty women, a benevolent King, laws founded on equity, within the range of everyone, and that we have few diseases, and you will find that, although you can flatter yourselves with a few advantages, you also have, by way of compensation, so many inconveniences and obstacles to endure, that the bitterness of the latter entirely effaces all the pleasure that one might attribute to the former."

"Let's leave it there," the King interjected. "However one looks at it, there is doubtless a measure of good and a measure of evil for all. A man is happy who accommodates himself to both, and is content with his lot." Addressing me, he said: "It seems to me that you are not satisfied with yours; I am sorry, because I like you; I hope that in time you will find it supportable, and if I can contribute to that I will do so with all my heart."

At those words I bowed profoundly, and then looked him in the face. "You fill me with confusion, Sire," I replied. "I am infinitely obliged to you for the kindness you testify toward me; I don't deserve it, and I assure you that I will be sincerely grateful for it for as long as I live."

"You shall see proofs of what I say to you," said the King, "and in the meantime, let us try to satisfy your request."

"Don't put yourself out, Sire," said the Colonel, then, "I know your history; it is catechism of children here; permit me, I beg you, to relate the broad narrative to this honest man. Bardan will be good enough to relieve my memory in places where he notices that it is playing me false."

"I consent," said the King, "but you're impetuous—at least, don't go too fast; when one is not expert in a language, one likes to hear it pronounced slowly."

"We are originally from Ogiria," Falmur—that was the Colonel's name—continued. "A bellicose nation, from a country situated between Europe and Africa, taking advantage of our mildness, caused by too great an abundance of everything, subjugated us, after having fled their own land to avoid the tyranny of their King Narsan, who was cruel and barbaric. We abandoned our homeland and went to seek our fortune elsewhere.

"Several other unfortunates, to whom fate had been no more favorable, joined us, among others the majority of the inhabitants of a famous city built at the foot of Mount Orson, which the earth had swallowed in its entirety, in accordance with a prediction made by a soothsayer fourteen years previously, which had caused the wisest to leave, while the incredulous and the stubborn perished.

"Russal assumed the leadership of that frightened troop, composed of eighteen thousand combatants and a considerable number of women, charged with children of all ages, and headed toward the Boreal regions of his continent. Their General was young and intrepid; he had intelligence, and was fortunate in his expeditions; people made way for him, there was no one, no matter how brave, who did not flee from his presence.

"The appearance of a wealth that they had not expected inflated their courage, and they began to treat the inhabitants of the regions through which they passed with the same arrogance that they had been treated in their own land. Those who refused to welcome them or to bring them what they demanded were sure to be punished by fire and the sword. There was no violence or crime that they did not commit in order to slake their vengeance or their passions.

"They were soon punished for their insolence, however, for scarcely were they the peaceful possessors of Dilson, an extremely fertile country where they had made unusual extortions, than those who had fled reassembled and, supported by their neighbors, who feared the same destiny, they were forcibly dislodged, and driven to the shores of the North Sea. After many battles and fatigues, which had reduced the adventurers to a mediocre number, they camped on a peninsula that was uninhabited, where the cold seemed intolerable to those who had been born in more temperate climes.

"Seven years later, at the beginning of summer, about four thousand years ago, there was a frightful earthquake, accompanied by thunder, lightning and such a horrible tempest that our forefathers had no doubt that the world was about to end. That extraordinary agitation broke the Isthmus that attached the small country to the continent, and the wind, which was blowing from the south, carried the island away with extreme violence.

"No one paid any heed to that prodigy to begin with; when the weather calmed down, they thought of nothing but diverting themselves and acting as before; a few Astronomers that we had among us were the first to perceive it, by virtue of the movements of the stars. It was found that the days, the nights and the seasons were different from what they had been before; that was confirmed by those who lived toward the extremities of the island, where they often caught sight of distant lands which subsequently disappeared, and by voyagers who no longer found the passages to go to other countries of which they had previously made use.

"Eventually, the good people were utterly astonished that, fifty-three years after they had abandoned Ogiria, they ran aground here; but either because the wind was furious then, or the waters high and extremely agitated, their land rose over the dunes and this one, as can still be seen by the inequalities, and principally the difference, of the terrain, which brought species of trees and animals here that are found in no other place I know.

"Their chief, Russal, was still alive; as soon as he learned what had happened to them, he gave orders to visit the place where they had ended up and see whether their lives, their liberty and their property were safe. Not all of those he sent forth on that expedition can have returned; the cruel monsters with which the country was filled had devoured some of them, and the rest arrived very alarmed, reporting that they would not have to battle against barbarians, since they had not encountered anyone, but against Demons; that they had seen beasts of frightful form, immeasurable size and an inconceivable avidity for prey everywhere.

"That warning obliged them to be careful. It was necessary, at the junction of the two lands, to erect barriers sufficient to forbid entry to those furious animals, and to make sure that while some were busy gathering provisions the others were not deflected from hunting and did not cease to work for the entire destruction of their redoubtable enemies.

"As the number of the monsters diminished, which required a great deal of time and difficulty, they advanced further and further, and made new discoveries. They found coal mines and iron mines in one place, and large areas filled with piths in another, little spongy roots that could serve as wicks in lamps; and a quantity of the good and useful things.

"What seemed particularly admirable was that while digging they discovered a soft, white, uniform material that cut as easily as leather and which, when exposed to the air, became within a month as hard as the most solid stone in our quarries without crumbling; when blocks were joined together, only being detachable by heavy hammer-blows, they remained united as if they were a single mass. That was to prove very useful, as much for the construction of buildings as for the fabrication of all kinds of jars and household utensils, no matter of what size, especially if they had to endure fire—as experience showed and as you have no doubt remarked since you have been here.

"In the meantime, Russal died; his son, named Sylfom, who succeeded to the throne, named the new land Russal, after his father, and immediately commanded, the season then permitting it, that they should try to establish themselves here. They spent a long time excavating the ground, and then commenced building and lodging themselves.

"Finally, little by little, over God knows how many centuries, this superb city was finished, to which, as you know, the name Cambrul was given, signifying *perfect*."

"But Monsieur," I interrupted, "can one be certain of everything that you've just told me?"

"Yes," he replied, "as much as one can be of a history as ancient as that one, and which has been handed down by tradition from father to son, for you ought to know that we are careful always to relate it in the same manner. One might wish, for greater certainty, that it had been left to us in writing, but that was not done. I don't know why not, unless the materials necessary for an execution of that nature were lacking. Perhaps they did not know how to prepare parchment; it might also be that they had no ink. We presently make use of the bile of the Arlan, which is a dark and luminous green, and which never freezes, but it was not very long ago that the small fish in question was discovered. There was always blood, however, which they could have used, so it appears that the art of writing was not in usage among them.

"At any rate, there is another tradition, by which it is claimed that the change that I have just mentioned came about by virtue of a universal deluge, which appears quite plausible to us, especially since navigation exposed the people of lands less northerly than ours to dangerous voyages, where, after having been shipwrecked, they were fortunate enough to find a refuge among us, as I have heard tell, and have seen myself in the most southerly of our cities. Those people assured us that a great continent they called America had been discovered about two centuries before, and, given that it was as rich and populous as it was, no one doubted that it had been detached from Asia or Europe by some extraordinary circumstance that was unknown to them."

"What!" I exclaimed. "You have seen other strangers than us?"

"Several times," he replied. "There are still some here now, unless they have died very recently, but all those who have come were obliged to remain, for the same reasons that will keep you here; because neither they nor we had any large vessels, and no one would dare to make a long journey in cockleshells like ours."

"It's true," I continued, "that there are people who have those sentiments with regard to that last part of the world, but there are also many others who imagine that it was once joined to Asia above the Japanese Islands. Those are conjectures; one cannot say anything for certain, either might be true. What is certain is that if it was connected to other parts of the world, there is no difficulty explaining why the Portuguese found it full of rich inhabitants, as ancient as the world, and that if it has been separated from them, it is easy to admit the opinion you have just cited, provided that by the universal deluge one means that a great inundation, like those of Deucalion and Ogyges, which occurred, the first six hundred and thirty-six, and the second eight hundred and twenty-four years after that of Noah.[25] According to us, that is the only one that can be called universal since it destroyed the entire human race except for eight people of the two sexes, who were saved in a vessel of excessive grandeur, in which, by order of the Creator, they had taken aboard, as well as the provisions necessary for a year, a male and a female of all the species of animals, without exception, that were under the Sun, and which subsequently repopulated the earth.

"On that subject, it has been expressly remarked that at the issue from that punishment of the human race, which had been attracted for frightful crimes, God made an alliance with humans and set the rainbow in the sky like a sacred seal, as a perpetual sign of that solemn treaty, by which he promised never again to make the earth perish by water, because he had been touched by compassion.

"We have Authors who sustain facts that are no less surprising than that one. They claim that the island of Antissa was once joined, in much the same manner as you have related of yours, to Lesbos. Zephirium, according to them, was carried as far as Halicarnassus, as well as Narthecusa, which became Cap Parthenio in Tartary, on the coast of the Major Sea. We find today that Hibanda was once an island in the Ionian Sea, from which it is now more than twenty-five miles distant. Siria was once an island, which is now far inland, near Ephesus. I could say the same thing about Derandes, Sophonia, Epidanus or Ragusa, and a great many others, if necessary. The world is subject to a thousand new changes. Those that are known have formed entire new islands of which no trace appeared before, as for example Rhodes, Delos, Anaph, Nea and others. In the fourth year of the hundred and thirty-fifth Olympiad, according to the Greek manner of counting, people were surprised to see the earth give birth, at a stroke, to the Islands Thera and Theresia, in the middle of the sea, between the islands of the Archipelago. And in the year of the Consulate of Junius Silanus and Lucius Balibus, Thia emerged from the sea two full hours from the shore.

"Plato, a celebrated philosopher reputedly as sincere as he was judicious, assures us, on the other hand, that the Atlantic Sea presently covers a country of immense extent, which was once very populous, and which, in my opinion, must have connected America to Europe—which would alleviate the scruple of those

---

[25] Ancient Greek mythology referred to several great deluges, which, according to Hesiod, ended the various Ages of human history. Plato attempted to date the various deluges in question and fitted his story of Atlantis to them. Attempts to accommodate the two deluges cited to Biblical chronology went back to the 16th century, and the historiographical endeavors of Nicolas Vignier.

who cannot comprehend how people passed over such a vast sea in times when no one knew what navigation was, to go and inhabit the Occidental parts of the earth.

"It is easy to see, if a little attention is devoted to it, how many fertile countries of the Mediterranean Sea have been swallowed up in Arcania and the Gulf of Patra, and how it has encroached on Greece. Similar accidents have occurred in Europe and in Asia, by the Propontis, the Black Sea, etc. There are few scholars among us who are unaware that Mount Cybotus, with Curites, a very famous city, have disappeared, without anyone knowing what became of them. Phigius, the highest mountain in Ethiopia, had the same fate, and was not the country between Gamalis and Galanes, filled with famous cities, swallowed up in an instant?

"Apart from that, there are floating islands, which could well have been transported from one place to another, without much difficulty. Similar ones have been found in the lakes of Cecubo, Rieti and Bassano. The Calamine islands in Lydia were carried by the wind, sometimes into one location and sometimes another. In Italy, on Lake Bracciano, one sees floating islands that, as they move, take on all sorts of shapes, which can be seen all the more easily because they are covered with forests.

"That being so, it would not be very surprising if your land had been one of these portable or ambulatory islands, which, after having stopped somewhere for some time, was detached by a great tempest and finally came to run aground here. Then I would be of the opinion that it was joined to Lapland, because toward its northern extremities  it still has a tongue of land which might well be the remains of the isthmus with which it made a junction.

"However, there is another reason that makes me doubt whether Russal has ever been inhabited in that manner. Those who have the slightest smattering of Astronomy or who only know the system of the world know that about two thousand years ago, the earth changed its situation considerably; that follows necessarily from the fact that, the Ecliptic and the Equator always having been the same distance from one another, and it being known that in the time of Hipparchus the Polar Star, which we see here at the Zenith, from which it is only two or three degrees distant, was then more than twelve distant. That difference might have been even more considerable in remoter eras.

"I admit that the world is new, in the sentiment of many people, but personally, I believe it to be very ancient. Several nations authorize my thinking, and although the sacred book of our holy laws, which I respect infinitely, seems to accord with those whose sentiment is contrary to mine, in fact that is only an appearance; the language of Moses is doubtless allegorical and filled with metaphors on the subject of the creation and the first humans. But even if that were not so, there is nothing more commonplace that to be mistaken in matters of Chronology.

"The Jews claim that the world only began three thousand nine hundred and forty-nine years before the coming of Jesus Christ; instead of which the Greeks take its age back to five thousand five hundred and eight years. They could as easily differ by a hundred thousand as by five hundred and fifty-nine years. How do we know that the first humans did not live for eight or nine thousand years, instead of eight or nine hundred, as the interpreters of the book of Genesis assure us? When writing passes through the hands of many copyists, it often runs the risk of being falsified. It is as unnatural for a human being to live a thousand years as ten or a hundred thousand; one is no more impossible than the other, and it would not be astonishing if the first people to transcribe the Bible imagined that the number of the years of the Ancients, which appeared to them to be exorbitant, was mistaken, and reduced it to a less considerable figure, in order that the assertions they were maintaining appeared less fabulous.

"Following that assumption, the globe we inhabit would have had all the time it needed to turn and twist in all manners, without diminishing in the least the force of the writings of our prophets. And to speak frankly, it seems that it cannot have been very long that the equator has been in the location that it now occupies, whatever system one follows, either that of Heavens that are eternally agitated or a mobile earth which is made responsible for all the movements that people are accustomed to attribute to aerial and celestial bodies.

"If it is the firmament that rotates in twenty-four hours, dragging with it the Sun, the Moon, and the Planets, it is evident that those luminaries, being of immense size, the day star alone surpassing the earth by at least four or five thousand times, there must be so considerable a tension at the place of their passage, which is that enclosed by the two Tropics, that the water, which is fluid ought to have been entirely placed into the most remote parts of the terrestrial globe, in order to fill the voids—instead of which we see seas in the environs of the equator and a great deal more dry land, proportionally, where the two Poles are. If it is the earth that rotates around its own center, nature shows us, by an infinite number of experiments, that the most solid parts ought to be encountered in the environs of the greatest circle is describes and the others toward the extremities of its axis."

"What!" interjected the King. "Are there Astronomers who imagine that the earth is moving?"

"Undoubtedly, Sire," I said, "and they are even the sanest. It would be easy for me to prove it to you, but as it is a science that depends on several other items of knowledge of which, according to your own admission, you are unaware, the explanation I could give you could only weary your attention and cause you difficulty. Let us rather conclude what we have said, that these changes being supposed, there is no difficulty in your country being inhabited, because, having once been in more fortunate climes, the people had gradually become accustomed to changes that had happened to them in an imperceptible manner, just as those who are on the equator have done to a heat that your ancestors would have been incapable of tolerating.

"If, instead, we reject that hypothesis, we would be obliged to admit the opinion that gave rise to our conversation, and which, although not impossible, does not seem to me to be plausible."

"Whether it is true or not, it's still certain that we are here," said the King, laughing. "It does not matter much in what manner our forefathers came here, when we know that the truth would not fill the smallest of our jars of pithson. Come on, let someone give me another cup, and let everyone empty his own in imitation."

That magisterial order gave the company pleasure; no one ventured to oppose it.

"However," I said, not being content with what I had just heard, "have you no written history of your nation?"

"Of course," replied the King. "We have it in good order, and very full, from four or five hundred years after our arrival in this land, until the present day."

"I beg Your Majesty's pardon, Sire," I went on, "if I dare to say that I would be curious to see memoirs of more than three thousand years."

"It is conserved in the Archives," said the King, "but our Chioux each have a copy, with the Laws of the State; you only have to look at it, whenever you wish."

"If that is so, Sire," I replied, "it is not necessary for this Monsieur to tire himself out any further in relating it to me. I shall take the liberty of addressing myself, in our name, to the master of my quarter, in order to have the volume in question. We now have leisure, and I can look at it at my ease."

"Very well," Ayamu said, "but I don't know whether you understand our manner of counting. How do you divide up time in your homeland?"

"In France, Sire," I replied, "we divide time into years, months, weeks, days, hours, minutes, etc. A minute is the sixtieth part of an hour, an hour the twenty-fourth part of a natural day, with is the time that the Sun employs to make a circuit of the world from the Orient to the Occident. A week is composed of seven days, a month of thirty, more or less, because some are longer, and twelve months make a year, which marks an entire revolution of the sun around the Ecliptic, from the Occident to the Orient."

"All those divisions are not necessary here," said the King. "We only consider the two spaces that the Sun travels, one on a circle almost parallel to the equator, when it is carried by the first movement, which we call a revolution, and that which extends from one equinox to the other, which is what we call a period—from which it follows that two of our periods equal one of your years."

"That's sufficient, Sire," I said. "I can easily regulate the calculation."

"Apparently," put in Falmur, who understood a little Astronomy and Horologeography, "what you call a month must relate to the course of the Moon, but as for your hours and minutes, I don't know what their origin can be."

"It's true, Monsieur," I said, "that we have lunar, periodic and synodic months, but they all differ from the months of the year. Twelve lunar months are only three hundred and fifty-four days, instead of which the twelve solar months contain three hundred and sixty-five and a quarter, approximately. That difference is what we call the Epact. That manner of counting was agreed because it was found to be convenient and easy.

"As for the week, many scholars claim that its duration comes from the seven planets: the Moon, Mercury, Venus, the Sun, Mars, Jupiter and Saturn, which the Ancients believed to have a great deal of influence over sublunary bodies, and to each of which they alternately attributed the power of governing a particular day, which are, in fact, distinguished from one another by their names in many languages. But there are entire nations that take the cause back to the Creation, based on the notion that God employed six days in making the universe and rested on the seventh, which is a ceremony we observe throughout Christendom, in that, following the example of that great worker, we work for six consecutive days on domestic or public affairs, in accordance with the professions we exercise, and employ the seventh for acts of religion.

"The hours were undoubtedly invented for the convenience of members of society. Waking and sleeping, and the other activities of life, might well have been fixed in order to have a determined time to which everyone could regulate himself—that is, at least, what we observe in my homeland."

"We do not render ourselves slaves of time," said the Colonel, "And if our solar quadrants, which you have doubtless seen, divide a revolution into four principal parts, which we distinguish by the terms first, second, etc., it's simply by virtue of a principle of curiosity, which often leads us to want to know how far we have advanced, or how long we have been attached to particular occupations, for otherwise, we no more have determined times for sleeping, eating or any other action, than for urinating, sneezing, yawning, etc. When we have an appetite, we take food, we drink when we're thirsty, and so on. That is our custom," he added, "but I don't think yours is bad, for any peoples who are eternally in difficulties, and involved in great and awkward affairs."

"It's more complicated than the usage you make here of quadrants in summer," I continued, "but what charms me are your hydraulic machines."

"The invention of some is very ancient," he replied, "but the others are no more than fifteen hundred periods old, as you'll see in due course in our history."

"To prove to you," said the King, then, "that we have empire over time, and don't pretend that it governs us, I'm hungry; let someone bring us food; no matter what sober people estimate, I need to have three or four good meals every revolution."

On those words I tried to withdraw, but I was obliged to sit down again. It was necessary during the rest of that session, which lasted for ten or twelve hours, and during which the table was set twice, to tell them about the various fruits, vegetables, kinds of meat and other foodstuffs familiar to us. They tried to hide it, but I clearly saw that the account often made their mouths water.

Shortly thereafter, the King wanted to go to sleep, and I therefore took my leave of the company.

I did not fail to take the first favorable opportunity to acquire the annals of the worthy people in order to read them. There was enough to burden a mule; every scroll contained the life of one of their Princes, written in a rather confused manner and with poorly-formed characters.

The history commenced with their second King, counting from Russal, four hundred and thirty-nine years after their leaving Ogiria. I applied myself to it for several days, without taking a great deal of pleasure in it, because I found nothing remarkable therein. Those Monarchs having no quarrel with anyone, and the people being perfectly good-natured, lived very quietly, without doing anything that merited being inserted in the work.

That lasted until the forty-seventh, named Eubron, who was as wicked and intolerable as his predecessors had been mild and peaceful. He took one of his sisters for a wife, notwithstanding the aversion she testified for a man who did not love anyone; but he soon became disgusted with her; he put our her eyes himself after they had lain together a few times and married another, named Daila, with whom he had two sons in the space of twenty months. Although that one loved him madly, the barbarian ordered his Lieutenant to strangle her.

The Officer, moved by that innocent victim's tears, let her escape and commanded those into whose hands he consigned her to hide her well. The King, unable to imagine that a subject he thought to be very affectionate could be capable of disobeying his sovereign, did not mention the matter again. He had a great deal of confidence in him, and marked the esteem that he had for him by asking for his daughter in marriage. Not being of the royal family, the match was very honorable, and infinitely advantageous, but the Lieutenant feared that he might treat her like the others, and with that thought, he refused without hesitation. The King was outraged by that, entered into an inconceivable anger, and without any form of legal process, sacrificed him incontinently to his wrath, in order to impress respect and dread upon his people by that swift punishment.

That example of severity did indeed have its effect; those who had been commissioned to guard the Queen were intimidated by it, and, fearing that they might be discovered and punished rigorously, went to the Tyrant and revealed the mystery to him. He seemed delighted by the fact that the Lady was still alive, but testified his bitterness against those who had had the audacity to join

232

forces with the King's Lieutenant to save her. He commanded others to go and fetch her, and bring her to him without delay.

During the absence of those timid vassals a young man, who had caught wind of what was being plotted to the Queen's disadvantage, came to warn her and advised her to put on one of his sets of garments and go to the other extremity of the city, where he would try to find people who would take her to a place of safety. It was only a few minutes after they had gone, that the men commissioned to come and fetch the poor woman came in, but after having searched fruitlessly, they returned and told the king that he must have been misinformed, since there did not appear to be anyone in the place to which they had been sent.

The Tyrant, who was violent, believing both groups to be culpable, put them in the hands of his guards, and employed other people to carry out his orders, with the threat that if they did not bring Daila back, dead or alive, he would infallibly cause them to perish. Those, being no more fortunate than the others, took care not to go back.

Eubron was desperate, and his patience had run out. His impetuous temperament did not often permit him to tolerate the failure to carry out an order immediately. The command and its execution, according to him, ought always to accompany one another. He had those whom he called criminals and disobedient individuals brought before him, who were fifteen in number, and commanded them to cut one another's throats in front of him, for fear that someone might impose on his credulity. To render himself even more redoubtable, he published a declaration that if those who were harboring his wife did not produce her within the space of a revolution, they and their children would have their eyes put out and their ears cut off.

Those rigorous threats were, however, fruitless; those who had the secret did not want to expose themselves to the rage of that madman, nor to be the cause of the loss of the Kingdom's fecund individual. Finally, the wrath of the superb King relented momentarily, and gave way to incontinence. He assembled his guards and ordered them to go and find the twelve most beautiful maidens in the city, in order that he might choose one to be his wife.

Although the example of the two predecessors intimidated the fair sex, they had no difficulty in finding the number of individuals demanded. The status of Queen effaced in their minds the impressions that the story of the Tyrant's cruelties were capable of making; the glamour dazzled them, and each one flattered herself that she had the art of pleasing to such an extent that she would not be running any risk of being maltreated.

All those who were taken to the King were charming, but there were two in particular who excelled in beauty and grace that, not knowing which of them to choose, he kept them both, on condition that he would marry the first who gave him a son and that the other would remain his mistress.

The older of the two, who was seventeen, consented to that proposition, but the younger did not want to hear of it. That refusal offended the King. "Well," he said, "I give you the choice: either conform to my will or die."

"O Tyrant," cried the virtuous maiden then, "so that is how you treat your poor people! Remember what I tell you: Heaven will never allow a crime of that kind to go unpunished."

"Ignorant girl," the King said to her. "Do you not know that your life and your death are within my power, and that I can avenge your insolence instantly on those who gave you the light of day?"

"And do you not know, Lord," she replied, "that you will attract by your violent and barbaric actions the malediction of your subjects, that the excessive crimes that you commit every day render you intolerable, and that it only requires one proud and enterprising man to render us liberty and put an end to your Tyranny with a single generous thrust?

"What have I done to you," she continued, "cruel as you are, to put my honor in compromise and expose to the inconstancy of fate what is most precious to me in all the world? You are the King, it's true, and I'm only the daughter of a commoner, I admit; the difference is great, it cannot be denied—but it does not come close, in my view, to the difference there is between and honest woman and an infamous concubine. I leave it to your disposition to take me for your wife or let me return to my parents; between those two extremities there is no other middle course than death, which it is up to you to give me."

The King, seeing the young woman's determination, tried to soften her and to make her comprehend the wrong she was doing to her own interests and those of her entire family, but his arguments were futile. The promises and the threats had no more effect than one another on her mind; she would rather suffer that she be locked up between four walls than take back a single word.

Eubron loved her, but he did not want to desist in case others followed her example. However, he could not resolve to take her life either, since by that action he would deprive himself of a benefit that he had not despaired of one day having the enjoyment, and he was afraid of attracting the punishment with which she had just threatened him. He decided to leave her there for a while and attach himself uniquely to the other, who also had fine qualities, and who, far from taking scruples to extremity, abandoned herself entirely to her destiny.

Although she had great presence, engaging manners and an infinite amount of love, people were surprised to see the King incontinently succeed the possession of such a rare and exquisite being with an inexpressible coldness. Helda enjoyed his embraces, it is true, but he burned uniquely for Sabeltine. He sent someone to talk to that beauty in secret, in the place of her detention, and subsequently went to see her himself. He employed all means imaginable, and attempted the impossible a thousand times to win her: ruses, threats and promises had no effect on her; one might have thought that the more he strove to give her evidence of his passion, the more she hated him.

That procedure ended up driving him to the last resort. No longer knowing what approach to take, he sent for her father, who was the foremost architect in the city, an honest man much loved by the inhabitants. In a few words, he made him understand what was at stake, and after giving him permission to go to see his daughter, he assured him that if, within half a period at the most, he had not persuaded her to accept the conditions he had proposed, it would be him who would answer for it—and without waiting for a response, he sent him away.

Sabur—that was the architect's name—went to communicate to his daughter the necessity that the King had imposed on him, under the threat of his indignation, in order to oblige her to obey. He showed her the advantages that she might obtain, and the danger to which she was exposing herself and all her relatives is she persevered in his obstinacy. In brief, he made use of the most forceful arguments and the most vivid expressions of which a father is capable with regard to his child, without it having any effect. The examples, the remonstrations, the prayers and all the most forceful representations he could make were unable to change her resolution. On the contrary; she protested that if he said any more, she would pierce her heart with her own hand, for fear that the right he had over her and the obedience that she owed him might make her forget her duty to herself.

While, on the one hand, Eubron excited hatred and scorn for his person in his faithful subjects, on the other, Rudomil, the protector of Daila, moved heaven and earth to provoke them to revolt...

I had reached that point when I was suddenly interrupted by a confused sound of voices, cornets and other instruments, which filled the entire city. The matter to which I had just been applying myself had made such an impression on my sense organs, and my imagination was so filled with disasters, that I thought at first that it was an armed uprising and that we were on the brink of being murdered, and that everything was going to be put to fire and the sword.

With that thought in mind I emerged from my apartment with my rifle and my sword, with the design of rallying to the stronger side, but I was quite astonished when I saw that what I had heard were cries and marks of rejoicing, because the day star, which had been absent for six months, was beginning to appear over the horizon.

It is a custom among those people, since time immemorial, that the first person who comes to inform the King of the return of the beautiful star, however small a part of it is visible, is exempt from work for a year. Everyone who can walk goes up to consider the beauty of the charming object that brings them light, with pleasure. Then they prostrate themselves on the ground several times. Three bears per year, which are nourished for that express purpose, are sacrificed in its honor, one in the middle and the others at the two extremities of the city. The people dance, sing and drink with such force that the Sun has sometimes made an entire rotation before they recover their equilibrium.

There is also some rejoicing every time they see the full moon, as at the summer solstice, and on days of birth, marriage and the coronation of their kings; apart from that there are no festivals.

After that little digression, let us pick up the thread of our story, and say that, in spite of the activity that Rudomil put into it, he had great difficulty in making the Partisans act. It seems that the glacial zones induce sluggishness, or that nature conserves a principally phlegmatic character. The peoples of the region have a great deal of moderation and patience; it is necessary to irritate them greatly to move them to anger, and it is easy to make them put things off.

The Tyrant was warned quietly that something to his disadvantage was brewing; with that he assembled the people, and after having divided the city into five districts or parishes he selected an equal number of venerable old men, to whom he gave the title of Chioux, as one might say watchmen, to whose guardianship he committed public tranquility and repose. As a result, instead of selected fathers of families judging disputes between individuals, as before, the Chioux became sovereign judges, each in his district, and had to take cognizance of all things and bring remedies to them, or, if anything bad happened as a result of their negligence, they would be held personally responsible.

That new regulation thwarted Rudomil's measures completely, the goal of which was liberation from Tyranny. No longer seeing a means to recover his liberty by the death of the governor, he resolved to procure it by removing himself from his presence forever. Often, change flatters us, and the hope that we have of finding more advantage in the possession of a benefit that only exists in our imagination sometimes causes us to scorn one whose enjoyment we already have. It did not take him long to sound out his friends in secret; he found a hundred young men and women ready to follow him wherever he wanted to take them.

Most of them were not unaware that forty or fifty leagues away, near the sea, there was a vast and dense forest filled with the most beautiful trees in the world. They were a species of oak, whose acorns, although they grew in great abundance, were the size of hens' eggs, tender and with an agreeable taste, to which only that of the chestnut can be compared. There were other commodities of life there, as considerable as could be desired in a region of that sort.

As the members of both sexes there are comparable to the best skaters in Europe, since there are some among them who can cover a distance of eighty leagues in twenty-four hours, they prepared fifteen or twenty sleds and as many small boats, with are usually between twelve and eighteen feet long, pointed in the bow and flat-bottomed, with two iron rails along their entire length, in order that they can be used on water, ice or snow, constructed of solid plants that are so light that two men can easily carry one of them. They loaded all of them with weapons, nets, food and earth-moving equipment, a few cooking utensils, and what they thought absolutely necessary to their new establishment.

Daila and the other women dressed as men, and under the pretext of going fishing as a company, as was done in those days, they left, without communicating their intention to anyone except a few venerable individuals who promised not to reveal their secret to anyone until it could no longer be disadvantageous to them.

Their voyage was fortunate; they arrived in good condition at the place destined for their retreat, but they found obstacles there that they had not expected. Although the season was advanced, the density of the trees had not permitted the Sun's rays to penetrate to their roots; the ground was still frozen, as in winter, and it was impossible to open it in order to make dwellings. In addition, that solitary place was the veritable lair of all manner of fierce and cruel animals; they were obliged always to be on their guard and continually burn entire trees, which they felled around their camp, in order to keep them at bay.

Finally, the ground softened and they had the opportunity to make crude provisional subterranean lodgings, the tops of which were covered with branches, which they believed to be adequate to protect them against the rigors of the imminent winter.

While they were working to form a small settlement and to make themselves secure against the effects of their common enemy, Eubron never ceased to move heaven and earth to gain the good graces of Sabeltine. He summoned her father again, and when that worthy man refused to speak to his daughter again because she had sworn that she would kill herself, he had his tongue cut out, in order that he would, indeed, never be able to talk to his child again. These inhumanities were unprecedented; no one had ever seen their like before.

Helda, meanwhile, despaired on seeing that she had not become pregnant and that the King was now treating her with the greatest indifference. She feared that her rival might profit from her disgrace, by accepting the bargain that had been offered to her so frequently, and labored thereafter to doom her. In order to forestall that disaster, she pretended to be passionately in love with one of Eubron's subaltern officers, and after having flattered him with the hope of possessing her and employing all his credit to mount the throne, she proposed to him to depose the Tyrant.

The man in question, who had ambition, and who know how much the public hated his master, did not hesitate for long over the path he should take. The first time he was on guard in the Palace he went into the Tyrant's apartment, which he had the liberty to do whenever he wished, and having found him unaccompanied, plunged his word into his breast and calmly went to rejoin his comrades, without letting the slightest semblance show.

A short while thereafter, the Colonel, wanting to go pay court to the King, found him drowned in his own blood. The spectacle made him shiver; he was penetrated by an inexpressible dolor, because he was perhaps the only one to whom new favors had been granted every day. The frightful cries he uttered at the sight of the horrible murder attracted all the domestics and soldiers in the vicinity. The murderer presented himself with the others and showed more astonishment than anyone.

A considerable reward was offered to anyone who discovered the murderer, but as there had been no witnesses, the deed remained hidden until the guilty party learned that the people were so overjoyed by it that many of them wanted to know their liberator, and there was even a considerable number who claimed that the smallest recompense that could be made for such a heroic action would be to put the crown on his head. Then he admitted overtly that he was the one who had struck the blow, preferring to risk his own life by taking that of the cruel and unnatural King, than to see an infinite number of honest people exposed any longer to his unjust barbarity.

Helda, in order to win the esteem of the citizens, applauded the arguments of which the instrument of her cruelty had made use, in order to advance her cowardly design, and said that since he had had the generosity and benevolence to deliver them from their common enemy, he would have no less grandeur of soul and capability to fulfill all the duties that must necessarily accompany the dignity of Monarchy.

Their plan did not, however, have the success that they anticipated. The Chioux, having assembled, remonstrated with the inhabitants of the superb city, that the Kingdom had been hereditary since its foundation until the present day, without interruption, that for five hundred years the scepter had not left that family, and that since the deceased King had a brother, it was only just that he should be preferred to all the other subjects. They extended themselves and great length, and broadly, on his good qualities and his conduct, which had always been above reproach; they spoke about the advantages that people had enjoyed under the government of his father and his ancestors. In the end, they were able to dispose hearts so well to the advantage of Humal that by common consent, he was elected King and Father of the Nation.

That choice gave considerable joy to the majority of the people; there was public rejoicing and there were few individuals who did not welcome it with pleasure. As soon as Humal had the scepter in his hand he confirmed the laws and regulations made for the wellbeing of his subjects, and swore an oath never to infringe them under any pretext whatsoever. He accorded new privileges to fathers of families, appointing them to judge differences that occurred between their domestics and their children, without the masters of the districts having any knowledge of them, in order that they would become more affectionate and obedient.

He dismissed his brother's murderer, as unworthy of his position, for raising his hand against the sovereign, but without imposing any other punishment on him, and took Sabeltine for his wife, with the consent of her parents, who were as delighted as she was that the young woman's confidence had been crowned with a recompense entirely worthy of her virtue. Helda, on the other hand, was obliged to return to her home, where she spent the rest of her life in the opprobrium and scorn of all her relatives and friends.

The people to whom the secret of the establishment of the new colony had been confided, knowing the tribulations that those poor folk were having to endure in a place far from any commerce, believed that it was their duty to make the new King party to it, in the hope that it would not be difficult to persuade him to recall them to their birthplace.

Humal, who knew the situation of the location, was surprised by such a bold enterprise, and immediately commanded that people should be sent with refreshments to sustain them and assist them to return, or, if they persist in wanting to stay where they were, to assure them of his protection and benevolence. He added to those orders that, the city being extremely populous, he would be glad to see other young people going to join them, in order to help them to extend their boundaries increasingly, and to enable them to exterminate the monsters that were depriving them of the diversions of going outside in the summer and of the advantages they might extract from many places if they could frequent them with more security.

I cannot lie; I expected, as I read the memoirs, to hear that the newly established had taken advantage without hesitation of the offer that had been made to them to receive them with open arms, but I was astonished to see that after having welcomed the advances of the envoys and received the presents from the King with the most evident marks of a just gratitude, they had sent them away shortly thereafter, instructing them to tell their master, after congratulating him on their behalf on his fortunate accession to the Crown, that they thanked him very humbly for the graces that he had been generous enough to make to them, that they would never forget it, but that since he gave them the choice of going back or staying, they begged him not to hold it against them that they would persevere in the resolution they had made to end their days together. They added the plea, however, that they could have free entry to his city and open commerce with the inhabitants of his Kingdom, since that might be advantageous to both of them, and that in time, they would not fail to communicate reciprocally by trading that with which Heaven, the Sea and the Earth furnished to each of them, which the other did not have.

That response charmed the new King; he took a particular interest in them, and did everything in his power to facilitate their enterprise, making available to them everything he had that was superfluous, and encouraging the youth of Cambul to follow their example and augment their number. As they had no lack of quarrymen, they did not take long to build houses and dig wells. They had no need to employ their time in other activities, since they were sent in abundance everything necessary that their land did not provide, they had no difficulty killing as such game as they wished, and the trees that surrounded them furnished them with more acorns in summer than they could consume in a hundred years. In addition to those advantages they lived in a harmony that would have been sufficient in itself to make many people envy their estate, although it had many other charms as well.

Each of the young men had taken one of his female traveling companions for a wife; they were married before the commencement of work on their establishment. Rudomil also possessed his dear Daila, who had only believed it possible to recompense the fidelity and services of her liberator worthily by giving herself to him entirely. The other, considering that she had already worn the diadem, had unanimously decided to reestablish her with the dignity of Queen and to constitute her as their absolute Mistress, without any restriction, but that offer having been refused, they awarded sovereignty to her spouse, and his descendants after him.

Following his wife's example, Rudomil did not want to assume a character that might cause envy and jealousy to his associates in the future; he contented himself with being their Protector and their Judge, on condition that they provided him with six Counselors and Assessors to supervise the conduct of the people, govern them and settle any disputes that might arise between them—in brief, to regulate everything in accordance with justice, equity and the laws, which they would agree together. Everyone admired Rudomil's modesty and applauded all of these proposals; and in order that there should be no subject of discontent among the others, he had them draw lots in order to determine who would be appointed to be Magistrates with him.

The Governor in question was then twenty-four years old. He was short in stature, but with a lively and penetrating intelligence, capable of great enterprises and possessed of a consummate prudence. The memory attributed to him was so prodigious that at the age of eighty, when he died, he knew all the inhabitants of his city by name. He had named the city after his wife, and it grew to number more than ten thousand inhabitants, according to those who had come to establish themselves in Cambul.

Nothing considerable happened during the reign of Humal, who was as good as his brother had been wicked, except that the King and Queen Sabeltine died a natural death at the same hour after having lived together for nine times nine years, to the day, without the slightest incommodity or disgrace.

His first three successors were no less blessed, but the fourth, whose name was Arbal, had no sooner succeeded to royalty than he began to spend all his days thinking of a means by which he and his descendants could appropriate the two cities of Russal, or at least lay claim to their sovereignty. He found no better means of furthering his hopes than to ally himself with the Protector of Daila. He knew that he had one sister who, in addition to the beauty with which nature had liberally favored her, had an infinite ambition, and asked for her in marriage.

Nothing similar had been seen before; amour had never taken anyone outside the limits of the city; everyone who lived outside the walls and ditches of their birthplace was considered to be a foreigner, and custom did not permit marriage to one of them. That being the case, it is unnecessary to be surprised that the Protector took umbrage at Arbal's request. Although he had sufficient penetration to see that it would not be advantageous to him, however, it was impossible for him to prevent it; the interested person had no sooner caught wind of it than she was personally disposed to consent to the Prince's request, with the result that the affair was concluded without any possibility of a delay.

The two newlyweds had once been together for a matter of days when they made one another reciprocally party to their deepest secrets. The king's plan was not the only one that he set on the table; the Queen applauded it immediately, and to demonstrate the lack of difficulty she found therein, she promised to persuade her brother, who was younger than her and had always had a particular regard for her, to render himself her husband's vassal.

With that, she sent an express message to Molion, which was the name of the Governor of Daila, to inform him that she ardently desired him to recognize her husband as the legitimate sovereign of everything that the Polar Circle enclosed, with the protestation nevertheless, that although it might be his duty, she did not want him to refuse, even if he only acted out of love for her, and that she would be able to recompense him; but in the case he were imprudent enough to refuse the Monarch, he would excite his hatred, and would by that excite a great deal of trouble.

Molion received the envoy very politely and showed him all the marks of esteem of which he was capable, but at the same time he made him understand that what he requested did not depend on him, that he would consult those who shared his regency and would willingly consent to whatever they decided. In the meantime he talked privately to his two principal Counselors, and then convened an assembly. The number of those individuals was small, and the affair was of the greatest importance, so they took the view that they could not, in all conscience, and without rendering themselves odious to the public, settle it without consulting the people, who had a veritable interest in it, since their privileges were at stake.

All the father of families received orders to appear at the Council. The Governor put the question to them in a manner so indifferent, and with so many marks of disinterest, that it was impossible for the cleverest among them to penetrate his thoughts and to know what he wanted. That great phlegm, however, did not temper the ardor of the assembly; there was one unanimous cry that they only recognized Molion as the Father of the Nation, that they wanted to live under his guidance, and that they would rather die than accept another while he remained alive.

The Envoy witnessed that declaration himself, with the result that he saw himself reluctantly forced to return without having obtained the advantage of his Master, although they were his Servants, and they begged him to have the generosity to continue to live with them, following the example of his ancestors, in perfect intelligence.

That response did not satisfy the King, and the Queen was piqued by it to her very soul; she thought of nothing less than avenging herself on her own brother, in order to intimidate by that means a handful of inhabitants who thought they could lay down the law to a man who could exterminate them in a moment, or call them to duty if he desired.

In order to carry out her pernicious resolution, she won over one of her former domestics, under the flattering appearance of putting him on good terms with her husband, who would entrust him with the highest responsibilities, and instructed him to pretend that, having been maltreated at Arbal's Court, he had found it appropriate to leave and to return to the protection of his former Master, in the expectation that they would do him the honor of admitting him to the number of his servants, in order that he could always be near him and would be able to murder him when he wished.

The man in question, who was bold and enterprising, was initially disposed to carry out Elide's orders—that was the name of Arbal's wife. As soon as he had arrived in Daila he went to find the Governor, and began by giving him the prearranged story, but when he saw the obliging manner in which he was received, and the kind offers that were made to him, his conscience was reawakened, in such a way that he did not feel capable of committing a crime of such black ingratitude, and exposing himself to the reproach that could rightfully be addressed to him that he had betrayed an innocent man who had declared himself as his benefactor; so he confessed ingenuously the reason for which the Governor's sister had sent him.

That cruel intention surprised Molion and horrified everyone who had the slightest acquaintance with it. Elide heard the news; she thought she might die of chagrin and said frankly to her husband that since remonstrations and stratagems had failed, it was necessary for him to employ force and to demonstrate boldly that he had the means to summon them to their duty.

Before going to that extreme, Arbal thought it appropriate to send a message to Molion to give him one last warning that if he would not see reason, he was resolved without further delay to set out on campaign, with the design of exterminating Daila and all its inhabitants. Misfortune determined that the courier, only being accompanied by the four guards who had been given to him for an escort, was attacked by a pack of wild beasts, which tore them apart, as the sad remains that were found shortly afterwards testified. They had only been given a term of ten days to go and return.

Arbal, who was horribly impatient, not hearing any news of his people, got it into his head that Molion had had them killed, or at least imprisoned. He assembled all the inhabitants of Cambul and selected ten thousand of the strongest, who had the reputation of being the best hunters among his subjects, and, having joined them with regiment of his guards, put himself at the head of the tumultuous troops, followed by a prodigious number of camp-followers charged with provisions and whatever was considered to be necessary for such an expedition.

Thos men, who had never made war, were immediately discouraged by the difficult march. They said frankly to Arbal that the dispute he had with Molion was domestic, and as it was of no concern of the public, they did not believe that they had any indispensable duty to expose themselves to the fatigues of such a long journey run the risk of perishing on the way, since the season was extremely advanced.

"We're going back," they declared. "It's up to you whether you continue with your regular troops; they're paid to guard your person, so we don't think they'll refuse to accompany you."

The King was extremely surprised to see himself treated in this way by people in whom he had had so much confidence, but it did not put him off. He made them understand that, notwithstanding the love and respect that they owed him, he did not want to force them to do anything, and that if there were none among them courageous enough to go with him to attack his enemies, then he would rather do it alone than have the shame of going back without having done anything.

Meanwhile, Molion's friends had sent dispatches in secret to warn him of what was happening to his prejudice, in order that he might take steps to defend himself and guard against being taken by surprise. The young man in question, who was tall and well-built physically, skilled with weapons and extremely strong and courageous, took five hundred volunteers with him, and went to confront Arbal, the number of whose combatants had shrunk to approximately two thousand.

As soon as they were within sight, Molion detached three of his bravest men from the troop and sent them to Arbal to say to him that, since their differences only concerned the two of them, there was no need to involve others in it and cause them to risk their lives for a cause whose only foundation was the pride and vanity of two mere mortals, and that if he wanted to come against him alone, or with one or two of his most skillful soldiers, then he would come alone to meet them, in order to conclude their quarrel by that individual combat.

Arbal had courage, and he knew by the silence of those accompanying him that the proposition was not disagreeable to them, with the consequence that before his immediate departure, they had only to go and tell his adversary that he was coming. His Lieutenant, seeing him about to depart, swore that he would never allow a delicate man, as he was, to go to fight alone with a mere Governor, who was moreover of gigantic stature.

With that there were great arguments, because the King imagined that his honor did not permit him to go with any second to fight a single man, however redoubtable he might be. Whatever he could say, however, that Officer did not want to abandon him, and preferred to be disobedient than disloyal.

As soon as Molion saw them coming he went to meet them, and tranquilly allowed them to unleash their arrows, one of which pierced his thigh all the way through.

That rude blow, which he had not expected, put him in fury, with the result that after having felled the Lieutenant with a single blow of his club, which was enormous, he drew his sword, parried the thrust the Arbal tried to deliver to his breast, and hurling himself upon him, seized him by the collar with one hand and by the leg with the other, and threw him over his shoulder to land ten paces away, so heavily that having fallen face down on the ground, the unfortunate fellow lay motionless.

As soon as he saw him in that deplorable state, Molion took pity on his destiny, and demanded of him whether he still had any pretentions upon him, or against the citizens of Daila. Receiving no reply, however, and thinking that he there was no need to strike the wretch again, from whose mouth blood was gushing freely, and who seemed bound to expire imminently, he went limping back to rejoin his men, and took the road homeward, extremely glorious, in spite of his wound, in the defeat of his enemy.

Arbal had been joined incontinently by his own people, who carried him back to Cambul, where he only lived just long enough to address bloody reproaches to his wife, because, instead of exhorting him to live in peace and concord with his subjects and neighbors, she had flattered his vanity and had engaged him in a dispute that had cost him his honor and his life.

Elide did not survive two months of that disgrace; she was so outraged that if she had not died of chagrin she would not have failed to use violent means to deprive herself of the light.

A hundred and forty-seven years later, a new colony was formed around a freshwater lake thirty-eight leagues from Daila. That small sea, which was a league and a half in circumference, was oval in form, never froze and was extraordinarily rich in fish. There was an island in the middle comprising about ten arpents of land, and some distance from its shore there was a chain of hills of firm, soft clay soil, very easy to work. At least five hundred people went there simultaneously from the two cities to settle in that agreeable location. It is true that they had some difficulty in establishing themselves to begin with, in spite of the continuous assistance of their friends, who were glad to see the foundation of a new retreat for animals of their species; but in the end they obtained such a good anchorage that their posterity became numerous and considerable in every respect.

The area between the lake and the dwellings that they hollowed out measured more than fifteen hundred paces. They found that it was a peat-bog—which is to say that the soil was sulfurous, mingled with bitumen and saltpeter, and burned very well, almost completely consumed. Immediately beyond the heights that they inhabited there were valleys, beyond which there were vast woods, where an abundance of yellow-tinted roots grew that were as large as beets and tasted rather pleasant, which could take the place of bread. Venison was very common. In brief, the place in itself, because of its situation, was delightful, and everyone there thought it charming. The man they elected as their chief took up residence on the little island; he lodged there with those of his family he thought to be necessary; the number was small at first but augmented considerably over time.

As the three Cities had continual need of one another, for as long as the summer lasted, the roads were hardly ever free of people, some going in one direction and others traveling in the other, in such a manner that large-scale commerce gave rise to the discovery of many things that had not previously been known, and which were of great utility, In addition, the country was gradually cleared of the ferocious animals with which it had been filled before then, and in consequence, the passages were much freer.

Finally, the number of inhabitants of the places I have named multiplied to the point that once again, a multitude of young people expressed a desire to quit their birthplace to go and establish themselves elsewhere. They chose for that purpose a place that they had already noticed at the extremity of their continent, between six and seven degrees from the Pole, situated on the edge of the sea, facing southwards. It was shaped like a crescent and rose in the form of an amphitheater over hills formed of a kind of brown stone as soft as chalk, which was consequently not difficult to put to work.

That entire terrain was intercut by little streams, which seemed to have their source on the summit of mountains that they bathed. That gave them the opportunity to fabricate an innumerable multitude of public drinking-fountains at the junctions of streets, in the markets and on the roads, and an infinite number in the principal private houses. They were all deep, and surrounded by coverts on all sides to prevent them from freezing in winter; and it was always necessary to keep the lights on for the convenience of those in quest of water. They also found a few mines of iron, coal and various minerals.

That abode was soon the most considerable and the most populous of the four of which the memoirs make mention. It was called Meralde, as the preceding one was named Persac. One of the most remarkable things about that famous city is that goats are bred there of an excessive size, so that some of the billy-goats surpass in size the largest English mastiffs. They have hair half a foot long all over their bodies, which enables them to resist the greatest cold. In the beginning there were very few of them, but now that the humans are established there and the monsters no longer prey on them their number has increased so vastly that the inhabitants obtain a prodigious quantity of milk from them, and use them to pull their sleds, in which role they are as effective as the best Friesian horses.

Their ordinary nourishment is a dry and insipid grass, which grows in the mountainous parts of the region, but they adapt just as well to pith roots, dried fish and the majority of human foodstuffs without every suffering any deterioration. It is alleged that those animals can go for a fortnight or three weeks without drinking. The males are quite rare in the city, and are kept there simply to cover the females, which usually give birth to no less than three kids at a time, and sometimes as many as five; but whether they are few or many, the master of the billy-goat always has the choice of one of the kids of the brood, and a large bucket of milk, as the price of his service.

I had reached that point in the Annals of Russal when the King was struck by a kind of apoplexy and died so suddenly that few people were even aware of his indisposition.

He had already disposed of the Crown in favor of the penultimate of his children, who appeared to him to have considerably more genius and to be much more apt for government than the others. The law authorized that choice, which was why there was no dispute between his brothers.

As there was only the Sovereign and his family, to the third generation, who were burned after their death, I had not yet had occasion to see the ceremony in question. We were in the heart of winter, so the body was opened up and the entrails drawn out, and after both had been salted, the cadaver was enclosed in a hollow stone in the form of a coffin until spring.

The Queen, the children and the brothers and sisters of the deceased were obliged, in accordance with custom, to weep once every period, for the space of half an hour, for ten years, not so much because of their proximity, but with a view to reminding the people of the loss they had suffered in the person of a Lord who had had such good qualities and had governed so equitably.

A month after the Equinox the body was taken from its sepulcher with much ceremony; the tears and exclamations of the spectators were not spared. That lasted for more than two hours, after which he was laid on a stretcher, which six Officers carried to the Senate, or the great courtyard of the palace, where he was paraded for a long time; for after they had made three circuits, six others took over, which was repeated four times.

When that procession was complete, the relatives came up one by one; the King's Lieutenant followed immediately afterwards, and then the guard corps, accompanied by all the Chioux and the principal citizens. When the convoy had arrived at the pyre, the cadaver was placed on a table, naked, which was enclosed, and having set fire to all four corners at once, those who wanted to withdrew. As there was a great deal of coal, the fire burned for more than twenty-four hours before it was entirely extinct. Then all the horns were sounded, as at the arrival of the Sun.

The College of the Masters of the districts assembled, and went ceremoniously to the apartment of the Monarch's Successor and brought him out into public, where he was saluted as the King, and exhorted to follow in all his actions the example of his Father of fond memory, and to maintain the laws in all their force and vigor. In his turn, he harangued his people, but with such Majesty and good grace that everyone was charmed by him.

The joy was universal; one might have thought that the pithson cost them no more difficulty than going in quest of wells; it was drunk in profusion, even by the fair sex, the majority of whom were still dazed three days later.

The following day, acting in our own manner, two of my comrades and I went to congratulate the new King. He treated us very kindly and assured us that he would have the same regard for us as his predecessor. He even did me the honor of appointing me, along with his Lieutenant, two Chioux and an escort of twenty guards, to go announce to the other cities the decease of his father and his succession to the Crown, to the prejudice of his elders, and to assure them of his amity and the desire he had to live with them in perfect intelligence.

I was sitting with Bardan in a cart pulled by four goats; the two judges were together in another, slightly smaller, pulled by three animals, and the others had little carriages with two beasts. We went at a rapid pace, by reason of the fact that the machines in question are light, the animals pulling them indefatigable, and the roads very straight, smooth and well-maintained. They are mostly divided between one city and another into demi-leagues of five hundred geometric paces, which seemed to me to be shorter than they actually were.

When we had crossed a quarter of the distance that we had to travel to the first city, we arrived at a place where there were subterranean dwellings, which are quite well-illuminated, where a few food supplies are always kept, safe from spoiling, for the convenience of travelers, which is done at public expense. We rested there for seven or eight hours, because our Ambassador was drowsy and wanted us to procure some repose.

At a similar distance from there, we found lodgings similar to the preceding ones, and so on until we reached Daila. When we reached the last way station, Bardan sent two of his men ahead to give notice of our arrival.

As soon as the Governor was alerted, he came out to meet us, accompanied by a dozen of the principal citizens and twenty-five or thirty archers. The moment we saw them, we got down and ran to meet them on foot, as they were coming toward us. Our Ambassador had a mark of distinction on his clothing, which was not unknown to the others, so the Protector went straight to him and assured him that he was very welcome. Afterwards he paid me the same compliment, and then also addressed himself to the Chioux. When these ceremonies were over, he took us to his most beautiful apartment; it was there that Bardan gave him an account of his Embassy.

All the residents were swiftly informed; they remained for an entire revolution in silence and inaction, as a mark of their mourning and their displeasure at the death of a Prince for whom they had much esteem. At the end of that interval, the instruments and cries of rejoicing were heard on all sides; people amused themselves and testified their joy that Yomaha—which signifies God—

had given Cambul a Grin, which is to say a King, and an ally, in accordance with their wishes.

At the conclusion of these ceremonies, during which we had been very well treated, we departed for Persac, without saying goodbye to anyone, because it would be necessary to pass that way again on our return journey.

It must be admitted that we had a great deal of pleasure there. The Governor's residence, which is, as I have already said, on an island in the middle of the lake around which all the inhabitants live, was where we were lodged. We were dealing with a lover of the good life who had nothing too precious when it was a matter of regaling his friends. He had more than a hundred gondolas made in various styles and sizes to divert them whenever the desire took them. He assured us that almost every day, as long as the weather was fine, he, his family and his Officers made use of those machines on the water as we might make use of horses on land and invent some new training routine. There were prizes for swimming, fishing and racing. Often, they staged little naval combats. In sum, they were never short of pastimes, which they procure by means of those agreeable conveyances, which had either two or four oars, and glided like the wind.

We witnessed four of those pleasure parties. At the first of them they extended a stout rope from one bank to the other, in the middle of which a goose weighing twelve for fifteen pounds was hung, which had been steeped in oil in order that it could slip between the hands of anyone who tried to grab hold of it, and they would not be able to get a grip. The Governor had nominated four young men, among whom there was one of his sons, to catch the animal, which was six feet above the surface of the water. Each competitor mounted a gondola with four rowers, sitting two by two and lightly clad.

The Protector's son went first, with an inconceivable rapidity, not by virtue of any privilege annexed to his person, but according to the right accorded by the casting of lots. When he arrived beneath the bird he leapt into the air, and having seized it about the body he remained suspended in the air for five or six minutes, but whatever efforts he made to carry it away by a foot or a wing, it was impossible for him to do so; the sticky beast escaped him and he fell into the lake, from which he was immediately pulled out by those who were set to look after him and had brought him there.

The second and third had no more luck than he; they were obliged to let go without the slightest advantage, except that a few feathers remained in their hands. The fourth tore away a leg with his teeth, the ninth or tenth another. Finally—I believe they had been occupied for at least four hours—one of the troop, who was a veritable Mopsus,[26] broke its neck and carried it away. The whole recompense that the victor received for his bellicose action consisted of a

---

[26] The reference is presumably to the Argonaut Mopsus, who understood the language of birds, and competed in the funeral games held in honor of Jason's father.

kiss that the Governor's wife, daughters and nieces, who were watching the spectacle, were obliged to give him, and to have the preference of the first course, if he wished, as often as he laid claim to it.

I laughed a great deal during the action, but I nearly choked when it came to distributing the prizes. The Governess, who was not old, and who still had a considerable residue of beauty, gave hers with a very good grace, and even presented her cheek to double the value; timidity and respect were the reason why the victor dared not take advantage of it. But when he approached the damsels, there was not one who did not receive him with a coldness capable of chilling the blood. His swollen face, his snub nose and his slack cheeks frightened them, and one might have thought that they had a fever.

He doubted that the cause was so serious, and, attributing it, with reason, more to his deformity than their modesty, he took hold of them one after another and, in spite of the resistance they put up, he defeated them so easily and completely that that act alone was worth as much the best comedy that Molière ever played in Paris. I cannot describe the pleasure that it gave the spectators in genera and our Ambassador in particular; there was nothing but continual jeering and bursts of loud laughter to be heard in all directions. Sometimes one extended her arms in one direction, sometimes another shoved with her hands in the other, and it is certain that those various gestures were no less diverting than the subject to which they owed their origin.

The second action that we witnessed only differed from the first in that, instead of a having to deal with goose, it was a man that it was necessary to attack. A fellow of twenty-five or twenty-six years of age, tall, strong and robust, who could leap like the most skillful rope-dancers in Paris, sat astride the taut rope, to which he gave continual wrenches, and never failed at each coming and going to provoke a tumble. As he held on tightly with both hands, and his clothing consisted of a tight pair of smooth leather trousers, all of a piece, and he was slick with oil from head to toe, it is easy to understand that he was difficult to reach. They only dared attack him one by one; often those who reached him failed because he was skillful at dodging, and when they contrived to seize him, either by an arm or a leg, he was so adept at slipping out of their hands that one can say in his praise that it was time and the continuous effort he was making, rather than his vanquisher, that eventually tipped him into the water, where he was so weak and exhausted that he would infallibly have drowned if people had not raced to his aid.

On the third day we had the Lancers, who, even though they were protected by good breastplates, often did one another harm; they tumbled into the lake all over the field, but they were usually so prompt to pull themselves out that their falls often went unnoticed. They also picked up rings, and contributed a good deal to our enjoyment.

Finally, at the last spectacle, a ten-month old bear was attached to a round table made expressly for that purpose, which was about thirty feet in circumference. The rope around its neck, which was attached to the center of that floating machine, permitted it to reach the rim but no further. Then barbet dogs were released to mount he first attack; after a quarter of an hour that number was increased by six more, and so on until twenty-four. Assuredly, I had never seen such a combat; it was long and bloody, with the result that eleven dogs were either killed or wounded before the ferocious beast was mastered, and it would have killed them all had not one that was bolder and more obstinate that the others, having had the honor of seizing it by the throat, held firm, not wanting to let go unless it was the first to die.

So many different pleasures, combined with the good cheer that we were given, had charms or me that made me reluctant to leave that agreeable place, and I swear to you that if it had depended completely on my choice I would have stayed there for the rest of my life.

Notwithstanding those advantages, it was necessary to move on and take the road to Meralde. I was surprised again by the situation of that place, where all the dwellings, overlooking the sea, from the top of the mountain to the bottom, being shielded from the north wind, were warmer and also better illuminated than elsewhere.

There is no need to relate here how we were received and treated, since the maxims of those northerly peoples were almost exactly the same; so it is sufficient to say that we wanted for nothing there, that they treated us with all imaginable respect, and that we were regaled with all the best and most precious they possessed.

While we were there the fishermen brought in a Monster, which was not entirely unknown to them but the like of which I had never seen. It had a head in the form of an olive some five feet eight inches in circumference. Its mouth, which was at the very end, was round, and opened to a width slightly greater than a dinner-plate. A foot from there, all around it, there were six eyes as large as a French écu, equidistant from one another. The animal had twenty-four feet, short and stout, which extended until half a brass from the neck, in such a way that it was almost indifferent as to which side it used for walking. The rest, from the navel to the end of the inferior part of the body, which could pass for a tail, was smooth and sticky, like the skin of an eel, always tapering toward the extremity, where there was a fin shaped like a bell, which rounded out or flattened as it pleased. The fish was about twenty-five feet long in total.

As it was good to eat, the Governor had it cooked in its entirety, in order that we should have the opportunity to taste all its parts, which were extremely different. The head had a taste reminiscent of mutton, the feet were closely analogous to our knuckles of veal, the body had flesh similar to that found in the claws of lobsters and the tail was very little different from our conger eels, except that it was not nearly so greasy.

The animal has no teeth, which makes me think that it lives entirely on water or some tiny soft fish that it swallows without chewing. The fishermen assured us that according to the multitude of their catches there must be a prodi-gious quantity of them, but that whales hunted them incessantly, and killed as many as they encountered, unless they had the good fortune to reach some nar-row grotto, whose smallness prevented them from being swallowed, but that that rarely happened.

On leaving we were each honored by a complete suit of clothes, and were given two more for the King, which were made of the finest and most precious skins that were found in that region, with bonnets constructed in a very artistic manner. We received similar presents in the other cities through which we passed.

On my return I found that one of my Dutch comrades had died and had been thrown by the roadside, as was customary in that country, in order to be eaten by ferocious beasts—which, as can be imagined, would otherwise have persecuted them even more. The rumor went around that he had been ensor-celled, with the result that the Master of the district carried out a widespread investigation; several people were accused of culpability and taken to the judge to be examined rigorously, but they denied the fact and were released.

Finally, an old woman more than eighty years old was arrested , whom the neighbors, who had suspected her for a long time, claimed to have seen entering the abode of the dead man with a forked twig in her hand, which she had hidden in his bedclothes like one of the pernicious instruments of which she ordinarily made use to cast her spells, after which, the Dutchman, having returned home, fatigued by hunting, had gone to bed to get some sleep and had immediately been gripped by a violent fever, which had carried him off the next day.

That declaration, formally made, with all the details, and supported with various examples, appeared so strong that, in spite of everything the old woman could say in her defense, in the disturbance that had been agitated, they were ready to try her and put her to torture, in accordance with the law of the nation, which ordered that sorcerers and murderers should be put to death.

The apprehension that I had that that rigorous sentence might be carried out caused me to talk to the King, whom I had only seen during a ceremonial visit since my return with the Ambassador.

My presence seemed to give him pleasure and he invited me to sit beside him and tell him in detail what had happened during our voyage. After having satisfied him somewhat, I raised the issue of the unfortunate woman and asked him if there was o means of exempting her from death.

"But how can she be disculpated," he asked, "if she has merited punish-ment? It is necessary that justice take its course."

"But it is also necessary, Sire," I said, "for there to be reasons sufficient to authorize its severity. I have examined the matter closely. The old matron does not deny that she was in my friend's apartment; it was not the first time; she had been there often to hear him talk about a thousand different things that happen in his country, which were new and charming to her and excited her curiosity to come to hear more every day. That reason alone, it seems to me is sufficient to justify her. In fact, I think she loved him, and that his death has touched her more than any of us.

"As for what was found in his bed," I continued, "you know, Sire, that idle people are not tolerated here; there is no one who dies not look at them with a malevolent eye. The poor woman being extremely old, but vigorous, occupies herself in order to avoid public hatred with making cords of gut, cutting forked sticks and constructing dormant fishing-lines. She came to see her child—for that is what she called him—with her materials in hand, in order not to lose time, and having learned, to judge by appearances, that he was about to return, she hid her work under his bedcovers for fear that it might go astray, with the intention of coming to collect it shortly and working for an hour or two in his company.

"With that, the pretext was found to accuse her, and the judge, who did not know that her accusers were her sworn enemies, because she is a pious woman and often took it upon herself to criticize them and administer lessons to them, condemned her without examining their depositions in depth, and would like you to approve the sentence that he has passed upon her."

"Can I be sure of what you're telling me?" the King interjected.

"It is quite true, Sire," I told him, "and I would dare to swear an oath that the poor woman is no more guilty than I am. But Sire, even if the proofs of her innocence were less evident than I have tried to make you see, and the depositions that people have taken care to envenom were stronger and more convincing than they appear to me to be, would it be necessary to deprive a reasonable creature made in God's image of her life?"

What?" said Benedon. "Let a sorceress live?"

At the manner in which he asked me that question I could not help laughing.

"What do you understand by sorceress?" I asked.

"I mean," he replied, "A wretch who has given herself to Demiotan"—which is to say, the Devil—"in order to be able to torment and afflict other people with impunity, and act with subtlety, feigning to be doing good, while applying herself with all her might to doing evil."

"That is an error," I said, "which the succession of time has spread throughout the world, but which many peoples have rejected, and which they are even beginning to mock openly in the majority of places where I have been. We certainly cannot deny that there is a Devil, since the book of our laws makes mention of him, although the Doctors are not in accord in all respects as to what is meant by the term in the original language, but even supposing that there is one, as the Religion I profess engages me to believe, I strongly doubt that the author of all things has given him the power and the faculties necessary to be able to present himself to us, render himself visible and lead us to give ourselves to him, and I deny that any rational human has ever had the idea or the desire of doing so."

"Which is to say," said the King, "that you do not believe that there are sorcerers."

"In the sense that you mean, no," I replied. "But if by that word you simply means thieves, poisoners or murderers—in a word, blackguards—inclined to commit crimes that are most hateful to society, yes. Expressions only have the significance one gives them, and one can as easily give it that one as any other."

"But if it were proved to you," Benedon interrupted, urgently, "that thousands of deaths are caused here every year by people who admit themselves that it in the sense that I mean, and who go to the Sabbat[27] every day, what would you say?"

"I would say, Sire," I replied, "that torture is capable of making an innocent person say anything you want, who would rather die at a stroke than be gradually cut into pieces; or that those to whom that had happened are mentally disturbed. That is a truth that I can confirm by incontestable examples, invented by design or discovered by hazard, which, I have no doubt, could easily convince you.

"It cannot be denied that we have a natural attachment to the marvelous; prodigious and extraordinary stories of invisible powers that act upon us and the malice of sorcerers please us, although our minds are often frightened by them. A force that we cannot resist is capable of tracing vestiges in the minds of many people, especially when they are ignorant or young, that time never effaces. We are weak enough to add faith to stories that are told to us, especially when they are confirmed by people of authority and maturity, in whom we have confidence.

"Given that, I dare say that if there were even one imagined sorcerer in an entire city, it is not impossible that there be a thousand of them before fifty years had passed, without the Devil being mixed up in it."

"You surprise me," said Benedon, "and you would oblige me by clarifying the matter with arguments powerful enough to prevent me from doubting them any longer."

"Imagine, if you please, a father of a family," I said, "who takes it into his head to be a sorcerer, as there are some people who are found who believe that they are God or that they have horns on their head. It is evident, Sire, that he will

---

[27] The narrator is presumably translating a Russalian term rather loosely into the word conventionally used to denote witch-meetings in Europe, as the Russalians have no week, and hence no Sabbath. Indeed, given that their history diverged from ours thousands of years before Christianity, it is very surprising that their beliefs about witchcraft should have so much in common with those fabricated by European inquisitors.

take pleasure in telling his wife and children what he has seen at the Sabbat, which his wounded imagination makes him believe that he has witnessed.

"He will tell them, for example, that the place is a palace, the splendor and beauty of which are so far beyond the natural that it is impossible to describe; that the one who presides there is tall, strong, robust, hairy all over his body, with horns on his head, which render him redoubtable, and long pointed ears; that he had a twisted and busy tail, which compels respect, thin legs and horses' hooves—in a word, something like the form of a satyr; that he is seated under a magnificent awning, in an armchair of exquisite workmanship, raised on a platform carried by four griffins, which is on a pivot that turns perpetually, in order that the Majestic Prince can examine, one after another, the faithful servants who surround him, and who come to kiss him, some on the feet, others on the thighs and the boldest on the backside, with the greatest veneration in the world…and a quantity of other circumstances that he will not fail to add to the fabulous tale.

"The disposition those innocent creatures have to hear such a surprising subject treated cannot fail to result in to the vivid images that have been represented to them imprinting traces of excessive depth in their weak minds, which make them afraid. The love and respect that those dependent and submissive members of the household have for its head does not permit them the slightest doubt regarding the astonishing facts to which he affirms that he has been a witness. They shiver to hear him, and yet they take pleasure in it, and become so accustomed to it that if he forgets something in his frequent repetitions they take particular care to remind him of it.

"The listeners receive traces that are ever more profound; the material gradually becomes familiar to them, and finally, the curiosity grips them to go to the imaginary Sabbat too. They rub themselves with the same grease of which they have seen their Master make use, and then go to bed and sleep. The agitation that has warmed them up, the vestiges that the animal spirits have had time to form in hearing so many marvelous tales open up, and cause them to see clearly the same objects and the same ceremonies that have previously been described to them—as it often happens to us to see in dreams the things about which we were thinking the previous day, especially when the organs of our senses have been vividly struck by them.

"And what I am saying, Sire," I continued, "is so true that these sorcerers have been found who, in spite of being woken up while they were asleep, and being convinced that they have not moved from their place, swear on execrable oaths that they have been to the Sabbat, body and soul, in places very different from the house where they live.

"In consequence, the best means of having no sorcerers is a country is not to persecute them and put them to death, but to treat them as lunatics. A thousand people will not take extraordinary offense if one calls them scoundrels, drunkards, card sharps, lechers, libertines or atheists, who would believe themselves to be deeply offended if one treated them as visionaries."

"What you say there," said the King, "seems quite plausible. I will, at least provisionally, have the person whose cause you are pleading released. As regards the rest, we'll see about it another time."

A short time afterwards, the King married Triola, his uncle's daughter, that being tolerated in their society; it is only a mother or sister that one is not permitted to marry. We were then at the commencement of winter, which is the season in which everyone shuts themselves away. I resumed the History of Russal, which I continued as far as Varinoul, who lived about eight hundred years ago.

One can say that the King in question was one of the worthiest princes who ever governed. He was handsome, well built, knowledgeable, inventive, judicious and perfect in political virtue. He ordered that the Chioux's tours of duty should rotate, and he assembled seven of them every revolution, at the first blast of the great cornet, to administer justice. He resolved to attend those assemblies often in person, which he convened when he wished in order to see how everything was going.

Because the Solar quadrants could only be used during summer, he invented a hydraulic machine for the division of time, which I thought admirable. He had noticed that millstones were made of an extremely porous rock, had one of them hollowed out and found, as he had conjectured, that water that was put in the resultant vessel penetrated it, to be distilled underneath drop by drop. In order that more would not pass through at one time than another, he had it lined with iron inside to a depth of two fingers, which was very cleverly imagined, since otherwise it was evident that, the stone being full of little holes, there would be a greater dissipation when the machine was full than when a considerable fraction had run out of it.

He also had a case made of another material, in the form of a calabash or a cone, broad at the bottom and tapering toward the top; then, having marked the place to which the water falling from the porous vessel rose up therein, in the space of a natural day, or one revolution of the Sun from the Orient to the Occident—which a easily observed in the fine season by means of a meridional line—he made a hole at that point in which a little tube was inserted, in order that the liquid falling from above would be obliged to flow out through it on to the wick of a lamp placed directly beneath it, which would thus be instantly extinguished.

That new invention was reiterated and calibrated with the Solar quadrants, until it was found that the hydraulic clocks were perfect. Varinoul gave orders that one of them should be placed facing every stairway of the palace courtyard, and beside a sentinel, one of the two hundred men who mounted guard every day. Those men were responsible for preventing disorders and sounding the horn at the moment the lamps went out. That lasted for a few minutes; there were other sentinels a considerable distance away who responded to them, in order that the entire city would learn simultaneously what time it was, and the judges would know when they ought to appear at the Senate in order to obtain cognizance of any differences that had arisen among the inhabitants.

The same Prince abolished polygamy, what then still practiced, forever, and ordered that every msn should have his own wife and every woman her husband, in order to avoid confusion and jealousy. He made a law on the subject of larceny, by which a person who had stolen anything whatsoever was obliged to pay double its value to the assembly of judges, who administered a harsh reprimand to him in the presence of witnesses. After a second offense the thief was held to be infamous; on the third, he was banished from all associations and those who came within two paces of him were allowed to give him a slap with impunity, or strike him on the back with a stick.

Another law decreed that orphans should be brought up by their nearest relatives, or, for lack of any, at public expense—which is to say, by means of the tribute that the inhabitants were obliged to give to the King for the maintenance of his family and his guards, buildings and similar things. Births and the attribution of names to children, as well as marriages, had to be made in the presence of four witnesses from among the nearest neighbors, not counting relatives, in order to prevent disorders and abuses, of which there had been unfortunate examples. And when someone died, not only were the neighbors to witness the fact, but also had an indispensable obligation to transport the corpse gratis, either to the water or the roadside, in order to be devoured there by fish or beasts of the fields.

No one was to wear any but uniform clothing, without any variegation or mixture of colors, men of one sort and women of another, with the sole exception of the King, who, as the Sovereign, had to be distinguished from his subjects. With regard to sick, infirm and old people, both in regard to the work that everyone was obliged to do and the other actions of life, there were regulations and ordinances that it was not permitted to infringe without incurring the censure or punishment associated with them.

All these laws, and many others that have considerable similarity to ours, and which I do not believe it necessary to report here, appeared so just and so reasonable that everyone, without distinction, applauded them and promised to observe them with all imaginable exactitude. So no reign was ever seen that was happier and longer than that Monarch's. He had four wives and twenty-eight children—seventeen sons and eleven daughters—the youngest of which was eighteen years old when he died, at the age of a hundred and sixteen years, after having governed for more than sixty. His history relates than when it was a question of burning him, he was put in a stone coffin in order that nothing of his body should be lost. The small quantity of ash that resulted was placed in a box, and when someone was afflicted by a unknown malady that could not be cured, he was made to take the hundredth part of a grain, which, it was alleged, never failed to have an admirable effect, and to render life to the dying, no matter how little faith he might have in it.

His successor followed in his traces, and was exact in having the laws rigorously observed—to the point that he had the forehead of a young man, who had refused to aid and bring up a little girl left an orphan at two years of age by his brother, marked on the forehead with a hot iron.

The latter's son, however, failed to imitate his father and grandfather, as much as they had tried to make themselves loved by the people, that enemy of the human race worked to attract the malediction of all the living. He was suspected of having poisoned his own father, in order to mount the throne sooner, to have committed two or three incests, and even of being a necromancer, although there were no convincing proofs of that. What was known for certain was that he was cruel enough to make the hair of those who read about his tyrannical actions stand on end.

He was a great lover of hunting and fishing, but woe betide those who were with him if he did not catch anything when he went out. As soon as he was a long way from Cambrul, they could be sure that if they encountered some furious beast on the way back, they would be obliged to fight it without weapons, and to kill it or be torn to pieces.

One day, when he did not catch anything, on the way back he spotted three prodigious bears in front of the company. That sight filled him with joy. "Go on, lads," he said to his followers. "You know my custom; it's a maxim that I wouldn't change for any man in the world. Arms are not in season here; it's necessary to be victorious or die; I intend, however, to be the last. If you all have the misfortune to succumb, you can see that there will be no means for me to escape; in consequence I'm risking as much as you are."

With that he detached twenty men and commanded them to hurl themselves full tilt at the enemy. One can imagine the carnage that those pitiless animals wrought among so many weak creatures. The knives, forks and other items they carried concealed about their person were incapable of saving them. In truth, they inflicted a few slight cuts; one bear lost an ear, and other had an eye punctured, the third the right forepaw pierced, so that it could not walk without limping, but all those wounds together were far from adding up to one mortal one.

The Tyrant watched that combat with pleasure; sometimes, a man was hurled ten paces away; a moment later, another would have an arm torn off; some were bathed in their own blood; they all had agonizing lacerations. Finally, the poor fellows all being dead or incapable of fighting, the King sent forth twenty more. It was necessary to obey, under pain of being accused of rebellion, which was a capital crime.

God determined that, as the latter party approached, uttering frightful cries to intimidate them, the bears were indeed frightened, and ran away. Some of the wounded men recovered, but nine died. That action caused a great deal of noise; many honest men murmured about it, and it nearly caused an extraordinary revolution. Matters did not go any further, however; no one dared talk about it, convinced that no one could do any more or less than himself about it.

Two years later there was another adventure similar to the preceding one. He was coming back without having caught anything, and, in consequence, chagrined, in a very bad mood. They were not far from the city when they saw a Blings on the edge of a marsh, which came directly toward them, as if issuing a challenge.

One of the ten who were detached to attack it had taken precautions; he had made a blade half a foot long, which had two sharp points at each end, about two inches apart, and which he always carried about his person in case of need. As soon as he was within ten feet of the animal, which was coming in his direction, open-mouthed, with a meaning expression capable of making the most fearless man in the world shiver, he took hold of his spur and, holding it couched lengthwise in his hand, presented it at arm's length, exciting it in order that it would advance to bite it. The Dragon eyed the prey, stretched out its neck and swallow the Soldier's arm—but it was trapped when, suddenly trying to close its jaws, it felt the sharp iron points entering its flesh above and below, which the intrepid hunter had lifted up at the moment when he saw that he was in danger of seeing his limb cut off by a set of teeth as long and pointed as awls.

The embarrassment in which furious beast found itself is incapable of accurate expression; it spun around and contorted its body in a hundred ways to give evidence of its pain. It reached into its mouth with its paws in order to pull that inconvenient torn out, which sank deeper as it moved. Meanwhile, its enemies were not keeping their arms folded; daggers thrust tellingly, and stones rained down on its body like hail.

The King watched that farce from a distance with astonishment; he could not conceive how a frightful monster like that one could allow itself to be struck down by blows without doing anything to defend itself except to keep its mouth eternally open. Finally, he was seized by confusion when he saw the Dragon, all bloodied, turn around and retreat precipitately into its miry marsh, toward the middle of which there was a pool of extraordinary depth, where it was impossible to follow it.

An honest man would have been charmed by the inventiveness and bravery of the man who had just performed a veritably heroic action; on the contrary, the Tyrant appeared so outraged that he hesitated more than once as to whether to take his life personally. He contented himself, however, with telling them all very emphatically that if it ever happened again, in violation of the prohibition that he had imposed on making use of anything whatsoever except their natural weapons, stones and anything else that came to hand on the way, to combat the ferocious beasts they encountered on the way back from a fruitless hunt, he would hack them into little pieces with his own hands.

Although he treated the citizens a little more humanely than his soldiers, he did not forgive them anything. When anyone let the lamp in front of his door go out, for want of oil, threw ordure into the street, or neglected to complain when someone had done him wrong, or took the slightest step that gave the Prince occasion to accuse him of a felony, he was certain to be severely punished. The punishment that the Tyrant imposed most frequently, and in which he took a singular pleasure, was that of sitting the victim on a rope, whose two ends were attached to the ceiling two feet apart, the middle of which hung down to a similar distance from the ground, of tying his arms and legs together in order to be able to swing him very easily, and to shove him, at each pass, against the wall, more or less forcefully, in accordance with the imagined magnitude of the crime he had committed, or the passion that dominated him.

That was how the malevolent King treated his people for the nine consecutive years that he reigned, after which he came to a tragic end. He had gone whaling, and had already taken several monsters when, as his men were occupied in dragging one on to the shore, a marine Dragon emerged from the water, seized him by one leg, and carried him away before he had time to shout for help. Several people saw the spectacle from a distance, but it was impossible for them to remedy the situation. The beast that had seized the Tyrant carried him off into the depths of the sea, and apparently made use of him as fodder; at least, he was never seen again. No one missed him; his own wife seemed delighted to be liberated.

As he had no male children, his brother succeeded him. His predecessor's example had rendered him sage, and people had every reason to praise his ways of acting. One might even say that he went from one extreme to the other, and that he was too good, or, at least that he lived too familiarly with the inhabitants of the city. There were few days on which he did not go out to the houses of individuals that he knew; he ate with them and invited them to his home, and treated them as his fellows most of the time. That had a marvelous effect on the minds of honest people, but there were some of lesser caliber who abused his generosity, entirely losing respect for him and seeming to be scornful of his person. It is very true that one can sin by default as well as by excess; there is a medium in everything, but not everyone is capable of finding it. At any rate, that good King was happy from the beginning of his reign to the end, and governed for some forty years without experiencing any reversal of fortune.

While I was occupied in reading the history, the King sent for me frequently in order to converse with me. He wanted me to tell him the slightest detail of the things I saw.

One day, as I was telling him the story of the life of Merac, the successor of Varinoul, he said to me: "You have in that man an example of virtue that has no parallel, although, strictly speaking, he did nothing worthy of note. He was known nevertheless for his extraordinary bounty, which made people speak of him as the consummation of centuries. What contributed most to conserve his memory, however, was something that is claimed to have happened during his time, which was as strange as anything you have heard in your life. I ought to tell you about it in detail."

"It would do me great honor, Sire," I replied, "if you would take the trouble; I will listen to you with pleasure."

"It was toward the end of winter," said the King, "and it was intolerably cold, as it usually is in these parts, when all of a sudden, everyone was surprised to hear someone knocking very forcefully on one of the doors of the palace and uttering frightful cries, like a person in extreme difficulties whose is in danger of perishing if someone does not run promptly to his aid. The Officer on duty came to inform the King. That easy-going Prince gave orders that someone should go immediately to find out what it was. Those who went to see, finding a man stiff with cold, did not think it was a time for lengthy interrogations, and began by helping him to descend, until he was better able to talk.

"As soon as he had been brought into the guard-room and placed beside the fire, he was recognized as one of the inhabitants of the city, who was believed to have died seven or eight months previously. That was reported to Merac, who had him brought to his room, gave him a cup of pithson, and invited him to arm himself and recover his strength—for although he was able to swallow he was not yet able to speak.

"The care that was given to the poor man eventually enabled him to pull himself together. As soon as the King perceived that, he said: 'Well, how are you now?'

"'As well as can be,' he replied. 'I did not think, Sire, that I would have the honor of seeing you again, for although I was in a good enough state when I reached the barrier, I had so much difficult in climbing it that if God, by virtue of a particular grace, had not given me the strength and, so to speak, carried me over it, it would have been a thousand chances to one that I would have perished.'

"'But where have you come from, then in this season when no one ever goes out?' Merac interjected.

"'I don't know that myself,' he replied. 'It's not, however, a dream that I've had. The adventure was utterly marvelous, I admit, but I find so much coherency in its contents that I can't help adding faith to it, and convincing myself that there is nothing but verity in it.'

"'Tell me, then, what it is,' said the King. 'I'm impatient to know; you've already delayed too long in telling me.'

"'It's impossible, Sire, for me to determine any time in the detail of the adventures that I underwent; the country that I've come from does not know any. All that I can say for certain is that the sky was serene and the season the most agreeable of the year when I went out with fifteen of my neighbors, all men from the Serdion district who were partial to hunting.

"'We had been beating the country for at least half a day, without having caught anything much, when finally having discovered a Eumale, I set off in pursuit of it with all my might. At the same time, my comrades were attacked by two hungry bears, and I heard the noise immediately, but at a distance. Unable to resolve myself to abandoning a rare animal destined for Your Majesty's usage, and imagining, on the other hand, that the number of our hunters would be able to reckon with those two ponderous beasts, I pushed on ahead, and was separated so distantly from my fellows that, the quarry having suddenly disappeared—I don't know how—and having reflected briefly on what had happened, I perceived that I could no longer hear them.

"'With that, I was gripped by fear; I was not unaware of the danger there was in being alone in a desert region, and, in addition to that, one might say that I had a presentiment of what was about to happen to me. In fact, I had not taken two hundred steps when the sight of a horrible monster, which presented itself before me as if it had emerged from the depths of an abyss, chilled my blood, to the point of no longer permitting me to put one foot in front of the other.

"'Fortunately, it stayed there, planted like a fence-post, without moving, content to grind its teeth at me and stare at me furiously with its sparkling eyes—which would have intimidated the most intrepid of men. That interval of time, which might have completed my distress, gave me the time to pull myself together and strength came back to me with courage. Having drawn my bow, I put myself in a position to unleash a forceful arrow if the desire took it to have a closer look.

"'The movements I made, passing in my crazed mind for threats, excited its wrath; it stretched out its neck, foaming at the mouth, and without postponing for an instant the execution of its pernicious design, it came toward me, growling, in order to tear me apart and eat me all the way to the bowels. I did not want to give it time to fall upon me; as soon as it was within range, I released my arrow, with all the more violence because my weapons were good, and pierced it through the body.

"'That wound, which probably ought to have deterred it, animated it further; it came forward more rapidly, although it was limping, because it was wounded in the hindquarters. I was not idle, however; I had drawn my bow again, before it was close enough to take its vengeance, and shot a second arrow. Unfortunately, I did not hit it. I dared not turn my back on that monstrous beast, however; I beat a retreat, always moving backwards, while it advanced toward me, moving more rapidly than me.

"'Finally, as I prepared to release a final arrow, and then try to escape by running if I missed, the ground vanished from beneath my feet, and I fell into a frightful precipice, which nevertheless had sufficient slope for me to roll, with the result that when I reached the bottom, I found that it was fear that had done me the most harm. That was consoling, on the one hand, all the more so because that fall had enabled me to avoid being devoured in a pitiless manner; but on the other hand, the situation was distressing, in that I could not see any human means of getting back up again.

"'The abyss was immense in its depth, and the heights that surrounded it all seemed to me to be equally steep. I made a tour several times, with a deathly sweat on my brow, without finding any place that favored an emergence. *My God, what have you done*, I said to myself, *to bring this punishment down on yourself? Have I offended my king or my neighbor in the slightest respect? No. Heaven is just, however, so I must have sinned in some fashion. If my dear wife and children knew, perhaps time would be able to console them, but what will they think has become of me, and what would my comrades say about my imprudence? The harm is done; there's no remedy for it, and it will cost me my life unless Providence contrives a miracle to get me out of this mess.*

"'As nothing escaped my research, and I examined rigorously all the objects that offered themselves to my sight, I noticed holes that appeared to me to pierce the inaccessible terraces that were an obstacle to my liberty horizontally. I visited several of them, one after another, without discerning anything that seemed to favor my exit, but after all, what can one do? When danger seems inevitable, one attempts the impossible in desperation. Already having death before my eyes, I thought that I might as well be buried alive as survive in such disgrace, and that the worst that could happen to me in plunging into one of the cavities would be to hasten my death by a few days, which would not be as bad as spending them in profound mourning and inexpressible misery.

"'The opening that I chose was, in truth, very narrow; my body had all the trouble in the world getting through it, and my legs were scarcely inside than I began to repent of having engaged into such a lugubrious passage. I had made such great efforts that my strength was exhausted, and I remained absolutely motionless, without being able to stir. When I had got my breath back, I wanted to go back, in the hope of finding a better discovery elsewhere, but finding that to be impossible, and sensing that the passage became broader as it extended, I made a new attempt and advanced about as far as I had the first time. Although that took much less effort, it had been such a long time since I had had any rest that I allowed myself to become drowsy and fall asleep.

"'I slept tranquilly until I was woken up by a thunderous voice, which said to me twice, in different terms: *Raoul, Raoul, what are you doing? Don't you realize that you're ready to faint? Go on, go forward, and you'll eventually arrive in the abode of the blessed.*

"'That language surprised me; I had no idea what to conclude from it. Sometimes I attributed the sound to a supernatural cause, sometimes I took it for an effect of my anxiety or a strong imagination, which could easily form chimeras capable of flattering me with a prompt and agreeable deliverance. It often came to my mind that the abode of the blessed ought properly to signify the state in which men find themselves when they emerge from this life, and to which my fatal destiny was impelling me, in order to increase the infinite number of the dead.

"'While I was giving myself the trouble of forming conjectures about the future, a sweet odor that embalmed the entire cavern made itself felt so agreeably that I changed my sentiment incontinently and conceived favorable hopes. So I began to drag myself along again with more courage than ever.

"'I advanced considerably, and I don't think I had covered a demi-quarter of a league when I found myself in an open space; I could easily support myself on my hands and knees. Sensing that I was less impeded than usual, I raised my head, and God knows with what astonishment I was struck when a faint light suddenly presented itself to my eyes; the joy I felt is assuredly inexpressible.

"'I had no doubt,' Raoul continued, 'that I had traversed the base of a mountain, which was open to daylight, and I believed that all the more easily because the region was filled with all sorts of strong and industrious animals. It was probably some of them that had opened the passage, as much to go their own way as to have a retreat from others more malevolent than them or to shelter from the rigors of winter. An objective so agreeable and unexpected redoubled my strength; close as I was, I nevertheless still had some distance to travel.

"'The light I had seen was augmented with every step I took; finally, I emerged from the long and arduous burrow. But O Heaven, how surprised I was when I saw that I was in an enchanted place, where the slightest object offered to my senses had inconceivable charms!

"'That ravishing abode had an extent much further than the range of my eyesight. Its floor was nothing but a tissue of all kinds of fine and brilliant stones, of which I did not know the name of a single one. The vault was enriched with precious pearls of an extraordinary size, as round as if they had been cast in molds. In the middle, a globe of fire was suspended, which rendered everything that could be seen in that beautiful place dazzling.

"'What I found most remarkable of all was that it was inhabited by a infinite number of little creatures with human faces, as naked as a hand, and scattered high and low, in the air, in the water and on the ground. My presence frightened all those in the vicinity, which moved away to a distance of two hundred paces without pausing, but having then turned round and considered me with application, a band of two or three hundred separated from the others and flew toward me.

"'Their number did not frighten me; people about two feet tall, devoid of clothing and offensive or defensive weapons, cheerful, agreeable and laughing, did seem to me to be capable of occasioning any dread.

"'As soon as they had joined me, the foremost of them said: "Who are you, my friend?"

""'I'm an honest man, my good child," I replied. "Your servant, your slave; I'm whatever you want me to be."'"

"Forgive me, Sire," I interrupted. "Is it history that you're telling me, or are you adding something of your own? To speak frankly, that dialogue is a trifle suspect; I have difficulty believing that people of such different estates could understand one another; it's doubtless to embellish the tale and render it more intelligible that they're being made to speak the same language."

"I'm relating word for word what is in the story," the King replied. "When all the inhabitants of Russal tell it to one another, they don't differ by a single syllable; that would a crime for which they would be responsible. What can be said about your objection is that at similar conjunctures, even if they only happen once, the blessed, who are apparently not unaware of anything, can accommodate themselves to the weaknesses of mortals, and that between themselves they express themselves in different manner—but let me continue."

"With all my heart, Sire," I said. "In any case, what I said was only to make you laugh."

"'You are very welcome,' the other said.'" the King continued, "'but I do not understand how a giant, a gross man covered in hair like a ferocious beast, has been introduced among us? Who brought you here?'

"'It's a mystery,' my dear child, Raoul continued. 'By your own confession, it is hidden from you; I swear to you that I even don't know, and that I don't understand anything about it. I can only say that I left my home in company to go hunting, that I was separated from my companions, that a terrible beast frightened me, and pursued me until I fell into a precipice, where I thought I would never reach the bottom, and in which, after having searched in vain for a way to get out, I finally found a hole, into which despair caused me to venture, and by means of which I reached this superb Palace, but to say by whom all that was directed, and for what end, is not within my power. But who are you, in order that I might know you?'

"'A fine demand,' said the other. 'Do you not see, or can you not conjecture? We are glorified humans, the Elect of Yomaha, and this is our abode, where we are to live eternally together; it is indeed the Palace of glory.'

"'What! You're adult humans!' said Raoul. 'I took you in good faith for children, and even for slightly deformed children.'

"'What do you call deformed?' replied the saint. 'Do you imagine that it is the size and arrangement of the parts of the body that make a human? It is the form, my friend, that veritably constitutes their essence. We have also once been citizens of Cambul or the other neighboring cities, and of a stature equal to yours; presently, we are small and inhabit this place here. Providence is wise, it makes everything in perfection; its works are always proportionate to the ends and uses to which it has destined them. When we were mortal, subject to a thousand different infirmities, and natural functions could often not be served without application, care, work and difficulty, we needed strong, large, robust bodies and organs appropriate to what nature indispensably demanded of us for our existence; today, when it is only a matter of enjoying the delights of an eternal bliss, that gross mass of flesh would be more harmful to us than advantageous.

"'Our little bodies, light and composed of porous and delicate parts; our slender hands, our short feet, long thin fingers joined by little webs of skin like those of geese; and these membranes folded in the form of folds of flesh that we bear, one around the head, another around the body like a girdle and the last around the ankle, and which, when deployed, extend for approximately half a foot around, enable us to walk, swim or fly with equal facility. If you stay here for some time you will see thousands assemble around the Simulacrum of Yomaha, the image of Providence, that beautiful flamboyant Globe whose penetrating rays extend for an infinite distance.

"'Others go to bathe in the streams of lively and silvery water with which the charming abode is intercut in innumerable places. You can amuse yourself by considering some of them taking pleasure in walking, wrestling, running or similar exercises. You will see others occupied in making garlands or bouquets of the rare and odorant flowers, the most exquisite and the most beautiful in the world, with which our flower-beds are always enriches. If you like Music, you will be ecstatically delighted to hear the melody of all kinds of strong, clear voices, which mimic all the instruments that humans have ever been able to invent—with the result that you will have reason to be entirely satisfied with what you took just now for small, poorly built figures.'

"This reproach threw Raoul into confusion. 'You're accusing me of a sin, fortunate strangers,' he said, 'of which I'm entirely innocent; perhaps a term escaped me that gave rise to your discontent, but I assure you that there was no malice in it; I have conceived nothing to your disadvantage.'

"'Don't make excuses,' the other replied. 'I admit that you have not entirely explained yourself orally on that matter, 'but you had it in mind; I was holding your hand then and I perceived it in your pulse, which is one of the means of which we make use in order to converse with one another when we have something to communicate in secret.'"

"Pardon me, Sire," I said, "If I interrupt you here to tell you that I have read several books by voyagers, who affirm unanimously the physicians of China do not pass for experts unless they can see clearly by means of their patients' pulses into all their interior parts and cannot immediately give an accurate account of their infirmities and their maladies, and even what they have eaten the day before, without obliging them to speak, as they are accustomed to do in all the countries of Europe."

"Both appear to me to be subject to caution," said the King. "It would be necessary for me to see it, and examine it closely, in order to believe it. But let's get back to our story.

"'If I had the thought that you attribute to me,' said Raoul, 'I had not reflected on it, and it was formed without any design of causing you chagrin, as I have already informed you, and at the moment when I saw that you had a different stature, and were slightly differently made, than humans normally are.

"'But tell me, pray,' he continued, 'do you know how long you have been here, and if one remains for a short or a long time before being introduced here when death removes us from the other world?'

"'We have no machine capable of measuring time,' replied the saintly individual, 'so it is impossible for me to reply positively to your question, in relation to the first point. Perhaps it is only a day, to speak in your fashion, but it might also be ten thousand years. We do not get bored at all; pleasures never weary us; nevertheless, there is nothing new, for which we are avid. As for the other, it appears very much as if there is no interval at all between the separation of the spirit from the sensual body and the junction of the same spirit with the glorified body, such as this one. At least, I did not perceive that my soul was devoid of a body for a single instant. It is made to act by means of various organs; it is improbable that it can do without them—but is it also futile to want to be always attached to the same ones; it is so accustomed to seeing a body make new evacuations and considerable losses by transpiration, which it is obliged to repair by drinking and eating; the changes and renewals to which it is subject are so familiar, and not unaware that when it has inhabited a body for fifty or sixty years it is possible that not the slightest particle remains of those that comprised its mass when it was first introduced thereinto, or even since the moment when it first saw the light of day, that the further change cannot cause it any difficulty. On the contrary; I am convinced that it must be indifferent to it.'

"'Since you say,' said Raoul, 'that you are from Cambul, that is evidence that you remember having been in our world. Do you not know, similarly, whether you have seen arrive since then others that you knew, and whose names are familiar to you? For if that is so, and if they are also of my acquaintance, knowing when they died, I would be able to satisfy myself immediately by calculation.'

"'I have already told you,' replied the blessed individual, 'that I might have been here since time immemorial, but even if it were only three days—or three minutes, if you wish—I would not know any more or less. Our joy is so perfect, and we are so replete with pleasures that that every instant furnishes us, that we are incapable of a sufficiently great distraction to think, either about you or about who we once were ourselves; in addition, the impressions that objects made on our senses during the other life are so worn away that almost no trace remains of them. How could that not be the case, since the brain and the whole machine of which it as a part have been destroyed? We have another, which is a veritable *tabula rasa*, in which we only think of engraving the images of things that are present to us here.'

"'I have nothing to reply to that,' said Raoul. 'It's a fact that you know by experience; what consoles me is that one day I shall know as much as you, although at present I know nothing. Another difficulty that surpasses me is that one can be sure that the terrestrial Globe is so large, and contains such a vast number of humans, and that one cannot express its duration, but in proportion to that I find very few people here.'

"'That question is easy to resolve,' the saint told him. 'If the earth is large, the universe that contains it is infinitely larger, and just as, in a city, there are not only streets but also houses, in each of which a family is accustomed to lodge, it is easy for Providence to lodge in the great City that extends from the depths of the abyss to the highest Heaven, every individual nation, or even to put in one society only the inhabitants of a single city, without the others perceiving it; and to speak frankly, I would be greatly mistaken if this republic is not composed only of inhabitants of Cambul, or, at the most, of the cities enclosed within the polar circle. In whatever place one is, on the route to the firmament or the center of the earth, the joy is always equal among the Elect; we do not know any chagrin, or anxiety, melancholy or care, and the tranquil state in which we find ourselves is what makes our happiness.'

"'But wait' Raoul interjected, 'did you not tell me just now that the Globe of fire that lights this place of delights is a symbol of the author of the Universe? If there are many similar abodes distant from this one, how can the Glory that you see be sufficient to communicate light to them?'

"'What a question,' said the blessed individual. 'Are not the Sun and stars that illuminate you as many simulacra, or images as you like to call them, of the one that is the source of the veritable light? Can he not make as many as he pleases?'

"'That's true,' said Raoul. 'I didn't think of that. It's necessary to attribute the cause of such a puerile interrogation to my ignorance. It isn't surprising, however, it seems to me, that a mortal is ignorant of the state is which he will be after death, just as he knows nothing of the state in which he was before the moment of birth. I've heard talk a hundred times, as a dubious matter, or as a poetic fiction invented expressly to hold people to duty, of a second life or an abode of the blessed, but I never imagined it as like this. I believed that if it were real, it must be vast, and common to all the living; that God himself dwelt there, instead of a Symbol, and that it was, in fact, his presence that made the felicity of the inhabitants.'

"'That thought is material,' said the saint. 'You doubtless know that God is a simple being, spiritual and infinite in every respect: infinitely wise, infinitely perfect, and so on. He is everywhere, he fills everything, he is everything; outside of him and without him, absolutely nothing exists. If he is everything, one therefore sees him in everything and by means of everything; it is, therefore, impossible to imagine him being more present in one place than another. That being so, it does not matter where one is, he is there in the state in which one ought to find him, when one takes on the character of the blessed.

"They had reached that point when they were suddenly surrounded by a numerous troop of the Elect, whose members were holding hands, and who began to dance and caper around them to an agreeably symphonic sound."

"You had broached a subject there, Sire," I said to the King, "that I would have liked to have been taken a little further; it also seems from what you have just made that saint say that God is simply the immanent cause, and not different and distinct from all beings, as we are obliged to believe—from which it follows that matter must be eternal as well as God."

"It is difficult," Benedon replied, "for a finite creature to have an accurate idea of an infinite being. For myself, when I examine the question closely, I find that God is not less a necessary cause of his works than his essence, for all eternity. I admit that one finds difficulty, and even contradiction, in accommodating two infinities, but if I'm not mistaken, that comes from envisaging the two things as independent of one another, instead of, as one ought to, representing them as parts of one whole, which are fundamentally inseparable, and cannot be divided, just as one cannot divide the infinite power of God from his infinite bounty, or his infinite clemency, which are all attributes that belong to him equally. I conceive of a God that thinks, a God that extends beyond the limits of the universe, a God who is everything and who does everything; in that manner I conceive a God who is something, instead of which, it seems to me that others make a God who, when one examines him closely, is fundamentally nothing but a phantom, a chimera, a pure illusion. But let's leave that matter, I beg you. It is beyond our range. Let is rather see what has become of our pilgrim."

"You left him in the midst of a company of dancers, Sire," I said.

"That's true," the King continued. "They wanted him to dance and sing like the others, but he could not hear either the cadence or the measure of that country."

"Who knows, Sire," I said, "whether, if the octave is double in this world, it might not be triple in the other? And if our Musicians, who claim that the fifth is like three to two and the fourth like four to three, would not make the sixth among those people? Music is only child's play by comparison with what it was in the time of Orpheus, according to the sentiment of many scholars in that profession; it's only necessary to pass from France to Italy to find a prodigious difference; it would not be surprising if there were an infinite and inexpressible difference between this place of corruption and that of immortality and glory."

"Those are closed letters," said Benedon. "One would need to have been there in order to reason about it with foundation, and one would still be very embarrassed if one were obliged to explain it on one's return."

"What you say there, Sire," I continued, "is confirmed by the sincere avowal of a holy Apostle, who, after having boasted of having been raised as far as the third Heaven—which is, according to us, the superb palace of God's Elect—confessed ingenuously that the things he saw and heard there were so admirable and so different from those that he had understood and considered elsewhere that it was not within his power to give us the slightest idea of them."

"Raoul, having got rid of those agreeable importunate individuals," said the King, "rejoined the first one who had spoken to him, and asked him to take a little stroll with him, in order to obtain from him all the instruction that he would need, in the examination he proposed to make of all things. In fact, there was nothing that was not worthy of remark; every new object that he discovered redoubled his admiration. The paths along which they passes were extended in linear fashion, and bordered by little trees laden with all sorts of fruits, beautiful, agreeable, and which seemed to be of excellent taste. Between each pair of those shrubs there was a rock of exquisite stone in the form of a pedestal, with a magnificent pot enriched with figures in relief, filled with flowers that were different from the others, with an odor that surpassed the imagination, and beneath these vases one saw a little stream of liquid trickling, red, yellow, clear, green or some other color, which seemed to have charms capable of exciting the soul most insensible to covetousness.

"'All this is charming,' he said to his guide, 'but what is the point of this abundance of good things and delicious refreshments, since none of you is using them?'

"'You're mistaken,' replied the blessed. 'We neither eat nor drink, I admit, but we nevertheless take great advantage of everything that fills our abode. The principal usage that we make of all these things consist of seeing them, considering them and admiring therein the works of Providence. The pleasure that you receive from them, in your manner, would be fleeting and extremely limited, instead of which, in each of us it is permanent and infinite in every way. However, we do not always limit ourselves to looking at them; we collect some, we wash and stroke others. Sometimes we amuse ourselves by braiding bracelets and necklaces, in which fruits and flowers, mingled together, find a place; those artificially-constructed works we use for frivolity; we attach them to pedestals, to tree-trunks, and often ornament ourselves, or make presents of them.'

"'That would have some foundation among us,' said Raoul, 'where gallantry is in vogue, and where the difference of sex causes a principal of amour to operate; in addition to that, certain objects are found to which one finds a singular pleasure in giving marks of esteem or distinction, and which it is a benefit to have by virtue of preference. Here, where I do not see any individual who is not made absolutely like all the rest, since everyone is equal and passions are not even known, I don't understand what the objective is that you are pursuing in these little games.'

"'It's true,' said the blessed individual, 'that we do not know here what male and female are; we all resemble one another in all things. Being in the entire possession of a life without limits, our principal aims are to profit from it by simple and innocent diversions, which are to the unique glory of the Sovereign Master of the world.'

"'Which is to say,' Raoul continued, 'that your felicity consists of being continually in a state of indolence, of having a soul always in the same affect, sensing no agitation, of being exempt from harm and taking pleasure in everything that presents itself to your senses. That state is happy, I admit, but I have known people among us who believe that they are not far from that state.'

"'To tell you the truth,' said the saint, 'I don't deny that one can commence to have in your world a foretaste of eternal bliss; and why should that not be the case, since the same God that governs there also has his empire here? We are his creatures everywhere, and he wants us to sense the tender effects of his bounty everywhere. When he grants a man the grace of a strong and robust complexion, of having all the parts of his body in a just proportion, healthy, entire and in good order; that his organs and senses performs their functions perfectly adequately; that with all that he is abundantly provided with wealth and fortune; that he holds an honorable rank in society; that he has what he needs to nourish himself, clothe himself and lodge himself honestly and comfortably; that he is not subject to any passions—I mean that neither adversities, nor prosperity, nor the loss of a part of his wealth or his dearest friends are capable of bringing any deterioration to his soul, or that notwithstanding the privation of the advantages I have just enumerated, he is always cheerful and always content with what he has and with whatever happens to him in any place or situation in which he finds himself—it is constant that he is happy, and that between his state and ours there is not as much difference as one might think...except that it is rare among you, and perhaps so rare that there is no example of it, instead of being ordinary among us, and cannot suffer any change.'

"'If ever I find a means of returning to my own world,' said Raoul, 'I shall profit from that lesson, to the extent that my constitution will permit, that will be all the more valuable in anticipation of the future, but I shall not say anything about it to anyone else, because vulgar individuals have other sentiments, although they do not give evidence of practicing them, and if I were imprudent enough to divulge what you have just assured me as a truth, it would undoubtedly find false devotees, who would not fail to blacken me and cause me trouble. But what is the significance of that affluence of people that I see over there?'

"'I don't know,' replied the guide, 'unless they're new recruits. I've never reflected on the matter before, but now that you've brought it to my attention, and we're conversing about the matter, it does indeed seem that they're dazed and discountenanced.'

"'I believe,' said Raoul, 'that it requires time for newcomers to get their bearing; I know from experience by what a vertiginous sensation one is struck when one arrives here.'"

"Excuse me for interrupting you so frequently, Sire," I said to the King, "but the History does not say whether there was then any significant mortality in Cambul.'

270

"Undoubtedly," Benedon replied. "Three or four hundred of our inhabitants had gone whaling; a storm caught them by surprise, which caused more than half of them to perish, and the rest scarcely reach land; then misfortune determined that they landed in a place filled with marine and amphibious monsters, which took advantage of their exhaustion, finding it all the easier because they were deprived of weapons for self-defense, because the launches in which they had escaped had sunk."

"Evident proof," I continued, "of the truth of what the Guide had said to Raoul regarding the new bodies that mortals acquire on emerging from this life. I would not have wanted you to omit that circumstance for anything, because I have often had disputes on that subject in France with obstinate individuals who take all the passages in the book of our Laws literally, imagining that the same body that falls in death is the one that must necessarily rise again one day in order to be recombined with its soul, without it suffering any change, diminution or augmentation of any of its parts."

"What!" said the King. "You also believe, in your homeland, that there will be another life after this one?"

"Undoubtedly, Sire," I replied. "We have a more than moral certainty about that. There have been a number of saintly men who, by virtue of a divine and very particular inspiration, have revealed that truth to us, which is no longer contested by anyone except a few libertines and strong minds, at whom people laugh and whom men of probity avoid like the plague, and on whom powerful men often impose rude punishments when they persist in their incredulity. The clergy, above all, cannot tolerate that they give any scandal to the faithful, if they involve themselves; otherwise, people are content to consider them as hypochondriacs."

"It's customary," said the King "to call those who do not see things as other do madmen, whether or not they are mistaken. All that is praiseworthy; I'm glad you have that opinion; I congratulate you on it and I say to with all the more sincerity because it cannot be other than infallible, since it is supported by the authority of more than a thousand venerable and ancient matrons of the celebrated city of Cambul."

"You seem to be joking, Sire," I said. "If you will listen to me briefly, I am sure that..."

"No, no," Benedon cut in. "Any discourse that you could make on that subject would be bound to weary us both; I've made my decision and am not a man to go back on it. Let us rather say that the crowd of newcomers approached Raoul, and, perceiving a stream of fresh water, infinitely clearer than those our rocks distill, following a slope with a thousand agreeable cascades caused by inequalities of its uneven bed, strewn with silvery pebbles of various shapes and sizes, they threw themselves into it head first, and, after having washed themselves well, started leaping and gamboling, striking poses and puling puerile faces, which testified naively to the simplicity of their innocent pleasures.

"The guide invited Raoul to imitate them, but he was cautious, unsure that he would emerge mortal, as he was, and in a state to return to Cambul if the opportunity ever arose. The design he claimed to exhort his good friends, when he returned among them, to render themselves worthy of such great happiness by a religious and exemplary life seemed to authorize the desire that he had to rejoin them, and not to attempt anything that might be capable of retaining him in a place whose beauties he would otherwise have been glad to entertain, but fundamentally, it was not that. He had a wife and children whom he loved; he was no enemy of real pleasures, and the table supplied a considerable fraction of his delights. All those advantages were lacking there, and that was why he could not accommodate himself to it.

"When those new guests had bathed, Raoul approached them and asked them a few questions, in vain; the only thing that they imagined that they knew, albeit in a rather confused manner, was that they had been honest people, and inhabitants of a city named Cambul; they were ignorant of everything else, and seemed so busy contemplating the new objected presented to them that they hardly deigned to reply to him. Feeling light and energetic, they set about flying; at the first attempt they found that they were masters of the art, and, having taken the route of the Globe of fire, they arrived there in a moment, with the design of examining its splendor and glory. Our pilgrim would have liked to follow them, but his heavy and fleshy body was not made for that.

"What was admirable was that he was not hungry, thirsty, drowsy, cold or hot; he felt no discomfort, except for the desire to find a way back to our world, and even that desire was often tempered by the novelty of the various objects that were continually presented to his eyes. One that occupied him for a long time was an inverted dodecagonal pyramid more than fifty brasses high made of solid gold and enriched with rubies and sapphires, the tapered summit of which was supported on the tip of one of the thorns of a rose-bush planted in the middle of twelve jets of water, formed by as many silver dolphins, covered on the spine by mother-of-pearl, each of them in an agate basin thirty feet in diameter in the form of a decagon."

"Permit me, Sire," I said, "to ask you a question. How did Raoul recognize the precious metals and minerals of which he speaks in such a plausible manner, given that he came from a country where he had never seen any?"

"It's a mistake," said the King, "to imagine that something is unknown because it has never actually been present to our senses. We do not have the opportunity to travel, but we know nevertheless that there are countries other than ours. We know the names of several, either directly, by the accounts of a few unfortunate strangers who, like you, have landed on our coasts, or indirectly, by tradition, which is a less recent means, but as infallible as the others, since it is impossible, morally speaking, for that which has been seen by our ancestors and reported so many times to their children and were afterwards written down, to be other than absolutely incontestable.

"Those people knew what gold, silver, pearls and diamonds were and everything most precious in the world; they did not keep silent about them, so it is not surprising that many of us have conserved the memory, as there are also some who, living in continuous indolence, are ignorant of many things, even the names of the things that ought to be the most familiar.

"Even if that were not the case, however, it is only necessary to consider the place where Raoul was, always in the company of a consummate philosopher, a very wise and skillful interpreter, to be convinced that it is impossible for him to be ignorant of anything. Everything there, as you will see in due course, was laid bare there, and the most hidden secrets were set in the clearest evidence.

"Raoul ought to have known everything, since he had set foot in the School of divine wisdom, but in your imitation, forgetting where he was, and his reason still being to some extent obfuscated by carnal and terrestrial thoughts, he did not understand how it was possible that such a heavy mass could be supported on a base to which it had such scant proportion. What redoubled his surprise was that the water emerging from the mouths of the aquatic animals entered the mysterious pyramid by means of an imperceptible opening in the center of the surface of each of its faces, without a drop falling to the ground, and one might have imagined that it stayed there."

"Indeed, Sire," I said, "one is delighted by admiration every time one considers that the terrestrial glob remains almost equidistant from the concave surface of the firmament, without discovering anything that supports it, but that, it is true, does not approach the prodigy about which you have just done me the honor of telling me, which is capable of embarrassing our reason so considerably, especially when we have the slightest smattering of mathematics and know the system of the world.

"The rapid course of the firmament, the appearance of comets, sometimes with a dragon's tail, often with an old man's beard and sometimes the tresses of a young man; the frightful rumbling of thunder, the origin of winds and the formation of meteors are trivial by comparison. If one descends from the highest of the heavens to earth, we shall also see that Babylon, with its superb gardens in the air and its formidable tower whose summit penetrated the clouds, the monstrous colossus of Rhodes, between the legs of which great sailing ships passed with ease, the great and solid pyramids of Egypt that neither time nor instruments made of the finest steel that art has ever invented can dissolve or damage—in a word, none of the rarest and most curious things in the universe—can compare with that marvel."

"Raoul's guide, who often left him," the King continued, "having come to rejoin him, could not prevent him from telling him about his difficulty. 'I suspected that,' he said, "and that's the reason I came back to you so soon. Once can see by that that you have not been initiated among us; as long as you are burdened with that heavy and corruptible body your mind will remain in a kind of lethargy, which will always prevent you from seeing clearly, where we do not perceive any obscurity. You can know what appears externally to your eyes, but anything that encloses the slightest mystery surpasses you; it's necessary to explain it to you, or you won't understand.

"'All the water that comes from those dolphins,' he continued, 'and enters into the sides of the pyramid, descends to its point, and after having passed into the spine that supports it, it flows through the trunk of the rose-bush to the flower-pot in which it is planted, and emerges in a seething flood from the pedestal, via subterranean conduits, which transport it to the dolphins, in order that they can spew it out again higher up, and which thus remains in continuous circulation.'"

"That, Sire," I suddenly exclaimed, "is the perpetual motion for which our scholars have been searching for such a long time. "It's to be hoped that Raoul was able to explain the secret."

"Patience," said the King. "You're not giving me time to finish."

"My mistake," I said. "I won't say another word."

"'With the consequence,' Raoul said," the King continued, "'that the water is continually in motion, and that it rises and descends without weight, without impulsion and without constraint; truly, that surpasses me.'

"'I don't doubt it,' the saint replied. 'You say it, but I find it admirable that you dare to think it—or, to put it better, that you're sufficiently innocent to hold to such language after the time you've been among us. Reflect a little on the past; enter into yourself—have you seen anything natural since you've been here? Isn't everything here extraordinary, surprising miraculous, admirable and beyond the range of the senses? Know that the one who presides here has infinite power, and that the least of his works surpasses the extent of our knowledge. Come, follow me and I'll show you something even more surprising.'

"Although Raoul was not as light and nimble as him, he was nevertheless indefatigable; he did nothing but run to the right and the left; he was always on the move, always active, but he did not even notice it. This time, it was necessary to make a long journey, but eventually they reached a pool whose edges were carpeted by a green lawn of grass as fine as silk, which he thought very pleasant. If was replete with gladioli and various other marshy plants, between which there were two rocks, diametrically opposed, a toise from the bank, which supported a Giant of excessive height, one of whose feet was placed on the tip one and the other on the tip of the other. From the base to the waist, it was made of jasper; the rest of the body, up to the shoulders, was ambergris, and the head as a single emerald.

"That enormous statue was holding a pelican in its arms, proportionate to its size, which was opening its breast with its sharp beak, in order to nourish its chicks, which were eight in number, each of which was supported on one of the giant's gingers, on its own blood. The giant was holding them and equal dis-

274

tance apart, and what was even more admirable was that the bird's blood was emerging from its breast with such impetuosity and in such great abundance that after having risen up an traveled a long way through the air, it fell far away as dew, or raindrops, in which the Sun, or the fiery globe, formed by the refraction of its rays as it passed through them a triple Rainbow, the vivid colors of which, with all their shades, could not be envisaged without being dazzled by them.

"Those colors were so bright that they visibly increased the light of that enchanted palace; but what contributed the most to that was a diamond cut into facets, in the form of a hemisphere, the base of which, nine feet in circumference, was supported on a cone of black marble, which always remained perpendicular to the inferior surface of the Simulacrum, and which consequently followed it wherever it went. The glare that the precious stone emitted was unbelievable; it would be necessary to have seen it to form an accurate idea of it.

"Raoul was not satisfied by seeing that beautiful Rainbow; he begged his guide to accompany him to the place where it appeared. As he drew closer to it, he said: 'What is that noise I can hear? One might think that it's the splashing of a great mass of extremely agitated water. Is there some sluice?'

"'You shall see what it is,' the blessed individual replied. At the same time, he discovered a crystal vat, so prodigious in its perimeter that it received all the bloody dew that the pelican was hurling to that distance. The vessel contained a soft white substance, rather like that from which glass is blown in factories, which was seething and making all the noise. Beneath it was a porphyry alembic, which served as its support, and which was surrounding by a large number of flasks, placed at different levels, the inferior parts of which were fitted with perpendicular tubes that plunged deep into the earth.

"'What is the meaning of all this?' asked Raoul.

"'It is one of the laboratories of the world,' his guide replied. 'As soon as fruits, leaves and flowers are no longer on their stems, unless we have employed them for some other purpose or other things happen to them, of whatever nature, that we believe to be good for some reason, they are thrown into that vat, where they are mixed with the blood that falls continually from above, act upon it, dilate it and cause that boiling and the noise that resounds in the atmosphere. From that composite, all the metals and minerals known to man emerge. The sulfurous parts, after being separated from the other, find an opening at a certain height that permits them to pass into one of the flasks; that those are to compose mercury flow into another, and so forth for all the rest. As soon as the corpuscles have reached their general receptacle, which is the earth, the descend rapidly, some more and some less, in accordance with their weight—for they all differ so considerably that, for example, between gold and iron, it requires a quarter of the former to be as light as the latter—they descend in a spiral described around its axis.

"They find no impediment in that because the terrestrial globe is hollow, and simply filled with a subtle and extremely agitated matter, which, apart from its own particular movement has a circular one from west to east, which is the same for all the bodies we inhabit, and which they are obliged to follow, with the result that they often do not often get half way from the Pole to the center, which they are already describing in a great circle. Thus it is that, when they reach the interior parts of the earth they enter into its pores and rise up from there in a straight line until they have entirely lost their momentum and remain anchored the places where humans digging down find them assembled, either in masses, veins or simply granules mingled with sand, depending on the disposition of the location or the area, where they encounter and extract them in order to employ them as they can for a thousand different purposes.'

"'Based on what you say,' said Raoul, it seems to me that there ought only to be mines between the two Tropics, but it cannot be denied that there are even some where we live, which is as far away as can be.'

"'If there were only our Laboratory,' the blessed individual told him 'there would scarcely be any mines except in the equatorial regions, but inasmuch as there are a number of others situated either around the polar circles or other parallels, it is necessary that they are found in all the habitable places on earth. The reason is that the particles emerging from their alembics, falling perpendicularly, or nearly so, toward the axis of the world, some have scarcely penetrated the crusts or different layers of the earth than they acquire a circular moment that they return soon afterwards at some other location to form the precious stores of lead, tin, copper, salt, saltpeter and other materials, of which Russal also has its small share.

"'Given all that, it is easy for you to conjecture that we are the ones who have the veritable philosopher's stone, in the quest for which so many chemists exhausted themselves in vain.'

"Having passed to the left of that, Raoul said: 'I thought that no one slept here, but here are thousands of people lying on beds of violets, jasmines and roses, who are not moving any more than if they were dead. Are they meditating? Are they dreaming? Do they need to do it?'

"'There are, in fact, people who sleep,' said his guide, 'but you should know that they are not yet counted among the blessed; they are sleeping because they have no lived well in the other world; it is a punishment imposed on them when they set foot in this one.'

"'How long does that last?' Raoul asked.

"'You often make me repeat the same thing, the Elect continued. 'I have already told you that we do not measure time here; it is evident that their sleep lasts in proportion to the sins they have committed. There are several that were already here when I arrived here; others have come since; it is impossible for me to say anything more positive about it. The perfect Sovereign Being is what occupies us; we do not think about anything else, because it would be unworthy of us.'

"As they were about to pass on, one of the sleepers, having suddenly awakened, stood up, and seemed very astonished to find himself surrounded by creatures that he did not remember ever having seen before, and who, like him, were so different from those with whom he had previously been acquainted.

"'Did you sleep well, my friend?' Raoul asked him.

"'Passably, comrade.' he replied, 'but if it's you who have woken me up, I'm not grateful to you; you'd have given me pleasure by letting me finish my slumber.'

"'What?' said Raoul. 'You're no more content to enjoy eternally the inexpressible pleasures in which you'll participate in this enchanted place than being immersed in a mortal sleep that deprives you of all the sweetness of life? Assuredly I find you admirable.'

"'I don't know what the sweetness you mentioned is,' the resuscitated individual continued, 'but I know the perfect wellbeing procured for me by the repose I've enjoyed from the moment I was introduced here. So long as I was conversing with mortals, I had nothing but cares and difficulties. My Master Eubron—I don't know whether he is still alive or not—did as much for me as he was capable of imagining, but I was obliged, in recompense, to accommodate myself to his caprice; he made use of me as a rod; I was the instrument that his rage employed to persecute his poor subjects incessantly, to the extent of killing my poor father because he opposed his interests and did not approve of my conduct. I was murdered in my turn at his whim, and transported to the place where I now find myself, where I was seized when I arrived by a torpor that rendered me insensible to everything, until now. I don't know what will become of me, and would have remained eternally ignorant if my sleep hadn't been interrupted.'

"'That reasoning is pardonable in a man like you,' said Raoul, 'who knows nothing of the delights of an eternal felicity; you'll soon change your mind.'

"'That might be so,' the other replied. 'However, I say once again that I would rather have been left as I was. It was sufficient for when I died, that I lived in eternal good cheer, replete with great imagination and convinced that in a little while I would be one of the of the foremost in Cambul. Those flattering thoughts have accompanied me to the tomb. Since that moment I have passed into the realm of forgetfulness, where I have tasted a sweet and tranquil repose, to which I do not think any other state can compare. I have experienced all the delicate foods there are, all the delicious liquors, games, instruments and conversations; there is nothing one can bring to mind for which one does not lose one's appetite in the end. Only repose is always sweet, always agreeable; the more one takes, the more one can take; one never wearies of it. Provided, when one lays one's head on the cushion that one has int...'

"'Let's go,' said Raoul, with that. 'The babble of this chatterbox is offending me. He's an ingrate, who doesn't merit the thousandth part of the grace that Providence is according to him.'"

"Raoul was right, Sire," I said to the King. "People as criminal as that one admit to having merited a punishment more severe than eternal sleep. Origen, who, in the admission of all scholars, passed for a great genius and one of the greatest men of antiquity, believed it appropriate, in the matter of what punishment and reproof ought to consist, that our religion condemns them to frightful torments that only end with eternity."

"Raoul had no sooner said, that," Benedon continued, 'than the resuscitated individual fell down, as if he had been struck by a thunderbolt, and re-entered the state that he regretted, until further notice, since he had shown himself to be unworthy of a better one.

"As they continued on their way, Raoul was curious to examine an object on which his gaze had happened to fall at closer range. It was a square table composed of all sorts of odorous wood, the feet of which were four eagle's claws and on which there as an imperial crown of coral, decorated with turquoises and enriched with flowers, whose periphery rested on the four corners.

"'Do you know what that is?' his guide said to him. 'It's the reef of the Mathematicians, the quadrature of the circle. The surface area of that stable and the contents of the circle of the crown supported thereon are equal in magnitude. The sides of the former are five scepters long; the diameter of the latter is twenty fleurons and its circumference a hundred and four pearls, with the result that their product is known, and in consequence, a hundred and four square palms measures the altar.'"

"All that and nothing," I interjected, "are the same thing. Raoul doubtless did not to care about the proportion between the circumference of a circle and its diameter; otherwise, he would have asked for an explanation of the magnitude of the measures that were being mentioned, and taken charge of them himself; that would have put an end to the difficult research that has been done on a question that had embarrassed many people and has cost many others sleepless nights, unless it has been resolved, as the rumor was running around when I left Holland that Monsieur Mallement claimed to have done it and promised to make the public party to it with an accurate demonstration[28]—but I beg you to take up the thread of your discourse."

"To speak frankly," said the King, "I'm beginning to get tired, so I don't want to tell you in great detail about an olive-tree in the form of a pine, with an olive at its summit as large as the egg of an ostrich, from which virgin oil flows constantly via four different conduits, like so many small fountains into a great

---

[28] Claude Mallement de Messange (1653-1723), the author of several books and monographs published in Paris, including *Nouveau système du monde* (1678) and, with relevance to the point at issue, *Le Grand & Fameux Problème de la Quadrature du Cercle résolu Géometriquement par le Cercle & la Ligne droite* (1686). The method did not survive criticism from contemporary mathematicians.

basin of carved porphyry, gilded at the edges, that surround the mystical tree, and with which those holy souls anoint themselves every time they approach the globe of fire with the design of rendering homage to the one of whom it is the image and the veritable symbol.

"Nor will I tell you about the chariot of fire with two wheels, pulled by twelve times twelve ardent cherubim for the amusement of the blessed. I shall also say nothing about the bath of musk- and amber-scented rose water in which they go to bathe as often as the desire takes them; an innumerable quantity of cedar-wood gondolas, gilded and enameled, for amusing themselves on the water; and a thousand other devices of a magnificence and neatness in which the eye alone takes pleasure. It is sufficient to add to this discourse that the various objects that Raoul had to consider in that beautiful abode occupied him so much that the time he employed in it went by insensibly without him even being aware of it.

"And it must not be imagined that the sight of them eventually became so familiar to him that he wearied of them; that was impossible, because, according to him, that marvelous theater changed its aspect at every moment; there was nothing but new decorations, new objects and new marvels. When, after having made a tour, he retraced his steps, everything had changed so much that he would have sworn that he had not passed that way before—so that, instead of ardent wishing, as he had at the beginning, to return home, be began to fear that his mortal body might eventually prevent him from staying any longer and become an obstacle to his eternal felicity.

"That which he feared happened to him; his presence there no longer being agreeable, they were surprised to see that the ardent globe was gradually darkening. The stones and the precious gems—everything that had been hard and polished, capable of reflecting its rays—ceased to gleam, because they were not receiving any. And just as a total eclipse of the sun causes the loss of daylight at midday, one might have thought that there was a threat of seeing the most penetrating light that there ever was succeeded by thick darkness.

"That saintly people were, in a way, alarmed by that; no one knew the cause of that baneful accident, which, even though they sensed within themselves that they would live forever, seemed to threaten them with an imminent end. After much reflection on what they were capable of conceiving on that subject, however, they became convinced that a change so prejudicial to their society, and which was unprecedented, could only come from that sinner, and discussed it among themselves for some time.

"What confirmed them in that idea was that since the moment they had taken the resolution to expel him, the light visibly acquired a new force. It needed no more to bring them to carry out their enterprise. His guide, who had shown him so much civility, was the first to order him to follow him and to withdraw as soon as possible. His protests were futile; it was necessary to obey; everyone was at his heels, and the moment he thought of slipping away and avoiding their pursuit, he was astonished to find himself, with snow up to his knees, in the middle of a hollow valley, without having perceived the place or the moment of his emergence.

"His return caused a great deal of noise; he told his story to everyone who wanted to take the time to listen to it. Some mocked him, others believed him, and it made such an impression on some that it deranged a considerable number of feeble minds, to the point that in the expectation of enjoying sooner the delights and pleasures of which Raoul had given them hope at the exit from that life, people were killing themselves every day, by means of the rope, the blades or any other.

"Merac was in despair at seeing so many misfortunes arrive, which desolated many families and deprived a thousand honest people of their relatives and best friends; in order to put an end to it he tried to represent Raoul as a hypochondriac, who had forged by design or adventure in his own unhinged brain the disreputable tales that he had told them. It was all to no avail. Everyone knew how long the man had been lost, that the region was uninhabited, that there was no safe retreat there, and not a single place in the entire country where a human creature could live for three days in the heart of winter. He had been seen to return with the aid of the twilight, in a season in which no one went out, in a very bad state in every respect, with a long bristling beard, and torn clothing apt to give access to cold and malady. So much evidence, of which not the slightest circumstance could be called into doubt without insulting a multitude of eyewitnesses worthy of faith, rendered them more stubborn, and caused them to form judgments that were disadvantageous to the less credulous, whom they called libertines, rascals and atheists.

"The King, seeing that his first strategy had not succeeded, devised another. He obliged Raoul to go out with him, accompanied by a company of the citizens' inhabitants and to show him the place where he claimed to have been during his absence. He did, indeed, lead them to the place where he had been attacked by the monster, and showed them the precipice into which he had fallen. He offered to show them the rest if they could take him any further. In order to overcome that obstacle, Merac put men to work building a stairway in the slope of the profound gulf.

"In some places there was rock; in others there was no purchase, with the result that it took time and a great deal of effort. When the work was finished, they found things at the bottom as he had described them. He had only to show them the hole through which he claimed to have passed, of which there was no sign, in spite of the fact that he showed them where it ought to be. And when he insisted that a turbulent wind, heavy rain or a landslide must have blocked the opening, they started to dig in several places, but some of them pierced the wall at the right height for twenty-five or thirty toises without being able to discover any empty space.

"Raoul said that it was not sufficient, that he was convinced that he had gone much further underground than the length of that tunnel, that they had not yet covered the tenth part of the distance he had had to cover before reaching the abode of the blessed, but the difficulties they had to overcome put them off, and thought it a sufficiently plausible pretext to decry the man who had caused such a futile and time-consuming search as an impostor.

"The King was again mistaken in his conjectures, however; the evil that he thought to avoid by that means was further increased, and it was to be feared that if it continued, the city would soon be entirely depopulated. Another expedient thus became necessary. Men were sent secretly to Daila who had orders to inform the Governor, and the King's behalf, about the dangerous consequences of certain sentiments that a number of the inhabitants of Cambul had about an eternal bliss after the present life in a new place, where a fanatical citizen named Raoul claimed to have been not long before, where he had seen inexpressible things; the extremities to which that erroneous opinion had taken thousands of simple and overly credulous people; that his own people would be at risk, following that example, of hastening their death in order to enjoy the same advantages with which they were flattering themselves, if news of a sentiment so prejudicial to society reached them, as it could not fail to do; and other arguments calculated to oblige the Lord not to refuse the help that was expected from him in those unfortunate circumstances.

"The emissaries carried out their commission perfectly, and were received better than they had dared to hope. They came back with several false witnesses, who sustained loudly in the presence of the King and the Court, in spite of everything that Raoul could say to the contrary, that they had seen him among them during the time that he had been away from his home. Several people were enraged by that and talked about tearing him apart, because of the profound mourning and considerable losses he had caused in a great many families. But he seemed so honest and sincere in his justification, brought forward proofs so convincing of what he had told them, and pleaded his cause with so much eloquence and boldness that the people continued to side with him, and the King, who was naturally good-natured, could not resolve to deprive him of his life—in addition to which he anticipated that, if he were to do that, instead of being efficacious, the remedy might aggravated minds rather than calming them down.

"In the meantime, Merac died. His successor, who was not as scrupulous as he was, seeing that the personal sacrifices were continuing, made a law, which still subsists, by which relatives of those who killed themselves, to the third generation, would be obliged to eat their flesh, raw or cooked, in the presence of four Chioux and two Officers of the King's household. That sentence, which was both cruel and inhumane, had an immediate effect. As soon as it was noticed that someone was showing the slightest disgust for this world and began talking advantageously about the other, the interested parties kept watch on them so closely that they found no opportunity the carry out their nefarious plan; to which it can be added the necessity that fathers saw of being devoured by their own children, or the children of being treated in the same way by those who had given them the light, filled them with such horror that the craze abruptly died down—and self-destruction has remained without a further example to the present day."

"With the result, therefore, Sire," I put in, "that no one has ever known whether what that good man had told them was true."

"No," the King replied, "except that he sustained until his dying breath that he would not take back a syllable of his account. However, many people were in mortal anxiety; they did not know what to believe, so the affair had consequences. It's one thing when it is a matter of life; one often expends a considerable part of what one has in order to prolong it for a few moment; but when it's a matter of a life that might never end, what would one not give the participate in it? And if it can be acquired by actions, of what would one not be capable?

"There had been a number of philosophers among us for a long time who maintained that a human being is composed of two different parts, one material and the other spiritual: of a body extended in height, breadth and depth, and a soul constituted by thought. The first of those parts, according to them, is mortal and subject to corruption, the other immortal and incorruptible; with the consequence that at the moment of their separation, one does not know what becomes of the spirit: whether it returns to the author of all things, from whom it is claimed to emanate; whether it enters into the body of another animal, of whatever species it can; or whether it goes to a particular place destined for its repose; but there had been no talk previously about the conjunction of that spirit with a new body, which remained hidden from other humans. That sentiment was new, and struck the ears of a few idiotic and simple individuals, who were delighted by astonishment and welcome it joyfully.

"Those who made fun of it, overtly denied the existence of the soul, and supported their opinion with the strongest arguments that they were capable of imagining, with the result that, in accordance to their principles, having nothing to expect after this life, they were obliged to put forward sufficient reasons to nullify a fact of which Raoul, who had always been reckoned a man of probity, swore that he had been the witness—which was difficult. Thus, it is not astonishing that they remained eternally divided.

"Some accepted that Raoul was an honest man, and claimed to be convinced of it, but sustained at the same time that his mind was deranged and capable of forming illusions that he mistook for realities. Others claimed, on the contrary, that he had sense and sound judgment, but that what he had seen and heard was nothing but a dream. And the remainder clung obstinately to the opinion that he was a vain and ambitious man who, having a strong imagination, had forged the system with the design of starting a new sect and immortalizing himself by becoming its leader.

"It is impossible to say positively which of the three sentiments is the true one, if they are not all equally false, so the question remains undecided at present. They all have their defenders, but it is still the case that the party that has taken Raoul to its heart is much larger than the others."

"I am not clever enough, Sire," I said to Benedon, "to judge definitively a difference of opinion that, as I understand it, has been debated for so many centuries, but if I am permitted to offer my sentiment by way of conversation, I admit frankly that I lean toward the side of those who make Raoul pass for a villain; that is plausible, and is the character of the majority of those who invent new systems in religion."

"Well," said the King, "is it not possible, after the misfortune that had overtaken him and the fatigues that he had suffered, that he entered into a long and profound lethargy, during which his imagination represented to him so vividly all that he recounted, that he believe it to be true himself?"

"I don't deny, Sire," I continued, "that we can be deceived by a dream; I have had several in life that I would not have taken for illusory if I had not, after a sincere examination, finally found that they could not be connected to what had happened to me before and afterwards, at a time when, it was impossible for me to doubt, by virtue of convincing proofs that I had, that I had not been awake. The difficulty would be much greater of being asleep for more than half a year, even though Christians talk about seven people who once slept for several centuries in succession without waking up as an incontestable face; that Pliny, in his history of the world, sustains that a man was once buried for more than fifty years before waking up from his torpor.

"I place no more faith in a story that was published about a sleeping woman in Toulouse. My father was in the city at the time; he heard it said that a devotee of between thirty and thirty-two years of age had slept for some eight years before waking up, having not taken an aliments. The worthy man was there, and deceived like the others, although he took precautions to protect himself. Great and small, scholars and ignorant people—everyone—wanted to witness that prodigy in order to bear witness to posterity, and to know whether it was a trick, and whether the woman really had been in that state, as her sisters, who watched over her continuously said that it was apparent to their eyes.

"Some of them put the most penetrating spirits under her nostrils; others tickled her, one pinched her so horribly that he carried away a piece of flesh; all that produced nothing; she as asleep, or at least put on a semblance of being so while patiently enduring all the harm that was done to her, as much to immortalize herself among humans as to amass enough to be able to remain in easy circumstances for the rest of her life. For you ought to know, Sire, that few people set foot in her house without giving a small present to the parents, for whom they felt sorry and did not have the leisure to do anything.

"That deceit lasted until someone decided to bring a ladder by night and look through the windows overlooking the street to see what was happening inside the room containing the pretended sleeper, and were astonished to see that she was standing up; on other occasions she was walking about, or sitting down at a little table, where she gave no quarter to anything that was presented to her. That was how the trickery was discovered, with the result that someone warned her to save herself, along with her accomplices, for fear that they might be put in a place where they could sleep peacefully without being interrupted by anyone.

"Notwithstanding that discovery, however, and supposing that someone could sleep for that length of time, would it be possible to live without eating or drinking? I will be told, perhaps, that dormice, tortoises, flies and a large number of insects can do so, and I don't deny it, but they can do so much better than humans, whose constitutions rebels against such abstinences.

"But finally, passing over all that, let someone give me examples capable of satisfying me that a human creature can subsist for an entire winter, lying on the ground, in a country where darkness then reigned continuously and the cold is so piercing that one can scarcely keep it at bay in a well-sealed house unless one has a god fire what never lacks fuel."

"What you say is forceful," the King said. "I have nothing to produce to counter it, but I don't claim to go that far; I only want to admit the possibility to a dream."

"By limiting yourself to a dream, sire, you are tacitly accusing your pilgrim of deception, for one of two things must be true: either he was outside during the rude season or he was enclosed in a space where nothing necessary to him was lacking. If he had been in the open he could not have remained alive, as I have proven; if he had hidden here and only gone out in order to cry out and complain of cold that had nearly killed him, in order to be better able to tell the story of his pretended adventures later, he was a rogue; there's no means of disculpating him."

"Oh, as to that," Benedon continued, "I've always taken the tale as fiction; and what I said was only to show you how far human credulity extends."

"There would be a means, Sire," I added, "of still saving appearances by another means, if the difficulties that I've reported were not insurmountable. It is not only dreams that are known among us, and are often thought to be true. We can also have visions and revelations. The book of our Laws, which is always holy and divine, is filled with examples that put the verity in question beyond doubt. Jacob, Daniel, Paul, John and many others, in sufficiently larger number, confirm what I say by the testimony they render and their own experiences.

"I know that there are impious individuals who treat as illusions what is said about so many saints. The Cerdonites, the Marcionites and other entire sects have had the impudence to put their lives and their writings on a par with the Sibyls and Aesop. The most sacred truths are subject to that. If I were as sure of the sanctity of Raoul as we are of that of the people I have just named, we would be obliged to receive the things he has told you as indubitable verities, without examining them to see whether or not they contain any contradictions, and to place them in the number of the Mysteries that God has revealed to his children, however extraordinary they might seem, since it is not our prerogative to put limits on the power of the Creator. He has made prodigies as great as those recounted, upon which no one in all Christendom casts doubt.

"We have had Prophets and Apostles who have been raised up to Heaven in the flesh and bone, who have rendered hearing to the deaf, speech to the mute, sight to the blind, cured maladies, resuscitated the dead, made a passage across the Red Sea for the people of God, rained bread and flesh from the clouds and a hundred similar miracles..."

"Have you known such people?" the King interjected, abruptly.

"I haven't known them, Sire," I replied, "but they were no less real for that; they have even left us accounts of their lives, their actions, relations of the history of the past and future since the beginning of the world to the end, and that has been approved and confirmed by so many other great and divine individuals, that there is no denying it."

"If that is so," said Benedon, "I'm of the opinion that we should also canonize Raoul; he lived without reproach, as I've already remarked, and he was away from home all the time that he was not seen here; that is evident from the fact that his wife, having learned from those with whom he went hunting that he had been separated from them, and not seeing him return thereafter, married someone else."

"That's a circumstance that says much in his favor, Sire," I said. "When Raoul returned, he found his wife in the arms of another man?"

"Yes, certainly," replied the King, "and that caused difficulties. She had loved her first husband, and had children by him; she did not hate the second, by whom she was found to be pregnant; she would have liked to keep both, and they did not want to surrender her. As no similar case had ever been seen, the King ordered that they should possess her alternately, taking turns every six weeks. They seemed content with that verdict and lived perfectly contentedly, but it didn't last long—the latter man died after a year and Raoul remained his beloved's sole master."

"In my homeland," I put in, "the law is formal. The woman would have been returned to Raoul without contest, if he had claimed her; if not, he would have left her to his rival and renounced her forever. But Sire, what did people in the other cities of Russal believe about Raoul's vision?"

"Everything that is believed here," Benedon replied. "Intelligent people make fun of it and the common people are so strongly edified by it that there is not one person in a hundred who is not convinced that on dying they will go straight to Raoulssult, or the field of Raoul—for that is what the imaginary abode of the blissful dead has been baptized—in order to enjoy the delights and advantages of the other world. The very people that Merac obtained to depose against Raoul were the first to go home to praise his merits, his probity and the miracle that had occurred to him highly. Promises of an eternal bliss are flattering, and the confession they gave of the false declarations that they had been persuaded to make in order to subvert it and to work for the reversal of such a consoling opinion lent a so much weight to their arguments that most people entered incontinently into their sentiments.

"At various times, large number of people even came to Cambul to have the honor and satisfaction of seeing the saintly Raoul with their own eyes and giving considerable presents to his wife and children. The most timid only dared look at him from a distance, for fear that their presence might soil him; others requested benediction at twenty paces; and those who were bold enough to approach him kissed his hands and knee with all the marks of an inexpressible respect and zeal, after which they went home as content as Kings."

Although the King had been yawning for an hour, our conversation would have lasted much longer if it had not been interrupted by the presence of a Chiou, who came to tell Benedon about a trick that had been played on him by one of the Palace guards

For three months he had not failed for a single day to come to find that political Officer, to tell him on behalf of the King that he had to give him a measure of Pithson that the physician had prescribed for him, until he was entirely cured of a stomach ache that was giving him no respite. He had taken the man at his word, but, thinking that it was going on too long had asked the name of the physician who had indicated the remedy and had found that it was all false—with the result that, as much because he had borrowed the Sovereign's name to carry out his deceit as for the sake of the beverage, which was precious, he imagined that such a procedure merited a small punishment.

The King, having been informed of the fact, could not help laughing, but he sent for the soldier, and, having told him what it was about, demanded to know what had led him to take such license.

"Nothing, Sire," he replied, "but a violent passion often to drink a liquor of which I had none, and which flatters the palate so agreeably that I would attempt anything one might wish and renounce all the pleasures of Raoulssult to have a portion every day similar to the one Your Majesty takes."

"You're not inconvenienced at all?" said the King.

"No, Sire," the soldier replied. "I'd be lying if I said otherwise."

"Well," Benedon continued, "I sentence you to dig the earth, in the season, for as much time as you've put into contenting your appetites, and to make restitution to the Chiou whose credulity you have abused, of twice the number of piths necessary to make as much pithson has you have consumed. If you fail, I shall make you take two measures of sea water mixed with vinegar, every day for six months; perhaps that penance will make you wiser on another occasion."

With that, everyone withdrew, and I went to resume my history.

The King who came after Merac had been married for six years when his wife became pregnant. She felt violent pains during her pregnancy, which no remedies were capable of soothing. The most skillful physicians despaired of her ever regaining perfect health.

Her fruit came to term, but in a manner that I could not read without shuddering. After frightful cries and howls, which lasted until the fourth day, she gave birth to two male children at one, who were locked in such an embrace that they could not be separated no matter what was done to them.

There was as much joy among the people in general and the court in particular as there had been sadness before that miraculous birth, in its wake. There were public celebrations, which surpassed all those previously held.

Twins usually resemble one another, but those two were so similar in every regard that it was not possible to identify the slightest difference between them. Not only were they similar in respect of height, girth, facial features, complexion and all other external qualities, but they were entirely the same with respect to their constitution, their appetites and all their inclinations, good and bad. As soon as one was eating, the other wanted to eat too, even if he did not know that his brother was having a meal. They slept, they wept and did everything, without exception, together, as if their two bodies were really only one. But what surpassed the imagination was that it was not only joy, dolor and sadness coming from within that were common to them; those that were caused by external and foreign objects were common as well, to the point that one of them having fallen on his face one day, injuring his nose to the extent that he lost a great deal of blood, a reaction but the other in the same state, and neither the bleeding nor the pain stopped sooner on the one hand than the other.

No one had ever heard talk of such a sympathy; it was the subject of the admiration and the conversations of all the inhabitants of Cambul. The Queen had no other children, and they had completed twenty-four years when their father died. Being equal in their inclinations, they both wanted to be King, or to stand aside in favor of the other, since the law only tolerated one Sovereign at a time, and they did not want to govern alternately. There were no other successors to the Crown, so there was a predicament, and no one knew what course to take to satisfy all the difficulties simultaneously.

After holding numerous conferences and taking advice from a thousand different places, it was concluded that the two young Princes, who had learned their exercises very well, would each fire a light arrow at one another at a distance of twenty-five paces, and the one who hit the other at a place that would be marked, over the heart, would be king; the other, on the contrary, would be obliged to do violence to himself and yield the Crown to his brother.

That condition seemed harsh to them, and it required nothing less than the entire city to engage them to lend themselves to it. Although they were very skillful, they could not avoid their fate; on either side they punctured the left eye, which was another subject of affliction among the people.

While there was a stalemate on the subject of the election of a Monarch, the nurse of the two young lords dreamed that she was on the seashore, amusing herself picking up little seashells, when she was surprised to see an enormous marine monster emerge from the sea, which had six legs and three heads, one large and two smaller one situated on the two sides. The head in the middle was covered by a tiara, the others each had a crown; but what astonished her more was that when the central head was awake the inferior ones slept, and their crowns, which were only attached by a kind of membrane, fell off and hang down over the forehead. Nevertheless, at the moment the eyes of the small heads opened, their crowns straightened up, and the middle head went to sleep, immediately allowing its tiara to hang down.

The nurse had the same dream on three separate occasions, and the fourth time, when the middle head went to sleep, the other two hurled themselves upon it and devoured it—and the beast disappeared while the wound was still very bloody.

The woman told several of her friends about the dream; the Queen caught wind of it, and as she had a penetrating mind, she perceived something therein that did not seem to be to her disadvantage. She sent for the nurse, who confirmed everything that she had been told, and related various details that she had not heard.

With that, the assembly of judges was convened, and all the other enlightened men and scholars that there were in the city also appeared. They were told about the miraculous dream and they were asked, individually, to reveal their sentiment and offer an explanation of it according to their whim.

As things have several faces, and can in consequence be viewed from different sides, and the men did not all have the same views and the same thoughts, it turned out that some of them claimed that the beast from the ocean represented Russal, its body Cambul, the big head Meralde and the two smaller ones the cities of Daila and Persac; that Meralde because of its extent, its situation and its beauty, would become proud and arrogant, that it would become scornful of the other two, would try to master them and constrain them to put themselves under its dependence, but that Daila and Persac, feeling themselves to be free and in a state to resist its violence, would employ their strength against it and finally defeat it.

Others understood by the big, fat and swollen head, an abundant and fertile year crowned by all the good things necessary for human life, and by the two small, meager and fleshless ones, two years of extraordinary famine, which would consume everything that the other had brought in, with the result that there would be absolutely nothing left.

There were others whose sentiment was entirely different, but the High Priest, who had not opened his mouth until then, imposed silence, and in the presence of the Queen and the Princes, who were also there, he raised his voice and adopted a tone of authority.

"Listen, inhabitants of Cambul, and you Princes," he said, "do not scorn my words; this woman's dream, which has nourished you with its own substance, has made you see yourselves. The great beast that she has seen is the innumerable multitude of citizens who live in this famous city; the three heads that it bears are three persons. The one in the middle, from which the lesser ones seem to emerge, being covered by a tiara, which is like a woman's headgear, represents the Queen, who will govern for a year. Those at the sides, with their crowns, are the twin sons, who will occupy the Royal seat for another, and be considered as if they were a single person; then the mother's turn will come again, and then that of the sons—and so on, alternately, until the large head falls, for she will die first. I dare not say in what manner that will happen, but I see clearly that we are threatened with seeing terrible changes among us; may it please Yomaha, in his infinite bounty, that the end is not tragic and we will not be called, justly, children of blood."

That explanation immediately obtained preference; absolutely nothing was found to say against it, so everyone applauded and recognized Nardisse as the Queen Regent and the Princes, her sons—Nardan and Nadran—as her associates in royalty.

That election pleased the mother; she seemed extremely satisfied. The children, on the contrary, murmured and gave incontinent signs of their discontentment. Fate, however, had spoken, the inhabitants had approved it, and it was necessary to move on, and to resolve to live for an entire year as citizens, under the absolute orders of a woman — which was a novelty thus far unheard of.

As soon as Nardisse had the scepter in her hand she ordered a day of celebration, on which she demanded that everyone should testify to their joy by public rejoicing, and that the ceremony should be renewed every year, in perpetuity, in order that it would be a kind of eternal monument to posterity. She also commanded the High Priest to draw up a formula of prayer, which would be given to every family, with the requirement for the heads to recite it every revolution at a certain hour, in the presence of their children, in which the person of the Queen and the entire Royal household should be recommended expressly to God.

Subsequently, she summoned the wives of the Chioux to the Palace, and placed herself on the throne. This is what she said to them, very nearly in these terms:

"Venerable Matrons, women distinguished among all others by your age, wisdom, conduct and singular virtues, you know the degree of honor to which Providence has been pleased to elevate me. It is a grace that I consider not so much in relation to myself, but with regard to all persons of my sex, whom I intend to feel that sweet and extraordinary influence.

"Heaven is just; it is weary of seeing the prolongation of tyranny that our superb husbands exercise over us, which has never been discontinued until today, prevailing by virtue of their strength in holding us in servile obedience and treating us like their domestics and children. Government, which they have arrogated, has been eternally in their hands; they have disposed political and mili-

289

tary responsibilities, and all honors in general, in their favor, to such an exclusion of our sex that it has not entered into the slightest consideration.

"That treatment is injurious, that yoke intolerable; I liberate you from it today, by giving you the same titles, dignities, honors, charges and prerogatives that your tyrant husbands have enjoyed until now. I shall hold Council every day; come to it with me, in the same order, and the same number and at the same hour as those observed by the men, in order that we can administer justice and obtain cognizance of affairs of state, from the greatest to the smallest, so that we can protect ourselves from the reproach that might be made to us of not governing with as much wisdom, equity and god order as our predecessors."

"We are infinitely obliged to Your Majesty, Madame," replied one of the oldest and most considerable of the venerable Matrons, incontinently, "for the honor that you are doing our sex in general, and those who compose this illustrious assembly in particular, for having sentiments so advantageous to its sufficiency and for wanting to constitute it Chief and absolute master in every regard of the one that has always governed, which I would not be sorry to see so badly situated that it has no just grounds for complaint—but I admit frankly, Madame, that the inversion in question does not have my approval, and I find it entirely to our disadvantage.

"It is a great pleasure to have authority in hand, to be in possession of its charges, and to govern as one thinks appropriate, but that pleasure is tempered by many inconveniences and bitter annoyances. Look at the cares, I beg you, that a veritable father of a family must have, only to talk about a single household and of domestic government: in what difficulty, labor and embarrassment does he not find himself continuously, in order to furnish his wife and children, with what he believes to be necessary to them. If he stays awake, it is to tire himself, to act, to expose his life to a thousand dangers, and he almost never sleeps without the convulsive movements of his body making it evident that his mind is not without anxiety.

"The cares that those must have whose hand is on the tiller for the conservation and salvation of peoples that have been committed to their care are infinitely more considerable; those two estates, so to speak, do not suffer and comparison. Believe me, Madame, our situation is far better than that of our husbands, and I am convinced that we would lose by the exchange.

"But even if that were not the case, let us speak sincerely: are we ordinarily capable of exercising the function of judge and Sovereign? Do we have enough enlightenment, knowledge, judgment, resolution and strength to fulfill all the functions and maintain ourselves in those positions? But supposing that, in measuring others by yourself, who have a great soul and are capable of anything imaginable, you will find us able to such undertake difficult and important matters, who do you expect to take care of our households? Will it be necessary for our husbands to do the cooking, clean our houses, look after our children, take care of nursing them and bringing them up with the patience, attachment, tenderness and sweetness that is our nature, and of which they have none?

"Leave things the way they are, Madame; let us continue to obtain vanity from the striking action of which those to whom we are joined in marriage are capable. It is not them alone who enjoy the honor, the dignity and the advantages that fall to them in preference to the opposite sex; we usually have a considerable share in it. There is no husband King whose spouse is not a Queen; the wife is everywhere considered as well as her spouse."

"You conceive things poorly," said the Queen, "and you credit us with only one item of possession, which is a husband, of whom you have only the shadow and the appearances. Look at the arrogance with which poor women are generally treated by their husbands; how they are excluded from any matter of importance; men have no scruples, but they consider it shameful to communicate the smallest secret. Are not the table, the most exquisite dishes, the strongest and most delicate liquors, gambling and gallantry, and everything pleasurable, entirely their preserve?

"All excesses are permitted to them; that is a truth than no one can contest. At the slightest license that we give ourselves, however, we pass for incontinent, for gluttonous, for wantons who no longer have any honor or reputation. Is it not them who, in addition to the empire they have over the general, take cognizance of everything that happens within the family? Have we the courage to make any expense, to dress or children, to entertain our friends, to go out—to make a move, so to speak—without consulting them and giving them knowledge of it?

"Our vanity leads us to hide these circumstances before others; we try to make them understand, of the relationship we have with the head of the household, that we share his authority and that everything is common between us— but admit it, whatever status you have, is not true that we are veritable slaves, in a base and servile dependence? This is a matter that is known to me, a subject that I have studied in depth, to which I have joined the experience. That is why we shall not talk about it anymore; what I have said is resolved; I shall be obeyed without contradiction; you shall be Chioux instead of your husbands.

"They will not give up heavy work for that; they will go fishing and hunting; they will work the land as before, and occupy themselves with everything necessary for the wellbeing of your household; there will be no difference except that instead of obeying, you will command, and that your husbands will be obliged to account to you for their actions, as you had to account to them for yours.

"However, you ought to know that my unique objective is to free you from servitude and not to abuse you; I am not inclined to force anyone; if you do not want to be clothed in the dignity that I am offering you, you may withdraw boldly. I shall find ten times as many who will be delighted to exercise the employment of judge in your place; I shall have no difficult doing that. But I will not grant any delay; it is necessary to determine things now, and not to go take advice from others, who did not give you the same grace in similar circumstances."

When the good Ladies saw that there was no means of warding off the blow, they preferred to follow the Queen's orders rather than to appear disobedient or scrupulous. In addition, it was in their interest to do so, not only because by that means, their household would conserve its luster and privileges, but also because they would be in a better position to work to return things to their former footing when the opportunity presented itself, and to obtain the necessary assistance to fulfill their responsibilities with honor from people who had already exercised them, and were therefore more capable than anyone else to furnish it in all kinds of circumstances.

Seeing that they were determined, she had them swear to be faithful and not to allow themselves to be corrupted in any fashion.

Such an extraordinary and unexpected change sowed consternation among the inhabitants; the men murmured in protest and the majority of women were not at all content. Able people were delegated by several districts to beg the Queen, with all the submission with which they were capable, to be kind enough to retract her edict and not to persist in such a sentiment, which troubled good order in its entirety, undermining the foundations of the foremost Laws of the State, and was no less than a cause of sedition that would cause the total ruination of the Realm.

All the arguments that were employed, far from being of any utility, acted so forcefully upon her mind that she went as far as the extremity of pronouncing that if anyone took the liberty of mentioning it to her again she would punish them in an exemplary fashion so severe that others would shiver in consequence. Those threats frightened them, and they resolved to keep quiet and be patient until the year had elapsed, or she died.

I do not know whether a man naturally has some mark of grandeur, Majesty and Sovereign authority, or whether custom has such a great ascendancy over the sex that it brings to have deference and respect for him, but it is certain, according to the historian's report, that the women were so well-behaved and respectful, in those circumstances, with regard to their husbands, that one might have that that there were express orders obliging them to submit to their obedience more than ever.

Meanwhile the two Princes took the trouble to inform themselves fully of what was happening in the city during their interregnum. Seeing that the families were tranquil, and that everyone was keeping within the rules of duty, they did not believe that it would be necessary to make new regulations when their turn came and to reestablish men in their former rights and privileges. They hoped that either the Queen would change her mind, or that things would gradually revert of their own accord, without their taking action that might mortify or irritate the woman who was the most capable in all the world of attempting the impossible in order to satisfy her ambition.

What was most extraordinary was that neither Nardan nor Nadran held any Council with the new Chioux throughout the year of their regency, and always made use of some specious pretext to dispense with them, with the consequence that when any matter of importance arose, it was necessary for them to settle it in their apartment.

Nardisse's turn having come for a second time, she was not content to confirm what she had ordered at the commencement of her reign; she made new Laws, by which she imposed rigorous punishments on women who did not command as Masters in their homes, and on husbands who did not obey them punctually. The High Priest was dismissed and a Priestess elected in his place; she also gave the command of her guards to a female Colonel. The King's Lieutenant was similarly obliged to transfer his employment to his wife. And in order to demonstrate her authority, she swore aloud that if she heard the slightest murmur, or if anyone took it into their head to complain about those changes, she would issue a perpetual and irrevocable decree in which she would declare that only females would be recognized as free and that men would remain slaves forever.

She concluded in addition that maidens would conduct amorous affairs henceforth in a formal manner; they would ask the mothers of bachelors for their hand in marriage, and command men expressly to love, honor and obey them, for better or worse. The young women acquitted their duty marvelously, and observed the orders of their Princess rigorously. Those who had only attained the age of thirteen or fourteen appeared no less skilled in amorous matters than many others had been at forty; they flirted with all comers and talked about nothing but gallantry. They sang and composed amorous verses; gifts, assemblies, dancing, instruments and all that went swimmingly; there was nothing but continual rejoicing throughout the city.

The men, for their part, had not sustained their personality so well; there were many who yielded to the first proposal of amity they received. The good thing was that the male sex, being clever and political, knew how to string things out, and only come to a decision after having amused themselves thoroughly for a time; otherwise, it is evident that within the space of a year there would have been no marriageable people left in Cambul.

With all that, it would not have taken much for the most well-behaved of people to become mutinous, and they were only restrained to duty by the promise that the young Kings would put everything in order as soon as the year came to an end. In the meantime, it was necessary to suffer a thousand impertinences. The extravagant Queen often invited Ladies to dine with her, in order to have the pleasure of having them served at table by their own husbands, whom she subjected to intolerable indignities, to the extent that if they were not sufficiently prompt in obeying her, or they gave the slightest sign of discontent, even if it were mechanical and intention played no part in it, she made them kneel before her and forced them to beg her pardon seriously—for lack of which rods would

293

come into play and their lives would be at risk. She also took pleasure in going in person to private houses in order to observe the rigor of the maxims that she had invented and which she never ceased to recommend carefully.

Finally, however, everyone being weary of a government so opposed to common sense and what nature dictates to us herself, as soon as the two Kings had return to their functions, they summoned all the political and military officers to the palace, where they were reestablished in their employments and dignities, with an express instruction only to be stripped of them by death. They also resumed their former authority, in relation to their families as well as public affairs. And for fear that those regulations might be annulled again, with unfortunate consequences, three officers of the guard were ordered by the Council, with the consent of Nardan and his brother, to go and strangle Nardisse.

No woman had ever testified to less aversion to death than that one.

"You're right," she said to her executioners, when they laid hands on her and acquainted her with their commission. "You're right to deprive me of life; I am the greatest enemy that your sex has ever had in the world, and it will not see another one like me in future. The changes that my sons have just made in the regency have caused me more pain than a thousand deaths would have done.

"They do well not to wait until I am in a position to avenge myself; they can be sure that they would not have been allowed to mount the throne again, and it would not have been my decision if you had not died with them. You are the tyrants of the fair sex; you have been since the beginning and you will be until the end. My design was to set limits to your empire and to make ours succeeded it forever.

"I have been poorly seconded in that great design; those who had as much interest in it as me were the first to betray me and to sustain the cause of my enemies; I abandon them now to their fury, that they may be scorned, beaten, and killed; they deserve no better; if they are content to live as slaves, I am delighted to die free."

The history of that heroine, who would have been veritably worthy to be Queen of the Amazons, is extremely long; I am only recounting it in abridged form, for fear of wearying those who might read it, because I know full well that men do not all have the same tastes. For myself, I can tell you that it gave me a great deal of pleasure, that I believe that I have read it twenty times over, with the same desire to read it another twenty, because nothing similar has passed through my hands, because the case is extraordinary, and because I wanted to be able to remember it, in order to be able to tell it.

Meanwhile, the time of our detention passed and we were easily able to agree to reopen the doors of our prisons. No one, however, undertook long excursions so long as the Sun was only crawling along the horizon; the air only began to warm up when it renounced the vicinity of the ground and it only made itself properly felt when it reached ten or twelve degrees of elevation. It was then that people began to take pleasure in the countryside, and the pleasure increased as the beautiful star approached the sign of Scorpio, although the season is even more beautiful on its return, because the warmth is then more sensible, lasts for longer, and Heaven and the earth have the leisure to warm up in that northern hemisphere where, having neither nights nor fresh winds to prevail there, there is nothing to interrupt it that is capable of diminishing it.

The cold and tenebrous winter that one has spent gives way to the bright gleam of spring, which one finds much more agreeable in consequence. I have already said that advantage is taken of the fine weather to lay in the provisions that will be needed in the rude season. Those who go whaling stay away for about a month, because they can live on fish, and they prepare the oil that they bring back in wooden vessels made expressly for that purpose.

During their absence I asked the King for permission to go and see the place where it was said that Raoul had fallen, and to give me someone to accompany me for fear of unfortunate encounters.

"I'll go with you," he said. "I have not yet been there myself, perhaps because I take all that for veritable old wives' tales and have never thought of doing so."

When we reached the place I found that things were, indeed, as they had been represented to me.

Having afterwards left the precipice to the right, we came to a little stream that could easily be crossed by a stride, we followed its course, and were surprised, after having covered some distance, to find a round pond that might have been three or four hundred paces in diameter, from which three other streams emerged similar to the first, equidistant from one another, of the same width, and flowing in opposite directions, in such a way that if they were prolonged in one direction they would have intersected at right angles, and in the other would have divided the sphere into four equal parts.

That observation caused me to judge that the pool must be situated exactly at the North Pole on the Earth, not only because the water descended from it all around it, but also and principally because there was a continual seething that could only be caused by the agitation of the subtle matter that must necessarily enter and emerge at the two extremities of the world, in view of what anyone can perceive wherever there is a spring of fresh water.

Benedon shared my sentiment as soon as I had explained my thinking. I subsequently found that my conjectures were not ill-founded, because, having returned to the same place again, with a ninety-degree quadrant—which, in truth, was perhaps not the most accurate—I took the height of the Sun as precisely as I could. I did the same twelve hours later, which is to say, when the star was exactly opposite, which is very easy to observe, and I was able to determine that there was no difference between the two elevations: evident and incontestable proof that we were as far away from the equinoctial line as possible.

Finally, our fishermen came back, as well furnished as one could reasonably hope. There was nothing very extraordinary about it, but what gave us a subject for astonishment was that they brought back a small boat, which they had found among the ice-floes, containing three dead men, whom they would gladly have brought back had they not been prevented from doing so by the unbearable stink they emitted. They had to be content with their clothing and a few petty possessions they had in their pockets, among which there was a watch and a few English coins, which led me to conjecture that they must be men of that nation, whose ship has sunk, or who had been separated from their crew and had not been able to rejoin them. Having finally died of hunger and disease, the wind had blown them all the way to Russal, where our men had found them.

The King was delighted to see silver money and a machine similar to those about which I had told him several times. It was necessary for me to show him how the chain is attached at one end to the spring that is enclosed in the drum, and at the other to a wheel; how that wheel is enmeshed with another, to which it communicates the movement that it obtains from the spring, which, being wound, tends continuously to relax, under the impulsion the subtle matter making an effort to pass from its convex parts, where the pores are wide open, toward the concave, where, because of the curvature of the steel, they are so narrow that there was no free passage; and finally, how, from wheel to wheel, one succeeds to the last, which is in communication with the pointer, which rotates and indicates the hours marked on the dial of the case.

After having carefully examined the physical and artificial causality of the watch, and having reset it and wound it up, I had the pleasure of seeing the admiration with which the King considered the different movements of its parts. He blessed a hundred times the man who had been the inventor of such a pretty and useful instrument, and wished him for a recompense a considerable rank in the fields of Raoul.

Immediately afterwards, he sent for the iron-workers who had the reputation of being the most experienced in the city, and charged them with employing all their skill to imitate that beautiful device, but they had absolutely no enthusiasm for it. I counseled the two who seemed to me to be the most skilful first to attempt something similar on a larger scale. I helped them personally, with all my industry. Finally, they brought it to a conclusion, and I can say that before my departure they were making chiming clocks that worked passably well, and were of considerable utility.

We then conversed about different kinds of money, their usage, and the necessity there is for a civilized nation to be well-furnished with it, for the convenience of the inhabitants. The King understood all that very well, but being deprived of the metals of which use is made for all kinds of coinage among us, he did not imagine that the thing was feasible in Cambul.

"That is not true, Sire," I told him. "There are places in Guinea where seashells provide all the inhabitants' money. We have seen the great Gustave, King of Sweden[29] make use of pieces of leather instead of silver and copper during the bloody and onerous wars that he fought with the Emperor, on which he had certain characters put which gave them the value he desired, and which were received without difficulty throughout his army.

"You have iron here," I continued. "it only remains for you to fabricate small pieces, round and flat, the size of a thumbnail, which will provided petty money, and will be worth, if you wish, one liard apiece. Those which are four times as heavy would have the value of a sou; you can make others of five, ten and twenty sous each, which will not be assessed by their weight or size but by the effigy that you have imprinted on them. For example, on the liards you can mark Cambul on one side and Liard on the other; for sous you only have to put the Moon on one side and Sou on the other; for five-sou coins I would put the Sun on one side and its value on the other; demi-florins might bear the effigy of the Queen, with her name around it on one side, and 'ten sous' on the other; and the francs, your portrait and name on one side and 'twenty sous' on the other.

"In order that the people should soon have the means of buying and selling, I would have them bring the scrap iron of which they made use in their houses and give them its value in coins in exchange. I would pay my guards, my political officers and my domestics in money instead of giving them food and clothing; reciprocally, I would tax the inhabitants in the same way, either so many coins per month or per year, instead of the tithes that you levy on all things. That way, everyone would have the liberty to do what he wanted, or what he could; as long as he lived peacefully, and paid you your due, you would have absolutely no criticism to make."

"I'm astonished," he replied, "that none of my predecessors have ever thought of that. I can see that nothing more convenient is imaginable, and that if the other cities do the same, it will be much easier for us to negotiate with one another than it was in the past."

"Not everyone is capable of inventing new things, Sire," I told him. "It's a particular grace that Heaven only accords to a few individuals. The invention of metal money was doubtless unknown when your ancestors came to settle in Russal; those who had metal bartered it in bars or pieces of irregular shape for the foodstuffs of which they had need, as is still practiced among savages and some of the inhabitants of the New World, and perhaps the foreigners you have received in these parts before me did not think of giving the instruction that I have given you to the Kings that governed here in their time."

That topic was the subject of our conversations for several days in succession, and it was concluded that work would begin on that great project as soon as the summer was over, since the greater part of society would then be huddling in idleness, and everyone would have the leisure to put his hands to his own

---

[29] Gustavus Adolphus (1594-1632) led Sweden to great military success during the Thirty Years' War before being killed at the Battle of Lützen.

work, which would not be disagreeable, inasmuch as it was for the public good and everyone would be beside the fire that is the most desirable company of all in winter.

But let us not bother with that, supposing it to be already done, and take up the thread of our Russalian history.

After the death of Nardisse, her two sons took care to revive the laws, returning their former vigor and putting everything back on the same footing that it had had since time immemorial, to the great contentment of the people, who did not express the slightest sadness at the Queen's tragic demise.

What was troubling was that the two Prince Regents had no inclination at all toward marriage; there was no means of making them resolve to take a wife, because there was never an object that pleased them both at the same time—with the result that, when they died simultaneously of apoplexy, they left no legitimate successors. Their uncles were dead; they had no nephews, cousins or any relatives at all who were not so distant that they could no longer be counted as members of the Royal family.

It was very difficult to make another King; several would have liked to be one, but those who had a right to election did not have any enthusiasm for it.

One clever and ambitious woman, who was beginning to incline toward old age, having learned about this predicament, summoned her six sons, who were aged between twenty and thirty.

"My children," she said to them, I have often heard your father recount that when his worthy mother was carrying him, she had a mysterious dream, which had always flattered her hopes extremely, all the more so because she was of Royal blood. She had, however, died without seeing anything great arrive in her household.

"It seemed to her," she said, "that she was on the summit of an ancient rock of excessive height, but which the weather and the waves of the sea, which bathed it, has so eroded and hollowed out that it was threatened with collapse, and that from there, she could see the entire ocean. After having considered that watery expanse for some time, she suddenly saw a small boat in the center of that circumference, which had not been there before, and which, in spite of the continual agitation of the waves that surrounded it, was at tranquil repose, absolutely unmoving from its position.

"That small boat," she added, "remained in that state for twenty years; in the twenty-first, she saw a worm emerge from it, of the same color as the boat, which was almost imperceptible. That tiny animal always remained in the same state, and never moved; it did not grow; one might have thought that it was not alive. Finally, she was surprised to see it suddenly swell up, becoming prodigious in size. It also grew wings, which covered a vast extend of the waters. Then it took the form of an eagle, which was holding a scepter in its beak, and a double-edged sword in its claws, with which it seemed to the threatening the Heavens and the Earth.

"If this dream is ever to have its accomplishment, my dear children," the good woman continued, "it is in the present circumstances. The throne is vacant, for want of heirs; one has only to be elected to occupy it. Your father is an honest man, beloved by everyone; I admit that he is only a sculptor, but a sculptor who excels in his profession; he is a citizen of Cambul, like the most high-ranking, and according to the law, no more excluded from Royalty than the Chioux and the most distinguished people.

"This is a matter that concerns you closely; the Kingdom is hereditary; if he were elected to it you would succeed him. Follow my advice; don't go to sleep; if you act according to my fantasy, I'm mistaken if you don't succeed. To bring my design to a conclusion, my opinion is that two of you should depart secretly and go down into Raoul's precipice. Let the other four make a hunting party with fifteen or twenty of their friends and lead then insensibly to that place. When the two who are hidden there hear them coming, one of them should cry out at the top of his voice: 'I am Yomaha, and it is my will that Helumac should be King of Cambul.'"

Those young men, being quite ready to work to fulfill their mother's plan, which was entirely advantageous to them, carried out her instructions, and did so with so much success that not one of those who heard the words in question would not have sworn that God himself had spoken to them in a thunderous voice. The entire city was immediately filled with the news of that prodigy.

Helumac, who knew nothing about the scheming of his wife and children, heard the story with marks of an extraordinary astonishment, but without wanting to profit from the circumstance that seemed so favorable to him and his family. On the contrary, when they attempt to persuade him that the thing was not impossible, that it was necessary to profit from the opportunity and that he ought not to neglect the possession of a privilege that Heaven had declared loudly to be destined for him and his family, he made fun of them overtly, and nearly became angry. He acted in the same way with all those who talked to him about it, which put back the affair considerably, all the more so as the most high-placed individuals were not at all inclined in that direction.

Seeing that, the woman showed her sons a crow that she had kept in a cage for a long time without anyone knowing about it, and which she had taught to say: "Helumac is King." She ordered them to take it secretly to the other side of the city and, having set it down in some isolated spot while no one was about, make themselves scarce and leave it alone.

The bird was to longer on the ground than it seemed very frightened; sometimes it ran, a moment later it fluttered; it hopped in one direction then launched itself in the other, not knowing where to go or what would become of it.

Eventually, someone came along casually, who, perceiving its confusion, could not help laughing, and laughed so loudly that the noise attracted other spectators. Everyone as surprised by the actions of the young crow, which, having been locked up in an obscure place, and never seen anyone. But it was even worse when, seeing itself surrounded by a group of people, it started repeating its old lesson aloud: "Helumac is King."

There was not a single person who suspected that it was a trick, but they made various judgments as to the quality of the animal that had saluted Helumac as the King. The ill-intentioned declared that it was a sorcerer, because it was black and had the form of a bird of ill-omen. Others took it for the Devil himself, who, being envious of their prosperity, wanted to give then as a Master and Sovereign a man devoid of any birth or character that distinguished him from the crowd. The greater number were, however, of the opinion that since Yohama had said the same thing from the depths of Raoul's Cavern, the bird, no matter what it looked like, could only be a divine messenger, sent by Yomaha himself to confirm what he had said and convince the incredulous of their disobedience in not wanting to acquiesce to what he had resolved in his eternal Counsel, with regard to the one man among all the inhabitants of Cambul that he thought worthy of wearing a Crown.

The number of those who shared this sentiment was considerably augmented in very little time, with the result that if the Chioux, who had immediately caught wind of it, had not just dispersed, they would have been capable of immediately going to find Helumac and carrying him to the Throne. The King's Lieutenant, the Colonel of the guards and several masters of the districts, however, were moving Heaven and Earth to succeed to that dignity.

For her part, Helumac's wife, whose name was Saya, was in despair that the means she had thus far employed had proved futile. She spent night and day racking her brains to invent further expedients. Finally, after having tormented herself considerably, she came upon the last, which had the success that she anticipated. It was then the commencement of winter; it had been three weeks since the day star had last shown itself.

"You have learned a composition of your father's," she said to her children, "which burns on wood and parchment as well as on stone for an hour or two before going out. Make a flying dragon and attach characters coated in that material to its tail, which spell out the words: *Helumac Grin, ausa Cambul truda*"—which is to say "Helumac King, or I burn Cambul—"and then go out secretly, two or three of you, and transport it to the side of the city from which the wind is blowing, taking enough gut-cord to make your kite fly so high and far that it will be visible over considerable parts of Cambul, and leave it suspended in the air, in order that the others, putting on a semblance of having things to do on the surface, can go up incognito, and have the opportunity to see the new prodigy, to which they will incontinently make others party. Afterwards, they will retire in favor of the multitude, which will not fail to carry the news everywhere, in order that we will not be suspected by anyone."

Although the movements they had previously stimulated had not had any effect, they had nevertheless shaken things up and disposed people to act in their favor; it was easy to see that, however slenderly the intrigue was continued, there was every appearance that they would see it crowned with success. With that thought in mind they did not hesitate to put their mother's plan into action and carried it out point by point, like the preceding ones, as much to give her evidence of their obedience as to have nothing for which to reproach themselves.

Hazard determined that the sky was cloudy and receiving very little twilight. As soon as the rumor went around of the sight of a new spectacle in favor of Helumac, of a speaking sign, of a comet whose tail had just announced the will of Yomaha with rude threats, not a single soul remained indoors. Everyone came out, the great and the petty, struck with the ultimate astonishment, saying with a common voice that it was necessary not to defer any longer electing for their Sovereign the man whom God had destined for that dignity a long time ago. The Council assembled, where Helumac was appointed King of Russal, to universal applause.

As the Prince was charitable, benevolent and extraordinary in his piety, there were few inhabitants in the city who were not delighted to have him for their Monarch. Saya's nature was very different from his; if he had wanted to listen to her he would not have followed his own inclinations so much as the examples of Eubron the Tyrant, or overturned the laws, like Nardisse. Incapable of violating the rules of equity, however, he always took a singular pleasure in exercising justice everywhere, in a manner that his clemency was often evident even in the cases that seemed to demand severity.

For all that, his reign did not last long; he only governed for the space of eight years, to the great regret of his subjects, who would have desired ardently that it had never come to an end. The eldest of his sons, named Zandor, succeeded him; immediately, Ambassadors were appointed, and, following the custom, went to inform the other cities of the change.

The Governors of those places did not neglect to send delegates from the body of their Magistracy to express to the court the sorrow they felt on the decease of the one and their pleasure in the elevation of the other. Among those who came from Meralde, misfortune determined that there was an individual of extraordinary height, a lively man with a great inclination to the truth, but very ugly, and who was constitutionally capable of any undertaking. After an audience with the King, who received him very politely and remarked particularly on the pleasure he had experienced in hearing him speak, he wanted to see the whole city, especially its curious sights, because he had never been there before.

The poor people, who are brutal everywhere, and of whose actions an honest man ought not to take any notice, never ceased insulting him, in spite of all those accompanying him could do to prevent it. Some called him lung-nose, others thin-back; there were a few who shoved him or threw dirt in his face. Finally weary of suffering all those impertinences, and seeing a carpenter who was shouting: "Why aren't you being hunted, Heron-legs?" at him at the top of his voice, and who made as if to trip him up, he was incapable of maintaining his self-possession any longer, and having drawn his sword, ran the man through.

That unfortunate incident excited the whole populace; everyone wanted to kill him, and it required all the difficulty in the world to get him out of their hands. Zandor learned the news with all imaginable chagrin; he would have liked to facilitate the Ambassador's retreat, but he did not know how to contrive that; he was afraid that he might be discovered or ambushed as he left, and that the carpenter's death would be avenged on his person. While he was reflecting on the inconvenient adventure someone came to tell him that the relatives of the dead man had assembled in the main street and all had sworn an oath either to avenge the wrong that the foreigner had done them in the person of the man he had killed, or perish.

The King immediately sent a Captain of the guard with sixty men, armed to the teeth, to command them to go home, with a promise on the part of the Sovereign that the Ambassador would be arrested and justice would be done. That promise contented them, but they asked the Officer to tell the king that they hoped of his bounty that he would give them the grace of not breaking his word.

At the same time the Envoy was brought to the Palace, where Zandor spoke dryly to him and made him understand that he had been wrong to allow himself to be carried away by passion; that he should instead have complained about the insults that he claimed to have been made to him, and that he would have had all the satisfaction imaginable; instead of which, he did not know what to do to protect him from those who were interested in the man—one of his subjects—whose blood he had shed.

The worthy man tried hard to justify himself and to throw the cause of the misfortune, about which he was in despair, on to the dregs of an insolent and insupportable people, who had tried his patience to the end. All of that was of no use, and the Chioux, who feared the consequences, counseled the King not to permit the Ambassador to leave without leaving behind four of the principal members of his retinue as hostages, who would be kept in Cambul until it was evident how things were going, or what satisfaction the Governor of Meralde would give to the blood-relatives.

However advantageous and honest that condition appeared, it was difficult to get the citizens to agree to it; they had it in for the Envoy, and that feared that once he was free, it would be difficult—as was, indeed, obvious—to make the innocent pay for the guilty.

It proved, in due course, that they were not mistaken in their conjectures. The Governor of Meralde having been informed, on the return of his envoys, of the unworthy treatment they had received, immediately sent a demand that the people detained in Cambul should be released immediately, with the threat that if they were not, there would be reprisals, which would teach people not to brutalize foreigners who had come expressly to offer them civilities.

Zandor, to whom those who had that commission addressed themselves, seemed surprised by a proposition as arrogant as that, and, not wanting to reply on his own impulse, assembled the masters of the districts and told them what had happened. With that, the delegates were sent the Senate, and after having expressed to them again the displeasure they felt at the indignities their Ambassador had suffered in their city, they were made to understand that the latter, for his part, had had the audacity to trespass upon the rights of the Sovereign, whose sole prerogative it was to punish those who committed a fault with the area of his jurisdiction, and there was reason to find it strange that their Protector was reckless enough to refuse to punish the guilty party in the manner most appropriate to the satisfaction of interests.

To that was added that, in order to make him see how little they cared about him and his threats, they had only to tell him frankly that if he did not to justice as soon as possible, the hostages, who had been well-treated thus far, would be exposed to the fury of the poor people, who would not fail to tear them apart and feed them to the dogs; which would doubtless cause a deadly war between them, in which much blood would be shed.

The envoys did not let it rest without retort; they pleaded their case eloquently, but, having been unable to obtain any other response than the one that had already been made to them, they returned home, extremely malcontent.

The Governor was so enraged to see that his threats had had so little effect that he did not even take the time to consult the Magistrates as to what he ought to do; he ordered the Commander of his Guard to depart immediately for Cambul and to tell Zandor that, since he did not want to live with him in good intelligence, he summoned him to be at the Cape of Rushes, half way between the two cities, in a fortnight's time, at the head of two hundred and fifty boats; that he would bring as many himself, and that they would settle their differences at sword-point.

The King accepted that challenge, reluctantly; he would rather have settled the quarrel amiably. The people, by contrast, were delighted to be able to come to grips with an enemy that was becoming more arrogant every day, and was putting a foot on their throat everywhere. If one had wanted to believe the greater number, the entire city would go forth to take part in that battle.

The word having been given, they worked at first on the equipment of the fleet. They put out to sea, and the two naval armies exercised so much diligence that they were at the named location at the appointed time.

As soon as the diminutive vessels were within sight of one another, the drums, horns and marine trumpets made the whole atmosphere reverberated with their sound. The two sides were draw up in battle order, and having approached with half bow-range they began the action with so much promptitude and courage that one might have thought that the Heavens were raining arrows.

The combat had scarcely lasted an hour when a thick fog rose up, which obliged both parties to advance, and they came so close, because the obscurity was deepening from one moment to the next, that the gradually came together. Then, making use not only of their cutlasses but also oars, sticks and everything that came to hand, they fought with so much fury, and so obstinately, that if a strong wind that blew up shortly afterwards had not constrained the to steer for the shore and avoid being swallowed by the waves, not one of them would have come back.

Eighty-nine boats perished, and the majority of the combatants were killed or wounded. Both sides had taken prisoners, with the result that one could not say positively that one of them had the advantage over the other, and victory could not be attributed to either. Zandor was mortally wounded in the battle, and no one knew what had become of three of his brothers. The legitimate successor to the Crown, whose name was Amander, had received a blow to the head, and the youngest one was the only one to emerge from the battle fortunately— without a scratch, as the saying has it.

Before passing on, I think that it is appropriate to remark at this point that one of the inhabitants of Meralde, a fisherman by profession, had, among other children, a daughter aged twenty, who had none but masculine inclinations. She liked the company of men, and only wanted to involve herself in the things they did. She was known as the Matelot, because her father dressed her in boy's clothing from the age of four and continued to make use of her has a servant for the heaviest labors of seafaring

That young woman resembled Amander as closely as his twin; they were almost exactly the same age, the same build and height, with coarse features, an aquiline nose, and—most admirably of all—Amander had no beard. As she had a martial heart, she had thought that she ought not to let a favorable opportunity escape, which might not present itself again in her lifetime, to see two armies at grips. She had joined the party without anyone thinking about it, because everyone was accustomed to see her undertaking difficult and dangerous actions.

Finding herself after the battle in the Cambulian ranks, she was delighted to find that everyone was calling her Amander and seeing everyone competing to take care of her wound. In the situation she was in she had the best excuse in the world for not saying a word; she allowed herself to be fawned over, bandaged, served and taken where they wanted, without giving evidence of the slightest surprise, as if they were only doing their duty. In sum, the Matelot had become the son and brother of the King; honors were deferred to her and she was taken to the Princes' house, where particular care was taken to make sure that she lacked nothing.

Her relatives, not seeing her return to Meralde with the others, and being unable to learn from anyone what had become of her, believed her to be dead, with the result that forgetfulness was the first place that was destined for the Matelot for her sepulcher.

The Governor of that superb city did not have the hostages as yet; he had not had the right to demand their return beforehand, and did not have any advantage over his enemies that would give him a means to constrain their return. He thought that while his people were still animated that he ought to offer a new challenge to Zandor to come to meet him on land with an army of two thousand men, on condition that the vanquished would be forced to give preference to the victor in the matter of the difference that had caused their rupture, in order that it should not have to be done twice.

It only required a few days to prepare for the new march. The season was agreeable, the roads good and smooth. They were divided, as we have previously described, in that every half mile between the cities there was a stone column on each side, twelve feet high and numbered, all the way to the first lodgments, where the numeration recommenced, finishing at the second, and so on, as long as the territory of Cambul extended, for an equal distance in all directions. From Meralde until that point, which was, in consequence, half way, the divisions were terminated by triangular pyramids of equal height, marked in the same fashion.

The King's Lieutenant, who was leading the Cambulian army, had as much maturity and experience as one can have in a country that has only ever been at war with wild beasts. He remarked, as he approached the Meraldians, that they had the Sun and a fairly strong wind in their faces—advantages too considerable to neglect. He charged them with all the pride of which a brave general is capable, and having given orders to his men to raise as much dust as they could, he attacked them so forcefully, sword in hand, while a cloud of sand robbed them of the sight of all the objects surrounded them, that they immediately began to flee in disarray.

Two thousand six hundred and fifty-five men were laid out on the battlefield; the Governor lost his life there and his eldest son was among the prisoners; with the result that the Cambulian forces returned home triumphant, but not swell-headed about their victory.

Zandor, on the contrary, in order to show all Ruffal evidence of his generosity, had the son of the late Protector of Meralde brought to him, who was the person due to succeed him in that high dignity. He expressed his displeasure at the tragic death of his father, and made him see that he had been the cause of all that misfortune and the death of so many brave men, without any cause, since the difference between them could have been settled by a simple submission, an apology or a slight penalty imposed on the guilty party, after he had declared that he would abide by the sentence that the Governor had pronounced himself in favor of the victim.

"I demand," he said to him, "that you eat with me, that you accept one of my best garments as a present, and that you return home with all those of your government who are here, all the hostages that that I have taken in the two battles. Go, may God guide you. If you become Governor of Meralde, I recommend you to love for your subjects and peace with your neighbors."

That compliment broke the honest hearts of all the foreigners; before their departure they gave a thousand sensible and respectful signs of their sincere gratitude, and protested that if the Ambassador—who was, however, built like a lion—had not perished in the recent action they would remit him in his hands at the first opportunity, in order that he might punish him as he saw fit.

The inhabitants of Meralde were also content with this procedure; they sent a new deputation of the most artful among them, to thank Zandor and to negotiate a perpetual alliance with him, which could not be broken under any pretext whatsoever.

That peace was a new subject for rejoicing; the entire city of Cambul testified to its joy. Only Zandor did not appear in public to add his own marks; his wounds were getting worse every day, and there was no means of curing them—with the result that his reign was of very short duration.

On the other hand, the Matelot became stronger from day to day; everyone endeavored to procure "him"[30] pleasure, and to render themselves necessary with regard to his person, in the hope that he would soon be in a position to recompense them and do them good. As he had intelligence, he had not failed to pay very close attention to everything that was said about him and the Royal family; he had even been able to obtain adroitly from the mouths of a thousand flatterers, who were eternally obedient to him, the information that was necessary to him to play his role well in circumstances of that importance. In consequence, immediately after the death of his supposed brother, he was elected without any difficulty and thus succeeded to the sovereignty.

Although, fundamentally, a King of that order has very little to do by comparison with the Monarchs that one has in all the nations of Europe and Asia, it is nevertheless quite considerable. He is the Figurehead of at least a million peo-

---

[30] In French, because "matelot" is a masculine noun, the pronoun that stands in for it is "il," without necessarily containing any absolute implication as to the actual sex of the individual thus designated, and the same is true of "Roy" [King]. Because English pronouns do not work in the same fashion, the substitution of "he" in such circumstances inevitably contains an unambiguous implication of sex, but as the story goes on, the French text takes on a positive implication of maleness in its use of pronouns to refer to this character, until the crucial juncture when it suddenly begins to substitute unmistakable references to her actual sex, although not without subsequent inconsistency. Thus, the evident eccentricities and confusions of the translation are not far removed from those of the original.

ple, whose property and lives he can dispose as he pleases, for no one there can make a case of conscience of opposing his will in any respect whatever, or even pt o a semblance of so doing.

That being the case, it would not be surprising to hear that the false Amander, having no society, no education and no birth, forgot what he owed to his character and abandoned himself to luxury, vanity and debauchery. Not at all; one might have thought, from his actions, that he had only ever frequented people of high rank. He was civil, generous and honest as could be, and with all of that he conserved a certain gravity that imprinted respect on all those who came close to him.

As he cast an eye over everything, and observed the slightest movements of his subjects, he thought one day that he had remarked that his pretended brother Merusol was having a affair with the wife of a Lieutenant of the troops, in that she rarely failed to come to see him when her husband was on guard duty, or if he was away from home for any length of time.

In order to clarify the matter, he put on clothing very similar to hers, lowered his heels by two inches because he was much taller than she was, and, having posted men as sentinels at a time when he suspected that the beauty would come to visit her gallant, he was delighted when they came to tell him that the Lady had indeed slipped into Merusol's room, alone. He sent a domestic to ask her to come immediately to speak to the King, who had something important to say to her in her own interest, with a promise that he would only keep her for a moment.

Believing as she did that no one had seen her enter the place where she was, she was nonplussed on hearing that message, but, having pulled herself together she said to the officer of the chamber: "Go tell the King that I will come to him immediately." At the same time, she got up, and left, but as she presented herself at the door of His Majesty's study, the same man who had just left her showed her into another apartment, saying that in the interval something had cropped up to which the King was obliged to attend without delay and that he had orders to beg her on his behalf to be kind enough to wait there until he had finished, when he would speak to her.

Meanwhile, the King had gone in disguise to find Merusol, who, as soon as he saw him come in, threw his arms around his neck and kissed him with an inconceivable ardor.

"I was impatient to see you again, Madame," he said. "The fire that your presence had lit, and that your charity was on the point of extinguishing when you received that fateful order to depart, is consuming me. Let's go, my Goddess, let's not waste time, for fear that some other similar inconvenience will interrupt once again the beautiful deign that Cupid[31] formed in his day for the wellbeing of two Lovers who love one another more than life."

He took him by the hand and pulled him toward the place where his passion dominated conduct.

The king did not say a word. He was so confused and nonplussed to be treated in that manner, in a dark place in which it was difficult to make out the most evident objects, that he could not utter a sound. As he was not insensible, his nature seemed to awaken, and to take some pleasure from that badinage, with the result that, the pleasure being combined with the vain curiosity that he had so far had as to the extent that those people pushed their intrigue, he made very little reflection on what was happening. He had so completely forgotten the duties to which his quality as a maiden engaged him—a maiden who had enjoyed so much success this far in playing the role of the Sovereign—that he had crossed the frontiers of the empire of amour before having perceived that he had set foot on its territory.

It was at that moment that his conscience began to awaken and to apprehend the consequences of that dangerous encounter.

"Let us whisper, Merusol," he said to that passionate lover. "I fear that there might be people spying on us here."

"To speak frankly," Merusol replied, "I had the same thought, when the King sent for you. It's easy to judge by the circumstances. What did he want with you?"

"What he wanted," Amander said, "was to tell me that, the Captain of the third Company of his guards having just died, he had already cast his eyes on my husband as a man of whom he was generous enough to think highly, and that, having heard from one of his domestics that I had come in here, he wanted to make my party to his benevolent sentiments for an officer who has always served him carefully and with an inconceivable fidelity.

"You can imagine that I was charmed by the compliment, not only because it was agreeable and advantageous, but because it furnished me with the means of satisfying a desire that he then expressed to know what I was going to do in his brother's rooms, and also arms sufficient for the defense of my honor, which was considerably at risk in such a case. As soon as he had finished speaking, I did not fail to thank him very humbly, I recommended the interest of my family to him, and declared that I had only come to see you with the intention of asking you to intercede on behalf of your old friend with His Majesty."

---

[31] The narrator might be substituting the name of the Roman god for a Russalian equivalent left over from their own ancient heritage and retained in poetic diction, but the presence of the term—subsequently supplemented by another of similar origin—could also add weight to the hypothesis that the author is inserting stories into his portmanteau narrative that had been written previously with a different setting.

"Assuredly," said Merusol, "that worked out perfectly, since you can use the same pretext for coming to see me more often than that one you used just now. It's twelve days since we last saw one another, and that interval seemed prodigiously long to me."

"I don't understand," said the King, still in a very low voice, "how that solicitation could be drawn out any longer."

"Yes indeed," replied Merusol. "It's a custom here, which has become a kind of law, that is only violated in extraordinary cases, such as when someone distinguishes himself in war, is intrepid, indefatigable and always fortunate in hunting, visibly risks his life to save the King from danger in which he would probably have perished, or renders a considerable service to the fatherland. That being so, it would obviously be a glaring injustice not to give the company with the vacancy to its Lieutenant. He is brave, he has nothing to answer for to anyone, but as he is old and presently confined to bed, in such a manner that hardly anyone imagines that he will get up again, it only remains to go to the King to speak in favor of your husband, and to prevent him disposing of the vacant post until the direction that the patient's malady will take becomes clear, in order to give no one grounds for complaint. Let me do it; I'll take care of all that."

"That's very well imagined," Amander replied. "We'll talk about it at greater length another time. I dare not stay here any longer; I'm going."

"Adieu, then, my lovely soul," said Merusol. "By the way, don't forget the gloves you left on that table just now."

"I was so troubled," said Amander, "that I didn't notice it until I was in the King's antechamber—but no harm was done; I had another pair in my pocket, which I presently have on my hands, as you see. I'll take the others, though; they're better than these, and I don't suppose you'd care to have anyone see a woman's gloves in your bedroom. Adieu."

As soon as the King had returned he changed back into his own clothes and summoned Sardanie, as the wife of the deceived officer was named.

"You've been kept waiting, Madame," he said to her. "I'm sorry about that, but something came up, which didn't permit me to join you sooner. Knowing that you were nearby, in the apartment of one of my relatives, I thought it would give you pleasure to tell you that I have cast an eye on your husband, to fill the post that the decease of Captain Melchor has just rendered vacant. I've sought information as to his conduct and have received good reports; in addition to that he has been recommended by several people for whom I have consideration."

Sardanie, delighted to hear that the matter in hand was of a nature entirely different than she had thought, expressed her just gratitude to the King with a thousand thanks. She added to that compliment, in order to save appearances, that it was in the design of doing that good work that she had taken the liberty of going to intercede with Merusol, whom she knew the King loved like his eyes, and concluded by recommending herself increasingly to his bounty.

"What?" said the King. "You went to solicit from my brother a charge that depends entirely on me, and which I give without anyone else taking cognizance of it? I would rather you had not told me that, notwithstanding the fact that I can clearly see that you thought by that means to pay court to me. That offends my honor; my glory is involved; I don't want anyone to address themselves to anyone but me when it's a matter of my favors—that would be the kind of means likely to make me to the opposite. However, as I'm persuaded that you have only acted on a principle of respect for my person and have sinned innocently, I'll willingly pardon you—but I forbid you in future to address yourself to anyone but me in your needs, and above all, to avoid seeing Merusol again as you would falling into the fire, under the penalty of my indignation."

The overture of the King's compliment was admirable, but the conclusion did not please Sardanie at all, although she gave no semblance of it. She even promised, with a smile on her face, to obey scrupulously the command he had just given her. Having made a profound reverence, she went away, scarcely imagining that the severe prohibition was the pure effect of the jealousy of a woman, who had become her rival without intending to, and did not want to share with her a benefit that she had not yet thought frankly about possessing.

The next day Merusol came to visit the King. He spoke to him about the Lieutenant and recommended him very earnestly.

"You're not unaware," the King said to him, "that I'm incapable of doing wrong to anyone; the post that is vacant belongs by right to the officer next in command in the same company. You know that as well as I do. However, I would like, for love of you, not to dispose of it as yet, inasmuch as the man concerned is ill, in order to see whether time will furnish us with an expedient in order to content you. Perhaps I love you more than you think, and I assure you that I shall always take a singular pleasure in giving you marks of my esteem."

"I am much obliged to you, my brother," Merusol replied. "You can rely on my fidelity, and be persuaded that for you, I would attempt the imp..."

"Enough compliments," Amander interrupted. "There's no need for you to explain yourself further; I believe that you're sincere, just as I am."

As soon as Merusol had withdrawn, the King reproached himself internally for not having retained him for a meal, in order to enjoy his company for longer. Although he had previously regarded him with indifference, he no longer considered him without pleasure. The young man's words, actions, gestures and attitudes all had charms, which excited in him an unknown passion that he had not felt before. His absence made him anxious, and he hesitated more than once as to whether or not he ought to go in quest him. He had enough strength to control himself, however; he sat down at his table pensively and went to bed in a melancholy mood.

His domestics thought that he was not well, and thought that there was no doubt about it when, on getting up again, he seemed paler than usual. In fact, he had hardly slept, and the little sleep he had enjoyed had been traversed by bad dreams, in which his health had deteriorated in some way.

As he had taken his butler into his confidence regarding the desire they had to amuse himself by discovering the intrigues of Merusol and Sardanie—because he was the one who had told him that they saw one another frequently—he told him that being chagrined, he wanted him to help him disguise himself as before, in order to go and visit Merusol, to see if he could make the fantasy pass by that means. The man, who was very fond of him, applauded his scheme, and helped him to go out by a hidden door so that no one would see him.

When Amander had entered Merusol's apartment he slipped quietly into his bedroom, where he found him alone, a large volume of the Laws of the land on his knees, that being his principal occupation.

The Prince seemed surprised by the sight of an object that, in truth, he loved like his eyes, but which he was not accustomed to seeing so frequently, because they took measures to protect one another and he had not been alerted in the usual way. That made him believe that some pressing affair had brought her, which would not suffer any delay.

"What is it, Madam," he asked, "that makes you come unexpectedly like this? Either something extraordinary has happened, or you need my help—or couldn't you find anyone to let me know, and to prepare to receive you without witnesses? I am, in fact, sometimes alone, but it's fairly rare, and I'd be embarrassed if anyone were to see you coming here repeatedly. You did so twice the day before yesterday, and now here you are again. I'm speaking with an open heart; I don't see you intimately as often as I'd like, but it's better, in my opinion, to enjoy pleasures soberly that we're capable of procuring for a long time than to be prodigal briefly, and see ourselves deprived of them permanently."

"You're right," Amander replied, in a whisper, "but my heart is heavy with what has happened since I have not seen you, and I had to come in order to unburden it on you; it's a secret that I dare not confide to anyone else. The king summoned me to the Palace a little while ago, and, under the pretext of taking all the measures necessary for the success of the plan regarding my husband, he has ordered me not to see you again, under the penalty of his indignation, because he wants to have the sole honor of befitting my family and does not want his brother to have any part in it. I dare not disobey His Majesty because of the consequences; he would be capable of avenging himself on us and our children. On the other hand, you are dearer to me than all I possess, so you can see that the penalty he has imposed on me is intolerable; it's a penitence that will be the death of me if I'm obliged to observe it unreservedly."

"The King doubtless said that as a joke," said Merusol. "He loves me too much to take offense because someone employs me to procure his amity and his favor."

"Not at all," Amander continued. "He was speaking very seriously, and I fear that something bad might happen to me if I tried to treat it as a joke."

"I'll sound him out on that," said Merusol, "the first time we see one another; meanwhile, use precaution."

"It's impossible for me to contain myself anymore," Amander replied. "My temperament and the inclination I have for you don't permit it."

"Do as you please, then," the Prince replied, "provided that you send someone to warn me of your plans."

"That's easy to say," Amander continued, "but don't you see that I'm risking as much by that as otherwise? If I come here directly, and don't find you, or you have company, I can get out of it by saying that I have something to say to you in private—a favor to ask you on behalf of my husband, for some soldier in his command, or some similar cause; that's common enough for the wives of officers. Otherwise, it's necessary to have trusted people for those kinds of messages, and it often happens that the more one hides, the more renders oneself suspect.

"Another expedient occurred to me, of which I hope you'll approve, which is that I only come here costumed as a man—a hunter, if you wish—and that will shelter both of us from malevolence and the danger that there would be otherwise that the king might perceive something. And if the case should arise that, being in the neighborhood, that I forget myself to the point of entering your apartment in female attire, or ask you for permission to do so, I beg you not to receive me, and to send me away without letting me speak to you—will you promise me that?"

"With all my heart," Merusol replied, "and I assure you that I shall hold you to your word, since I think your scheme very reasonable."

"Adieu, then, it's agreed," said Amander then, getting up and making as if to depart.

"What are you doing?" said Merusol, abruptly. "I don't think you wanted to leave me so soon. Come on, be sweet, don't we know one another any longer? Or did I moralize too much when you arrived? Don't think, rascal, that I love you any less for that; on the contrary, it's the fear of losing you that made me take that tone."

At the same time, he takes her hand, kisses it, extends the caresses and, believing that the efforts made by Amander, who is not yet entirely stripped of modesty—which is quite natural in the fair sex—are only feigned in order to excite his amorousness, he draws her into the lists, so to speak, and half by inclination and half by force he obliges her to joust with him, twice over, unrestrainedly.

After which, Amander went out, more satisfied with that tender violence that he wanted to appear.

The butler was delighted to see the King return in such a good mood; he testified that by expressions that further augmented his joy, and advised him to take advantage the same diversion often.

"Assuredly," said the King, "it's necessary to admit that Merusol is a gallant man; I played my part perfectly with him, but I can clearly see that it requires a clever and virtuous woman to resist the assaults of a champion like him."

At the next meal that was served to the King he invited Merusol to keep him company, and gave him so much pithson that he seemed tipsy, in order to have the opportunity to get him started on the chapter of his mistress; but no matter which way he approached the subject, he could not get anything out of him on that score; he even protested that she had only set foot in his apartment on two or three occasions with regard to matters related to her family in which she needed his assistance.

"The woman has slanderers, then," said the King. "I've been assured that she sees you frequently and that she was in your apartment only yesterday."

"Well, Sire," he retorted, "to shut those people up, I won't see her again, whatever pressing reason she gives me."

"I think you would do well," said the King. "A woman has to be careful in order not to scandalize anyone and to prevent her husband from maltreating her or having her punished in accordance with the rigor of the law."

Two or three days later, Amander went to see Merusol, who treated her in the most passionate fashion in the world and redoubled his urgencies and attentions in her regard. He also praised her for her presence of mind and her genius in sheltering them from slander.

"We would have been doomed," he said to her, "if you had continued to come here in the clothing appropriate to your sex. Someone was spying on you, nothing is more certain; the King could not help telling me the last time I ate with him; he knew that you had been to see me on a particular day and that you had left your gloves on my table the time before."

"Is it possible?" said Amander. "See, I beg you, to what extremity I would soon have exposed myself. I came back dressed in my own fashion, and was only twenty paces from your door when I remembered the plea that I had made to you no longer to give me access in that outfit.. Once again, I beg you, keep my word. Passions are sometimes so strong that they blind us; if I'm seen here again, someone might report it to my husband; you know him, he's a violent man who would be capable of doing me excessive harm."

"There's no danger," said Merusol. "I'll make sure for both our sakes that no misfortune over takes you."

Amander, who was beginning to get a taste for the visits he rendered to Merusol, secretly applauded himself for having distanced such a dangerous rival from his cherished lover; he went home more content than ever, resolved to continue the tender commerce and to profit as much as he could from such a favorable combination of circumstances.

Indeed, having no more discretion to exercise, they saw one another almost every day, to the great contentment of both.

The officer's wife, by contrast, enraged by no longer being able to enjoy the company of her former admirer, whom she believed so impatient to see her, and desiring ardently to see him, made an attempt to content herself. She went back and forth past his house several times, and, having finally remarked that no one appeared to be about, she ran inside recklessly. A domestic who perceived her came to ask what she wanted.

"Let me pass," she said. "I need to speak to Merusol; I want to go and find him myself."

"He's not visible," the valet replied.

"He always is for me," she went on, proceeding on her way as she spoke.

"All the same," the servant said, "we're not in a place where any violence is permitted, but withdraw, Madame, I beg you. No one can see My Lord at this hour, and even if that were not the case, I have orders no longer to permit you to enter his apartment."

"You're mistaken, my friend," said Sardanie. "You're doubtless mistaking me for someone else."

"I'm not mistaken," he replied. "You're the wife of an officer; I've known you for a long time; once again, withdraw, and don't oblige me to constrain you."

Sardanie was nonplussed by that turn of events; she did not know how to account for it.

*What have I done to that perfidious individual,* she wondered, *for him to treat me as the least of creatures? Is it because the King has forbidden him to see me, since he found out that I had been to his apartment, under the pretext that he does not want others to meddle in his affairs, or to avoid the scandal that the visits of a married wan to a young man might give the public? No, there's doubtless some mystery in this. The traitor loves someone else; some newcomer has appeared, who has dazzled his eyes and effaced in his mind the brilliance he saw in my person. It's common for men to be inconstant; they like change. Whatever it is, I can't remain silent; it's necessary to reproach his perfidy, or give him an opportunity to explain this cruel treatment, which I don't think I've deserved.*

She was still occupied with reflections on what might have happened when she arrived home. Being impatient to seek information on the subject that had caused it that she picked up a pen and wrote the following letter:

*To Merusol,*

*What have I done to you, most inconstant and cruel of all men? You have pursued me and persecuted me for two years; threats against my husband and*

*promises of benefits to my relatives have entered into play; there is no imagina-*
*ble means that you have not employed to vanquish me, and it was only after a*
*thousand reiterated protestations of loving me eternally that I yielded to your*
*amour. I have betrayed my duty, I have been unfaithful to a husband who loves*
*me like his eyes, and I have put myself in danger of being punished in accord-*
*ance with the rigor of the Law to please you, and after having given myself to*
*you entirely, you abandon me in a cowardly fashion, you scorn me and forbid*
*me entry to your door. I ask you to judge yourself whether anything could be*
*more insulting and mortifying. Well, you shall not see me anymore, ingrate; the*
*resolution is made, but if you have not entirely renounced humanity, at least add*
*to my sentence the reason for which you have signed my condemnation, in order*
*that, if I am guilty, I can punish myself, and if I am innocent, I can justify myself,*
*and make you see that Merusol is veritably unworthy of your former lover*

*Sardanie.*

This note was confided to a young servant, who delivered it by hand, without saying who it came from, because he did not know himself. Merusol opened
it immediately, but with what astonishment did he not feel himself gripped when
he began to read it?

*I'm awake, though,* he said to himself. *I'm not being deceived by a dream,*
*and I haven't indulged in any excess that might make me lose the usage of my*
*senses and my reason. This discourse is conceived in its form; it's strong and*
*it's urgent; but all things considered, it can't be serious; it's doubtless a joke,*
*some gallantry invented to amuse me. On the other hand, when I consider the*
*matter more carefully, I can't see that there's any foundation for all this, since*
*it's such a short time since we saw one another, and nothing has happened that*
*could give rise to any complaint, however pretended or apparent.*

With that, he called his servants and asked the one who was performing the
function of doorkeeper that day what kinds of people had set for in his antechamber. After a scrupulous examination, he learned that someone had come,
out of breath and very alarmed, demanding to speak to him, but that, in accordance with the order that he had given, she had been refused entry.

That incident annoyed him, but as there was apparently nothing in it that
was not in conformity with their agreement and the plea that she had made herself, he concluded that her memory had betrayed her and that she alone as the
cause of the inconvenience. He did not think, however, that it was appropriate to
quarrel with her; on the contrary, he thought he ought to make his apologies
simply recommend her to be more circumspect another time, by means of a note
whose tenor was as follows:

*To the Beautiful Sardanie,*
*You complain of a disgrace, Madame, for which you ought only to blame*
*yourself; you know the conditions which we have agreed for seeing one another.*

*You commanded me yourself only to receive you in future in male garb, because of the consequences, if you had forgotten. If, having changed your sentiment, you thought you could relax your resolution, I should have been informed. My domestics have been told to follow your commandment rigorously. I admit to you, however, that if I had met you at the door when you entered my house, I would have spared you the chagrin that you have been obliged to endure in being turned away unsatisfied. As a result of this misunderstanding I shall no longer obey; come henceforth in whatever clothing and manner you like; you will always be very welcome, and I shall make you see that I am, as much as ever, your very faithful lover*

*Merusol*

As the bearer of this note, which he was holding in plain sight, set off for the Palace, he had the misfortune to encounter Amander in disguise. The Prince, who knew him to be his brother's domestic, beckoned to him and asked him where he was going and what he had in his hand, on which the young man became troubled.

Amander perceived that. "Tell me the truth," he said. "I'm your master's friend; he has no secrets from me."

The servant having explained, the King protested that he was the very same Sardanie, that he had put on male garb as a joke to play a little trick on someone, so he had only to give him the letter he was carrying and simply tell Merusol that he had delivered it with his own hand.

The King, whose intention was to go to see his brother, being uncertain of what the note contained, retraced his steps and went back to his study in order to read it, in order to discover what had happened between the two former lovers and to be able to take precautions in case anything as brewing to his prejudice.

As soon as he had seen it he resealed it and sent it to Sardanie by an unknown messenger, better instructed than the previous one, who was to take care only to hand it over if the circumstances were appropriate. After that, Amander resumed the route of Merusol's house.

That passionate lover was delighted to see his beloved mistress again, whom he had thought lost. He sent away several other people who were with him, under the pretext that he had matters to settle with the newcomer that could not be deferred. As soon as he was alone with Amander he did not hesitate to express the displeasure he had with regard to her disgrace.

"Let's not talk about it anymore," said the King. "It's my fault, I confess; another time, I'll think more about what I'm doing, so long as love, which blinds poor mortals, leaves me the liberty to do so,."

"Oh, my beautiful Angel," exclaimed Merusol, "how agreeable that expression is to me; I shall never forget it, and were you to make the silliest of blunders, you will always have a reputation for wisdom, since you attribute its cause to a God who does not fail to inspire sentiments worthy of him to those who abandon themselves to his Laws and depend absolutely on his empire."

With that there were a thousand further protestations on either side to love one another reciprocally until death, which were couched in good and due form in the tablets of the Mother of amours, and sealed with the seal of the Chancellery of Cupid, to the great contentment of the parties, who only separated with regret and with the hope of seeing one another within a short time.

Sardanie, by contrast, was unable to maintain her self-possession, and, understanding nothing in the note that she had received, she composed another.

*To Merusol,*

*It is very disgraceful of you to treat me in such an unworthy manner, since I have not merited any punishment, if not by virtue of having loved you too much, but it is infinitely worse for you represent me overtly as chimerical and hypochondriac, given that I have given you no reason. On that basis, I do not merit a more ample explanation of the different roles that you claim I play in order to see you, and for the execution of which you say that I have given my consent, which is gibberish, for which I have no taste, and which makes me doubt whether you are even in your right mind; there would be no point; it is sufficient that you do not want to see me anymore, and there is no need for you to receive any further letters from me. If the displeasure that I experience at such an insulting procedure is violent, it will not be long in recompense, since it is impossible that I shall survive a disgrace that forbids me the means any longer to call myself your beloved*

*Sardanie*

While Sardanie was occupied in writing to Merusol, the King sent for her husband, in order to tell him that he was still thinking about him and that his fortune would assuredly be made, if not on the present occasion, in which it seemed that the ailing Lieutenant was not yet able to resolve to die, then infallibly on another—but that he warned him once again not to give him the chagrin of soliciting others, as it appeared that his wife had done and was continuing to do, since he was charitable enough not to judge that it was any other motive that led took her to his brother's house and elsewhere.

As the worthy man tried to disculpate himself, the King continued: "Don't dispute that, I beg you. I have certain knowledge of what I am telling you. Look, this pair of gloves, which belongs to her, and which I found in the apartment of a man of consideration, where she had forgotten them, is proof of it. Here they are; you have only to return them to her and seek information of the matter; she will not deny it."

The Officer remained confused by this speech, and had absolutely no idea how to respond, except to say that he knew nothing about it, and that he would make sure that his wife did not commit the same fault again.

Needless to say, as soon as he returned home, he took Sardanie to task. She tried to deny the actions of which she was accused, but had to change tack the moment her husband showed her the gloves.

"It's true," she said, then. "I've been to Merusol's apartment, to beg him urgently to have the kindness to remember your long service and recommend you to the King. That was done in his Antechamber, in the presence of several witnesses, whom I can name. That's the only time that I've been there, and the only one on which I spoke about your affairs."

"But Madame," the husband said, "is it the fashion to go with bare hands to present oneself to distinguished persons, or to take one's gloves off in a place where there is neither food not drink, when it is only a matter of imploring the protection of the Brother of our Monarch? What have you done in that Prince's home? Have you played games, or been required to put your hands on something?"

"Nothing like that," she replied. "Having felt, before going in, that one of my garters was undone, I took off my gloves in order to reattach it, and, flustered as I was, on going to present myself to a Lord to whom I had never spoken before, I forgot to put them on again. I went in, and it appears that I let them fall out of my sleeve, where I had put them, without noticing. I couldn't imagine what I had done with them and searched for them for a long time, fruitlessly, in my chests, not realizing that I had lost them. It's a small accident that won't happen again, come what may; I shall leave the care of our affairs to you, since, in any case, my solicitation had no effect."

The Officer, who was unaware of his wife's intrigues and had always believed her to be honest in her conduct, took that at face value, and did not mention it again. However, it was still the case that the circumstance completed the ruination of Merusol in Sardanie's mind; she was invincibly convinced that he had taken the King into his confidence with regard to the nature of their relationship, since there did not appear to be any other means for him to have got hold of her gloves—with the consequence that if her letter had not already been sent she would probably have conceived another in terms that would not have failed to be even stronger and more shocking. It was out of her hands, however, and she contented herself with breaking entirely with the Prince and making an oath never to set foot in his house again.

For his part, Merusol did not take much account of Sardanie's letter; as they were in a very different state he imagined that its principal objective was to amuse him. He mentioned it, however, to Amander the first time he came to see him, after having told him about the receipt of his pretended letter, but the latter was able to change the subject so adroitly that they did not linger upon it for long. They were taking so much pleasure in more substantial occupations that they did not take the trouble to examine it closely.

Amander and Merusol were no longer worried about anyone, thinking of nothing but procuring new amusements every day; they made that their study, and nothing else was worthy of their application. As there is no perfect happiness in this world, however, and joy ordinarily precedes sadness, which hardly ever abandons it by more than a few steps, and that which appears permanent and accomplished is very often the most imperfect of all and the most subject to the vicissitudes of chance, Amander was utterly astonished when he perceived one day that he was threatened by a swelling, which, although it was not mortal, was nevertheless dangerous and capable of giving him a great deal of annoyance.

That unfortunate accident alarmed him; he did not know of any means appropriate to remedy it, and did not see how he could avoid being dethroned as soon as it became known. The catastrophe by which he was menaced was terrible, and the opprobrium that he would receive in consequence, in all likelihood, made him shiver every time he thought about it. No matter where he went, he no longer had any repose; the mere idea of his downfall filled the entire capacity of his mind during his slumber, and, not daring to confide in any of his subjects for fear that they would betray him, he resolved to write to his father, to attempt to dispose him to come to find him with his mother, his brothers and his sisters, in the hope that if they remained in Cambul they could help him give birth secretly without anyone else even catching wind of it.

This is what he wrote:

*To Resan, father of Amander, or the Matelot,*

*I am sure, my dear father, that you have long thought me dead; it is a misconception, however; I am full of life and health and in a condition very different from that in which you would ever have imagined seeing me. I have wealth, I have power and I have credit. The King and I live in perfect intelligence; he loves me like his eyes; we have but one heart and one soul, and I can tell you that he would despair of attempting anything without my entire approval. Judge, in consequence, of what I am presently capable: employment, honors and the wealth of the state all depend on me. I am speaking seriously, there is no hyperbole, and nothing in this that smacks of fiction.*

*Take advantage of such a favorable circumstance, I beg you; leave as soon as you can, and come to find me with your family and those you will have taken as our relatives. I shall raise you to the highest rank in the city, without anyone protesting as long as I remain unknown, for it is necessary for you to know that I am passing for someone other than who I am, and that people are even unaware of my sex.*

*On arriving here come directly to the Court, and address yourself to the King, under the pretext that you have left Meralde in order to establish yourself in Cambul, where you will need his protection. Do not forget to bring a present of Raf, Rekeling, Caviar and Esliguer; he loves all that passionately. I shall*

*make arrangements on the meantime to receive you honestly and to do every-*
*thing imaginable for your benefit. I have already spoken to him about you sev-*
*eral times, and I am not lying when I say that it is really him who is sending you*
*the bearer of this letter, in my consideration, who will tell you personally of the*
*desire that the Prince has to embrace you.*

*Leave immediately, by the first convenient means; I await you with impa-*
*tience, in order to give you convincing proofs of the zeal with which I am verita-*
*bly all yours.*

*The Matelot*

A week later, a Caravan departed, which was joined by the man he charged with delivering the letter, and to whom he gave instructions that he had not dared put in writing. The messenger acquitted his commission perfectly, but he was met with gibes and mockery. It did not appear very plausible to them that the Matelot was still alive, and even less that he had had enough intelligence to obtain the ascendancy over a King that he claimed, but even if all that was true, they were so accustomed to living a rude and private life that they would have preferred it to the most dazzling position in society: employments, dignities and the Court were objects of scorn to them, because they often engendered the hatred of the public and gave birth to nothing but hard labor and anxiety. Thus, the poor man was forced to return without having accomplished anything to the advantage of his master.

Amander had not expected that; he had counted so firmly on his parents that since sending the letter he had fallen into a kind of indolence, which had rendered him insensible to all kinds of events. The moment that his chagrin became visible again, Merusol noticed it, and asked to know its cause; all that he could reply was that he was not feeling very well, and was threatened with dying soon of dropsy.

"My illness," he said, "commenced a few months ago, with heart trouble and fainting fits; I'm often thirsty but I rarely have an appetite. Eventually, it passed, and I thought I was better, when I noticed by my clothes that my body was gradually swelling. I consulted my physician then, and I've employed several remedies, but nothing helps; on the contrary, the illness is getting worse every day."

Merusol loved him, not because he believed him to be his brother but by virtue of another principle, the cause of which he did not know himself; that reason determined that he did not abandon himself in the least to what was possible; he did everything he could to divert him, either by singing or playing instruments, or by means of gallantries, and finally with history, and the most remarkable adventures that had ever happened in Russal, of which he possessed an inexhaustible fund.

"It's necessary to admit," he said to him one day, "that something very extraordinary happened once in Persac, which merits your attention. It was a devout woman who told me the story and who, she told me, had it from people who were eye-witnesses.

"A rather well-to-do Marshal—which is to say that he possessed a lot of iron, tools, good clothes, fine furniture and houses, and who had shares in mines, quarries and pith-fields, for that is, as you know, what the wealth of that region mainly comprises, as does ours, except for the woods that we do not have, and in which he had no part—well, this Marshal, being old, a widower and without children, made a will by which he declared the universal and legitimate heir of all his wealth to be the first son that one of his two remaining nephews had, but that if they only had daughters, the wealth would pass to relatives of his wife, to whom he had great obligations.

"The hope of such a fine acquisition caused the two young men to marry at the age of fifteen or sixteen years. The wife of the first remained sterile; the wife of the other had six daughters one after another, and at the seventh pregnancy, the husband and wife resolved to work together to corrupt the midwife and to make sure that whatever child the woman gave birth to, she would end up with a boy. They were able to persuade the matron so well, seasoning the speech they addressed to her with such a considerable present, that she assured them that they would not lack a son.

"Things were arranged with that in mind; the pregnant woman had already delivered well before anyone went in search of the neighbors and relatives, because, it was said, the child came before it was expected. It was, in fact, another female, which was immediately taken away, and in whose place a male three days old had been substituted.

"That new guest brought much joy into the household and mortified extremely the party interested in the opposite result; but it was, after all, a settled matter that could not be changed. A fortnight or three weeks after the birth, a further exchange of children was effected.

"The mother took such good care of the pretended boy that no one ever imagined that it might be a girl. Not only did she wear clothing appropriate to the male sex, she even learned the exercises more appropriate to that sex, and succeeded in them so well that everyone had reason to be content.

"Thinking that there was no difference between herself and other men, she sought their company everywhere, and one might almost have thought that she had a distaste for the other sex. That changed with time, however, and she eventually began to talk about marrying. Her parents and the midwife, who knew her better than she knew herself, always deflected her from that thought, but as they alone were party to the secret, they were soon unable to prevent the young man from searching for a wife in the incontinent desire to establish a household.

"The woman he had selected was from an honest family, beautiful and shapely, and in very god health; for his part, he was just as well turned-out. Everyone looked forward to seeing their children. They wished in vain, however; none arrived. His friends often remarked on it; sometimes he laughed about it, bit more often he seemed mortified. For his part, the poor child was ignorant of the function of a husband; his wife, either out of modesty or innocence, always testified that she was perfectly content.

"Her mother was more afflicted than she was, with the consequence that when it had gone on for four years, and the delicacy of the features and complexion of the young man rendered him suspect to many people, who had remarked that no hair grew on his chin, she talked to her in private one day, and informed herself so cleverly as to how her husband was made that they took hold of him together and discovered the whole mystery.

"With that, the father in law addressed himself to his son-in-law, who told him ingeniously what the situation was. He protested that he had never known what the difference as that distinguished the male from the female, and that he did not understand why his mother had passed him off for what he was not. He might have got out of it at the cost of breaking the marriage; there had been no malice on his part and it would have been an injustice for the Magistrate to impose the slightest penalty on him. What was more troublesome was that his uncle's relatives on the maternal side, having learned of the metamorphosis, did not remain idle. They immediately brought the case before a judge, who pronounced in their favor without any difficulty and gave them the right to have everything usurped from them by that deceit returned."

"Indeed," said Amander, "that is a very curious case, but here is another, which ought to surprise you no less. A famous fisherman of Meralde had several children, including a daughter, whose inclinations were diametrically opposed to those of her sex. Her actions were male, and her vivacity had nothing ordinary about it. Scarcely was she able to walk than she sought out all the boys with whom she could play in their manner; subsequently she enjoyed hunting, fishing, exercises with arms and everything suitable to the sex opposite to her own. From her childhood, her father accustomed himself to that libertine life; he began to take the child with him from the age of four, and in order that her clothing should not inconvenience her, he dressed her as a boy.

"No one looked at her very closely when she was still young, but when she began to grow up, she was dressed as a girl in winter, for fear of causing scandal, and all summer, when she was at sea, she wore her old garments.

"I won't bother relating all the circumstances of that girl's life, which would doubtless please a mind less solid than yours, because my goal is to skip straight to the heart of the matter, so I will only tell you what became of her at the age of twenty-five or thirty year.

"It came about the Government of Meralde had some quarrel with the inhabitants of Daila; the matter went so far that war was declared, and it even came to a pitched battle. Our heroine—let's call her Sciola—was among the combatants, and as the victory was dubious, there were prisoners taken on both sides and also a great many people killed. One of the most important Chioux was mortally wounded and several of his sons lost their lives. Sciola resembled one of those young men as if they were identical twins. The Amazon was wounded, and because the clothing of the inhabitants of this country is uniform, without exception, only the Governor dressing in another manner, as you know, it is not surprising that a mistake was made.

"Effectively, the same care was taken of the young woman as would have been taken of the person they mistook her for; she was called by his name, she was taken to the house of that man of justice, and was treated like a Queen. Being clever and wily, she was careful not to give herself away, and took advantage of the circumstances, playing her role to well that when the Chiou died of his wounds, she was glad to see that, as the eldest son of a man who had sacrificed his life for the homeland, and in recompense for what she had done so well, she became a Chiou in Daila.

"She had not been exercising that responsibility long when she imagined by virtue of a few plausible indications that her putative brother must be having an affair with the wife of an officer who was much the same age and height as her. It was necessary to use various ploys to discover whether her conjectures were well-founded or not, and whether anything criminal was occurring in their commerce. She employed spies, who compensated her handsomely for their trouble, and then disguised herself, put on clothes like the woman's and went to see her brother in that outfit. Playing the role of the other with great skill, she pushed curiosity so far that she found herself taken.

"Yes, my dear Merusol, the unfortunate woman became pregnant; I leave it to you to imagine her anguish when she perceived it; she trembled every time she thought that when the time of childbirth approached, she would be on the brink of being covered with opprobrium, confusion and ignominy. However, she dared not reveal to the pretended brother that she loved him with all her heart, and in what their relationship consisted, for fear that he would mock her, and would be delighted to discover by that means an opportunity to solicit, with reason, a dignity to which, in accordance with the Law, he could only aspire while the person who was thought to be the issue of the same father actually had possession of it.

"The poor woman was a foreigner, and in consequence devoid of support; there was not a soul in the entire city to whom she could confide her predicament without running the risk of ruination. She had need of advice, however, in that dire circumstance. Finally, after having tormented herself to no avail, and having looked at the situation a thousand different ways, she resolved to go to the source and to reveal herself to the person who was the true cause of her misfortune, to see whether he would have the generosity to marry her and not abandon a poor wretch who had given herself to him without reserve.

"As I reached that point, the cornet sounded, and I woke up."

"What!" said Merusol, "is this a dream, then, with which you are entertaining me?"

"Undoubtedly," said the King. "However, I swear to you that I would very much like to have known, because of the rarity of the fact, the gallant's response. I would have liked to go back to sleep in order to see whether I could pick up the thread of the adventure, but it has been impossible for me."

"I don't know," said Merusol, "what response Morpheus would have made to you in sleep, but I can easily tell you in what terms equity would have wanted it to conclude, and how I would pronounce if I were in the same situation."

"Let us see, then, how you would have handled it," said the King.

"A bagatelle, Sire," replied Merusol. "Let's leave it there; it's only a dream, and a chimerical dream at that, which does not even have plausibility for a foundation."

"I admit," said Amander, "that perhaps nothing similar has ever happened, so it's not for that reason that I'd like you to explain yourself; it's simply because you pass in my estimation for a cold, insensitive man to whom everything is indifferent."

"You know me very poorly, Sire," said Merusol. "I have, on the contrary, an extremely tender nature. I do not think that anyone has more compassion than I have for the afflictions of his neighbor, from which it is easy to judge what I would do for a poor young woman who abandoned herself to my love, and for whom the most precious thing she had in the world depended on my will."

"By the example of others," said the King, "I know you; there is no honor or reputation that holds when it is a matter of our interests. You would have given her a kick in the rear, in the hope of enjoying her responsibilities and finding another mistress, either more accredited or more agreeable than her."

"No," replied, Merusol. "Joking apart, these are bagatelles with which we're entertaining yourself, but I swear to you that if a similar affair happened to me, a young woman would be able to count on me as on herself, were she the dregs of the people and as ugly as the night, I would take her for my wife even if I were refused the situation of which she was in possession, and I had to work like a slave with her to earn our living."

"You're an honest man," said the King. "I esteem you more. Give me your hand. You'll take me for your wife? I consent to that with great joy, and I congratulate you at the same time on the Royalty that will not be contested by anyone."

"Courage," said Merusol. "That's the conclusion of the dream; if someone heard us joking as we are, they might indeed believe that we're asleep."

"No, my love, we're not asleep," Amander continued. "I've told you a true story, except that instead of a King, I introduced a Chiou on to the stage, for fear that you might perceive the deception. I am the daughter of the fisherman of Meralde, who was brought here instead of your brother, who was doubtless killed in the last battle that we delivered against the inhabitants of this superb city. It is me who, in consequence of that proximity, has been elevated to the Throne in your father's place, and it is also me who supplanted Sardanie and introduced myself to your presence in her stead. Finally, it is me who is pregnant by Merusol, who, according to the word that he has just given me himself, ought to become my husband, and thus conclude all my hopes."

At this speech, Merusol almost fell over. He remained there for a long time without saying a word, but having recovered a little of his self-possession, he said: "Yes, Madame, you shall be my wife, and Queen of Cambul; that you shall not lack—but in the name of God, give me, I beg you, a more detailed account of all your adventures. What you have told me is scarcely sufficient to know you, and it's necessary to hear you at length and broadly, if you are to content my curiosity."

"We shall have time for that, Merusol," replied Amander, whom we shall call henceforth the Queen of Cambrul. "Let us think of something else; I'm ready to give birth, and it's necessary not to wait for that extremity to reveal the mystery of my sex."

"You're right," said Merusol. "Convene the grand Council for that, and tell them how things are as frankly as they happened."

It is not necessary to report here exactly what happened at an assembly in which no one expected to see an instant metamorphosis of a King into a simple foreigner, the issue of a professional fisherman, and pregnant by a man who had previously passed for her brother The surprise was so great that everyone had difficulty recovering from it, but notwithstanding the difficulties that some had in giving their hands to an Alliance so disproportionate, seeing the two parties content, it was necessary to consent to it and accompany it with the customary rejoicing.

Delegates were also sent to the other three cities to make them party to the accession of Merusol to the Crown and the celebration of his marriage. The Queen took care to charge one of her domestics with a letter in which she gave her father a conciliatory account, fully detailed and without any disguise, of what had happened to her since she left Meralde, and to invite him once again to bring all his family to settle in Cambul, where she could make his old age happy.

The matter was deliberated, and after much argument, the mother, who wanted to see her daughter, was able to plead her cause so well that the worthy people decided unanimously to come and congratulate the newlyweds. But the season was well advanced and they dare not set forth; it was necessary to defer the journey until the following summer.

In the meantime, the sick Lieutenant died and the vacant Company was given to Sardanie's husband, to console her for the injury that the false Amander had done to her amours by stealing Merusol from her.

Three weeks after the marriage the Queen gave birth successfully to two perfectly beautiful children, a boy and a girl, to the great contentment of the King, who was the only remaining child of his father, and had feared not having an heir to succeed him.

Finally, the winter passed, and the Envoys from Meralde arrived, bringing the Queen's father with them, accompanied by his wife and five children. The King lavished a thousand kindnesses on them, and created his father-in-law the President of the Chioux, in place of the one that had just died, as if to make that place available to him. The rest of the family also received sensible marks of his amity.

I found that part of the history of Cambul so singular that I read it three or four times in succession, with the result that I knew it so well by heart that when Benedon, with whom I was conversing one day, and had almost forgotten it because he had not seen it since his childhood, asked me to help him recall it to mind, I recited it to him, so to speak, word for word.

He praised me for my memory, and claimed that I must know good things, since I read willingly, and that according to what he had heard me say, people in my homeland had the convenience of finding books on all kinds of subjects without exception. I apologized for my negligence, which had been much greater in my youth than it would have been had I had the opportunity to study.

"It's true," he told me, "that you don't have the opportunity here of acquiring new enlightenment in the sciences, but at least you can exercise those you know, otherwise you run the risk of forgetting them."

"Not easily, Sire," I said to him. "My foundation is Physics, which requires precious instruments, difficult to construct and mostly made of materials that are not found here, in order to carry out experiments that render demonstrations evident."

"You have sometimes told me about beautiful phenomena of Astronomy," said Benedon. "Does it also need many mysteries for its treatment? All human knowledge has its principles and commencements; you could teach our children that commodity, and you have our permission for that. In winter, there is not a great deal to do; it would be an agreeable pastime, you would obtain pleasure from it yourself and you would be held in greater esteem because you were rendering yourself necessary."

"If it's only a matter of that, Sire," I continued, "We can set up a school whenever it pleases you, and take it as far we can. However, there would be a few expenditures to make, and inasmuch as the humor that I know you to have will often lead you want to witness our exercises, it seems to me that, in order not to give you the trouble of going out, it might not be a bad thing were we to create a little observatory above one of your apartments.

"It would have the form of a dome twenty or twenty-five paces in diameter, with windows all around that can be opened or closed, and in the middle of which we can have a hearth with a chimney, where you can have a good fire, in order that the place can be tenable for some time. I shall have no difficulty making instruments to calculate elevation, and I can easily describe, on two large spheres of wood or stone that I can appropriate for that purpose, the circles that are the most necessary to provide, for beginners, a general idea of the system of the world. What is unfortunate is that we have no telescopes in order to see the different phases, either of the moon when it is eclipsed, or other planets, in accordance with where they are situated relative to one another or their distance from the terrestrial globe."

"What we do not have," said the King, "we shall have to do without. You have only to begin by making a model of the place you need. It will be built as soon as possible, and I will give you all the other things you need that are within our scope."

"Very good, Sire," I replied. "I could not ask for anything more."

Benedon had such a passion to see me in action with those who has the curiosity to hear me reasoning about the movement of the stars that he immediately set hands to work, and the work was done with so much diligence and success that everything was soon ready but me.

Meanwhile, not a day went by when I did not visit the King in his apartment; he was absolutely in that demand, and as he wanted to be among my pupils and wanted the honor of surpassing all the others, he obliged me to give him private lessons in order to have a start and to be ready to respond in my Colleges to all the questions that I might put into the minds of those who attended them.

In conversing together about the primary matter, its divisions, the different shapes of its particles and its movements, and its simple components, we gradually came to what is known as the weight and lightness of terrestrial substances. He did not believe in the beginning that it was even worth the trouble of asking why certain substances rise while others fall, since, according to him, it was evident that that it came from the fact that, by a natural and immutable law, everything tends toward its center and to unite with the mass from which it has been taken, on which it depends as a part to its whole.

That did not last long, however; the objections I raised to it soon obliged him to change his sentiment, and the difficulties finally increased to the point at which he did me the honor of ordering me to give him the pleasure of relieving them by means of explanations that were within his range.

"I am unable to do that right away, Sire," I replied. "It's necessary that I think about it in order to acquit myself worthily. I will do so tomorrow, if you please, or, if you think it appropriate, that subject can be the subject of my first public lesson, as we ought to begin soon."

"I'm content with that," Benedon told me, "and in order that there will be enough room for the audience, which will doubtless be very large, because it's a novelty and everyone will be curious to hear you, I intend that the Palace will serve as your auditorium and my throne as your pulpit. The places of the Chioux will be for people of distinction who will be there; the others can stand."

"Which is to say, Sire," I said, "that you will never come to hear me? For otherwise, it would be glorious enough for me to exercise my function as Professor to either side of you."

"On the contrary," replied the King, "I certainly want to profit from your teaching and to serve as the very example of your disciples; I shall be there, among their number. It would not be just, in that quality, that I appear above you as King and Judge; the most eminent place befits you, and I intend that you should occupy it for as long as you are playing the role of Master and Doctor. Custom does not provide for that, I know, but it is my sentiment that, there being nothing nobler than science, scholars ought to be the peers of Princes and Kings, since it is always advantageous for a People to see the palms and the laurel with the Scepter and the Crown."

"It would be wrong for me to prescribe the Law to you, Sire," I said to him. "That is for you to give, and my duty engages me indispensably to submit; I shall carry out your orders—you would consider it disobedience if I did not— but that does not prevent you from retaining the right to resume the place that you are ceding to me whenever the desire takes you."

"Well," said Benedon, "Prepare yourself to begin in six days. I shall notify the Council of the dignity to which I have now raised you; I intend that they will approve and will congratulate you for it."

At those words I bowed profoundly to mark my gratitude and retired, in order to give him the leisure to work on the affairs that he had in mind, and also with the design of preparing myself for the day of my inauguration.

When the hour of that ceremony had come, the King took the trouble to come to my apartment, which was not far distant from his, accompanied by all the Chioux. He commanded me to come out, and then placed himself to my right, while the President set himself to my left; the others came after us three by three.

As soon as we had arrived in the Palace, the King did indeed set me on his Throne and sat beside me, as he had said. I immediately remarked the astonishment that that great deference caused the audience, which was very numerous, and imprinted them with far more respect for me than they had had in the past; but after all, I was not the cause of it; the master wished it thus, and it was necessary for the inferior to comply with it.

The moment we took our places, cornets, musical instruments and the voices of the most accomplished singers make themselves heard, just as they had at the King's coronation. That coarse music, in the style of the country where we were, having faded away, I stood up and pronounced the following:

*Concise Discourse on Weight*
*In the form of an Inaugural Speech rendered in the*
*Palace of Cambul, Capital City of Russal, situated*
*at the Arctic Pole, in 1696.*

Great and redoubtable King, gentle, clement, pious and indulgent Prince, Sovereign Monarch of a people as numerous as the stars in the firmament and most fortunate of men;

Sage powerful and most honorable Lord, the King's Lieutenant and the second person in the flourishing Kingdom;

Prudent, discreet and equitable Lords, the President and the Chioux of the superb city of Cambul;

Brave, valiant and intrepid warriors, Military Officers of His Ruffalian Majesty;

Rich, Opulent and Magnificent citizens, inhabitants and soldiers of the city, all of you who have node me the honor of coming here to hear me, it is to you that this discourse is addressed.

It is an astonishing thing that among so many thousands of people who are on the surface of the earth, one cannot find two who are so similar that, no matter how much one examines their height, their hair or the features of their face, one cannot easily distinguish them, and find in one certain marks or qualities that are not perceived in the others. But it seems to me far more surprising to see, when one pays a little attention to the matter, that all the minds which animate that innumerable host of bodies are different, that it would be quite impossible to encounter two that had the same thoughts, and which formed the same judgments, in every regard, of all the objects of which we are capable of thinking.

I say that that is more surprising because, however little knowledge one has of the structure of bodies, and in versed in chemistry, one knows that, matter being a mass of an infinite number of tiny imperceptible particles of different shapes and sizes, the bodies composed of them must necessarily have something of that mixture. The parts whose principal particles are cubic cannot be very similar to those in which pyramids or cylinders intervene. In addition, the constitution of humans is so diverse, and the complexion of one creature so different from that of another, that it is not astonishing that the greater or lesser quantity of food that they take for their nourishment causes such a considerable diversity in their entire bodies.

One cannot say the same thing of minds, since they are constituted by thought alone, which is the same in substance in all animals endowed with reason, and which is exempt from changes, to which bodies are indispensably subject by their nature. However, it is those minds, so uniform, which differ so much in their sentiments. Although we cannot see hearts as we see faces, and it is not in the power of a Metaphysician to examine or thoughts naked, as a Geometer measures the dimensions of our bodies, we can nevertheless be sufficiently persuaded of this truth by the diversity of opinions that we know to reign over all things of which we have the slightest idea: as many individuals, as many sentences. Never do two Jurisconsultants, or two Physicians, agree in every respect on the difficulties one deigns to propose to them, and there is no Philosopher who is not contradicted in the explanation he gives of causes.

The world is filled with books, which are as many irreproachable witnesses of what I have just advanced; it is not necessary to produce many examples. It is sufficient, Messieurs, to prove the point, that the simplest subject in the word, the cause of the weight or lightness of bodies, has generated as many disputes between Physicists as they have had occasions to discuss it.

The different opinions that scholars have had on this subject are incontestably numerous, but the principal ones can nevertheless be reduced to six.

The first of these opinions holds absolutely that bodies have weight because of the inclination they have to reunite with the center of the universe, which its supporters claim to be the same as that of our terrestrial globe, to which they do indeed tend, and push with effort everything that opposes their descent.

The second asserts that in of all bodies there are some that, by virtue of a certain sympathy, tend toward the surface of the earth, while others, by virtue of a contrary inclination, draw away from it with all their force.

The third establishes it as a constant that all bodies, in general, have a penchant to descend, but that, some having more of it than others, they move ahead of them, and consequently force them to rise in order to take their place.

The fourth, which is exactly opposite to the previous one, supposes that all matter tends to rise, but that there are certain parts that prevail in their movement, and consequently constrain others to take a contrary route

By the fifth, one undertakes to demonstrate that the bodies that are called heavy and light do not have the qualities that the vulgar attribute to them capable of making them descend or rise, but that the veritable cause of these different movements must be sought in the mass of the earth, which has the virtue of attracting them to a greater or lesser extent, depending on the disposition of their parts.

Finally, the last is the one that only admits as the cause of the phenomenon one simple and natural movement.

The first five of these opinions are absurd and impertinent; only the last is true; that is what I am going to show you, as clearly as the subject matter and the time fixed for our exercises will permit.

To begin with the first of the sentiments that I have just listed, and which we are going to examine in the same order, it is necessary to remark that those who have proposed that free bodies, or which float, so to speak, in the air at some distance from the mass of the terrestrial Globe, are really only descending to get as close as possible at its center, believed that the center in question was also that of the Universe.

God, they said, is a Sovereign Being perfect in every respect, who has been throughout eternity and is without beginning and without end; the world, on the contrary, is limited in every manner, as much in relation to its extent as its age;

that Providence extracted it from nothingness in a certain time. He did not think it appropriate to leave such fine work deserted and unknown, and populated it with a countless host of all kinds of creatures, among which humans, which he formed in his image and resemblance, endowed with judgment and reason, in order that he might admire the structure of it, is incontrovertibly the most noble and perfect.

It is really for love of those intelligent and rational creatures that everything that has been made has been made. The earth in particular is destined for their dwelling, and it is therefore just, so these clever philosophers say, that it occupies the place of honor, the most eminent place, and that place of honor can only be the center of the immense space that enclosed everything possessed of dimension, of whatever nature it might be.

Now, the terrestrial bodies that are vague and detached from all mass, they continue, being of the same matter that is, in general, the Globe that we inhabit, it is evident that they must tend to reunite with it, and that the moment that the cause that has drawn them away from it and is doing them violence ceases, they are forced by a natural and inherent Law to move toward the common Center and to approach, in consequence, the whole of which they are only very tiny parts.

However scantly one examines this sentiment, one finds more vanity and pride in it than probability and plausibility. In fact, is it not very presumptuous to want to assign limits to Divine omnipotence and determine the form of a work as vast as the Universe—for, after all, who has revealed to us the manner in which it is constructed? If it has the form of a sphere, like the inferior and concave vault of the heavens, how far can we take our view in representing it; is it so because it contains more than any other and is more susceptible of movement? Or if it is a cube, as Saint John, one of our great men claims in his Apocalypse, is it so because six, which is the quantity of the faces limiting that body is a perfect number, according to the definition that Mathematicians give? How do we know that it is not a dodecahedron, in view of the mention in the sacred book of our holy Laws of twelve doors through which the elect will enter into the celestial Jerusalem, to employ the language of Christians? That there were twelve patriarchs among the Jews, twelve Apostles of Jesus Christ, that the Moon makes twelve revolutions in a year, that the Zodiac contains twelve signs, that the Heavens, the Planets, the Firmament, the two Crystallines, the *prima mobile* and the abode of the blessed make up the number twelve, etc? Or if one can compare it to some other regular body, whatever it might be—although it must necessarily be regular, since if it were irregular, it would be impossible for its center to be common with that of the terrestrial Globe?

Far from determining, Gentlemen, either the shape or the Center of that great all, it is certain that we have no idea of its extremities, and I am convinced personally, as a man like others, that there is no one in the world who, after having placed himself as far as his imagination is capable of extending them, can prevent himself from wondering: what is there beyond that? Let us not be obstinate, however, in disputing that point with them; let us grant it if you wish. Let us not even contest with them the preeminence of humans, against which we would nevertheless have good grounds to protest.

As to whether the Center is the most honorable place in the world, that is something I cannot conceive. I know that in civil society, when three men walk together, the one that is in the middle occupies the place of honor, but I don't know whether that formality, instead of being universal, might by different, or at least indifferent, elsewhere. The right is here the more honorable position, in Turkey it is the left; in a room, it is not the middle that is the foremost. There is similarly less honor in being in the center of an army than being in the rearguard or at its front. And if in public Assemblies, when the women come in, they are ordinarily placed in the middle, it is rather to surround and protect them than to honor them with the best place.

Perhaps one might say that the examples I am putting forward are inapplicable to the subject in question, since, supposing the heavens to be round and the luminaries placed in circles that they travel for the utility of the human species, it is obvious that we could not be in a more advantageous and more comfortable position than the one that is equidistant from all sides. But in addition to the fact that we can consider the earth as a woman or the baggage of an army, it is not true that the circles the Planets describe are concentric with the Globe we inhabit. Even Ptolemy was of a contrary sentiment in his Astronomical System, and we understand things very differently if we give audience for a moment to Copernicus.

However, I shall, by complaisance, also let that pass. But tell me, then, by what means the parts of the earth know the Center of the Sphere, from which they are sometimes detached and what gives them the faculty to act and to push themselves, when nothing opposes the penchant they are claimed to have for approaching it. Do simple things, stones, metals and minerals, have intelligence? Are they endowed with mentality and reason? Is a material and inanimate substance capable of following, like a dog, by means of smell, hearing or whatever other sense one might wish, the thing on which it depends? A vegetative soul is attributed to plants, as a sensitive one is given to beasts, but I have never heard of a stone being assigned a motive or following soul, by which it is able, for example, to act like a child following his mother when he needs her help or wants to be picked up.

That opinion is therefore absurd, ridiculous and unworthy of longer discussion. What we have said proves that evidently, and time, which is passing insensibly, obliges me to pass on to another.

The authors of the second sentiment that we have to combat admit four Elements as the principles of all corporeal beings without exception, to wit, Earth, Water, Air and Fire. The first of these Elements must be the hardest and most solid, since it forms the foothold of humans, the most excellent of animals. Water, which is also of very great utility to them, comes next. Air is third in rank, in that they breathe, and it tempers the vehement heat of their blood, and floats over the previous one. And the fourth, which is Fire, composes, they say, a Heaven or a region that is situated immediately above the Moon.

These Elements, which are arranged in layers one atop another, are very different from one another in nature. The first is cold and dry; the second cold and humid; the third warm and humid; and the fourth hot and dry. It is impossible, in view of this great diversity, that the particles of one can combine with the particles of another; they are incompatible, with the result when they are separated from their mass they are forced to abandon the place they occupied previously and to fly with all possible promptitude to rejoin and augment the volume of their quantity. That happens by virtue of a certain antipathy with regard to those from which they flee and sympathy with regard to those of which they go in search, which are natural to them, and with which God imprinted them when he created them

Hence it is that stones, water and all the bodies that we generally call heavy, having an aversion for the Air, when they find themselves surrounded by it and at some distance from their fellows, quit it precipitately, falling with violence until they encounter some other impenetrable body, which stops them and opposes their downward curse. And it is for the same reason that the igneous particles that fire, in great agitation, detaches from wood, coal or some other combustible matter rise up, and tend with so much rapidity toward the Heaven from which they have been separated, or to which they belong, and for which they never ceased to have an inclination that cannot be expressed.

That opinion, which has been followed by most of the great men of antiquity and which many men of our century have not yet rejected, appears to me as ill-founded as the preceding one; for, in addition to the fact that it supposed purely material substances to be capable of discernment and choice, it establishes for the elements and principles of natural things the most compound things in the world—which, far from being admitted, dos not even merit being refuted.

The two following sentiments are, in truth, a little simpler than the others, in that they only suppose a single appetite in bodies, which is either that they all want to descend, or are all inclined to rise—but that slight difference does not give them any advantage over their predecessors, so that one is obliged to reject them for the same reasons that have already been put forward.

Let us remark, Messieurs, before passing on, that according to the four opinions about which I have had the advantage of speaking to you, the cause of the fall of bodies or their tendency toward the parts most distant from the terrestrial Globe is attributed to themselves. In the fifth, which is the one on which we shall pause shortly, it is claimed that they have absolutely no part in it, but that the mass of the earth must be considered as the mother of the parts detached by some cause or other, and which has the power to recall them and force them to rejoin her, as to their principal object, there to remain.

The reason for that attraction, they say, is the same as the one exerted on a fragment of iron by a magnet; because that stone contains in its pores a large quantity of tiny particles, which, being in constant motion, extend over a certain determined distance, if it happens that a particle of iron is within the sphere of their activity, they hook on to the imperceptible fibers that compose it, and as they return they drag it, little by little, until it sticks to the mysterious little stone. That is visible; it is a fact that cannot, without temerity, be called into doubt, but although the other cannot be perceived with the same evidence, it doubtless acts in the same manner. The earth is a vast magnet, the particles of which have the faculty of attracting a stone, for instance, when it is separated from it, and is not retained where it is by the water or air that surrounds it.

In order to comprehend this truth, they continue, let us suppose that a blind man is supporting a lump of iron weighing one pound in his hand, for the first time; unknown to him, someone else is holding a magnet below it, which has the virtue of attracting a weight of one pound; it is evident that the weight ought to appear heavier to the blind man in proportion to the efficacious attraction of the magnet—which is to say that what would seem to another only to weigh one pound will seem to him to weigh two. The result would be that if the man has never handled iron without being deceived in the same manner, he would have a different idea of its weight from the one we have, and would sustain, at the risk of his life, that it was heavier than any other metal, although it is, on the contrary, the lightest of them all.

We are all blind, say these Messieurs, with regard to the principal operations of nature; we do not perceive the air in which we exist because we are born in it, it is too subtle to disturb our organs, in which it makes no more and no less impression than water makes on fish, which are also ignorant of its density and do not sense in their movements that it puts up the slightest resistance to them— as long as either of them is in their natural state and the air and water are not agitated by extraneous causes.

The Matter that we respire might escape our senses but the curious research that we have carried out into its different qualities have enabled us to understand that as well as extension it also has weight, that it can perhaps be considered, fundamentally, as a liquid composed of gross particles. Let us say once again that it is the earth that is the cause of the fall of all bodies, in that it attracts them toward it, because it is beneath them, and when our hand is between it and a stone for example, that we hold above it, we can easily imagine that the virtue does not come from there, instead of which we sense considerably the violent effort that the stone is making, by its weight or it impulsion, to approach the mass from which it has been separated, which it continues to do until the obstacle that prevents it from descending is entirely removed.

A man whose has never seen nature naked, who only considers her excellent works through thick veils, with which she affects to cover herself in order to hide from us the simplicity with which she produces them, or who refers blindly to those who pass in Society for scholars and have arrogated the title of Learned, cannot avoid admitting that this reasoning is strong, that one could not speak more justly, and that it is impossible to invent an explanation for the cause of the weight of bodies more subtle, more coherent and which squares better with appearances than the one we have just reported to you. However, it remains the case that if we reflect a little, as veritable Philosophers, and examine its ins and outs carefully, we will infallibly find much ignorance in it, or an infinity of malice, and I do not even know whether one can refrain from attributing both to it simultaneously.

In fact, is it not to be ignorant and malevolent to make use with impunity of one mystery to explain another mystery, and to operate ingeniously to alleviate one difficulty by means of another, which, from the commencement of the world to the last century, and one can even say this one, has been hidden from the most clear-sighted? The ancients never knew the truth of the virtue of the magnet; they were ignorant of its effects and knew absolutely nothing of their causes. They saw that the stone in question was capable of attracting iron, or that two magnets placed close to one another approached one another when they were in a certain situation, and fled from one another as soon as they were placed in another, but the manner in which that happened was always a secret for them, which they were unable to penetrate. In consequence, they were obliged to have recourse to Sympathy, to occult qualities and other similar sticking-plasters appropriate to cover a crass ignorance to which they did not want to admit.

There were some among them who were not content with the mysterious terms that I have just cited, and preferred to say that since a magnet only attracts iron within a certain determined distance from its ends, it follows necessarily that a subtle matter emerges from that stone, which forms threads capable of insinuating themselves into the pores of iron, serving as arms and hands to draw it gradually until it meets up with the stone. The advantage that they claimed to have over the others by that reasoning is not very considerable, however; what they advance is merely an ill-founded conjecture, so distant from the truth that it does not even have the appearances of it.

For, in addition to the fact that these imaginary threads are, by their own admission, contiguous, or composed of tiny particles detached from one another, even when they are continuous, like as many little roads making up one piece it is not possible to imagine that the magnet could be capable of withdrawing them voluntarily and, in consequence, drawing nearer the iron, in which their most distant extremities must necessarily be hooked or embedded, unless one attributes to the magnet a cognizant soul and imagines in its parts that emerge from it spirits, nerves, muscles tendons, or something equivalent to what we see in animals for carrying out such operations. For that reason, I do not think that we have yet reached the idea that is needed.

Let us nevertheless grant them, notwithstanding the invincible obstacles, that the world being full, these radiations of subtle matter are so directed that only the ones emerging from the center of the magnet go in a straight line toward the iron, the others all entering sideways, in proportion to the distance of the parts from which they come, and that the particles of that matter, not being pushed or agitated by others that follow them immediately or cut across them, are like as many little darts, which only emerge and reenter, which gives rise to the pretended attraction. How can this state of affairs be extended when it is a matter of the case in which two magnets placed next to one another, in such a way that the poles with the same name are facing one another, flee from one another and draw away to a certain distance? Personally, I don't know whether they have even tried to offer the slightest reason, and that the cleverest among us might be constrained to have recourse to antipathy, which is enough to make the weakness of all their reasoning evident.

With all that one can say that it is from muddy source and a false and misconceived principle that they claim to draw the strength of the argument that they employ in order to sustain their hypothesis.

The terrestrial Globe, they say, is a magnet, as we have already remarked, which has the same power with respect to all bodies in general that the magnet has with regard to iron in particular, and an incontestable proof of that verity is that the closer a stone, for example, falling from a height, approaches the earth, the more its movement increases and the more impetuous its fall becomes—which can only come from the fact that the magnetic radiations of the earth are more efficacious low down than high up and that their force diminishes as they get further away.

It is constant that if one lets a stone fall from a height of a hundred rods, and if it falls in a third of the time a distance, for example, of one rod, then it will travel three rods in the second third, five in the third, seven in the fourth, and so on, always two rods more until the end of its course. From that it follows that the sum of the distances that a body travels in falling is exactly the square of the time that the same body takes to descend—which is to say that as the first moment is the root of the first rod, the second added to the first will give two, the root of four, which is the sum of the first rod and the three further rods that the body has fallen during the second moment; in the same was, the first three moments added together make the root of the nine rods that have been traveled in that time, being one in the first, three in the second and five in the third—and so on for the others.

But what demonstrates that the good people are ill-founded in what they allege, even for example, is that if one lets a stone fall from a height of only one rod, it will not fall faster in the first instant than it will if one lets it fall from a hundred, or a thousand rods; since it is certain that if the rapidity of the fall were caused by an attractive virtue of the earth, the bodies that fall close to its surface ought to descend more rapidly as those that come from a great height. And it is necessary not to imagine that there are exceptions to this rule; it is incontestably general, for the most complicated movements as well as the simplest—which is to say that when a body is chased and displaced by an impetuous gust of wind, or descends along the roof of a house, as well as when it falls perpendicularly to the ground.

Curious individuals in the majority of the kingdoms of Europe have convinced themselves of this verity, and it is easy to assure oneself of it by means of a few tubes or shafts of glass divided in the same proportion that I have indicated above—or, for want of glass, which you do not have here, take tubes of iron or wood pierced from end to end—for then one can see with pleasure little balls or other similar objects that one pass through them, and observe rigorously the same rule in those which are leaning and those which are vertical, even though they fall much more slowly in some than others, in proportion to whether their inclination is great or small. That inclination can almost approach so close to the horizontal that a body needs as much time to traverse a space of one inch as another falling vertically takes to cover a hundred feet.

To do the experiment it is only necessary to draw a circle of a wall of any size that one wishes, and having taken an indefinite number of points on its circumference, arrange tubes of different length in such a way that one of their extremities ends at one of these points and the other at the point of the circle that touches the horizontal plane on which it rests, or the end of the vertical diameter; all the pellets that one throws at the same time into these different tubes, some of which are, if you wish, ten, a hundred, a thousand times longer than the others, reach the ground at the same moment, or traverse them in the same quantity of time.

It is for the same reason that the times of the vibration of a pendulum are always equal, however different its excursions, or coming and goings, are. If, for example, having attached to a plank a string three feet two inches in length, at the other extremity of which a little ball is hanging, that device is set in motion, by drawing it from its original situation, it will be found at the beginning as well as at the end—that is to say, when the ball extends as far as the cord to which it is attached permits and when it is very close to its rest position, each coming and going will take precisely one second, or the sixtieth part of minute of time, which, is, in the majority of healthy and robust men, very nearly one pulse-beat.

Although that is very curious, and of great utility in society, it is nevertheless easy enough to comprehend, since one has only to imagine that the nail to which the pendulum is attached is the center of a circle of which it forms the radius, and of which the ball describes large or small arcs, or parts, according to the rapidity or slowness in which the ball descends on one side or the other, as if it were a pellet descending in one of the tubes that we supposed extending from the circumference of a circle to the touching point or extremity of its perpendicular diameter; in effect, they are both the same thing.

I will add, superfluous to all that has been said, that it is not very probable that the magnetic virtue of the earth would be uniform and that it would act equally at the same distance. The surface of the globe that we inhabit is too uneven and composed of too many different parts to be capable of the same effect everywhere. One can make a fire of excessive magnitude and maintain it in a state that always seems the same, but it will always act differently, in accordance with the different bodies that are exposed to its action, and as it will, for example, more easily agitate and heat a vessel containing four inches of water than one four feet deep, and more easily melt an ingot of lead than one of gold of equal size, it is inconceivable that the pretended small parts of the earth that had to attract bodies would have the same attractive power after having traversed three or four hundred brasses of sea water, which is often profoundly agitated, as if they encountered nothing but sand or some other similar fixed material composed of particles that leave fairly considerable intervals between them to accord them free passage.

The earth itself, unified as it appears to us when it is considered as the principal and efficient cause of all the aliments that serve to nourish animals, produces plants of a single species so different from one another that they often resemble one another as little as the most distant and different climates. Its virtue is therefore not equal everywhere; however, the fall of bodies is the same no matter where in the world one goes; everywhere, the same proportion is observed. Galileo assures us of that by the experiments he made in different places, and it has been confirmed by so many great men after him that it is not permissible to doubt it if one wishes to pass for reasonable.

All those opinions being sufficiently refuted, it remains to be seen, Messieurs, in what the veritable cause of weight and lightness consists, and to demonstrate that the sixth sentiment, which we shall now examine, is the only sustainable one, and confirms to the laws of motion from top to bottom and from bottom to top.

In order to make that verity comprehensible it is necessary to establish as constant what experience confirms every day, to wit, that all bodies that rotate tend to move away from their common center, or the circle they describe, in proportion to their shape, their solidity and their agitation. To convince oneself of that it is only necessary to make use of the example of the sling, since it is evident that according to whether the stone one places in it is heavy or light, and whether its periods and slow or rapid, the person rotating it around his hand and around the circumference that it is describing, can feel directly whether the effort that it is making to fly away is great, small or mediocre, and that one corresponds perfectly well to the other. In consequence, if the stone is light and it escapes from a sling whirled slowly, it might perhaps only fly six feet, whereas it might cover a hundred if the stone is heavy and the action that excites it is violent.

The same thing can be observed in the wheels of carts that pass along dirty and muddy roads, in that the mud that sticks to them falls to the ground almost vertically when they are rotating slowly, and by contrast, it flies away and covers a considerable distance when the movement is very rapid.

Let us suppose in addition that the earth rotates about its center in twenty-four hours from west to east. That is a supposition that is very easy to make, since it is now only ignorant people and a few preoccupied individuals stubborn in old opinions who are not convinced of the verity of that hypothesis, which is demonstrated at present, so to speak, Mathematically, instead of which there are absurdities in others that render the ridiculous. It is certain that the particles of fire, which are the most agitated, must pass ahead of those of air, which nonetheless follow them; then those of water come next, and finally the terrestrial particles, as the slowest moving, are forced to remain as close to the center of that great mass as possible.

Things being disposed in that fashion, our question is resolved, and there is no need to say any more.[32] I am sure that there is none of my listeners who is incapable of making the application. To save you the trouble, however, Messieurs, let us do an experiment.

Let us take a stone and dispose ourselves to hurl it into the air with all the strength of which we are capable. You will see that the force we employ to distance it from ourselves will open the passage and make it rise with sufficient rapidity; but that progress will only be sustained briefly, far from extending to infinity, as would infallibly always be the case if the whole extent were a void. Instead of which, there is no space that is not absolutely full; thus, the stone will no sooner have left our hand that every part of it will collide with a countless host, which, although extremely subtle, nevertheless constitute an obstacle to it, gradually slowing its movement down, in the same diminishing proportion that I have cited above as augmenting in all heavy bodies, as long as they are descending, until they prevail, in accordance with the law of nature that informs us that a body that is agitated communicates its movement to those it encounters until it entirely loses its own, depending on circumstances, which vary, and are, in fact, very different.

Then, in the column of air in which the stone is located, having less force to draw away, the quantity of movement that it has being less than an equal volume of subtle matter, the others infallibly move ahead, constraining the stone to

---

[32] Given that Mésange is close to the North Pole, one would think that it might have occurred to him that the rotational effect of the earth about its axis would be markedly different there than at the equator, and that if "centrifugal force" really were the sole cause of weight, it would not be having the same effect on him as on the folks back home—contrary to the observations he has just cited of the invariability of the seeming centripetal force that draws objects toward the Earth's center.

move closer to the ground, in order to occupy their space, which would otherwise remain void, until it has reached the surface.

That rule is general, in water as well as air. In fact, a stone thrown from the bottom of a pool by a diver, toward the surface, only descends after having encountered in its passage and infinite quantity of little aqueous particles that have slowed its course, and the column of water in which it is located, having less movement that other similar columns, to draw away from the bed, similarly tends upwards when, the quantity of a volume of stone being less than an equal volume of water, it cedes to the other, for then it is necessary that the stone returns to the place from which it was violently launched.

This is so true that if, instead of a stone, one takes a piece of oak, or some other heavy wood, a certain quantity of which—a cubic foot, for example—and weighs in a balance an equal volume of water, it will remain in the place in the liquid where one puts it, or float in the fashion that one of its surfaces in level with the surface; instead of which, if the wood has less solidity one will see that it projects above the water, in proportion to the quantity of its own matter it contains.

Let us remark in passing that, as there are many kinds of wood, which differ so considerably that, as well as some being heavier than water, so that they go to the bottom, there are, by contrast, some so light that they protrude almost entirely from the water into which one plunges them.

In the same way, one observes such a great difference between human bodies that, whereas some sink to the bottom, others float and remain naturally on top, in fresh water as well as salt water. The reason for this difference, in my opinion, is not difficult to comprehend, if one reflects a little on the construction of the human body, for it is constant that, depending on whether the flesh, the bones, the sinews and other parts are thick, compact and solid, and whether the lungs are large or small, or the belly had a small or large capacity, the mass considered as a whole must be either equal, heavier or lighter than an equal volume of water, and must float or sink according to the proportion between them.

Given that, it is necessary to admire the ignorance of certain peoples who condemn to death as so many unworthy sorcerers those who, on the mere accusation of their enemies, being tied up and thrown in the water, are unfortunate enough to remain on the surface, from which their condemnation ensues, whereas they would have been absolved had they been a few ounces heavier. I have bathed several times in the Rhine in Holland with a gentleman from the province of Utrecht who always floated, no matter what posture he adopted, and I have seen another with my own eyes weigh a mere six ounces in the Saone, which is a famous river in my homeland, whereas he weighted a hundred and fifty-six livres when put in a balance on land—from which it appears that if his particles had been a little more porous, and that if within the same volume he comprised he had been eleven or twelve ounces lighter, it is obvious that he would have floated on the surface of the river, and could, like the previous example, have been placed in the rank of sorcerers in Westphalia, and burned alive.

From all this we can draw various consequences for the good intelligence of hydraulic machines; I shall content myself for the moment with enabling you to see how easy it is, in accordance with the principles we have established, to know the weight, not merely of one of your launches but one of your merchant vessels, or a warship with all its crew, without needing weights and balances, when it is in water deep enough to carry it; for, since the volume of water that a floating body occupies must be equal in weight to its entirety, including the part that is above the level of the water and the part that is below; it is evident that there is no difficulty in measuring by the rules of geometry the volume of the vessel that is below the surface, and it is similarly easy to calculate the weight of that volume of water, and, in consequence, the weight of the boat.

Let us suppose, for example, to satisfy our curiosity, that, having examined the length, width and depth of the part of a vessel that is below the water-line, one finds that it contains twenty-four thousand cubic feet. Let us also remember that it is a determined fact that a cubic foot of salt water weighs seventy livres; if one multiplies the two numbers together, the product, which is one million six hundred and sixty-eight thousand livres, will incontestably be the weight of the boat and all of its contents.

And let no one tell me that this law of nature, invariable as I claim it to be, is often belied by experience, as when little needles of glass or steel, which are incontestably heavier than water, nevertheless float on that liquid instead of immediately sinking to the bottom, since such contradictions are only apparent and are incapable of doing the slightest harm to the rules that we have just established. In fact, if one takes the trouble to search for the cause of that rare phenomenon, one will find that it only consists of the coarse air conserving a free passage between those little bodies and the surface of the water, which thus sustains them and prevents them from sinking to the bottom;[33] which is so true that, as soon as it is lacking, it is not possible to make a single one float.

Moreover, just as the air of fish, which is water, is extremely gross, by comparison with that we breathe, I believe that there is a prodigious difference between that terrestrial air and that which is above our atmosphere, and that whereas a body that is light enough not to make itself felt in water is a considerable burden on land, it is apparent that a mass of horrible weight in that pure air very distant from us would not enter into any consideration in that which refreshed our lungs.

Let us conclude, Messieurs, that what I have said here about a few bodies in particular must also apply to all the others in general, when one considers

---

[33] The correct explanation of surface tension would not be discovered for nearly two hundred years, and requires a much more sophisticated understanding of physics, so Mésange's fudge is forgivable.

them, like those, in their natural state; for otherwise, they might have certain borrowed and artificial qualities that would produce effects very different from those we have just put forward as examples. It is thus that a bomb, which is a machine of which use is made among us to burn and destroy the cities of our enemies, being well filled with powder and other similar combustible materials, which, drawn by the weight of its mass of iron, will infallibly fall to the bottom of water in which I suppose it to have fallen by accident, for reasons which are sufficiently deduced from those above—but if one set fire to it there, for which its composition has perhaps prepared it, its agitation will become so violent that not only will it extract itself but it will fly up into the air.

Experience also teaches us that a cannon-ball can be driven so high that it might never return to earth—but the explanation of such a curious and extraordinary phenomenon merits discussion another time in a particular discourse, inasmuch as it is time to bring this one to an end. Only permit me, Messieurs, to remark to you that as bodies are forced to descend by a Law from which they cannot dispense themselves, spirits, on the contrary, generally have a penchant to rise and to elevate themselves above the center of all things.

God, being unable to rise any higher, rises as far as himself, and limits himself to considering with pleasure the immense grandeur of his infinite perfections. The Angels and the blessed Spirits, rise up as the Throne of that Perfect Sovereign, and are so dazzled by the bright radiance of his glorious face that they are constrained to cover it with their wings, in order to avoid being incontinently consumed.

Finally, humans have the inclination to quit the earth and transport themselves toward the Heavens, not only as toward the place of their eternal dwelling, but because, being the seat of wisdom, where no impurity or ignorance resides, it seems that our minds are in a perpetual desire continually to discover new verities, to extend their enlightenment every day, and by that means to get closer, so to speak, to the one who is the source of all the knowledge in the world.

It is true that that desire for knowledge is not equally great in all mortals; just as there are bodies that descend much more rapidly than others, there are also minds that make very particular efforts to rise above those of their species. Speaking for myself, I can say without vanity that I am of the number of those who cannot envisage any height that they do not aspire to reach. Since my most tender youth I have had a penchant for the sciences; my parents not having the means to fulfill my ambitions, I made an early resolution to quite society and devote myself to Religion.

Providence did not judge it appropriate for me to finish my days there; it took me out at a time when I was more enthusiastic than ever to continue my studies. I have taken advantage of my vigor, my age, and the opportunity I had in one of the foremost universities in Europe to consult very skillful individuals. Heaven blessed my efforts and I considerable augmented in Holland what I had only sketched out in my homeland. I admit frankly, however, that whatever progress I made in Mathematics, I never had the presumption to think about the Professoriat; I found that Employment too elevated for a man of my range and ordinarily envisaged it as an eminent degree only destined for scholars of the first order, to whom nature has given very particular talents to advertise.

The King alone is the cause of my elevation, and he is the one that has put the palm in my hand and who wants the least of his subjects and disciples to have henceforth in his estates the glorious function of Doctor and Master. Yes, Sire, it is to you that I owe the honor that I have today of taking a veritable Giant's stride, and extending my flight to the clouds. You have wanted, like a strong, vigorous Eagle accustomed to breathe a free air far from the base parts of the earth, to permit me, who can only be compared to a wren, to rise to the favor of one of your wings, higher than my imagination had ever been capable of bearing me. It is a singular grace that I do not deserve, but of which I shall try to render myself worth, and for which I thank you from the utmost depths of my heart.

Your interests, my dear Audience, engage you to have the same gratitude; I shall only have the glory of it; you and your children will have all the profit; I shall have the difficulty of teaching, and you the pleasure of learning. I only ask you, as recompense for my labor, diligence, competition and a little esteem. On that condition you can boldly frequent my private and public lessons, and I shall strive to give you all the satisfaction to which you can legitimately aspire.

As soon as I had finished my discourse, the music recommenced, after which the King came to tell me that he applauded himself for the choice that he had made of me to teach science publicly. He made use on that subject of several expressions that I would be embarrassed to recite, and that some people would have difficulty believing to have emerged from the mouth of a sincere man. After having congratulated me formally he stepped back and made a sign to the others to come and do likewise.

When those ceremonies were complete, we returned in the same order as we had come, without any difference, except that instead of going to my apartment, the King wanted to take us back to his house, where we were agreeably surprised to find the table set and a magnificent meal awaiting us.

Benedon treated us like Princes, and in order that the feast should be complete, he had us drink so much pithson that all of us had difficulty finding our way home.

The following summer the King informed the inhabitants of the other cities that he had a Philosopher in Cambul, whom he had honored with the title of Professor, that he had never seen such a great man, and that if they wished to send him their young people in order to take his lessons, he was convinced that they would have all the satisfaction imaginable.

In fact, at least a hundred came at first, who, combined with those I had already, made a College as considerable as any I had seen at Louvain. Every day we spent two hours in private, and from time to time I gave a public lesson lasting about forty minutes. Although everyone was very assiduous, the progress they made was not proportionate to my efforts. The people had good judgment, but heavy minds, and could only conceive the things with which I attempt to inculcate them with extreme slowness and difficulty. I saw many of them repeat an argument three times before being able to understand it in its form, and to see if they could deny one of its limbs with some appearance of reason; from which it appeared that they were worthless in debate and that Metaphysics was not their strong suit.

Several among them learned Arithmetic well, to know the stars in the firmament, to take their heights and calculate their distances; in brief, they saw clearly enough everything that was associated with a figure or which could strike the senses; whereas, to the extent that the things with which they were dealing were abstract and detached from the material, they seemed discomfited and it took them a long time to form an idea of it, which was often confused and imperfect.

Nevertheless, they were as content as kings with the scant enlightenment they obtained by my means. They had all the respect imaginable for me, and cited the slightest words I pronounced as maxims and oracles, which it was not permitted to contradict. Unfailingly, when it was a matter of some dispute in science, the question was terminated them moment when, following the example of the disciples of Pythagoras, someone took it into his head to say "the Master has spoken." There was no pleasure they did not try to procure for me; no day went by without my being invited to several places, either to a formal meal or a beautiful light snack; with the result that I had reason to be the most contented of men.

However, when I came to reflect on my work, on the distance of my homeland and the impossibility there was of ever amassing a sou in a land where wretched iron coins were only just beginning to appear in commerce, I often found myself in a mood to risk a thousand lives, if I had had them, to try to regain the place from which I had come.

In the meantime, something happened that nearly terminated all my cares and put me in shelter from all my anxieties.

I was lying down and sleeping rather deeply, because I was fatigued by staying awake for a long time, having not had any repose for thirty hours, when the frightful noise of a large number of people crying "Fire!" at the top of their voice woke me up with a start.

I leapt out of bed, but the smoke, which had already reached my bedroom, was becoming thicker with every passing moment, hiding the majority of objects from my view, and I was beginning to have difficulty breathing. I finally reached the door, but when it was a question of going any further, I could not find any issue anywhere and had absolutely no idea where I was.

In that embarrassment I began to shout for help. One of my pupils, to whom I will be indebted as long as I live, heard my plaints in the distance, had pity on his Master, and without any regard for the danger to which he was exposing himself, came to me and took me by the hand.

"Follow me, Master," he said, "and move quickly, or you run the risk of being burned."

Indeed, we had difficult saving ourselves; however diligent I was, I could not avoid passing through an ardent flame, which took away all the fur from my garments, but from which my body did not receive any considerable inconvenience. As luck would have it, we soon found a staircase by which we could go up and reach a place where we had the liberty to breathe.

Having recovered myself somewhat, I asked what the cause of the frightful conflagration was, but could not discover anything positive. I was told subsequently that the storehouse of the provisions of wood and coal for the King's household and the Guard had caught fire, without anyone seeing how. A domestic of the Court, who had been maltreated by the Colonel in the King's name, was suspected, because he had been heard to say afterwards that he would have his revenge. He was interrogated, but he denied everything and it was only one young man of eighteen who accused him; there were no other witnesses.

What is pitiful in those sorts of circumstances is that one is shut in, and consequently in danger of being choked by smoke, which kills more people than the fire itself, and which renders everyone incapable of action. They opened all the doors to the upper levels and the ventilation shafts, but that was almost the same as doing nothing; the fire only went out when everything around it had been consumed. Sixty-five people perished in it, and if they had not taken care to break up and carry away immediately everything combustible in the vicinity of the storehouse, the King's House would have been t risk of meeting the same fate, which would incontestably have cost the lives of many people.

Benedon had as much difficulty as I had in saving himself, because he was in a place from which, when he was warned, there was no other exit than the passage I had taken to get out of trouble.

The danger that the Prince had been in caused him to make a Law by which any man who set fire to any place whatsoever in whatever fashion would be publicly whipped or have his right ear cut off, in order to render people more careful, and thus prevent similar misfortunes from occurring so frequently in the city. The first time I went to see him after that I praised him highly for his prudence, and told him that I agreed in that matter with the wisest and most civilized peoples of Europe, who also imposed penalties, or heavy fines, even on those who set fire to their own houses, or anything else.

That subject gave us the occasion for conversation for some time afterwards, above all I did not forget to wax lyrical about leather seals, ladders, hooks, syringes and the various other devices that are employed in the Low Countries to remedy the largest conflagrations promptly and prevent further consequences.

"Speaking of machines," he said to me, "that remains me about one that you mentioned in passing at the end of your speech, from which you claimed that a cannonball could be fired that would rise up high enough not to fall back to earth. Was that a joke, an enigma or the outdated opinion of some enthusiast of the olden days, or was it an allusion to something previously cited to which I did not pay any heed? Which is it? What did you mean by it? Explain yourself frankly, I beg you, for, to speak frankly, I don't understand it at all."

"It's true, Sire," I replied, "that it appears paradoxical even to those very experienced in the knowledge of the arts; for myself, I was so surprised the first time I heard mention of it that I didn't even deign to reply. However, I subsequently found out that it was a question of fact, which is clearly demonstrable, and which has been confirmed by experience several times."

"Well," said Benedon, "I won't let you go now, until you've satisfied my curiosity on the subject, which is assuredly admirable, but I'll expect you to keep your word and inform the public about it, as you promised. I can't hide it from you. I love to see you in the chair, you enunciate very well, you're clear, there's nothing in your style that embarrasses your audience and you have an enthusiasm and gestures that delight. All of that makes a powerful impression on my mind. I admit that if I encounter some obstacle then, one doesn't have the liberty of asking you to alleviate the difficulty by means of some familiar example or greater discussion, but that's a minor point. We see one another every day, and it's good to have something to enquire about in the conversation; it's always agreeable when it's a little animated and it's permissible to quibble."

I'm delighted that I have the good fortune to amuse you, Sire," I continued. "I don't attribute the cause to myself, however; I think it's more an effect of generosity and prejudice that you admire everything I do. I'll make preparations for it, Sire, and tomorrow, at our accustomed hour, I'll try to content you on the matter in question."

"Good," said the King. "I'll come to the auditorium early, for fear of making you wait. But at least be concise—when matters are difficult and one needs to stretch one's intelligence to understand them, it's tiring, and I have a headache for two days thereafter."

As soon as I had quit the King he sent, unknown to me, warnings to all the Chioux and Officers of what was to happen; they communicated it incontinently to others, and thus, all of Cambul was informed of my intention two hours before I was in a state to carry it out. In consequence, when it was time to go to the appointed place to give my public lecture, the streets leading to the Palace Court were so full of people that I could not get through.

The King was beginning to get impatient when I arrived, and he would infallibly have gone home of I had taken another ten minutes to appear. I could tell as I approached him that he was not at all content, by the way he looked at me, but that only lasted a moment. I approached him and told him why I was a few minutes late. Then I went up to my chair, wearing a great robe of the most beautiful local furs, which Benedon had had made for me of his own accord, after having heard me talk about the manner in which Ecclesiastics and Learned men of the first rank were dressed in other countries, and I recited the following:

*Discourse by which I demonstrate why a cannonball*
*fired perpendicularly toward the zenith*
*does not fall back to earth.*

Sage, powerful and redoubtable Monarch, etc.

So many men have judged the effects of nature by appearances, and if, far from consulting reason, they have only envisaged the world simply, with bodily eyes, it is certain that that they have always judged falsely. Their best reasonings are nothing but conjectures and they are often obliged to admit that the majority of things that happen in the Universe do so by means of secret virtues that are hidden and absolutely unknown to them. But once one has determined to make use of the eyes of understanding, and one is not content to envisage from afar and rather tranquilly in the theater-stalls of the great All, the artificial movements of subtle and natural machines that the Supreme and incomparable mechanician of the world causes to act on the stage of his opera, having penetrated behind the curtain that has so far limited our view, one discovers the strings, weights and wheels that activate so many different objects and cause such great admiration to the spectators. One has found the secret of explaining clearly that which one once passed for supernatural and incomprehensible, and often even for magic.

In the times of the Ancients, nature employed great thrift in her designs, and an extraordinary magnificence in her operations; by contrast, one remarks today that she executes at very little expense the greatest and most magnificent designs. There is no longer anything hidden, so to speak, in physics; that which once passed for a paradox has become an axiom. The magnet only works overtly, the ebb and flow of tides no longer embarrasses Philosophers. The movements of Comets have become regular; the origin of winds is known, as if the cause of thunder and the formation of meteors. In brief, everything can be explained, and if hazard first informed us that when one fires a cannon perpendicularly toward the zenith, the ball that emerges from it does not return to earth, Philosophy furnishes strong and evident reasons to indicate the cause of the phenomenon, which appears so contrary to the opinion that the majority of people have.

It is that beautiful and rare subject with which I have resolved, Messieurs, to entertain you for a few moments. As I consider that it has never been fundamentally explained by others, however, I believe that to give you a clear and distinct idea of it, it would not be a bad idea to examine nature in herself a little, and consider the causes attentively before coming to effects.

But, one might say, will the explanation that you are about to give be a real proposition or simply chimerical? I admit that at first, I took it for a fiction, although I presently believe it to be incontestable. The reason I have for that is that the author of a certain book, which is well-known in the world under the title *Récreations de Mathématiques*,[34] speaks of it as a fact that cannot be called into doubt. Several celebrated writers have the same sentiment. The Reverend Father Mersenne has carried out the experiment several times, as it appears in the seventy-sixth, a hundred and sixth and a hundred and eleventh letters of the second volume of Monsieur Descartes, who had solicited it from him forcefully.[35] Finally, after a serious examination, I find that it squares so well with the principles of Philosophy of that modern and extensive Author that it is impossible that one could subsist if the other were not veritable. To be convinced, with me, of that verity, let us go to the source and look at things from a distance.

Imagine, if you will, that Providence, having in its eternal Counsel to produce and to extract, so to speak, from the bosom of nothingness, a visible world, first created matter, and, having divided it up into an innumerable host of tiny particles of the same form, or nearly so, imprinted it with a certain quantity of movement, which it has conserved until the present moment. That thought is simple, natural and implies no contradiction. One consequence that I draw from it is that, there being no void in nature, it is evident that none of those particles was able to move in a straight line, with is the simplest movement that one can represent, if the others with which it went to take its place were only moving in circles, in coming to occupy the place it held before; and thus a circle was formed, of greater or lesser quantities of these particles, depending on whether he first had little or great force in advancing along the route that it had taken,

---

[34] The reference is obviously to Jean Leurechon's oft-reprinted book of mathematical puzzles *Recréations Mathématiques* (1627; tr. as *Mathematical Recreations*), initially published under the pseudonym Hendrik van Elten, shortly after the author was ordained within the Society of Jesus. Problem LXIII—titled, in the English translation "Of Cannons or Great Artillery"—poses, among others, the question of whether a cannon pointed at the zenith should fire with greater violence than one directed at an angle; it does mention that cannonballs fired in that manner have sometimes not been found, but the author suggests, very sensibly, that the projectiles might simply have fallen too far away to be observed or located.

[35] In fact, the experiment suggested by Descartes to Mersenne was to direct a cannonball horizontally in a north-south direction, to see whether the Earth's rotation could be demonstrated by its deviation from that line (it cannot, for reasons that Jacques Massé explained to the King of the austral land described in the earlier text).

and of several similar circles, immediately joined together, a sphere, a spheroid or, if you wish, a vortex.

From that it appears probable that from a large number of particles that began to move in a straight line, a considerable quantity of these swirls was formed. If one follows that thought step by step, it is easy to see that the particles of matter, incessantly colliding because of that continual movement, eventually lost their angles and all became round. There were then, therefore, two sorts of bodies, to wit, spherical, very proper, rotating around their center and in several other different fashions; and others, originating from the first when, in collided with one another and rubbing against one another, they were rounded out, losing their angles, being extremely subtle, flexible and capable of filing exactly all the intervals that several rounded bodies necessarily leave between them, in whatever manner they are joined.

I contend that although a similar divisibility, which extends almost to infinity, is not easy to conceive, it is not impossible. There is no Geometer, however scantly versed in his métier, who does not know that the smaller a body is, the larger its surface area is in proportion to its mass, from which it follows that when it is agitated, and transported from one place to another, it encounters many more bodies, whose effort, which it cannot absolutely resist, is so considerable that they break it and cause it to suffer new divisions continually. These two forms of the particles of matter are the first two elements of everything that exists in the world.

If we now apply ourselves to considering precisely the place that these particles must necessarily occupy in their turbulence, we find that the most subtle, or those that we have said to be the scrapings of the others, and which we shall call in future the particles of the first element, are for the most part, assembled in its center, in the place where the smallest number are placed in the intervals or small spaces between round ones, and that the spherical ones, or particles of the second element, fill the other spaces of that turbulence, approaching the extremity in proportion to their size and agitation—which is confirmed by experience in what we see every day that the more solid a whirling body is, the more effort it makes to move away from the center of the circle it is describing.

If we want to be fully convinced of that verity, let us take a round, flat-bottomed vase of white stone whose edges are only an inch or two thick; let us fill it half way with eater and throw into that water iron filings and powdered red or yellow earth; and let us then fit the vase with a wooden lid in which there is a hole in the middle, in order to be able to see what is happening in the vessel, which it is necessary to coat with clay around the edges so that the water does not escape when it is agitated. Finally, let us attach that machine to a potter's wheel that rotates on a pivot and set it in motion. First we will see, with pleasure, that the particles of iron, being the most solid, will flee the middle in order to arrange themselves around the inner surface of the vessel, while those of earth, which are much lighter, will only approach as close as those permit. By contrast, the moment that the rotation stops, the iron, whose motion slows down first, will gradually approach the middle, the earth will be arranged immediately above it all around and the water, which, as a liquid, still remains agitated, extends alone to the rim.

This is the point at which, if I'm not mistaken, it will be very appropriate for me to draw your attention to two things. The first, of which perhaps not everyone has yet become aware, is that the system attributed to Ptolemy, in which the earth is considered as immobile, is absolutely unsustainable, since it follows from what we have just said that if the prima mobile rotated from east to west in the space of twenty-four hours, as the great Astronomer claims, the Globe that we inhabit, the Planets in general and everything that has more solidity than the subtle matter would be hurled impetuously toward the concave surface of the parts most distant from us. The second is that it is really in the tension of those particles of the second element, or in the effort that they make, so to speak, to draw away from the center of their turbulence, that the nature of light consists, in that it is by that means that the middle of each particular accumulation of matter, up to a certain distance, appears luminous to us and is represented to the eyes if those who are some distance away, like a Sun or a fixed star.

But that is not the question. Let us rather consider that by an indispensable law, and the invariable rules of movement, of all the swirls in the Universe, the poles of some turn, as much as they can, toward the equators of the others that surround them. That situation is necessary, as much for their conservation, which would otherwise be of short duration, since, if their particles take a similar path and have occasion to mingle, they would be swiftly confused and we would not see any resistance between them, as because the particles of subtle matter, which are positioned in the vicinity of the greatest circle that each swirl describes, sometimes being drawn by their extreme agitation beyond the limits of dependency, are within range and find it convenient to enter into others via the Poles. Which nevertheless, I shall note in passing here, cannot happen easily, these particles being so soft and flexible that they cannot take on the form of a screw because the spaces that three Globes of the second element leave between them, through which it is necessary to pass, are triangular and continued at an angle or aslant.

That change of shape does not prevent them from being able to conserve the name of first element, so long as they are not augmented in their mass, but it happens quite often that, their embarrassing form ensuring that they are unable to act with the same liberty as the others when they reach the Center of their new swirl, they attach themselves easily and form on the body of a star the patches that we sometimes remark on the surface of the sun by means of our best telescopes, sometimes in such great abundance that, the rays are unable to penetrate them well and become considerably less bright. However, that dissipates in time, just like the froth of liquids that come to the boil in a pot, when it is inverted or precipitated downwards by the impetuosity of the rising bubbles.

It is then that the fluted or spiral particles of which the froth is formed on the outer surface of a star, which are nothing but aggregations of particles of the first element, which are imprisoned in the middle of a swirl, take on another name. Because several remain tangled together, their volume becomes considerably larger, which means that one can justly attribute to them the qualities necessary to the third and final element of which earth and air are composed. In the same way, when the patches which we were speaking just now are annihilated and the particles composing them, reduced to their original state, it can also happen that they become so massive, dense and prodigious in extent that they eventually cover the entire surface of the star that has served for their production, to which the sparse subtle matter that the surrounding swirls send to it can contribute greatly.

In the same way, after the formation of that initial crust or cover, if the neighboring swirls send it more particles of the first element than usual, it can become comparable to a box, or the banks of a stream, which cannot contain the matter that one tries to cram into it, which finds coverts therein, envelops and surrounds it in all directions. That flow of subtle matter above the surface of a luminous body cannot help rendering it harder and more polished over time, although it never goes as far as closing to the fluted particles the passages that they have made since the beginning. That being so, the same causes that have concurred in the production of a first rind can also produce a second, a third and several others, so that instead of a luminous body, which a star was before that first envelope, and which it might have remained if the matter of the first element had remained fluid on the surface without forming a second, it becomes an opaque body, which only provides light by reflection.

Let us add to that, Messieurs, that if the weight of those crusts diminishes, the force of the swirl, which they imprison, and whose situation between those surrounding it raises some obstacle to them in their movement, it will inevitably be gradually undermined and finally borne away impetuously toward the most powerful of them, the course of which it will be content to follow, conserving nevertheless the faculty it had of rotating around its own axis, by means of the subtle matter remaining in its interior—which is to say, under the first of the patches that covered it over—with the consequence that it will continue to rotate in a certain time about itself, as the earth does, for example, in the space of twenty-four hours, and also rotate in another around the one that is the center of the swirl into which it has descended, as the earth similarly does around the Sun in three hundred and sixty-five days, five hours, forty-five minutes and sixteen seconds, while one of its poles inclines to a greater or lesser degrees toward the equatorial plane of its principal, to which it is constrained by the matter of the first element, which emerges from the middle of the two swirls that corresponds most closely to its Poles, and in the course of which its adjusts itself more easily to receive it, as does the planet we inhabit with regard to the Sun, over the plane of the equator, from which the axis inclines in our century by twenty-three and a half degrees—which is the cause, as everyone knows, of the changing of the seasons and the difference in the days and nights for all the people living above or below the equinoctial line.

Furthermore, it is also necessary to remark that when a swirl is thus carried away by a more powerful one, it must, in accordance with the laws of motion and what we have said previously, be necessarily pushed toward its center while it is less agitated than the particles that surround it, until it is at such a distance that the respective action and weight of the corresponding column of matter are counterbalanced. If, on the contrary, it is very solid, by virtue of the quantity or thickness of its crusts, and simultaneously in great agitation, it will no sooner be in the enclosure of the one that has swallowed it than it will rise up again rapidly and pass from one swirl to another, becoming what we call a comet; whereas, if it remains further down, as I have just said, it will bear the name of wandering star, or Planet, or earth.

All that has happened since the commencement of the world, according to the knowledge we have, to sixteen different heavenly bodies in our swirl, to wit, Mercury, Venus, the Earth, the Moon, Mars, Jupiter, Saturn and nine others, which have no other name except Guards or Satellites, because there are four that revolve around Jupiter, as the Moon revolves around the Earth, and five more around Saturn. If these heavenly bodies had been of the same size, or solidity, and in an agitation proportionate to their mass, having descended into the swirl of the Sun, they would all have remained equidistant from its Center, which would doubtless have caused confusion, but that was, humanly speaking, impossible, as it has only happened to a few of them, and then with some difference.

Mercury, being the smallest and least solid, went to place itself closest to the Center of the Sun. Venus, a little larger, is considerably more distant from it. The Moon and the Earth, gradually found themselves on the same path, but the Earth being about forty times heavier, absorbed the Moon into its swirl, the course of which it still follows, completing its monthly period in twenty-seven and a half days, while the other planets were each borne away by the dependant matter of the Sun, which surrounds them. Mars, although smaller than the Earth, is nevertheless more distant from the common torch that illuminates them, which it is not necessary to find strange, since it is quite ordinary to see bodies containing much more matter than others have that are nevertheless superior in size. Jupiter with its Moons comes next, and Saturn, accompanied by its own, is the most distant.

It is necessary to add to all this that each swirl, rotating around its own center, has the same effects, with regard to the matter composing them, as that of the Sun with regard to its own, and the Planets in floating therein, since, as has been said, all the bodies that rotate around their common center tend to draw away in proportion to their size, their solidity, their agitation and their form.

From that I draw, in passing, the consequence that gold, which is found in the superior crust of the Planet on which we live, being composed of hard but flexible particles incapable of elasticity, which have little force to continue moving in a straight line, ought to be closer to the Center, and the other metals ought to come afterwards according to the proportionate degrees of their composition; that earth made of gross and irregular particles ought to be at a greater distance; that after the earth should come water; and finally, the air we breathe, which is really a tissue of tiny particles, branches and delicate, ought to find its place above all the others, of which it is nevertheless a part, and not of our general swirl, in the middle of which is the Sun—in the same way that the water is evidently part of the same earth, although it is really the air of fish—and which, if one measures its height above the surface of this great body by means of the water enclosed in aspirant pumps, or, in my homeland, tubes filled with quicksilver, makes it obvious that it weighs upon us, which it would not do if it tended as strongly to draw away as all the particles above it.

Now, the reason why the metallic parts have less force to continue their movement is that the matter of the first element, which is their true motive cause, finds fewer obstacles in passing through the earth or all the inferior crusts that precede it, and which cover our heavenly body, than those tiny particles, which allows them to move ahead, abandon them and thus force them, as a consequence to retreat and descend, which they do with all the more rapidity the more solid they are. On the contrary, if the same metallic particles, large or small, in bars or in the form of cannonballs, can be raised above our atmosphere, where they will no longer be submerged, except in subtle matter, it is evident that their movement must increase, and perhaps even surpass that of the matter surrounding them, as one sees heavy bodies in great waves, such as a boat, a wooden beam or something similar, continuing their movement, at the turning point, with more impetuosity, in a straighter line than the water that carries and surrounds them.

All of that being explained in that manner, it only remains, in order to come to the nub of our question, to imagine that the entire earth is a ball, which, instead of falling toward the Sun, had been driven away from it violently, since it comes to the same thing; it is no longer supported by anything, there is nothing from which it is suspended, and yet it remains almost the same distance from the star.

It is a truth that leaps to the eyes, of which reason informs us and which experience confirms, in whatever place in the world one goes, east, west, south or north, where thousands of Europeans have been, the air is equally free, and everything else, in that regard, is disposed there in the same fashion. That being so, let us now make an exchange, substituting the Earth for the Sun and our cannonball for the Earth. It does not matter that there is a disproportion in their sizes, since there is none in the columns of matter that hold them in equilibrium; pumps that are a foot in diameter carry thirty-one feet of water just as well as those that are only an inch in diameter, and air similarly sustains twenty-seven and a half inches of mercury in a square tube with a six-inch root as in a triangular one whose sides are only a fraction of an inch.

By making that substitution it is easy to conclude that one thing is no less possible than the other, and that if a Planet remains at a particular distance from the Sun because of the column of matter that counterbalance it, a cannonball, once outside our atmosphere, can similarly circulate and remain as if suspended in the air, at a certain distance from the earth.[36]

The greatest difficulty one can find, if I am not mistaken, is that of causing a cannonball to rise above the air, to the region where meteors form, but it seems to me that since the experiment has been carried out and repeated several times by people worthy of faith, one ought to be persuaded of its verity, and not imagine that because an ordinary canon, being directed horizontally, cannot achieve a distance of a league or two, which is, at the most, the distance above the earth occupied by the fluid matter that serves continuously to refresh the mass of our blood, it might not be able to do it when aimed perpendicularly.

There are convincing proofs and very good reasons that assure us of the contrary, on which I do not think, however, that it is necessary for me to stop on a question that is purely a matter of fact, all the more so as there is no Physicist who might contest them. If we can believe the Historians of the Low Countries, a cannon that I have seen with my own eyes in the Armory of Papenbril in Boisleduc, sawn through in the middle—which a cannoneer moved by good will for the people of the States of Holland and ill-intentioned toward his master, the King of Spain, had advised them to do, on the pretext that being shorter, the powder would lose less force and would carry the bullet much further than it had—sent a cannonball all the way to the town of Bomel, at least two and a half leagues distant in a straight line, which is further than is necessary to settle our question.

Finally, someone might perhaps tell me that the cannonball, not having within itself the principles of a circular movement, as I have supposed in the Earth and the other Planets, in which I have enclosed a great mass of subtle matter that makes them turn around their Center in a certain precise time, cannot stay for long at the same distance from the center of the swirl to which the rapidity of its movement and the subtle matter had carried it. I admit frankly that that is a strong objection, but one ought to know that if a round ball of a well-polished metal, placed between two points of a circumference can remain in motion, after a single impulsion given to it, for two and a half-hours, as has been done experimentally hundreds of times, it is probable that a cannonball, agitated by the violent fire of several pounds of powder, and which one supposes to be

---

[36] This "demonstration" of the possibility of putting artificial satellites into orbit is an interesting example of extrapolating a sound conclusion from false premises.

surrounded by mater so subtle that it provides almost no obstacle to its movement, ought to last not only for hours but days months and perhaps years.

In any case, if the cannonball were to begin to fall, it might as soon be on another Planet as on the earth. In addition to which, that does not lessen the force of my demonstration, and the rarity of the phenomenon, in the least, since the objective of the question was to make it evident why a cannonball fired in the said manner would not fall back incontinently to earth, in accordance with the nature of all heavy bodies that one throws into the air, of whatever sort.

That, Messieurs, in brief, is the solution to our proposition, on which I would incontrovertibly be able to extend myself further, if I did not fear rendering myself obscure by too much enlightenment and too long a speech, and abusing the attention of my listeners. It only remains for me to make the remark to lovers of the sciences that, in order to resolve this difficulty, it is necessary first to consider the extent, how that extent of matter can by divided into separate particles, and the forms that their agitation produces; that although the simplest movement is straight, numerous particles are forces to move in circular lines; that these different movement form swirls and so on, always composing, following the method of Geometers, which hold it is constant that it is always necessary to begin with the simplest things, examining all their parts and rendering themselves familiar, before passing on to the more complex things on which they depend.

Now, it is difficult to observe these rules exactly, if one has not first learned the art of making the comparisons necessary to discover the relationships between figures and numbers. That is a truth that was not unknown to the ancients, since they took care to educate their children in Arithmetic, Geometry and Algebra. They doubtless knew that those sciences render the mind capable of a penetration that cannot be acquired by other studies; that they regulate the imagination and give it a certain extent of justice that drives and conserves the clarity of the mind, all the way to the most awkward difficulties in the world. That is apparent in all the beautiful and subtle questions that great men have resolved by means of them, including the one that I have just rendered evident to you, and it will appear even more evidently if, following my example, you young people wish to engage seriously in the study of these noble sciences and take the opportunity of accepting the offer that I have made and an reiterating now, to serve as your guide and director, with all the zeal of which I am capable.

The King, who seemed extremely content, on seeing me leave the chair, beckoned to me and ordered me, on the pretext that I had been brief, to accompany him to his House and to bring with me his Lieutenant, the President of the Chioux and the Colonel of the Guards. We were very well fed again that day.

While we were at table, the talk that I had just given was the subject of our conversation; they talked about nothing else. If they had given ne another time to express all their sentiments, each of them would have talked at great length, but even though they were all talking at the same time, I realized immediately that none of them had understood me. The matter was entirely new to them, so it is not surprising that they only had a confused idea of everything that I had said; thus, they only raised puerile and ridiculous objections, to which it as very easy for me to respond. Those petty and rather ill-founded disputes, of scant importance, nevertheless gave Benedon, who had talked least of all, considerable overtures for the intelligence of the question.

"Your explanation pleased me," he told me, "but I realize now how far I was from understanding it; I'm only beginning to see clearly, but I flatter myself that now that we've talked about it in private, I won't any longer find anything that will stop me."

"I can say that same as you, Sire," added the President. "It's certain that however attentive one is, it's impossible to follow a orator for long who is treating an abstruse matter of which one has never heard mention before; there is nothing like a familiar conversation to obtain some fruit therefrom; as every difficulty presents itself one can pause and request clarification, and if the Teacher does not smooth them out the first time, one can raise different objections and requests to which he is obliged to respond, and, for his part, to offer so many examples and turn things in so many different ways, that in the end it becomes intelligible to the most stupid of Listeners."

"There is no need," the King said, "for our Professor to wear himself out with so many replies; it's as clear now as it will ever be, and if he makes himself seem naïve by his actions and the terms in which he expresses himself, he knows what he's doing and that the ideas that he had are clear and distinct." And he improvised a rhymed couplet: "*Mésange adelai, ramel tamelaion; Duia Memel, aten simala peiteion,*" which meant: "In good qualities Sire Mésange abounds/He is the greatest Doctor there ever was."

"That, Sire." I said, "is an impromptu in my praise worth infinitely more than the speech made on the cannon, which you praise so highly, since that has been an object of my mediations for some time, whereas the two excellent lines that we have just heard are an effect of your knowledge, your presence of mind and the extent of your genius, given that you pronounced them while chatting, without the slightest application."

"I've never done so much in my life," replied Benedon. "I'm no poet, and I must attribute the cause of that enthusiasm to your presence, which apparently gives intelligence and knowledge to those who have the good fortune to enjoy it. Our city is glad to have you, and if you live here for only another ten years, all our inhabitants will be Mathematicians and Philosophers."

The rest of the session was only spent in reciprocal compliments; they strove, each in turn, to sing my panegyric and exalt my supposed talents. For my part, I extended myself on their personal merits and the generosity they had shown in treating a foreigner so charitably. In consequence, we parted more content with one another than ever.

Although I was extremely occupied with teaching, I nevertheless continued riffling through the History of Cambul. The children of Merusol did nothing remarkable, nor did several of his other successors. Good things were said of them but I did not find them worthy of imprinting on my memory or copying them in writing. Nevertheless, I cannot pass over in silence the fact that the fourth King after that Monarch was a man eleven feet tall and whose body measured nine in circumference around the waist. His name was Hermenon. His wife was proportionately tall and stout; never had such monsters been seen. That Queen gave birth four times, each time to three children; the first and last sets were boys, the others girls.

That was singular enough, but what rendered the story a trifle suspect is that the writer affirmed positively that those dozen children, having reached ages between twenty and thirty, remained so small that it excited the curiosity of the father to weigh his entire family, and he found that he weighed seven hundred and fifty pounds, his wife four hundred and forty-five, his sons a hundred and twenty-five and his daughters sixty-five—from which it appeared that the king alone equaled the weight of his sons and the Queen that of her daughters; in consequence, the father and mother together weighed exactly as much as all their children, who were nevertheless adults.

I could not help telling Benedon one day that the account appeared to me to be a tale invented for amusement and that the Historian, having nothing notable of which to inform his readers that thought it appropriate, lest they should yawn, to reawaken their languishing attention with a detail of his invention, into which the marvelous entered.

"Don't think that," said the King. "The Author is recounting nothing but the truth; the thing is recent, and it wasn't so long ago that the king in question died that tradition represents him to us other than he was. My great grandfather, who I knew, had talked to old people who had heard the same thing from eye-witnesses. All that you see therein is nothing; many other things are said about that Monarch that was not written down, for fear that our History might pass for a romance in the minds of our descendants.

"Everyone claims that he had sixteen teeth in his mouth, his wife eight and his children two each, which were exactly the same size, that they chewed and ate in proportion, and that in consequence, he needed enough food for eight persons in his meals, his wife four; if they were short by as much as an ounce, they would have perceived it immediately. Their sleep was regulated in the same fashion. The eyelashes of the father and mother equaled in number those of all their children, and if decorum permitted it I could mark the relationships and proportions there were between other actions and parts of those giants with those of their parents and children, which surpass the imagination, and which no one can call into doubt because they are facts that have been seen and known by an infinite number of irreproachable witnesses.

"No one was unaware long after that king lived that on certain days of recreation he but braces over his shoulders that hung down so far, in the form of stirrups, that when his wide put her feet in them and stood up straight, with her back turned to her husband's that their heads were at the same height. Then their hair was combed, and braided together, so that the two heads became one, which seemed to have two faces, one in front and the other behind. That being done he put on a long robe, which covered him from his feet to his shoulders, and at the bottom of which there were six inside pockets, into which his six sons entered, passing their heads through opening made expressly for that purpose, in such a way that spectators could only see their faces. Higher up, and also all around, at equal distances, there were similar facilities to lodge the six daughters, so that when the giant walked in that outfit, either sideways, as he sometimes did, forwards or backwards, one saw only one body, but which as surrounded by fourteen faces.

"Often, it happened that after having been for a stroll in that manner, he picked up another young man in each hand, whom he held at arm's length, and then a square hat was placed on his head about two feet high, with four children inside, each facing a different way. A burden of that horrific weight did not alarm him; he danced with all of it as if he were wearing nothing but his clothes.

"He rarely carried weapons when hunting; on several occasions he encountered a powerful Bear, which attacked him; he grabbed it by the throat and strangled it with his two hands, or, if he could take it by the legs he tore it in two without any difficulty. In brief, he was a man like none that had ever been seen in the land; at least, the Histories make no mention of any, and I doubt that more than one had been seen."

"Alas, Sire," I said, "if one were forced to add faith to all the things that are repeated every day as incontestable verities, which have reached us via tradition, or were written by our ancestors, we would be very subject to being mistaken. We have rooms full of books in my homeland, which, with all the assurances of verity in the world, contain everything that the human imagination is capable of inventing of the grotesque and the fabulous. The histories of Kings as well as commoners are filled with stupidities, bagatelles, absurd circumstances, controversial facts and impertinences that leap to the eyes of the greater number of readers.[37]

"Each Religion, even, ancient or modern, has its mysteries, its oracles, its laws, its constitutions, which those who make a profession of them believe to be holy and divine, to the exclusion of everything that the others say, to the point of suffering martyrdom and signing with the last drop of their blood the testimony that they render with their infallibility, at which those of an opposing party laugh uproariously, and which Authors contemporary with those who left us the beau-

---

[37] The allegation that cannonballs fired toward the zenith do not fall back to the ground, for instance?

tiful things in question make no mention, contradict or deny with much foundation.

"In consequence, all those different parties decry one another and treat as madmen, wretches and libertines, or at least incredulous, those who write from certain viewpoints that the persons who read them do not have; and it has often happened that writers have composed fictions to pass their time, to divert their friends or to show the world that nature has endowed them with the faculty of imagination, which, several centuries later, have passed for the dogmas of a sacred cult, which have caused bloody wars and the total ruin of those who have been bold enough to call them into doubt or speak of them with derision.

"I have heard it said in Holland of a man from Sedan named La Feuille, a clockmaker by profession, and an eccentric, recounted an adventure that he claimed to have had during a voyage, which is similar in character to the one I have just reported, and which is in consequence rather appropriate.

"He was in a coach that was taking him from Sedan to Paris, where he had business; on the way his traveling companions seemed surprised to see two beautiful tall, upright trees of an extraordinary girth, planted a hundred or a hundred and fifty feet apart in a bare landscape where, as far as the eye could see, no steeples, houses or bushes were visible; there was absolutely nothing but heather and a few brambles of the same height.

"Everyone, having formed conjectures different from those of others, argued about that endlessly as to which was the most probable. 'Well,' said La Feuille, finally, who had listened to them with pleasure and had not yet opened his mouth on the subject, addressing one of them, 'you're speaking Latin; you've read books and you can only spit sentences.' To another he said: 'You're an Officer, you've frequented the Court, you doubtless know the map.' He turned to the third and continued: 'And you're a merchant, who, having no fixed abode, so to speak, does nothing but go back and forth over land and sea. You're people interested in the world, and yet you're equally ignorant of the veritable cause of why those two trees have been planted here. Assuredly, that's admirable; there's not a nurse in our city who doesn't entertain her nursling with it every day, and all the children amuse one another with it in their schools.'

"La Feuille's apparent surprise increased their astonishment further; they admitted frankly that they knew nothing about it, and begged him not to leave them in secrecy, if it was worth the trouble of them knowing it.

"'About nine hundred years ago,' he said, 'there were four beautiful villages here, which formed a perfect square, which situated directly toward the four cardinal points: east, south, west and north. The first was called Lenon, the second Tourcoing, the third Avane and the last Brussier. In the exact center of those four villages a magnificent château had been built, of great extent, which was named Garcy, and where a giant of monstrous height lived, with his entire family.

"'That extraordinary man, who was known by the name of the Invincible, had rendered himself redoubtable by this strength and his unusual cruelty, which everyone feared; many people trembled merely on hearing his name, and it happened more than once that the sight of him afflicted young women with fever and caused pregnant women to miscarry. He held all the peasants in the vicinity of his house under contribution; it was necessary that they provide him with everything, and he needed  great deal of food, not only because he ate enough himself for a company of Swiss Guards, but because he kept a good table, had a magnificent retinue, and his domestics surpassed in number those of many Sovereign Princes.

"'The villagers finally wearied of his extortions and refused to put up any longer with the taxes he imposed in them. With that he issued terrible threats, massacred a number of them and sent word to the others that if they refused again to recognize him as their legitimate Lord, he would run them all through with his sword and burn their houses to the foundations.

"'At these threats, the inhabitants of the villages that I have just named armed themselves, and having fixed a day they went out to an appointed place, with the design of taking him by surprise and giving him no quarter. Their enterprise had been secret, and it was executed with so much order and prudence that the Invincible had no warning until they were no more than seven or eight hundred paces from his house. He emerged incontinently with his club, which was made from one of the tallest oaks of the forest of Ardennes, and with which he alone was capable of defeating a numerous arms, especially when he had put on armor—this was in the times when there were not yet any firearms.

"'As soon as the poor folk saw him, his presence frightened them, and they started running away as fast as they could, imploring his mercy with loud cries. "No, wretches that you are," he said to them, "A crime of this nature is not pardonable. To lose respect for me, to violate my rights and attempt my life, no, one more blow, there even if there are ten thousand in the plain, and you the last of the living, not one will carry the news home. You shall all perish, such as you are; death is the just recompense for rebellion."

"'Things did not go as he planned, however; as he ran after them, fortunately for them, he carelessly placed his foot in a large, deep trap that was artfully covered, which a wolf-hunter had constructed to catch carnivorous beasts, which were desolating the region, with the result that, suddenly collapsing into that ditch to a depth of eight or ten feet, he fell full length on the ground and wounded himself dangerously.

"A woman who was eight months pregnant but who had the courage of a Lion and who had come out of Tourcoing with her husband, swearing an oath never to return until she had seen the Giant die, seeing the pitiful colossus lying at her feet, so stunned by his fall that he did not know where he was, threw a large stone she was holding at his head with so much violence that it opened a huge gash on his left temple, which completed his distress. The blood gushed out from the mortal wound in great spurts, as water ordinarily emerges from a fountain.

"'With that he began to utter terrible screams, which made all those who heard them tremble; he turned and twisted in all directions; he reached out his arms; his body made a thousand contortions, which evidently revealed the state he was in. "What are you waiting for, wretches?" cried the bellicose woman, however, at those timid peasants, who only dared approach him trembling. "Are you waiting, pray, for our redoubtable enemy to recover his wits, and come round? Be in no doubt; indubitably, he won't pardon anyone; your tears, your sighs and you supplications would soften a rock more easily than him. If he gets up, not one of us will remain alive. While we have the advantage over the monster, let's take advantage of the opportunity and not give our descendants reason to complain of having cowards and effeminates for ancestors. Let's go! Forward, as quickly as possible; the moment is pressing; it's time to finish him."

"'At these reiterated cries the most timid individuals plucked up their courage; the shame of being excited to be liberated from slavery by a person who ought naturally to exhort them to obedience and submission made them advance diligently, and after raining a hail of stones on the Titan, who was bloodied all over, they hurled themselves at his body and pierced it with a thousand blows of daggers and knives, without meting any resistance.

"'His wife and children suffered the same fate; it was necessary that the race be entirely wiped out, or they would not have been content. The domestics, who were mostly their own people and who had been ordered not to go out but simply to guard the château and its contents, were all spared; no one offered them the slightest insult.

"'That memorable action demanded a perpetual monument, which would renew it in the memory of their descendants. A number of different species were proposed, but after much debate, it was eventually concluded that the Giant's house would be razed to the foundations, the master buried under the ruins, and two trees would be planted at his head and feet, which would mark his height exactly. King Pepin, who was then reigning, having heard this news, was infinitely pleased, because that prodigious man was beginning to make him jealous, in that he was becoming stronger by the day and extending the limits of his dominion further. In recompense for such a great good he ennobled the sin of the woman who had been its cause, desired that he bear the name of the village, of which he appointed him Lord in perpetuity, and that his arms should be argent with a sable cross, charged with five golden pebbles, which were mistaken later for bezants.'

"That tale, invented on the spur of the moment, so detailed and related with such composure, made such an impression on the minds of those simple and credulous travelers that they were completely convinced by it. They recounted thereafter, everywhere they went, as an incontestable History. They added to it, to support their testimony, that they had seen the trees between which the Giant as inhumed with their own eyes, that they knew the family of the Tourcoings very well, who did indeed have the same arms,[38] and as for the villages, it was not surprising that they no longer existed after the terrible and continual wars that had since raged in the region, which had often put everything to fire and the sword.

"Eventually, it was passed on to children, and there are few places thereabouts where people will not tell you the story very seriously, although there is no foundation to it but a fiction, which is perhaps not one of the best imagined."

"You can say all that if you please," said Benedon, "But I am sincere, and in order that I do not affirm anything of which I cannot be as certain as if I had seen it myself, I receive easily as verities everything that other honest men advance as such."

"If you were a Christian," I continued, "you would make a very good Catholic. The majority of those who profess that religion, which is very ancient and preferable to all the others, give themselves blindly to all sorts of puerilities, as long as the authority of our priests intervenes therein. We have a heavy burden of Legends, filled with fables so gross that they make all reasonable people who take that communion ashamed. The Authors of those books have had the impudence to attribute to the pretended saints whose lives they describe, feats that are not only beyond the range of any human being but which surpass nature, and even what the Messiah did.

"According to them there are people who have been transported to Paradise, others to Hell or Purgatory, three different abodes destined for the souls of the dead. It is claimed that they have traversed seas dry-footed, flown through the air, cured all sorts of maladies and infirmities without exception, enabled the lame to walk, rendered sight to the blind, hearing to the deaf, speech to the mute, sated thousands of hungry men with two or three loaves, resuscitated the dead, vanquished demons, commanded angels and conversed with God as their peer. And what is admirable is that all of that is often recounted in a manner that is either so innocent or so bold, that I suspect that it is necessary to be mad to admit it, and impudent to sustain it.

"And yet, it is on the word of those honest people, who had doubtless for the most part been pagans, who can only have had it in view to decry Christianity, that an incredible multitude of relics is conserved in the thousand different places in Europe, for which superstitious and idolatrous people have an infinite veneration, to the point of putting more faith in them than in God himself. Some boast, for example, of having the skull of Saint John, the blood of Saint Etienne, a jawbone of Saint Jacques, an ear of Saint Francis, a piece of the robe of Saint

---

[38] Tourcoing, a commune in the far north of France on the outskirts of Lille, does, in fact, have the coat of arms described by the storyteller, although the yellow circles on the black cross presumably really are bezants [heraldic coins] rather than pebbles.

Laurent, one of Saint Anne's slippers, etc. Others maintain that they have in hand, as a sacred deposit, the Holy Virgin's milk, holy hay from the stable where she gave birth to her blessed son, the tears of Jeremiah, or a tip of Araon's rod. And to complete the abuse, instead of the three nails, according to some authors, or four, according to the sentiment of others, that were used to attach Jesus to the cross, and one shroud on which the image of his faith is imprinted, there are enough to load a mule in different countries, cities, churches and chapels, of which those who guard them all insist equally strongly that theirs are the true ones, and try to decry the others, to make them pass as fakes, in order to attract devotees who make pilgrimages there and bring money to enrich the Convents and to help the Monks live in luxury.

"With all that, there are places like Italy, Spain, Portugal and similar places, where, if an individual were imprudent enough to declare that he doubted the verity of the most absurd of these tales or the slightest of these bagatelles, he would run the risk of being put to the Inquisition, where he would infallibly be condemned to death, or at least to spend the rest of his life between four walls."

"Everyone is left at liberty here to believe what wishes," said the King, "but people like everyone, nevertheless, to conform to the common opinion; when one does not, one often attracts the scorn of some and the hatred of others, who accuse them indirectly of stupidity or weakness, or of too little penetration to discover the falsity of what they are asked to envisage as evident and infallible."

"At that price, Sire," I continued, "I believe the History of the Giant King and all his family; I would be in despair to cause scandal to anyone whatsoever, as I am accustomed in my voyages never to do so to anyone. I am not naturally inclined to make myself conspicuous, and to want to pass for cleverer than others; I accommodate myself to everyone, and desire that everyone accommodates themselves to me. In any case, we have the custom here, as I have heard it said elsewhere, of 'throwing our books in the fire,' so to speak, during the vacation, which begins and ends with the summer; from one Equinox to the other, we devote ourselves to domestic affairs."

As Benedon had not been whaling since his accession to the throne, the desire took him to go and partake of that diversion. I usually participated in his pleasure-parties; he would have thought that that one would not be a success if I had not put my name down first as those who were to accompany him on the expedition.

A fine crew was put together for it; there was no lack of men or provisions. The first fish we discovered seemed at a distance to be an island. The King was then in one launch and I was in the other. He immediately gave the order that we should head straight for it, and we followed he fishermen at close range. As soon as they found themselves, on one side and the other, in the vicinity of the neck of the monster, two of them sank their harpoons into its back simultaneously, with so much violence that they each penetrated to a depth of a foot and a half.

The animal, feeling itself thus pricked, gave a thrust of its tail and dived, which agitated the water so prodigiously that seven skiffs were overturned, among which was the King's.

That misfortune caused general alarm. Everyone raced to secure the sacred person of their common Monarch, so it did not take long to pull him out of danger. While they were taking off his wet clothes in order to cover him with a dry robe until he could be taken to the shore, where fires were ready, as much because they were accustomed to incidents of that sort as for cooking, someone shouted that no one knew what had become of one of the harpooners, who had disappeared when the whale dived and had not been seen since.

Benedon wanted one party of his men to remain there in order to be able to help the man if he returned to the surface, while the other, releasing the rope, followed the mighty fish with all the rapidity that the vigor of the rowers could produce as it fled with all its strength from the place where it had received two mortal blows.

After having been under water for a full quarter of an hour, it appeared on the surface again, and with it the unfortunate fisherman, for love of whom so many sentinels had been posted. The monster, seeing people approaching, dived into the sea for a second time, but the harpooner remained on the surface; the boats raced toward him as quickly as possible, and he was seized as he was about to go under again, which made it seem unlikely that he could survive.

The poor fellow had lost consciousness, and some of those holding him in their arms doubted that he was still breathing. A few drops of pithson were put on the palms of his hands, on his temples and under his nostrils, and a little of it poured into his mouth, which was open, as if he were dead; that brought him round.

When he was on land, he was sat down next to a good fire, and such care was taken of him that he recovered consciousness entirely. The King was delighted, expressed his joy to him and asked him how he had been able to remain under water for so long.

"When I hurled my harpoon into the body of the fish, Sire," he replied, "my sleeve caught in the ring through which the rope passed, which was open, so that when the monster dived it dragged me with it without anyone noticing. I remember very clearly that I tried for several minutes to free myself and get myself out of that bad situation, but it was impossible for me; there was every appearance that it couldn't be undone when I was lifted out of the water again."

As no harm had come to him, and he had got out of it with a scare, the King could not help laughing at the adventure and taking the opportunity to tell the fisherman that he must be more circumspect on another occasion.

Meanwhile, the whale was tiring, and had also lost a good deal of blood; it was finally brought to the place where Benedon was. Like me, he was struck motionless by the sight of the excessive size of the prodigious animal. Two hundred and forty-five barrels of oil were extracted from it, which I had never seen before.

The next day we caught another, which was about a third smaller, after which the King withdrew, with a small number of men to escort him, and left the others to finish their operation.

On the way we talked about the age that the first fish we had caught must have been. He told me that the fishermen had very different sentiments on that subject. "There are some," he continued, "who imagine that a whale grows without interruption from the age of one until it dies, increasing in length by an inch and a half every twelve moons. Others think that it increases every period by eight lignes. Some claim that they gain half a barrel of oil every year—from which it would follow that our big fish would have been four hundred and ninety years old. In my opinion, the most plausible are those who assert that there are fish in the sea like beasts in the fields and trees in the forests, which, although born on the same day differ by half or more in weight, girth or length after a few years.

"Of pips from the same fruit, one will be more rounded, better-furnished and much healthier than the others; if that one is planted in suitable and well-cultivated soil, where it has enough nourishment and the seasons are favorable to it, and, on the contrary, the others are put in meager and gravelly soil where they lack humus and they are also exposed to cold winds and other similar inconveniences, one finds that the difference between the plants they become will be so considerable that in a thousand people who see them there would scarcely be one who believes them to be of the same race and of the same age.

"There are few brothers, even though they are the issue of the same father and mother, who have the same constitution and who resemble one another in every respect. One respires a certain air, which is neither of the same place or the same time as the other; the aliments with which they are nourished are different, and they do not take them in equal quantity; they are no more uniform in the actions, their work, their late nights, their sleep, nor anything that concerns them; they are, therefore, unlikely to resemble one another, either with regard to the size of their body or the strength of their mind."

"I believe that you're right, Sire," I replied, "and I can tell you without vanity that it was very nearly the same argument of which I once made use against the Dutchmen who sustained unanimously that the pike, which is a river fish of our regions becomes heavier every year by exactly a pound. At any rate, it is probable that the marine monsters that are fished in our seas must be very old, but I don't think their age can be determined by any mark, as one can determine the age of oxen and cows by the rings around their horns, and the age of horses by certain marks that appear until the age of four on their teeth.

"We have curious individuals in my homeland who put collars on deer and rings on carp in order to know when they are caught again how long they have lived, and inasmuch as it is claimed that the experiment has been carried out several times, one can be sure that the latter animals live for a hundred years and the former easily surpass ten; but it wouldn't be so easy to assure oneself of that verity with regard to whales, because instead of them being enclosed in parks or ponds, where one can see them again whenever one wishes and cares to take the trouble, they have a free range that had the extremities of the world for its limits, where a thousand might be marked and not one ever seen again.

"Of domestic animals, the majority die quite soon; there is only the elephant that reaches a very considerable age; I have read more than once that the King of Persia had, among others, a white one more than four hundred years old, without any perceptible marks of old age."

"Those animals are more fortunate than us," said Benedon. "As soon as we have reached the age of sixty or eighty years we become decrepit, weak and subject to a thousand infirmities; even the mind manifestly loses its strength; the entire machine goes into a decline, and it's rare to see a man live for a hundred and fifty years."

"At the beginning of the world, Sire," I said, "people lived a very long time. The History of the Creation, which I have often mentioned to you, tells us of several men who surpassed nine centuries. God had his reasons for abridging our years, but the fact that we would have been eating one another if we had all lived so long would have been enough. The world is well populated as it is, but it would then be too much; the earth could not provide nourishment for such a large number, unless they ate no more than one does in the fields of Raoul."

That idea made the King laugh. He wanted to turn to ridicule what was said about the long lives of the ancients, but he was diverted by occupations that seemed more agreeable. In fact, as we had been fortunate in fishing, we had the same luck in hunting, as we went along the coast, since, while only rarely deviating far from our route, we killed more game than we could carry home. Among others, we killed a gray bear, which is very rare in that country, where one almost never sees any but white and ruddy ones.

We had three hundred and twenty-eight woodcock; they were in prodigious quantities then, and on the point of migrating. The King was very fond of birds of that kind, and ate almost no other meat during the season; I saw them brought to his table for some three weeks; toward the end they had such a strong carrion smell that only he could stomach them; he never left any, even if they were half-rotten.

A few days after our arrival in Cambul, I went to see the King. As soon as he saw me he asked me how far I had got with the History of his country.

"I'm within sight of the end, Sire," I replied.

"Well, what have your retained?" he asked.

"Not very much," I continued. "The further I've advanced, the fewer things I've found worthy of my attention. Hermenon died and his children only survived him by a matter of days. He had had two brothers, who were both deceased; the son of the elder one was only fifteen, while the son of the younger was thirty. The King's two nephews, Helial and Talmusel, both aspired to the Crown. The Laws authorized the younger one; age, intelligence and experience gave the other license not to let go of his pretentions. The inhabitants of Cambul were divided as to which of the two to choose.

"The Chioux unhesitatingly came out in favor of Talmusel, but the people and the warriors, joined by the King's Lieutenant, supported Helial. The two parties were considerable, one by virtue of its authority, the other by virtue of its strength. The masters of the districts, fearing a revolt, demanded that conferences be held. Commissioners were appointed by both sides, who assembled regularly every day, but instead of the differences being concluded peacefully there, the arguments became more heated every day.

"When the Judges saw that, they surreptitiously delegated two of the principal members of their body and sent them to the other three cities with an escort of fifty men in order to set the justice of their pretention before them and implore their assistance. The delegates acquitted their mission perfectly. Daila, Persac and Meralde all shared the same sentiment. If the fathers of the two claimants were alive, they said, it is incontestable that the elder would have been preferred to the younger, but since it was a matter of their children, it was necessary to pay attention principally to age and then to capability."

"They were right," the King interjected. "For, suppose that when the Giant and his children died, Talmusel had not yet been born; would they have deferred giving the crown to Helial, and if he had once been in possession of it, would it have been taken away when his cousin was born because he was the issue of an uncle older than his father? You can see that that could not have happened, and that it would have been an unparalleled injustice."

"I beg your pardon, Sire," I said, "if I take the liberty of telling you that it is what you assert that cannot be, and which is unparalleled, for according to you, your Kingdom is not elective, and has always been hereditary. If the fathers of the two competitors had lived, the elder would have succeeded the Giant by natural right, which could not be contested by anyone, as the other cities knew perfectly well; in default of the elder the Crown belonged to the younger; the younger being dead, having left a son, it was necessary that the older should also be deceased, since there would not have been any confusion between him and the son of his younger brother; and if he was deceased, how could he give birth to a son to dispute Royalty with the son of his father's younger brother?"

"I admit," said Benedon, "That I am mistaken in my reasoning; I had not envisaged the veritable nub of the question clearly. But after all, it still would not be unparalleled, as you claim, Sire Professor. Talmusel would not have been the first son to be born after the death of his father, since his mother could then have been pregnant with him."

"It's true, Sire," I replied, that in a similar case one would have waited until after the lady had given birth to dispose of the vacant dignity, for fear of a blunder of which there might have been cause to repent in future. Here, the two fathers having been dead for some time, the younger of the competitors having reached the age of fifteen, it was therefore just, or at least it is the law of our regions, that the son of the elder be honored with the Scepter that his father would have carried had he lived."

The neutral cities of Russal, however, were not of that sentiment. They assembled all their troops and gave them orders to muster in Daila, which was the assembly-point from which they would leave together for Cambul with all possible diligence. That plan, which was of the greatest importance, was carried out so secretly and with so much promptitude that no one in Helial's party was alerted until they were four leagues from the gates.

The Colonel of the Guards was the first to hear the news. He thought that he ought not to waste time consulting his friends as to what he ought to do in that dire circumstance; he went out with ten of his soldiers, stopping three men on the way who went to warn the Chioux as to what was happening. Having approached the foreigners, he demanded to talk to the man in command.

"The city of Cambul," he said to him, "is in combustion, within two fingers of its ruin; its inhabitants are infinitely obliged to you, Sir, for having undertaken such a long journey in order to cam their troubles and return peace, but before deciding anything in favor of one or other party, are you well-informed regarding their difference? Do you know that the interest of two individuals is the sole and unique cause of it? What fundamental need is there for us to sacrifice ourselves for them?

"You have four or five thousand men of good troops, all intrepid fellows incapable of recoiling, I have no doubt; but you must also know that you'll have to fight a rude battle. I command a corps that cedes nothing to any other in the world; I'm assured in addition that the best part of the citizens, whose weapons are ready as I speak, and who are only waiting for the agreed signal to take them up.

"Your people are weary and fatigued; if you'll take my advice, let's give them some rest, let's avoid a frightful massacre and terminate this difference by means of a prompt accommodation. I'll go, supported by my friends, who are waiting for me, to assemble the Judges and everyone in Cambul who has the slightest authority; stay here, I beg you, until you are summoned, and instead of declaring yourselves for Helial or for Talmusel, simply say that you have come to provided support to Hegbaton, the Lieutenant of the late King, and that you have no doubt that his person is agreeable to them, because of the thousand good qualities that are justly attributed to him, of which it will be easy for you to make an ample deduction."

"I admit," said the General to the Colonel, "that I came here reluctantly, and that I would be delighted if everything were to happen amicably. The proposition you have made to me is reasonable, to avoid the terrible consequences of animosity on both sides, which will never want to concede, but what you request of me is absolutely not in my power. I have orders to employ myself for Helial; my masters would punish me if I took a contrary course."

"I can see," replied the Colonel, "that you have measures to take; well, all that I ask of you is that you accommodate yourself as best you can to the sentiments of those who appear to you to be the most reasonable. I shall go set my hand to work while you march with your men as slowly as possible; trust me, I give you my word that no harm will come to you; the expedient I've just imagined, cannot fail to be successful."

As soon as the Colonel had returned he had the Horn sounded, as was still the custom in extraordinary circumstances, upon which everyone went to the Palace. The Captains and Soldiers appeared; the Chioux took their places according to their rank, and at the moment when the President opened his mouth to ask the reason for the extraordinary assembly, the Officer advanced, and, having bowed profoundly, said to them:

"This is not the place, Sires, where it is my prerogative to speak, but I have something to propose to you that is of such great importance and requires so little delay that I have taken the liberty of having the alarm sounded to warn you incontinently.

"All of our allies' troops are at our gates, and I have come myself from seeing them in an array capable of striking terror to all those not of their métier. One might think by their appearance that they have been brought up in fire and carnage; their lugubrious physiognomy presages nothing but ruin for our inhabitants. Under the pretext of coming to cam our troubles they are capable of pillaging our houses and doing violence to our wives and daughters. They are already preparing to shed rivers of our blood.

"For myself, I have no fear. God is my witness that if it only required one victim for the conservation of the State, I would be ready to offer myself in sacrifice. If it comes to combat, I have brave officers and my soldiers are no less well-disciplined than they are valiant and intrepid; not one of them fears danger—but in the end, what can a handful of men do against a numerous and formidable army? And when we have all been hacked to pieces, who will protect you from the fury of your enemies?

"You are wise, Sires, and you are prudent; be political too. For the moment, set equity aside, whether you would now like to choose Helial for your Sovereign, or whether you prefer Talmusel; that is a matter on which you will never agree, the parties being too animated against one another. The common interest needs you to agree and, in order to avoid your ruination, to cast your eyes on a third party, whom no one with then deny. The King's Lieutenant, here present, is incontrovertibly already the foremost in the city; he has the age, the experience, the probity and all the other necessary qualities to govern a kingdom well. Elect him immediately, and if you love your property and your repose, cry at the top of your voice with me, 'Long live King Hegbaton, Long live King Hegbaton!'

The warriors, who were not far away, hearing a loud voice repeat several times "long live King Hegbaton!" and imagining that it was by order of the Council, imitated it with all their might. Several others did the same, with the result that it passed from house to house and from street to street. Everyone was astonished to know, in the farthest parts of the town, that Hegbaton had been created King.

The Chioux were delighted by the Colonel's expedient; they thanked him for the efficacious means of which he had made use, with so much success, for the advantage of the Fatherland, and confirmed his election. The foreign troops were advancing, however; instead of having their General come in order to consult him as to what he was going to do, they sent three delegates—two Chioux and the Colonel—with orders to thank him on behalf of everyone for the trouble he had taken, and his generosity in having come so far with the design of facilitating their agreement. They added that they had now agreed to take Hegbaton for their King and that it only required to make their allies' Protectors aware of the fact.

The whole militia was brought into Cambul and, after having feasted well for ten days, it was permitted to return, with all the provisions necessary for the journey and charged with a thousand blessings and thanks.

As soon as Hegbaton was on the Throne he promoted the Colonel, who was the sole cause of his elevation, to the position of King's Lieutenant that he had occupied himself, and promised him firmly to be his friend as long as he lived. He also made Helial the Colonel of his Guards, as much to bring him on to his side as to throw dust in the eyes of the Chioux who had supported him, and having brought Talmusel close to him, not only did he designate him as his successor to the Crown, since he had no children, but obliged all the Political and Military Officers to approve his choice, and drew up an irrevocable edict for fear of further dissent after his death.

He need not have taken the trouble. The poor young man died before him, with the result that Helial still succeeded to the Royalty, in spite of all that Hegbaton's nephews could do, who claimed the right to occupy the Throne after their uncle.

As soon as the Sun had bid us adieu, we recommenced our exercises.

Benedon had a female cousin who, after having often attended my public lectures, also wanted to witness our observations. In spite of the precautions we had to take, only exposing the pupils of our eyes to the air, the cold often being intolerable in our observatory, the Lady would gladly have spent several revolutions there, if I had let her have her way, talking about all sorts of Astronomical phenomena. It did no good to tell her, in order to weaken her appetite, that in the genealogy of the Sciences, whereas Poetry is said to be the daughter of Amour, drawing and painting the daughter of hazard and afterwards of Invention, and Geometry the daughter of necessity, Astronomy only had idleness for a mother, in that it had been invented by the shepherds of Chaldea, who had applied themselves to studying the stars while watching their flocks by night and made remarks on their different movements; it was incapable of putting her off. She had conceived a distaste for everything neighboring the earth, which she thought unworthy of the least of her meditations; the army of the Skies charmed her, and she wanted to familiarize herself with its march, its exercises, its maneuvers, and everything a mortal could know at such a prodigious distance.

What caused her difficulty for a long time was why the Sun, that star so beautiful and so admirable, and at the same time so necessary, hid itself for six months, and then remained for such a long time on the horizon, but always at unequal distances, whereas the fixed stars and all the constellations, whose names I had taught her, always rotated in circles parallel to the equator.

Another difficulty that shocked her and caused her to find disorder in the works of nature was seeing that the celestial torches rotated around us. She thought that it would have been more appropriate had they risen on one side, passed overhead and set on the other. When I told her that there were, in fact, entire peoples to whom that happened, and that others lived directly under our feet for whom they rotated in the same fashion as us, but with the difference that while we could see the Sun, the Moon, Mars, Jupiter, Saturn and the other Planets, they were out of range of their eyes, and that reciprocally, they were visible to their eyes when we could not see them; and that with regard to the fixed stars, we could never discover those that were over their hemisphere, and they were absolutely deprived of those that appeared over our horizon every winter—or, at least, that their appearance differed very little during a human lifetime, because those luminaries only advanced from west to east in circles parallel to the ecliptic by about one degree every century, all of that appeared to her mind as so many paradoxes. She could not see that it was possible, supposing the earth to be round, that it could be inhabited on all sides, and that there were nations diametrically opposed to one another.

All those obstacles were however, smoothed over in time. She had only been studying for three years when she understood Physics quite well, and Copernicus would have taken pleasure in hearing her argue formally against the partisans of systems different from his. What spoiled everything was that her great soul had the weakness of allowing itself to be vanquished by the one passion to which I believed it to be least susceptible. I was not at all surprised to perceive that the esteem she had for her master was transformed into amity; that is natural enough, and I could cite a thousand examples of it; but I was dumbstruck when I first realized that that honest and moderate amity had been succeeded by an indiscreet and violent amour, which no longer permitted her to sleep or to eat.

In the beginning, she made efforts nevertheless not to let it show. Before, when I had spoken to her, either about indifferent things or matters concerning the sciences, she looked me boldly in the face; one might have thought that she did not understand what I was saying, her eyes being fixed on mine; afterwards, on the contrary, she kept her eyes lowered, hardly darting a glance at me any longer, and only when I was not paying attention.

That procedure, so different from the first, rendered me suspicious. Several of my pupils noticed it, as well as me, and congratulated me on it several times. I always remained cold; on the one hand, I put on a semblance of not knowing that she was only thinking about me, and on the other, I replied to my friends in a manner that should have made them understand that, even though I was convinced that they were mistaken and that the Lady was too wise and too well aware of her interests to ally herself with a wretched stranger, it was nothing to do with me.

In the meantime, the poor woman, who had been rather shapely, became skeletally thin. I confess that I felt sorry for her, but what could I do with a woman in a country like that one, when I was always hoping, in spite of the apparent unlikelihood, of leaving it eventually, and a woman, moreover, who was not beautiful and for whom I did not feel any inclination? She was blonde, it is true, and had perfectly beautiful hair, which hung half way down her legs, but she had a low and wrinkled brow, small round eyes, a snub nose pierced by two holes that bore more resemblance to buttonholes than nostrils, flat cheeks covered in freckles, a mouth with white gums and pale, thin lips, which pursed every time she laughed, a pointed chin, a long neck, a bosom as flat as a hand, large buttocks, and one shoulder higher than the other. She was short of stature, with a slight limp. In sum, she was a young woman of whom one could say in truth that to the same extent that her mind was fine, subtle and penetrating, her body was badly-constructed and disagreeable.

I would have liked with all my heart to find a means of making her disgusted with my person; for that reason I often neglected to comb my hair, wash my hands and face or trim my fingernails. I affected indecent postures and mannerisms, like crossing my legs, picking my teeth, yawning, stretching, putting my elbows on the table, sniffing, licking my lips and making a noise when I ate or drank; I talked to her about my age and the infirmities by which I was beginning to be threatened, and especially about a childhood fall from which I pretended to have never fully recovered, which made it difficult for me to hold my water; I added that I was subject to hemorrhoids, which produced an intolerable stink. I spoke to her brusquely and appeared indifferent to the most urgent of her caresses.

All that did not put her off; the pretext of my knowledge, combined with a great preoccupation, opened wide scope for her to make me new compliments every day and to entertain the others with a thousand observations in my praise.

"You're fortunate, Mésange," she said to me sometimes, "in that Heaven has favored you with so many graces. One finds people who look good, who are well turned-out, well-built, who have beauty and utterly engaging manners; one finds others who have penetration, or vivacity, or judgment, or a good memory, or some other spiritual quality; you possess both to an eminent degree; you are the summary and the digest of all the perfections.

"There are singular gifts to which you have not contributed, but what is admirable about you, and infinitely to be praised, is that you have added art to nature. You have made full value of the talents of which Providence has made you the depository. You owe the one to your star, but you owe the other to your effort. Indeed, how many languages do you not know?

"And you know the History of the entire world; there are no Empires unknown to you, no States of which you do not now the origin, the birth, the alliances, the deaths of great men, the revolutions that have occurred in Monarchies, the wars, the troubles, the changes of religion, the plagues, the famines—nothing is hidden from you; you are not ignorant of their times or their circumstances.

"If one talks about Jurisprudence, you cite the Laws of the majority of the peoples of the World and religiously observe those of equity. There are no kinds of contracts, obligations, testaments and writings of any tenor or nature one desires that you cannot draw up formally, and you plead like an Advocate. You understand the fundamentals of the science on a large scale. There is no Philosopher to match you.

"Drawing is extremely familiar to you, I have seen specimens of it, which are inimitable; to be convinced of it, it is only necessary to cast an eye on your Portrait of the King, whose delicate features, drawn with a simple pen, are so similar to his, that it only lacks speech to be a second self. You sing delightfully, and play all sorts of instruments to perfection.

"You know about lice, about urine, about the symptoms of different invalids and the causes of their illnesses; you give them medicaments, emetics, purgatives, sudorifics and everything that is capable of easing their ills and restoring them to health. In sum, you are universal, and I doubt that one could find your peer in all regards."

As I have never like flattery, I gave very little consideration to the veritable motive for so many insipid compliments, and I only saw their profusion with chagrin. Often, instead of replying with something similar, as civility and kindness required, I tried to interrupt her by talking about something else or turning my back on her. She suffered that harshness patiently, as if it were a compliment that she ought to receive as a considerable recompense. If I thought about it afterwards, I hardly ever did so without a sensible regret, and feeling sorry for her with all my heart.

The last time she talked to me in such language, I said to her, "I don't like incense, Zemire"—that was her name—"and I'm incapable of burning it on your altars; you're mistaken if you're praising me with that intention. When I say something good about someone, I say it in their absence, for fear of causing them confusion or vanity. I know your worth, and my infirmities are not unknown to you. If I've acquired a little knowledge, it's by the sweat of my brow; you know yourself what it costs those who cultivate the sciences; you claim that they're extremely familiar to me, and that I treat them with more facility than the majority of Doctors; perhaps so, but it does me harm to glorify me, and you'd give me pleasure by refraining on another occasion. When we're together it is to talk about our affairs; raise objections, show me the progress you have made, the difficulties that have impeded you; I'll respond to everything—but once again, let's not touch on personal qualities; if they're criticized, it irritates me, and if they're exalted, what's said of them always seems suspect."

Zemire appeared utterly mortified by that speech, which she took for a reproach or a correction, and to which she did not say a single word in reply. She was content to bow profoundly and to quit the company, which did not appear any more edified by what I had done.

An hour later I was surprised to see a young boy enter my room, who gave me Zemire's compliments and handed be a manuscript, which I took, and in which a found the following:

*Letter to Mésange,*

*You can protest, my dear Mésange, against the just eulogies that I make of your person and protest about the wrong that you claim is being done to you by talking to you about your perfections, but I take that as an effect of your modesty, which cannot suffer being applauded in public. I hope, now that I am speaking to you in secret, that you will be more flexible and less rigid than you have appeared to me incontinently. But even if it annoys you further, I shall tell you what I think, without any intention of criticizing you. There is nothing about you that I do not admire; everything that you do pleases me; I hold you in esteem; I love you; I cherish you; I adore you. If you are insensible to a declaration of that nature, I confess that you are less perfect than I imagined, since it is only natural to incline in the direction of someone who inclines toward you. But even if that is the case, I shall nevertheless always have respect and tenderness for you. It is not worldly views or individual interest that leads me to that, but only a principle of gratitude and sincere movements of the passion with which I am veritably entirely your*

*Zemire*

I laughed as I read that letter, but at the same time I feared its consequences; I knew the extent to which a woman scorned is capable of taking her fury. No matter how ardent amour might be in the most passionate individual, indifference chills it, and rarely fails to cause it to be succeeded by a mortal hatred, which neglects nothing to avenge itself. I was not dealing in this instance with a daughter of the common people; she belonged to the aristocracy of the city, and was a person with whom I had to take precautions.

With that thought, this is what I felt indispensably obliged to reply:

*Letter to the Scholar Zemire,*

*You are right, amiable Zemire, to attribute to the presence of a multitude of witnesses, often indifferent and jealous, the cause of the coldness with which I have responded to the obliging praise that you have given me. Although everything that you have said on that subject appears to my mind to be an effect of your preoccupation in favor of a man who does not merit it, I am nevertheless infinitely obliged to you for it. You can be assured that I have no sentiments less than advantageous in everything that regards you.*

*Since you have been a pupil you have not ceased to give me evident marks of the extent of your fine mind; at the slightest opening that I have made for you in abstract and horny propositions, you have rarely been wanting in finding the solution, drawing advantageous consequences therefrom, and making use of them to discover verities of which I had not thought, or which I thought to be beyond human range. Those fine qualities are estimable in themselves, but they receive an even greater brightness from the sublime virtues with which you accompany them, and which veritably no more abandon you than your shadow.*

*That is the veritable motive that attracts all my esteem to you; so I have preferred you to all those who have been party to my teaching—that is a fact of which you cannot be unaware. I take Heaven for my witness that I have not hidden from you anything I know, and in taking pleasure in enlightening you in the most difficult matters, I have always considered myself well-rewarded by the fact that you have applied yourself with zeal and labored with success.*

*I want to tell you, however, that I have often affected not to give you praise proportionate to your merits and not to give you evidence of the sincere affection that I have or you, for reasons that I cannot explain to you. I shall observe the same maxims in future; I shall love you without publishing the fact; I consent that you similarly have the most advantageous sentiments for me, provided that you hide them from me, and that you will nevertheless remain persuaded that I am your humble servant,*

*Pierre de Mésange*

The next day, Zemire came to the College as usual, but even more disconcerted than before. From day to day she was seen to change visibly; one might have thought that she was becoming stupid. She was so distracted that she often had to be asked a question three or four times before she replied. It was impossible, in that state, for her to make any further progress in the sciences, so she no longer talked about it with my other disciples, whom she had once held in suspense, without which they would have had little or no competition. Although I was insensible by nature, that caused me chagrin, as much by virtue of the distress in which I could see that the poor young woman was in as because I was the cause of it, and I could not resolve to apply the remedy.

That was not, however, the end of it; the following summer, I had the misfortune to fall down the staircase of the Great Hall and to break my right arm a little way above the wrist. That annoying accident, which obliged me to keep to my room for a long time because of the fevers that accompanied it and various other symptoms, which made many of my friends doubt my recovery, prompted visits from all the honest men in Cambul.

Zemire was not the last to come to express her sorrow at my misfortune. She did it with a great deal of modesty, but with expressions that showed clearly enough that she was suffering with me the dolors that I felt. I do not know what slant I adopted to mark the obligation that I felt toward her, but I perceived very clearly that it effaced from her memory all the ill-treatment to which I had previously subjected her, and that she conceived new hopes therefrom.

This is the letter that she wrote me the following day:

*Letter to Sire de Mésange,*

*I take Heaven as my witness, my dear Mésange, that the sorry state in which I found you yesterday moved me to pity, gripping me so strongly in the heart that I suspect that I am suffering from it more than you are; however, I do not know whether what has been unfortunate for you might have done me good. In the space of a revolution you have changed. While you were healthy and sheltered from ill-fortune, you appeared to me to be insupportably arrogant: always rude, always austere, always malevolent. By virtue of all the rights of which you availed yourself, to which your role as Master gave you over your pupils, I came to be no longer able to look you in the face or open my mouth before you. Today you are entirely humanized; you are civil, you are honest; I know no gentle and affectionate terms seasoned with actions and graces that you did not believe you ought to render to those who are presently visiting you.*

*Why is it, Mésange, that you can only be in a good humor when suffering? Is it necessary to wish you harm is order to live on good terms with you, and instead of the ardent wishes that I have made for your prosperity, which have never attracted anything but your disgrace, to implore heaven for punishments to humiliate you? God forbid that my satisfaction should engage me in such a crime, and simultaneously cost you so dear. No, if you have to hate me more than ever, I shall pray incessantly for your convalescence. I shall see you; I shall serve you; I shall watch over you every time that it might be necessary, and I shall force you to admit that I am veritably your friend,*

*Zemire*

I was in such a bad state when I received that note that I did not even feel capable of reading it; I had thrown it down on my coverlet, and did not remember it until the following day, when Zemire came herself to enquire as to the state of my health. Scarcely had she greeted me than the letter appeared to her eyes in the same state in which she had sent it to me—which is to say, folded and sealed with a little patch of gum, in the local fashion.

She went pale at the sight of the object and remained nonplussed for a moment or two, after which a flush rose to her cheeks.

"What, Sire Professor?" she said to me. "I thought you metamorphosed to my advantage. And on the contrary, I now find that, not content with disdaining my person, you scorn that which is sent to you on my part, so far as not even wanting to take the trouble to look at it. Assuredly, that's too much."

She reached out her hand, and would have seized it if I had not been prompt enough to prevent it. Seeing that I had it, I tried to make my excuses and offer my apologies, but she hardly gave me time to utter a word; she left abruptly, refusing to listen to me. "Adieu, ingrate!" she cried, as she went out "You shall never see me here again until you have changed your maxims and put at my discretion the just punishment that you deserve."

Although, fundamentally, I had done nothing wrong, I nevertheless criticized my imprudence, and made an effort to write to her in spite of my extreme debility.

This is what I said to her:

*Letter to the Charming Zemire,*

*You are right, Zemire, but you are also too precipitate in your judgments; I have often noticed that in your public disputes, and the last one you have just made, in consequence of which you impose on me the insupportable penalty of being banished from your presence forever, confirms me in the conviction that I was not mistaken.*

*Believe me, I am not as guilty as you make me out to be. Appearances have told you that, and the appearances were so imprinted with the image of verity that I do not think one could be deceived by them. I confess that; but that is not sufficient for a Philosopher to make a decision and draw a final conclusion. If you had had the patience to listen to me before you fled as you did, I flatter myself that you would not have wanted me to say more than three words in my defense.*

*Yes, Zemire, I will tell you. nevertheless; the truth is that I did not have the strength to look at the person who came to deliver your letter and if it cost me my life I could only say by conjecture whether it was a boy or a girl; pain obsessed me so strongly that it was only permissible to ask them to drop it in my bed until my illness gave me sufficient release to look at it, and to beg that person nevertheless not to forget to give you a thousand thanks on my part.*

*Some time afterwards I felt a little better, and as I was exhausted, I drifted off to sleep without having had the leisure to reflect on what had happened. That slumber lasted three or four hours, and I swear to you that I had only just woken up when you came into my room. The precipitation with which you advanced*

*your hand toward me made me understand what was in question, and the appre-*
*hension I had of missing my opportunity rendered me sufficient presence of mind*
*and promptness to take possession before you did of what you believed to be the*
*object of my scorn, and which veritably has all my esteem.*

*I have since seen at my leisure that charming letter; I have kissed it and*
*praised a thousand times the hand that formed its strokes I cannot reply to you,*
*Madame; I do not have sufficient strength for that and my left hand, which I am*
*using to disculpate myself, is not sufficiently accustomed to wielding a pen to*
*permit me to make more use of it for the moment; what it is doing presently*
*ought to pass for a prodigy, since it has never tried before.*

*Judge by that, Madame, of what I am capable to avoid your wrath and to*
*conserve your amity, but allow me to put an end to this discourse; I assure you*
*that I can do no more. Come to see me as quickly as you can, if you wish, and I*
*shall try to persuade you orally that if anyone in the world merits the continua-*
*tion of your concern it is your very humble servant,*

*Pierre de Mésange*

That letter did not fail to have its effect; my mistress came, and even offered me an apology for having allowed herself to be deceived by appearances
and condemned my procedure without having heard me.

If it is necessary to tell the truth, I am obliged to admit that no young
woman ever took better care of an unfortunate foreigner than that one took of
me, until I was entirely recovered. She did not neglect for a single day, for the
nearly three months that I kept to me room, to come to see me once or twice,
often spent entire hours with me, and employed the rest of the time searching the
homes of her friends the best things they had and the most appropriate to stimu-
late my appetite. She was not content to see that the King took pleasure in sharing with me the best things that came to his table; it was necessary for her to add
something of her own.

With all that, it is necessary that I say to my shame that I nevertheless remained insensible, and was entirely healed without having felt the slightest amorous affliction.

Benedon, seeing that matters still remained in the same state, could not
help expressing his astonishment.

"Assuredly," he said to me one day, "you must have a very singular temperament, or a great enmity for the fair sex. For several years now, to speak
honestly, my cousin has been in love with you, without you having responded to
her persistence with anything but complete coldness. What do you want, or what
don't you want? Why, I beg you, don't you make her your wife?"

"My wife, Sire?" I replied. "It's not very probable that she's thinking of
that; she's too wise to make an alliance of that nature. At least, I've assumed
until now that I would offend her if I so much as remarked that that was my sentiment."

"Don't say that," said Benedon. "I know full well that she loves you, and that, notwithstanding your manner of acting, which should have put her off a long time ago, she still lives in hope of one day having you for her husband. There are many people who would be glad to see it, and to speak frankly, I wouldn't be sorry about it."

"I believe everything you say, Sire," I replied, "if only to amuse you, but supposing that it were true, it would not be in my power to respond to the desire that you both have to render me happy. I was a monk in France, and all those of the Order to which I consecrated myself and are initiated into its mysteries are excluded from that sacrament—or, if you prefer, that ceremony. The vow that I made still subsists; my absence does not dispense me from it; even though I am outside the Convent I am nonetheless subject to ecclesiastical discipline, and that being so, I cannot avoid observing rigorously the holy Laws of celibacy that I embraced in voluntarily accepting the habit of a Franciscan."

"If that is the case," said the King, "you are wrong not to have told her about that obstacle; there have been a thousand occasions when you might have done that appropriately without anyone perceiving your design."

"I do not know whether I have or not, Sire," I replied. "At least, I did not think that it was necessary in a place where I did not see any possibility that a young woman like that might honor me with her love. Perhaps it's too late, but I'll try once again to remedy the situation."

In fact, the first time that I saw the Lady in private, I said to her: "I owe you my life, Zemire; without you, I would no longer be. I'm delighted to have such a great obligation to a pupil, whose virtue is proven, and whose merits are above what can be imagined, but I am in despair that I am impotent to recognize it. I do not possess anything worthy of being presented to you; my own body does not belong to me; it has been pledged to another. Even if I were reckless enough to offer it to you, such as it is, I would not have the credit of delivering it to you; many years ago, I gave it to God; it is his; it is no longer of this world; I would be committing a sacrilege by taking it away from him, which would never be forgiven."

"Everything that you have just said to me," she replied, "is an obscure enigma, of which I do not understand either the words or the meaning. Explain yourself, I beg you, if you want me to understand. Speak with an open heart, don't prevaricate; I give you the liberty to say everything to me that is in your heart; you must not be afraid that I will complain."

"Well, Madame," I responded, "since you wish it thus, it is necessary for me to declare that I am in despair at not being able to propose myself as the re-ward for the care that you have taken of my person during my indisposition and everything else that you have done for me. I have made a vow never to marry, and it is not permissible for me to retract it; I could not take a wife without damning myself, and my soul is too precious to me to lose; on the contrary, there is nothing in the world I would not do to save it. In recompense, I offer you my services very humbly; dispose of me, I implore you, as an item of property that belongs to you; speak, and I will listen; command, and I will obey."

"To speak the same language as you, Mésange," she said then, "and take away the mask entirely, is that the coin in which you intend to pay me in recompense for all the movements that I have made to please you? You have made me suspect it for a long time, but I have always lived in hope of triumphing one day over your insensible heart. Presently, I believe that it has come to an end; you are having recourse to a chimerical vow, by virtue of which a legitimate marriage to a woman, who is your equal in every way, is forbidden to you.

"Admit it frankly—it will be neither more nor less so for it—is it not true that that procedure is unjust and utterly unworthy of a Philosopher? What, because you had recklessly given your word to God to kill a man, you would not leave his life to someone who abandoned himself to your mercy? Or because you had sworn not to drown, you would persist stubbornly in the resolution not to drink a drop of water as long as you live? Assuredly, that is ridiculous."

"There is a great deal of difference between one and the other, Madame," I replied. "The Society of which I am a member does not permit me to soil myself; celibacy is a penitence attached to my Order, which is perhaps only agreeable to the Omnipotent; whereas I could not, without becoming a criminal, propose formally to take the life of my fellow, let alone carry it out..."

"I think what you are trying to say," she interrupted, "is that circumstances alter cases; when one is at war, it is a virtue to exterminate one's enemies; on another occasion, it would be a crime deserving of exemplary punishment. One can also never form a household; that is not forbidden here at present, as it once was, but I deny that it is permissible to make a solemn vow not to marry. Man and woman were created for one another; nature demands that they join together by marriage, and I firmly believe that Yomaha expresses himself clearly on that matter; he commands all the animals carefully to observe that Laws of union, which he seems to have imprinted in the hearts of all living creatures. If you have Societies of men in your homeland who deprived themselves of the company of women deliberately, I swear to you that if I had the authority, I would put them in a state that would oblige them, perhaps against their will, not to violate their promise,"

One of her neighbors, who came in abruptly at that point to have a word with her, prevented me from bursting into laughter on hearing that Turkish sentence, which would build Seraglios on the ruins of all Convents, and which would not want Eunuchs by will but by effect. I was glad to see a discourse interrupted at that point that could not have continued without chagrin on either side. For fear of its resumption, I took advantage of that visit to leave.

The first time I saw the King thereafter I gave him an account of the conversation I had had with his cousin. He told me quite frankly that he shared her opinion. He treated our Monks and Nuns as idle bellies, useless burdens on a

State, leeches who live on the substance of widows and orphans, hypocrites, rascals and everything scornful and worthy of the hatred of honest men.

I tried in vain to persuade him that the sanctity of those devoted souls appeased the ire of God, excited by the enormous sins of the other inhabitants of the earth, who, but for that, could never avoid being exterminated and reduced to nothingness; that by their works of supererogation, they earned paradise for millions of poor sinners who merited eternal death; that they never ceased to pray for the dead and he living; and that, in consequence, there could never be too many in a country. He mocked me overtly and only neglected to spit in my face.

"I esteemed you once for your knowledge," he told me, "but in future I can no longer regard you as anything but a fanatic."

"Don't get carried away, Sire," I said. "You were born in one religion; I was brought up in another; the difference between them is the cause of the diversity of our sentiments, but although that diversity often engenders hatred, that is usually only among the common and the ignorant. You are too wise to imitate them in that, and I cannot imagine that you can have scorn for a man who has thus far been the unique object of your esteem."

"It is true that I have loved you as myself," he continued, "but that was for want of having considered you from all sides. I did not know that you affected maxims that are detestable in themselves. In fact is it not horrible to hear from the mouth of a miserable mortal, who puts himself among that number, that there are animals with human faces capable of sustaining with impunity that their actions ought be held in account before the Being of Beings, that they are meritorious works, not only for themselves but generally for all those who employ them or pay them for that?

"We do not nourish ourselves on chimeras; that is reserved for hypochondriacs like Raoul, you or your fellows, who penetrate the future and flatter yourself that you have glimpsed immense treasures there, which you ought to enjoy throughout eternity. We content ourselves with temporal goods, of which Providence gives us a share in this lie; they are not comparable to others, but however simple they are, we admit frankly that we are unworthy to possess them, and that if the Author has given them to us, it is nothing but pure generosity, a very particular grace.

"Oh, ingrate," he added, "how grateful you should be for the cares of a poor woman, who has risked death in order to conserve your life, not to mention the protection of a King who has honored you with all his esteem, and has rendered you honors that are only due to him alone, since you have had the insolence to claim that the Sovereign Monarch of the Universe, after having extracted you from nothingness and given you a share of a thousand good things thus far, owes you much more? Assuredly, that makes one shiver."

"Forgive me Sire, if I tell you..."

"There is nothing Sire can do," he interrupted. "So long as you plead for such a detestable cause and do not change your sentiments, I will not listen to you anymore, and you will give me the pleasure of no longer presenting yourself before me."

*Is it possible*, I asked myself, privately, *that there is so little foundation to a man that he is capable of passing from one extreme to the other in such a short time?*

I went away from there to complain of my misfortune to a Chiou who had always seemed to me to be one of my friends.

"I'm not astonished by what has happened to you." he said. "The King has had this marriage in mind for you for some time. He has lived until now in the hope that you would finally have regard for someone he considers highly and is even his relative. Now you have refused flatly to marry her; he imagines that can only come from a principle of scorn and concludes that it is a very poor recognition of the obligations you have to him."

"I admit," I replied, "that Benedon has had a regard for me of which I am entirely unworthy, and which I shall remember as long as I live, but does it follow therefrom that he must become my Tyrant? Why does he want to force my inclinations and oblige me at the same time to break an oath that I made never to unite with a woman?"

"There are people," he said, "who are madly in love on the first day of their marriage, who hate one another mortally thereafter, whereas others, who regarded one another yesterday with indifference and coldness, cannot live today without going to extremes to give tangible marks of their tenderness. The inclination that you do not have as yet might come with time, and as for the oath with which you want to authorize your procedure, it's a pretext that is not receivable here."

"It is however, that which poses the greatest obstacle to this proposed marriage," I continued, "and it is so great that, for from lifting it, I would prefer to leave Cambul forever than even heave the thought."

"If that is so," said the Chiou, "I advise you not to stay; without the protection of the King, who has treated you like a brother, there would be no great pleasure for you. The Queen has fortunately given birth to two sons, as you know, and it will be necessary to inform the other cities of that happy event. If you'll take my advice, you'll ask for permission to go with the embassy, and in passing, you can stay in the place that suits you best, or the one that gives you the best welcome."

"If I leave here," I replied, "I shall go to live in Meralde, which is, in my opinion, the most beautiful place in the continent. But before I undertake the voyage, oblige me by speaking to the King, and discovering whether my going away would give him more pleasure than my presence."

"There is no need," he said. "Those who know Benedon know very well that he can cease to love, but that he never forgives. I'll go, however and I'll bring you his reply myself."

The Chiou was right; two days later he came to confirm his thought, and added as an extra affliction that the King wished me a pleasant voyage and more prudence in the future than I had shown with him. That compliment, from a man with whom I had lived on such familiar terms, and of whom I was as fond as I was of myself, appeared so harsh that I thought I might die of displeasure; I kept to my bed for three days, but finally, having reflected on the inconstancy of things of this world, I pulled myself together and got ready to go and seek my fortune elsewhere.

A short time afterwards we left, without my saying goodbye to any but my most intimate friends.

At the first resting-place, I was the most disconcerted of living beings when the Lieutenant of the Guards, who was commanding our escort, took me to one side and looked me in the face.

"Zemire has instructed me to murder you on the road, Sire de Mésange," he said, "and it was necessary for me to promise to do it, but I would be very sorry to keep my word. However, in order that I can give her an excuse and tell her that you disappeared first, having not given me time or an opportunity to content her, ask five or six of my soldiers to go on ahead with you as far as Daila, in order to get there ahead of me, and hide in some place where I cannot see you. Then, when our Ambassador is no longer there, you can establish yourself there or wherever you please."

I thanked him very humbly for his generosity, and profited from his salutary advice, but not without reflecting seriously on the damnable resolution of Zemire, who wanted nothing less than my blood to avenge herself for the scorn that she imagined I had had for her love.

Although I was given a good welcome in that place, I only stayed there for a month or so; a convenient opportunity arose to go to Persac, and I thought that I ought not to neglect it. Afterwards I passed on to Meralde, as the most beautiful and best situated city in Russal, where I would have stayed in retirement for a long time if the person of Benedon and my own had not been present in my mind as inseparables. On arriving there I went I search of two of my old comrades, one Dutch and the other a Walloon, named Pierre and André, who were living together and who would surely invite me to share their lodgings. I knew that they were still alive, and everyone knew them, with the consequence that I did not have to search for long.

Then I went to pay my respects to the Governor. He was perfectly well informed of the reason why I had left Cambul and not unaware of my footing there prior to the moment of my disgrace.

"You were wrong to quarrel with Benedon, my friend," he told me, "over a matter that could only have worked to your advantage—or you could have confessed to him frankly that you are impotent and not made use of vain pretexts that could only annoy your benefactor."

"Impotent, Lord?" I replied. "I'm not..."

"Let's leave it there," he interrupted. "That's a matter between the two of you; it doesn't affect me. You're protected from a similar incident in this city, where you can remain as long as you please without running any risk of being molested by anyone, since you're known and you'll be under my protection. As we live in a community of property, so to speak, you will lack nothing, provided that you have some occupation, for we do not like idlers. Until you have obtained one you do not have to go elsewhere; my house and my table are at your service; you may dispose of them as you please."

"I'm infinitely obliged to you, Lord," I said, "for the kind offers that you're making me, and I thank God that, in my misfortune, he has caused me to fall into such good hands; I have both, until I can apply myself."

"The dignity to which Benedon had raised you," said Emega—that was his name—"dispenses you from the fatigues and heavy work to which the common people are subject. Since you are well versed in the highest sciences, it is permitted to you to cultivate them. I have relatives myself who would be very glad to confide the education of their children to you; you will have an occupation, therefore, and the opportunity to make friends."

"My goal, Lord," I replied, "is to oblige all honest men, and although there are no treasures to amass in this land, I shall nevertheless occupy the best part of my time, if that is necessary."

Before quitting the Governor, he invited me to eat with him, which is the usual mark in the land by which one testifies to a man that one has a particular consideration for him.

Scarcely a month passed before I had a very considerable audience; many men came to hear me, and although they were extremely jealous, several of them had no difficulty in bringing their wives with them, thinking that I belonged to Queen Candace.[39] Among others, a Chiou named Seneha, who lived next door to us, rarely came without his. He loved her passionately, and inasmuch as what he heard me say gave him pleasure, he did not think his joy complete unless he shared it with his dear Spouse.

The Lady in question had intelligence; she entered into my sentiments much better than her husband, and if she had had more judgment she would have been capable of greater penetration. With that, one can say, without hyperbole, that she was consummately beautiful; I had not seen in my entire life, in France, Holland, or Germany, a better-made, better turned-out and better-mannered human being. Her complexion put the lilies of the field to shame; roses, as vividly as my imagination could represent them in a place where they could only be seen in the mind's eye, paled by comparison with her pink cheeks and coral lips. Her beautiful large, dark, well-separated and prominent eyes; her

---

[39] A Biblical reference to Acts 8:27: "And behold, a man of Ethiopia, a eunuch of great authority under Candace, Queen of the Ethiopians, who had charge of all her treasures..."

straight and perfectly shaped nose, her small mouth, furnished with rows of even, pearly teeth as white as snow; her fleshy chin, her round and well-furnished throat; her alabaster breasts; her nacreous fingernails; her slender arms and, in brief, all her limbs, were so perfect; her bearing had something majestic about it; her voice was so soft and her diction so polished, that one could have taken her for nature's masterpiece and the most beautiful work that had emerged from the hands of Rhea.[40]

An object so rare surprised me; the strongest resolutions I had made to abandon amour forever vanished in her presence, and, thinking more of the future than the past, without making any reflection on my years, I resolved to work incessantly to make a conquest of her.

In order to reach my objective, I began by affecting a grave and composed air; I only conversed with everyone about serious matters; I preached morality in any company in which I found myself. In sum, no Tartuffe ever counterfeited an honest man in the theater of Molière than I did under the auspices of Comega.[41] Those saintly and compassed manners attracted everyone's affection; people only spoke of me with respect, and the Ladies were so convinced of my probity that they trusted themselves alone with me without rendering themselves suspect to the slightest evil though even on the part of those who were the most interested in them, and who naturally ought not to have taken it in good part. I alone was the depository of my design; my own comrades had no knowledge of it.

By dint of frequenting my lessons, Marolde—that was the name of the beauty I adored—became accustomed to me; she saw that I took infinite trouble with her. I encouraged her, complimented her and excited her competition as much as was possible. I talked about her merit and the considerable progress that she was making in Philosophy everywhere I went, whenever the opportunity presented itself; I had her explain to the others difficult and abstruse matters on which I had given her extended particular instruction, which few others understood.

That attracted praise to her that delighted her and by which her husband was charmed. The cause of it could, however, be simply attributed to her Professor, and it would have been ungrateful for them not to mark their gratitude. In fact, those good people had nothing that they did not share with me; we often ate together and the only thing that was not common between us was the one at which I was aiming. I went to work slowly, in order not to make any mistake, and I'm mistaken if I did not frequent that charming person for two full years without saying a single word, or committing the slightest action, that might have

---

[40] A Minoan mother-goddess assimilated, like the Anatolian Cybele, to the Greek Earth-Mother Gaia.

[41] This reference is enigmatic but probably has something to do with the shape of the lower case of the Greek letter omega, $\omega$, the initial C being added to signify negation or emptiness

given rise to suspicion, when it came to mind to try to persuade her that all the heavenly bodies were in a single Heaven, or arranged on the concave surface of the firmament, and not at different stages one above another, in order to have the opportunity to make a pass at her collar.

The question was no sooner proposed than she raised several objections, to which I had difficulty responding without resorting to gross sophistry, because they were founded on the system that I had taught her.

"It is evident," she said to me, "according to our observations, that the Sun advances from the Occident to the Orient, in the plane of the ecliptic, every day, by nearly one degree; the Moon travels in the same direction a circle that cuts the preceding one at an angle of five degrees, in such a way that it covers about thirteen degrees in twenty-four hours. All the principal Astronomers, according to what you have often told me yourself, maintain that the Sun is several thousand times larger than the Moon; the difference in their movements is not in proportion to the difference in their grandeur; that being so, it appears, by the rules of motion, that when the Moon reaches the Sun at times of conjunction, which are at the head or tail of the dragon-which is to say, at the points where the circles they travel intersect—it ought incontestably to rebound and return to the place whence it came, without having lost any of its rapidity. Now, everyday experience informs us that that is not the case, so it is not true that those luminaries are in the same Heaven."

"That is what is called accurate reasoning, and in consequence of antecedents or principles that we have posed as constant and indubitable," I said. "But who has told you, beautiful Marolde, "that the bodies in question are equally solid? Everyone agrees that the Moon is a solid and opaque body, but as for the Sun, there are few people who are not persuaded that all its parts, subtle, detached and in continuous agitation, compose in sum a liquid whole. If that is the case, you can clearly see that as a stone easily opens a passage through the air or water, the beautiful Diana scarcely finds any difficulty in hiding herself for a few moments in the entrails of her brother Apollo and traversing him clean through rather than rebounding and retracing her steps."

"What you say there," she replied, "would perhaps not be impossible, if it were true, as you pretend in this trial, that they are equally distant from the Earth, but an evident proof that that is not the case is that during their conjunction, one perceives over the body of the Moon a faint light that it receives infallibly from the Sun, by means of the reflection that the terrestrial Globe sends back to it. That would not happen if it were enclosed and that whirlpool of fire."

"I could employ other arguments," she continued, "drawn from the different apparent sizes of the Moon, when it is eclipsed, to prove what I say more amply, but there is no need, and the last, if I'm not mistaken, ought to content you entirely."

"And it might not be difficult for me," I said to her, "to demonstrate to you that the Sun, being a transparent body, could no more hide from our eyes what is passing through its center from one extremity to the other than the clear water of a spring hides from our sight a fish that is swimming at a depth of several feet, and that during eclipses of the Moon, it is the Earth that draws nearer or recoils from it, not it from the Earth; but I shall show you mercy and only employ this single reason, which must infallibly close your mouth.

"This is what really happens: every time the Moon reaches the Sun in a straight line, it passes by turning around it in this manner"—and with that, I applied my right ear to her left, and rotated my face over hers, which I pressed with all my strength, especially at the location of the mouth, where I paused briefly.

"It was hardly necessary," she exclaimed, laughing very pleasantly, "to use that gross trick, which obliges you to suppose that the Moon rotates around its center in order to overtake the Sun, when we see, on the contrary, that it always has one side turned toward us, in order to steal a kiss from me, which I would have given to you if you had asked me."

"That you would have done that, divine Marolde," I interjected, "is what I would never have been able to believe without being convinced by experiment."

"Be assured, Mésange," she replied, "that I'm not an ingrate; that is a vice that I have always hated. I'm not talking about the kiss—that is a bagatelle; my gratitude ought to extend much further, but I assure you that my husband and I have nothing in the world that is not at your service. He has told you that several times, and I reiterate it to you today; it only remain to convince you whenever you wish."

A declaration so frank, and at the same time so advantageous, would have given me the opportunity to make a great deal of ground in a very short time if a small boy that she had, five or six years old, had not come in to say that his father had sent word that he had a appetite and to set the table s quickly as possible.

In fact, he appeared a moment later, and after having greeted me warmly, invited me to eat with him. A gander, which he had had caponized before being fattened, and which was served to us roasted, gave him the opportunity to tell us that the Council had just had a case to decide that had embarrassed the judges considerably.

"A woman," he told us, "has come to complain of the impotence of her husband and has asked us several times to annul her marriage and to permit her to remarry another man. 'What proof have you,' the President asked her, 'of the fault of which you accuse the one you have now?'

"'I have a convincing one,' she said, 'but in addition to that, I have been living with him for ten years, and we have not yet been able to do anything worthwhile; on the one hand, people mock him, and on the other, they never cease to commiserate with me.'

"'Do you talk about your affairs to everyone, then?' she was asked.

"'Is it necessary, Sires,' she replied, 'to divulge something that leaps to the eye? Doesn't the entire city know us? And no one is unaware that we have had no children together.'

"'Is that the misfortune of which you're complaining?' I asked.

"'Of course,' she continued, 'and not without reason, for if I grow old without having any, I run the risk of being exposed to the mercy of the public or my relatives, who will treat me at their whim; instead of having breadwinners at home, I'll be obliged to anyone whatsoever.'

"'You're right,' said the President. 'I didn't understand at the beginning what you meant. But my good woman, there are many other families who have no heirs, who are nevertheless in a state to have them, had Providence wished to give them to them. It's necessary not to complain; you're still young enough to have as many as you wish. It's necessary that the other reason, which you assure us is convincing, is of a nature different from the preceding one; would you be good enough to enlighten us as to that one, as you have explained the other?'

"'Sire,' she replied, 'I do not want to be crude; you have only to take the trouble to seek information, and you will find that on my side, as far back as we can go, which is fifteen or twenty generations, there has never been a wife who has not given birth; it is a essential quality attached to our family; whereas, on my husband's side, there are sterile marriages in large number. In addition to which I have heard my mother-in-law say a thousand times, talking about her son, when he was still a child, that he was never good for anything. At any rate, I don't want to stay with him, I need to be given another, or to choose one at my whim.'

"'We don't want to hear any threats,' said the President, then. 'Withdraw; we'll inquire more particularly into the subject of your complaint, and justice will be done.'

"To begin with, two delegates have been appointed, who have orders to go and find the father and mother of the man in question, in order to find out whether they have ever noticed that he is lacking something. If they say no, it will be necessary to examine the two parties, to see whether there is innocence in their actions, whether they lack instruction, or if there is hatred and malice; and in accordance with the report that is made, a verdict will be pronounced."

"I don't know what I ought to think about all that," I said to Seneha, "but it seems that the good woman doesn't understand the subtleties of the matter, and I fear that the obstacle might come from her side. There was a time when similar complaints were often made to the Courts of Justice in the realm of France. A Law made expressly to settle these sorts of differences, which was known as the Law of Congress, was the principal cause. As soon as a gallant woman became dissatisfied with her husband and fell in love with someone else, under the pretext of not having children with him she took her complaint to the Council and demanded Congress. The majority of those put to that proof failed the test, the marriages were dissolved and the woman married someone else."

"That's not surprising," said Seneha, "and I'll wager that of ten husbands indignant against a wife who offered them the atrocious insult of challenging them to demonstrate their sufficiency in the presence of witnesses, there would scarcely be one who did not fail."

"That was exactly the reason for the abrogation of that law, made in favor of the fair sex," I told him. "Skillful Advocates were so well able to represent the state of the most vigorous man in such circumstances that a woman who demanded Congress nowadays would pass for mad or indecent, and that it might only be necessary for the husband to enclose himself without any form of trial, either with persons of his own sex in formal..."

"I have children," Marolde interrupted, "but even if I had not, it would never enter my head to complain about my husband, for fear of rendering myself suspect of knowing more about the facts of marriage than I ought."

"I say the same of you, my wife," said Seneha. "We are content with one another—at least, I declare frankly that I am, for my part, and I hope that you are for yours."

"Until now I have been," said Marolde. "I can't answer for the future as I have for the past. Mésange gave me a kiss just now which seemed to me so sweet, that it might well cause me, if I conserve me memory of it, not to take so much pleasure in yours."

"What, Sir?" said Seneha to me. "You amuse yourself kissing my wife in my absence, and without asking my permission? That would be capable of putting a hammer to my head." He paused, and continued: "You're blushing. Have you been falsely accused, or has there been some criminal thought involved?"

"Thank God, Sir," I replied, "you know me. Madame only said that in order to laugh; had there been any evil intent she would have been careful not to mention it to you. I'll tell you myself how it happened. We had no globe to hand and it was a matter of the movement of the Moon and the Sun for..."

"I have only to know your movements," Seneha interrupted abruptly. "Kiss as much as you please; you'll kiss a long time before I protest. I know my wife and I have faith in you; be assured that in whatever manner you act, you won't give me any umbrage."

I tried to respond twenty times to his kindness, and the wife, for her part, was enthusiastic to finish her story, but there was no means; he interrupted us repeatedly, and was absolutely determined not to talk about anything but drinking.

When I saw that he seemed insensible to a procedure that I had envisaged as injurious and ought naturally to excite his jealousy, I said: "You're right, Seneha," to trust your wives, as it's impossible to hold them to duty when they have a penchant for debauchery; it's human nature to apply more zeal to that which is expressly forbidden them.

"If Turkish Ladies were not imprisoned in Seraglios, and those in Italy so closely observed, perhaps they would not be more coquettish than others, but the jealousy of their husbands is so exorbitant that it drives them to discover the reason for it and to conclude that their qualities must be far inferior to those of the persons from they take care to keep them away with so much exactitude. The French know that the veritable means of holding their wives to duty is to make them sensitive to their honor and abandon the care of their conduct to them, giving them entire liberty. That means seems to them more efficacious for sheltering them from the disgrace to which marriage renders them subject.

"It is true, however, that if the former are punished for their extreme severity, the latter are not entirely exempt from the unfortunate consequences that stem from granting faith too great a license. Here is an example that will substitute for all the others and will serve to illustrate a middle way. I had it from a French Officer named Monsieur Jammet, who told us the story one day in The Hague, swearing that it had happened recently.

"He was in Paris, he told us, when a certain Monsieur Quevilli, a merchant in porcelain and glassware to the King had a daughter who was the joy of the house. He and his wife never talked about anything but her virtue and good qualities. She got up early every day to say ardent prayers; all the books that she had were of Orisons, Hymns, Spiritual Songs and the Lives of Saints, and everything that might furnish material for her piety. She fasted two or three times a week, frequented Churches and never failed for a single day of the year to go to the Hôtel-Dieu at nine o'clock in the morning to help the nuns at the hospital to serve and care for the poor invalids, who had need of her help, in order to gain by those good works the approval of honest folk and a place in paradise.

"So many saintly actions, which had lasted from the age of thirteen to eighteen years of age, had established her reputation so firmly that a very worthy man, among others, came to ask for her hand in marriage. She did not want to listen. 'Me,' she said to him, 'join with a man, enter into a household, where the cares of pleasing a husband, bringing up children and running a house would occupy me entirely and scarcely give me any leisure to think about my salvation? God forbid that I should ever think about it. Jesus Christ is my Spouse; it is for him alone that I feel love, him that I want to please, his house that I must frequent; the poor, who are his limbs and his children, re those whom it is necessary to serve all my life. I have renounced the world, the flesh and its covetousness; I hope that the Lord will grant me the mercy of never giving them any access to my heart. That is why we should not mention it again; that language shocks me, I cannot abide it; if you talk to me about such vanities again, you will have to resolve yourself to never appearing in my presence again.'

"That refusal seemed harsh to the lover, and he complained of it to her father. Monsieur Quevilli had been in military service for a long time; the scars with which his body was covered and his face, blue with gunpowder, testified sufficiently to that; in addition, he was violent by nature and scarcely proffered three words without taking God by the hands and feet twice. He summoned his daughter, and after having remonstrated with her very calmly, in his own manner, that the party she was disdaining was very eligible, and that she would doubtless have reason to repent of it one day, he made her understand that he would be very glad to see the young man, for whom he had a strong inclination, enter into his family.

"The tone of voice in which those words were pronounced disturbed the beauty, who began to weep. 'What, Father?' she said to him. 'Can it be that you, who have always loved me with all possible tenderness, now want to exercise violence upon me, to be the cause of the ruination of my soul? Don't you know that I have renounced all sorts of voluptuousness? Have you forgotten that, in accordance with the vow that I have made, that no man will ever do anything with me, and that if it had not been for love of you and my mother, I would be in a convent now? Don't force me, I beg you, since you would oblige me to do things of which I would have reason to repent thereafter.'

"'It's impossible, my daughter,' her father replied, 'given the humor that I know you to have, and to judge by your constitution, that you can be insensible; doubtless you have cast your eyes upon another object, which you are hiding from me, and you are making use of a vain pretext to avoid the choice that I have made of an honest man, but by death, you shall not toy thus with me; belly, blood nor head, the reproach will never be addressed to me that a daughter laid down the Law to me and lived in spite of me according to her own caprice. You will take the person who is asking for you, or the Devil will get mixed up in it.'

"Threats of that force intimidated the poor devout girl; it was necessary for her to consent to her parents' tyrannical propositions. She was married immediately. 'Violence has been done to me for love of you,' she said to her husband. 'I do not wish you any harm; the thing is done; I have no regret; on the contrary, I intend to live with you in perfect intelligence. I shall love you; I shall cherish you; I shall serve you with all the zeal of which I am capable; but in the name of God, have the kindness for your part to permit me to spend a part of my time in prayers and orisons, and most of all, suffer that I go as usual every day to exercise my charity by serving the poor invalids at the Hospital, whom the Lord recommends so expressly to our cares. Those works of piety will substitute for the stains and soilings to which one is indispensable subject in marriage; thus, on the one hand, I shall not be neglecting your interests, and on the other, I shall be working for my salvation.'

"The young man consented to her request without difficulty, in the hope that his company and the occupations that she would find in his shop and in the house, would divert her, with the result that those daily excursions would soon become burdensome to her. He was, however, mistaken in his conjectures; she took a great deal of care of his person, not did she neglect that which was committed to her care, but she preferred to work by night provided that she could go out by day.

"All that would have been perfectly fine, but eventually she had a child, and as the young people's business grew, the master, who had important business to handle, could not absent himself often because of his wife's absence; he was obliged to remain at his counter as his maidservant was to the cradle. Sometimes he complained to his wife, and recalled her to her duty, but seeing that those arguments were futile and that it was impossible for him to keep her at home whatever necessity there was for her to remain, he became suspicious, and resolved to follow her the next time she went out, to see where she went.

"After many turnings and detours, which did not lead to the Hôtel-Dieu, he thought he was falling from a height when he saw her enter one of the dirtiest and vilest places in the City. He made a decision on the spot and went in immediately behind her. 'Is there a means of spending an hour or two of time agreeably here?' he asked the landlady, to whom he had asked to speak. 'But at the least, I need a young person, who is not very tall.'

"'I have what you need,' she replied. 'Go into that apartment, and you'll be immediately accommodated.'

"He had not made three circuits of the room to which he was taken when his dear little wife was brought to him. I leave it to you to imagine, Seneha, how surprised that unfortunate woman was to find herself in view of a man who ought to be her judge and her profession. She threw herself at his feet and begged his pardon for her sin, and, dissolving in tears, swore that she would be good and never to undertake such escapades in the future.

"'The place where we are, pious and virtuous wife,' he said to her, 'does not permit me to explode and tell you my sentiments regarding your way of life; come on, let's return to our home.'

"As soon as they were in the house, the young man sent for his father-in-law. He told him what had just happened, and told him frankly that he had to take back his daughter, since it was impossible for him and a wanton to live together any longer. I shall not bother to describe to you the quarrels, outbursts and threats on the one side, and the apologies, accompanied by a thousand promises to live better in future on the other, that were the substance of that surprising scene. It will be sufficient for me to say, if I'm not mistaken, that the conclusion was, under the penalty of having the heads of both the husband and the wife broken by the tempestuous old man, to bury all of it in forgetfulness, on condition that he sent them a sum of two thousand écus, which he had to do.

"'I knew those people,' Monsieur Jammet added, 'and I can tell you that since then, nothing had been heard to the disadvantage of the young woman, who lives very quietly and perfectly well with her husband.'"

"I believe that wherever one goes,' Seneha said, "one finds all sorts of people; there are women who need to be watched, because they render themselves suspect by their conduct, and there are others whom one cannot suspect, because they are careful to behave tactfully on all occasions, and have given convincing proof of their virtue in various encounters. I have said, and I confirm once again, that with regard to my wife, I am convinced that her honor is dear to her and that what she does in private she could not do before everyone."

Our conversation lasted until the pithson began to take effect and it was necessary for us to take our repose.

Eight or ten days later I found the opportunity to talk to Marolde without witnesses, and did not fail to address reproaches to her for the fact that her imprudence has nearly exposed me to the hatred of her husband and, in consequence, deprived me forever of her presence, which would have been the greatest misfortune that could befall me.

"You're joking," she replied. "My husband jealous of someone else? He has too good an opinion of himself and of me for that; I have proofs of that which I cannot doubt. At least with respect to you, Mésange, I give you my word that there is absolutely nothing to fear, in addition to which I don't think that ether you or I would dream of giving him any reason for discontentment."

"That's true, Madame," I said. "However, it isn't necessary that he knows everything. I have been maltreated by the King of Cambul for not having wanted to love his relative; who knows whether Seneha might not be in despair and capable of discharging his fury on me if he learned that I am consumed with passion for Marolde? Certain marks have appeared on my fingernails for some time that do not prognosticate anything advantageous; I hope that the good God will protect me from further disasters. Do you see this triangle, Madame, and this circle on the line of the heart? That signifies nothing but misfortune, a mortal wound and insupportable dolors."

With that, I took off one of her gloves. "Let us examine your hand a little," I said, "and compare it with mine, to see whether we have anything in common to dread or to hope for. There are little appearances on the mound of Venus, which threaten you with being hated and abandoned by your husband, because you will be loved by someone else."

"I don't care about all these prognostications," Marolde interjected. "My husband loves me; he is incapable of the slightest cooling, on seeing me show affection to a man of merit to whom I have as much obligation as I have to you."

"What? You love me, Madame?" I said, kissing her hand in a manner that marked my passion.

"Certainly," she replied, "I love you; in that I am following my penchant and, I believe, doing my duty."

"If that is true," I went on, "I am the best recompensed of all mortals, but you will permit me to doubt it until sufficient testimonies have confirmed the truth of it."

All that was said while making progress—which is to say, while pressing or tickling the knees, and kissing the throat and the face; I was surprised myself by that young woman, who appeared to be an example of chastity, allowing herself to be stroked in that fashion, without giving evidence of the slightest reluctance.

Eventually, as I was thinking of pressing the point and taking advantage of the favorable circumstance, even though I was not in a safe place, the husband suddenly came in.

"Well, Mésange," he said, "are you giving my wife a lesson?"

"Yes, Seneha," I replied, "or, at least, we're amusing ourselves chatting."

"That's very good," he said, "but I fear that you might render her too knowledgeable; it's not good for a wife to know more than her husband."

"To get as far as that," I said, laughing, "it would be necessary for her to change master, or for me to become your disciple, and even then I would not be would not be able to catch up with you, let alone precede you."

"No mockery, if you please," he replied. "I'm an ignorant man; everyone knows that—and you're a knowledgeable man; that's a fact that no one disputes."

"The thought is too advantageous to me for me to contest it," I said. "I prefer to withdraw. Adieu, until the next time."

From that day on I was astonished not to see Marolde anywhere. She avoided the places I frequented, and when she saw me at a distance in the street she turned her back on me. Not knowing to what to attribute the cause of such a precipitate change, I thought I ought to beg her to send me a word by letter, in order that I could take measures in conformity with what I learned and remedy the situation, if that was in my power. This is what I wrote:

*Letter to the Divine Marolde,*

*I am in despair, most beautiful and most perfect of all women, at having offended you, and not knowing where, when or how. As much as you once ran after me, you now flee my presence. Are you scornful of me because you have become more knowledgeable than me, or have you begun to hate me because I love you? You are not ingrate enough to indulge in the former of those two vices, and you have too much equity to suffer that the latter has the slightest access to you. Your charming hand threatened me with this disaster; I have told you that; you owe it to yourself to remember.*

*The Heaven that warned us of this evil has not inspired me with sufficient prudence to avoid its unfortunate consequences. For after all, it is necessary that I say to you, since the thought has come to me in writing to you, that your husband has doubtless learned something of out innocent familiarities, either from your son, in front of whom we scarcely hide, or directly, by observing our actions himself. With that he will have caught fire, and let himself be carried away by anger, and you have undoubtedly been forbidden to see me again.*

*That is a conjecture, Marolde, which seems to me to be well-founded, and by means of which I discharge you from all culpability, in order to attribute it entirely to another. Tell me, I beg you, whether I have guessed correctly or not, in order that I can regulate myself in accordance with circumstances: whether I*

*can live, if I can remain in the hope of always enjoying your amity; or kill my-*
*self, if I am forced to lose it.*

*Yes, Madame, no other hand than mine will pierce my heart, which only*
*burns for you, from the moment that I learned that the good intentions you had*
*for me have changed to indifference, since death will be infinitely more support-*
*able to me than the dolors I would feel in seeing myself deprived of the right that*
*you have given me to be able to call myself, without criticizing you, your very*
*humble and very obedient servant,*

*Mésange*

I had to languish for several days without knowing my destiny; I heard no more mention of Marolde than if she had never been in the world. I loved her, though, and I can say that I loved her madly, and that without prompt help, I might indeed have been running the risk of succumbing.

My comrades did not know what was the matter with me; I became somber and melancholy; most of the time I sent my pupils away without having given them a lesson, and when I tried to talk to the about science the terms *Marolde, passion, love, rage, despair* and others of a similar sort escaped my lips so often without my perceiving it that some of them warned me about it and advised me to rest for a week or a fortnight, since it appeared that the machine had broken down and that my blood was corrupted.

That mental upheaval caused so much talk that it reached Marolde's ears. She was keenly afflicted by it, and, not wanting to leave me without consolation, she took the time to come and tell me exactly what had happened in her home with regard to me.

As soon as I saw her come in I threw my arms around her. "You are bringing me back to life, charming Marolde," I said. "I have nearly died of chagrin since I last spoke to you. Tell, me, in the name of God, what have I done for you to abandon me as you have?"

"What have you done, Mésange?" she replied. "You have done what you could easily have left undone. Your tears, your gestures, your exclamations, your grimaces and all the other extravagances that you have not discontinued making in my presence for some time had made such an impression on my son, who saw the best part of them, that he told his father everything, who then began observing us so closely that what he saw with his own eyes told him more than I would have wanted him to know.

"I learned the sad news of that with great dolor as soon as you had left us on the day of our last conversation. 'So this is the way, Madame,' he said to me, with his eyes inflamed with anger, 'that you live with your master; for some time already I have perceived the little liberties he takes with you and which made me suspect him, and I have just confirmed the thought that I had that you are living in an unedifying manner by means of the amorous dialogue in which you were indulging for half an hour while I was at the door, watching what you were doing through a crack. Assuredly I was scandalized by such a procedure; I do not understand myself what can have possessed me, and how it is that I did not make a fuss. I do not know of what I might be capable another time; to prevent a misfortune, I advise you to have no more rendezvous, and even less any private meeting, with that seducer, who is only seeking to compromise our honor and to make everyone point fingers at me.'

"'I admit,' my husband, 'I replied to him, that I have permitted Mésange to kiss me and tickle me and to put his hands on my body, sometimes in one place and sometimes another, because I noticed that he liked bantering with me; it seemed to me, given that I could content him with so little, that I would be ingrate to the supreme degree to refuse him that, after all the obligations that we both owe him. What he did with me was the veritable play of a child with a doll, a girlish or boyish pastime, which no one criticizes because the pleasures they obtain are so innocent. In any case, if there was evil in what we have done, it is to you that it's necessary to attribute the fault; you have told me a hundred times that I had no more measures to take with that man than with a woman, since everyone knows that he is a sexagenarian, and in addition, a mown field, and that you had no apprehension of a disarmed enemy.'"

"Well," I interjected, what did he reply to that?"

"Nothing," she continued, "except that all that was true, but that he would not have thought that things would go so far; and in addition, that all those lascivious embraces, those facial lickings, that vain badinage and a thousand idle things that accompanied them far surpassed the bounds that decorum prescribes to honest men. To speak frankly, you have played the fool too much, and you would have been able to control yourself if you had wanted to."

"That's easy to say, Madame," I replied, "but it's very difficult for a man who is always with you and whom your charms have ensorcelled to moderate himself."

"It will, however, be necessary to do so in future," Marolde replied. "And it might even, in order to have peace, be necessary for us to say an eternal Adieu."

"What, Marolde?" I said, precipitately. "You want to abandon thus, and cast into despair, a man who adores you?"

"Not so soon yet," she replied. "You had begun to explain to me, for the second time, the formation of meteors; it's necessary for us to finish that, and we'll see thereafter what it is necessary for is to do."

"But Madame," I continued, "when and where will our discussions take place?"

"That's what I've had difficulty in finding," she replied, "but finally I thought of an expedient, which should shelter us from my husband's suspicions and evil popular gossip. I don't know whether you've observed that our houses were once large caverns, which art, nature or perhaps both had excavated in the rocks. As the inhabitants of the large and popular city have increased in number, they have been obliged, gradually, to concentrate themselves, so to speak, and lodge themselves more narrowly than their ancestors once did. That is, at last, the common opinion—which I believe to be true, because it appears likely that those vast dwellings once served an entire family composed of several generations, who lived in community in all things, and which the oldest member governed with absolute authority; and that, eventually wearying of that tumultuous and servile way of life, each father wanted to govern his own wife and children as he pleased, and retired for the purpose into an apartment cutting off communication between that and the others.

"At any rate, it's still incontestable that there are many places where dwellings are separated from one another by a simple partition. Fortunately, there are only wooden boards between your bedroom and the one where we sleep, and in order that that should not be manifest, a larder has been constructed on either side, in such a way that if you take the trouble to make a hole therein through which you can pass, it will only be necessary to do so every time that a convenient opportunity presents itself."

"Assuredly, beautiful Marolde," I said, then, kissing her hand, "it must be admitted that you're fertile in fine inventions. Let me do it; love is ingenious and skillful in al métiers and will not abandon me in need; as long as it aids me, I shall carry out your plan so well that you'll have no reason to complain."

"That's enough," she replied. "I'll go, for hear that someone might catch me here with you."

"Adieu, my soul!" I exclaimed. "Conserve your amity for me always."

As we were then in the fine season, my comrades were hardly ever in the city; they were eternally hunting or fishing; and Seneha was often at the Council, or occupied with public affairs, with the consequence that it was easy for me to set to work. Several days passed before it was finished, however, because I dared not make a great deal of noise and it was necessary to listen carefully at all times, to see whether there was anyone in Marolde's house—for although she had promised to knock loudly on her cupboard door at the moment when I had to stop work, I did nothing without trembling, for fear of being caught in the act.

A pointed knife with a sharp edge was the only tool I employed for removing from the planks that prevented us from seeing one another a piece fifteen inches wide and a foot deep, and in order that it might serve to hold the narrow gap closed I made two holes at the top, two inches from the extremities, and as many in the plank above, through which I could pass a stout cord of gut, which I knotted firmly, in such a manner that it could take the place of two hinges. I attached a small piece of leather on me side, to the bottom of my hidden window, in order to be able to open it easily by tugging on it, and that it would only remain for me to pass through it when necessary.

No joy was ever similar to mine, when I tried it out for the first time—but that joy diminished prodigiously when I only found the charming Marolde disposed to hear me talk about physics.

"Let us keep to the solid," she said to me, immediately, "and banish the trivial from our midst, since it has given people occasion to find fault and would retard the progress of my studies."

As there was no finesse in her actions, and her speech was ordinarily grave and serious, I leave it to you to imagine how a language so opposed to that which I was expecting mortified me. I remained nonplussed for a few moments; one might have thought that I had lost the power of speech. In fact, that session passed rather coldly; the state in which Marolde had put me was so different from the one in which I had set out that, instead of talking to her about the flame of my passion, I only talked about hail, sow frost and ice.

In spite of that, I nevertheless lived in hope, and provided that when I saw her she permitted me to kiss her beautiful hands from time to time, I seemed already o have fulfilled all my desires.

The time passed, however, like lightning; I was always at risk of being caught, and I was not advancing in my affairs.

Eventually, the following summer, while Seneha was at the Council, a woman came to complain that, one of her neighbors having entered into a dispute with her husband on the matter of a dish of small fish that they had eaten together shortly before, he had launched such a furious blow of a lever against her left shoulder that she thought that the bone had broken. 'The one uttered frightful cries,' she said, 'on the subject of the pain she felt; the other had fled, believing that he had committed murder. I demand justice, and I beg the Magistrate to send a surgeon to visit the patient, and the expense to the man who will be judged to have done wrong.'

The master of that particular district was dying; he could not be sent in search of information and to arrest, if possible, the one who had struck the malevolent blow. The Governor delegated Seneha for that expedition, and had him accompanied by two soldiers, who were to give him assistance. It was a long way from the Palace to the place in question and it was necessary for him to go past his house in order to get there. Not knowing how much time he would be obliged to remain outside, and feeling hungry, he proposed to the two men that they come in and have a bite to eat with him.

Meanwhile, about a quarter on an hour before, Seneha's sister, feeling indisposed, had send someone to ask Marolde to come and see her, because she had something urgent to communicate to her which she could not entrust to someone else. I was with her then, and when I saw that she wanted to go out, I got ready to go back to my own room.

"No," she said to me, "I won't stay long where I'm going, and it's only a few steps away. I'll be with you shortly; so many comings and goings will tire you out, and there's no danger in waiting for me."

The amiable woman's words made a great impression on me. I allowed myself to be easily persuaded. I can say, however, that no sooner had she gone than I was awaiting her return impatiently and repented of not having returned to my own room. My heart was beating horribly, and a great emotion that I felt throughout my body seemed to me to be presaging some disaster.

While I was in that cruel anxiety I heard the door open; that noise focused my mind and I directed all my senses in that direction, but alas, instead of the joy that I anticipated receiving at the sight of the object of my hopes, I was gripped by a mortal fear when I saw Seneha accompanied by two men armed to the teeth.

If I had been thinking clearly I would not have budged from my place and there would have been no legitimate pretext to maltreat me, but, my design being criminal, far from giving myself time to reflect on the consequences, I resolved immediately to flee from the fury of my enemy, and with that I leapt into the cupboard, which I had left open deliberately, shoved the plank with my head and dragged myself over the edge of my larder in an instant.

It was a trifle dark in that corner, and in the manner that I went, it did not appear to me that anyone could have heard me. I was mistaken in my conjecture, however. One of the soldiers, on coming in, had darted a glance in my direction, and seeing something move, advanced promptly and seized one of my legs. His comrade, to whom he called for help, grabbed the other, and as they made an effort to pull me to them, the trapdoor that I had lifted up, taking the place of a valve, pressed so firmly into my back, consequently narrowing the passage, that it was necessary to be still, or be cut in half before being torn out of there.

They did not know me and I did not want to say anything.

"Hold on to this fellow," said one of those scoundrels to the Chiou. "It's necessary that I teach him to talk, and not to enter into people's houses like a thief."

At the same time he took a knife out of his pocket, slashed a large gash in my trousers, cut my purse and furiously tore away the only two testers[42] that I had in the world, which I still had from my father, and which I had always conserved as preciously as the apple of my eye, without those who held me having perceived them, nor even having the thought of what might come from such an operation.

The blood, which began to flow, alarmed them.

"What have you done?" said Seneha.

"I've put him out of a state to excite your jealousy," he replied. "You have a beautiful wife, and I suspect that we have here the Frenchman who, it's said, has been making love to her since he arrived in the city. Let him go now. I have

---

[42] The literal reference of *teston* [tester] is to a coin, but the "purse" to which this sentence refers is metaphorical, and the English "testers" is thus only one supplementary letter removed from the more brutal intended reference. The consequent dialogue leaves no room for error in construing the intended *double entendre*.

in my hand what will convince you that if he hasn't been chaste in the past, he will be in future."

"What?" said Seneha then. "It's Mésange that you've mutilated? You're mistaken; he's been a eunuch since birth, or has at least passed for such in the minds of all those who know him."

"He's the devil," said the soldier. "Those effeminates don't have the appearance that he has. He's healthy, vigorous, well-built, well turned-out, bearded like a billy-goat and has a ruddy complexion. Believe me, if he's passed himself off as what you think, it can only have been with the design of imposing on your credulity and succeeding more easily in his ends."

"It's necessary that I know that," said Seneha—and, emerging from his house, he went into mine, where he found me lying in my blood, devoid of consciousness of sentiment. I had been in such great agitation when held on one side, I felt myself pressed so tightly in the black on the other, that I had not felt the cruel operation that the guard had just performed, with the result that as soon as they let me go, I had advanced so hastily in the direction of my retreat that, having lost my balance, I had fallen head first onto the floor and had made a large gash above my forehead.

Seneha, seeing me in that sad state, took pity on me and hastened to bring me round.

When he saw me open my eyes again he said: "I'm sorry, Mésange, for the misfortune that has overtaken you; you have brought it on yourself; your passion has blinded you. The views that you have are doubtless bad, but you have been duly punished for them. If I had recognized you, however, it would not have happened; the men I had with me have availed themselves of the law, which authorizes an inhabitant of the city to treat at his discretion those he finds entering furtively into his house, or leaving in the manner in which you were trying to leave mine, because they are considered in such encounters as murderers or thieves. But it's no longer a matter of the harm that has come to you; it's now a matter of healing it, and of commencing by applying appropriate remedies. For the last of your wounds I'll give you a sovereign plaster, and for the other I have an ointment, which will get you out of it in a matter of days.

In the meantime, Marolde had returned to the house. The cupboards had remained open; there was a considerable quantity of blood on the plank, and she heard her husband in my room, all indications threatening that I had been taken by surprise in her room and that blows had been struck.

"Are you there, Seneha?" she cried.

"Yes," he replied. "Come—come and see the fruits of your fine studies and what has happened to your master."

She tried in vain to constrain herself; as soon as the poor woman was informed of the particularities of my disaster, she started weeping so bitterly that I was a thousand times more touched by it than by the dolor I felt. Her distress did not take away the usage of her reason, however; she conserved enough presence of mind to reproach Seneha forcefully, in the presence of the two soldiers, that he had given rise to the great familiarity with which she had lived with me; to which she added several execrable oaths that she had always believed me to be incapable, but that nevertheless, in order to remove from him and others any subject of scandal, she herself had imagined that communication window, in order to give me access by that route, and to finish instructing her in a few sciences for which she had a considerable inclination.

I was hardly in any state to talk, much less to make a long speech, so I contented myself with taking Heaven as my witness to Marolde's innocence, and rendering testimony to her virtue in the strongest expressions of which I was capable.

With that I was bandaged, and to avoid shame for me on the one hand and the difficulties that might have been caused to the rogues who had maltreated me on the other, in case matters were examined rigorously, it was concluded— and everyone swore an oath—that nothing would be divulged and that no mention of it would be made to anyone.

From that moment on I conceived such a disgust for the accursed land of Russal that, notwithstanding the care given to me by Seneha and his wife, I resolved to leave at any price whatsoever.

I told my comrades of my design as soon as they returned from fishing, some three weeks or a month after their departure. In the beginning, they mocked me, saying that it was as impossible to carry out as to attain the Heavens, but in the end, I insisted so frequently, and was able to persuade them that the danger we would run of not reaching one of the first inhabited islands of our knowledge were objects unworthy of the apprehension of three men like us, who were old, poor, foreigners, without the slightest support, eternally occupied and often exposed to the fury of the marine monsters and ferocious beasts that had devoured the other Christians that Providence had brought here with us, that they determined to accomplish whatever came to my mind.

We had passed the Summer Solstice and were in the most beautiful season of the year; and another great advantage, which I preferred to that one, was that we had in that place around eighty-three or eighty-four degrees of boreal latitude, which would abridge or navigation considerably.

I had one of the largest boats we could find prepared, on the pretext that I wanted to go and amuse myself with my hosts, taking care to stockpile food for twelve or fifteen days. We made a hole in the middle of one of the benches, in order to be able to plant a little mast therein, to which we had attacked a yard-arm and a sail made of perfectly sewn hides. We added to that weapons, two sledgehammers, two hatchets, four oars, hooked poles, several ropes of gut, a good quantity of pithson and everything else we thought absolutely necessary to attempt our voyage.

When everything was ready and I was about to leave the house go to the harbor, a soldier came in and asked me very politely to accompany him to the house of the Governor, who had a few words to say to me. I tried to excuse myself and to postpone the visit until another occasion, but there was no means of getting rid of the man, who, having changed his tone, told me in a rather arrogant fashion that he would not quit me before I had been to the assigned place.

At those words I was gripped by dread.

"What's the matter, my friend?" I said to him. "I'm not accustomed to being treated in such a high-handed manner. Has something happened to my disadvantage, or am I to be given some commission that will not suffer any delay?"

"I don't know what you expect me to say," said the guard. "I don't know what he wants with you; I was ordered to fetch you, and I obeyed. Now you have to go with me."

"Let's go, then," I said to him. "Let's see what he wants with us; we probably won't be hanged."

As soon as I appeared before the Protector, he said: "Well, Sir Philosopher, it seems that you take pleasure in playing some trick of your métier wherever you go. Do you want to render yourself odious to the whole world, or to have yourself torn to pieces by the inhabitants of Russal?"

"Me, Sire?" I replied. "You're surely mistaken; I've done nothing anywhere that I cannot justify, and I have no views capable of bring the slightest prejudice to anyone."

"Poor man," he continued. "You thought you were acting very secretly in fitting out a vessel in which to flee, but I've known your plan as well as you know it yourself for a week. Have you no shame, to want to pay with the blackest ingratitude there ever was for the benefits that you have had and the kindness that has been shown to you in our city? Does your science lead to this and does your religion authorize such pernicious maxims? You merit being imprisoned between four walls for the rest of your life, or being allowed to die of starvation."

"May God punish me if I know what you mean," I said.

"You don't know?" said Emega. "Do you still have the impertinence to lie to my face—or, to put it better, dare you deny a fact for which your conscience is making your reproaches that are visible to my eyes? Which is to say that you want me to explain myself; well, is it not true that you have loaded a boat with everything necessary to go to Sea?"

"Yes, Sire," I replied.

"With what design, pray?" he continued.

"With the design," I said, of amusing ourselves—my comrades and I—and spending a few days fishing."

"Your intentions are limited to that?" the Governor asked me.

"Assuredly, Sire," I replied.

"All evil intentions are deniable," he continued, shaking his head. "You'll soon sing a different tune. At the same time he called out, and the same man who had brought me to him took me into another room, where he ordered me to stay until further notice.

Emega immediately sent for four of the members of his Council and two witnesses who were to depose against me. When those people had come in I was summoned and I was asked whether I knew the two individuals who were there and with whom they wanted to confront me.

"Very well," I replied. "They're my neighbors, honest folk with whom we often converse."

"Too much," the Governor interjected. "Let us see presently whether you will deny before them that you desire to return to your homeland, like a traitor, and to bring your Sovereign to send swarms of Brigands against us in order to subjugate and destroy us?"

"Is that the great evil that I have committed, Emega?" I said, then. "That certainly wasn't worth the trouble of interrupting our little voyage and giving yourself so much unnecessary trouble. It's true, Sires, that I have often made these good people comprehend that I would be delighted to return to my homeland one day, and I have even talked to them, when it seemed appropriate, about the forces of several Princes of Europe. I've said many other things about them to Bencdon. Because we have a King of France who puts armies of two or three hundred thousand men on campaign, as many in Flanders as in Germany, Italy on the coasts of his kingdom and various other places; and in addition to that, a prodigious number of warships at sea, charged with firearms and warriors capable making law all over the world, you think I want to sell and deliver your country? The consequence is not just.

"Even if I had formed such a chimerical plan, however, I tell you frankly that it would not be in my power to carry it out. It would already be a hundred chances against one that we could reach some safe haven with a boat like the one that we have prepared. Another difficulty, no less considerable, would be to return to these waters with a fleet sufficient to obtain mastery of Russal. Since it has been possible to equip vessels for whaling, there are a hundred Dutch ships that have advanced to within ten, nine and perhaps eight degrees of the Boreal Pole; I do not know that they have got any further. That is not very distant from your parallel, I admit, but that which has happened to one ship at a time will never happen to a number sufficient to exterminate you. Impetuous winds, currents, ice and other similar obstacles would separate them before they could get within a hundred or a hundred and fifty leagues of your continent.

"But let us suppose that the dangers are not so great; do you seriously imagine that all you possess is worth a fraction of the expense that it would be necessary to make to come here with forces superior to ours? What do you have, pray, since you're obliging me to speak, that could give any Monarch the desire to disturb you?

"The Estates General of the United Provinces have made conquests in the East Indies that have cost them immense sums of money; they possess a vast land there which is more than three thousand leagues from theirs; they keep armies on land and sea there, in their hire; the trading posts that they have established there for commerce are so considerable that the most junior Officers they employ there become rich in a very short time. One can only go there with a great deal of risk, passing over terrible seas, in journeys that take eight or ten months; but in recompense, they extract immense treasures. The precious stones, pearls, amber, coral, gold, silver, silk, porcelain, spices and all the beautiful and precious items that they bring back in a single year are worth more than everything there is in the four cities of Russal.

"Believe me, it isn't for the fine noses of the inhabitants of Mexico that the Spaniards and the Portuguese made such great efforts to subjugate America; gold, which was more common there than iron is here, was the unique cause, although the climates there are very different from the one that you inhabit. It is only interest that makes the Powers act; so long as you have no other riches than those you have, I can assure you that you will be left in peace, and that not a single soul will think of molesting you.

"Sweden alone can furnish as much iron as we require; yours would be superfluous. The people who have need of furs find them in their own lands, or, if they lack something, Muscovy and Poland supply it. Your pithson is excellent, it cannot be denied, but we have liquors of numerous sorts that are worth as much, and are so common that even poor people never lack them. All the rest is not worth the expense of transport; as for fishing, we don't have to go so far for that.

"No, Sires, I can tell you, as a man of honor, that, far from wanting to do you any harm, I wish you all the good imaginable. These worthy people who have alarmed you have misunderstood my reasoning; they have mistaken for threats what was only told to them to give them an idea of the grandeur and power of the Potentates under the direction of whom my comrades and I were born."

The Governor did not know how to respond to all that. His Councilors looked at one another, shrugging their shoulders; I could see that they would have preferred not to attract that mortification.

"What have you to say against what you have just heard?" said Emega, finally, to the accusers. "Is it true that he has not said positively that he wanted to incite enemies against us?"

"Yes, Sire," they replied, "but having heard the rumor that he was equipping a boat, we thought, given what he had told us about the insatiable avarice and cruelty of several Princes, combined with the petty discontents that he claims to have received among us, that it could only be to go and inform some powerful Monarch of the discovery he has made and excite him to subjugate us to his Laws.

"If that is not so," they said to me unanimously, "go in the name of God, amuse yourselves, but don't take too many risks. We're sorry for having delayed the execution of your plan for a few minutes."

"It's nothing, Sirs," I said. "I hope that our fishing will be so fortunate that we can regale you on our return with an excellent platter of fish, in order to persuade you that we bear no rancor."

With that I took my leave of them and went to rejoin my friends, who were still waiting for me with the greatest possible impatience, because they did not know what had become of me.

That little hitch, which caused us some chagrin, saved our lives by way of recompense, because, just as we were about to cast off, a storm blew up so prodigious that none like it had been seen in living memory; all the boats that were at sea in the vicinity perished. Buildings, trees, and everything else rising above the level of the ground were badly damaged; edifices groaned under the pressure, earthworks collapsed and people penetrated with dolor and dread had no doubt that the world was about to end.

Although the tempest only lasted for two hours, the ocean was so agitated by it that it was not navigable for three days thereafter. It was not until then, the weather being quite beautiful and the wind mild and favorable for steering a southerly course from Meraldo, that my two old friends and I embarked, recommending ourselves to the protection of the Omnipotent.

We made use of the oars until we were about a league from the harbor we had quit, after which we raised the sail. The rapidity with which we cleaved the waters is inconceivable; our boat passed over them like a crossbow bolt.

In less than twelve hours it seemed to me that we had covered at least forty leagues. There we were stopped by mountains of ice; there was no point of issue no matter which way we turned; we were obliged to remain at the place that seemed to us to be the lowest point. We unloaded our baggage and then transported the hull on to the ice, with an indescribable labor. We set about hauling it slowly over the least uneven places, most appropriate to the continuation of our route.

Heaven, which did not want our doom, granted us the mercy, after we had covered about a league and a half, of finding another great extent of sea. As soon as we had hoisted our sail we each had a bite to eat, and while one of us manned the tiller the other two attempted to get a little sleep.

The journey we made that time was not as considerable as the first; scarcely had we crossed a degree that we found ourselves in the same predicament, but which lasted for such a long time, in which we suffered so horribly, that we despaired of our salvation.

We got out of it, however. Finally, God granted that on the seventh day after our departure we discovered, at the extremity of our visual range, a vessel that had no sails hoisted, from which we were separated by frightful heaps of ice, which seemed to be augmenting rather than diminishing. It took us more twenty-four hours of effort before we were able to reach it.

When those commanding the ship saw us, a thousand or five hundred paces away from them, they sent four sailors to meet us, each armed with a rifle, to see who we were. They took us at first for inhabitants of Greenland, because we were clad like them in animal skins, with the consequence that, ignorant of our intentions, they started shouting at us and questioning us from a distance.

"Who are you?" I said to them. "We don't understand what you're saying." Then we made deep bows and, extending our arms, tried to make them understand that we were imploring their mercy.

With that I heard one of them pronounce the word "Frenchman."

"They're English," I said to my companions.

Indeed, I was not much mistaken. We found, having arrived on board, that it was a ship out of Edinburgh, the capital city of Scotland. The pilot, who had traveled a great deal, knew a little French, and several of the sailors were not ignorant of Dutch; that gave them the opportunity to ask questions about our homelands and the place from which we were coming; it was necessary to content their curiosity.

The Captain would dearly have liked to be able to talk to us; he often gave time to others to listen to us say a few words whose meaning he wanted to know. If we could believe what he said, he would have tried to reach the country that we had just left, but he soon changed his sentiment, when he learned that the difficulties to overcome were insurmountable and that, in addition, there was nothing there capable of enriching a voyager.

Although the crew had advanced a long way and exposed themselves to evident dangers over and above the weather and the season, in the hope of good fishing, they had only caught small fish. That decided the master of the ship to set a course for Iceland on the return journey, which he had visited several times before, to see whether he could find merchandise to carry back to his homeland capable of compensating himself and his associates for the expenses they had been obliged to make for an expedition that had had such scant success.

The poor man did not have to take the trouble. Those of the Reformed Religion believe in predestination; we are of a contrary sentiment—but after what happened to us, it is necessary to admit that the most penetrating and understanding man is a stupid animal when it comes to reasoning about the works of Providence.

I do not think that there ever was a navigation more fortunate than ours; the air, the sea and the wind were all favorable. We advanced considerably without perceiving from the movement of the vessel that we were even changing location. That lasted until we came within sight of the island where we had decided to land. We were only four or five leagues distant at the most when all of a sudden, as if machines made expressly to sink us had been employed by all the infernal powers, we went down like a stone without anyone having remarked that there was anything amiss with our vessel, which was no more than four years old.

At that moment I was mounted on a ladder, from which I was watching what was happening outside, in such a manner that only half my body was in the aft chamber. The door to the place was hung very loosely, by means of two strap-hinges and two smaller hinges. That door, which might have been two feet wide and more than three long, remained on the surface of the water, and I, the most disconcerted of men, found myself beside it, without any other object than the sky and the element in which I was floating, presenting itself to my eyes.

As I knew perfectly well how to swim, I advanced into the middle of that plank, and under the protection of God, I allowed myself to be carried away by the waves of the sea. We had the wind behind us, and were drawn directly toward Iceland. An hour after our shipwreck, the waves brought alongside me two sailors from our vessel, who were being carried by a large hatch. We remained as close together as we could, talking about our unfortunate lot, and encouraging one another reciprocally to hold on for as long as we could, until it pleased God to cast us on to dry land, as there was every appearance that it might happen soon if the wind remained as it was.

Indeed, twelve or fifteen hours after our disaster, either because there was a current or because the tide took us in, I felt the bottom. One of the other two had died of the cold a few moments before.

Several islanders saw us emerge from the water, came toward us, and looked after us very well. First they lit a big fire, thanks to which we took off our clothes and put on others that they gave us. They also brought us the best they had to eat, which was not, in truth, very much.

I was surprised to see that the island, which, I learned, is about four hundred leagues around, situated under the polar circle, is more sterile than Russal. The soil there is good for nothing, and nothing grows in it but a few junipers, with the consequence that the inhabitants have no other wood than that washed up on the shore by the sea and the ice-floes, so it is principally those locations that are inhabited. Their ordinary aliments consist mainly of fresh or dried fish, and what is surprising is that their cattle, which have no horns, and can only find enough grazing in the open country for three months of the year, have adapted to it as well as them.

Since the King of Denmark has taken possession of the land, the islanders have embraced the Lutheran religion, but as the people there are generally simple and crassly ignorant, one can veritably say that the majority of them do not really know what they are. The Devil, who takes pleasure among the ignorant, enjoys himself greatly there, from what they say. Few days pass without one of them having some vision or other, or being maltreated by demons. They do not know whether or not there are several Hells, but they claim to have certain knowledge that the place where their own damned suffer is in the region of

Hecla, which is a famous mountain, eternally covered in snow at the summit and often completely on fire toward the base.

That fire is not, however, always equally violent; at times it is only mediocre, and at others is it frightful, being accompanied by the whistling of a prodigious wind and rumbles like thunder, which seem to threaten the world with its end. The impetuous movement of the sulfurous particles contained in that mountain open gulfs from which stones emerge, which fall as far as a mile away.

I did not want to take the trouble to go so far to examine that prodigy, because I was assured that it is not possible to get close to it; there are great heaps of ash everywhere in the surrounding area, and sometimes glowing lava underneath, into which people plunge who are attracted there by curiosity or interest, in search of deposits of sulfur, of which there are inexhaustible mines. It is principally that mineral, as well as whale-oil, leather and butter, that comprises their trade, and on which they are obliged to subsist. They live for the most part in community of everything, except for their wives, of whom they are more jealous than the Turks, especially since they have begun to frequent foreigners, who have deceived them a thousand times over, and have taught them vices that were absolutely unknown to them before.

What I have just said about their jealousy is so true that they are insensate enough not to want to survive a mere suspicion that they have of the infidelity of their wives. Here is an example that happened in Hola some time before I arrived.

The Governor's wife, feeling the pains of childbirth, sent in quest of neighbors and others of her acquaintance. One of the most familiar having assisted in the long and arduous labor, which lasted fifteen or twenty hours, was so debilitated and exhausted that she asked for permission to go home. They did not want to permit her to do that, and she was invited to go into a little room where there was a bed, on which she was obliged to lie down in order to get a little sleep.

Her husband was then out hunting, and he returned in the interim, well laden with game, including a hare. As those sorts of animals are quite rare there, he thought that he could not do better than take it to the house of the local chieftain, who had often showed him particular kindness. Having reached the door he asked to speak to him in person; a child who happened to be there told him to follow him, and took him to where he had seen his father go in shortly before in order to fetch a book.

As misfortune would have it, the innocent woman, who was in the same apartment, on hearing the voice of her husband, who was conversing with his guide, sat up in bed. The unfortunate man came in by one door just as the Governor was going out by the other. That sight disturbed him immediately, to which the condition of his wife—pale, unclad and unkempt, contributed not a little. He had no doubt that, profiting from his absence, she had abandoned herself to the man he had just seen disappearing—with the result that, without examining the matter more closely, he went out and went away, and hanged himself out of chagrin.

The Viceroy, or Governor General, who lived in the manor of Bestede, having heard mention of me as a man who had lived for a long time among Peoples hitherto unknown to anyone, summoned me, and forced me to choose his house for my refuge. I cannot describe the cares that he and his wife lavished upon me; they hid nothing from me; everything they possessed as at my service, and I wanted for absolutely nothing. We spent the greater part of the day together conversing about everything I could remember until my last shipwreck. I had no sooner finished the tragic story of my misfortunate life than it was necessary, out of complaisance, under the pretext that they had forgotten the best part of it, that I begin again incontinently.

That had being going on for a long time when the Governor, having drunk more than usual that day, said to me: "Mésange, you're no longer young, I admit, but cannot know what your end will be. You have had bad days, and you have also had good ones. A man's life is subject to a thousand different revolutions; the changes that overtake us should not astonish us; if they are to our advantage, it is necessary to take pleasure in them; when they are unfortunate, God wants us to support them patiently, convinced that it is for our own good, or in the hope that we will be happier in future, and the graces that we have to come will recompense us doubly for our past miseries.

"Between you and me, there cannot be a man on this island of viler extraction than me, who has been more maltreated by fortune, and who has finally succeeded to the utmost heights of felicity. It is a secret that must remain between the two of us; my own wife knows nothing about it, and there is not another soul who is not unaware of it; that is why I forbid you ever to divulge it, as I shall also keep to myself several circumstances of your life that you have confided to me.

"My father was Greek, small of stature, pale, rather unhealthy and very ill-tempered. By contrast, my mother, Egyptian-born,[43] was tall, well made, strong, vigorous, good and as intriguing as any woman in the world could be. As, following the example of their ancestors, they never remained long in one place, they had a son in Cairo, which is perhaps the largest, richest and most populous city in the world, and where it is free to everyone to reside and life as he pleases. There are Indians there, Ethiopians, Persians, Barbarians, Americans, Scythians, Tartars, Assyrians. Libyans, Jews, Greeks, Latins, Moors, Arabs, and principally Turks, who are the masters there at present.

"Although my parents had every reason to be content there, in the abject and wretched profession they exercised of drawers of horoscopes, it was impossible for them to stay. They passed into Europe, where they exercised their trade

---

[43] This might be meant literally, although it is certainly also meant in the sense that Roma were one called "Egyptians" or "gypsies."

successfully. I remember, among other adventures that happened to them, having been told several times by my brother, that, having arrived in Rome, they went to lodge in a disreputable tavern, which was the refuge of everything rascally and malevolent in the neighborhood. Everything was known there, and whenever anything happened, there were always long and wide-ranging conversations about it. They were then on the heels of a local female shopkeeper, still unmarried, whose last gallant had died suddenly when their banns had been published. All the circumstances of her life were discussed, up to the unfortunate incident that had just occurred.

"My mother, whom nothing escaped, did not fail the morning after to go in search of her and, while buying pins and a wretched boxwood comb, engaged her in conversation. 'You're sad, Mademoiselle,' my mother said to her. 'Are you unwell, or is business not going as well as you would like?'

"'Neither, replied the tradeswoman. 'I'm in good health, and I'm selling as much of my produce as I could reasonably wish.'

"'There is something, however,' my mother said, 'that is causing you anxiety. It's impossible for me to divine it, but if I could see your hand I'd know what it is.'

"'What?' said the damsel. 'You can read in my hand what is in my heart, and the cause of what is, according to you, rendering me somber and melancholy? I doubt that strongly, unless I have been in error for as long as I've lived. Here, take my hand; see what you can't find out.'

"'You're exactly thirty years old,' said my mother.

"'That's true,' she replied, 'but how do you see that?'

"'One can see it in your life line,' said my mother, 'here, where your days are marked; there are infallible rules for that. You lost your father when very young, your mother died of phthisis three years ago; thirteen years ago you fell downstairs and broke your right arm, but it healed so well that no inconvenience remains. Wait, here's what seems to me to be an alliance, almost effaced...yes, exactly. You were to be married three weeks from tomorrow, but death has taken away your lover. I can see that you're subject to toothache; you often have headaches. You have no brothers or sisters, all those you had having died young.'

"'Everything you're telling tell me is exactly true,' the young woman interrupted. 'It seems to me that one couldn't know it without being a sorceress, or knowing me very well. Have you been in the city long?'

"'Since yesterday evening,' my mother replied, 'and I've never been here before. Why do you ask me that? Do you imagine that I've asked questions about you. I don't know a soul in the city. I've already told you; our science is certain; only freethinkers and skeptics have no faith in it and try to decry us. To give you convincing proof, I dare to say that you presently love a widower, a master hat-maker by trade, with as much passion as you did the previous one; you won't marry him, though; there's a more considerable party reserved for you, but first you'll make another fortune, which will enable you to quit your trade. Do you have any desire to change residence?'

"'No,' replied the tradeswoman.

"'Permit me, then, to enter a little further,' the chiromancer said.

"'You'll soon have covered my entire dwelling,' said the other. 'I'm in a place of passage here; a trader has to pay more attention to her merchandise than to comfort. Follow me; I only have one room down below, with a meager and tiny kitchen.'

"'That's sufficient,' my mother went on. 'The odor I seek has already reached my nose; there's a treasure here; do no spirits come here?'

"'We've been living here for forty years, without me every hearing that my parents have seen anything at all,' said the young woman.

"'I'm surprised by that,' said my mother. 'Ordinarily the Devil takes possession of gold and silver that have been buried for nine times nine years, and it's nearly a century since this one as buried by a miserly old woman who was afraid of some troubling revolution. I see no lines in your hand that can determine the exact sum; all that I can see is that it's considerable; it must be at least twenty thousand écus, to judge by what there is...'

"'But do you know where this pretended treasure is?' the damsel interrupted, brusquely.

"'Not yet,' my mother replied. 'I'll only know that after a serious examination and certain ceremonies, which require time and expense.'

"'Well, if you can indicate it to me,' continued the other, 'I'll make you a present that you'll remember for a long time.'

"'I'm not self-interested,' my mother told her. 'I'm content with very little when I render a service to honest folk, but I would never undertake an affair of this importance unless you first swear an oath to keep the secret, because if it came to the ears of the law, above all here, where there's an Inquisition, I'd infallibly be punished, not only as an enchantress but as an accomplice to a crime of peculation, in that I'll have given you the opportunity to take possession of property that belongs to the Prince, or the Church, or to the owner of the foundations in which it's contained.'

"'Well, as to that,' the damsel said, 'you don't have to take the trouble; you'd undoubtedly be safe without an oath, since it's in my own interests to say nothing,'

"'Well,' said my mother, 'on those conditions, give me two hundred écus and your affair is settled.'

"'I'll give you a hundred,' the tradeswoman replied, at first.

"There were many arguments on either side before they fell into agreement on the sum of three hundred and fifty francs. The bargain having been struck, she told her that it was necessary for her to go to buy drugs and make the necessary preparations for a work of that importance. She came back two hours later, and advised her to invite to her home some woman of her acquaintance that she could trust and who was capable of looking after the shop, because once the ceremony had begun, it was impossible to interrupt it without spoiling everything. In the apprehension she had, however, that the mine might be discovered, she told her that she would rather defer the execution until the evening, when the shops were closed, since then, if anyone came, she could pretend to have gone out, as happened quite often, and thus oblige the customers to come back another time.

"Having returned at the appointed time, the coins were counted out, on which they went down together to the cellar, where the enchantress, in order to exercise her magical art formally, made a quantity of grimaces, which the other did not relish at all. She sent her upstairs twenty times in quest of things that she pretended to need. During her absence she buried an écu between two stones, in such a way that she alone could perceive it.

"Finally, she drew a large circle, the circumference of which had to be eight feet five inches and four lignes, so she said. She traced Arabic characters in the center of that figure, which she had learned expressly to make use of them in similar circumstances, and then, having placed her within it, with her face turned in a particular direction, and striking a certain pose that she claimed to be essential to the ceremony, she forbade her to budge from that spot nor to move a hand or foot until everything was finished, under penalty of seeing the Devil, who would not, in truth, do her any harm, but might give her such a fright that she would regret it for the rest of her life.

"With that she set fire to a sweet-smelling perfume, and a moment later, transported by joy, she cried: 'Good! Everything is going well. Look there, you can see the coins already rising up of their own accord, to assure us of the verity of the fact.' And, bending down, she picked up in her presence the coin that she had set in the ground a little while before.

"The damsel seemed delighted by such a fortunate beginning, and promised once again to recompense her better for her trouble. 'Patience,' said my mother, 'I don't see anything more coming yet; there's apparently something missing here.' At the same time, she took a little book out of her pocket. 'I suspected s much,' she went on. 'I've forgotten in my composition a quarter of a grain of ambergris and two drachms of lodestone; it's necessary that these be added, or we won't get anything worthwhile. Don't move from where you are, I warn you, lest something bad happen to you; I'll run to the druggist who lives just down the street to get them, and a little more incense; I'll be back incontinently.'

"As she went out she grabbed a large packet of perfumed frangipani seeds and a few pieces of Avignon ribbon that were on the counter and ran back to her lodgings with all possible diligence. It if it permissible to conjecture, it is highly likely that in the meantime, the dupe was in such deep distress at that nocturnal ceremony, and the many different grimaces had left such an impression on her mind, that she was incapable of making any reflection on what was happening.

Two or three hours having passed without her seeing anyone return, however, it is quite probable that she began to have doubts, and, fearing that she might have been abused, went upstairs. She soon realized that not only had she lost the money she had counted out but that more than a hundred francs' worth of merchandise had also been taken.

"What confirms me in this idea is that my father went past her door just then, also returning from some little expedition, as she opened it, uttering sighs that made even him feel sorry for her, and having looked in both directions along the street, closed it again, perhaps for fear that something worse might happen, for it was late, everyone had retired, and there was no longer anyone about.

"To tell you whether she divulged what had happened to her, or whether the fear of being openly mocked caused her to keep quiet, is impossible for me; I only know that our people slipped away early the next morning, with the booty that each of them had acquired.

"After having traversed Italy, their objective being merely to pass through the country, as their parents had done, they went to Paris, to lodge in one of the Faubourgs. First, my father went to buy a second-hand scarlet-trimmed suit, which he brought to my mother, who disguised herself in it, left the children with other Egyptians she knew and went to the other extremity of the city to take lodgings in a good-quality inn, with her husband, who posed as her valet. She passed herself off there as a Cévennois Captain, who, having business at Court, had also come to gather recruits.

"She had furnished herself with a trunk filled with old clothes and a few bags full of pebbles and rounded pieces of slate, which her domestic took care to show off at every opportunity, by shifting them around or seeming to search for something, or putting something away, with the consequence that in a matter of days, everyone in the neighborhood knew that there was an Officer there who must have considerable lands, or be in possession of the key to the public treasury, since he had more gold and silver than he would have needed to enlist all the water-carriers in the city.

"In the meantime, the Captain suddenly fell ill. The tailor who had furnished him with a complete outfit to the value of at least three hundred écus was obliged to leave it in her room, without being paid, because it was necessary that Monsieur try it on first. It was also said that the wig-maker left several valuable perukes in the hands of the valet, in order that the invalid could choose one or two at her whim as soon as the fever gave him a brief remission. Gold watches were similarly brought, with beautiful cases, from different clockmakers, which he wanted to try out. At the same time, two diamond-studded cuff-links arrived, and the jeweler brought a ring worth forty pistoles. In sum, everyone, being avid for profit, furnished everything he could, in order to make a greater breach in the sacks, even including the Apothecary, who, in order to show off a medicine to better advantage, sent it in a beautiful silver goblet.

"All of that was done with the greatest confidence in the world, because the landlord, who had been asked on several occasions whether there was any danger with the man that nobody knew, believed him to be sufficiently rich to say frankly that he would gladly be his guarantor.

"Finally, having accumulated and abundance of everything precious, my father carried the luggage away, little by little, including the Captain's suit, and, my mother put on her female attire again, which they had been careful to bring with them, and she chose a time to slip out one evening when there was no one around the door. Shortly afterwards, my father went to tell the landlord that, as he was obliged to go out for half an hour, he begged him not to permit anyone to go into his master's apartment for fear of waking him, as he was sleeping tranquilly, unless he called out for something to be served to him.

"What they had amassed there was considerable, and far surpassed their captures in Rome. They did not profit from it, however; they spent their wealth as fast as they earned it, with the result that often, in spite of all their subtleties, they went without bread—which was principally due to the fact that my father gambled, and was exceedingly unlucky."

"Those sorts of tricks are common enough in big cities," I interjected, "And it's surprising that the inhabitants allow themselves to be taken in by them. I heard the story in Leyden, from an aristocrat who was one of my pupils, of a trick played in his time on a young foreigner, which makes me laugh every time I've thought about it since, and which merits being told to you now, while we're on the subject of the knights of the industry. A good bourgeois of Verdun, a place renowned in France for the excellent sugared almonds made there, had a rich sister who lived in Paris with several of her children. None of the family had yet seen him, although they had been invited several times; they lived a long way apart and none of them liked traveling.

"Finally that honest man having decided to send her his son, aged between sixteen and eighteen, went to the Courier with him and strongly recommended the young man to him, whom he had provided with good clothes, fine linen, a watch and a purse of a thousand francs in gold, as much to furnish the expenses of the journey as to keep up appearances in company where it was necessary to put his hand in his pocket. He had also given him a horse, and several nice presents for his nephews and nieces. The Courier, who had experience, saw no difficulty in taking charge of the individual, and promised to put him in the hands of his relatives, with the result that they separated equally content with one another.

"Our travelers amused themselves very well on the way, and arrived in good health in the Metropolis of the most beautiful Kingdom in the world, at Carnival time, when the city as swarming with masquerades. Everything that the Novice had heard recounted elsewhere was nothing by comparison with what he saw there himself. He was charmed by the various objects that were presented to his sight. His guide pressed him to continue his route, but he stopped continually, either to look at the houses or to read the signs, in such a way that there was no means of making him advance.

"A few wily individuals, who were making use of the opportunity to amuse themselves, having observed him from a distance, resolved to take advantage of his innocence. The waited, masked, in front of a tavern. 'What are you looking for, Monsieur?' one of them, who knew the Courier, said to him when they approached. 'You're coming from Verdun, from what I see; we're waiting for someone from there, might it be you?'

"'I don't know.' the young man replied. 'My name is such-and-such, and I've come here expressly to see an aunt and cousins, of whom I only know the name, which is such-and-such.'

'Didn't I tell you that it must be him?' cried another. 'There's definitely a certain family resemblance, which would have enabled me to recognize him at five hundred paces.'

"'I don't believe it,' said the Novice. 'You would have been informed by letter of the day of my departure, you know my approximate age, and the Verdun courier is not unknown to you.'

'All that is true,' said the masquerader, 'but even without that, I swear to you that I'd have bet a hundred pistoles to one that you were related to us. So it's you, my dear Cousin,' he went on, embracing him. 'You're very welcome, and how is my dear uncle, my aunt and all the children?'

"'All the children?' the young man put in. 'Don't you know that I'm an only child, and that my mother has never had any others?'

"'Damn it, you're right,' said the pretended cousin, bursting out laughing. 'I said that without thinking about it, because it seemed to me that it must be the same in your house as in ours. But come on, come on, we're wasting time miserably here that could be better employed elsewhere. It's not at home, but at a tavern where we've had a meal prepared; help us expedite it promptly, and as soon as that's done, we'll go to find my mother. She'll be delighted to see you, the good woman; there's not a day goes by when she doesn't talk about you a hundred times, as the only son of a brother she's loved passionately all her life.' With that, he tried to help him down from his horse.

"'Not so fast, Messieurs,' exclaimed the Courier, who suspected, from certain indications that rendered those fellow dubious to him, that his man was falling into bad company. 'Monsieur has been confided to my care, and I can only let go of him on good evidence; I need to take care of his person, and I intend either that those who claim him should address themselves to my lodgings, in order that my host can take cognizance of them, or that I accompany him myself to the home of his relatives, in order that I shall be able, on my return to give his father and exact account of what he has done with me and what has become of him.'

'I'm very much obliged to you, said the young man to his guide. 'Those precautions would be good elsewhere and in other circumstances, but they're not necessary here. I'm not a child, and you can see that, already being with the people I'm looking for, and for love of whom I've come expressly to this place, it would be ridiculous to go with you.'

"The Courier wanted to reply to that, but with discretion, for fear of starting trouble with people who seemed to him to be light of hand, but all his arguments were futile, and it was necessary for him, reluctantly, to leave the unfortunate fellow prey the rogues who, notwithstanding the prudence with which he talked to them, were beginning to threaten to punish his temerity if he persisted any longer in treating them indirectly as dishonest men, and their innocent cousin as if he did not have sufficient judgment to look after himself.

"As soon as Monsieur set foot on the ground everyone embraced him again and took him to a room, where there was indeed food and drink; his horse was carefully put in the stable. Needless to say, while they plied him with drink they made every effort to worm information out of him. It was not necessary to make great efforts or to employ much subtlety to make him say more that it was necessary for them to know.

"Having been well instructed, one of them went to a bawdy house, where the brothel-keeper, who was almost the same age and build that the young man's aunt ought to be, and primed her to play that role; in the same way, two whores were found to play his two female cousins. When everything was ready he was taken there. As they had been informed of things that he had said without realizing it, he was surprised to find them so well instructed in the affairs of his family that he would have been more like to think that Pegasus had metamorphosed into a bronze horse than suspect them of the slightest artifice. The women received him in the most affectionate fashion in the world; they seemed to want to eat him, so much joy did they claimed to have in seeing him.

"Finally, although delighted with the good welcome that they had given him, fatigued by the journey and falling asleep, he asked to go to bed. They were careful, before consenting, to give him a small glass of a certain liquor, which was supposed to relax him and do him the world of good, but which was in fact a beverage calculated to upset his stomach. When they put him to bed the female cousins told him, in case he needed anything during the night, to call them, because their room was next door to his and it would be easy for them to hear him and get him whatever he wanted.

"Shortly thereafter the medicine took effect; he remained for a while in the hope that it was only wind, or that he could at least hold on until the Sun rose, but before much longer, he felt an attack of colic so violent that he was obliged to call for help. At those cries, one of the female 'cousins' who was on sentry duty, appeared. 'What's the matter, my dear cousin?' she said. 'I usually stay up late reading and I hadn't yet gone to bed. Is there something I can do for you before I go to sleep?'

"'Oh, Cousin,' he replied to her, 'I can't go on any longer. I have a colic that is killing me; I've never had one similar; one might think that I had vipers in my belly which are ripping out my intestines. Show me the facilities, I beg you; it seems to me that if I could empty my bowels, that would be a considerable relief.'

"'Alas, my dear Cousin,' the beauty replied, 'we're of the number that don't have a privy in the house; it's an inconvenience that's rather common in the city, but here's a door that which we let you out at the back, where there are only stables. Take off your underpants quickly, and set yourself against the wall. I'll wait here until you're done.'

"As soon as the young man had gone out, the young woman locked the door and withdrew very quietly. It was cold, in accordance with the season, and the wretch had to stay out there for a long time. Having finally relieved himself, he groped his way back to the place where he had been let out into the street. He pushed and pulled, feeling frozen by the cold, and started crying out with all his might: 'Aunt, Aunt...my Cousin, my dear Aunt...have pity on me, my Cousins, I'm freezing...I'm dying...in the name of God, let me in.'

"As he began to despair of shouting a porter who had been up late drinking and as retuning home, seeing a white body in the distance, feared that it might be a phantom; the plaints and cries that it was uttering, however, caused him to take a few steps forward. '"Who's that shouting?' he said.

"'It's me,' the young man replied. 'Come closer I beg you, and show me the door of my Aunt's house. I came out to do my business, and I can't find it again.'

"At those words the porter advanced, and after having been fully informed, he said: 'The place you're showing to me, Monsieur, is well-known to me. It's a house of ill-repute, a veritable cut-throats' den; you're lucky to have got out in one piece. Come with me; I'll take you to the lodgings of the Courier who brought you.'

"It was around midnight, and the man they sought had been profoundly asleep for three hours. He had to get up in order to hear all about the adventure, for which he had no other remedy than to counsel patience and recommend him to form the resolution to be more careful another time."

"It's a good story," said the Governor, "doubtless as good as the one that I told you, but let's continue. "Our people having quit Paris went on to Germany, where they played a hundred more tricks, which I shall leave out for fear of never seeing the end of them. Finally, they went as far as Poland. Having arrived in Krakow they were obliged to stay there for some time because my mother, who was reaching the term of a pregnancy, expected to give birth any day. It was there that I came into the world. My brother, who had been given the name of Beronice, might have been six or seven. I was named Constance.

"The lying-in having been completed, we left the city, because peasants, being simpler and, in consequence, more superstitious that well-to-do people brought up in society, are easier to take in and the desire to know the future causes them to tolerate fortune-tellers, who would be forced to hide elsewhere in order to avoid being maltreated. After having roamed the area for a few days, our parents, embarrassed by two burdens that seemed quite useless to them, were staying in a shepherd's tawdry hut near the high road. After waiting for us to go to sleep they got up very quietly and abandoned us to the mercy of whoever had sufficient charity to bring us up.

"The next morning, having been woken up by the frightful cries that I was making, my brother shouted for my father and mother a thousand times, but they did not respond. He was accustomed to being alone, but having compassion for me, and not being able to understand where my nurse, who was the one I wanted, was staying away for so long, he shouted with all his might for an hour, and ran like a lost soul to the right and he left without being able to discover which way she had gone.

"Finally, two good bourgeois women, fairly well off, who had property in the area, and had come to give instructions to their farmers, having got up early in order to go back to the city, happened to pass by. Seeing them approaching, Beronice threw himself on his knees in front of them and begged them to have pity and him and me. Well-intentioned as they were, they feared that rogues might be making use of the child to draw them away into a trap, so they were very reluctant to go to the place where he wanted to take them, where they could indeed hear me crying in a pitiful manner. Perceiving two peasants and a woman in the distance, however, who were on their way to work, they called to them and asked them to go with them to see what the matter was.

"As I resembled my mother, they were no less charmed by my beauty than touched by my misery; they immediately ordered the other people to take us to their house, with the promise of recompense for their trouble until those to whom we belonged came back. A week went by without any news, and the villagers, fearing that we might remain with them, which would have inconvenienced them greatly, took us to the homes of the Ladies who had recommended us to them, one of whom was the wife of a grocer and the other the window of a goldsmith.

"That sight surprised them; they believed that we were far away, and that they had settled their account for good and all by giving a few sous to those to whom they had committed our care—with the result that there was then a dispute, not only on the subject of the pretention of the poor people but also with regard to the children for whom no one wanted to take responsibility.

"The widow, who was the older of the two, being the first to se reason, said to the other: 'Listen: we have friends here; it's only necessary to employ them with the Magistrates; they will doubtless have no difficulty in furnishing the upkeep of two poor little creatures abandoned by the very ones who gave them light.'

"Having come to an arrangement with the peasants, who were content with very little, in order to be relived of a burden that was embarrassing them terrible, they sent them away, and neglected nothing in order to put us, at the expense of the public, in a place where someone would have the charity to bring us up. All their credit, however, and that of their friends, was to no avail; they were told that they ought to have left us where they had picked us up. They were also told that it was known throughout the world that the Egyptians are rogues, the dregs of society, a race of thieves and very nasty people, that our parents confirmed that verity by the inhuman action they had just committed with regard to their own children, who would be no better than them.

"Be that as it may, however, since they had taken charge of us, there was no middle way; it was necessary for them to nourish us until we were in a state to earn our living. That sentence, which was in accordance with the Law, seemed harsh to them, but there was no appeal unless they went to bend the ear of the King, who would not, in all likelihood, want to get mixed up in an affair of that nature because of the possible consequences.

"The widow, who had no children, took me and had me cared for until I was one year old by a nurse, after which she took me into her house. My brother remained with the grocer, who made use of him to begin within his shop. In the beginning he was treated rather harshly, and given work to do that was beyond his strength, but he did everything with so much zeal, so adroitly and with such good grace, that the merchant was charmed by him. After six months he loved him more than his own children.

"The hope of eventually getting considerable services out of that apprentice led him to send him to school, where he learned to read in a matter of days. Writing cost him no more difficulty. Everything the he saw he grasped, and in addition, one could say that everything that he read once he was capable of reciting by heart, word for word. His master, who talked to everyone about him as a marvel, and who diverted company with a thousand different exploits that the child swore he had seen before arriving at his adoptive cradle, and which he remembered as if it had been the previous day, was advised to end him to College, where he probably would not fail to acquire enlightenment that would please him, and which might be the cause of my brother's fortune and elevation in the world. He did not hesitate for a moment over what to do in that matter; he put him incontinently in the hands of a regent, to whom he recommended him exactly as if he were his own son.

"At first, the child distinguished himself as he had elsewhere; he learned with ease twice what the others could only imprint on their minds with obstinate hard work. Then he acquired judgment; his transcendent genius found the most abstruse matters facile and intelligible. In brief, he promised all that could be expected of a finite but rational and intelligent creature, such as a human being is. However, it all came to nothing. At the age of fifteen or sixteen, when he knew languages thoroughly, s well as history and several fine sciences, he abandoned everything at a stroke to libertinage, and notwithstanding the remonstrations of his adoptive father, who would gladly have spent his last sou to make him continue his studies, he was imprudent enough to join a troop of Savoyard chimney-sweeps, and to go with them without bidding us adieu.

"His Master and Mistress thought they would go mad; they search for him everywhere, advertised for him and offered considerable rewards to anyone who brought him back, but he was so well able to avoid their pursuits that they did not see him again and I don't know whether they ever heard mention of him. You can believe that, for my part, I was not insensible to that loss, young as I was; I knew very well to what extent he influenced me, and if it had been my choice whether to stay where I was or to go with him, I would undoubtedly have abandoned everything."

"But Monsieur," I interrupted, "what does he look like?"

"It's impossible for me to tell you. At the age I was then, things present themselves differently to our senses that when one is grown up. I remember very well that those who appeared to me as giants when I was a child became pygmies as soon as I was a man. To judge by the idea that that I have conserved of him, he ought, if he still lives, to be of mediocre height, with brown hair and an aquiline nose."

"I have seen a Beronice," I said, "very similar to the man you have described, who was, without hyperbole the foremost man in the world for the humanities: eloquent, clever, agreeable in conversation, there was no language, living or dead, that he did not know, and he was also a chimney-sweep, without wanting to be anything else, whatever offers were put to him."

"And you have known him?" asked the Governor.

"I was in his company on two or three various occasions in Leyden," I went on, "but it was said that he did not stay long in one place; his inclination and the profession that he exercised to satisfy himself did not permit it. He resembled the Wandering Jew, and did nothing but circle the earth."

"It was surely the same person," exclaimed the Governor, "that a German who had traveled in Holland told me had unfortunately fallen into the water between Leyden and Harlem, where he was found dead a few days later."

"About that I can say nothing," I said. "That must have happened after I left the country, or I would doubtless have heard the news. But you, Monsieur, what was your destiny?"

"My patroness," he replied, "did everything imaginable for me. She taught me to read and write; then I was sent to College, but I confess that whatever trouble the masters took, I did not make any considerable progress. I was worth no more for a métier. I spent six months in a sculptor's studio, and a year with an engraver; my last apprenticeship was the shortest—I believe it lasted about six weeks. A master embroiderer who had hired me chased me out of his shop with blows of the fist because I did not want to do anything.

"A nobleman from Warsaw named Ludoviski had come to Krakow in the meantime, and a means was found to place me in his household; I was then thirteen years of age. As I was only the errand-boy of one of his senior domestics, I rarely had occasions to be in his presence. More than a year later, he arrived back from the country, where he had gone to amuse himself in the home of a gentleman of his acquaintance; as he found no one else within range to serve him, he said to me as he lifted his leg: 'Here, can you pull off my boots.'

"'Yes, my Lord,' I replied. 'I pull off my master's, who is twice as fat as you.'

"My reply made him laugh; with that I set to work, and acquitted myself so well to his whim that he gave me that employment in perpetuity. In fact, from that day on did not want to suffer anyone else to anticipate me in my rights, and would have found it inconvenient. It was not only in that respect that I pleased him; the others, according to him, were mere bumpkins compared to me. I did everything, he said, with good grace, and I had an air about me that charmed people. So he treated me very humanely, and with many favors that he never showed to anyone else.

"Five years passed like that.

"The King, who knew that Ludoviski was one of the most artful politicians in his Realm thought he ought to make use of him to handle a matter of importance at the Court of Denmark; he honored him for that purpose with the title of Ambassador Extraordinary. Being inseparable from his person, he was careful not to forget me; I was one of the first marked on the list of those who were to accompany him.

"As soon as we arrived in Copenhagen, he requested an audience with the King, which was immediately granted to him. He came back therefrom full of chagrin; I perceived that clearly when I saw him at table, because he was very pensive and ate nothing; he did nothing but drink. The man who was serving him having gone away, I thought that I could perform his function temporarily without any risk, if necessary.

"In fact, it happened that my master demanded a wine; as I had seen, it seemed to me, that he was always served a Pontac, I brought him the same; whereupon, without looking to see who had presented him with his glass, he said: 'What, rogue! I ask you for white and you bring me claret? I'll teach you to listen to what I say,' and, making up a large table-knife that he was holding simply in order to toy with it, he hurled it at my head so furiously that the gash it made horrified all those who witnessed it.

"I fell flat on the ground after that rude blow. I was lifted up unconscious and put into the hands of a skillful French surgeon. The wound was dangerous, but I was fortunate enough to recover from it, against the expectations of the man who had dressed it. When I saw that I was out of danger I ran away, and went to hide in the home of a cook whose acquaintance I had made. He was kind enough to keep me in his house until the Ambassador had gone.

"As soon as I knew that he had left Copenhagen, I employed my benefactor to find me another position. His métier gave him access to all the honest men in the town, so it was not difficult to satisfy me. He placed me with a merchant, where I was infinitely better off than I would have been in my own father's house, and who gave me the name of my former master. I served him with as much zeal as affection, and mingled in all his business affairs.

"Eventually, I believe that I had reached the age of twenty when a considerable different arose between him and his correspondents in Iceland, where he did a considerable amount of trade. It was a matter of a capital of sixty or eighty thousand écus; there was no means of settling the matter at a distance; their accounts were confused and it was necessary for him to determine, in order to sort out the affair, to send his son there. Although he was a consummate businessman, it was nevertheless thought appropriate to send me with him, as much to keep him company as to assist him with my advice.

"We had not yet arrived here when we could no longer stand one another. The young man was hasty, proud and vain; he treated me with much more arrogance than his father ever had and that did not suit me. We nevertheless came together to the house of the Governor, my predecessor. That nobleman was only a year and a half older than me, and I resembled him as one drop of water resembles another. As soon as he had seen me, and learned that I had fallen out with my master's son, he proposed that I should come and live in his house in the capacity of his business manager. I accept the offer without hesitation, and did not even bid adieu to the other.

"As soon as I was in his house, he instructed his people to treat me with particular respect, and he treated me himself on many occasions as if I were a relative; it gave him pleasure when anyone testified amity toward me. That lasted for seven whole years without interruption; at the end of that time the worthy man fell ill, and three weeks later he died. His wife, who had let him expire without witnesses, came to find me in my room.

"'Ludoviski,' she said to me, you know that throughout the time that you have been living in my house, from the moment that you entered it, I have had for you, I don't say amity, inclination or esteem, but a veritably inexpressible passion. You know, however, that I have never given any evidence of it. I am an honest woman; that is a testimony that I can render myself, and of which everyone is convinced. I knew what I owed to my husband, and I was not unaware of what I owed to myself; I did not wish to stray over the bounds of decency and expose myself to the rigor of human and divine law. Now that the dear man is no more, I am free, and I no longer have any measures to take...'

"'What, Madame?' I exclaimed, interrupting her. 'My Master is dead?'

"'Quietly,' she said. 'It's necessary to observe silence here, until I know your sentiment. Yes, he is dead; he has just rendered his spirit in my arms; no one else but me knows it; I have hidden it from everyone and if I am confiding the secret to you, it is only with the aim of making you happy.'

"'You want to make me happy be telling me about the decease of the one man in the world that I loved as much as myself? Be assured, Madame, that it is rather the veritable means of causing me to die, or at least to trouble my mind;

the loss that I suffer in him is so great that I cannot survive it without being the most unhappy of all creatures. You, Madame, who excited jealousy among all the inhabitants of this region, will become the object of their mockery, and it will be a great deal if those you have treated as legitimate slaves are content to regard you with indifference or scorn; you would not be the first that they have, in such circumstances, stripped of all her wealth and force to flee for her life.'

"'My God,' she said to me, 'we're wasting time that we ought to be employing more usefully for your repose. Don't interrupt me again, I beg you; let me finish speaking, and if you don't approve of my plan, it will then be time to complain and to seek other expedients to avoid the accidents that you apprehend. Once again, I have loved you madly for seven years; I am not ashamed to tell you so today. You are so similar in every respect to my late husband that are closest friends are deceived by it. You also know all the affairs of the house, and the manner of governing the people is no longer unknown to you. Your master is no more; there is no one but you and me who knows that. What difficulty is there in putting him in the ground and you in the bed in his place? After a fortnight or three weeks, you can begin to show yourself; if, by any chance, anyone notices any change in you, which I don't expect, there will be no danger of discovery because of that; it will be the malady that has caused it. Not one of our subjects will have the slightest suspicion.'

"'That is all very well,' I replied, 'but what will become of me in the mean time?'

"'Three days ago,' she continued, 'the Governor, having become disgusted by your conduct, gave you the sack, and you left yesterday in secret for the nearest port, with the intention of taking advantage of the first available opportunity to return to your homeland.'

"The plan was too good and too advantageous to be rejected; we executed it with care, and as fortunately as could be. A year after I made the voyage to Denmark, where the King lavished a thousand kindnesses upon me. One day, when he was in a good mood, and we were dining together, I took the opportunity to tell him my story, under borrowed names, as if it had happened in Greece two or three thousand years ago. He laughed at it, and told me that the singularity of the fact merited that the man in question succeeded to the dignity of his predecessor.'

"'What, Sire?' I said to him. 'You approve of such a trick?'

"'Yes, certainly,' he replied. 'And what is more, I would give the succession to his son, if he had one, in order to eternalize his memory and not to give any subject to those people to live in concubinage with one another, which might attract the malediction of God on them and their children.'

"'Well, Sire,' I whispered in his ear, ' here is the man to whom that happened, and I hold you to your promise; have the generosity to confirm me in the charge that I have exercised thus far, and as soon as I return home, I shall marry, in order not to sin, as I have been doing until this moment.'

"The King granted my request incontinently, and for my part, I did not neglect to acquit the duties to which I had pledged myself. So, my dear Mésange, you see that it is necessary never to despair of one's happiness. I am, as I've already said, of the vilest extraction in the world, and by virtue of a fortuitous circumstance, which there was no reason to expect, I have become the Leader, so to speak, of a people who inhabit a very great Land."

"That is rare, my Lord," I said. "Histories, however, make mention of adventures very similar to that one, if we except the circumstances, which vary, and are for the most part different from one another. A Joseph, a Moses or a David is elevated from nothing to greatness. There were Emperors among the Romans whose birth was so obscure that they were never known to anyone. Whence was the issue of Mohammed, who did not know how to read or to write, and nevertheless succeeded to the glorious Empire of the Turks? What was that of Tamerlane, whose conquests infinitely surpasses those that were attributed to the like of Caesar and Alexander? But not to go back so far, no one is unaware that Masaniello, simple fisherman as he was, became Viceroy of Naples.[44] Jan de Weert, who commanded entire armies, was the son of a poor village innkeeper.[45] And Tromp and de Ruyter, in Holland, simple matelots as they were and issues of the dregs of the people, rose as far as the dignity of Admiral of the most numerous and most redoubtable fleets in the world.

"I could cite you others in large number and talk about the means by which numerous men of singular merit made use in order to acquire the foremost responsibilities of State, but this is one example that will substitute for all the others, and which, although it does not take its hero very far, nevertheless appears to me to be extraordinary. I got it from a worthy old man named Monsieur Farquet, who was an eye-witness to it, according to what I heard him say to a company that he was entertaining one day in Amsterdam.

"A certain Marquis du Blosel, he told us, having been suspected in Paris of the crime of lèse-Majesté, did not wait for some to come to put him in the Bastille; he ran away to Geneva, where he put himself under the protection of the Magistrate. The King of France, having heard that, sent a Honneton there to fetch him back.[46] Du Blosel, who had friends, was warned on the eve of his arrival, when he was at a ball that was being held by one of the principal inhabitants of the town in a room overlooking the Rhône.

---

[44] "Masaniello" (Tomas Aniello) became the leader of a populist revolt in Naples, then ruled by Spain, in 1647; he rose to the rank of Captain-General—not Viceroy—but his triumph was brief, and he was rapidly assassinated.

[45] Jan de Wert became better known as Johann von Werth when he became a German cavalry general in the Thirty Years' War.

[46] A honneton (or hanneton) is literally a cockchafer beetle, but the metaphorical reference is to men-at-arms.

"That news, which naturally disconcerted him, did not even cause him to change color. Coolly, he ordered one of his people to find a boatman and tell him to come as soon as possible and station himself beneath the windows of the apartment, through which a man would be lowered whom he was to take to the far side of the take, to the lands of the Duc de Savoy, and who would pay him generously for his trouble. He ordered as well that a rope should be attacked to the frame of the window corresponding to that conveyance, and that it should be left ajar in such a way that no one would notice it.

"When everything was ready, the same domestic gave him the signal that they had agreed. He was then holding the hand of a lady with whom he was dancing; when he saw the place where he needed to be, he slipped away and made his exit at the appointed place, so swiftly that no one knew what had become of him. All that went very well, but he had the misfortune that the rope broke and he fell from a height into the boat, and broke a leg.

"That unfortunate accident prevented them from carrying out their plan. As soon as they had crossed the water, the man the boatman had brought to help him, in order to go more rapidly, loaded the Marquis on to his shoulders and carried him to a mean tavern that was not far away. There he put him in a chair and told the tavern-keeper to go fetch a surgeon urgently.

"'What is your name and your profession?' du Blosel asked him, charmed by his promptitude and the authority with which he spoke.

"'My name is Essiva, Monsieur,' he replied. 'I was a coal-heaver for some ten years, before I married a woman who had relatives that procured me this petty employment. I would be able to live on it if I were alone, but having two children, and my family, in consequence, consisting of four people, we're obliged to eat as meagerly at Carnival as during Lent.'

"'Well,' said the Marquis, 'I'm going to raise a cavalry regiment in Savoy; if you want to enter my company and conduct yourself well, I promise to take care of you and recompense you for the services you're rendering me presently.'

"Essiva was delighted by that offer and accepted with joy. As soon as the Colonel was healed, he went with him, unknown to all those who knew him. His absence gave rise to a great deal of comment; some people imagined that he had drowned himself, others claimed that he had abandoned his wife in order not to have to live with her any longer; several believed that he had another woman, saying that he had run off with a girl from the Faubourg Saint-Gervais who had disappeared at the same time. In sum, everyone gossiped as they liked.

"Twenty-two years passed without any mention of him being heard; in the meantime he was so completely forgotten that even his wife no longer spared him a thought. However, everyone was very astonished so see him appear again, in a state very different from the one he had been in when he left. He was in command of a regiment of mounted Cuirassiers of between two and three thousand men, in the troops of the Emperor, who was then at war with Sweden.

"Essiva had been assigned to a garrison situated on the Rhine, and, seeing himself within range, had asked for leave in order to spend three months in Geneva, under the pretext that he had urgent business there, and giving an assurance that he would return to duty before the campaign began. Having arrived in his birthplace he chose the Écu de France for his lodgings; he had no sooner entered than he saw that the landlord he had known was still arrive, and called him over.

"'Shut the door, Monsieur such-and-such,' he said, calling him by name. 'Sit down here with me; I have a few words to say to you in private, and we have to drink a glass of wine together; it's a long time since I wanted that. Do you know who I am?'

"'No, Monsieur,' he replied. 'I don't remember ever having seen you before—but so many different faces come in here that it's impossible for them to make sufficient impression on my senses for me to retain an idea of them.'

"'There's a difference between someone passing through and a man one sees every day,' the Colonel said. 'I've been in your establishment a hundred times, and you've given me more glasses of wine to drink. Did you never know a man named Essiva?'

"'Monsieur,' he replied, 'we once had a man named Essiva here, who was a coal-porter, and hence a negligible person; I don't know that I've seen any other.'

"'Well, that's me, said the Officer. 'It's me who brought you a thousand sacks of coal at one time.'

"'You doubtless want to laugh at others, Monsieur,' the landlord replied, 'but the bait is too gross for me to take; one doesn't fool me so easily—it takes more than that.'

"'I'm not trying to make fun of you,' Essiva said. 'What I'm telling you is the simple truth; nor is it in order for you to admire the condition I'm now in that I'm revealing myself to you. If I had no better reasons than that, I'd never have done it, for fear that the revelation might harm my fortune, which is not yet at the point to which I intend to push it—for although it's more honorable for a man to owe his elevation to his virtue than his birth, and fundamentally there's no comparison between the man who ennobles his descendants and the man who borrows his luster from his ancestors, people often have the weakness of giving a gentleman of mediocre merit more consideration than a commoner who excels in good qualities.'

"'But Monsieur,' said the landlord, 'how can I believe what you're telling me? You're stout and powerful, you have a highly-colored face; I see you accompanied by a trumpeter, a valet and two burly lackeys in livery; you're wearing a coat covered in gold braid, and besides, if I dare mention it, you have a limp—and you want me to take you for a man who had none of those qualities, who was from the dregs of the people? Even if you were to knock me down, I'd never believe until forced by proofs more convincing than those that have appeared so far.'

"'It's true,' Essiva said, 'that good food has changed my build and my complexion, that a musket-ball has shattered my knee and left me unable to walk straight, and that my retinue, of which you see a small sample here, and the expense I'm obliged to make, have nothing in common with the figure cut by a poor townsman, but I'm nonetheless Essiva for all that. Monsieur le Marquis du Blosel, whom I helped to escape from here to avoid falling into the hands of one of the creatures of the King of France, as you ought to remember, was the cause of this change. But it's not presently a question of that; we'll talk about it another time, I'm only here for a few days. I beg you to tell me how my wife and daughters are.'

"'How they are, Monsieur,' replied the other, 'if it's true that they really belong to you, as I'm beginning to suspect, although with the greatest astonishment in the world, is reduced to beggary. A wretched grain-loft, open on all sides, where the four winds meet, is their dwelling; the mother works day and night spinning silk, from which she doesn't earn enough to have bread, and the daughters lead a life that isn't edifying..'

"'Is it possible?' the Colonel interrupted. 'That's unfortunate—but it's necessary that I see them. It's getting dark; ask your wife to take the trouble to find mine and bring her here, under the pretext that there's and Officer here who has news to give her of her husband, who is very well, and who has charged him to put a few pistoles into her own hand.'

"The hostess was immediately dispatched to deliver that agreeable message. She went to look for Madame Essiva, but she had a great deal of difficulty bringing her back, and had it not been for the hope of touching the coins had had been promised, she would never have been extracted from a place from which the shame of being seen in the sad state in which she was in only permitted her to go out in extreme circumstances.

"As soon as she appeared, Essiva cried: 'Come in my good woman, I beg you. I have good wishes to give you from your husband Essiva; he is hale and hearty—much better than you, I can assure you—and so much changed to his advantage that you would not recognize him if you saw him.'

"The poor woman, ashamed, remained at the door, however; it was almost necessary to use violence to make her come forward and oblige her to sit down. She did not know what countenance to adopt, and strongly suspected that the others were mocking her; with that thought she began to weep.

"Her husband, who was extremely moved, unable to dissimulate any further, threw himself upon her. 'What, wretch?' he said. 'You don't recognize your own husband? It's me, Essiva, who married you on such-and-such a day, in such-and-such church, by whom you had such-and-such children, and whom a left in such-and-such a manner.' To which he added, in whisper, many details that no one else but the two of them could know. 'God, who does everything for a reason, having ordered it,' he continued, 'you are now the wife of a man who has a rank in society. I have a considerable income in my responsibility as a Colonel, and have already amassed enough to nourish you for the rest of your days, in case I die before you.'

"For some time, the good woman was ecstatic to hear such an unexpected story; she did not know whether it might be a dream, a performance, or a comedy; it was impossible for her to find the denouement. Essiva, who wanted to sleep with her that night, immediately sent out to purchase new linen; he had simple and precious fabrics brought, in order to have clothes made as quickly as possible for the three unfortunate women, who were clad in rags rather than garments, and accommodated them in such was way that in two days they were no longer recognizable.

"From the next day onwards that rare adventure was the subject of all the conversations of the inhabitants of Geneva. Essiva went out to make a grand tour, expressly to be seen; afterwards, he made the acquaintance of the most important people in the city, and resolved, at their suggestion, to put five or six hundred pistoles in the corn exchange, at eight per cent interest, in order that if any harm came to him, his family would have enough to live on without being indebted to anyone.

"When his time ran out, he went away, to the great regret of his friends, who had a presentiment that he would never return. He was, in fact, killed, in the first battle in which he took part. The man had not yet reached the top of tree, but one can say that the fortune he had made was quite considerable since he had only quit the lake at the age of thirty-five.

"You can see from that. my Lord, that there are other examples of elevation than your own, although it is no less extraordinary for that, and so much so that I can't conclude anything to my advantage. There's such a difference between what you were then and what I am now; you were only thirty, and I'm over sixty; there's no longer any fortune waiting for me at that age. All that I desire, before dying, is to return to Holland, where I might earn my living educating pupils, among people where I could live more comfortably than in cold climates inhabits by people who have, for the most part, nothing humans about them but their faces."

"All that I have is at your service," said the Governor. "My house, my purse, my table and my credit: you may use them as your own, as I've told you before and I repeat today. Alternatively, it's up to you to withdraw whenever you wish—unless you'd like to come with me to Denmark; I've resolved to go next year in order to see my homeland once more; I don't want to die before that."

"You do me great honor, my Lord," I replied. "I'll take you at your word, and you'll have the generosity of suffering me in your home until you undertake that voyage—on the condition, however, that you do me the grace of employing me in the business of your household, in everything that is within my scope."

Three-quarters of a year later, which was in the month of June 1702, we traveled to Denmark. Once there, he invited me to accompany him as far as Warsaw. The obligations that I had, combined with the inclination that I felt to see Poland, prevented me from refusing.

I expected to see the residence of a powerful King, a beautiful abode, well constructed and full of monuments worthy of my curiosity, but I was very surprised to find nothing but a wretched village that is not even enclosed by walls. There are entire streets where there is no pavement, the houses there are twenty, thirty or fifty paces apart. The inhabitants are dirty and improper, to the point of making their ordure in public outside their doors, and in places that their Sovereign passes every day. All those filthy habits, as well as the bitter cold that reigns there, obliges people always to go booted and to build perrons three or four feet high in front of their dwellings; otherwise, they would be eternally buried in mire.

I would never have thought that there were people as poor and wretched as that in Europe. The peasants there are as stupid and ignorant as beasts, so they are treated neither better nor worse than horses and dogs are treated in France and the other countries where I have been. Their liege lords, who are usually great landowners, make use of them as they please, for all sorts of labor, and when the head of a family dies they take half of everything he leaves; if the husband and wife both die, they take possession of everything, to the last wooden bowl; if the cottage is full of children, they have no compunction in throwing them out and letting them die of starvation.

All that does or prevent them, however, from being as poor as church mice, because the crops that constitute their principal income are sold cheap and they like eating well. We visited the homes of several of those gentlemen, who had twenty or thirty domestics, but who would have been greatly embarrassed if they had had to find fifty écus in hard cash. Their ready money ordinarily consists of a small quantity of copper plaques, one of which, up to four feet in diameter and an inch or two thick, might be worth five ducats at most, in accordance with their size and weight—with the result that when it is a matter of a payment of twenty or thirty écus in such coinage, it requires strong men to drag it from underneath the table, where they keep it, and load it into a wheelbarrow or a cart. In consequence, they never give money to their domestics, and only pay them in grain, fruits, vegetables and whatever their land produces.

One strange custom they have is that when they want to eat supper, they have a servant commissioned for that purpose, who cracks a huge whip five or six times to summon all the comrades, who never fail to hasten incontinently to the place where they are to take their meal. As soon as they have finished, the same man chases before him, like a flock of sheep, into a barn, a fold or something similar, twenty, thirty or forty servants of both sexes—as many as there are—where they lie down in the straw pell-mell, and into which he locks them with a key until the following morning when he goes to open the door in order that they can all go to work.

Personally, I do not think that anything good can come of that mingling of the sexes; it is inevitable in consequence that the young people give themselves entirely to debauchery, unless they have a virtue proof against anything, or the penalties imposed on the guilty are so terrible that the mere fear of being subjected to them is capable of holding them to duty.

Another considerable abuse of the Poles is that in every village where there is a church there is a tavern next door, which they call Heaven and Hell respectively. That drinking-den always belongs to the parish priest, who keeps it as well-stocked as he can. Thus, I can say as a man of honor, having seen it many a time with my own eyes, that those miserable peasants, who are in any case idolaters of their priests and devout to the extent of superstition, almost never fail, on coming out of mass, to go into that den of debauchery and get drunk like beasts, on hydromel or grain alcohol, which are their favorite beverages, others being too weak or too expensive.

The Ecclesiastics have as despotic a domination over their souls as the Nobles have over their bodies; the first damn them or save them at their whim, the others let them live or kill them as they please. When they kill one, they have only to put half an écu on his body in order to have him buried, and are quits for that; no one ever mentions him again, as if his mother had never brought him into the world.

As they are pitifully poor, they are obliged to be extremely laborious, and it seems that necessity gives them industry; thus, they make with their own hands almost everything of which they make use in the house, most of which is made from wood: dishes, plates, ladles, bowls, chairs, benches, cupboards, chests, beds, racks, doors, windows, etc. Carpenters do not see a sou of their money.

One thing that delighted my admiration at the beginning, however, was seeing a woodcutter and his son, with a huge cart laden with wood, in a forest that they had entered two hours earlier with their horses alone, each holding an ax in his hand. They begin by cutting stout branches of ash or some similar wood, which they bend into a circle, and which they join up, attaching the ends together by means of a few pegs of the same material and the bark that they have stripped from it. The hub and the spokes are ready in a moment. When the wheels are made, they pass axles through them and fix them at whatever distance apart they please, with the aid of two ladders, which they attach to the two sides over the axles. In all that there are no cords or nails—not iron whatsoever. When the machine is loaded with wood, they make harness the same way, putting their animals in front, and leading them at a walk for one, two or three leagues—and having sold all that they have on it, they return home with their nags and fifty sous more or less.

We remained in that region for about six weeks, and from there we went to Brandenburg, where things were beginning to go somewhat better, with regard to villagers, who are not entirely enslaved as in Poland.

What they have in common, although of different religions, is that they are equally infatuated with the idea that their country is filled with sorcerers, and in that conviction, they sacrifice to their ignorance an infinite number of wretches who are neither more or less criminal than me. As soon as a few cows or mares abort, ewes die or the hens no longer want to lay, it is the Devil that has caused it, and it is necessary to make an exact search for the accursed instrument of whom the enemy of the human race is making you to exercise his infernal malice against people.

If a miserable peasant has only one envious individual who holds him in slight discredit, he is sure to be accused as the guilty party, whereupon he is seized, put to the question and tormented so much that he is forced in the end to attribute a thousand deeds to himself of which he has never thought, in order to spare himself as much as possible from the rage of the torturers.

One day, we found ourselves in the company of a Lieutenant-Colonel, who assured us that he had known a rascal of a High Sheriff, who was enraged that, being on the edge of the grave, he had only burned ninety-nine sorcerers; he feared that he might die before setting fire to the hundredth. "I've served in Holland," he continued, "but I didn't notice that people there were infatuated with such a stupid opinion. It's true, however, that when I was garrisoned at Grave a few years ago, a poor woman was accused of witchcraft in a hole called Borkelo, in the vicinity of the province of Münster, with which it still sympathized in relation to many errors. Those who wanted to doom her were so many in number, and the evidence they alleged of several pernicious deeds that were imputed to her seemed so plausible to the public, that it was impossible to avoid imprisoning her.

"The judge, embarrassed as he was, and not wanting torture to be applied to her, which can make anyone say more than is the case, said that in accordance with a Law, which people claim that the Emperor Charles V invented on that subject, her thumbs should be attached to her big toes and that she be thrown naked into the river to see what happened. Misfortune determined, contrary to the sentiment of the Legislator, the Judge and the ordinary constitution of human beings, who normally sink incontinently, because a human body is usually heavier than a similar volume of water, that the innocent woman floated.

"With that, everyone raised a terrible hue and cry and picked up stones with which to lapidate her, for fear that she might soil the ground with her feet if she were permitted to walk on it—with the result that it required all the difficulty in the world to appease the multitude, and that objective was only achieved by telling them that, the crime being so atrocious, it merited a more severe punishment than the one to which they wanted to limit themselves—in addition to which it was necessary that the law take its course and that everything be done in order.

"The woman was put back in the cell from which she had been taken and held there for some time; finally, she was enabled to escape by night via the door of the place of her detention, which it was asserted that she had forced. Which makes it evident," the Officer added, "that even though a few petty individuals are simple enough to believe in sorcerers, the Magistrates and enlightened people in those countries have no faith in it."

Finally we traversed Saxony and went to Bremen, where Ludoviski had business. There we said adieu, in a manner that testified adequately to his affection and my just gratitude. In quitting me he put another twenty ducats of good gold in my hand and wished me good luck and a long life.

During the seven or eight days that I stayed there to rest from the fatigues of such a long and difficult journey, I heard of an unfortunate incident that seemed to me to be singular in every respect, to which I cannot refuse a place here.

We were at table, and had almost finished eating, when a French merchant named La Vigne came in, out of breath. "I can do no more," he told us. "Assuredly, Messieurs, I've just witnessed the most tragic action that I ever heard of in my entire life. I had business with a local citizen; after settling it, we didn't want to part without having drunk a bottle together. He took me to the Ange, where he claims that the best gourmets go. The room we were in was crowded; among others, there was a venerable old man there whom everyone addressed as 'Bailiff,' who was chattering like a one-eyed magpie and amusing all those who were listening to him. He had been at the inn for three days, and hadn't ceased to procure pleasure, under the pretext that the affairs he had to expedite, and for which he'd come to Bremen, weren't urgent.

"The presence of the worthy fellow held everyone there; otherwise, we would have left two hours earlier. As we were in the middle of laughing, and everyone was trying to furnish the conversation, another man came in, decrepit in age, who attracted the attention of everyone there because of his gigantic stature and because he was as gray as a pigeon. He ordered a half-liter of wine and took a seat with everyone else. As soon as the Bailiff saw him sit down he went to sit next to him, in order to be able to chat about old times with someone who must have seen more of them than any of the others.

"'You're laden with the weight of many years, my dear friend,' he said to him. 'You're like me, your memory doubtless goes a long way back. Where are you from, if you please?'

"'I'm seventy-eight years old,' the stranger replied, 'and I've been living in Berlin for half a century.'

"'We're about the same age,' the Bailiff said.

"'It's necessary, then, Messieurs,' I said, 'that you're very different in constitution; you're as fit as one another, and no one would never judge you to be as old as you are, but it's certain that the Bailiff seems younger by a quarter, and I'll wager that I'm more worn out than he is.'

"'Worn out or not,' said the Brandenburger, 'I'm robust, healthy and have a good appetite. To give you proof of that'—he raised his voice—'Landlord, do you not have a slice of cold meat with which I can make my supper?'

"He has brought the remains of a ham, with butter and cheese. While eating, he continued chatting with the Bailiff, who wanted do know his name—one might have thought that he was interested in getting to know him thoroughly. His curiosity went so far that he learned that the man to whom he was speaking was the son of a man who had been his father's sworn enemy.

"'What?' said the Brandenburger. 'Your father was the Bailiff of Renhaus? Mine made me promise, when he died, to avenge the wrong that had been done to him, on him or his children. It's necessary...'

"And, as he pronounced those words, he stretched out his arm and cut the Bailiff's throat with a large knife that he was using to slice up his ham. The other, meanwhile, had grabbed a pewter tankard that was in front of him, and at the moment that the hand had been raised against him he had raised his own, in such a way that as the first one acted, he brought the tankard down furiously upon his head, at the temple, which laid him out dead on the floor. The Bailiff also gave up the ghost a moment later.

"With that, I went to the door, trembling, and I swear to you that I'm still so upset that I can't collect myself."

"Great God!" cried the mistress of the lodging-house, who had hastened toward us to hear the story of that fatal adventure. "Can it be that sane men have so little empire over their passions that they can think of avenging themselves on the brink of the sepulcher?"

"Vengeance is a possession that has no peer, my good Lady," said a ship's captain who was also in our company. "That's a proverb that applies to all places and all times. Italy, above all, furnishes rightful examples of it. There's nothing more commonplace than seeing a rascal stab an innocent man under the pretext that one of his ancestors had insulted one of his own ancestors. Their hatred is handed down from father to son until the race is extinct. They never forget and never forgive. Although that's rarer in this region, where society is considerably less vindictive, we've nevertheless seen it happen to those two old men, and I remember an almost similar incident, which I think I ought to relate to you, since it's very relevant and merits your attention.

"You all remember," he continued, "the glorious enterprise of William III, Prince of Orange, in the British Isles in 1688. The States furnished for that effect a numerous and formidable fleet; I was part of the expedition. On the vessel on which I was performing the function of pilot, we had a German General named the Graf von Solms. As he was quite familiar, and chatting to other gentlemen who were not far distant from the King, the conversation gradually turned to the same subject about which we've just been talking.

"'There can be nothing more extraordinary,' said that Hero, 'than what happened one day to my own father. Two German Princes had a few differences; the Emperor intervened to settle them, but one of the two being too difficult, he sent two fine cavalry regiments to help the other. The older of the Colonels commanding them directed his march in such a way that he and his associates came to lodge one evening in the town where we lived. My father, who was very generous, and who knew in advance that the people were coming, had prepared a very fine supper, two which he invited all the Officers of both corps.

"'The Commandant was placed at the top of the table. The first glass of wine that was drunk was to his health. When the round was finished, instead of thanking the company, he said to my father: "It's you, Graf, who introduced that toast, and it's also to your consideration alone that I won't drink it."

"'At the same time, he threw the glass, which shattered into a thousand pieces. "What do you mean?" my father said. "You have the audacity to insult me in my own house? That's the first time that anyone has ever ventured to humiliate me in that fashion; whoever you were, I will not suffer it, or you'll tell me the cause of it."

"'The Colonel replied: "I'm an honest man, and I'll give you whatever satisfaction you demand, but not now. Let's eat while the food is hot; let's drink without mentioning your health or mine, since I can't answer for it. As soon as supper is finished, I'll tell you my reasons."

"'To that, my father replied: "No. No one will ever reproach me for having calmly had a meal with a man who treated me in such an insulting manner, infinitely beneath my quality; it would be impossible for me to swallow a mouthful. First tell me what you have in your heart, what I have done to you, or whence that sally comes, and then I promise you, wrong or not, to contain myself for this evening and settle matters with you as you desire,"

"'After many protests, however, it was necessary to get up. As soon as they had gone into another room, the Colonel said: "Do you remember, Graf, having had in your service about thirty years ago a woodcutter named Daniel?"

"'"No," my father replied. "I change domestics so frequently, and have so many, and it's such a long time since then, that it's not surprising that I've forgotten. But in any case, what has that to do with our quarrel?"

"'"A great deal," said the Colonel. "It's the most essential part of it. Pay a little attention, if you please. You then had such-and-such a butler, such-and-such pages, such-and-such valets; it was in the time when such-and-such things happened."

"'"I'm beginning to have some idea of it," said the Graf. "This Daniel, if I'm not mistaken, was the son of one of my farmers, a rather well-made fellow, who didn't lack intelligence, but who made such poor usage of it that I threw him out for various misdeeds. His parents haven't heard mention of him since, poor folk..."

""""Well, Sire," the Officer interrupted, "I am that woodcutter."

""""What? It's you?" said my father. "You're joking, it seems? Let's talk as sensible men, please, and not amuse ourselves talking nonsense."

""""What I'm telling you," the Colonel went on, "is the truth. I am that Daniel, who spent four and a half years in your house, who served you faithfully, who kept watch continuously over the actions of my comrades, and by virtue of that excited their jealousy and attracted their mortal hatred. They accused me of such enormous deeds that, after having had me beaten with sticks, you commanded me to leave your house immediately and never to come back. That manner of action was unjust; I was innocent and you treated me as if I were guilty. I was no more insensible then than I am now, but I could only avenge myself by murdering you. Instead of going to that extremity, about which I thought several times, I preferred to abandon my homeland and to bid an eternal adieu to all my friends. I entered the service in which I have been fortunate enough to rise to a rank that permits me to demand satisfaction from you for the injury you did me, and I demand that you give it to me before I leave in the morning."

"'My father remonstrated with him in vain,' the Graf continued, 'that there was no proportion between a master and a servant, between a person like him and a miserable woodcutter; that, according to his own admission, he had been abused by the testimony of envious individuals whose multitude seemed to merit belief; and that, in addition, it was unbecoming of an Officer of his merit to want to avenge a wrong that he claimed to have been done to a mere servant; there was no means of appeasing him. He sustained loudly that a superior Christian, however grand he might be, ought never to treat his inferiors as slaves, not chastise them without having heard hem, convinced that they had committed the sins imputed to them. It was necessary, in spite of my father's reluctance, to promise to fight him when they awoke in the morning.

"'With that they went to join the others, and as if nothing had happened, they spent the rest of the evening in formal debauchery. The next day, the Colonel was at the rendezvous at the time fixed for the duel; he remained there for a whole hour, with the greatest impatience in the world, without the Graf appearing. A Captain, imagining that my father dared not come out, or that he had the intention of insulting his Commandant, offered to reproach him for his negligence; he was given permission to do so.

"'The valet to whom he addressed himself in order to discover the cause of a delay that was causing them so much inconvenience told him that his master was still asleep and that he dared not disturb him until he rang. "I'll go to him myself," said the Officer, and, having been shown the door to his room he went in and made an angry din, shouting, swearing and raging.

435

"'The racket woke my father up. "Who is it," he said, in a menacing voice, "who is bold enough to disturb my sleep? Can't it wait until I've finished?"

"'"No," replied the Captain. "My Colonel is impatient to see you; our two regiments are under arms; he wants the difference between you to be settled before going. Do you want to delay his march? Do you not know what you promised?"

"'"Certainly," said my father, "but I drank so much wine yesterday evening in order to set my guests a good example, that I've been so profoundly asleep since that I was no longer in a state to think about the matter. Wait, please; I'll be with you in a minute."

"'With that he rang, he got dressed and instructed that his best pistols should be brought in order that he might load them himself at his whim. They moved quickly, but all that was not done with as much promptitude as the Captain would have wished, and he never ceased urging everyone to hurry. Finally, he said so much that my father told him bluntly to go away, and made him understand that if it had not been for consideration for his Commandant, he would have thrown him downstairs.

"'At these words things became heated on both sides, and gross words were exchanged, the conclusion of which was that it was necessary to begin the dance with the two of them. At the first shot my father fired, he did not fail to hit the target. Thereafter he ran to find the Colonel, who made him frank reproaches for making him wait for at least two hours. "I'm sorry," my father said, "but I was asleep. But I'm even sorrier that you sent an Officer to wake me up brutally, who pushed me to the limit. From words we came to blows, and I've had the misfortune to shoot him in the head."

"'"What, Sir?" said the Colonel. You've killed that young Cavalier? That's unfortunate. Heaven, annoyed by our procedure, apparently demanded a victim. Perhaps it might be appeased by his blood, but even if Heaven is appeased, I'm not. It's necessary for us to settle our quarrel. Let's see what fate decides."

"'After separating by two or three hundred paces, they turned and rode toward one another at a gallop. The colonel fired first and perforated the brim of my father's hat, who, for his part, cut the bridle of the Colonel's horse. He quickly perceived that, the animal being impetuous, it was impossible for the other to control it, with the consequence that, in order not to lose time, he ran toward him, put the barrel of his other pistol to his opponent's ear and said: "Your life is in my hands. I could take it without any difficulty, but God forbid that I should profit from my advantage in such circumstances. I am your friend, if you will oblige me by never speaking again about the quarrel between us."

"That generosity warmed the Colonel's heart. They embraced as if they were brothers, and both wept with joy, that Providence had directed matters so well to their advantage that they had not even been touched. They made many protestations of amity, but I doubt that they ever saw one another again.'

"Well, what do you think of that story?" the ship's captain concluded.

"It's remarkable in every respect," I replied, "And as you said, I think it well worthy of being told. Even so, I'd like to know the veritable cause of the implacable hatred there was between the fathers of the two unfortunate men who have just murdered ne another so miserably."

"I can satisfy you in part," the host interjected, "because it made a great deal of noise at the time; no one as talking about anything else. The father of the man who passed here for a Brandenburger once lived in this town. He was a leather-worker by trade and a dealer in leather, whereas the son became a horse-dealer in Berlin. One of his brothers, who was an old bachelor, whose sole heir he was, having just died, he found among his effects an obligation for a thousand écus to the charge of the Bailiff of Renhaus, the father of the man whose throat has just been cut.

"Having need of money to expand his business, and knowing, on the other hand, that his debtor had the reputation of not doing too well in his affairs, he went to find him and told him that he wanted to have the money, which he asked him to have ready when the year expired. 'Very well,' said the Bailiff, 'come here at such-and-such a time and I'll pay you.'

"Having returned at the appointed time, the Judge said to him: 'Where is your obligation? Give it to me, so that I can see it.' He turned it this way and that, looked at it and read it. Eventually, a domestic came to whisper something in his ear. 'Is it possible?' he cried. 'Here,' he said to the Merchant, 'here's your script,' returning it to him folded. 'Some business has come up, the execution of will not suffer any delay. We'll examine things at leisure another day. Come back in a week, if you please; I shall unfailingly be at home.'

"On the second visit the Merchant made, he gave orders to tell him that he had visited his papers, where he had found that the obligation for which he was claiming payment had been acquitted, and thus he had nothing to settle with him. Our man was astonished; instead of going to consult a prosecutor he summoned his party before competent judges.

"The President listened to them and demanded to see the obligation. He had no sooner cast his eyes over it than he returned it with disdain. 'Go away, ill-advised as you are,' he said to the leather-worker. 'You must be very bold or very ignorant to dare to produce before a tribunal a false document like this, on which there is neither a name nor a date, in order to claim a sum of two thousand five hundred francs from an honest man. You merit being treated in another manner.'

"The poor man did not know what al that meant; he went out utterly nonplussed, and found that the rogue of a Bailiff, having doubtless moistened his thumbs, had erased the signature and the most essential part of the obligation when he had taken it to him and the other had handled it in his presence. That detestable action angered the Merchant so much, not so much because of the loss he had suffered as because many people imagined that he had not acted in good faith, that in private he made rude threats against the Bailiff and swore to kill him the next time he found him alone outside the town.

"He died without being able to content himself, but with the precaution that on his deathbed, he made his son swore to avenge the insult, on him or his children, when he found the opportunity. The son kept his word to with regard to that vindication, but as we've seen, it cost him his life."

As I feared making too much expenditure while traveling, I sought every favorable and cheap means to take me in the direction of the Low Countries. One person who knew that told me about a horse-dealer who was to depart the following day for Minden with several horses, one of which he would allow me to use for a bagatelle.

The opportunity was too good to neglect, and I went out immediately in search of the merchant to see whether there was a means of reaching an agreement with him.

It was raining lightly when I set out, but on the way I was caught in a prodigious downpour, which obliged me to stop under an awning until it passed, under pain of being soaked to the skin. Opposite the place where I was standing there was a rather fine house with a split door, the upper part of which was open, allowing a master wearing a violet satin robe with a black velvet bonnet on his head to look me up and down from head to toe.

"What are you doing standing there, my friend," he said to me. "Come here, come in and sit down; I fear that the rain will continue and you might be forced to stay there for a long time."

The street was not very broad and I could hear him distinctly, so I bowed and thanked him for his civility. That did not satisfy him, and it was necessary for me to go into the antechamber, where he made me sit down next to him.

As soon as I sat down he said: "You're French, if I'm not mistaken; one can tell by your pronunciation."

"That's true," I replied. "I'm from Viviers."

"You're from Viviers?" he continued, giving evidence of astonishment. "What is your name, if you please?"

"My name is Pierre de Mésange." I told him.

"Once a Franciscan?" he asked.

"Indeed," I said. "How do you know that, pray?"

"I know it for a reason that I hardly dare tell you," he replied. "Don't you recognize me? Has Jacques Surcel changed so much that there are no longer any features in his face capable of giving you an idea of it?"

At those words I changed color; the evils that I had suffered, of which he had been the cause, came back to mind, and made me look at him with indignation. I would have liked with all my heart not to have had such a lugubrious encounter.

He perceived my disturbance.

"You're much changed," he told me. "In the name of God, let's forget the past. Providence, which governs all things, decided, for the good of my soul and my body, that I deprive, unfortunately and without intention an innocent man of life, whom curiosity alone had led him to see the author of the apparitions about which you had doubtless confided in him. I can see from the state that you're in, that that has been to your misfortune, but console yourself that I am presently in a position to render you fortunate for the rest of your days. I swear to you that, if you wish, I will share everything with you, down to my last sou."

With that, he sent for a bottle of wine, and whatever I could say, it was necessary, half by persuasion and half by force, that I help him to empty it. In the meantime, I recovered my spirits somewhat, and a residual desire for vengeance gave way to the curiosity that gripped me to know the cause of the changes that I remarked in a man issue from the dregs of the people.

"Is it possible that this is you, Monsieur Surcel?" I said. "By what fortuitous circumstance do you come to be in this country, and what means have you used to establish yourself as you appear to be? Tell me that, I beg you, but go back to the beginning, and tell me what became of you after we left the convent, under the pretext of going to seek remedies for our dying friend?"

"I went straight to the house of Master Jean the shoemaker," he replied, "Who, as you know, was one of my old acquaintances, in whose shop I had worked in my youth. I had only been there for an hour when someone came to look for me, on the Superior's orders, who told me that I had only to return without remedies, that there was no more need for them, and that all was well.

"I trusted his word, because he had always shown me a good deal of friendship, but I had no sooner returned than I recognized that I had been deceived by that stratagem. I was immediately imprisoned, and the following day I was rigorously examined. Far from being evasive, I recounted the incident frankly as it had happened.

"'If that is true,' I was told, 'as seems very plausible, you had no quarrel with the dead man; it was not out of animosity that you killed him; it was the effect of a rigorous destiny, which determined to make use of your hand, as of an instrument of God's ire, to take away the life of a saintly man who had not merited it. However, although there was no malice in your action, you are nevertheless guilty and worthy of punishment. It is necessary, on the other hand, that this does not cause a scandal, because of the consequences, so you will not be handed over to the secular arm. In order not to attract the ire of the Lord upon our Society, however, you are condemned to six weeks of penitence, which will consist of your living for that time on bread and water and flagellating yourself, in the presence of three Monks, six Fridays in succession until the blood flows from your body.'

"I pleaded my case, but it was necessary to submit to that punishment if I wanted to reenter into grace. I fasted, as I had been ordered to do, and I whipped myself twice, but it was impossible for me to wait until the third time; a maceration of that nature suited my constitution so poorly that I could not have continued without succumbing. I picked my time, and ran away for a second time to my former master, who had the charity to hide me so well that I was not discovered.

"It took me more than three weeks to get better; when I had recovered my vigor, he gave me money and a poor suit of clothes, with the aid of which I fled, and went straight to Paris, as a society where I thought that I could best avoid the pursuits of my torturers, with a view to exercising there the métier that I had learned in my youth. I found, however, that I had forgotten so much of what I had known that I was obliged to go to a placement bureau to see whether there was any means of finding me a master of quality whom I could serve as a valet. In the meantime I thought I ought to profit from the time I still had to myself to go and see the most beautiful things there were in the Metropolis of the Kingdom of France.

"One day, while I was going to Saint Denis, where the sepulcher of the Kings and Princes of the Land is, I was surprised while passing a tavern that was on the way, when a rogue adroitly seized my hat and threw it into the house. Ignorant of the deceits that men of war use to trap soldiers, I was about to go in to search for it when a peasant who happened to be passing by, and who knew about those sorts of ruses, warned me not to do so, for fear that harm might befall me.

"When those who were on watch saw that I was staying outside the door, two of them came out, seized me by the arms and tried to drag me inside. While resisting, I fell to the ground; they threw themselves upon me, and began to labor me with their fists.

"Fortunately, a Page of the Court arrived, who made us get up, asked about the subject of our quarrel. I told him what had happened, whereupon he drew his sword and gave those scoundrels a beating. 'So this is the way, rogues that you are,' he said to them, 'that you abuse the right that had been given to you to impress men into His Majesty's service. I'm not astonished that we receive complaints every day, and that everyone deserts as soon as they're enrolled. It's mendicants, vagrants and such rabble that the King wishes to be taken in that manner, because the public is inconvenienced by them; he doesn't intend you to do violence to passers-by and honest people. If it happens again, you'll be taught a lesson.'

"That little inconvenience prevented me for a while from going out into the city, but finally, in order to prevent similar incidents, I resolved to do of my own free will what they had tried to make me do by force. I enrolled voluntarily in an infantry regiment.

"God knows the extravagances that I committed in the company of those rascals, who, for the most part, were nothing but veritable pillars of houses of debauchery, where they often helped to maltreat and rob those who had the misfortune to fall into their hands, either by surprise or deliberate deception. I won't bother telling you about the tricks and stratagems of which they and their concubines made use to lead the unfortunates into traps, of which I was often the witness; that wouldn't be appropriate here, and I can't recall such things without exciting the remorse of conscience, which racks my poor mind horribly.

"Leaving that matter aside, then, I'd rather tell you that, Paris being a place where one finds people from everywhere, I did not neglect opportunities to inform myself secretly as to what was happening in Viviers. I learned, among other items of new appropriate to your subject, that your father was put in bed shortly after your departure, and that the poor man died of chagrin after six months. Your mother survived him by a year and a half.

"Eventually, the King of France declared war on the Dutch, and I found myself in several battles, from which I fortunately emerged unscathed, until the battle of Sénef in 1674, where I received a musket-shot that left me lame, as you can see. A Sergeant from a German regiment, having also been wounded there, was taken to the same place as me in order to be bandaged. He was accompanied by his wife, who lavished all the cares imaginable on him. Nevertheless, he died of his wounds. After his death, his widow did not leave my side. She served me, nursed me and, in brief, treated me as if I were her own brother. That made no small contribution to my recovery.

"Having nothing more precious than my person, I offered it to her, in recognition of so much kindness, adding that it was all that I had in the world. 'I'll take you at your word,' she said, 'such as you are, I have the means of earning bread for both of us, if, in exchange, you will go with me to my own country and embrace the Lutheran religion.'

"'I'll go wherever you wish,' I said, 'but as for changing my sentiment with regard to religion, that I can't promise you. I want to see what it is, and if I can make my salvation there, I'll make that decision; if not, I'll remain a Catholic.'

"'That's sufficient,' she said. 'You have intelligence; when you've had a little instruction, you'll soon be ours.'

"With that she collected her things, and we went to get married in Brussels, and then came here. She had a house here, where her father had kept an inn; she embraced the same profession. Out affairs went very smoothly; we made a living, but little beyond that. Fortune determined that I had a superior wife, who took care of everything, which gave me the leisure to pass my time elsewhere. I made the acquaintance of a florist, who had all sorts of plants. Although I only had a very small garden behind my lodgings, the cultivation of flowers seemed to me to be such an innocent diversion, and at the same time so agreeable, that I devoted myself o it wholeheartedly.

"My friend accommodated me with everything I wished; I took great care of what he gave me, and everything changed visibly in my hands, especially my tulips, which became more beautiful every year. I sowed the seeds, and nothing finer, more bizarre and better marked had ever been seen that what they brought me. Whereas I worked in the beginning for my pleasure, afterwards I occupied myself entirely out of interest, and no longer had flowers except to make money. One day, I sold a tulip bulb for a hundred écus, the next a fifty franc plant.[47] Hardly a day passed when my counter didn't resound with some new influx.

"In sum, I can tell you that in less than ten years I've made more than seventy thousand livres. When I saw that I was in a situation to live without doing anything, I had my wife shut up shop and bought the house in which you see me presently, where we live very comfortably with a valet and a maidservant, for as to children, I have none."

"I'm delighted by your good fortune," I interjected. "You're rich and I'm poor. I've been very fortunate if I've even been able to earn an honest living, and I'm going to Leyden to do that. May it please God that things go as well there as they did before."

"It's not necessary," Monsieur Surcel replied, "to go so far in search of what is close at hand. I've told you, and I repeat, that I have enough wealth for both of us; it only requires you to enjoy it at your will. You won't have to change religion, as I have done, if you don't want to. I don't even insist that you live with me, although I can accommodate you with two beautiful well-furnished rooms. Lodge here, lodge elsewhere; eat and drink here or wherever you wish; my purse will pay for everything. I can't say any more than that, unless I add that if I die before you, as I might, being a few years older, I'll leave you enough to live honestly for the rest of your days."

"I'm much obliged to you," I replied. "I've never directly been a burden to anyone, and I don't intend to be, except in extremity. If I can't do anything where I'm going, perhaps I'll take advantage of your generous offer, but I dare to flatter myself that I won't have any need of it."

"I can't force you to do anything," he said. "If you stay, you'll please me; if you go, I'll pray to God that he blesses you. Permit me, however, to ask you whether you have money and clothing for the journey."

"As for clothing, I have only what you see on my body," I replied, "and for money, I only have a little remaining; I hope that Heaven will provide for everything."

With that he stood up, and went to fetch a complete suit in good iron-gray cloth, which was still as good as new, and ten ducats, which he made me take by force."

"I'd give you more," he said, "but I'd prefer it if necessity obliges you to come back."

---

[47] The Dutch craze known as "tulipomania," which peaked in 1637, was long past by the 1670s, but tulip bulbs—whose cultivation is a painstaking process requiring considerable expertise—nevertheless remained a significant commodity and exotic blooms often fetched high prices throughout northern Europe.

God forgive me, I had a heart so swollen by the trick he had played on me, from which so much disgrace had ensued, and above all the death of my father, about which I only knew thanks to his honesty, which fundamentally merited a good deal of gratitude, that, notwithstanding his insistence that I should at least stay for supper, I quit him rather abruptly, to make him see that I was capable of conserving the memory of a bad turn for a long time. I went to find my horse-dealer, with whom I departed the following morning when the gate opened.

I repented a thousand times on the way having treated Monsieur Surcel so coldly, and resolved to link myself to him by means of letters as soon as I was settled in Holland.

From Minden, where I did not stay overnight, I went to Munster, and two days later I left that place for Zutphen.

Eating that evening at the host's table in a lodging-house, several people, curious to know me, asked where I had me from and where I intended to go. I replied modestly to their questions, and gave them to understand that my design was to spend some time in Leyden, where I had once lived, with a view to teaching the French language there, and a little Mathematics.

An individual named Monsieur Unia, who was in the company, thinking that it might not be advantageous to me, started shaking his head. "You're ill-advised," he told me. "Since the revocation of the Edict of Nantes, Holland is overflowing with French refugees, who are dabbling in teaching all sorts of languages and faculties, especially in the Academies, where foreigners go to study. If you'll take my advice, you'll go to establish yourself in Leeuwarden. It seems that the Friesians have acquired a taste for Geometry and Fortification since they've remarked that those sciences have caused the advancement of Baron van Koehoorn.[48] The French language has become much more familiar there than it has been in the past; everyone wants to learn it. In consequence, I have no doubt that you'll find the means in that Court of sending your days at your ease."

I thanked him for his kindness, and decided to follow his advice. The following day, I went to visit Monsieur de Wintsum, the Burgomaster of that place, because I had been told that he was a Mathematician. He kept me with him for more than two hours, and swore to me that if he had still been young he would have asked me to stay in his house to help him to improve his Algebra, in which he had taken a great deal of pleasure, but being old, and absorbed in affairs, he could no longer think about an occupation of that nature. When I left, he put a Spanish pistole in my hand, which he absolutely insisted that I kept, and wished me every prosperity.

---

[48] Menno, Baron van Koehorn (1634-1704), an officer in the army of William II of Orange—who took over the English throne in 1688—published *Nieuwe Vestingbouw op een natte of large horisont* (tr. as *A New Method of Fortification*) in 1685.

Monsieur Unia gave me two letters, one for Councilor Jorsma, the other for the Advocate Leli, after which I bid him adieu and took the road to Deventer. I lodged there in the hostelry at which the coach arrived, near a gate at the extremity of a large square named Brink, in the middle of which is the customs office and guard-post.

The next day, as I was going along a rather dirty street, I heard a voice like a man preaching, and wondered what it was. Someone told me that it was a Professor giving a public lesson. I went into his auditorium and saw that he was explaining the Elements of Geometry. He was on the thirtieth proposition of the sixth book of Euclid, in which the Author explains how to cut a straight line in the extreme and mean ratio. He did so perfectly well; his demonstration was accurate and clear; he spoke well and with good enough grace. Afterwards he showed a few usages for which a knowledge of that problem was necessary, but what finished giving me advantageous sentiments regarding the enlightenment of the learned individual was that he informed his readers of a method quite different from that of the author he was treating, which he claimed to be his own invention, as I believed it to be.

The people I asked about him held his in considerable esteem, and spoke of him as a man of intelligence, consummate in his profession and capable of reasoning well on all matters.[49] I would undoubtedly have taken the liberty of speaking to him, but he did not finish his lesson until midday chimed, and the time was not convenient then. In addition, I needed that which remained to me to have a bite to eat and to run to catch the regular coach that was to take me to Zwol.

There I did not have the leisure to speak to a single soul. I arrived there in the evening and left again at nine o'clock the following morning for Sneek.

Finally, I reached Leeuwarden, but the gentlemen to whom I addressed myself old me frankly that they could not do anything for me. The Councilor seemed sorry that I had made such a journey on the word of a man, who could not really do very much, and who was less of a politician than a gourmet, although me made up for that defect with a liberality worthy of a man of his rank. The Advocate, who was a Catholic, had his Church give me fifteen francs. I went away with that and went on to Franeker.

At that University I only saw Monsieur Fulenius, the Professor of Mathematics, whom I also found to be a very clever man, but his manner of demonstration did not please me as much as that of the man in Deventer, who em-

---

[49] The author, who was teaching in Deventer at the time indicated by the narrator, is presumably referring to himself; the reader will remember that Mésange had already met Simon Tyssot de Patot long before, and had first gone to Leyden on his advice, but given the continual difficulties that he and many other people in the narrative have in recognizing people, it is perhaps unsurprising that the name does not spring to his mind.

ployed absolutely nothing but lines, following the example of the greatest philosophers of antiquity, whereas he made use of characters and only worked with equations. The pupil might well be convinced by that of the verity of the thing, but he is not entirely enlightened; that method narrows the mind, so to speak; it limits views to a lesser extent, whereas they ought to be expanded, and made to see all the relationships that a proposition entails at once, since that is the most beautiful fruit that scholars obtain from the cultivation of the sciences, whose object is grandeur.

He showed me, among other curiosities, a complete carillon of little bells that he had made himself, of which the greatest Musicians thought very highly. As I was leaving his house he suggested that I go to see a village situated a few leagues away named Molqueer, which he thought entirely worthy of my curiosity. I went there, on his word, and found, indeed, that one could not imagine anything more singular.

One might have thought that the houses there had been built with the intention of constructing a Labyrinth; there was not a single road or street that did not end at one of those Peasant dwellings where one is obliged to turn right or left when one wants to pass on, and from there one finds another similar obstacle, with the result that one if one does not fix one's sights on, for instance, the Church, or another building easy to distinguish, with the aid of which once can return to the place from which one has come, or one has a good guide, one risking wandering for a long time.

In addition to that, it must be remarked that the Molquerians dress in a manner very different from their neighbors, even those not far from the village. They also have a dialect quite different from other inhabitants of the same region. Their mores, their maxims and, in general, everything about them has so little relationship with what one sees in the rest of the population that until now, it has been impossible to know the cause of such a great diversity, where those people came from and when they established themselves in a place of such small extent.

The next day I found a convenient means of getting to Stavoren, and after that one that took me to Ijmuiden. I was addressed there to Monsieur Scagen, who also advised me resolutely to continue on my way. The cleanliness of the town caused me to stay there for two whole days; on the third I took the coach to Hoorn, which is one of the principal places in the north of Holland. Although the three-league road from one town to the other is paved, well-maintained and bordered all along the route by houses, as if it were a street comprising four or five villages, we nevertheless had the misfortune to overturn precipitately and very violently, although I did not feel any discomfort.

The other passengers, who also escaped the fall with a fright, got out. There was only me who remained there, and who could not help laughing on seeing all of them as pale and distressed as if they had sustained some serious injury.

"Come on, laugher," they said to me, "Let's see whether we can turn the carriage right way up and continue on our way."

"I don't know what's wrong with me," I replied, "but I seem to be nailed to the spot. It isn't in my power to move."

As I spoke, I was still laughing.

"The old man is mad, or drunk," said the driver. "Move, then—what the Devil are you doing still there?"

At those words, making an effort to raise myself up, I perceived my disaster.

"Oh God!" I cried then. "I'm doomed!"

"What, you're continuing to play the clown," they said, "and you have no fear that God will punish you another time?"

"There's no mockery here," I went on. "I can't move my leg, and it's beginning to give me an unbearable pain; it's impossible that it isn't broken."

With that, I fainted.

They came forward, and having placed me on a stretcher, they carried me to a tavern that was nearby on the road. A surgeon from the village, who was sent for immediately, came to see me, and after a thorough inspection they found that I had broken the right thigh-bone a short distance above the knee.

"If that's so," I said, "I'll never permit you to bandage me alone; I want someone else with you; that which one won't understand, the other might, and I have enough to pay both of you.

The landlord, who was already looking at me with respect, inevitably thought that I was a man of means, and hastened to carry out my orders, making sure that I was very well served.

I had a sound heart, and I had fallen into the hands of very honest people who had served at sea for a long time and who conducted themselves in a manner that made me understand that they understood their métier. In fact, five or six weeks after my fall, I was lifted up every day and set in an armchair, in front of which I had a chair with a cushion on which to rest my leg, which did not inconvenience me a great deal.

As I often lacked company and the time seemed to me to be extremely long, it came to my mind to make new memoirs of the principal events of my life and what had happened to me in my voyages, to the extent that my feeble and unsteady memory permitted me to remember it.

I occupied myself with that work for the space of four and a half months, at the end of which it turned out that I had finished the rough draft. It was then that my wound reopened and I felt greater pain than ever. Several bone-splinters emerged, and with that a bad fever ensued, which made me doubt that I would recover.

I told my host to keep that manuscript, which was very imperfect, as much in terms of style as the arrangement of materials and with concern to certain events where I have perhaps been too concise or too confused, for lack of time and enough freedom of mind, until it pleased Providence to put me in a condition to revise it, and with the prayer that in case I die he would not fail to impart it to any public whatsoever.

# SF & FANTASY

Adolphe Alhaiza. *Cybele*
Alphonse Allais. *The Adventures of Captain Cap*
Henri Allorge. *The Great Cataclysm*
Guy d'Armen. *Doc Ardan: The City of Gold and Lepers*
G.-J. Arnaud. *The Ice Company*
Charles Asselineau. *The Double Life*
Henri Austruy. *The Eupantophone; The Olotelepan; The Petitpaon Era*
Barillet-Lagargousse. *The Final War*
Cyprien Bérard. *The Vampire Lord Ruthwen*
S. Henry Berthoud. *Martyrs of Science*
Aloysius Bertrand. *Gaspard de la Nuit*
Richard Bessière. *The Gardens of the Apocalypse; The Masters of Silence*
Albert Bleunard. *Ever Smaller*
Félix Bodin. *The Novel of the Future*
Louis Boussenard. *Monsieur Synthesis*
Alphonse Brown. *City of Glass; The Conquest of the Air*
Emile Calvet. *In a Thousand Years*
André Caroff. *The Terror of Madame Atomos; Miss Atomos; The Return of Madame Atomos; The Mistake of Madame Atomos; The Monsters of Madame Atomos; The Revenge of Madame Atomos; The Resurrection of Madame Atomos; The Mark of Madame Atomos; The Spheres of Madame Atomos; The Wrath of Madame Atomos* (w/M. & Sylvie Stéphan)
Félicien Champsaur. *The Human Arrow; Ouha, King of the Apes; Pharaoh's Wife; Homo-Deus*
Didier de Chousy. *Ignis*
Jules Clarétie. *Obsession*
Michel Corday. *The Eternal Flame*
André Couvreur. *The Necessary Evil; Caresco, Superman; The Exploits of Professor Tornada* (3 vols.)
Captain Danrit. *Undersea Odyssey*
C. I. Defontenay. *Star (Psi Cassiopeia)*
Charles Derennes. *The People of the Pole*
Georges Dodds (anthologist). *The Missing Link*
Charles Dodeman. *The Silent Bomb*
Harry Dickson. *The Heir of Dracula; Harry Dickson vs. The Spider*
Jules Dornay. *Lord Ruthven Begins*
Alfred Driou. *The Adventures of a Parisian Aeronaut*
Sâr Dubnotal *vs. Jack the Ripper*
Alexandre Dumas. *The Return of Lord Ruthven*
Renée Dunan. *Baal*
J.-C. Dunyach. *The Night Orchid; The Thieves of Silence*
Henri Duvernois. *The Man Who Found Himself*
Achille Eyraud. *Voyage to Venus*
Henri Falk. *The Age of Lead*

Paul Féval. *Anne of the Isles; Knightshade; Revenants; Vampire City; The Vampire Countess; The Wandering Jew's Daughter*
Paul Féval, *fils. Felifax, the Tiger-Man*
Charles de Fieux. *Lamékis*
Louis Forest. *Someone is Stealing Children in Paris*
Arnould Galopin. *Doctor Omega; Doctor Omega and the Shadowmen* (anthology)
Judith Gautier. *Isoline and the Serpent-Flower*
H. Gayar. *The Marvelous Adventures of Serge Myrandhal on Mars*
G.L. Gick. *Harry Dickson and the Werewolf of Rutherford Grange*
Delphine de Girardin. *Balzac's Cane*
Léon Gozlan. *The Vampire of the Val-de-Grâce*
Edmond Haraucourt. *Illusions of Immortality; Daah, the First Human*
Nathalie Henneberg. *The Green Gods*
Eugène Hennebert. *The Enchanted City*
V. Hugo, P. Foucher & P. Meurice. *The Hunchback of Notre-Dame*
Romain d'Huissier. *Hexagon: Dark Matter*
Jules Janin. *The Magnetized Corpse*
Michel Jeury. *Chronolysis*
Gustave Kahn. *The Tale of Gold and Silence*
Gérard Klein. *The Mote in Time's Eye*
Fernand Kolney. *Love in 5000 Years*
Paul Lacroix. *Danse Macabre*
Louis-Guillaume de La Follie. *The Unpretentious Philosopher*
Jean de La Hire. *Enter the Nyctalope; The Nyctalope on Mars; The Nyctalope vs. Lucifer; The Nyctalope Steps In; Night of the Nyctalope; Return of the Nyctalope; The Fiery Wheel*
Etienne-Léon de Lamothe-Langon. *The Virgin Vampire*
André Laurie. *Spiridon*
Gabriel de Lautrec. *The Vengeance of the Oval Portrait*
Alain le Drimeur. *The Future City*
Georges Le Faure & Henri de Graffigny. *The Extraordinary Adventures of a Russian Scientist Across the Solar System* (2 vols.)
Gustave Le Rouge. *The Mysterious Doctor Cornelius* (3 vols.); *The Vampires of Mars; The Dominion of the World* (w/Gustave Guitton) (4 vols.)
Jules Lermina. *Mysteryville; Panic in Paris; To-Ho and the Gold Destroyers; The Secret of Zippeliu; The Battle of Strasbourg*
André Lichtenberger. *The Centaurs; The Children of the Crab*
Listonai. *The Philosophical Voyager*
Jean-Marc & Randy Lofficier. *Edgar Allan Poe on Mars; The Katrina Protocol; Pacifica; Robonocchio; Return of the Nyctalope;* (anthologists) *Tales of the Shadowmen 1-11*
Xavier Maumejean. *The League of Heroes*
Joseph Méry. *The Tower of Destiny*
Hippolyte Mettais. *The Year 5865; Paris Before the Deluge*
Louise Michel. *The Human Microbes; The New World*
Tony Moilin. *Paris in the Year 2000*
José Moselli. *Illa's End*
John-Antoine Nau. *Enemy Force*
Marie Nizet. *Captain Vampire*

C. Nodier, A. Beraud & Toussaint-Merle. *Frankenstein*
Henri de Parville. *An Inhabitant of the Planet Mars*
Gaston de Pawlowski. *Journey to the Land of the 4th Dimension*
Georges Pellerin. *The World in 2000 Years*
Ernest Pérochon. *The Frenetic People*
Pierre Pelot. *The Child Who Walked on the Sky*
J. Polidori, C. Nodier, E. Scribe. *Lord Ruthven the Vampire*
P.-A. Ponson du Terrail. *The Vampire and the Devil's Son; The Immortal Woman*
Edgar Quinet. *Ahasuerus; The Enchanter Merlin*
Henri de Régnier. *A Surfeit of Mirrors*
Maurice Renard. *The Blue Peril; Doctor Lerne; The Doctored Man; A Man Among the Microbes; The Master of Light*
Jean Richepin. *The Wing; The Crazy Corner*
Albert Robida. *The Adventures of Saturnin Farandoul; The Clock of the Centuries; Chalet in the Sky; The Electric Life*
J.-H. Rosny Aîné. *Helgvor of the Blue River; The Givreuse Enigma; The Mysterious Force; The Navigators of Space; Vamireh; The World of the Variants; The Young Vampire*
Marcel Rouff. *Journey to the Inverted World*
Léonie Rouzade. *The World Turned Upside Down*
Han Ryner. *The Superhumans; The Human Ant*
Pierre de Selenes: *An Unknown World*
Angelo de Sorr. *The Vampires of London*
Brian Stableford. *The New Faust at the Tragicomique;The Empire of the Necromancers (The Shadow of Frankenstein; Frankenstein and the Vampire Countess; Frankenstein in London); Sherlock Holmes & The Vampires of Eternity; The Stones of Camelot; The Wayward Muse.* (anthologist) *News from the Moon; The Germans on Venus; The Supreme Progress; The World Above the World; Nemoville; Investigations of the Future; The Conqueror of Death; The Revolt of the Machines*
Jacques Spitz. *The Eye of Purgatory*
Kurt Steiner. *Ortog*
Eugène Thébault. *Radio-Terror*
C.-F. Tiphaigne de La Roche. *Amilec*
Louis Ulbach. *Prince Bonifacio*
Théo Varlet. *The Golden Rock. The Xenobiotic Invasion; The Castaways of Eros; Timeslip Troopers* (w/André Blandin); *The Martian Epic* (w/Octave Joncquel)
Paul Vibert. *The Mysterious Fluid*
Villiers de l'Isle-Adam. *The Scaffold; The Vampire Soul*
Philippe Ward. *Artahe ; The Song of Montségur* (w/Sylvie Miller) *Manhattan Ghost* (w/Mickael Laguerre)

## MYSTERIES & THRILLERS

M. Allain & P. Souvestre. *The Daughter of Fantômas*
A. Anicet-Bourgeois, Lucien Dabril. *Rocambole*
A. Bernède. *Belphegor; Judex* (w/Louis Feuillade); *The Return of Judex* (w/Louis Feuillade); *The Shadow of Judex*
A. Bisson & G. Livet. *Nick Carter vs. Fantômas*

V. Darlay & H. de Gorsse. *Arsène Lupin vs. Sherlock Holmes: The Stage Play*
Séamas Duffy. *Sherlock Holmes in Paris*
Paul Féval. *Gentlemen of the Night; John Devil; The Black Coats ('Salem Street; The Invisible Weapon; The Parisian Jungle; The Companions of the Treasure; Heart of Steel; The Cadet Gang; The Sword-Swallower)*
Emile Gaboriau. *Monsieur Lecoq*
Goron & Emile Gautier. *Spawn of the Penitentiary*
Paul d'Ivoi. *Around the World on Five sous* (w/Henri Chabrillat)
Rick Lai. *Shadows of the Opera: Retribution in Blood; Sisters of the Shadows: The Curse of Cagliostro*
Steve Leadley. *Sherlock Holmes: The Circle of Blood*
Maurice Leblanc. *Arsène Lupin vs. Countess Cagliostro; Arsène Lupin vs. Sherlock Holmes (The Blonde Phantom; The Hollow Needle); The Many Faces of Arsène Lupin; The Island of the Thirty Coffins*
Gaston Leroux. *Chéri-Bibi; The Phantom of the Opera; Rouletabille & the Mystery of the Yellow Room; Rouletabille at Krupp's*
Richard Marsh. *The Complete Adventures of Judith Lee*
William Patrick Maynard. *The Terror of Fu Manchu; The Destiny of Fu Manchu*
Frank J. Morlock. *Sherlock Holmes: The Grand Horizontals; Sherlock Holmes vs Jack the Ripper*
Jean Petithuguenin. *The Adventures of Ethel King*
Antonin Reschal. *The Adventures of Miss Boston*
P. de Wattyne & Y. Walter. *Sherlock Holmes vs. Fantômas*
David White. *Fantômas in America*
Pierre Yrondy. *The Adventures of Thérèse Arnaud*

Victor Margueritte. *The Bacheloress; The Companion; The Couple*

## SCREENPLAYS

Mike Baron. *The Iron Triangle*
Emma Bull & Will Shetterly. *Nightspeeder; War for the Oaks*
Gerry Conway & Roy Thomas. *Doc Dynamo*
Steve Englehart. *Majorca*
James Hudnall. *The Devastator*
Jean-Marc & Randy Lofficier. *Royal Flush*
J.-M. & R. Lofficier & Marc Agapit. *Despair*
J.-M. & R. Lofficier & Joël Houssin. *City*
Andrew Paquette. *Peripheral Vision*
Robert L. Robinson, Jr. *Judex*
R. Thomas, J. Hendler & L. Sprague de Camp. *Rivers of Time*

## NON-FICTION

Stephen R. Bissette. *Blur 1-5. Green Mountain Cinema 1; Teen Angels*
Win Scott Eckert. *Crossovers* (2 vols.)
Jean-Marc & Randy Lofficier. *Shadowmen* (2 vols.)
Randy Lofficier. *Over Here*

www.ingramcontent.com/pod-product-compliance
Lightning Source LLC
Chambersburg PA
CBHW020249030726
47499CB00001B/124